DARKNESS DESCENDING

Also by Harry Turtledove from Earthlight
Into the Darkness

DARKNESS DESCENDING

HARRY TURTLEDOVE

EARTHLIGHT

LONDON · SYDNEY · NEW YORK · TOKYO · SINGAPORE · TORONTO

www.earthlight.co.uk

First published in Great Britain by Earthlight, 2000
An imprint of Simon & Schuster UK Ltd
A Viacom Company

Simon & Schuster UK Ltd
Africa House
64–78 Kingsway
London
WC2B 6AH

Simon & Schuster Australia
Sydney

A CIP catalogue record for this book is available
from the British Library.

ISBN 0-684-85827-4

1 3 5 7 9 10 8 6 4 2

Typeset in Bembo by SX Composing DTP, Rayleigh, Essex
Printed and bound in Finland by WSOY

DRAMATIS PERSONAE

Algarve

Almonio	Constable in Hwinca in Forthweg
Balastro	Count; Algarvian minister to Zuwayza
Bembo★	Constable in Tricarico
Clovisio	Trooper in Trasone's squad
Domiziano	Young dragonflier; squadron commander for Sabrino
Dosso	Jeweler in Trapani
Evodio	Kaunian-speaking Algarvian constable in Oyngestun
Fronesia	Sabrino's mistress
Galafrone	Tealdo's company commander
Gismonda	Sabrino's wife
Lurcanio	Colonel on occupation duty in Priekule
Mainardo	Mezentio's brother; new King of Jelgava
Mezentio	King of Algarve
Mosco	Captain on occupation duty in Priekule
Olindro	Dragonflier; squadron commander for Sabrino
Oraste	Constable in Tricarico; Bembo's partner
Orosio	Dragonflier; squadron commander for Sabrino
Panfilo	Sergeant in Tealdo's company
Pesaro	Constabulary sergeant in Tricarico
Raniero	Mezentio's cousin; named King of Grelz
Sabrino★	Colonel of dragonfliers; wing commander
Saffa	Constabulary sketch artist in Tricarico
Sasso	Constabulary captain in Tricarico
Spinello	Major in occupying force in Oyngestun
Tealdo★	Footsoldier in invasion of Unkerlant; Trasone's friend
Trasone★	Footsoldier in invasion of Unkerlant; Tealdo's friend

Forthweg

Brivibas	Vanai's grandfather
Conberge	Ealstan and Leofsig's sister
Daukantis	Kaunian olive-oil merchant in Gromheort
Doldasai	Kaunian girl in Gromheort; Daukantis' daughter
Ealstan★	Student in Gromheort; Leofsig's brother
Eanfled	Woman in Gromheort
Elfryth	Ealstan and Leofsig's mother
Elfsig	Felgilde's father
Ethelhelm	Band-leader in Gromheort
Felgilde	Leofsig's girlfriend in Gromheort
Hengist	Sidroc's father; Hestan's brother
Hestan	Ealstan and Leofsig's father; Hengist's brother
Leofsig★	Laborer in Gromheort; Ealstan's brother
Oslac	Laborer near Gromheort
Peitavas	Kaunian laborer near Gromheort
Penda	King of Forthweg
Sidroc	Ealstan and Leofsig's cousin in Gromheort
Tamulis	Kaunian apothecary in Oyngestun
Vanai★	Kaunian girl in the village of Oyngestun

Gyongyos

Alpri	Istvan's father
Arpad	Ekrekek (ruler) of Gyongyos
Batthyany	Istvan's great-uncle
Csokonai	Istvan's cousin in Kunhegyes
Fenyes	Soldier in Istvan's squad
Gizella	Istvan's mother
Horthy	Gyongyosian minister to Zuwayza
Istvan★	Sergeant in the Ilszang mountains
Jokai	Sergeant on the island of Obuda
Kanizsai	Trooper in Istvan's squad
Korosi	Villager in Kunhegyes
Kun	Corporal in Istvan's squad; former mage's apprentice
Szonyi	Trooper in Istvan's squad
Tivadar	Captain; Istvan's company commander

Ice People

Abinadab	Follower of Elishamma
Eliphelet	Follower of Elishamma
Elishamma	Tribal chieftain on the austral continent
Gereb	Follower of Elishamma
Hepher	Follower of Elishamma
Machir	Follower of Elishamma
Pathrusim	Scout in Yaninan service

Jelgava

Ausra	Talsu's younger sister
Donalitu	King of Jelgava
Gailisa	Grocer's daughter in Skrunda
Laitsina	Talsu's mother
Talsu	Ex-soldier; tailor's son in Skrunda
Traku	Talsu's father; tailor in Skrunda

Kuusamo

Elimaki	Pekka's sister
Heikki	Pekka's chairman at Kajaani City College
Ilmarinen	Elderly master magician
Joroinen	One of the Seven Princes of Kuusamo
Kuopio	Professor Heikki's secretary
Leino	Mage in Kajaani; Pekka's husband
Louhikko	Mage in the customs service
Olavin	Banker in Kajaani; Elimaki's husband
Parainen	One of the Seven Princes of Kuusamo
Pekka★	Theoretical sorcerer in Kajaani
Rustolainen	One of the Seven Princes of Kuusamo
Siuntio	Elderly master magician
Uto	Pekka and Leino's six-year-old son

Lagoas

Affonso	Second-rank mage on austral continent
Brinco	Grandmaster Pinhiero's secretary
Diniz	Commander aboard the *Implacable*
Fernao★	First-rank mage visiting Kuusamo

Fragoso	Captain of the *Implacable*
Gradasso	Aide to Colonel Lurcanio in Priekule
Junqueiro	Commander of Lagoan forces on austral continent
Peixoto	Colonel in the Ministry of War
Pinhiero	Grandmaster of the Lagoan Guild of Mages
Vitor	King of Lagoas
Xavega	Second-rank mage in Setubal

Sibiu

Barbu	Lumberman on Tirgoviste
Brir.dza	Cornelu and Costache's baby daughter
Bureoistu	King of Sibiu
Cornelu★	Leviathan-rider in Tirgoviste
Costache	Cornelu's wife
Giurgiu	Lumbermen's gang boss on Tirgoviste
Levaditi	Lumberman on Tirgoviste
Vasiliu	Naval officer exiled in Setubal
Vlaicu	Lumberman on Tirgoviste

Unkerlant

Addanz	Archmage of Unkerlant
Alboin	Soldier in Leudast's company
Annore	Garivald's wife
Ansovald	Unkerlanter minister to Zuwayza
Chlodvald	Retired general
Dagulf	Peasant in Zossen; Garivald's friend
Euric	Cavalry colonel
Garivald★	Peasant in Zossen
Hawart	Leudast's regimental commander
Kyot	King Swemmel's twin brother; deceased
Leuba	Garivald's daughter
Leudast★	Corporal in Unkerlanter army
Magnulf	Leudast's sergeant
Merovec	Marshal Rathar's adjutant
Morold	Dowser east of Cottbus
Munderic	Leader of irregulars in Duchy of Grelz
Ortwin	General near the town of Wirdum

Rathar★	Marshal of Unkerlant
Roflanz	Leudast's former regimental commander; deceased
Swemmel	King of Unkerlant
Syrivald	Garivald's son
Vatran	General fighting in the south
Waddo	Firstman in Zossen
Wimar	Sergeant in the western Duchy of Grelz

Valmiera

Bauska	Krasta's maidservant
Dauktu	Peasant and irregular near Pavilosta
Gainibu	King of Valmiera
Gedominu	Peasant and irregular blazed by Algarvians
Krasta★	Marchioness in Priekule; Skarnu's sister
Merkela	Widow to Gedominu; Skarnu's lover
Negyu	Farmer near Pavilosta
Raunu	Skarnu's former sergeant; irregular
Sefanu	Duke of Klaipeda's nephew
Simanu	Count over Pavilosta; the late Enkuru's son
Skarnu★	Captain; irregular against Algarve; Krasta's brother
Valnu	Viscount in Priekule

Yanina

Broumidis	Colonel of dragonfliers on austral continent
Iskakis	Yaninan minister to Zuwayza
Tsavellas	King of Yanina

Zuwayza

Hajjaj★	Zuwayzi foreign minister
Ikhshid	General in the Zuwayzi army
Kolthoum	Hajjaj's senior wife
Lalla	Hajjaj's third wife
Muhassin	Colonel in the Zuwayzi army
Qutuz	Hajjaj's secretary
Shaddad	Hajjaj's former secretary
Shazli	King of Zuwayza
Tewfik	Hajjaj's majordomo

MAP

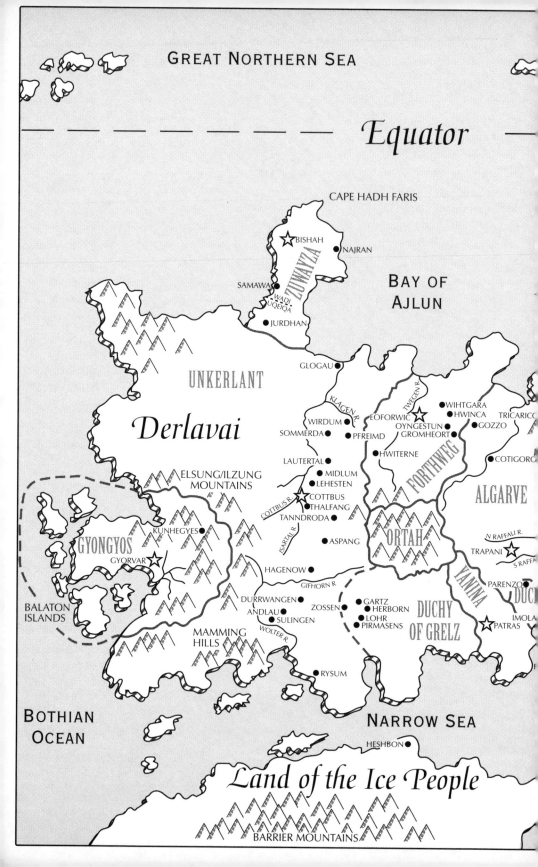

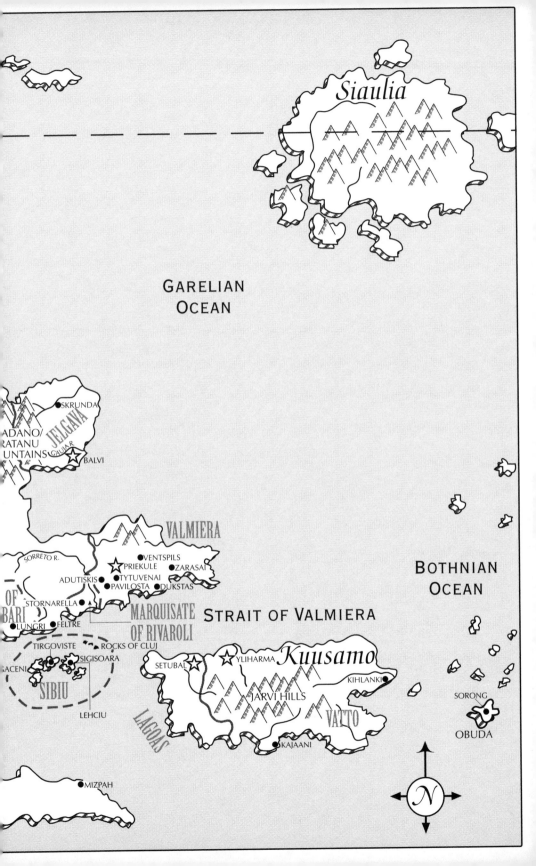

One

Tealdo slogged west across what seemed an endless sea of grass. Every so often, he or his Algarvian comrades would flush a bird from cover. They'd raise their sticks to their shoulders and blaze at it as it fled. They were ready to blaze at anything.

Sometimes they would flush an Unkerlanter from cover. Unlike the birds, the Unkerlanters had a nasty habit of blazing back. The Unkerlanters also had an even nastier habit of staying in cover till a good-sized party of Algarvian soldiers had gone by, and then blazing at them from behind. The ones Tealdo and his comrades caught after stunts like that did not go east into captives' camps, even if they tried to surrender.

"Stubborn whoreson," Sergeant Panfilo said, dragging one such soldier in rock-gray out of his hole once he'd been stalked and slain. His coppery side whiskers and waxed mustachios were sadly draggled. "Don't know what he thought he was doing, but he isn't going to do it any more."

"He wounded two of ours, one of them pretty bad," Tealdo said. "I suppose he figured – or his commanders figured – that's fair exchange." His own mustache and little chin beard, about as red as Panfilo's, could also have used sprucing up. No matter how fastidious you wanted to be, you couldn't stay neat in the field.

From up ahead, Captain Galafrone called, "Come on, you lazy bastards! We've got a long way to go before we can take it easy. Unkerlant isn't much of a kingdom, but it's cursed big."

"And that's the other thing this fellow was doing," Tealdo said, stirring the dead Unkerlanter with his foot: "slowing us down, I mean."

Panfilo swept off his heat and gave Tealdo a sardonic bow. "I thank you for your explanation, my lord Marshal. Or are you perhaps pretending to be the king?"

"Never mind," Tealdo said. Arguing with his sergeant didn't pay. Neither did showing Panfilo up.

They started marching west again, toward a column of smoke that marked a burning village. A young lieutenant with soot streaking his face came up to Galafrone and said, "Sir, will you order in your men to rout out the last of those miserable Unkerlanters in there?"

Galafrone frowned. "I don't much like to do it. I'd sooner leave 'em behind and push on. If we fight for every miserable little village, we'll run out of men before King Swemmel does."

"But if we pass them all by, they'll harass us from behind," the lieutenant said. Then he noticed that Galafrone, while wearing a captain's badges, had none that proclaimed him a noble. The young officer's lip curled. "I don't suppose commoners can be expected to have the spirit to understand such things."

Galafrone knocked him down. When he started to get up, the veteran knocked him down again, and kicked him for good measure. "I don't suppose they teach juniors to respect their superior officers these days," he remarked in conversational tones. "But you've just learned that lesson, haven't you?"

"Sir?" the lieutenant wheezed, and then, "Yes, sir." When he got up again, Galafrone let him. He took a deep breath before resuming, "Sir, you may not care for my tone" – which was, Tealdo judged, a pretty fair understatement – "but the question remains: how can we leave the Unkerlanters behind us?"

"They'll wither on the vine once we pass them by," Galafrone said. "We've got to knock this whole kingdom flat, not fight through it one village at a time."

"If we don't capture the villages, sir" – the young lieutenant was careful now to speak with all due military formality, but did not back away from his own view – "how are we going to knock the kingdom flat?"

Despite the fellow's earlier insolence, Tealdo thought it a decent question. Galafrone didn't hesitate in answering it. Galafrone, as far as Tealdo could see, rarely hesitated about anything. "We've got to smash the big armies," he said. "These little village garrisons are just nuisances, and they'll be bigger nuisances if we let them." He waved to indicate a path around the village. "Come on, men," he called, raising his voice. "We've got to press on."

"Captain," the lieutenant said stiffly, "I must protest, and I shall report your conduct to higher authority."

Galafrone gave him a wave of invitation so elegant, any noble might have envied it. "Go right ahead. If you care to let people know your favorite way to knock down a stone wall is by ramming it with your head, that's your affair." He waved again, this time getting his company moving in the direction he judged best. The lieutenant watched them go, his hands on his hips, the picture of exasperated frustration.

Coming up alongside of Trasone, Tealdo said, "I hope those Unkerlanters don't break out of there and kick us in the arse when we're looking the other way."

"Aye, I can think of things I'd like better," Trasone agreed. He pointed ahead toward a tangled wood of oaks and elms. "I can think of things I like better than heading through that, too. Powers above only know what the Unkerlanters have got lurking in there."

Several unpleasant possibilities crossed Tealdo's mind. Evidently, they crossed Galafrone's mind, too, for the captain ordered a halt. Now he looked unhappy. "They could have a whole regiment in among those trees," he said. "I don't care to bypass them, not even a little I don't." His face grew longer still. "Maybe that cursed lieutenant wasn't as stupid as I thought."

Now Tealdo did see him have trouble making up his mind. Before he could give any orders, a man emerged from the woods. Tealdo threw himself flat and had his stick aimed, ready to send a beam at the fellow, before noticing he wore tunic and kilt of light brown – Algarvian uniform – not an Unkerlanter's rock-gray long tunic.

"It's all right," the soldier called in Algarvian with a northwestern accent much like Tealdo's. "They threw us out of here day before yesterday, but not for long. A few of the whoresons may still be running around loose off the paths, but you shouldn't have any trouble getting through."

"That sounds good enough," Galafrone said. He waved his company forward. "Let's go! The sooner we're through, the sooner we can hit the Unkerlanters another lick."

Tealdo rapidly discovered the Algarvian soldier who'd told him the woods were mostly clear of Unkerlanters was a born optimist. Some paths through the woods were clear. The Algarvians already in among the trees kept those paths clear by posting guards along them. One of the guards called, "You go off the road to squat in the bushes, you're liable to get blazed or get your throat cut or have something worse happen to you."

"Who does hold these stinking woods, then?" Tealdo called back.

"Wherever we are, we hold," the guard answered. "Eventually, they'll run out of food and they'll run out of charges for their sticks. Then they'll either surrender or try and pretend they were peasants all along. In the meantime, they're a cursed nuisance."

Galafrone swore. "Aye, maybe that lieutenant did have a point." A moment later, though, he snorted and added, "Besides the one on top of his head, I mean. Thought he was a noble, so his shit didn't stink." He turned back to his men. "Hurry along, you chuckleheads, hurry along. Got to keep moving."

"Got to keep moving is right," Trasone grumbled. "Sounds like we're nothing but targets if we don't."

They turned out to be targets even when they did keep moving. A beam slammed into the trunk of an oak in front of Tealdo. Steam hissed out of the hole charred in the living wood. It would have hissed out of a hole charred in his living flesh the same way.

He threw himself off the track and behind a log. Somewhere behind him, a comrade was screaming. Off to the other side of the path, the Unkerlanters were shouting: hoarse cries of "Urra! Urra!" and King Swemmel's name repeated again and again. More beams hissed through the air above Tealdo's head, giving it the smell it had just after lightning struck.

From behind a nearby bush, Trasone called, "I'm sure glad we cleared the whoresons out of these woods. They must have been standing on each other's shoulders in here before we came through and did it."

"Oh, aye." Tealdo hunkered down lower behind his log as the shouting on the other side of the path got louder. "And now they're going to try and throw us out again."

Still shouting "Urra!", Unkerlanters swarmed across the path. Tealdo blazed one down, but then had to scramble back frantically to keep from being cut off and surrounded. All at once, he understood how the Forthwegians and Sibians and Valmierans and Jelgavans – aye, and the Unkerlanters, too – must have felt when King Mezentio's armies struck them. He would sooner have done without the lesson.

Mezentio and the Algarvian generals had outplanned their foes as well as beaten them on the battlefield. The Unkerlanters here in this stretch of wood showed no such inspired generalship. All they had were numbers and ferocity. Tealdo tripped over a root and fell headlong. Those were liable to be enough.

"Rally by squads!" Captain Galafrone shouted, somewhere not too far away.

"To me! To me!" That was Sergeant Panfilo. Never had his raucous voice seemed so welcome to Tealdo.

As Tealdo made his way toward Panfilo, Galafrone shouted again, this time for his crystallomancer. Tealdo's lips skinned back from his teeth. One way or another, the Unkerlanters were going to catch it.

He only hoped he didn't catch it first. Along with Trasone, he found Sergeant Panfilo. They all had to keep falling back, though, ever deeper among the trees. Tealdo began to wonder if they would run into still more Unkerlanters there. He would hear cries of "Urra!" and "Swemmel!" in his nightmares as long as he lived. He hoped he lived long enough to have nightmares.

He cheered when eggs started falling among the Unkerlanters who'd broken the Algarvian grip on the path. He cheered again when shouts of "Mezentio!" rang out from the east, and yet again when the Unkerlanters started yelling in dismay rather than in fury.

As Algarvian reinforcements struck the Unkerlanters, the pressure on Galafrone's company eased. "Powers above be praised for crystallo-mancers," Panfilo said, wiping sweat from his face.

"Aye." Tealdo and Trasone spoke together. Trasone went on, "Say whatever you want about these cursed Unkerlanters, but going up against them isn't like fighting the Jelgavans or the Valmierans. We'll lick 'em, aye, but they don't know they're licked yet, if you know what I mean."

"That's the truth." Tealdo turned around, still nervous lest some Unkerlanters come at him from behind. "Uh-oh." He caught a glimpse of light brown kilt behind a bush. By the way the Algarvian soldier lay, Tealdo knew the fellow had to be dead. He looked around, but all his companions – all the men who'd rallied to Sergeant Panfilo – were still standing. He took a few steps forward, then stopped in his tracks.

Panfilo and Trasone followed him. Trasone gulped. "Powers above," Panfilo said softly.

The Algarvians, half a dozen of them, looked to have been dead for a couple of days. Maybe they'd been caught in the earlier Unkerlanter counterattack in the woods. The guard on the path had had the right of it. They hadn't been blazed. They hadn't had their throats cut. They'd been gruesomely and systematically mutilated. Most of them had their kilts hiked up. What the Unkerlanters had done down there . . .

In a sick voice, Trasone said, "We haven't fought a war like this for a long time."

"Well, we are now," Tealdo said grimly. "I don't think I want to be taken alive, doesn't look like. If I can't find some way to kill myself, I'd sooner have a friend do it than go through . . . that." One by one, the other Algarvians nodded.

Waddo strode out into the middle of Zossen's village square. Garivald, watching from the edge of the square, found the stocky village firstman's walk curious: half the limping swagger he usually used, half a nervous, almost slinking step, as if Waddo also feared the pride he so often displayed.

Garivald, for once, felt a certain sympathy for the firstman. Waddo had been reporting the iniquities of the Algarvians, all of them lovingly detailed on the crystal that had recently come to the Unkerlanter village. Like everyone else in Zossen, Garivald had expected the next bombastic announcement would be of the Unkerlanter invasion of Algarvian-occupied Forthweg, and probably of Yanina as well. Instead, a few days before, the crystal announced that the Algarvians had without warning attacked Unkerlanter forces engaged in no warlike activity. A palace spokesman had declared that the Algarvians would be beaten. He had not said how.

Since then, silence.

Silence till now, silence that let fear build, especially among the older villagers who remembered how the Algarvians had hammered Unkerlant during the Six Years' War thirty years before. Gossip and rumor filled Zossen – and doubtless filled every other peasant village throughout the vast length and breadth of Unkerlant. Garivald had taken part, cautiously, with people he trusted. "If things were going well," he'd said to Dagulf, "Cottbus would be shouting its head off. It's not. That means things can't be going well."

"Makes sense to me," scar-faced Dagulf had said, also cautiously, looking over his shoulder to make sure no one, not even his wife, could overhear.

Now Waddo stood in the center of the square, waiting to be noticed. He struck a pose that guaranteed he would be noticed. "My friends," he said in a loud voice. A couple of people looked his way, but only a couple; he didn't seem to have a lot of friends in the village. Then he spoke again, even louder: "People of Zossen, I have an important announcement. In one hour's time, I shall bring our precious crystal from my home to the square here, so that you may listen to an address by our famous, glorious, and illustrious sovereign. His Majesty King Swemmel will speak to you on the state of our war against the barbarous savages of Algarve."

Off he went, trying to look important. He had a right to look important: through *his* crystal, the king would speak to the village. Garivald had never imagined such a thing. If he got close enough to the crystal, he might actually see King Swemmel, though the King would not see him.

That was exciting. But, try as Waddo would to walk with the best swagger he could with his bad leg, that nasty, slinking hint of fear stayed in his step. It had nothing to do with the limp, either. Garivald didn't like it. If Waddo was afraid, he probably had good reason to be afraid. Garivald wondered what the firstman had heard on the crystal and then kept to himself.

Whatever it was, Garivald couldn't do anything about it. He hurried back to his own house to tell Annore and Syrivald the astonishing news. "The king?" his wife said, her dark eyes going wide. Like Garivald, like most Unkerlanters, she was solid and swarthy, with a proud nose. She repeated herself, as if she couldn't believe it: "King Swemmel will talk to our village?"

"Powers above," Syrivald added around a crust of black bread. Leuba, a toddler chewing on another crust, was too little to care whether Swemmel spoke to Zossen or not.

"I think he's going to be talking to the whole kingdom," Garivald said, "or to as many places as have crystals, anyhow."

"Will we go see him?" Syrivald asked.

"Aye, we will," his father answered. "I want to find out what the truth is about this miserable war we've got ourselves into with Algarve." After he'd spoken, he paused to wonder how much of the truth King Swemmel was likely to tell.

Annore said, "If we're going to go, we'd better go now, so we can get up close to the crystal." Suiting action to word, she scooped up Leuba and carried the toddler out of the house. Garivald and Syrivald followed.

They weren't the only family with the same idea. The square got as crowded as Garivald ever remembered seeing it, and then a little more crowded than that. Not everyone in Zossen had heard Waddo's announcement, but no one could miss friends and neighbors and relatives heading for the square. People jockeyed for position, stepped on one another's toes, and loosed a few judicious elbows. Garivald caught one, but he gave it back with interest.

"I don't know what we're squabbling about," somebody said. "Waddo's not even here with the crystal yet." That comment produced a brief, embarrassed pause in the pushing and shoving, but they soon resumed.

"Here he comes!" Three people said it at once. Everybody surged toward Waddo, who carried the crystal on a cushion whose cover his wife had embroidered. "Make way!" That was three different people.

Waddo hadn't had such an eager, enthusiastic reception since . . . Thinking back on it, Garivald couldn't remember the firstman ever getting such a reception. But, of course, it wasn't really for him; it was for the crystal he bore.

"Don't drop it!" someone told him.

"Set it on a stool," someone else said. "That way, more of us will have a chance to see."

Waddo took that suggestion, though he ignored the other one. "It won't be more than a few minutes before his Majesty speaks to us," he said. "He will set our minds at rest about the many things that trouble us."

Garivald doubted whether Swemmel would do any such thing. But he shouldered his way through the crowd till he stood in the second row and could peer at the crystal over the shoulders of the people in front of him. Inactive at the moment, the crystal might as well have been an ordinary ball of glass.

Then, abruptly, it . . . changed. Garivald had heard stories of crystals in use, of course, but he'd never seen one work till now. First, light suffused it. Then, as the brief glow faded, he saw King Swemmel's long, pale, narrow face looking at him. By the other villagers' exclamations, they all saw the king looking at them, too, even though they surrounded the crystal. After the magic that made the crystal work, Garivald supposed the one that let it be viewed from any direction was a small thing by comparison. It impressed him just the same.

Swemmel stared out as if he really could see the peasants gaping at him from one end of the kingdom to the other. After Garivald's first astonishment and almost involuntary awe faded, he saw how haggard the king looked. Beside him, Annore murmured, "I don't think he's slept for days."

"Probably not since the war started," Garivald agreed. Then he fell silent, for King Swemmel had begun to speak.

"Brothers and sisters, peasants and townsmen, soldiers and sailors – I am speaking to you, my friends," Swemmel said, and Garivald was astonished yet again: he had never imagined that the king would address his subjects in such terms. Swemmel went on, now with the first-person plural instead of that astonishing, riveting first-person singular: "We are invaded. The vile hosts of King Mezentio have plunged their dagger deep into us, and Algarve's dogs, Yanina and Zuwayza, course behind their master. The enemy has stolen much of that part of Forthweg which we reclaimed for our kingdom summer before last. Our own long-held territory farther south also groans under the foe's heels."

Swemmel took a very visible breath. "But we must also tell you that only on our territory have the Algarvians, for the first time, met with serious resistance. If a part of that territory has nevertheless been occupied, let that serve as nothing more than a goad to our recovering it. The Algarvians, may the powers below eat them, caught Unkerlant by surprise. Let all Unkerlanters now take the accursed redheads by surprise as well."

Garivald raised an eyebrow at that. He thought King Swemmel had been getting ready for a war with Algarve. But Swemmel, after sipping from a crystal goblet of water or pale wine, was continuing: "Our kingdom has entered into a life-and-death struggle against its most wicked and perfidious foe. Our soldiers are fighting heroically against heavy odds against an enemy heavily armed with behemoths and dragons. The main force of the Unkerlanter army, with thousands of behemoths and dragons of its own, is now entering the battle. Together with our army, the whole of our people must rise to defend our kingdom.

"The enemy is cruel and ruthless. He aims at grabbing our land, our wheat, our power points and cinnabar. He wants to restore the exiled followers of Kyot the usurper, and through them to turn the people of Unkerlant into the slaves of Algarvian princes and viscounts.

"There should be no room in our ranks for whimperers and cowards, for deserters and panic-spreaders. Our people must be fearless and fight selflessly for Unkerlant. The whole kingdom now is and must be for the service of the army. We must fight for every inch of Unkerlanter soil, fight to the last drop of blood for our villages and towns. Wherever the army may be forced to retreat, all ley-line caravan cars must be taken away and the lines wrecked. The enemy must be left not a pound of bread nor an ounce of cinnabar. Peasants must drive away their livestock and hand over their grain to our inspectors to keep it out of the Algarvians' hands. All valuable property that cannot be moved must be destroyed.

"Friends, our forces are immeasurably large. The insolent enemy must soon become aware of this. Together with our army, our peasants and our laborers must also go to war against the treacherous Mezentio. All the strength of Unkerlant must be used to smash the foe. Victory will be ours. Onward!"

King Swemmel's image faded from the crystal. Light filled it again for a moment. Then it was, or seemed to be, simply a round lump of glass once more. Garivald shook himself, like a man awakening from a deep, dream-filled sleep. Instead of seeing the whole kingdom, as Swemmel had made him do, he was back in tiny Zossen, filled with the village he'd known all his life.

"That was a great speech," Waddo said, his eyes shining. "For the king to call us his friends . . ."

"Aye, he sounded strong," Garivald agreed. "He sounded brave."

"He did indeed." That was Dagulf, who had no great use for the king.

Neither did Garivald. Neither, so far as he knew, did anyone in the village, save possibly Waddo. Even so, he said, "I may fear Swemmel more than I love him, but I think the redheads will come to fear him, too."

"He is what the kingdom needs right now," Annore said.

"We will fight them," Waddo said, sounding very fierce for a heavy man with a bad ankle. "We will fight them, and we will beat them."

"And once we have beaten them, we will make songs about it." That was Annore again. She glanced over toward her husband in confident anticipation.

No song rose up in Garivald right at the moment. He began sifting words in his mind, looking for rhymes, looking for smooth flows from one thought to the next. He frowned. "I don't know enough yet to make any songs."

"Nor shall you learn," Waddo said, "for surely our brave warriors and fliers shall drive back the Algarvians long before they enter Zossen." He looked toward the east with complete certainty.

"So may it be," Garivald said from the bottom of his heart.

Unlike so many Zuwayzin, Hajjaj was not fond of the desert for its own sake. He was a city man, most at home in Bishah or in the capitals of the other kingdoms of the continent of Derlavai. And he loathed camels with a loathing both deep and passionate, a loathing based on more experience than he cared to remember. Riding on camelback through the desert, then, should have been nothing but ennui and discomfort.

Instead, he found himself smiling from ear to ear as he rode along. This waste of thornbushes and sand and yellow stone had been seized by Unkerlant more than a year before. Now it was back in Zuwayzi hands, where the Treaty of Bludenz said it belonged – not that King Swemmel had paid any attention to the treaty when he invaded Zuwayza. That made it worth seeing, worth riding through, even if it was full of scorpions and lizards and bat-eared foxes just like any other stretch of desert.

Hajjaj's escort, a colonel named Muhassin, pointed to corpses from which vultures and ravens reluctantly flew as the camels ambled past them. "Here, your Excellency, the Unkerlanters made a stand. They fought bravely, but that did not save them."

"They *are* brave," Hajjaj said. "They are mostly ignorant, and ruled by a king half a madman, but they are brave."

Muhassin adjusted his hat, which bore four silver bars – one broad, with three narrow ones beneath it – to show his rank. Zuwayzi officers had trouble making themselves as impressive as did their counterparts in other kingdoms, being limited to their headgear as an area for display: like Hajjaj, Muhassin wore hat and sandals and nothing else covering the brown skin between the one and the others. "They are dead now," Muhassin said, "dead or fled or captured."

"It is good," Hajjaj said, and the colonel nodded. The Zuwayzi foreign minister stroked his neat white beard, then went on, "Do I understand correctly that they were not here in great strength?"

"Aye, your Excellency," Muhassin replied. "Of course, they are somewhat occupied elsewhere. Otherwise, I have no doubt, we should not have enjoyed such an easy time of it."

"Powers above be praised that we did catch them unprepared to fight back hard," Hajjaj said. "Perhaps they did not believe everything Shaddad told them. My own secretary! Powers below eat the traitor! I had a scorpion in my own sandal there, and did not know it. But he did less harm than he might have."

"Perhaps it did not matter so much whether they believed him or not," Muhassin said. Hajjaj raised an eyebrow. The broad brim of his hat kept Muhassin from seeing that, but the colonel explained himself anyway: "If you were about to fight Algarve and Zuwayza at the same time, where would you place most of your warriors?"

Hajjaj considered that for a moment, then chuckled wryly. "I don't suppose King Swemmel crouches under his throne from fear of our parading through the streets of Cottbus on these ugly, mangy, ungainly brutes." He patted the side of his camel's neck with what looked something like affection.

Muhassin stroked his camel with what was obviously the genuine article. "Don't listen to him, Sunbeam," he crooned. "Everyone knows you're not mangy." The camel rewarded that limited endorsement by twisting around and trying to bite his knee. He smacked it in the nose. It let out a noise like a bagpipe being horribly murdered. Hajjaj threw back his head and laughed. Muhassin gave him a wounded look.

A column of glum-looking Unkerlanters came toward them. Naked Zuwayzi soldiers herded the men in rock-gray along. The Zuwayzin were in high spirits, singing and joking about the victories they'd won. They also made comments their captives were lucky they could not understand.

"Stop them for a moment, Colonel, if you'd be so kind," Hajjaj murmured to Muhassin. The officer called orders. The captives' guards shouted in broken Unkerlanter. The light-skinned men halted. In Algarvian, Hajjaj asked, "Does anyone speak this language?"

"I do, sir," an Unkerlanter said, stepping forward.

"Don't you wish your kingdom would have let mine alone?" Hajjaj asked him.

"I don't know anything about that, sir," the captive said, bowing low as he would have to one of his own nobles. "All I know is, they told me to come up here and do my best, and that's what I tried to do. Only trouble is, it didn't turn out to be good enough." He looked warily at Hajjaj. "You won't eat me, will you, sir?"

"Is that what they tell you Zuwayzin are like?" Hajjaj asked, and the Unkerlanter nodded. Hajjaj sighed sadly. "You don't look very appetizing, so I think I'll be able to do without." He turned to Muhassin. "Did you follow that?"

"Aye, I did," Muhassin answered in Zuwayzi. "He's no fool. He speaks Algarvian well – a better accent than I have myself, as a matter of fact. But he doesn't know anything about us." He chuckled in grim anticipation. "Well, he'll have his chance to find out."

"So he will. There's always work to be done in the mines." Hajjaj gestured to the column of captives. "They may go on now."

Muhassin spoke to the guards. The guards shouted at the captives. The captives shambled forward again. Muhassin turned back to Hajjaj. "And now, your Excellency, shall we go on toward the old frontier, the frontier we are restoring?"

"By all means, Colonel," the foreign minister said. His camel wasn't so interested in going on, but he managed to persuade it.

"Here and there, we're already in position to cross the old frontier," Muhassin said. As if to underscore his words, a squadron of dragons flew by overhead, going south. Muhassin pointed to them. "We couldn't have come so far so fast without help from the Algarvians. Unkerlant hasn't got but a few dragons up here in the north country."

"Cross the old frontier?" Hajjaj frowned. "Has King Shazli authorized the army to invade Unkerlant itself? I had not heard of any such order." He wondered if Shazli had given the order but not told him for fear of angering or alarming him. That would have been courteous of the king

– courteous, aye, but also, in Hajjaj's view, deadly dangerous.

To his vast relief, Muhassin shook his head. "No, your Excellency: as yet, we have received no such orders. I merely meant to inform you that we have the ability, should the orders come. A fair number of folk south of the old frontier – and east of it, too – have dark skins." He ran a dark finger along his own arm.

"That is so," the foreign minister agreed. "Still, if a small kingdom can take back what rightfully belongs to it, it should count itself lucky, the more so in these days when great kingdoms are so mighty. We would need something of a miracle to come away with more than we had at the beginning."

"It is with feuds among kingdoms as it is with feuds among clans," Muhassin replied. "A small clan with strong friends may come out on top of a large one whose neighbors all hate it."

"What you say is true, but the small clan often ends up becoming the client of the clan that befriended it," Hajjaj said. "I do not want us to become Algarve's clients, any more than I wanted us to be Unkerlant's clients back in the days before the Six Years' War, when Zuwayza was ruled from Cottbus."

"No man loves this kingdom more than you, your Excellency, and no one has served her better," Colonel Muhassin said, by which flowery introduction Hajjaj knew the colonel was about to contradict him. Sure enough, Muhassin went on, "We have had the accursed Unkerlanters on our southern border for centuries. Our frontier does not march with Algarve, and so we have less to fear from King Mezentio than from King Swemmel. Is this not your own view as well?"

"It is, and Mezentio is a far more sensible sovereign on his worst day than Swemmel on his best," Hajjaj said, which made the colonel laugh. But the Zuwayzi foreign minister continued, "If the war goes on as it has been going, would you not say our frontier is liable to march with Algarve's before long?"

"Hmm." Now the corners of Muhassin's mouth turned down. "Something to that, I shouldn't wonder. The Algarvians are moving west at a powerful clip, aren't they? Still and all, they'll make better neighbors than Unkerlanters ever did. Aye, they wear clothes, but they have some notion of honor."

Hajjaj chuckled under his breath. It wasn't that Muhassin was wrong.

It was just that what the Zuwayzin and the Algarvians had in common was a long tradition of fighting their neighbors when those neighbors were weak and fighting among themselves when their neighbors were strong. It wasn't that the Unkerlanters didn't fight; they did. Zuwayza would not have been free but for the Unkerlanters' Twinkings War, when both Swemmel and his brother Kyot claimed to be the elder, and so deserving of the throne. But Unkerlanters did not fight for the sport of it, as both Zuwayzin and Algarvians were wont to do.

"Come on, your Excellency," Muhassin said. "The encampment is over that rise there." He pointed and then booted his camel back into motion. The beast's complaints at having to work once more sounded as if it had been given over to the King of Jelgava's torturers. Hajjaj also got his camel going again. It too sounded martyred. He had little sympathy for it. Though descended from nomads, he greatly preferred ley-line caravans to obstreperous animals.

But the Zuwayzin had done their best to sabotage the ley lines as the Unkerlanters drove northward. King Swemmel's sorcerers had repaired some of the lines, only to sabotage them in turn when the Zuwayzin began pushing south once more. These days, naked black mages worked to undo what Swemmel's wizards had done. Nobody could sabotage a camel; the powers above had already taken care of that. However revolting the beasts were, though, Hajjaj would rather have gone by camel's back than by shank's mare.

At the encampment, a comfortable tent and a great flagon of date wine awaited him. He drank it down almost in one long draught. In Algarve, he'd learned to appreciate fine vintages. Next to them, this stuff was cloying, sticky-sweet. He didn't care. He always drank it without complaint whenever it was served to him in Zuwayza, as it often was. It put him in mind of clan gatherings when he was a child. Visiting Algarvians might turn up their noses at the stuff, but he was no visiting Algarvian. To him, it was a taste of home.

Colonel Muhassin's superior, General Ikhshid, greeted Hajjaj after he had begun to refresh himself. The general gave him more date wine, and tea fragrant with mint, and little cakes almost as good as he could have had in the royal palace. Hajjaj enjoyed the leisurely rituals of hospitality for the same reason he enjoyed the date wine: lifelong familiarity.

Ikhshid was not far from Hajjaj's age, and quite a bit paunchier, but seemed vigorous enough. "We drive them, your Excellency," he said when small talk was at last set aside. "We drive them. The Algarvians drive them. Down in the south, even the Yaninans drive them, which I would not have reckoned possible. Swemmel heads up a beaten kingdom, and I am not the least bit sorry."

"Few in Zuwayza would sorrow to see Unkerlant beaten," Hajjaj said, and then, meditatively, "I would like our allies better if they ruled less harshly the lands they have conquered. Of course, I would like the Unkerlanters better if they were less harsh, too."

"When you have to choose between whoresons, you choose the ones who'll give you more of what you want," Ikhshid said, a comment close in spirit to Muhassin's.

"That is indeed what we have done," Hajjaj said. He looked toward the east, the direction from which the Algarvians were advancing. Then he looked toward the south, the direction in which the Unkerlanters were retreating. He sighed. "The most we can hope for is that we have made the right choice."

When the ley-line caravan in which Fernao was traveling reached the border between Lagoas and Kuusamo, it glided to a halt. Kuusaman customs agents swarmed aboard to inspect all the passengers and all their belongings. "What's this in aid of?" Fernao asked when his turn came, which did not take long.

"A precaution," the flat-faced little inspector answered, which was more polite than *None of your cursed business* but no more informative. "Please open all your bags." That too was more polite than a barked order, but left the Lagoan sorcerer no more room to disobey. When the Kuusaman customs agent came upon the letter of introduction from Grandmaster Pinhiero to Siuntio, he stiffened.

"Something wrong?" Fernao asked with an inward groan; he'd hoped the letter would save him trouble, not cause it.

"I don't know," the Kuusaman answered. He raised his voice: "Over here, Louhikko! I've got a mage."

Louhikko proved to be a mage himself: probably, if Fernao was any judge, of the second rank. The spells he used to examine Fernao's baggage, though, had been devised by sorcerers more potent than he. He spoke to the inspector in their own language, then nodded to Fernao and left.

"He says you have nothing untoward," the customs agent told Fernao. He sounded reluctant to admit it, and demanded, "Why do you come to see one of our mages? Answer at once; don't pause to make up lies."

Fernao stared at him. "Is this Kuusamo or Unkerlant?" he asked, not altogether in jest: such sharp questions were most unlike the usually easygoing Kuusamans. "I've come to consult with your illustrious mage on matters of professional interest to both of us."

"There is a war on," the Kuusaman snapped.

"True, but Kuusamo and Lagoas are not enemies," Fernao said.

"Neither are we allies," the customs agent said, which was also true. He glowered at Fernao, who made a point of staying in his seat: a lot of Kuusamans did not care to be reminded that they ran half a head shorter than Lagoans. Muttering something in his own language under his breath, the Kuusaman went on to search the belongings of the woman in the seat behind Fernao.

The inspection held up the caravan for three hours. One luckless fellow in Fernao's car got thrown off. The Kuusamans paid no attention to his howls of protest. Only after they got him out of the car and on to the ground did one of them say, "Be thankful we didn't take you on to Yliharma. You'd like that a lot less, believe me." The ousted man shut up with a snap.

At last, the ley-line caravan got moving again. It glided across the snow-covered landscape. The forests and hills and fields of Kuusamo were very little different from those of Lagoas. Nor should they have been, not when the kingdom and the land of the Seven Princes shared the same island. The towns in which the caravan stopped might for the most part have been Lagoan towns as readily as Kuusaman. For the past hundred years and more, public buildings and places of business had looked much alike in the two realms.

But, when the caravan slid past villages and most of all when it slid past farms, Fernao was conscious of no longer traveling through his own kingdom. Even the haystacks were different. The Kuusamans topped theirs with cloths they sometimes embroidered, so the stacks looked like old, stooped grannies with scarves on their heads.

And the farmhouses, or some of them, struck Fernao as odd. Before the soldiers and settlers of the Kaunian Empire crossed the Strait of Valmiera, the Kuusamans had been nomads, herders. They'd learned farming fast, but to this day, more than fifteen hundred years later, some of their buildings, though made from wood and stone, were still in the shape of the tents in which they had once dwelt.

The day was dying when the ley-line caravan pulled into the capital of Kuusamo. As Fernao used a little wooden staircase to descend from the floating car to the floor of the Yliharma depot, he looked around in the hope that Siuntio would meet him and greet him; he'd written ahead to let the famous theoretical sorcerer know he was coming. But he did not see Siuntio. After a moment, though, he did spot another mage he recognized from sorcerous conclaves on the island and in the west of Derlavai.

He waved. "Master Ilmarinen!" he called.

Ilmarinen, he knew, spoke fluent and frequently profane Lagoan. Here this evening, though, the theoretical sorcerer chose to address him in classical Kaunian, *the* language of magecraft and scholarship: "You have come a long way to accomplish little, Master Fernao." He did not sound sorry to say that. He sounded wryly amused.

Ignoring his tone, Fernao asked, "And why is that?" If Ilmarinen told him the reason he was bound to fail, perhaps he wouldn't.

But Ilmarinen did no such thing. He came up and waggled a forefinger under Fernao's nose. "Because you will not find anyone here who knows anything, or who will tell you if he does. And so, you may as well turn around and go back to Setubal." He waved a mocking goodbye.

"Can't I eat supper first?" Fernao asked mildly. "I'd gladly have you as my guest in whatever eatery you choose."

"Going to quibble about everything, are you?" Ilmarinen returned. But, for the first time, he seemed amused with Fernao rather than amused at him. Stooping, he picked up one of the bags at the Lagoan mage's feet. "That may possibly be arranged. Suppose you come with me." And off he went. Fernao grabbed the other bag, slipped its carrying strap over his shoulder, and followed.

He had to step smartly; Ilmarinen proved a spry old man. For a moment, Fernao wondered if the Kuusaman was trying to lose him and make off with the bag – it was the one in which he'd brought what little sorcerous apparatus he had. He didn't think Ilmarinen could learn much from the stuff, but Ilmarinen wouldn't be able to know – he didn't think Ilmarinen would be able to know – that in advance.

As they were leaving the large, crowded depot, the Kuusaman

theoretical sorcerer looked back, saw Fernao right behind him, and said over his shoulder, "Haven't managed to make you disappear, eh?" Was he grinning because he was joking or to hide disappointment? Fernao couldn't tell. He didn't think Ilmarinen wanted him to be able to tell.

Fernao looked around. Yliharma wasn't one of the great cities of the world, as Setubal was, but it stood in the second rank. Buildings towered ten, some even fifteen, stories into the air. People dressed in almost as many different styles as they would have been in Setubal crowded the streets. They hurried into and out of fancy shops, sometimes emerging with packages.

As most Kuusaman towns did to Fernao, it all looked very homelike – except that he could not read any of the signs. He spoke Sibian and Algarvian, Forthwegian and classical Kaunian. He could make a fair stab at Valmieran. The language of the principality next door to his own kingdom, though, remained a closed book.

"Here," Ilmarinen said, still in Kaunian, after they'd walked a couple of blocks. "This place isn't too bad." The words on the sign hanging above the eatery were unintelligible to Fernao. The picture, though, made him smile: it showed seven reindeer in princely coronets, sitting around a table groaning with food. He followed Ilmarinen inside.

In Priekule, the capital of Valmiera, the waiter would have fawned on his customers. In Setubal, Fernao's home town, he would have been more stiffly servile. Here, he might have been Ilmarinen's cousin. He addressed Fernao in singsong Kuusaman, a mistake made all the more natural by Fernao's narrow, slanted eyes – Lagoans, though primarily of Algarvic stock, had some Kuusaman blood in them, too. Fernao spread his hands. "I'm sorry," he said in Lagoan. "I don't speak your language."

"Ah. That makes you easier to gouge," the waiter answered, also in Lagoan. His grin, like Ilmarinen's, might have meant he was joking. On the other hand, it might not have, too.

The menu also turned out to be incomprehensible Kuusaman. "Three specialties here," Ilmarinen said, now deigning to speak Lagoan himself. "Salmon, mutton, or reindeer. You can't go too far wrong with any of them."

"Salmon will do nicely, thanks," Fernao answered. "When I was in the land of the Ice People, I ate enough strange things to put me off them for a while."

"Reindeer is better than camel, but have it as you will," Ilmarinen answered. "I'm going for the mutton chop myself. Everyone calls me an old goat, and this is as close to eating my namesake as I can come without horrifying the Gyongyosians." He waved to the waiter and ordered for both of them in Kuusaman. "Ale suit you?" he asked Fernao, who nodded. Ilmarinen turned back to the waiter, who also nodded and went off.

Fernao said, "I shouldn't think offending the Gyongyosians would worry you, not when Kuusamo is fighting them."

"Because we're fighting them, they're too easy a target," Ilmarinen replied, which made an odd kind of sense to Fernao. The waiter returned with a large pitcher of ale and two earthenware mugs. He poured each one full, then left again.

"Good," Fernao said after a sip. He looked across the table at Ilmarinen. "It struck me as odd that none of the top theoretical sorcerers in Kuusamo has published anything lately. It struck Grandmaster Pinhiero as odd, too, when I pointed it out to him."

"I've known Pinhiero for forty years," Ilmarinen said, "and he's so odd himself, it's the normal that looks strange to him." He studied Fernao. "I'm too polite to explain what that says about you."

"No, you're not," Fernao said, and Ilmarinen laughed out loud. After another sip of ale, Fernao went on, "And I had expected to see Master Siuntio, not you."

"He sent me," Ilmarinen answered. "He said I was better at being rude than he was. Bugger me if I know what he meant." His chuckle displayed uneven yellow teeth.

"Why would you want to be rude to me?" Fernao asked.

"That's just it – I don't need a reason, and Siuntio would." Ilmarinen's eyes lit up. "And here's supper." For a while, he and Fernao paid attention to little else. Fernao's salmon steak was moist and pink and flavorful. He did not enjoy it so much as he might have, though, for he'd become convinced he wasn't going to learn anything on this journey. He'd also become convinced there were things he badly needed to learn.

"More ale?" he asked Ilmarinen, hefting the pitcher.

"Oh, aye," the Kuusaman mage answered, "though you'll not get me drunk." Fernao's ears burned, but he poured anyway.

"What would happen if I ignored you and did go to see Siuntio?" he asked.

Ilmarinen shrugged. "You'd end up buying him supper, too. You'd be even less likely to make him drunk than you are me – I enjoy it every now and again, but he's an old sobersides. And you still wouldn't find out anything. He'd tell you there's nothing to find out, the same as I'm telling you now."

"Curse you both for lying," Fernao flared.

"If Pinhiero's curses won't stick to me – and they won't – I'm not going to worry about yours, lad," Ilmarinen answered. "And I say I am not lying. Your own research will prove the truth of it, as the exception proves the rule."

"What sort of research?" Fernao asked.

Ilmarinen only smiled again, and said not a word.

These days, Vanai feared every knock at the door. Most Kaunians in Forthweg did, and had reason to. She had more reasons, far more, than most. Major Spinello had kept his part of the bargain: her grandfather no longer went out to labor on the roads. And she had to keep her part of the bargain, too, whenever the Algarvian officer chose. For Brivibas' sake, she did.

It no longer hurt, as it had the first time. Spinello was not cruel that particular way. In fact, he kept trying to please her. He would caress her for what seemed like forever before doing what he wanted. She never kindled. She never came close to kindling. She despised him far too much for that. Even resignation wasn't easy, though at last she managed it.

Instead of by wounding her in the bedchamber, Spinello took his nasty pleasure by ostentatiously leading her to that chamber and closing the door in Brivibas' face. He didn't bother barring it. Once, in a transport of impotent fury, Brivibas had burst in. "Come to watch, have you?" Spinello asked coolly, not missing a stroke. Vanai's grandfather reeled away as if blazed through the heart.

It was after Major Spinello left that the fights would start. "Better you should have let me die than to do such a thing!" Brivibas would shout. Vanai knew he meant it, too, which was twisting the knife.

She always answered the same way: "In a while, this will be over. If you died, my grandfather, that would be forever, and I could not bear it."

"But how does this make me look?" Brivibas cried one day. "Preserved alive because my granddaughter gives herself to an Algarvian barbarian? How am I to hold my head up in the village?"

He spoke in terms of himself, not in terms of Vanai. His selfishness infuriated her. She said, "I have not been able to hold my head up in Oyngestun since you first grew friendly toward the Algarvian barbarian – which is not what you called him when he began meeting with you – *how* he admired your scholarship! I shared your shame then. If you share mine now, is it not part of the bargain you made?"

Brivibas stared at her. For a moment, she thought she'd made him see things through her eyes. But then he said, "How, after this, will I be able to make a proper marriage alliance for you?"

"How, after this, do you think I would ever want another man to touch me?" Vanai retorted, at which her grandfather flinched and retreated to the safety of his study. Vanai glared after him. He hadn't thought about how she might feel about being married, only about the difficulties her behavior might cause him. A poisonous thought sprouted in her mind, tempting and lethal as a death-cap mushroom: *I should have let him labor till he dropped.*

She shook her head violently. If she blamed him for thinking only of himself, how could she let herself do the same? By all the logic Brivibas had so carefully taught her, she couldn't. And, once in the open, the thought sickened her. However much she wanted it to, though, it would not go away.

When she had to go out in the streets of Oyngestun, she held her own head high. That stiff, straight carriage – and the trousers she wore, still stubbornly clinging to Kaunian styles – drew howls and leers from the Algarvian soldiers who passed through the village these days, marching west toward the fight with Unkerlant down roads her grandfather had helped pave. The men of the small local garrison, though, stopped bothering her. She wished she could be happy about that, but she understood why all too well: they knew she was an officer's plaything, and so not for the likes of common soldiers.

Only little by little did she notice that the Kaunians of Oyngestun were slower to curse her or turn their backs on her than they had been the summer before. When she did notice, she scratched her head. Then all she'd done was eat some of the food Major Spinello lavished on her grandfather and her in the hope of getting Brivibas to say how happy he was with Algarvian rule. Now she was indeed Spinello's plaything, was the harlot she'd been accused of being then. The villagers should have hated her more than ever.

She got part of the answer one day from Tamulis the apothecary. Brivibas had sent her forth because he was down with a headache – he seemed to come down with headaches ever more often these days – and they had no powders in the house. Handing her a packet, the apothecary remarked, "I'm cursed if I think the old buzzard is worth it."

"What? Headache powders?" Vanai shrugged. "We can afford them – and, except for food, there's not much to spend silver on these days."

Tamulis looked at her. After a moment, he said, "I was not talking about headache powders."

Vanai felt the flush climb from her throat to her hairline. She couldn't even say she didn't know what he was talking about. She did. Oh, she did. She looked down at the dusty slates of the floor. "He is my grandfather," she whispered.

"By all the signs I've seen, that's his good fortune and none of yours," the apothecary said, his voice rough.

Tears filled Vanai's eyes. To her mortification, they began dripping down her cheeks. She was powerless to stop them. She'd spent so long and put so much effort into inuring herself to the villagers' scorn, sympathy struck her with double force. "I'd better go," she said thickly.

"Here, lass – wait," Tamulis said. Blurrily, she saw him holding out a square of cloth to her. "Dry your eyes."

She obeyed, though she didn't think it would help. Her eyes would still be red and swollen, her face blotchy. When she handed the cloth back, she said, "These days, we all do what we have to do to get through."

Tamulis grunted. "You do more for that long-winded old foof than he would ever do for you."

Vanai had a vision of a statuesque, brassy-haired Algarvian noble-woman demanding that Brivibas – whose own blond hair was heavily streaked with silver – make love to her to keep his granddaughter out of a labor gang. She held that vision in her mind for a couple of seconds . . . but for no more than a couple of seconds, because after that she exploded into laughter almost as involuntary as her tears had been. Try as she would, she couldn't imagine an Algarvian noblewoman with such peculiar tastes.

"And what's so funny now?" Tamulis asked.

Somehow, explaining to the apothecary why she'd laughed would have embarrassed Vanai more than having the whole village know Major Spinello spread her thighs whenever the fancy struck him. Maybe it was that she couldn't do anything about Spinello, not if she wanted Brivibas to stay safe in Oyngestun. But maybe, too, it was that explaining would have meant admitting she'd had a bawdy thought of her own. She took the headache powders and left in a hurry.

"What kept you?" Brivibas demanded peevishly when she gave him the powders. "My head feels as if it were on the point of falling off."

"I brought them to you as quickly as I could, my grandfather," Vanai answered. "I am sorry you are in pain." She kept her voice soft and deferential. She'd been doing that around Brivibas for as long as she could remember. It was harder now than it had been. She sometimes felt he ought to keep his voice soft and deferential around her, considering who owed whom what at the moment.

She shook her head. Brivibas had been father and mother both to her since she was no more than a toddler. All she was doing when she lay still for Spinello or sank to her knees in front of him was paying back a small part of that debt. So she told herself, over and over again.

And then Brivibas said, "Part of my pain, I have no doubt, comes from my grief and sorrow at your fall from the proper standards of Kaunian womanhood."

Had he said, *at what you are enduring for my sake*, everything would have been well. But that was not how he measured things. To him, the standards were more important than the reason for which they were broken. Vanai said, "I can meet your expectations, my grandfather, or I can keep you alive. My apologies, but I do not seem to be able to do both at once." She turned on her heel and walked away without giving him a chance to reply.

They did not speak to each other for the next several days.

They might have healed the rift sooner, but Major Spinello chose that afternoon to pay Vanai a visit. Brivibas retreated to his study and slammed the door. Spinello laughed. "The old fool does not know when he is well off," he said. As if to declare the rest of the house his to do with as he chose, he took Vanai on the divan in the parlor, under the eyes of the ancient statuettes and reliefs displayed there.

Afterwards, sated, he ran his hand along her flank. She wanted to get up, to wash away the feel of his skin slick against hers, but his weight still pinned her to the rather scratchy fabric of the divan. With a wriggle and a twist, she let her exasperation at that show. She'd seen he didn't mind, or not too much.

This time, though, he didn't let her go free right away. Looking down at her face from a distance of about six inches, he said, "You were wise to yield yourself to me. The whole of Derlavai is yielding itself to Algarve."

All Vanai said, rather faintly, was, "You're squashing me."

Spinello took more of his weight on his elbows and knees. He stayed atop her, though, his legs between hers, imprisoning her. "Forthweg is ours," he said. "Sibiu is ours. Valmiera is ours. Jelgava is ours. And Unkerlant crumbles. Like a child's sand castle when the tide rolls over it, Unkerlant crumbles."

Boasting of his kingdom's conquests excited him; she felt him stir against her inner thigh. He bent his head to her breast. She realized he was going to have a second round. With a small sigh, she looked up at the rough plaster of the ceiling till he finished.

As he got back into his kilt and tunic, he went on, "The war is as good as over. You need have no doubt of that. Our time, the Algarvian time, is come at last, the time of which our forefathers dreamt even in the days when they dwelt in the forests of the distant south."

Vanai only shrugged. What seemed a golden dream to Spinello was her nightmare brought to life. She shuddered to think of Algarvians free to torment Kaunians for the next hundred years. She also shuddered to think of Spinello free to come back here tomorrow or the next day or a week from now to make her do whatever he wanted.

She could do nothing about Spinello. She could do nothing about the war. As the Algarvian major had boasted that his kingdom's armies were overwhelming the Unkerlanters, so the war had overwhelmed her.

Spinello chucked her under the chin – one more liberty she had to let him take. "Until I see you again," he said with a bow, as if he imagined she might want to see him again. "And do give my best regards to your ever so learned grandfather." Out he went, laughing and whistling.

He was happy. Why not? He'd satisfied himself, and Algarve's armies stood everywhere triumphant. Vanai, despised by the large Forthwegian majority in her own kingdom, despised even more by its conquerors, went off to get a rag and a pitcher and to do her best to scrub the memory of his touch from her body. She despised herself most of all.

Marshal Rathar had come down into the south to see with his own eyes how the Algarvians were making such headway against the Unkerlanter armies there. He had gone to the north, to the border with Zuwayza, to take charge of the fight in the desert when it was going badly. That had been an embarrassment for Unkerlant. If this fight went badly, it would be a catastrophe.

His first lesson was very nearly his last. He had just got out of his ley-line caravan car in the medium-sized town of Wirdum, a good twenty miles behind the battle line, when flight after flight of Algarvian dragons appeared overhead. By the time they got done dropping eggs, the local depot was burning. So were the baron's castle and much of the center of town.

He didn't realize he was bleeding till someone offered him a sticking plaster for the cut on his cheek. He declined with a shrug: "I thank you, but no. I don't want the soldiers to think I hurt myself shaving." The joke would have been better if he hadn't had to say it three times, each louder than the one before, till the fellow with the plaster finally got it. The rain of eggs from the sky had stunned everyone's ears.

Strong, hook-nosed face set in a frown, he rode forward toward General Ortwin's headquarters. That was no easy trip, either. The Algarvians had already given the roads hereabouts the same sort of pasting Wirdum had just taken. Rathar's horse had to pick its way through the fields to get around the craters in the roadway. Soldiers and horses and unicorns and a few behemoths lay sprawled in death; the stink of rotting meat that rose from them was very strong. Flies rose from them, too, in great humming, buzzing clouds. Rathar's horse flicked its tail this way and that; the marshal swatted and fumed.

Turning to the soldier guiding him to General Ortwin, he demanded, "Where are our own dragons? We need to pay the enemy in his own coin."

"We didn't have as many to start with as the cursed redheads did," the man answered. "The ones we did have are mostly dead by now."

Closer to the line of battle, egg-tossers concealed from the air with nets hurled destruction back at King Mezentio's men. Rathar grunted in some satisfaction when he saw that. "The Algarvians aren't having it all their own way, then," he said.

"Oh, no, my lord Marshal," his escort replied. "They pay a price for every mile they move forward."

"They've already moved too many miles forward," Rathar said, "and the price they've paid hasn't been nearly high enough." The soldier riding with him grimaced and then, with obvious reluctance, nodded.

After what seemed far too long, the marshal reached the tent from which General Ortwin was conducting his defense. Ortwin, who was very bald on top but, as if to compensate, had tufts of white hair sprouting from his ears and nostrils, shouted into a crystal: "Bring that regiment forward, curse you! If we don't hold the line of the river, we'll have to fall back past Wirdum, and King Swemmel will pitch a fit." He glanced up and saw Rathar. In a voice full of defiance, he said, "If you want to haul me away for lese majesty, my lord Marshal, here's your chance."

"I want to halt the Algarvians," Rathar said. "That's the only thing I want, and I'm not fussy about how I do it."

Ortwin snorted, which made his nose hairs quiver like grass in the breeze. "Why aren't you shorter by a head?" he asked with what sounded like genuine curiosity. "Everybody thought you were going to be, this past fall."

Rathar shrugged. "His Majesty believes I do not want to be king, I think. Powers above know it's a true belief. But I came here to escape the court, not to gossip of it." He strode forward. "Show me how you are doing."

"None too bloody well," Ortwin answered, which would have served as commentary for the entire Unkerlanter fight against Algarve. "When you set out, we still had a decent force on the east side of the Klagen. This morning, though, the cursed Algarvians threw us back over the river, and powers below eat me if I see how we're going to keep them from crossing." He pointed to the map to show what he meant.

"Why didn't you reinforce your men on the east side?" Rathar asked.

"My lord Marshal, what do you think I tried to do?" Ortwin retorted. "I haven't got a fancy hat with a feather in it like an Algarvian general, but I'm not stupid – not too stupid, anyhow. I tried. I couldn't. Their dragons kept dropping eggs on the fords of the Klagen, and their behemoths thundered right through the line our men put up."

"Where were our behemoths for a counterattack?" Rathar inquired.

"Spread too thin to do much," Ortwin told him. "They bunched theirs, and they broke through with them."

Rathar exhaled angrily. "Shouldn't that have given you a hint, General? We're going to have to learn to fight like the Algarvians if we intend to throw them back."

Ortwin said, "My lord Marshal, I didn't have enough of the beasts to make any great counterattack with them, anyhow." He held up a hand whose back was gnarled with veins like old tree roots. "And before you ask why I didn't get some from the north or the south, the redheads are driving back our armies there, too, and no general has enough for himself, let alone to spare any for his neighbors."

"That is not good," Rathar said, an understatement if ever there was one. "We must be able to concentrate our behemoths, as the Algarvians are doing, or else they will go right on smashing through us."

"You are the Marshal of Unkerlant," Ortwin said. "If anyone can make it so, you are the man." He cocked his head to one side. "Listen to the way the eggs are falling. Sure as sure, Mezentio's men are trying to get over the Klagen." Rathar cocked his head to one side, too. Ortwin was right. Most of the bursts came from the southeast, where the Unkerlanters were fighting to hold the line of the river. One of the crystallomancers turned and spoke urgently to the general.

"I came here to see the fighting," Rathar said as he started out of the tent. "I am going up toward the line there."

"Crystals," Ortwin called after him. "We need more crystals, too. Seems as though the stinking Algarvians have 'em on every behemoth and every dragon, and we've got regiments out there without any. They fight smoother than we can, if you know what I mean."

"I do know," Rathar flung back over his shoulder. "The sorcerers are working night and day to activate more. But we have to keep so many of them busy turning out sticks and eggs, we can't do as much with crystals as we'd like." Unkerlant was a bigger, more populous kingdom than Algarve. King Mezentio's domain, though, had more trained mages and artisans than did King Swemmel's. Algarve spent matériel and sorcerous energy lavishly. To stop the redheads, if they could be stopped, Rathar feared Unkerlant would have to spend men lavishly.

He shouted for a fresh horse. When he got one, he rode toward the Klagen at a rapid though bone-jarring canter. Unkerlanter egg-tossers were flinging relentlessly, straining to hold back the Algarvians. Even as Rathar watched, though, Algarvian dragons dove on a knot of tossers. The fliers released their eggs at just above treetop height, so they could hardly miss. Most of those egg-tossers fell quiet. No Unkerlanter dragons challenged the ones painted in red and white and green.

Men in rock-gray tunics streamed back toward the west. "Stand, curse you!" Rathar shouted. "Stand and fight!"

"The Algarvians!" three of them shouted at him in return. "The Algarvians are across the river." One soldier added, "Our officers say that if we don't get out now, they'll cut us off and we won't be able to get out at all."

Their officers might well have been right. Rathar rode toward a farmhouse where a captain was pulling together a rear guard to hold off the redheads while their comrades retreated. The young officer gaped, goggle-eyed, at the large stars on the collar of Rathar's tunic. "Carry on, Captain," the marshal said crisply. "You know the situation and the ground better than I do."

"Uh, aye, sir," the captain said, staring still. He ordered his men – more than a company's worth – with no small skill.

But then, from the east, another shout rose: "Behemoths!" Rathar grinned in fierce anticipation; he'd come a long way to see the fearsome Algarvian behemoths in action. Only belatedly did he realize that, having seen them, he was liable not to be able to make the long journey back again.

Far from thundering down on the farm in a great rampaging charge, the behemoths paused out of range of a footsoldier's stick and began methodically pounding the Unkerlanter strongpoints to bits. Eggs fell on and around the holes the Unkerlanters had dug for themselves. Heavy sticks set the farmhouse and its outbuildings ablaze, flushing from cover the soldiers who'd sheltered there. After they'd battered the position, Algarvians in short tunics and kilts snaked forward to finish off their foes.

"My lord Marshal, get out while you can," the young captain called to Rathar. "We'll hold them off here while you get away." A cheer rose from the Unkerlanter line. One of the troopers had been lucky enough to blaze a behemoth in the eye. As the beast toppled, it crushed a couple of the Algarvians who'd been riding it.

Rathar realized the captain was right. If he was going to get out, he had to do it now. He saluted the soldiers who would cover his retreat, then remounted and rode off toward the west. A couple of Algarvian behemoth crews lobbed eggs after him. They burst close enough to frighten his horse, but not close enough to knock it over.

More Algarvian dragons flew overhead. Again, they had the sky to themselves. They did not bother with a lone man on horseback, but saved their attention for larger groups of soldiers and horses and unicorns. Rathar had seen the gruesome results of that tactic on the ride up from Wirdum. Now, as he retreated along with the mass of Unkerlanter soldiery, he saw those results again, rather fresher this time.

On came the Algarvians behind them. All through their fights against earlier foes, they'd advanced as smoothly as a ley-line caravan. Nothing he'd seen here made it look as if things would be any different – till he thought of that young captain. And there, ahead of him, another officer was shouting at the men around him to form up for another rear-guard action. The men obeyed, too, though they must have known they were unlikely to last long.

This far south, darkness came late. A little bit further on toward summer and it would hardly have come at all. When at last twilight deepened, Marshal Rathar lay down in a hole in the ground and slept like a worn animal. The Algarvians hadn't come far enough to scoop him up before he woke. Nor, for a wonder, had anyone stolen his horse, which he'd tied to a bush close by. He rode west again.

General Ortwin greeted him with a cry of glad surprise when he rode up to the headquarters. "Powers above be praised you're here, my lord Marshal," the general said. "We've got to pull back soon – can't hold here much longer with the redheads over the Klagen; I told you that already – and you're urgently ordered back to Cottbus."

"What?" Rathar said irritably. "Why?" Only too late did he wonder if he really wanted to know.

Want to or not, he found out. "I'll tell you why," Ortwin said. "The Gongs have stabbed us in the back, that's why. They've started up the war in the far west again."

Two

After so long on the island of Obuda, the Ilszang Mountains, the borderland between Gyongyos on the one hand and Unkerlanter on the other, seemed almost like home to Istvan. As a matter of fact, the valley where he'd been born and raised lay only a couple of hundred miles southwest of the hillside path along which he marched now. He scratched at his long, thick, tawny beard. Stars above! He could even think about going home on leave, something unimaginable out in the middle of the vast Bothnian Ocean.

"Come on, you mangy sons of goats," he called to the men in his squad. "The stars have never once looked down on such a pack of lazy wastrels as you."

"Have a heart, Sergeant," Szonyi said. "Back on Obuda, you were a common soldier yourself, you know."

Istvan raised a hand to brush its back against the single white hashmark embroidered on his collar tab. Sure enough, on Obuda he'd hated Sergeant Jokai's petty tyranny. He still wasn't so harsh as Jokai had been, but now, with rank of his own bestowed on him for good service, he better understood why Jokai had acted as he did. "The boot was on the wrong foot then," he answered. "It's on the right one these days – so step lively."

"I don't know why you're worrying, Sergeant." That was scrawny, bespectacled Kun, still as argumentative, as fussily precise, as he had been back on the island. His wide wave almost knocked Istvan off the path and down the hillside. "I don't think there are any Unkerlanters for miles around."

"I'm worrying because worrying is my job," Istvan told him. "And that's why we're moving forward so easy, too: because the lousy goat-eaters have their hands full way off in the east, I mean. Pick up your clumsy feet, like I told Szonyi. Let's grab with both hands while we can."

Not even the former mage's apprentice had a good comeback for that. On he tramped, with Istvan, with the rest of the squad, with the rest of the company, with the rest of the regiment, with the baggage train of horses and mules. Istvan wished there were a ley line anywhere close by. But ley lines were few and far between in this stars-forsaken country, country so little traveled that wizards surely hadn't yet mapped all the ones there were.

Szonyi grinned at Kun, and at the other troopers in the squad from the coastal lowlands or from the Balaton Islands off the coast. "Even if there aren't any Unkerlanters around here, you've got to look sharp. Otherwise, a mountain ape'll sneak down, tuck you under his arm, and walk off with you."

Kun stared at him over the tops of his spectacles. "The only mountain ape I see in these parts is you."

"Oh, you won't see them, Kun," Istvan said, nodding toward Szonyi. "No, you won't see them. But sure as sure, they'll see you."

"Bah!" Kun kicked a pebble. "If they didn't keep the cursed things in menageries, I wouldn't even believe in them. And I'll bet you anything you care to name that nine stories out of every ten the old grannies tell about 'em are lies. I'm no superstitious fool, not me." He puffed out his weedy chest and looked wise, or at least supercilious.

"Have it your way," Istvan answered with a shrug. "One thing the grannies say is that whoever calls someone else a fool names himself, too."

With an angry grunt, Kun kicked another pebble down the steep hillside. Istvan ignored the little show of pique. His eyes were on the slopes above the path. Somewhere up there, mountain apes *were* liable to be staring hungrily down at his companions and him. Years – centuries – had driven them up into the desolate heights and taught them wariness when it came to man. That did not mean they would not sneak down and raid, only that they picked their spots with care.

One of the lowlanders newly attached to the squad, a broad-shouldered fellow named Kanizsai, said, "I heard a savant claim once that mountain apes weren't really apes at all, not like the apes in the jungles of Siaulia. What this chap said was, we ought to think of them as really stupid people instead."

That notion kept the next couple of miles light and full of laughter. Everybody had his own candidate for who should be reckoned a mountain ape, starting with childhood rivals and ending up with King Swemmel and most of the population of Unkerlant.

"And what about us?" Szonyi added. "If we had any wits, would we be tramping through these miserable mountains just because somebody told us to?"

"Oh, now wait a bit," Kanizsai said. "We're warriors, by the stars. This is what we're supposed to be doing." The argument took off from there, like a dragon taking wing. Istvan and Kun sided with Szonyi. Most of the new men, men who hadn't yet seen action, ranged themselves behind Kanizsai.

"You'll find out," Istvan said. "Aye, we're warriors. That means we know how to fight and we're not afraid to do it. Ask anybody who's seen real war if he likes it, though, and you'll hear some different stories." Now Kun and Szonyi supported him.

"But there's glory in crushing the foes of Gyongyos," Kanizsai declared. "The stars shine brighter when we show ourselves to be true men."

"Where's the glory in huddling in a hole in the rain while the enemy tosses eggs at you?" Istvan returned. "Where's the glory in sneaking up behind a Kuusaman who's squatting in the bushes with his trousers around his ankles and cutting his throat so you can steal whatever food he's carrying?"

Kanizsai looked revolted. Having been through the course that hardened recruits into warriors, Istvan knew it stressed ferocity. That was all very well – to a point. He wanted men at his side who would not give way in battle. But he did not want men at his side who would endanger themselves and him by rushing ahead when they ought to hold back.

Today, all that hardly mattered. The Unkerlanters offered no resistance to the advance. Maybe the war in the east did preoccupy them. Maybe they just didn't care about losing this stretch of mountains. Had it belonged to Istvan, he wouldn't have cared about losing it, either.

When evening came, the squadron encamped on the flattest stretch of ground Istvan could find. It wasn't a very flat stretch of ground, or very large, either. "We'll keep two men on watch," he ordered. "Three shifts through the night." He named the sentries for each shift. One of the best things about being promoted to sergeant was that he didn't have to take a turn on sentry-go himself. As he rolled himself in his blanket, he smiled at the thought of sleeping till morning.

Someone shook him. He came awake at once, as he'd learned to do on Obuda. Men who couldn't rouse quickly and completely there often never roused at all. The dying embers of the campfire gave the only light. "What is it?" he asked, his voice a thin thread of whisper.

"Sergeant, someone's coming," Kun whispered back. "I can't see anybody, but I know."

"Your little piece of magecraft?" Istvan asked. Kun nodded, the motion next to invisible in the gloom. He'd used that trick he'd learned from his master before, back on Obuda. Istvan seized his stick and got to his feet in one smooth motion. "All right. You'd better show me." The squad was *his*. This was the price he paid for not having to stand guard or do some of the other things common soldiers did.

"Follow me," Kun said. Istvan did, as quietly as he could, up the side of the hill above the encampment to a boulder from behind which Kun could keep an eye on the slope that ran up higher still. When they got there, Kun mumbled to himself. He played what looked like a child's finger game. After a moment, he raised his head and looked at Istvan. "He's still out there, whoever he is. Coming closer, too, or the sorcery wouldn't spot him."

"Aye," Istvan said. "An Unkerlanter spy, I'll lay, maybe with a crystal, so he can let his friends know what he sees." *A brave man*, he thought. No one but a brave man would dare come spying on his enemies when they were here in numbers and he alone, so very alone.

Istvan peered up the slope. He wished for a moon; the stars, however beautiful and potent they were, did not yield enough light to suit him. The pale stones seemed dark, the inky shadows impenetrable. King Swemmel's men could have concealed not just a single spy but a battalion up there. But for Kun's little sorcery, no one would have known till they attacked.

"Sergeant—" Kun began.

"Wait." Istvan's answer was an almost voiceless whisper, but it slapped the mage's apprentice into silence. Istvan leaned forward, ever so slightly. One of those inky shadows had . . . moved? As if Istvan's stick had a life of its own, it took aim at that shadow, which was now so still, he doubted whether he'd seen what he'd thought he saw.

He waited. Patience hard won on Obuda came in handy now. He

tried not to hear his own soft breathing, or Kun's. All of him was pointing toward that shadow, waiting for it to do something, to do anything. If he'd imagined the motion, the Unkerlanter could be sneaking up on him from another direction.

The shadow moved again. Istvan blazed. His finger found the blazing hole before he was consciously sure he'd seen the motion. The bright beam tore at his dark-adapted eyes.

From up the slope, a harsh cry rang out. Istvan dashed toward the place from which it had come. Kun pounded at his heels. Now the silent waiting game was over. He heard scrabbling among the rocks, and blazed again. Another cry rewarded him, this one, he was sure, of mortal agony.

"Have a care, Sergeant," Kun panted. "He might be shamming."

"If he is, you'll avenge me," Istvan answered. The cries had roused the other soldiers in the squad. He heard them coming up the hillside behind him. *After glory*, he thought. All he wanted was a dead Unkerlanter, or perhaps a live one from whom answers could be ripped by someone who spoke the easterners' ugly language.

Kun pointed. "There!"

Istvan was already hurrying toward the form from which the stink of burnt meat rose. And then, all at once, he stopped short. "I'll be a son of a goat," he said softly. "You may not have much believed in mountain apes, Kun, but your magecraft did, and took it for a man."

"Is it dead?" Kun asked in an unwontedly small voice.

"Not yet, I don't think," Istvan answered. As if on cue, the mountain ape writhed. He blazed it once more, this time in the head. It groaned, as a man might have done, and lay still. Istvan turned to the oncoming soldiers in his squad, calling, "Somebody start a torch and fetch it up here. I want a good look at this beast."

Unlovely in life, the mountain ape seemed even more unlovely sprawled in death under the flickering torchlight. It was bigger than a man, and its long, coarse, shaggy reddish hair made it look bigger still. Its low brow, broad nose, and mouth full of enormous (though not very sharp) teeth turned it into an embarrassing caricature of mankind. Was that a club fallen from its huge hand, or just a branch that happened to lie close by? Istvan couldn't be sure.

Kun turned away in fastidious disgust. "Abominable creature," he muttered. "Simply abominable."

"I suppose so," Istvan said. "It's dead, and it didn't hurt any of us. That's what counts." He looked east into the night. "When we do finally run into the Unkerlanters, they'll have more with them than clubs, worse luck."

In the dark quiet of the second-story farmhouse bedchamber, Merkela moved slowly, delicately, above Skarnu. "Oh," he said in a soft voice, still astonished at the joy she could wring from him.

He peered up at her. Her face, inches above his own, was half intent, half slack with pleasure. The tips of her breasts brushed the bare skin of his chest as she sat bent above him. Somehow, that excited him almost as much as anything else she was doing. He ran a hand down the smooth curve of her back till he clenched one meaty buttock. The fingers of his other hand tangled in her golden hair as he pulled her mouth down to his. He found her lips sweeter than honey, sweeter and more intoxicating than the finest fortified Jelgavan wine.

All at once, she moaned and strained and bucked against him, delicacy forgotten. She clenched him inside her, as if with a hand. He cried out; he could no more have held back than he could have stopped himself from breathing. Merkela cried out, too, a curious, mewing wail, almost like a cat's. Then, spent, she slumped down on to him.

And then, as she did after every time they joined, she began to weep as if her heart would break. No – as if it were already broken. "Gedominu!" she wailed. "Oh, my poor Gedominu!"

Skarnu held her and stroked her and waited for the worst of the sorrow to pass, as he knew it soon would. There were jokes, there were sayings, about the chances a man took when he consoled a new widow in her bedchamber. Discovering she still loved her dead husband was not the least of them. Her tears felt hot as molten lead against the side of his neck and the hollow of his shoulder.

"I can't bring him back," Skarnu said once the sobs had ebbed to sniffles. The Algarvians had blazed Gedominu, as they'd blazed a good many other Valmieran hostages, to punish resistance against their occupying army. "I wish I could, but I can't."

That was true, even if it meant Merkela would not be giving herself to him now. It might not have meant anything of the sort; what had smoldered between them might have caught fire even with Gedominu still limping around his farm. "He was a brave man." That was also true. Skarnu would have said it even were it not, to honor the dead.

"Aye, he was." Merkela's head came up. From grief, she swung quickly to rage. Tears still streaked her cheeks, but her eyes glittered with fury. "He was brave, and the redheads blazed him down like a dog. Powers above spurn them. Power below eat them through all eternity." Her voice held an incantatory quality, as if she truly had the power to make her curses bite deep. "They will pay. How they will pay."

"Aye." Skarnu kept stroking her, gentling her, as if she were an unbroken unicorn. "They will pay. They are paying. You're helping to make them pay."

Merkela nodded. The thought might have come from her own mind, not Skarnu's. While Gedominu lived, she'd been content to wait at home and let him carry on the clandestine war against the redheads. After they executed him, she'd gone out on every raid Skarnu and his sergeant, Raunu, and the handful of stubborn local farmers and villagers had put on. Skarnu's greatest fear was not that she would be unable to hold her own but that she would get herself killed from foolish eagerness to throw herself at the foe. It hadn't happened yet. In time, he hoped, she would get her common sense back.

"And you, Skarnu, you are a brave man," she exclaimed, suddenly seeming to remember he was there even though she'd been lying mostly on top of him, her naked, sweaty flesh pressed tight against his. "When they took him, you tried to go in his place."

Skarnu shrugged. She'd been watching them. He could think of no other reason why he'd offered himself to the Algarvians instead of Gedominu. Had they taken him, had they blazed him, would Merkela now be mourning him, naked in this bed with her old lame husband? Skarnu shrugged and shivered, both at the same time. No one could know such a thing – and just as well, too.

He reached for her, to hold away what might have been. She was reaching for him, too, perhaps to hold away what had been. Only noblewomen in Valmiera were said to know what she knew and used to get him ready quickly. He'd learned before that what people said and what was so often had no connection to each other. Soon, she arched her hips to receive him. "Hurry," she whispered, there in the darkness.

When her pleasure came this time, she groaned as if it were pain. A moment later, Skarnu groaned, too, and spent himself. Merkela wept again, but only for a little while. Her breathing grew deep and slow. She drifted off to sleep without bothering to put on the loose tunic and trousers she wore at night.

Getting into his own clothes was a matter of a moment for Skarnu. Merkela let him share her bed when they joined on it, but she would not let him sleep with her in the literal meaning of the words. He slipped down the stairs and out of the farmhouse, closing the door behind him. He'd grown very used to sleeping on straw in the barn. A mattress, by now, would probably feel too soft to be comfortable.

"Hello, sir," Raunu said quietly. Straw rustled under the veteran – Raunu had fought in the Six Years' War – as he sat up.

"Oh, hello, Sergeant," Skarnu said in dull embarrassment. Raunu had kept him afloat when, thanks to his being a marquis, he'd taken command of a company in Valmiera's failed war against Algarve. They'd stayed together after the formal fighting ended, too. Now, since he hadn't been here, Raunu could hardly help knowing where he had been and what he'd been doing. "I didn't mean to wake you."

"You didn't," Raunu answered. "I was wakeful anyhow." He didn't say anything else for a little while after that. Skarnu could see his face but not make out its expression; the inside of the barn was darker even than Merkela's bedchamber had been. At last, Raunu resumed: "Are you sure you know what you're doing, sir?"

"Sure?" Skarnu shook his head. "No, of course not. Only fools are sure they know what they're doing, and they're commonly wrong."

Raunu grunted. Skarnu needed a moment to realize that was intended for laughter. Raunu said, "All right, sir, fair enough. If she'd chosen to look at me, I don't suppose I'd have looked away, either."

"Ah." Skarnu didn't want to talk about it. He pulled off his boots. He'd also got used to sleeping in tunic and trousers, to keep the straw from poking him so badly. His yawn might have been a bit theatrical, but he thought it would serve.

Here on the farm, though, sergeant and captain, commoner and noble, were far closer to equals than they had been in the tightly structured world of the army. Raunu did not back off. He said, "Did you know, sir, that Gedominu knew she'd started looking your way before the redheads hauled him off and blazed him?"

That had to be answered. "No, I didn't know," Skarnu said slowly. "Nothing happened between us before then." It was true. How long it would have kept on being true, he didn't know. He'd started looking Merkela's way, too. He'd started looking her way from the moment he met her.

He wondered if she mourned Gedominu so extravagantly because she felt guilty about having turned her eye elsewhere before the Algarvians seized her husband. He doubted he would ever know. He could hardly come right out and ask.

Raunu's thoughts had traveled along their own ley line. "Aye, he knew," the sergeant said. "It was always one thing after another, he said to me once – that was how he looked at the world. He was sure Algarve would go after Unkerlant next. With Forthweg and Sibiu and us and the Jelgavans down, Unkerlant was the next duck in a row."

Skarnu didn't care about Gedominu's theories. He yawned again, louder and more stagily than before, and lay down in the straw, which rustled as it compressed under his weight. He felt around till he found his blanket, then wrapped it around himself.

"I hope everything turns out all right, sir, that's all," Raunu said, apparently resigned to the idea that he wouldn't get many more answers from his superior.

But Skarnu gave him one more after all: "Everything's turned out fine so far, hasn't it, Sergeant? Our armies will be in Trapani next week at the latest, and Gedominu should have a fine harvest come fall. Or have you heard something different?"

"Well, I walked into that, didn't I? I only wish we were in the Algarvians' capital and not the other way round." Raunu lay down, too; the straw rustled once more. The sergeant sighed and said, "I'll see you in the morning, sir."

"Aye." Now that Skarnu was off his feet, his yawn had nothing forced about it. He fell asleep almost as fast as Merkela had, up in her room.

In the morning, he drew up a bucket of water from the well and splashed it over his face and hands. Raunu used some, too. Then they went into the farmhouse. Merkela fed them fried eggs and bread and butter and beer: all from the farm, nothing bought in town but the salt that went on the eggs.

Thus fortified, they went out to tend the crops and the cattle and sheep, leaving Merkela behind to bake and wash clothes and weed the vegetable garden and feed the chickens. She and Gedominu had got a good enough living from the farm. Skarnu marveled at that. He and Raunu together had trouble doing as much as Gedominu had managed by himself.

"Ah, but there's a difference, sir," Raunu said when Skarnu grumbled about it, which he did every now and then. "The old man had a lifetime to learn what he was doing. We've had not quite a year."

"Aye, I suppose so." Skarnu glanced over toward the veteran. Raunu had had a lifetime to learn how to be a soldier . . . and then Skarnu, with a good deal less than not quite a year's experience, had been set over him. *I ought to count myself lucky he didn't betray me to the Algarvians, the way so many Jelgavan soldiers did with their officers*, he thought. Raunu might have been better off had he decided to turn traitor.

Skarnu was weeding – somewhat more expertly than he had the year before, if not with Gedominu's effortless skill – when a couple of Algarvians came riding along the path that ran by the fields. They dismounted not far away. One of them nailed a broadsheet to an oak tree. The other one kept him covered, which meant that, for most of the time he was busy, the fellow pointed his stick not quite straight at Skarnu. Once the broadsheet was in place, the Algarvians swung back up on to their unicorns and rode away.

Only after they were out of sight did Skarnu amble over to see what the broadsheet said. In rather stilted Valmieran, it offered a reward for information leading to the capture of soldiers who had gone into hiding rather than surrendering, and a double reward for information leading to the capture of officers.

He stood rocking back and forth on his heels, the picture of rustic indifference. Then, with a shrug more convincing than his yawns had been the night before, he went back to work. Maybe someone in the countryside knew what he and Raunu were and felt like turning a profit on his knowledge. Whether that was so or not mattered little at the moment; Skarnu couldn't do anything about it. He could do the work. If he didn't, no one would.

When he and Raunu came in for their midday meal – big bowls of bean soup, with more beer to wash them down – he mentioned the broadsheet. Raunu shrugged. "Figures the redheads would try it sooner or later," he said. "But not many people like 'em well enough to talk with 'em for money."

"Someone will," Merkela said. "Someone will want silver, or will remember an old quarrel with Gedominu or with me. There are always people like that." She tossed her head to show what she thought of them, a gesture even Skarnu's sister Krasta might have envied. Skarnu wondered how many of the people who'd had quarrels with Gedominu were jealous of him for taking such a woman to wife.

He chuckled. He hadn't imagined farmers might have feuds as serious and as foolish as those of the nobility. "Can you think of anyone in particular?" he asked Merkela. "Maybe someone needs to have an unfortunate accident."

Her eyes flashed. Skarnu would not have wanted that wolfish smile aimed at him. "Or even a fortunate one," she said.

Captain Hawart said, "Gather round, men." Corporal Leudast and the other Unkerlanter survivors from his regiment obeyed. They might have filled out three full-strength companies. Hawart was the senior officer still alive. Colonel Roflanz hadn't lived through the counterattack he'd stupidly ordered against the Algarvian invaders.

Leudast marveled that he himself was still breathing. The regiment had been encircled twice during the grinding retreat through Forthweg. Once, the men had slipped through the Algarvian lines a few at a time under cover of night. The other time, they'd had to fight their way clear – which was one reason so few of them gathered to listen to Captain Hawart.

He pointed back toward the village in eastern Unkerlant through which they'd retreated the day before. The Algarvians held the place now, or what was left of it: a breeze from out of the east blew stale, sour smoke into Leudast's nostrils. "Men, we have to retake Pfreimd," Hawart said. "Once we do it, we can form a line along the western bank of the stream that runs by the other side of the town and have some chance of really stopping the redheads."

That stream was hardly more than a creek. Leudast hadn't bothered looking for a ford before wading across it, and the water hadn't come above his waist. He didn't think it would prove much of an obstacle to the Algarvians. As a matter of fact, it *hadn't* proved much of an obstacle to the Algarvians.

"We'll have reinforcements coming in behind us," Hawart promised. "They'll give us the men we need to make a proper stand on the river line." It wasn't a river. Not even in flood could it be a river. But the regimental commander had met Leudast's most urgent concern.

In any case, Hawart gave the orders. Leudast's job was to obey them and see that the men in his squad did the same. He glanced over to Sergeant Magnulf. Magnulf shrugged, ever so slightly. He had to obey orders, too. After a moment, Leudast also shrugged. Going straight at the Algarvians was only slightly more perilous than falling back before them.

"Let's get moving," Hawart said. "Advance in open order. Use whatever cover you can find. If you can manage it, Unkerlant needs you alive. But Unkerlant needs dead Algarvians even more. Come on."

"Open order," Magnulf repeated. "Spread it out as wide as you can. We want to get into the village, we want to clear out the Algarvians, and we want to keep on advancing to the line of the stream. And Leudast here," he added, pointing toward the corporal, "wants to keep the redheads as far away from his home village as he can."

"Aye, that's so," Leudast agreed. He turned his head to look westward. His village couldn't have been more than twenty or thirty miles west of the battle line, though he was rather south of it, too. "Too many villages lost already."

"Well, let's take one back," Magnulf said.

Leudast did his best to force fear to one side. He couldn't keep from feeling it. As long as he kept from showing it, though, he could hold his head up among his comrades. Maybe they felt it, too. He hadn't asked. Nobody'd asked him, either.

He trotted forward through fields of growing wheat that might never be harvested. He wished he were dressed in green, not rock-gray. How far forward had the Algarvians moved their outposts during the night? One way to find out was to get blazed by a redhead. Somebody was liable to find out that way. He hoped he wouldn't be the one.

Eggs started falling on the advancing troops. The Algarvians were demons for making their egg-tossers keep up with the rest of the army. Here, though, they were tossing a little long, so they did less harm than they might have.

Before they could correct their aim, flashes of sorcerous energy came from inside Pfreimd. Leudast let out a glad, startled whoop, then turned it into words: "We've got egg-tossers of our own in the fight." He shook his fist in the direction of the village. "How do you Algarvians like it, curse you?"

He didn't think Algarvians liked it at all. Dishing it out was always easier than taking it. The eggs the Unkerlanters flung at the redheads must have put a couple of their tossers out of action, for the rain of eggs down on to the advancing Unkerlanter regiment slowed.

Leudast waved men forward as he himself ran on. Maybe Captain Hawart hadn't been trying to get what was left of the regiment killed after all. Familiar-looking thatch-roofed houses – some amazingly intact, others nothing but charred ruins – swelled in Leudast's sight as he drew near them.

"Unkerlant!' he yelled. "King Swemmel! Urra! Urra!"

More Unkerlanter eggs fell on Pfreimd. They would make the Algarvians holed up in the village keep their heads down. With a little luck, that creek on the other side of Pfreimd would become the front line once more. A barricade of Algarvian corpses might keep the defenders safe.

Troopers started blazing at the nearest houses, houses in which the redheads might be lurking. Where beams struck it, thatching began to smolder. So did some of the timbers. Before long, those houses would catch fire. The Algarvians would have to come forth or roast.

In the meanwhile, though, they fought. Beams began cutting down the Unkerlanters advancing on the village. A near miss charred a line through the grass by Leudast's feet. He threw himself down behind a rock that wasn't really big enough to shield him and blazed back.

After a moment to gather himself, he was up and running again. Then he was in among the houses of the village, and discovered that the Algarvians hadn't merely taken cover in them. The redheads had also dug trenches and foxholes by the houses and in the village square. They resisted with everything they had, too, and seemed not in the least inclined to give up Pfreimd.

Well, if they won't, we'll have to take it away from them, Leudast thought. He blazed at a redhead in a hole. The fellow reeled back, clutching at himself.

"Surrender!" an Unkerlanter officer shouted in Algarvian. That was a word Leudast had learned.

"Mezentio!" was the only answer the officer got. The Algarvians intended to fight it out in the village. Captain Hawart had said reinforcements were coming to help the regiment he commanded these days. Leudast wondered if the redheads expected help from their friends, too.

If they did, best to finish them now, before that help arrived. "Follow me!" Leudast shouted to his comrades, and leaped down into the trenches. To his vast relief, the Unkerlanters he led did follow. Had they hung back, he wouldn't have lasted long.

As things were, he'd never found himself in such a vicious little fight. The Algarvians might have been used to overwhelming all the foes in their path, but they did not shy away from combat with the odds against them. Nor did they hang back from fighting at close quarters. Some of the work Leudast did was with his stick used as a club and with his knife: warfare as it had been in the days of the Kaunian Empire, and even before.

The last few Algarvians threw down their sticks and surrendered. They looked as frightened as Leudast would have had he been trying to yield to them. "They aren't nine feet tall and covered with spines after all," he said to Magnulf.

"No, so they're not," Magnulf agreed. He was tying a rag around his arm. Blood soaked through the wool; one of the Algarvians had had a knife, too. "Not too bad," he told Leudast. "Should heal well enough — and that cursed redhead isn't going to stick anybody else, believe you me he won't."

"Good," Leudast said. He thought he'd come through without a scratch till he discovered a cut on one leg. He had no idea when he'd got it. In the heat of battle, he hadn't noticed it till now.

Villagers — those who hadn't fled or been killed — began coming out of their battered homes to shake the hands of the Unkerlanter soldiers. Some of them held out jugs of spirits. "We would have had more," one of them said, "but these redheaded swine" — he spat in the direction of the Algarvian captives — "stole everything they could find. Still, they did not find it all."

An old woman pointed to the captives. "What will you do with them now?"

"Send them off to a camp, I suppose," Captain Hawart answered. "We start killing them in cold blood, they'll do the same to our men."

"But they deserve to die," the woman shouted angrily. "They killed us. They took a couple of our girls to enjoy. They stole. They burned."

Captain Hawart's smile was hard and unpleasant. "They'll have a thin time of it, granny, I promise you that."

"Not thin enough." Stubborn as an ox, the old woman stuck out her chin.

Hawart did not argue with her. He detailed a couple of men to take the captives back to the rear. As the Algarvians stumbled away, glad to keep on breathing, he waved his own men forward. "Up to the stream," he told them. "See? It went just the way we planned it."

So it had. Leudast scratched his head. He wasn't used to things going as planned. Even retreats had been botched lately. Now the regiment had successfully advanced against the Algarvian army, the army that had thrown all foes back in confusion. Did that mean the line of the stream would hold after all? Leudast was willing to find out.

A couple of Algarvian behemoths came up toward the eastern back of the stream. Leudast suddenly got less optimistic about holding the position the regiment had just gained — to say nothing of living much longer. He hoped the redheads would come close enough to let him blaze them off their great beasts. But they were too warwise for that. They started tossing eggs at the Unkerlanters defending Pfreimd and the streambank from a range at which Leudast and his comrades could not hurt them.

But the Unkerlanter egg-tossers that had lobbed packets of sorcerous energy at the redheads in Pfreimd now shifted their attention to the behemoths on the other side of the stream. By chance, one of their eggs burst right on top of one of the beasts. That burst all the eggs the behemoth carried. Leudast shouted himself hoarse. More eggs burst all around the other behemoths and wounded or killed one of the men atop it, but it trotted away from the stream faster than it had advanced.

"Powers above. We held them." Leudast knew he shouldn't have sounded astonished, but he couldn't help himself. Magnulf nodded, looking astonished, too.

Less than an hour later, a messenger ran up. After listening to him, Captain Hawart cursed furiously. "Pull back!" he shouted to his men. "We've got to pull back."

Leudast cursed, too. "Why?" he burst out, along with many others.

"Why? I'll tell you why," Hawart answered. "The redheads have broken through in a big way farther south, that's why. If we don't pull back now, we'll have to try to fight our way out of another encirclement. How many times can we stay lucky?"

Wearily, Leudast got to his feet. Wearily, he tramped back through the wreckage of Pfreimd. The villagers cursed him and his comrades for retreating. He couldn't blame them. The regiment had done everything it was supposed to do, and done it well. Even that hadn't helped. Here he was, retreating again. Head down, he slogged on.

Looking down from his dragon on the Unkerlanter landscape far below, Colonel Sabrino smiled. From the day the Algarvians began their campaign, it had gone better than the nobleman dared hope. Columns of behemoths broke through one Unkerlanter defensive line after another, and footsoldiers flooded into the gaps the great beasts tore. The foe either found himself outflanked and surrounded or else had to flee for his life.

Sabrino peered back over his shoulder at the wing he commanded: sixty-four dragons painted in the Algarvian colors of green, white, and red. He wished he were wearing a hat, so he could wave it – like almost every Algarvian ever born, he delighted in theatrical gestures. Taking off his goggles and waving them didn't have the same flair.

He contented himself with a wave of the hand. When he looked back over his shoulder again, half – more than half – the dragonfliers were waving back at him. His smile got wider, and fonder. They were good lads, every one. Few had more than half his fifty-odd years; he'd fought on the ground in the Six Years' War a generation before. One stretch of soldiering in the mud had convinced him he never wanted to go through another. Thus, dragons.

His mount twisted its long, snaky neck this way and that. It let out a fierce shriek that tore at his ears. It was looking for Unkerlanter dragons to flame out of the sky or – better yet, from its point of view – to claw and tear with its taloned forelegs.

It shrieked again. "Oh, shut up, you cursed thing," Sabrino snapped. The only people who romanticized dragons were those who knew nothing about them. Like any dragonflier, Sabrino scorned the beasts he flew. Bad-tempered, stupid, vicious . . . No, dragonfliers never ran out of bad things to say about their mounts.

He looked down once more, looked down and spied a long column of wagons moving up toward the fighting front through the dust they kicked up rolling along a dirt road. He pointed to it, and also spoke into his crystal: "Let's make sure those whoresons never get where they're going."

The crystal was attuned to those his squadron leaders carried. "Aye, sir, we'll do it," Captain Domiziano, one of those squadron leaders, said with a grin. "It's what we're for – it's what we've been doing all along." He seemed altogether too young and eager to hold his rank . . . or maybe that was just a sign Sabrino was getting old.

"Down, then," Sabrino ordered, and used more hand signals to pass on the command to the dragonfliers who didn't have crystals. His squadron leaders were relaying the order, too, in case the men watched them and not their wing commander.

From his seat at the base of his dragon's neck, Sabrino leaned forward to tap out the command that would send the beast stooping like an out-sized hawk at the wagons and draft animals below. The dragon ignored him, or possibly didn't notice the signal he'd given it. That was why he carried an iron-tipped goad. He gave the command again, this time with force that probably would have felled a man.

He did get the dragon's attention. It screeched in outrage and twisted its head back to glare at him with great yellow eyes. He reached out with the goad and whacked it on the end of the nose. It shrieked again, even more angrily than before. Dragons were trained from the days when they were no more than new-hatched lizards with evil dispositions never to flame the men who flew them. But they were also very stupid. Every once in a while, they forgot.

Not this time. After a last scream, Sabrino's dragon folded its wings and plummeted toward the Unkerlanter supply column. The wind whistled in Sabrino's face. One more glance behind him showed that the rest of the wing followed.

Down on the ground, the Unkerlanters had spotted the dragons diving on them. Sabrino laughed as he watched them mill around. Not many could hope to run far enough or fast enough to escape the flames of destruction. Unkerlant, by all the signs, had been getting ready to attack Algarve before King Mezentio's men struck first. Now the enemy was discovering what a mistake he'd made, imagining he could stand on equal terms against the greatest army the continent of Derlavai had ever known.

Here and there, footsoldiers marching with the column blazed at the Algarvian dragons; Sabrino spied the flashes from the business ends of their sticks. They were brave. They were also foolish. A footsoldier couldn't carry a stick strong enough to bring down a dragon unless he hit it in the eye, which required as near a miracle of blazing as made no difference. He might also hit a dragonflier, but Sabrino preferred not to dwell on that.

The Unkerlanters swelled from specks to insects to people with astonishing speed. Similarly, their wagons stopped looking like toys. They ripped the canvas cover off one of those wagons. Sabrino wondered what they were doing, but not for more than a heartbeat. To his horror, he saw they'd concealed a heavy stick in the wagon. Soldiers in calf-length rock-gray tunics brought it to bear on one of the Algarvian dragonfliers.

"No!" Sabrino cried in dismay as the beam spat upward. To his frightened eyes, it seemed bright as the sun, wide as the sea. No dragon's scales, not even if they were silvered, could withstand a beam like that at close range. The beam lashed out again.

But the stick had not been aimed his way. Since he was in the lead, he couldn't tell whether it had struck one of the beasts behind him – no time to look back, not now. The stick slewed toward him as the Unkerlanters swung it on its mounting. If it blazed once more, it was death.

Sabrino slapped his dragon a different way. This time, the beast obeyed without hesitation, not least because he was ordering it to do what it already wanted to do. Its great jaws yawned wide. It belched forth a sheet of flame that engulfed the Unkerlanters' heavy stick and the men who served it.

Fumes reeking of brimstone blew back in Sabrino's face. He coughed and cursed, but he would rather have smelled that odor just then than his mistress' most delicate perfume. Those fumes and the flames from which they sprang had just saved his life.

Nearer the head of the column, the dragon flamed again, incinerating a wagon and the horses that pulled it. Sabrino whacked it with the goad to make it gain height and come round for another run. As its great wings worked behind him – he could feel the mighty muscles contract and loosen, contract and loosen, with every wingbeat – he craned his neck to see how the rest of the dragonfliers had served the supply column.

He waved the goad with glee. Great clouds of black smoke rose into the sky, the pyre of dozens of wagonloads of food, clothing, eggs, sticks – who could guess what? – that would never reach the Unkerlanters struggling to hold back the Algarvian footsoldiers and behemoths.

A good many Unkerlanter soldiers and drivers had burned, too. So had a good many horses. Not all of them, men or beasts, died at once. A burning horse ran madly through a wheatfield, spreading fire wherever it went. It galloped close to half a mile before falling over.

And two dragons lay not far from the wreckage of the Unkerlanter column. That meant two Algarvian dragonfliers surely dead. Sabrino cursed; the Unkerlanters had caught him by surprise there. They fought hard. From what he'd seen, they fought harder than either the Forthwegians or the Valmierans. Already, the word had gone through the Algarvian army – don't let yourself get captured behind the enemy's lines.

Sabrino spoke into the crystal once more: "We've done what we came to do. Now we can head back to the dragon farm and get ready to do it all over again tomorrow."

"Aye, sir," Captain Orosio said. "I'm already bringing my men up into formation." And so he was. Though a good deal older than Domiziano, he hadn't commanded a squadron for nearly so long as the other man. *Poor fellow*, Sabrino thought. *His family connections aren't all they might be.* Now that Orosio had the squadron, he handled it with matter-of-fact competence. *Too bad he couldn't get it sooner.*

Orosio's squadron was, in fact, the first one to re-form. Because of that, Sabrino ordered that squadron up above the rest, to cover them from attack by Unkerlanter dragons as they flew east. Here and there below them, knots of Unkerlanter troopers still held out against the Algarvians. Elsewhere, though, Algarvian behemoths, some carrying egg-tossers, others with heavy sticks mounted on their mail-covered backs, trotted west with next to no one even to slow them down. By all the signs, it was a rout.

But when the wing flew over land where there'd been fighting, Sabrino saw, as he'd seen before, that things weren't so simple. The Unkerlanters had fought hard in every village and town; most of them were little more than charred rubble. And the corpses of men and behemoths, unicorns and horses, scattered through fields pockmarked with craters from bursting eggs proclaimed how hard they'd fought in open country, too.

"Dragons, Colonel!" Captain Orosio's sharp warning snapped Sabrino out of his reverie. Dragons they were, half a dozen of them, painted in Unkerlanter rock-gray that made them hard to spot against the hazy sky. They were flying back toward the west, which meant they'd been raiding behind the Algarvian lines.

They could have escaped Sabrino's wing and fled into the all but limitless plains of Unkerlant. Instead, no matter how outnumbered they were, they flew straight for the Algarvian dragons.

For Sabrino, it wasn't a question of urging his mount on. It was a question of holding back the dragon, of making the attack part of an organized assault on the Unkerlanters rather than a wild beast's headlong rush. With the dragon goad in his right hand, he used his stick with his left. Aiming from dragonback was tricky, but he'd had a lot of practice. If he blazed an enemy flier, the fellow's dragon would be nothing more than a wild beast, as likely to attack friend as foe.

He'd fought Unkerlanters in the air before, and had a low opinion of their skill. Seeing six assail sixty or so, he also had a low opinion of their common sense. But, as with the comrades on the ground, he'd never been able to fault their courage. Here they came, as if they outnumbered his dragonfliers ten to one instead of the other way round. They couldn't have hoped to win, or even to escape. They intended to sell themselves as dearly as possible.

For his part, he wanted to dispose of them as fast as he could. He sent several of his dragons after each of theirs, to give them no chance for heroism. Somebody blazed one of their fliers almost at once. That dragon, suddenly on its own, flew off. Another one plunged to the ground when an Algarvian got in back of it without its flier's knowing and flamed it from behind.

Inside a couple of minutes, all the Unkerlanter dragons were out of the fight. Sabrino himself blazed the dragonflier his group of Algarvians attacked. But one of King Swemmel's men got a measure of revenge. A couple of Algarvian dragons had flamed the one he flew. It was horribly burned, and so, no doubt, was he. Still, he made it obey one last command: he flew it straight against an Algarvian dragon. They smashed together and both tumbled out of the sky.

"That was a brave man," Sabrino said softly. A moment later, as an afterthought, he added, "Curse him." Save for the Algarvians, the heavens were empty. Sabrino waved the wing back toward the dragon farm where they and the handlers would tend to their beasts. But now they had one more slot that wanted filling.

Ealstan looked up from the page of bookkeeping questions his father had set him to find his cousin, Sidroc, grinning a most unpleasant grin. "I'm done with *my* work for the night," Sidroc said. "But then, I only have what the school dishes out. I told you you'd end up stuck with more."

"Aye, and you've *been* telling me, too – telling me and telling me," Ealstan said. "Why don't you shut up and let me finish?" He wished Leofsig, his older brother, were around. But Leofsig had gone to hear music with Felgilde, whom he'd been seeing even before he went in King Penda's levy.

Sidroc went off. He did his best to look insulted, but he was chuckling, too. Ealstan felt like chucking the inkwell after his cousin. Instead, with a sour frown, he buckled down and finished the rest of the problems. After rising, he stretched till his back created; he'd been sitting there a long time. It certainly seemed a long time.

He took the problems into the parlor, where his father and Uncle Hengist were sharing a news sheet. His father turned away from the sheet. "All right, son," he said, "let's see what you've done with this lot."

"Let's see what this lot's done to me," Ealstan returned. Uncle Hengist – Sidroc's father – laughed. Ealstan's father smiled for a moment and started checking the work.

Sidroc must have got his habit of interrupting from Hengist, who set the news sheet on his lap and said, "Looks like the Unkerlanters are finished, eh, Hestan? Algarve's going to be top dog for a long time to come."

"What was that?" Hestan asked; his mind had been on the questions. Sidroc's father repeated himself. Hestan shrugged. "The only news the Algarvians let into Gromheort – into any of Forthweg – is what makes them look good. If anything goes wrong, we'll never hear about it."

"Nobody's said the Unkerlanters are calling the redheads liars, and the Unkerlanters call people liars even when they're telling the truth," Hengist replied.

Hestan only shrugged again. He tapped Ealstan's paper with a fingernail. "Son, you reckoned simple interest here. You should have compounded it. A client would not be happy to find that sort of error in his books."

"Which one, Father?" Ealstan looked down to see what he'd done wrong. He thumped his forehead with the heel of his hand. "I'll fix it," he said, "and I'll remember next time, too." He hated making mistakes, in which he was very much his father's son. The only real difference between them was that his dark beard was still thin and wispy, while gray had started to streak Hestan's. Otherwise, they could have come from the same mold: broad-shouldered, swarthy, hook-nosed, like most Forthwegians and their Unkerlanter cousins.

"Let me explain again when you use simple interest and when you must compound," Hestan began.

Before he could explain, Hengist interrupted once more: "Looks like the Algarvians and the Zuwayzin are both heading toward Glogau. That's the biggest port the Unkerlanters have up on the warm side of Derlavai. Cursed near the only port up there, too, except for a couple way out to the west. What do you think of that?" He waved the news sheet at Hestan.

"I think it would matter more if Unkerlant didn't have such an enormous hinterland," Ealstan's father answered. "The Unkerlanters need things from the rest of the world less than other kingdoms do."

"They need sense, is what they need, though you can't haul that on ships." Hengist pointed toward his brother. "And you need some sense yourself. You just hate the idea of Algarve winning, that's all."

"Don't you, Uncle Hengist?" Ealstan spoke before Hestan could.

Now Hengist shrugged. "If we couldn't beat the redheads, what difference does it make? Things won't be too bad, I don't expect. It's not like we were Kaunians, or anything like that."

"Remember what the Algarvians are letting your son learn," Hestan answered. "Remember what they aren't. You're right, they save the worst for the Kaunians – but they do not wish us well."

"They ruled here when we were boys – have you forgotten?" Hengist said. "If they hadn't lost the Six Years' War, if the Unkerlanters hadn't fought among themselves, we wouldn't have gotten a king of our own back. The redheads treated Forthwegians better than the Unkerlanters did farther west, that's certain."

"But we *should* be free," Ealstan exclaimed. "Forthweg is a great kingdom. We were a great kingdom when the Algarvians and the Unkerlanters were nothing to speak of. They had no business carving us up like a roast goose, either a hundred years ago or now."

"Boy has spirit," Hengist remarked to Hestan. He turned back to Ealstan. "If you want to get right down to it, we aren't carved up any more. King Mezentio's men hold all of Forthweg these days."

Ealstan didn't want to get right down to it, not like that. Without waiting to hear when he should use simple interest and when compound, he left the parlor. Behind him, Hestan said, "In the old days, a Forthwegian or even a blond Kaunian could get ahead in Algarve – not as easily as a redhead, but an able man could make do. I don't see that happening now."

"Well, I don't want a Kaunian getting ahead of me – unless she's a pretty girl in tight trousers." Uncle Hengist laughed.

That's where Sidroc comes by it, all right, Ealstan thought. Instead of going back to his room, he went into the kitchen, intending to hook a plum. He hesitated when he discovered his older sister Conberge in there kneading dough. Since hard times and the Algarvians came to Gromheort, his sister and even his mother had grown stern about making food disappear like that.

But Conberge looked up from her work and smiled at him. Thus encouraged, he sidled up. Her smile didn't disappear when he reached toward the bowl of fruit. She didn't swat him with a floury hand. He took a plum and bit into it. It was very sweet. Juice dribbled down his chin, through the sparse hairs of his sprouting beard.

"What have you got there?" his sister asked, pointing not to the plum but to the paper in his other hand.

"Bookkeeping problems Father set me," Ealstan answered. With a little effort, he managed a smile. "I'm not wild about doing them, but at least he doesn't switch me when I make mistakes, the way a master would at school."

"Let me see," Conberge said, and Ealstan handed her the sheet. She looked it over, nodded, and gave it back. "You used simple interest once when you should have compounded."

"Aye, so Father told—" Ealstan stopped and stared. "I didn't know you could cast accounts." He couldn't tell whether he sounded indignant or astonished – both at once, probably. "They don't teach you that in the girls' academy."

Conberge's smile turned sour. "No, they don't. Maybe they should, but they don't. Father did, though. He said you never could tell, and I might have to be able to earn my own way one day. This was before the war started, mind you."

"Oh." Ealstan glanced back toward the parlor. His father and Uncle Hengist were still going back and forth, back and forth, but he couldn't make out what they were saying. "Father sees a long way ahead."

His sister nodded. "It was a lot harder than writing bad poetry, which is what my schoolmistress set me to doing, though they didn't know it was bad. But I think better because of it, do you know what I mean? Maybe you don't, because they will teach boys some worthwhile things."

"They *would* – till the Algarvians got their hands on the school," Ealstan said bitterly. But he shook his head. He didn't want to distract himself. "I didn't know Father had taught you anything like that, though."

"And up until not very long ago, I wouldn't have told you, either." Conberge's grimace made Ealstan see the world in a way he hadn't before. She said, "Men don't usually want women to know too much or be too bright – or to show they know a lot or they're bright, anyhow. If you ask me, it's because most men don't know that much and aren't that bright themselves."

"Don't look at me like that when you say such things," Ealstan said, which made his sister laugh. He grabbed another plum.

"All right, you can have that one, but that's all," Conberge said. "If you think you'll get away with any more, *you* aren't that bright."

Ealstan laughed then. Perhaps drawn by his amusement and his sister's, Sidroc came in from the door that opened on the courtyard. Seeing Ealstan with a plum in his hand, he grabbed one himself. Conberge couldn't do anything about it, not with Ealstan eating one. As she turned back to the bread dough, Sidroc asked, "What's so funny?" His voice came blurry around a big mouthful of plum. He looked a good deal like Ealstan, save that his nose bore a closer resemblance to a turnip than to a sickle blade.

"Getting stuck with bookkeeping problems," Ealstan answered.

"Men," Conberge added.

Sidroc looked from one of them to the other. Then, suspiciously, he looked at the plum. "Has this thing turned into brandy while I wasn't looking?" he asked. Ealstan and Conberge both shrugged, so solemnly that they started laughing again. Sidroc snorted. "I think the two of you have gone daft, is what I think."

"You're probably right," Ealstan told him. "They do say that too many bookkeeping problems—"

"Compounded quarterly," his sister broke in.

"Compounded quarterly, aye," Ealstan agreed. "Bookkeeping problems compounded quarterly cause calcification of the brain."

"Even you don't know what that means," Sidroc said.

"It means my brain is turning into a rock, like yours was to start with," Ealstan said. "If the Algarvians had let you take stonelore, you would have found out for yourself."

"Think you're so smart," Sidroc kept smiling, but his voice held an edge. "Well, maybe you are. But so what? So what? – that's what I want to know. What's it gotten you?" Without waiting for an answer, he pitched his plum pit into the trash basket and stalked out of the kitchen.

Ealstan wished he could ignore the question. It was too much to the point. Since Sidroc hadn't stayed around, he turned back to Conberge. "What *has* being smart gotten me? Or you, either? Nothing I can see."

"Would you rather be stupid? That won't get you anything, either," Conberge said. After a moment's thought, she went on, "If you're smart, when you grow up you turn into someone like Father. That's not so bad."

"No." But Ealstan remained unhappy. "Even Father, though – what is he? A bookkeeper in a conquered kingdom where the Algarvians don't want us to know enough to be bookkeepers."

"But he's teaching you anyhow, and he taught me, too," Conberge reminded him. "If that isn't fighting back against the redheads, what is?"

"You're right." Ealstan glanced toward the parlor. His father and Uncle Hestan were still arguing. Then he looked at Conberge, as surprised as he'd been when he discovered she knew how to cast accounts. "Sometimes I think I don't know you at all."

"Maybe I should have gone on seeming stupid." His sister shook her head. "Then I'd sound like Sidroc."

"He isn't really stupid, not when he doesn't want to be," Ealstan said. "I've seen that."

"No, he's not," Conberge agreed. "But he doesn't care about the way things are right now. He's happy enough to let the Algarvians run Forthweg. So is Uncle Hengist. All they want to do is get along. I want to fight back, if I can."

"Me, too," Ealstan said, realizing his father might have been teaching him more than bookkeeping after all.

"Milady, he is waiting for you downstairs," Bauska said as Marchioness Krasta dithered between two fur wraps.

"Well, of course he is," Krasta answered, finally choosing the red fox over the marten.

"But you should have gone down there some little while ago," the maidservant said. "He is an Algarvian. What will he do to you?"

"He won't do a thing," Krasta said with rather more confidence than she felt. Standing straighter and brushing back a stray lock of pale gold hair, she added, "I have him wrapped around my little finger." That was a lie, and she knew it. With a younger suitor, a more foolish suitor, it might well have been true. Colonel Lurcanio, though, to her sometimes intense annoyance, did not yield himself so readily.

When Krasta did go downstairs, she found Lurcanio with his arms folded across his chest and a sour expression on his face. "Good of you to join me at last," he said. "I was beginning to wonder if I should ask one of the kitchen women to go with me to the king's palace in your place."

From most men, that would have been annoyed bluster. Lurcanio was annoyed, but he did not bluster. If he said he'd been thinking of taking one of the kitchen wenches to the palace, he meant it.

"I'm here, so let's be off," Krasta said. Lurcanio did not move, but stood looking down his straight nose at her. She needed a moment to realize what he expected. It was more annoying than anything he required of her in bed. Grudgingly, very grudgingly, she gave it to him: "I'm sorry."

"Then we'll say no more about it," Lurcanio replied, affable again now that he'd got his way. He offered her his arm. She took it. They went out to his carriage together.

His driver said something in Algarvian that sounded rude. Had he been Krasta's servant, she would have struck him or dismissed him on the spot. Lurcanio only laughed. That irked her. Lurcanio knew it irked her and did it anyhow, to remind her Valmiera was a conquered kingdom, and she a victor's plaything.

After the carriage began to roll, she asked him, "Have you ever been able to learn what became of my brother?"

"I am afraid I have not," Colonel Lurcanio answered with what sounded like real regret. "Captain Skarnu, Marquis Skarnu, is not known to have been slain. He is not known to have been captured. He is not known to have been among those who surrendered after King Gainibu capitulated. It could be – and for your sake, my lovely lady, I hope it is – that the records of capture and surrender are defective. It would not be the first time."

"What if they aren't?" Krasta asked. Lurcanio did not reply. After a few seconds, she recognized the expression on his long, somber face as pity. "You think he's dead!" she exclaimed.

"Milady, there at the end, the war moved very swiftly," the Algarvian officer replied. "A man might fall with all his comrades too caught up in the retreat to bring him with them. Our own soldiers would have been more concerned with the Valmierans still ahead than with those who could endanger them no more."

"It could be so." Krasta did not want to believe it. But, with most of a year passed since she'd heard from Skarnu, she had a hard time denying it, too. As was her way, when a painful fact stared her in the face, she looked in another direction: in this case, around Priekule. "I don't see so many Algarvian soldiers on the streets these days, I don't think."

"You are likely right," Lurcanio said. "Some of them have gone west to join in the fight against King Swemmel."

"He's a nasty sort," Krasta said. "He deserves whatever happens to him, and so does his kingdom." Civilization, as far as she was concerned, did not run west of Algarve. Not so long before, she would have said it did not run west of Valmiera.

Someone shouted at her from a dark side street: "Algarvian's hired twat!" Running footsteps said the fellow who'd yelled had not lingered to note the effects of his remark. In that, no doubt, he was wise. Had she been able to catch him, Krasta would not have been gentle.

Colonel Lurcanio patted her leg, a little above the knee. "Just another fool," he said, "so take no notice of him. I do not need to hire you, do I?"

"Of course not." Krasta tossed her head. Had Lurcanio offered her money for the use of her body, she would have thrown everything she could reach at him. He'd done nothing of the sort. He'd simply made her afraid of what might happen if she said no. (She chose not to dwell on that; she did not care to think of herself as afraid.)

"Ah, here we are," Lurcanio said a little later, as the carriage came up to the palace. "An impressive building. The royal palace in Trapani is larger, but, I think, less magnificent. One can imagine ruling all the world from here." After that praise, his laughter sounded doubly cruel. "One can imagine it, but not all that one can imagine comes true." He descended from the carriage and handed Krasta down. "Shall we pay our respects to your king, who does not rule all the world from here?" He laughed again.

"I came here the night King Gainibu declared war against Algarve," Krasta said.

"Then he still ruled some of the world from here," Colonel Lurcanio said. "He would have done better to keep silent. He would have gone on ruling some of the world. Now he has to ask the leave of an Algarvian commissioner before he takes a glass of spirits."

"If Algarve hadn't invaded the Duchy of Bari, he wouldn't have had to declare war," Krasta said. "Then everything would still be as it was."

Lurcanio leaned over and brushed his lips across hers. "You must be an innocent. You are too decorative to be a fool." He began ticking points off on his fingers. "Item: we didn't invade Bari; we took back what was ours. The men welcomed us with open arms, the women with open legs. I know. I was there. Item: Valmiera had no business detaching Bari from Algarve after the Six Years' War. It was done, but, as with wizards, what one can do, another can undo. And item: things would not still be as they were." Just for a moment, long enough to make Krasta shiver, he might have been one of his barbarous ancestors. "Had you not gone for us, we would have come after you."

Krasta turned and looked back toward the Kaunian Column of Victory. It still stood in its ancient park, pale and proud and tall in the moonlight. Unlike during the Six Years' War, no damage had come to it in this fight. Even so, the imperial victories it commemorated had never seemed so distant to her.

"Well," Lurcanio said, "let us in, then, and pay our respects to your illustrious sovereign." He spoke without discernible irony. In the wink of an eye, he'd pulled the cloak of polished noble courtier over whatever lay beneath.

In the palace, King Gainibu's servitors bowed to Lurcanio as they might have to a count of Valmieran blood, or perhaps even as they might have to a duke of Valmieran blood. They fawned on Krasta as if she were duchess rather than marchioness, too. That went a long way toward improving her mood.

At the door to the reception hall – the Grand Hall, Krasta realized, the hall in which Gainibu had declared his ill-fated war – a uniformed Algarvian soldier checked Lurcanio's name and hers against a list. After affirming they had the right to go past him, he stood aside. He and Lurcanio spoke briefly in their own language.

"What was that about?" Krasta asked irritably.

"Making sure neither of us is an assassin in disguise," Lurcanio answered. "Still a few malcontents loose in the provinces. They've murdered some nobles who cooperate with us, and some of our men, too. If they managed to sneak a murderer in here, they could do us some harm."

He thought of harm to his kingdom. Krasta thought of harm to herself. When she looked around the room, she found it odd to realize Algarvians were more likely to keep her safe than her own countrymen. She made a beeline for the bar and got herself a brandy laced with wormwood. She tossed it back as if it were ale. The sooner the world got blurry, the better she'd like it.

Lurcanio took a glass of white wine for himself. He drank. He enjoyed drinking. Krasta had seen that. But she'd never seen him fuddled. She doubted she ever would. *Foolishness*, she thought. Anything worth doing was worth doing to excess.

"Shall we go over and greet his Majesty?" Lurcanio asked, glancing toward the receiving line at whose head Gainibu stood. His mouth tightened. "Perhaps we should do it now, while he will still remember who we are – and who he is."

Gainibu held a large tumbler half full of amber spirits. By the way he stood, by the vague expression on his face, he'd already emptied it a good many times. Krasta remembered Lurcanio's sardonic comment outside the palace. The Algarvian commissioner must not have given the king any trouble about refills.

Krasta and Lurcanio worked their way up the receiving line. It was shorter than it would have been before the war. Not all the guests bothered presenting themselves to Gainibu. He was not the most important man in the room, not any more. Several of Lurcanio's superiors possessed more authority than he. Again, Krasta had the sense of ground shifting under her feet.

Gainibu's decorations, honorary and earned, glittered on his chest. Lurcanio saluted him as junior officer to senior. Krasta bowed low. "Your Majesty," she murmured.

"Ah, the marchioness," Gainibu replied, though Krasta was not sure he knew which marchioness she was. "And with a friend, I see. Aye, with a friend." He took another sip from the tumbler. His eyes followed it as he lowered it from his mouth. Before the war, his eyes had followed beautiful women that way. They'd followed Krasta that way, more than once. What was she now? Just another noblewoman on a conqueror's arm, less interesting than the spirits that swirled in his glass.

Lurcanio touched Krasta's elbow. She let him lead her away. Behind her, King Gainibu mumbled something courteous to someone else. "He is not the man he was," Lurcanio said, hardly caring whether Gainibu heard or not. In a different tone, it might have been pity. It was scorn.

To her surprise, sudden tears filled Krasta's eyes. She looked back toward the king. There he stood, impressive, amiable, drunk. His kingdom was a prisoner of Algarve. And he, she thought with a burst of insight that surely came from the wormwood, was a prisoner within himself.

"Now we have done our duty," Lurcanio said. "We can enjoy ourselves the rest of the evening."

"Aye," Krasta said, though she had seldom felt less like enjoying herself. "Excuse me for a moment." She hurried over to the bar. An expressionless servitor gave her another glass of the wormwood-flavored brandy. She gulped it down with reckless speed.

"Have a care, there," Lurcanio said from behind her. "Will I need to carry you up the stairs to your bedchamber tonight?" An eyebrow quirked. "I do not think I need to make you pass out drunk to have my way with you."

"No." Melancholy and insight were not natural to Krasta. Ingenious lubricity was. She ran her tongue over her lips, tilted a hip, and gazed saucily up at the Algarvian officer. "But would you enjoy it that way?"

He considered. Slowly, he smiled. "Once, perhaps. Everything is interesting once." Krasta needed to hear no more. She turned back to the bar and began to drink in earnest.

Three

Pekka was beginning to hate knocks on her office door. They always seemed to come in the middle of important calculations. And the last thing she wanted was to discover Ilmarinen, or even some other theoretical sorcerer, standing on his head in the hallway, as she had once before. Maybe it would be a Kajaani City College student. She could, she hoped, get rid of a student in a hurry.

She got up and opened the door. That done, she had to fight back a gasp of dismay. The smile that appeared on her face was an excellent job of conjuring. "Professor Heikki!" she exclaimed, for all the world as if she were delighted to have her department chairman visit her at that moment. "Won't you come in?"

Maybe Heikki would say no. Maybe knowing Pekka was here and working would satisfy her. But she said, "Aye, I thank you," and strolled in as if it were her office and Pekka the visitor. Pekka, in fact, waited for her to sit down behind the desk. But Heikki planted her rather broad bottom in the chair in front of it.

Retreating – and it felt like a retreat – to her own chair, Pekka brushed a strand of coarse black hair away from her narrow eyes and asked, "What can I do for you this afternoon?"

Whatever Heikki wanted, Pekka was sure it had nothing to do with the project that had engrossed her for so long. Heikki had got to be the chairman of the Department of Sorcery more for her bureaucratic talents than for her magecraft. Her specialty was veterinary sorcery. In unkind moments, Pekka thought she'd chosen it to make sure she knew more than her patients.

"I am disturbed," Heikki said now.

"In what way?" Pekka asked. By the chairman's expression, it might

61

have been dyspepsia. Pekka knew she would get herself in trouble if she suggested stomach bitters. Knowing just made the temptation harder to resist.

"I am disturbed," Heikki repeated. "I am disturbed at the amount of time you are spending in the laboratory of late, and at the expense of your recent experiments. Surely theoretical sorcery, being, uh, theoretical, requires less experimentation than other forms of the art."

In lieu of picking up a vase and smashing it over the department chairman's head, Pekka replied, "Professor, sometimes theory and experiment have to go hand in hand. Sometimes theory proceeds from experiment."

"I am more concerned about our budget," Heikki said primly. "Suppose you tell me what the nature of your experiments is, so that I may judge whether they are worth the time and money you are expending on them."

Pekka had not told her about the assault on the relationship between the laws of similarity and contagion. No one without the most urgent need to know heard anything about that project. All the theoretical sorcerers working on it agreed that was too dangerous. And so, doing her best to look regretful, Pekka murmured, "I'm very sorry, but I'm afraid I can't do that."

"What?" Heikki leaned forward. Had the matter been less important, she might have succeeded in intimidating Pekka. As things were, Pekka had to fight hard not to giggle. The department chairman spoke in portentous tones: "When I ask a simple question, I expect an answer."

You don't know any other kind of question, Pekka thought. She smiled sweetly. "No."

"What?" Heikki said again. "How dare you refuse?" Though her skin, like Pekka's, was golden rather than pink, a flush darkened her cheeks. Pekka said nothing more, which seemed to disturb the chairman further. "If that is your attitude, your laboratory privileges are hereby revoked. And I shall bring your insubordination to the attention of the academic council." She got to her feet and made a stately exit.

That vase sprang into Pekka's mind again. But chasing Heikki down the hall and braining the department chairman would only get her talked about. A different revenge, more vicious if less bloody, occurred to her. A distant ancestor might have smiled that smile just before he sneaked into an enemy clan's camp to slit a warrior's throat. Pekka activated her crystal, spoke briefly, and then went back to work.

She had not been working long when another knock on the door made her set down her pen. The fellow waiting in the hall was Professor Heikki's secretary. "And how may I help you today, Kuopio?" Pekka asked with another of those sweetly bloodthirsty smiles.

"The chairman would see you in her office right away," he answered.

"Please tell her I'm busy," Pekka said. "Perhaps day after tomorrow would do?"

Kuopio stared at her as if she'd suddenly started speaking one of the clicking, coughing languages of tropical Siaulia. She looked back without another word. Shaking his head, the secretary departed. Pekka returned to her sheet of numbers and abstruse symbols.

If she'd miscalculated – not on the problem of the two laws, but on the knottier one of the Kajaani City College bureaucracy – she'd be in hot water. When a third knock came, she jumped, then hurried to the door. There stood Professor Heikki. "Hello again," Pekka said. She'd know in a moment.

Heikki licked her lips. She looked even more dyspeptic than she had earlier in the afternoon. From that, Pekka knew she'd won even before the department chairman said, "Why did you not tell me your experiments had Prince Joroinen's patronage?"

"I could not tell you anything about them," Pekka answered. "I cannot tell anyone anything about them. I tried to tell you that, but you would not hear me. I wish you did not know I was experimenting at all."

"So do I," Heikki said bitterly. "Such ignorance would have spared me a great deal of the abuse I suffered just now. I have been instructed to tell you" – she spat out each word as if it tasted bad – "that the department is to offer you every possible assistance in your work and – and to accept unchallenged any budgetary requisitions you submit." Plainly, that hurt worse than anything else.

No one this side of the princely mints had such untrammeled access to money. For a heady moment, Pekka wished she were a woman of extravagant tastes. But Joroinen would not have given what he gave had he reckoned her likely to abuse it. She said, "What I want most is to be left alone to do what I need to do."

"Then that is what you shall have." Heikki backed away, as if from a dangerous animal. And Pekka *was* a dangerous animal. Had she not been, could she have caused one of the Seven Princes of Kuusamo to turn on the department chairman, who reckoned herself a princess within her realm?

Pekka stood in the doorway and watched Heikki retreat. That helped turn the retreat into a rout. By the time Heikki reached a corner, she was all but running – and was looking over her shoulder as she went, so she nearly slammed into the far wall.

After Heikki did successfully negotiate the corner, Pekka went back to her desk, and got some of her calculations to an interesting point before yet another knock on the door, this one from her husband, ended the day's work. When she opened the door, Leino looked at her with curiosity flashing in his dark eyes. "What did you do to our distinguished chairman?" he asked as he and Pekka walked across the campus to the caravan stop.

"Kept her out of my hair," Pekka answered. "These are modern times. There are cures for head lice."

Leino snorted. "I think your cure was to drop an egg on her. I saw Kuopio in the hall. He flinched as if he thought I'd hit him, too."

"I didn't hit him. I just told him no. He's not used to that." Pekka smiled again. "I did hit Heikki – with Prince Joroinen."

"Ah, so you did drop an egg on her," Leino said, and then he said no more. Pekka blessed him for having better sense than Heikki – not that that made much of a compliment. But Leino, himself a mage of a more practical bent than Pekka's, could not help knowing she was working on an important project. Her trips to Yliharma proved it. Ilmarinen's recent visit to Kajaani proved it. But he hadn't asked questions. He knew her well enough to know she'd tell him what she could. If she didn't tell him anything, she couldn't tell him anything.

They bought a news sheet from a hawker at the caravan stop. Leino frowned at the lead story. "Curse the Gongs, they've sunk half a dozen of our ships off Obuda. We've thrown more into that fight than they have, but they keep hanging on." With reluctant admiration, he added, "They are warriors."

"They're stubborn," Pekka said, and then wondered if there was any difference between her words and her husband's. She pointed to a smaller story about a bigger battle. "The Unkerlanters are counterattacking against Algarve."

"They say they're counterattacking, anyhow," Leino answered. "They've said that before, too, but they keep getting driven back." He turned the news sheet over to read the rest of the story. "The Algarvians say there's heavy fighting, but they're still going forward." As the caravan came gliding up the ley line toward them, he asked, "Who do you hope wins that fight?"

Pekka considered. "I hope they both lose," she said at last. "Unkerlant is Unkerlant, and Algarve is bent on taking vengeance on everyone who ever wronged her. As best as I can tell, that means the rest of the world."

Leino laughed, then shook his head. "That's one of those things that would be funny if only it were funny, if you know what I mean." He stepped aside to let Pekka get into the caravan car ahead of him.

The sun still stood high in the southwest as they walked from the caravan stop up the hill toward their house and that of Pekka's sister. In high summer, it dipped below the horizon only very late, and briefly. Even then, no more than the brightest stars came out, for twilight would linger till it rose again early the next morning. Kuusaman poets wrote verses about the pale nights of Kajaani.

High summer did not incline Pekka toward poetry. It inclined her toward tearing her hair. Her six-year-old son was never easy to get to bed at any season of the year. With the house light at almost all hours of the day and night, getting Uto to bed turned as near impossible as made no difference.

Elimaki handed him over to Pekka and Leino with every sign of relief. Leino's laugh was rueful; he knew what his sister-in-law's frazzled expression meant. "The house is still standing," he remarked, as if that were some consolation.

Some, perhaps, but not enough, not by the way Elimaki rolled her eyes. "I didn't stuff him in the rest crate," she said, as if that proved her extraordinary virtue. "I was tempted to, but I didn't."

"And we thank you for that," Pekka said, giving Uto a glare that bounced off him like a beam from a stick off a dragon's silvered belly.

"I don't thank her," Uto said. "I want to see what it's like in there."

"Aunt Elimaki keeps her rest crate locked when she isn't using it for the same reason we keep ours locked when we aren't using it," Leino said. "The magic in there is to keep food fresh. It isn't to keep little boys fresh."

"Aye – you're fresh enough already," Pekka told her son. As if to prove her right, Uto stuck out his tongue.

Leino swatted him on the bottom, more to gain his attention than to punish him. Elimaki rolled her eyes again. She said, "He's been like that all day long."

"We'll take him home now," Pekka declared. Uto hopped off the porch and down the walk like a frog. Pekka's knees ached just watching him. With a sigh, she turned to Leino. "Some kinds of magic haven't got anything to do with magecraft." Leino considered, then solemnly nodded.

In days gone by, Cornelu had strolled through the streets of the shore town of Tirgoviste in his uniform or in tunic and kilt of the latest style and the softest linen, always perfectly pressed and pleated. He'd been proud to put himself on display, to show off who and what he was: a commander in the island kingdom's navy.

Coming into Algarvian-occupied Tirgoviste now, he still wore his best clothes, such as they were: a much-patched sheepskin jacket over a sleeveless undertunic, with a wool kilt that had long since lost whatever shape it might once have owned. He looked like a shepherd from the inland hills down on his luck. Three days of ruddy stubble on his cheeks and chin only added to the impression. The first Algarvian soldier who saw him tossed him a coin, saying, "Here, you poor beggar, buy yourself a mug of wine."

By his accent, he came from the far north of Algarve; Algarvian and Sibian were closely related tongues, but a real shepherd from back in the hills probably wouldn't have understood him. But the small silverpiece carried its own meaning. Cornelu bobbed his head and mumbled, "My thanks." Laughing, nodding, King Mezentio's soldier went on his way, for all the world as if Tirgoviste were his own town.

Cornelu hated him for that despite his casual kindness. Cornelu hated him all the more because of his casual kindness. *Toss a Sibian dog a bone, will you?* he thought. Not showing what he felt ate at him. Algarvians played at feuds, made them into elegant games. Sibians nursed them, cherished them, never let them go.

A broadsheet pasted on a brick wall drew Cornelu's eye. It showed two bare-chested, sword-swinging warriors from ancient days. One was labeled ALGARVE; the other, younger and half a head shorter, SIBIU. Below them was the legend, SIBIANS ARE AN ALGARVIC FOLK, TOO! JOIN THE STRUGGLE AGAINST UNKERLANTER BARBARISM! Below that, a line of smaller type added, *See the recruiter, 27 Dumbraveni Street.*

Fury filled Cornelu. After a moment, it leaked away. A slow smile spread over his face instead. If Mezentio's minions were trying to get Sibians to fight for them, how many men were they losing? More than they could afford, evidently.

But men hawking news sheets did their best to tell a different story. They shouted about one Algarvian victory in Unkerlant after another. By what they said, Herborn, the biggest city in the Duchy of Grelz, was on the point of falling. Even if that proved a lie, that the Algarvians had come far enough to make the claim did not speak well for the fight King Swemmel's men were putting up.

Another Algarvian soldier strolled by, this one arm in arm with a girl who spoke Sibian with a Tirgoviste accent like Cornelu's. They didn't always understand each other, but they were having fun trying. The girl's face shone as she looked up at the man who had helped bring her kingdom to its knees.

Again, Cornelu had to fight to keep from showing what he felt. He'd already come into the city a couple of times since swimming ashore after Eforiel, his leviathan, was killed, and had seen the same kinds of things then. They tore at his heart. Some – too many – of his countrymen were willing to accept that they had been conquered.

"Not I," he muttered under his breath. "Not I. Not ever."

He made his way along the hilly streets till he came to an eatery that had been fine once but had gone down in the world. He nodded as he set his hand on the latch. He'd gone down in the world himself.

Inside, the place was cool and dim. It smelled of fish and the oil in which the cook fried them. A couple of old men sat at one table nursing glasses of pear brandy. A fisherman was demolishing a platter of fried prawns at another. The rest were empty. Cornelu sat down on a stool at one of those.

A waiter came over with an expectant look. Cornelu glanced at the bill of fare chalked on a board behind the bar. "Fried cod, boiled parsnips and butter, and a mug of ale," he said.

"Aye." The waiter went into a back room. He didn't come out right away; maybe he was the cook, too. He didn't have so much trade that he couldn't be both.

Presently, the door from the street opened. Cornelu started to leap to his feet. A tired-looking fisherman came in and sat down with the fellow eating prawns. Cornelu sank back on to his stool.

Out came the waiter, with his supper on a tray. He set it down, then took his new customer's order. That fellow wanted prawns, like his friend. Cornelu started eating his fish. It wasn't bad. He'd had better, but also worse. He sipped the ale. Like the fish, it was middling good.

He ate slowly, stretching out the meal, making it last. That wasn't easy. He felt hungry as a wolf. He'd come up on to the island without a copper banu to his name, and stayed alive doing odd jobs. He really had herded sheep for a while. He'd spent a lot of time hungry.

Coins clinked as the old men paid for their brandy. They got up and left. The waiter scooped their money into a leather pouch he wore at the front of his kilt. Cornelu raised a forefinger and asked for another mug of ale. The waiter looked him over, then raised an eyebrow. He understood the challenge, and set silver on the table. Mollified, the waiter gave him what he wanted.

He'd almost finished the parsnips and was halfway down that second ale when the door opened again. A worn woman pushing a baby carriage paused in the doorway and looked at the handful of customers in the eatery.

A worn woman pushing a carriage . . . for a moment, to his shame, that was all Cornelu saw. He salved his conscience by noting she'd needed a moment to recognize him, too. Then he did leap up, as he'd started to do before. "Costache!" he exclaimed.

"Cornelu!"

He'd expected his wife to run to him. In his dreams, that was how it had been. His dreams, though, had left out the carriage. Carefully pushing it ahead of her, she made her way to his table. Then he embraced her. Then he kissed her. As if from very far away, he heard the fishermen sniggering. He didn't care. As far as he was concerned, the powers below could swallow them both.

At last, Costache asked, "Do you want to see your daughter?"

What he wanted was a chance to start another child then and there. He knew he couldn't have that. As naturally as he could, he looked down into the carriage. "What is her name?" he asked. He'd been able to write to his old address, to the house where Costache still lived, but he'd had no address of his own, drifting from one place to another. Till this moment, he hadn't know whether his child was boy or girl.

"I called her Brindza, after your mother," Costache answered.

Cornelu nodded. It was good. It was fitting. He wished the baby could have been named Eforiel, but that would have been wrong. The leviathan had still been living when she was born.

"And what would milady care for today?" the waiter asked. He might have been standing there for some time, waiting to be noticed. Had he not spoken up, he would have kept on waiting quite a while, too.

"Whatever my husband had there will be fine for me, too," she answered, sitting down on the stool next to Cornelu's. She sounded dazed, as if she didn't want to think right now. Cornelu understood that; he felt dizzier, drunker, than if he'd swallowed a tun of ale. The waiter shrugged and went off to the back room.

Costache pointed a finger at Cornelu, as if in accusation. "I thought you were dead."

"I was out to sea when the Algarvians came," he answered. "They'd already taken the harbour when I got back." He spoke in a low voice so the fishermen couldn't overhear: "I didn't want to surrender, so I took Eforiel over to Lagoas. I've been there ever since, along with the rest of the exiles, doing what we could to fight Mezentio."

Now that Costache wasn't in his arms any more, wasn't pressed against the flesh that had missed her so, he took a longer look into the carriage. The baby sleeping in there had a thin, short fuzz of reddish hair. "She looks like you," Costache said softly.

"She looks like a baby," Cornelu said. As far as he was concerned, all babies looked more or less alike – oh, maybe not Kuusamans or Zuwayzin, but the rest. And yet, even as that thought went through his mind, he was trying to find his nose, his chin, on those small smooth features.

The waiter set down Costache's supper. If he found anything remarkable about a father staring at a daughter more than a year old as if he'd never seen her before, he kept it to himself. Costache ate absently. She kept staring from Cornelu to Brindza and back again, as if reconnecting the two of them in her mind.

"How have you been?" Cornelu asked her.

"Tired," she answered at once. "If you have a baby, you're tired. You can't be anything else. And times have been hard. No pay, no pension, no money to hire a nurse to take care of Brindza so I could make money on my own." She shook her head. "Tired," she repeated.

"I wish I could have let you know sooner that I was all right," Cornelu said. "Some . . . friends of mine were finally able to post that note." He wondered if the Lagoan raiders were still on the island. He had no way to know, not now.

"I almost fell over in a faint when I recognized your script," Costache said. "And then the other notes started."

"They wouldn't have, but I got stranded here." Cornelu shook his head. "Poor Eforiel took all the energy from an egg."

"Ah, too bad." Costache also shook her head. She sounded sad. But she did not understand, not really. No one but another leviathan-rider could have understood. Cornelu had been more intimate with his wife, but not a great deal.

Intimate with his wife . . . It had been so long. He took a last swig from the second mug of ale. "Can we go home now?" he asked, confident he knew the answer.

But, to his astonished chagrin, Costache shook her head again. "I dare not bring you home," she said. "I have three Algarvian officers billeted on me. They have been correct in every way," she added hastily, "but if you came there, you'd go into a captives' camp the instant you walked through the door."

"Three Algarvian officers?" Cornelu echoed in tones that couldn't mean anything but, *Three men I have to kill*. He thought pain and outrage would choke him. Clapping a hand to his forehead, he exclaimed, "Has it come to this, then? Do I have to make an assignation to sleep with my own wife?" He barely remembered to keep his voice too low for the fishermen to hear him.

"Aye, I fear it has come to that, and even assignations won't be easy," Costache answered. Cornelu felt the veins of his neck tighten with fury: fury at the Algarvians, fury at her, fury at everything that kept him from taking what he'd wanted so much for so very long. Before he could bellow like a bull, Brindza woke up and started to cry. Costache gave Cornelu a weary smile. "And here you have one of the reasons assignations won't be easy." She scooped the baby out of the carriage.

Cornelu stared at his daughter. He did his best not to see her only as an obstacle standing between him and taking Costache to bed. She looked back at him out of eyes that might have been her mother's. With some effort, he smiled. She turned her face back toward Costache, as if to ask, *Who is this person?* What she did say was, "Mama?"

"She's shy with strangers right now," Costache said. "People say they all are at this age."

I am not a stranger! Cornelu wanted to shout. *I am her father!* That was true, but Brindza had no way of knowing it. A new thought cut him like a dagger from out of the night: *I wonder if she's shy with the Algarvians living in my house.*

"I'd better go," Costache said. "They will be wondering where I am at this hour." She leaned forward and brushed Cornelu's lips with her own. "Keep writing to me. We'll meet again as soon as we can." Brindza up on one shoulder, she pushed the carriage with the other, as she'd obviously had practice doing. She used the carriage to butt the door open. It closed behind her. She was gone. Cornelu sat by himself in the eatery, more alone in his home town than he had been in exile in Setubal.

As soon as Bembo walked into the constabulary station in Tricarico, Sergeant Pesaro's face warned him something was wrong. The plump Algarvian constable searched his conscience like a man ransacking his belt pouch for spare change. Rather to his surprise, he found nothing.

But, no matter how innocent he was, or thought he was, Pesaro — who was much rounder than he — pointed a fleshy finger at him and growled, "You had to be so cursed smart, didn't you?"

"What? When?" Bembo asked. "Usually you call me an idiot." The only time he could remember being smart lately was catching Kaunians with their hair dyed. He hadn't gotten in trouble for that; he'd earned a commendation. Even pretty little Saffa had liked him — for a bit.

"You *are* an idiot," Pesaro said. "Even when you're smart, you're an idiot."

"Tell me what you're talking about, anyhow," Bembo said, starting to get angry now. "I'd like to know what kind of idiot I am."

Pesaro shook his head. His flabby jowls wobbled. "I'll leave it to Captain Sasso. No patrols today, except for a few lucky bastards. The rest of us have to assemble at midmorning. Then you'll find out."

Wondering if Sasso was going to order him executed before the assembled constables, Bembo tried to pry more out of the sergeant, but had no luck. Cursing under his breath, he went back to the offices to see if anyone there knew and would talk. Saffa sneered at him and tossed her fine head of fiery red hair when he walked in. He ignored her, which no doubt left her disappointed. He ended up disappointed, too; if anyone did know what Sasso would say, he wouldn't admit it.

Nothing to do but wait and worry and fume till midmorning. Then, along with the rest of the constables, Bembo trooped out to the scruffy lawn in back of the station. The summer sun beat down on him. Sweat rolled down his face and started to darken his tunic. *Stewing in my own juices*, he thought.

Captain Sasso strutted up to the front of the assembled men. Without preamble, he announced, "King Mezentio is taking a contingent from every constabulary force in Algarve into his service, to control captives, to round up criminals and undesirables in the newly conquered lands, and to free up more of our soldiers for the fight against the kingdom's foes."

A low murmur ran through the constables. Pesaro mouthed, *Now do you remember?* at Bembo, and Bembo had to nod. He'd seen the need a year before the authorities had, but his opinion of the authorities' cleverness was low.

Sasso hadn't finished. "From Tricarico, the following constables have been selected for the aforementioned service . . ." He pulled a list from a breast pocket and began reading names. Pesaro's was on it, which explained why he was irate. And then, a moment later, Bembo heard his own name. Sasso went through the whole list, then continued, "Men named here will report in uniform to the caravan depot at noon tomorrow, for transportation to your new assignment. Bring all necessary constabulary gear, but no more personal effects than will fit into your belt pouches and one small pack. I know you will acquit Tricarico well, men." He spun on his heel and marched away without so much as calling for questions.

"Tomorrow?" Bembo howled. His was far from the only cry of amazement and dismay. He raised his hands to the uncaring sky. "How can we go tomorrow? Powers above, how can we go at all?"

"Southern Unkerlant is lovely in the wintertime," said a constable who was staying in Tricarico. He kissed his fingertips. "So white! So fair! And winter there doesn't last more than three fourths of the year."

"Your wife is lovely in a whorehouse bed," Bembo snarled. He kissed his fingertips, too. "So white! So fair! And your daughter the same. They both charge more than they're worth, though."

With a curse, the other constable hurled himself at Bembo. Normally no braver than he had to be, Bembo was ready to brawl. Before either of them could throw more than a punch or two, though, their comrades got between them. "When you come home, wretch, our friends will settle where we can meet," the other constable said.

"You haven't got any friends," Bembo retorted. "Ask your wife to help. She has dozens. Hundreds."

Sergeant Pesaro shoved Bembo away before the fight could flare again. "Let it go," he said. "Getting in trouble won't keep you off the caravan." Bembo hadn't thought of that, and wished he had. Pesaro went on, "We aren't going to Unkerlant, anyhow. Some other poor whoresons get stuck with that. We're heading for Forthweg. The weather will be better, anyhow."

"Huzzah," Bembo said sourly. He cocked his head to one side. "How do you know where we're going?"

Pesaro only smiled. After a moment, Bembo realized it was a foolish question. Pesaro was fat and slow and a long way from young. If he didn't know things, what good was he? He thumped Bembo on the shoulder. "Go on. Go home. Get ready. We're stuck with it. If you're not on the caravan car with me tomorrow, you're a deserter during wartime." He sliced a thumb across his throat.

Thus encouraged, Bembo went back to his flat. Packing didn't take long, not with the limits Captain Sasso had imposed. He drank his dinner. For good measure, he drank his supper, too. With nothing better to do, he went to bed early.

He woke with a pounding head and a taste in his mouth like the river downstream from the sewage works. A glass of wine helped dull both complaints. He still felt lethargic and abused, but he'd felt that way before. Shouldering the few belongings he could bring, he made for the depot.

He got there at the same time as his frequent partner, Oraste. Pesaro checked off both their names. Oraste was quiet and looked somewhat the worse for wear, too. Maybe he'd spent his last night in Tricarico the same way Bembo had.

Bembo was climbing up into the caravan car when someone – a woman – called, "Wait!" Saffa came running up. She threw herself into his arms and gave him a kiss that made him forget his headache. Then she slipped away and said, "There! Is that because I'm sorry you're going or because I'm glad? You'll never know." She headed back toward the constabulary station, putting everything she had into her walk.

"Don't stand there gaping with your tongue hanging out," Pesaro told Bembo. "Go on; get aboard." Bembo didn't move till Saffa was out of sight. Then, as if a spell were broken, he shook himself and obeyed.

But for the constables from Tricarico, the ley-line caravan carried no passengers. As soon as the last man climbed into the car – with curses from Pesaro for being the last – the caravan began its long glide west. The Bradano Mountains sank below the horizon. Wheatfields, meadows with cattle and sheep grazing in them, vineyards, and groves of almonds and olives and citrus fruit slid past outside the windows. Before long, Bembo got into a dice game and stopped worrying about the scenery.

Just after noon, the caravan stopped in a medium-sized town along the ley-line. Half a dozen irate-looking men in constable's uniform filed aboard. "Hello!" Bembo said. "Misery loves company, looks like."

The caravan stopped several times during the afternoon. At each stop, another contingent of disgruntled constables got on. By the time the caravan began to near what had been the Forthwegian border, all the cars were full. Bembo doubted there was a happy man in any of them.

Pesaro pointed out the window. "Look at all the behemoths feeding there. And we saw even more unicorns a little while ago."

"Behemoths. Unicorns. Constables." Bembo shrugged. "All animals that get ridden off to war whether they want to or not."

At what had been the border with Forthweg, the caravan halted again. By then, lamps – dim ones, in case the Unkerlanters managed to sneak a few dragons through – were shining in every car. An Algarvian army officer bounded up into the car in which Bembo rode. "On behalf of his Majesty, King Mezentio, I thank you for entering his service," he said. "With you to patrol the towns and villages of Forthweg, we can use the soldiers who were on garrison duty as soldiers should be used: in the fighting. If constables are constables, then soldiers can be soldiers."

That sounded good. It even impressed Bembo – till he remembered that the officer was as far behind the lines as he was. "Where in blazes are we bound, anyway?" he asked. He saw no need to treat the officer as he would have a superior in his service, in spite of the fellow's fancy talk.

A scowl said the officer realized that, too. But he answered mildly enough: "Constables in this car will get off at Gromheort, not far from here." He coughed. "Some of them may be fortunate they are replacing the army there and not elsewhere. On the other hand, army discipline might improve them."

Bembo did not rise to that. One narrow escape was enough. The caravan slid along the ley line toward Gromheort. He tried to remember if he'd ever heard of the place. He didn't think so. It would have been under Algarvian rule before the Six Years' War, so it might not prove too bad, but he wouldn't have bet more than a copper on that.

Nor did his first glimpse, by moonlight, send him into raptures. The depot was battered, and about one building in four between it and the barracks where the constables would spend the night had been wrecked. "The Forthwegians fought hard here," explained the officer, who guided them to the barracks.

"Why haven't they repaired it since?" Bembo asked, safely anonymous in the darkness.

"They have," the army officer answered. "If you think it's bad now, you should have seen it just after we took it." He pointed ahead, to a low, squat building that once must have housed cattle or Forthwegian soldiers. "Go through the curtains one man at a time, to keep light from spilling out."

Inside, the barracks were as bad as Bembo had expected. After a day spent traveling across northern Algarve, he didn't care. He hurried to a pallet, set his pack under his head in lieu of a pillow (he labored under no delusions about his fellow constables, who were bound to have some light-fingered souls among them), and went to sleep.

Next morning, glum-looking Forthwegians served up bread and olive oil and harsh red wine. Another Algarvian army officer came in and distributed maps of Gromheort to those constables who would patrol it. "Things are pretty quiet," he told the newcomers. "Just keep 'em that way and everything will be fine." He offered no suggestions on how to achieve that laudable end.

Without enough breakfast to suit him, without a bath, without really knowing his way around, Bembo was thrust out on to the streets of Gromheort. Forthwegians in long tunics glared at him or tried to pretend he didn't exist. Kaunians got out of his way in a hurry. That, at least, felt right and proper.

No one did anything in the least untoward. All the same, he walked far more warily than he would have back in Tricarico. There, only the rare desperate fool would take on a constable. Here, in a sullen conquered kingdom, who could say? He didn't want to find out the hard way.

At midmorning, feeling peckish, he stepped into an eatery and demanded an omelette. The proprietor made as if he didn't understand Algarvian. Bembo's gut told him the fellow was bluffing. He hefted his club and growled – and got his omelette. He didn't care for the cheese the Forthwegian used, but it wasn't too bad. Patting his belly, he walked out.

"You pay!" the proprietor exclaimed – he knew some Algarvian, all right.

Bembo only laughed. If he wouldn't have paid for a meal back in Tricarico – and he wouldn't – he was cursed if he'd do it here in a land Algarve had won by the sword. What could the Forthwegian do if he didn't? Not a thing. He snapped his fingers and went on his way.

In summer, a cold bath looked better to Leofsig than at other seasons of the year. After a day of building roads in the sun, he took himself to Gromheort's public baths to wash off the sweat and dirt before he went home. He paid the attendant at the door a copper, hung his tunic on a peg in the antechamber, and, naked, hurried toward the pools and plunges beyond. He tested the water of what had been the warm plunge with a toe.

"Not too bad," said an older man already in there. "Could be chillier than this and feel good on a day like today."

"Aye, that's so." Leofsig slid into the water himself. He rubbed at his hide. By the time he got through, he was three shades lighter than when he'd begun. The plunge wasn't so warm as to make him want to linger, though, as it would have been in happier times. He climbed up the steps and headed for the soaping room.

The liquid soap in the troughs wasn't what it had been before the war, either. It was cheap and harsh with lye and smelled nasty. When he rubbed it into a little cut on his arm, it burned like fire.

An enormous tub stood in the rinsing room. He grabbed a bucket with a pierced bottom, filled it in the tub, and hung it from a hook at a level above his head. As the water in it streamed out through the holes, he stood under it and let the soap run off down the drain. A man in a hurry could make do with one bucket. Tonight, Leofsig used two.

On the other side of the brick wall, women were rinsing. As every man of Gromheort had surely done, Leofsig imagined that wall suddenly made transparent. Imagining Felgilde, his almost-fiancée, bare and wet and slick made the water seem warmer than it was. Imagining the screech she'd let out if the wall did turn transparent made him laugh. He set the bucket back by the tub for another bather to use, then got a towel from a Kaunian attendant who'd been there as long as he could remember – and as long as his father could remember, too.

When Leofsig was younger, he'd once said, "Maybe he's been handing out towels since the days of the Kaunian Empire."

Hestan had laughed, but then, precise as always, he'd shaken his head and said, "No. People bathing together is a Forthwegian custom, and an Unkerlanter one, too, but not a Kaunian one."

Dry and clean now, Leofsig threw his towel into a wickerwork basket and went up to the antechamber to get his tunic. He hated to put it back on; it was grimy and smelly. But he was no Zuwayzi, to walk unconcerned through the streets of Gromheort without a stitch on. *I'll change when I get home*, he thought.

He'd gone only a block or so when a chubby Algarvian in tunic and kilt of cut somewhat different from the army's spoke to him in Algarvian. "I don't know your language," he said in Forthwegian. That wasn't quite true, but, unlike his brother Ealstan and cousin Sidroc, he hadn't had to learn it in school. Plainly, the redhead didn't follow him, either. Leofsig tried classical Kaunian: "Do you understand me now?"

No sooner were the words out of his mouth than he wondered if he'd made a bad mistake. The Algarvians despised everything in any way connected to Kaunians. But this fellow, after frowning, answered in halting, thickly accented Kaunian: "Understanding little. Not using when . . . after . . . *since* school." He beamed at coming up with the right word.

Leofsig nodded to show he understood, too. "What do you want?" he asked, speaking slowly and clearly.

"Not finding," the Algarvian said. After a moment, Leofsig realized he meant *lost*. The redhead pulled a sheet of paper out of a tunic pocket. It turned out to be a map of Gromheort. He pointed. "Going here, please?" *Here* was a barracks where soldiers had been garrisoned. The Algarvian waved, one of his people's extravagant gestures. "I now where?" He made a comic display of frustration and embarrassment.

"I will show you," Leofsig said. He'd started to help before remembering he hated the conquerors. He had trouble hating this particular one, who was rumpled and funny and had asked for help instead of demanding it. And so, instead of sending him the wrong way, Leofsig traced the route back to the barracks on the map.

"Ah." The Algarvian swept off his hat and bowed as deeply as his rotund frame would allow. "Thanking." He bowed again. Leofsig nodded in return; Forthwegians were a less demonstrative people. Peering at the map, the redhead went off down the street. Maybe he would find the barracks. He was headed in the right direction, anyhow. He looked back to Leofsig and waved. Leofsig gave him another nod and headed on toward his own home.

He mentioned the affable Algarvian over supper. His father nodded. "That must be one of the constables they're bringing in," Hestan said. "If they use constables to keep order hereabouts, they can put more soldiers into the attack on Unkerlant." He glanced over to Uncle Hengist, as if he'd just proved a point.

By the way Hengist fidgeted, maybe Hestan had. Hengist said, "They're still moving forward. By the news sheet, they've trapped a big army west of the capital of the Duchy of Grelz – forget the cursed place's name. After a while, Unkerlant will run out of armies."

"Herborn," Ealstan put in.

"Unless Algarve runs out first," Hestan added. Hengist snorted and gestured dismissively, almost as if he were an Algarvian himself. Hestan sipped from his cup of wine, then turned back to Leofsig. "And what was this constable like, son?"

"He didn't seem too bad a fellow," Leofsig answered: about as much as he would say for any Algarvian. "He thanked me when I showed him where he ought to go. None of their soldiers would have."

"All their soldiers were good for were pinches on the bottom," Conberge said.

"I never had that happen to me," Leofsig observed.

"You'd best be glad you didn't," Sidroc said archly. Everyone laughed. It was easier and more comforting to think of the Algarvians as women-chasers – which they were – than as warriors who had overwhelmed all their opponents – which, unfortunately for their neighbors, they also were.

"Would anyone like more of this beans-and-cheese casserole?" Leofsig's mother asked, reaching out to touch the spoon in the bowl. "There's plenty, for once; I went to the markets early, and got the cheese before it all disappeared."

"I'll take more, Elfryth," Hestan said. Leofsig and Ealstan and Sidroc pushed their plates toward her, too. If his mother hadn't said there was plenty and plainly meant it, Leofsig would have made do with one helping. He'd grown resigned to being hungry a lot of the time. Feeling full, as he did after his seconds, seemed strange, almost unnatural.

After supper, Ealstan came to him for help with a bookkeeping problem their father had set him. Leofsig looked at it, then shook his head. "I know I ought to know how to solve it, but I'm cursed if I can remember right now." He yawned enormously. "I'm so tired, I can't even see. That's how I am, most nights. You don't know how lucky you are that Father decided to keep you in school."

"It doesn't teach much, not any more," his brother answered. "I'm learning a lot more from Father than from the masters."

"You're missing the point," Leofsig said. "You could be out hauling rocks instead. Plenty your age are. Then you'd be too tired to think, too."

"Oh, I understand that," Ealstan said. "What makes me sizzle is watching Sidroc not even working at the watered-down pap the Algarvians still let the schoolmasters teach."

"If Sidroc wants the masters to stripe his back, that's his affair," Leofsig said. "If he wants to try to get through life on gab, that's his affair, too. I don't know why you're wasting your time worrying about it."

"Because he goes off and does what he pleases, and I have the masters' work and Father's, too, that's why," Ealstan snapped. Then he paused and looked sheepish. "It could be worse, couldn't it?"

"Just a bit," Leofsig said dryly. "Aye, just a bit." But he paused, too. "It could be worse for me, too, now that I think on it."

This time, Ealstan did not miss the point even for a moment. "Of course it could," he said. "You could be a Kaunian." He lowered his voice. "At least you know. So many people don't even want to, or else say the blonds have it coming." He looked around, then spoke more softly still: "Some of those people are right in this house."

"Aye, I know that," Leofsig said. "If you ask me, Sidroc wishes he were an Algarvian. Uncle Hengist, too, though not so bad."

Ealstan shook his head. "That's not it – close, but not right. Sidroc just wants to be on top, and the Algarvians are."

"If he wants to be on top—" Leofsig broke off. Ealstan hadn't been through the army, and didn't take crudity for granted. Leofsig shrugged. "You know him better than I do – and you're welcome to him, too, as far as I'm concerned."

"Thanks," his younger brother said in a way that wasn't thankful at all. They both chuckled. Then Ealstan grew serious once more. "I'd like to pop him right in the face for the way he rides me about the problems Father sets me, but I don't quite dare."

"Why not?" Leofsig asked. "I think you can thump him – and if you have trouble, I'll pitch in. A set of lumps'll shut him up."

"Maybe I can, maybe I can't, but that's not it," Ealstan said. "And if I ever do mix it up with him, I want you to stay out of it."

Leofsig frowned. "I'm not following this. What are big brothers for, if they're not for thumping people who give little brothers trouble?"

Ealstan licked his lips. "If you thump him, he's liable to go to the redheads and remind them nobody ever let you out of that captives' camp. I don't know that he would, but I don't know that he wouldn't, either."

"Oh." Leofsig pondered that. Slowly, he nodded. "When you lift up a rock, you find all sorts of little white crawling things under it, don't you? That he'd do such a thing to his own flesh and blood . . . But he might, curse it. You're right. He might." He rubbed his chin. His black beard was a man's now, thick and coarse, not soft fuzz like Ealstan's. "I don't want him having that kind of hold on me. I don't want anyone having that kind of hold on me."

"I don't know what we can do about it," Ealstan said.

"I've frightened him once or twice already, when he started blowing in that direction," Leofsig said. "If I put him in fear of his life . . ." He spoke altogether matter-of-factly. Before going into King Penda's levy, he'd been as mild as anyone would expect from a bookkeeper's son. Now the only thing holding him back was doubt about how well the ploy would work. He clicked his tongue between his teeth. "The stinking worm might just run straight to the Algarvians."

"I was thinking the same thing," Ealstan said. "I don't know what to do. Maybe sitting tight and waiting would be best. It's always worked pretty well for Father."

"Aye, so it has." Leofsig gnawed at the inside of his lower lip. "I don't like it, though. Powers above can't make me like it, either." He pounded a fist down on to his thigh. "I wonder if Uncle Hengist would sell me, too."

Ealstan looked startled. "He's never said anything—"

"So what?" Leofsig broke in. "Sometimes the ones who don't blab beforehand are more dangerous than the ones who do."

In Skrunda, as in so many Jelgavan towns, ancient and modern lived side by side. A couple of blocks beyond the market square stood an enormous marble arch from the later days of the Kaunian Empire celebrating the triumph of the Emperor Gedimainas over the Algarvian tribe known as the Belsiti. Below a relief of kilted barbarians being led away in chains, Gedimainas' inscription declared to the world what a hero and conqueror he was.

Talsu took the arch and its inscription as much for granted as he did the oil-seller's shop next to it on the street. He'd walked under it a couple of times a week ever since he'd got big enough to go so far from home. He rarely bothered looking up at the relief or at the vaunting inscription below it. He could barely make sense of the inscription, anyhow; he hadn't studied classical Kaunian in school, and Jelgavan, like Valmieran, had drifted a long way from the old language.

He headed toward the arch this particular morning because he was carrying four pairs of trousers his father, Traku, had made for a customer who lived half a mile down the street the monument straddled. A crowd had gathered under the arch. Some were Jelgavans, some Algarvians in their broad-brimmed hats, tight tunics, kilts, and knee stockings.

"You can't do that," one of the Jelgavans exclaimed. Several of Talsu's countrymen nodded. Somebody else said, "That arch has stood there for more than a thousand years. Knocking it down would be an outrage!" More Jelgavans nodded.

"Why do they want to knock down the arch?" Talsu asked somebody at the back of the little crowd. "It's not doing anything to anybody." He consciously noticed it for only the third or fourth time since coming home to Skrunda after the Jelgavan defeat the year before.

Before the fellow could answer, one of the Algarvians did, in Jelgavan accented but clear: "We can destroy it, and we will destroy it. It is an insult to all the brave Algarvians of ancient days, and to the Algarvic kingdoms of today: to Algarve, to Sibiu, and even to Lagoas that is misguided enough to be our foe."

From the middle of the crowd, a woman called, "How is it an insult if it tells the truth?"

"Algarvians went on to triumph," the redhead officer replied. "That proves all the vile things this Kaunian tyrant said about our ancestors were false. They have stood too long. They shall stand no more." He turned to a mage. Looking over the people in the crowd, Talsu saw that eggs had been affixed to the pillars upholding the arch. All of a sudden, he didn't want to stand right there.

The oil seller didn't like his shop standing right there, either. Bursting out of it, he cried, "You people are going to drop a million tons of rock right through my roof!"

"Calm yourself," the officer said, a startling bit of advice from an excitable Algarvian's mouth. "Buraldo there is very good at what he does, very careful. You should come through fine."

"And if I don't?" the oil seller shouted. The Algarvian shrugged one of his kingdom's extravagant shrugs. The oil seller shouted again, wordlessly this time.

Talsu shouldered his way through the crowd. A couple of Algarvian soldiers swung their sticks in his direction. They were only alert, though, not dangerous. He'd seen the difference on the battlefield. Holding up the trousers, he said, "Before you do whatever you're going to do, can I get by to deliver these?"

"Aye, go on," the officer said, and waved him through with a laugh. He was glad of the arch's shade against the summer sun; that was about as much attention as he usually paid it. More Jelgavans stood on the far side, some of them also grumbling about what the redheads were on the point of doing to the monument. He pushed his way past them and up the street.

"How can you be so uncaring?" a woman with yellow hair like his demanded.

"Lady, I don't want the redheads to knock it down, either," Talsu answered. "But I can't do anything about it, and neither can you. If you have the time to stand around and moan, fine. Me, I've got work to do."

She stared at him. By the cut and cloth of her clothes, she had more money than he. A tailor's son, he could make a good guess at how much anyone made by what he wore on his back. These days, her wealth only meant the Algarvians could steal more from her than from Traku and his family.

Behind Talsu, the redheads started shouting, "Back! Everyone back! If you don't go back, it's your own cursed fault!"

"Shame!" somebody shouted. One by one, the crowd of Jelgavans took up the chant: "Shame! Shame! Shame!"

If the Algarvians felt any sense of shame, they didn't let it stop them from doing what they had orders to do. Talsu hadn't gone more than another few steps when a roar of bursting eggs made him want to dive for cover – again, reflexes honed in the field. An instant later, chunks of masonry thundered down like an avalanche in the mountains.

He turned to see what the redheads had wrought. Wind from the falling marble rustled his hair. The familiar square shape was gone. A cloud of dust kept him from seeing any more than that. When the dust settled, the street would be as unfamiliar to the eye as his lower jaw might be to the tongue after losing a couple of teeth. No one was shouting "Shame!" any more. He wondered if the collapse of the arch had caught any Jelgavans in it, or, for that matter, any of the Algarvian soldiers. He shrugged. He'd find out on the way back. Delivering the trousers came first.

Silver jingled in his pockets as he headed home. By then, the dust was gone, and so was the arch. The Algarvians had been clever about dropping it; the marble lay in the street, but did not seem to have wrecked the houses and shops nearby. Talsu couldn't see the oil-seller's place, which lay on the far side of that great pile of rubble. Small boys had already started playing king of the mountain on top of it.

Their game did not last long. The Algarvian officer who spoke Jelgavan shouted, "Get off!" He followed that with some choice colloquialisms that set the children giggling as they scampered down. Then, to Talsu's dismay, the officer and his soldiers (none of whom seemed to be missing) started pulling men off the street to get rid of the hill of debris. One of the troopers nabbed him before he could make himself scarce.

He called, "Is this a paying job?" to the officer.

After a moment, the Algarvian nodded. "Aye, we'll make it so."

For the rest of the day, Talsu carried baskets of broken marble under the boiling summer sun. He dumped them into freight cars on the ley-line caravan that could get nearest the arch. That meant going halfway across town; people hadn't known about ley lines in the days of the Kaunian Empire, and so hadn't set their big buildings near them. The Algarvians didn't stop him when he went into a tavern to buy a mug of ale, but one came in after him to make sure he didn't linger or slip out the back door. He muttered curses under his breath; he'd had something like that in mind.

As evening twilight fell, he lined up to get his pay. He was worn and battered. Bruises covered his legs; he walked with a limp because a stone had done its best to smash his right foot. He had a couple of mashed fingernails, too, and half a dozen cuts and scrapes on his hands. "By the powers above, we earned whatever they give us," he said.

When he got to the head of the line and held out an abused hand, the Algarvian officer slapped a couple of shiny new coppers into it. They bore the sharp-nosed image of King Mainardo, King Mezentio's brother and now, by grace of Algarve, lord of Jelgava. Talsu looked from them to the redhead. "Go on," the officer snapped. "Go on, and count yourself lucky you're getting anything."

Talsu stared at the coppers. They might have paid for an hour's labor. Most of a day's? He shoved them back at the officer. "Keep 'em, pal," he said. "Looks like you need 'em worse than I do."

"Do you know what I could do to you?" the Algarvian demanded.

"It might last longer than what you just did, but it couldn't hurt much more," Talsu answered with a shrug. "You had a chance to make people like you – like you better than our own nobles, anyway. This isn't how you go about it."

"Like us? What difference does that make?" the redheaded officer asked in surprise. "All that matters is that you obey us." He offered Talsu the coins once more. "Take them. You earned them."

"I *earned* six times that much," Talsu said, and walked away. He waited for the Algarvian to order him seized. It didn't happen. He scurried around the first corner he came to, trembling from fatigue and reaction both. He'd been a fool to talk back to the occupiers. He'd got away with it, but that made him no less a fool.

"Where have you been?" Laitsina, his mother, cried when he came into the shop above which the family lived and slept. Then she got a good look at him and cried out again, this time in horror: "And what were you doing while you were there? Have the Algarvians beaten you with sticks?"

"No. They just caught me in the street and set me hauling broken rock – one of their sorcerers wrecked the old arch past the market square." Talsu scowled. "Hard work, and then they cheated me at the end of it. About what you'd expect from the cursed redheads. I didn't even bother taking their lousy coppers." He didn't bother telling his mother how he'd rejected the coins, either.

His father slammed a pair of shears down on the counter beside which he was working. "They wrecked the imperial arch?" Traku said. At Talsu's nod, the older man muttered something pungent under his breath.

"That must have been the crash we heard this morning," Laitsina said. "I wondered what it was. If business were better, somebody who knew about it would have come in before this and told us."

"If the Algarvians weren't here, business would be better," Traku said. By the look he sent his son, he still blamed Talsu for the collapse of the Jelgavan armies. "And if the Algarvians weren't here, they wouldn't have been able to knock down the arch, either. Curse them, it's stood since imperial times. They've got no business wrecking things that have stood for so long."

"They won the war," Talsu said. At the moment, he regretted that more than he had at any time since he'd marched off to oppose the redheads. "That lets them do as they please. And they're turning out to be a worse bargain than our own nobles. Who would have thought anyone could be?"

Laitsina and Traku both glanced around nervously, though they were the only ones who could have heard what Talsu said. His sister chose that moment to come downstairs. "Who would have thought anyone could be worse than what?" Ausra asked.

"Worse than our nobles," Talsu answered defiantly. "The Algarvians are." He repeated the story of what they'd done to him and to the monument.

"That's terrible!" Ausra said. "Are they doing the same thing all over the kingdom? If they are, there won't be an arch or a column standing before long."

"They're jealous of us, that's what it is," Traku said. "We Kaunians were civilized while they still chased each other through the woods. They don't want to be reminded of that, and they don't want us reminded of it, either."

"Some people may think more about things that are missing than they ever did about things that were there." Talsu looked down at his battered, filthy, bloody hands. "I know I will."

Garivald didn't know why the impressers hadn't marched him out of Zossen as part of the draft they took for King Swemmel's army. Maybe they'd intended to scoop him and the other men they left behind into their net later. If so, they miscalculated, for the Algarvians overran the village before they could return.

Waddo kept reporting good news coming in over the crystal: Swemmel's forces advancing, the Algarvians and Yaninans and Zuwayzin falling back in disorder. The firstman even brought the crystal out into the village square several more times so the peasants of Zossen could hear the news for themselves. He hadn't misrepresented it; it always sounded good.

But then, one day, dragons painted in green and white and red flew by to the north of the village. They dropped no eggs, they did no harm, but they were there. They spread fear and, worse, they spread doubt as well. "If we're kicking the Algarvians' tails, how did those ugly flying things get here?" Dagulf asked Garivald as they were weeding in the fields outside of Zossen.

After looking around to make sure no one but his friends could hear him, Garivald answered, "If you expect the crystal to tell you the truth all the time, you probably think Waddo tells you the truth all the time, too." Both men laughed, each warily. After a moment, Garivald added, "I wish the king would speak to us again. He pulled no punches. I liked that."

"Aye." Dagulf nodded. "Some of these city men with their fancy accents who lie straight-faced, though . . ." He spat into the rich, black soil.

Less than a week later, soldiers in rock-gray tunics started falling back through Zossen. Some of them had fancy city accents, some used the almost Forthwegian dialect of the northwest, and others talked like Garivald and his fellow villagers. However they spoke, they all told tales much different from those the villagers heard on the crystal.

"Aye, Herborn is fallen," one of them said to Garivald as he gulped water and gnawed on a chunk of black bread Annore had given him. He was skinny and filthy and looked wearier than a peasant near the end of harvest time. "Powers above only know how many men the redheads cut off west of there, too. All I can tell you is, I'm cursed lucky I wasn't one of them."

"The crystal said we were still fighting hard there," Garivald said. Losing Herborn, the capital of Grelz in the days when Grelz was a kingdom and not a subordinate duchy of Unkerlant, was like taking a knife in the chest. He didn't want to believe it.

But the soldier said, "Bugger the crystal. If we still held Herborn, if the cursed Algarvians hadn't nipped in behind us like a crayfish nipping with its pincers, you suppose I'd be here now?" He stuffed what was left of the bread into his pack, drained the mug of water, wiped his dirty face on his equally dirty sleeve, and trudged off toward the west. Other Unkerlanter troopers retreated through the fields, careless of the crops they were trampling.

A couple of peasants ran out into the fields to try to preserve those crops. One of them, the soldiers simply ignored. The other, a cousin of Waddo's, might have thought his connection to the firstman gave him special authority. The soldiers thought otherwise. When he annoyed them – which didn't take long – they knocked him down and beat him. He got up again sooner than they wanted. They knocked him down again and beat him some more. He lay there for quite a while then before rising and limping back to the village.

"They told me they'd blaze me if I said one more word," he exclaimed in disbelieving tones.

After getting a good look at his bruised face, Garivald murmured to Dagulf, "You ask me, he'd already said too much by then." His friend nodded.

Later that afternoon, a company came up the road from the east. They were retreating, too, but in good order. They paid for it. Garivald had seen Algarvian dragons flying by. Now he saw them in action, and wished he hadn't. They dropped eggs on the Unkerlanter soldiers, then swooped low to flame those the bursts of sorcerous energy hadn't slain. Shrieks rose. So did the stench of burnt meat.

A stray egg burst on one of the houses at the edge of the village. Nothing much was left of it, nor of the woman and three children who'd been inside.

Waddo stared at the carnage the space of a few minutes had seen. "We ought to bury the poor brave fellows," he said, pointing out toward the slaughtered soldiers.

"What if they'd been in the village instead of just outside when the dragons came?" Garivald asked. "Who'd bury us then?" Waddo turned that horrified stare on him, then limped off without answering.

About noon the next day, four horse-drawn egg-tossers set up near the edge of the woods outside Zossen and started flinging death at the Algarvians farther east. For a little while, their solid presence cheered Garivald. Then he realized the enemy had drawn within egg-tosser range of the village. And then the Algarvians started tossing eggs back at that detachment.

Earth leapt skyward from the fields. Now Garivald watched in a different sort of horror: those were the crops on which Zossen would get through the winter – if it got through the winter. An older man, a fellow who'd fought in the Six Years' War, shouted at him and the other gawkers: "Get down, you cursed fools! A burst close by'll pick you up and smash you flat against the closest wall that doesn't fall over." He lay on his belly – he believed what he was saying.

Garivald did, too. He got down flat. He wished he could dig a hole. That was what soldiers did. When an egg burst behind him, it rolled him over and battered him with its force. Others who hadn't listened to the veteran were down and screaming – except for one woman who lay with her head twisted at an unnatural angle and would never get up again.

Before long, the Unkerlanter egg-tossers fell silent, beaten into submission by the redheads. A couple of men from their crews ran off into the woods. Garivald had a hard time blaming them when all their comrades were slain or wounded.

More and more soldiers in rock-gray tunics streamed through and past Zossen. By then, the villagers had nothing left to give them but water from the wells. The next morning, an officer declared, "This is a good enough place for a stand. We'll make the redheads pay high for it, by the powers above. You peasants head off to the west. If you're lucky, you'll get away."

"But, my lord," Waddo quavered, "that will mean the end of the village."

The officer pointed his stick at the firstman's face. "Argue with me, wretch, and it'll mean the end of you."

He started giving orders that would have turned Zossen into the best fortress he could make of it. Before he'd got far, though, his crystallomancer cried, "Sir, the redheads have broken through south of the woods. If we try to hold in the front, they'll take us in flank."

"Curse them!" the officer snarled. "That stretch of line should have held." He ground his teeth; Garivald clearly heard the sound. The officer's shoulders sagged. "Whoever was commanding down there ought to have his neck stretched, but no help for it. We've got to fall back again."

His men had already begun trickling off toward the west. They'd been through this before. Garivald wondered if they'd been through anything else.

"Firstman!" the officer shouted. Waddo hobbled toward him, looking apprehensive. The officer's lip curled. "Oh. You. Listen to me: if you've got a crystal in this miserable place, bury it deep. You won't like what happens to you if the Algarvians find it." Without waiting for an answer, he tramped off. He had more fight in him, but Garivald wasn't sure whether he'd sooner take on King Mezentio's men or his own side.

"Garivald!" Waddo called.

"Aye?" Garivald answered, all too sure he knew what was coming next. With his bad leg, Waddo couldn't dig.

And the firstman did not surprise him. "Fetch a spade and come with me," Waddo said. "We'd better get the crystal out of sight. I don't think we have much time."

Wishing Waddo had picked someone else, Garivald shouldered a shovel. The firstman went into his house – which eggs had left untouched – and came out with the crystal. Garivald followed him to a yard-deep hole in the middle of a vegetable plot where an egg had burst.

"Bury it at the bottom of that," the firstman said, pointing. "With the ground already torn, some more digging won't show."

"Fair enough." Garivald got into the hole and went to work. He might not like Waddo, but the firstman wasn't stupid. Garivald kept looking over his shoulder as he dug. Some people in Zossen liked Waddo even less than he did. If they told the Algarvians what the firstman had done, the redheads would do something to Waddo. While they were about it, they were liable to do something to Garivald, too.

Thinking thus, Garivald hid the crystal, covered it over, and scrambled out of the burst hole as soon as he could. He hurried to put away the spade. He'd just come out of his hut again when the first Algarvian behemoth trotted into the village.

He stopped in the doorway and stared. He couldn't help himself. He'd never seen a behemoth before, not in the flesh. The size and power of the beast astonished him. The iron sheathing its great horn and the heavy mail that protected it were rusty and had seen hard use. The mail jingled at every stride the behemoth took. The animal had a strong odor, something like a horse's, something like a goat's.

The behemoth bore on its back a heavy stick and four Algarvians – the first Algarvians Garivald had seen in the flesh, too. Two more behemoths followed close behind. They escorted a couple of squads of kilted footsoldiers. The Algarvians ran taller and leaner than Garivald's countrymen; to him, it gave them the aspect of coursing wolves.

One of the men atop the lead behemoth shouted in what he thought was Garivald's language: "Unkerlanti soldieri?"

"Not here." Three peasants said it at the same time. Two of them pointed west, to show where King Swemmel's men had gone.

Laughing and nodding, the Algarvian translated for his comrades. They grinned, too. *They're stupid, not to figure it out for themselves*, Garivald thought. But the redheads weren't so stupid as to take anything on trust. The footsoldiers fanned out through the village in pairs, searching every house – and seizing the chance to feel up any woman they found pretty. Several indignant squawks rose, but the Algarvians did nothing worse than let their hands roam free. Once they'd satisfied themselves no ambushers lurked nearby, they relaxed and seemed friendly enough – for invaders.

Before long, an unmistakable Algarvian officer strode into Zossen. He owned even more arrogance than had marked his Unkerlanter counterpart not long before. He also owned a real command of the Unkerlanter language, barking, "Where is the firstman for this stinking, miserable pustule of a village?"

Leaning on his cane, Waddo limped forward. "Here I am, lord," he quavered.

With a curse, the Algarvian pushed him over and kicked him. "You're not Swemmel's dog anymore. Have you got that? You're King Mezentio's dog now. And if you try any funny business, you'll be a dead dog. Have you got *that*?" He kicked Waddo again.

"Aye, lord," the firstman gasped. "Mercy, lord!"

Out of the side of his mouth, Garivald whispered to Annore, "So it's going to be like that, is it?" His wife's hand stole into his. They squeezed each other, hard.

Four

From the air, the battle below had for Sabrino the perfect clarity granted to footsoldiers only on maps after the fact. He watched with some anxiety the development of the Unkerlanter counterattacks toward Sommerda, a city from which King Mezentio's men had driven the enemy a couple of days before. The Unkerlanters lost fight after fight, but seemed too stupid to understand they were losing the war. They kept hurling new soldiers into the fray and striking back as best they might.

Nor could Sabrino blithely hurl his wing of dragonfliers at the men in rock-gray on the ground, as he had in the first days of King Mezentio's assault on Unkerlant. Dragons painted an unromantic rock-gray were in the air, too, their fliers intent on doing to Algarvian soldiers what Sabrino and his comrades had done to the Unkerlanters since the war was new.

Those boring gray paint jobs made Unkerlanter dragons cursed hard to spot, especially against cloudy skies or smoke coming from the ground. A squadron had got below Sabrino's wing before some sharp-eyed Algarvian flier spied them and spoke into his crystal, alerting the whole wing.

"They'll pay for that!" Sabrino whooped. "Domiziano, your squadron, and yours, too, Orosio. The rest of you, stay on top to make sure they don't try to bring any more of their little friends down on us."

He urged his dragon into a dive. He was wing commander, but he was also a fighting man. The dragon screamed in anger at being ordered about, but then screamed in fury at sighting the Unkerlanter dragons. Its great muscles surged beneath Sabrino, almost like an ardent lover's; its wings beat hard.

Unkerlanters, whether on the ground or in the air, carried far fewer crystals than did the Algarvians. If any of their fliers spotted Algarvian dragons dropping out of the sky on them, he could do little to alert his fellows. It might not have mattered much anyhow. The Unkerlanters were outnumbered close to two to one.

Sabrino flew out of the westering sun down on to the tail of an Unkerlanter dragon. He didn't bother raising his stick, but let his own beast have the pleasure of flaming the foe from the sky. The Unkerlanter flier had no notion of aught amiss till fire washed over him. He and his dragon tumbled toward the ground.

More rock-gray dragons plummeted, too. So did a couple of Sabrino's men and their mounts. He cursed when that happened. He cursed again when a few of the Unkerlanters managed to escape his trap, flying off toward the west with the last desperate energy their dragons had in them.

"Pursuit, sir?" Captain Domiziano asked, his image tiny in the crystal.

Regretfully, Sabrino shook his head. "No. We did what we came down here to do: We held them off our men on the ground. And night's almost on us. We'd better head back toward the farm. We'll want our beasts fresh come morning, because the powers above know we'll be flying again."

"Aye, sir." Domiziano seemed regretful, too, but obedient. Sabrino approved of the combination. He wanted aggressive subordinates, but not so aggressive as to set their will above his.

He led the wing back to the latest temporary dragon farm, which lay at the edge of a good-sized estate a little east of Sommerda. The manor at the heart of the estate hadn't suffered; the Algarvians had taken it by surprise, overrunning the area before King Swemmel's men could decide to use it for a strongpoint. They'd fought hard in Sommerda itself. Spiraling down toward the farm, Sabrino could see how his own countrymen had had to level half the town before finally clearing it of the stubborn Unkerlanter defenders.

On the ground, he was glad to let the handlers tend to his dragon. The beast liked them better than him, anyhow: he worked it hard, while they gave it the meat and brimstone and quicksilver it craved. It liked no one very much, though. Sabrino knew dragons too well to have any doubts on that score.

He ate hastily roasted mutton himself, along with hard bread, olives, and a nasty white wine the cooks who ran the field kitchen should never have bothered stealing. "Too sweet and too sour at the same time," he said, staring at his cup in dismay. "Tastes like a diabetic's piss."

"If you say so, sir," Captain Domiziano said innocently. "Myself, I wouldn't know." Sabrino made as if to throw the mug at him. He almost did it for real; it wouldn't have been a waste of the wine. But he was laughing even as he reared back, and so were the officers who ate with him.

"Hello!" Captain Orosio pointed toward the manor house. "Looks like the old boy in there has finally decided to come out and see what we're up to."

Sure enough, an elderly Unkerlanter approached the dragonfliers. Sabrino had ordered the manor house and whoever lived in it left alone, except for taking what he needed from the flocks to keep men and dragons fed. Until now, the Unkerlanter noble – for such Sabrino assumed him to be – had also ignored the Algarvians.

He was straight and spry and, for an Unkerlanter, tall. He wore a bushy white mustache, a style outmoded in his clean-shaven kingdom since the middle of the century, the days before the Six Years' War. And he proved to speak excellent Algarvian, saying, "I never expected to see your folk come so far into my land."

Sabrino got to his feet and bowed. "Here we are, sir, nonetheless. I have the honor to be the Count Sabrino: very much at your service." He bowed again.

A small, bitter smile crossed the Unkerlanter's face as he returned the second bow. "In my younger days, I had some considerable experience with Algarvians," he said. "I see the breed has changed little during my retirement."

"And you are, sir?" Sabrino asked politely.

"I doubt my name would mean anything to you, young fellow," the Unkerlanter replied, though Sabrino was not so young as all that. "I am called Chlodvald."

Not only Sabrino but some of his officers exclaimed at that. "Powers above!" the wing commander said. "If you are that Chlodvald, your Excellency" – and he had no doubt the old man was – "you were the best general your kingdom had during the Six Years' War."

"You compliment me too highly. I had good fortune," Chlodvald said with a shrug. In his place, an Algarvian would have preened and boasted.

"Will you give us the privilege of dining with us?" Sabrino asked. Several of the junior officers added eager agreement.

Chlodvald raised an eyebrow. "Generous of you to offer to share with me what is mine."

"Sir, it is war," Sabrino said stiffly. "Did you never feast from the fruits of victory?"

"There you have me," the retired general admitted, and sat down among the dragonfliers. His kingdom's enemies fell over one another to give him food and drink. When he tasted the wine, that eyebrow rose again. "This did not come from my cellars."

"Your Excellency, with all my heart I should hope not," Sabrino said. After Chlodvald had eaten and drunk, the wing commander asked him, "How is it that you live quietly here, sir, and are not engaged in helping Unkerlant against us?"

"Oh, I have lived quietly here a good many years, and I did not expect King Swemmel to call me into his service even when war broke out anew," Chlodvald replied. "You may not recall, but I fought for Kyot in the Twinkings War."

"Ah," Sabrino whispered.

Captain Orosio blurted what was in Sabrino's mind: "Then how come you're not dead?"

Chlodvald smiled that bitter smile again. "King Swemmel didn't spare many. I'd known both the young princes well back in Cottbus, of course, before their father died and they went at each other. Maybe that had something to do with it. I don't know; he slew others he knew as well as me. But he said he was letting me live because of my earlier service to Unkerlant, which partly excused my madness. Anyone who opposed him was and is in his mind mad."

"What is in himself, he sees in others," Sabrino said. Chlodvald did not disagree.

Captain Domiziano said, "Algarve is the broom that will sweep him away. King Mezentio will arrange this kingdom as it should be."

For the third time, the strange smile appeared on Chlodvald's face. "If only you had come twenty years ago, we should have welcomed you with open arms. But now it's too late. We were just getting back on our feet after the Six Years' War and the Twinkings War, and now you come and throw us back so we shall have to start all over again. Now we are fighting for Unkerlant, and in that cause we are all united."

Sabrino eyed his officers. They all looked amused, as he felt amused. Politely inclining his head to Chlodvald, he said, "Your Excellency, Unkerlant may be united, but we would not be here by Sommerda were that doing King Swemmel any enormous amount of good."

"Perhaps not," the retired – forcibly retired – Unkerlanter general replied. "But then again, while you are winning, you have not yet won. Tell me: has the fight been easy for you?"

Sabrino started to nod. In some ways, the fight had been very easy. The Unkerlanters weren't skilled, either in the air or on the ground. They blundered into traps that would have fooled no Valmieran or Jelgavan officer. Sometimes, though, they battered their way out of those traps, too, as the Valmierans or Jelgavans would not have even tried to do. They fought hard all the time; if they were doomed to defeat, they did not admit it even to themselves.

"You have not answered me, Count Sabrino," Chlodvald said.

"Easy enough," Sabrino said, and tossed an egg of his own: "How is it that all of Unkerlant's neighbors have joined against her? That speaks volumes about how well King Swemmel is loved throughout Derlavai."

"All of Algarve's neighbors joined against her, too," Chlodvald observed. "And what does that say about King Mezentio?"

"Yanina marches with us!" Captain Domiziano blurted.

Chlodvald raised his snowy eyebrow and said not another word. After a moment, Domiziano turned red. Sabrino had all he could do not to laugh at his squadron leader. He still wasn't sure having the Yaninans as allies helped Algarve more than it helped Unkerlant.

Chlodvald got to his feet. Rather stiffly, he nodded to Sabrino. "You Algarvians were a polished lot when you fought us in the Six Years' War. I see that has not changed. But I will take the liberty of telling you one thing more before I leave you: Unkerlant is a kingdom – Unkerlant is a land – that rubs the polish from invaders no less than from its own folk. Good night." He turned away.

"Good night," Sabrino called after him. "We may not meet again: before long, we shall be advancing once more."

Chlodvald did not reply; Sabrino wondered if the old man heard. He watched Chlodvald walk through deepening twilight back toward the manor house and go inside. No lamps showed at the windows; the

Unkerlanter general was too courteous to try to betray his foes in such a way. Even so, Unkerlanter dragons came over that night, dropping eggs all around the Algarvian dragon farm. They killed only a couple of dragons and no fliers, but their stubbornness made Sabrino thoughtful.

Lalla stamped her foot. The angry gesture set her bare breasts bouncing prettily. "But I already ordered that emerald necklace!" she said. "What do you mean, I can't have it? The jeweler will deliver it soon."

"No, he won't," Hajjaj said wearily. "As for 'you can't,' my dear, don't you speak Zuwayzi? I told you before you went and ordered it that you might not have it, for it cost too much. If you ignore my instructions, you must expect me to ignore your desires. I have had too many of these scenes with you."

His third wife set her hands on her hips. "Old man, you have been ignoring my desires since our wedding night. You might expect me to minister to the pleasure of your body, but you will not even let me adorn mine. Please?" She went from vicious to cajoling in the space of a couple of sentences.

Hajjaj eyed her body. It was well worth adorning: broad-hipped, wasp-waisted, full-breasted. He'd wed her in the hope of sensual pleasure, and he'd had more than a little from her. But he'd also had more than a little – too much more than a little – aggravation from her. Because she pleased him in the bedchamber, she'd grown convinced he was assotted of her and would grant her every wish, no matter how extravagant. Anyone who had such ideas about the Zuwayzi foreign minister knew him less well than she imagined.

With a sigh, he said, "I am an old man. Whether you grasp it or not, however, I am not necessarily a fool. If I were a fool, I would let you buy that necklace even after I told you not to do it. Instead, I shall send you back to the head of your clan. You may see how well you cajole him."

Lalla stared, realizing too late that she'd gone too far. "Have mercy, my lord, my husband!" she cried, and threw herself down on her knees before him, beseeching and inviting him at the same time. "Have mercy, I beg!"

"I have shown you too much mercy – and too much cash," Hajjaj replied. "I shall pay out your divorcee's allowance till you remarry – if you do. If you want more than that, you may either earn it or pry it loose from your clan chief. Since custom and law forbid him from touching you, you will have fewer inducements than you did with me."

"You wicked old scorpion!" Lalla cried. "I curse you! I curse the powers above for setting me in your hands! I—"

She scrambled to her feet, snatched a vase from a wall niche, and threw it at Hajjaj. Rage made her aim poor; he didn't even have to duck. The vase shattered against the wall behind him. The crash brought servants running to see what had happened. "Do escort her away," Hajjaj said, "and make everything ready to return her to the house of her clan head."

"Aye, lord," the servants said. By the way they smiled, they'd hoped for that order for some time. Lalla saw as much, too. She cursed them and then kicked one of them. They escorted her away much less gently than they might have otherwise.

Tewfik made his slow way into the chamber. He bowed as well as age and decrepitude allowed, then said, "My lord, Count Balastro of Algarve awaits without. He craves audience with you."

"By all means, Tewfik, let him in." Hajjaj's joints clicked as he stretched; he knocked one of the pillows on the floor aside with his foot. "I suppose you have a kilt and tunic waiting for me somewhere. Gauzy ones, I hope."

The longtime family retainer coughed. "Mufflings will not be necessary today, sir, the count having chosen to affect the habiliments of Zuwayza: hat – an Algarvian hat, but the brim is wide enough – sandals, and only himself between."

"And he's waiting outside, you said? Powers above, he'll bake! He's light-skinned, and not hardened against the sun." Hajjaj hurried to the entranceway. He was not so nimble as he once had been, but still easily outdistanced Tewfik.

From behind him, the majordomo called, "A suggestion, my lord."

As usual, Tewfik's suggestions had the force of commands. "And that is?" Hajjaj asked over his shoulder.

"Until the wench Lalla returns to her clan head's house, she ought not to be alone, lest valuables of this house go thither with her," Tewfik told him.

Till that moment, Lalla had been *junior wife* in Tewfik's mouth, and used as respectfully as either of the wives senior to her. Hajjaj wondered whether the majordomo was finally expressing his own opinion or echoing what he presumed to be his master's. Then he wondered if Tewfik saw any difference between those two. Either way, he gave good advice. "Aye, see to it," Hajjaj said.

"As you say," Tewfik replied, though he'd done the saying. "I presume you will entertain the Algarvian minister in the library?" He did not bother waiting for an answer to that, but continued, "I shall have tea and cakes and wine sent there directly."

"I thank you," Hajjaj said, still over his shoulder. Almost to the entranceway, he paused. "Algarvian vintages for the minister, not date wine."

"Of course." Tewfik sounded offended that his master should judge he needed reminding.

Hajjaj threw open the strong-barred door – like many clan centers, his home could double as a fortress. Sure enough, there stood Balastro, bare and pale and sweating in the sun. With a jaunty gesture, he swept off his hat and bowed. "I am pleased to see you your Excellency," he said.

"I am pleased to see you at least had the sense to travel here in a closed and covered coach," Hajjaj said. "Come inside, before my cooks decide you're done and put you on a serving platter."

"You follow my customs when you call on me at the ministry," Balastro said. He did sigh with relief when he stepped into the shade; the thick mud-brick walls fought the heat as well as anything could. "I thought it the least I could do to follow yours while visiting you."

"Aye, you've been known to do it before," Hajjaj agreed. "You are the only diplomat who ever does – Algarvian panache, I daresay. But truly, your Excellency, you are not equipped with a hide of the proper color . . . and yours will take several improper colors if you stay out too long." He could not quite take Balastro's nudity for granted, as he did nudity among his own people. Not only was Balastro the wrong color, as Hajjaj had said, but he also displayed the distinctive Algarvian mutilation. Hajjaj's eyes kept coming back to it; it made the redhead look deformed. To cover his queasy fascination, the Zuwayzi foreign minister added, "All your hide."

"Ah." Balastro took the point. "Can't have him sunburned, can we? He's got better things to do."

He followed Zuwayzi custom in the library, talking about books with Hajjaj instead of coming straight to his real business. He did not read

Zuwayzi, but was as apt to choose a classical Kaunian title as one written in Algarvian. He seemed to have as much regard for Kaunians of imperial day as his kingdom had little for modern ones. That puzzled Hajjaj, who longed to ask him about it, but could not: it was too serious to discuss before the rituals of hospitality were completed.

No sooner had Balastro sunk to the cushions than serving wenches brought in the inevitable refreshments. As part of his perfect care for his master's guest, Tewfik had chosen a couple of the prettiest women to wait upon Balastro and Hajjaj. They eyed the Algarvian minister with no small curiosity and looked to be fighting giggles, perhaps because of his race, perhaps because of the ritual of manhood he'd endured.

He eyed them, too, with interest that soon became visible. That made them giggle more. After they'd left the room, he asked Hajjaj, "Powers above, your Excellency, how do you keep from, ah, rising to the occasion whenever you see a comely wench?"

"I am old," Hajjaj said, remembering Lalla's taunt.

Balastro sipped wine. "Not so old as that, and you know it cursed well."

Hajjaj inclined his head; the Algarvian was right. "If you see something often enough, it loses its power to excite."

"I suppose that's so," Balastro said. "Seems a pity, though." He nibbled at a cake. "These are the nuts called cashews, aren't they? Tastier than walnuts and almonds, I think."

"Generous of you to say so," Hajjaj replied. "Not many of your countrymen would agree. I think you are right, but I grew up with cashews." He chuckled. "Of course, I grew up with date wine, too, but I know better than to serve you that."

Balastro's fastidious shudder could have played on the stage. "For which mercy, your Excellency, I thank you."

Presently, with tea and wine drunk and cakes diminished, with books and nudity talked dry, Hajjaj could with propriety inquire, "And what brings you up into the hills today, sir?"

"Past the desire for good wine and good company, you mean?" Balastro asked, and Hajjaj nodded. The Algarvian minister answered, "I was hoping we might get more aid from you Zuwayzin for the assault on Glogau than we've had thus far."

Hajjaj frowned. "And you come to me for this? Surely it is a matter for your military attaché to work out with his Majesty's officers down in Bishah."

Now Balastro looked annoyed, a genuine expression rather than the play-acting he'd used before. "I pray you for both our sakes, your Excellency, do not be disingenuous with me. You must know that your officers have dissembled and delayed and done their best to keep from answering aye or nay. This reluctance must spring from the king or from the foreign ministry: from you, in other words, in either case."

"If you think I lead King Shazli around by the nose, I must tell you that you are very much mistaken," Hajjaj said.

"Aye, you must tell it to me, for your honor's sake and your sovereign's, but must I believe it?" the Algarvian minister to Zuwayza returned: a toss with a good deal of justice in it. "Let us here – merely for the sake of argument, if you like – imagine that you are the author of your kingdom's treatings with its neighbors."

"For the sake of argument, as you say." Hajjaj steepled his fingers and fought against a smile. He liked Balastro, which made the fight harder. "I might say, in that case, that Zuwayza, by now, has avenged herself in full against Unkerlant – in full and more. Glogau has never been ours; few if any Zuwayzin dwell there, or ever have."

"Zuwayza is our ally, and needs must aid our cause," Balastro said.

Hajjaj shook his head. "No, your Excellency. Zuwayza is your cobelligerent. We war against Unkerlant for our own reasons, not yours. And, since this discussion is hypothetical, I might add that the vengeance you are wreaking on your neighbors leaves me somewhat relieved not to be one."

"We have been foes to the cursed Kaunians for time out of mind," Balastro said with a shrug. "Now that we have the whip hand, we shall use it. Tell me you love the Unkerlanters. Go ahead – I need a good laugh today."

"We have been known to live at peace with them," Hajjaj said, "even as you Algarvians have been known to live at peace with the Kaunians."

"Peace on their terms." Balastro had no bend in him (and was, Hajjaj knew, forgetting long stretches of his homeland's history). "Now it is peace on our terms. That is what victory earned us. We are the valiant. We are the strong."

"Then surely, your Excellency, you will not need much in the way of help from Zuwayza in reducing Glogau, will you?" Hajjaj asked innocently.

Balastro gave him a sour look, got to his feet, and departed with much less ceremony than was customary. Hajjaj stood in the doorway and watched his carriage start back toward the Algarvian ministry back in Bishah. As soon as it rounded a corner – but not an instant before – the Zuwayzi foreign minister let himself smile.

Istvan eyed the pass ahead with something less than delight. "There'll be Unkerlanters up yonder," he said, with as much gloomy certainty as a man eyeing dark clouds billowing up from the horizon might use in saying, *There's a storm on the way.*

"Aye, no doubt." That was Szonyi. "And we'll have to pay the bill for digging them out, too."

"There won't be very many of them." Kun, of all people, was looking on the bright side of things.

"There won't *need* to be very many of them." Istvan waved a hand at the steep-sided jumble of rocks to right and left. "This is the only way forward. As long as they hold it, we aren't going anywhere."

Szonyi nodded, looking no more happy than Istvan felt. "Aye, the sergeant's right, Kun. Ever since the Unkerlanters decided they were going to fight after all, this is the game they've played. They aren't trying to stop us. They're trying to slow us down, to give us as little as they can till winter comes."

"And winter in this country won't be any fun at all." Istvan eyed the sun. It still stood high in the northern sky at noon, but a tiny bit lower each day. Winter was coming, as inexorably as sand ran through the neck of a glass and down into the bottom half.

Trouble was coming, too. From the strong position they'd set up for themselves in that pass, the Unkerlanters started tossing eggs at the advancing Gyongyosians. Their aim wasn't particularly good; many of the eggs, instead of bursting on the paths Istvan and his countrymen were using, smote the mountainsides above them. Before long, Istvan discovered the Unkerlanters knew what they were doing after all. One of those bursts touched off an avalanche that swept several soldiers and several donkeys off a path and down to their doom.

"Whoresons!" Istvan shook his fist toward the east. "That's a coward's way to fight."

"They have no honor," Kanizsai said. "They do nothing but toss eggs and blaze at us from ambush."

"That's *because* there aren't very many of them here," Kun said, as if explaining things to an idiot child. "They can't afford a big standup fight with us, because they're in the middle of a big standup fight with Algarve."

"No honor," the young recruit repeated.

"Whether they do or whether they don't, we still have to shift the goat-buggers," Istvan said. As if to underscore his words, an egg burst close by, hurling a big chunk of stone past his head.

Kun asked a question Istvan wished he would have kept to himself: "How?"

Since the whole squad was looking at him, Istvan had to answer. Since he didn't know, he said, "That's for the officers to figure out."

"Aye, but it's for us to do," Szonyi said. "We do the work, and we do the bleeding, too."

"We are warriors," said Kanizsai, who, not yet having been in any big fights, didn't realize how quickly most of them could become dead warriors if they rushed a strong position manned by stubborn troops.

The officers set over them did seem to realize that, for which Istvan blessed the stars. Instead of the headlong rush he'd dreaded, the commanders in charge of the advance into Unkerlant sent dragons against the enemies blocking the pass ahead. Eggs fell from under the bellies of the great beasts. Having endured more rains of eggs on Obuda than he cared to remember, Istvan knew a sort of abstract sympathy for the Unkerlanters there to the east.

Szonyi had endured attack from the air, too. If he knew any sympathy for the Unkerlanters, he concealed it very well. "Kill the whoresons," he said, over and over again. "Smash 'em up. Squash 'em flat. Don't leave enough of any one of 'em to make a decent ghost."

Kun cleared his throat. "The notion that a ghost resembles a body at the moment of its death is only a peasant superstition."

"And how many ghosts have you seen with your beady little eyes there, Master Spectacles?" Szonyi demanded.

"Stuff a cap in it, both of you," Istvan said, rolling his eyes. "We're supposed to be fighting the Unkerlanters, not each other."

And the Unkerlanters, to his dismay, kept fighting back. They must not have saved all their heavy sticks for the fight against Algarve: they blazed a pair of Gyongyosian dragons out of the air as the beasts stooped low to drop their eggs precisely where their fliers wanted them to go. The rest of the men flying the brightly painted dragons urged them higher into the sky.

"Stars guide the souls of those two," Szonyi murmured, and glanced over to Kun as if expecting the mage's apprentice to argue with him. Kun simply nodded, at which Szonyi relaxed.

Eggs did keep falling on the Unkerlanter strongpoint, if not with the accuracy the Gyongyosians could have got by going lower. But eggs also kept falling on the footsoldiers waiting to assault the strongpoint, for the dragonfliers had not been able to wreck all the Unkerlanter egg-tossers.

A whistle shrilled. "Forward!" shouted Captain Tivadar, the company commander. He went forward himself, without hesitation. A commander who was not afraid to face the foe brought his men with him.

"Forward!" Istvan called, and trotted after the captain. He did not look back over his shoulder to see if his men followed. He assumed they would. If they didn't, their countrymen would do worse to them for cowardice than the Unkerlanters would for courage.

Here, at least, he could see the position he was attacking. Back on Obuda, he'd often blundered through the forest without the faintest notion of where the Kuusamans were till he or his comrades stumbled over them. The disadvantage here was that the Unkerlanters knew where he was, too. He used what bushes and boulders he could for cover, but felt as if he were under the eyes of King Swemmel's men at every stride.

Still under assault from the air, the Unkerlanters were slower than they might have been to shorten the range on their egg-tossers. That made life easier for Istvan and his companions . . . for a little while. But then flashes of light began winking from behind the piled-up stones at the mouth of the pass as the Unkerlanters brought their sticks into play.

Istvan blazed back at them. "By squads!" Captain Tivadar shouted. "Blaze and move! Make them keep their heads down while we advance on them!"

He wasn't the only officer shouting similar orders. The Gyongyosian soldiers who'd seen war before, either in the mountains against Unkerlant or on the islands of the Bothnian Ocean, obeyed more readily than the new recruits. Running past a corpse with tawny yellow hair, Istvan shook his head. Living through a couple of fights improved your odds of living through more than a couple.

A moment later, he shook his head again. If you didn't live through your first couple of fights, you were unlikely to live through any after that.

"Swemmel!" the Unkerlanter soldiers shouted. "Swemmel!" They shouted other things than their king's name, too, but Istvan couldn't understand those. To his ears, the Unkerlanter language sounded like a man in the last stages of choking to death.

A beam hissed past his head, so close that he could feel the heat and smell the sharp lightning reek it left behind in the air. He threw himself flat and scrambled toward the closest rock he could find. He peered out from behind it. In their gray tunics, the very color of the mountainside, the Unkerlanters were cursed hard to see.

When he did spot one, he took careful aim before blazing and then whooped as the fellow slumped bonelessly, stick falling from his fingers. "Good blazing, Sergeant," Tivadar called, and Istvan puffed out his chest: nothing like doing well when a superior was watching.

Then he had no more time to dwell on such trivia, for he and his comrades were in among the Unkerlanters, forcing the enemy back more by weight of numbers than by skill at arms. Some of King Swemmel's soldiers seemed glad to flee, running east down the valley toward the distant land where most of them were born. Others, though, held their ground as stubbornly as if they too sprang from a warrior race. And, indeed, it was not through want of courage that some of the defenders finally did give way, but only through being overwhelmed by the swarming Gyongyosians.

"By the stars," Istvan said, shaking his head in wonder as he finally made his way toward the end of the Unkerlanters' defensive works, "if this were great army against great army and not a regiment of ours thrown at a couple of companies of theirs, Gyongyos and Unkerlant would both run out of men."

"Aye." That was Kun, who limped along after him, having taken a light wound from a stick. The mage's apprentice still had his spectacles on, whether through some protective magic of his or thanks to an out-

and-out miracle Istvan couldn't have said. Kun pointed ahead. "One more little fortress of theirs up there, and then we can go on."

"So we can," Istvan said. "And then, a few miles farther east, they'll choose another pass we have to go through, and they'll entrench themselves here. At five miles a day, how many years are we from Cottbus?"

Kun wore a faraway expression as he calculated. "Three," he said, "or rather a bit more."

Istvan, who had only sketchy schooling, did not know if he was right or wrong. He did know the prospect struck him as gloomy. And he also rapidly realized that the Unkerlanters in the little fortress ahead had no intention of letting his comrades go any miles farther that day. They blazed away at the Gyongyosians with such ferocity across such level ground that to approach or to try to go around their strongpoint was an appointment with death.

Only after Gyongyosian dragons returned and dropped great swarms of eggs on the fortress did the blazing from it ease enough to let the foot-soldiers mount an assault. Even then, Unkerlanter survivors kept fighting in the wreckage until, at last, almost all of them were slain. Only a couple of dark-haired men came out of the works with their hands held high.

And when Istvan went into the battered fortress, he discovered something that set him shouting for Captain Tivadar. After a while, the company commander picked his way through the wreckage and stood beside his sergeant. "Well," he said at last, "now we know why they were able to blaze so well for so long."

"Aye, sir," Istvan said. "So we do." Ten Unkerlanters lay side by side, each of them with his throat cut. The Gyongyosians had not done that; the Unkerlanters' own countrymen had. "Do you suppose they volunteered, or did their officers draw straws, or would they just pick the men they liked least?"

"I don't know," Tivadar answered. "Maybe the captives will be able to tell us." He gulped, looking for something more to say. At last, he managed, "It was bravely done, though. See? – none of them has his hands tied. They gave themselves up so their comrades would have plenty of sorcerous energy in their sticks to keep blazing at us."

"So they did." Istvan looked down at the neat if bloody row of corpses. He gave them the best tribute he could: "They died like warriors." He wondered how many Gyongyosians would have yielded themselves up for their fellows' sake like that. Then he wondered what the Unkerlanters would do at the next position they chose to defend with all their strength. And then he wondered if he'd be lucky enough to see the Unkerlanter stronghold after that.

Seen from Setubal, the Derlavaian War had a curious feel, almost as if it were happening in a distant room. The Strait of Valmiera protected Lagoas from invasion. So did Algarve's enormous fight with Unkerlant; thus embroiled, King Mezentio's men could not afford to do much against the Lagoans. Occasional dragons dropped eggs on Setubal and the other towns of the northern coast. Occasional warships tried to sneak in and raid the shoreline. Rather more Lagoan dragons flew against the Algarvian-held ports of southern Valmiera. Other than that . . .

"They fear us," a second-rank mage named Xavega said to Fernao as the two of them sat drinking fortified wine in a dining room of the Grand Hall of the Lagoan Guild of Mages.

Fernao bowed in his seat, an almost Algarvian courtesy. "I thank you, milady," he said. "You have proved, without leaving the tiniest particle of room for doubt, that being a woman does not keep one from being a fool."

Xavega glared at him. She was in her early thirties, a few years younger than he, and had a fierce scowl somehow made fiercer by her being quite good-looking. "If Algarve did not fear us," she said, "Mezentio would have tried settling accounts with us before turning his eyes westward."

"You've never traveled outside Lagoas, have you?" Fernao asked.

"As if that should make a difference!" Xavega tossed her head. Her mane of auburn hair flipped back over her shoulders.

"Ah, but it does," Fernao said. "You may not believe me, but it does. People who've never left Lagoas have no sense of . . . of proportion – I think that's the word I want. It's true of anyone who hasn't traveled, but more so with us, because our kingdom is only the smaller part of an island, but we naturally think it's the center of the world."

By Xavega's expression, no other thought had crossed her mind. And, by her expression, she wasn't interested in having other thoughts cross her mind. The thought of bedding her later in the evening had crossed Fernao's mind; he suspected he'd just dropped an egg on his chances. She said, "Setubal contains the world. What need to go farther?"

That held some truth – some, but not enough. "Proportion," Fernao repeated. "For one thing, Mezentio couldn't very well jump on us when Swemmel was ready to jump on him from the west. For another, if he did jump us, he'd bring Kuusamo into the war against him, and he can't afford that."

"Kuusamo." Xavega waved her hand, as Lagoans had a way of doing when they thought of their neighbors on the island.

"Kuusamo outweighs us two or three to one," Fernao said, an unpleasant truth his countrymen preferred to forget. "The Seven Princes looked east and north for gain more than they do toward us or toward the mainland – easier pickings in those directions – but they don't have to."

"They're Kuusamans," Xavega said with a sneer, as if that explained everything. For her, evidently, it did. Pointing to Fernao, she went on, "Just because you have their eyes, you don't need to take their part."

Fernao got to his feet and bowed stiffly. "Milady, I think you would find yourself more at home in Mezentio's kingdom than in your own. I give you good evening." He stalked out of the dining room, proud he hadn't flung the last of his wine in Xavega's face. By her looks, she might have been of pure Algarvic stock. But, like most Lagoans, she also probably had Kaunians and Kuusamans somewhere down the trunk of her family tree. Scorning people for their looks was bad manners in most Lagoan circles – although not, evidently, in hers.

He wondered how many did share her view. If Lagoas became a kingdom where a man with narrow eyes or a woman with blond hair couldn't go out on the streets without fear of being insulted or worse, would it be the sort of kingdom in which he cared to live? No sooner had that thought crossed his mind than another followed it: *where else could I go?*

Nowhere on the continent of Derlavai: that was certain. He'd been to the austral continent, and heartily hoped never to have anything to do with it again. He hadn't visited equatorial Siaulia, but had no interest in doing so. It was as backward as the land of the Ice People, and the war that blazed through Derlavai sputtered there, too, as Derlavaian colonists and their native vassals squabbled among themselves.

The scattered islands in the Great Northern Sea were even less appealing, unless a man aimed to forget the world and make sure the world forgot him, too. That was not what Fernao had in mind. If Lagoas went bad . . .

As he left the Grand Hall, his head turned, almost of itself, toward the east. Odd to think of Kuusamo as a bastion of sanity in a world gone mad. It was odd for most Lagoans to think of their short, dark, slim neighbors any more than they had to.

Fernao hurried up the street to the caravan stop. Because of his own interests, he was not like most Lagoans. Maybe his interest in Kuusaman magecraft – and his curiosity over whatever the Kuusamans weren't talking about – had led him to take Xavega's crack about his looks more to heart than he would have otherwise.

A ley-line caravan glided by. A couple of passengers got off; a couple got on. Fernao stayed at the stop – this wasn't the route he needed. *And maybe she's just a nasty bitch*, the mage thought sourly. He glanced at the people hurrying past him: Regardless of the hour, Setubal never slept. One in five, maybe one in four, had eyes like his. If Xavega didn't care for them, too cursed bad.

Another caravan car came to the stop. Fernao climbed aboard and tossed a coin in the fare box: this car would take him to within a street of his block of flats. He sat down next to a yawning woman who looked to have a good deal more Kuusaman blood than he did himself.

Coming into his building, he paused at the pigeonholes in the lobby to see what the postman had brought him. Along with the usual advertising circulars from printers, dealers in sorcerous apparatus, nostrum peddlers, and local eateries, he found an envelope with an unfamiliar printed franking mark. He held it up to his face so he could read the postmaster's blurry handstamp over the mark.

"Kajaani," he muttered. "Where in blazes is Kajaani?" Then he laughed at himself. He'd been guilty of the crime for which he'd taxed Xavega: he'd thought of Lagoas first, to the exclusion of everyplace else. As soon as he stopped doing that, he knew perfectly well where Kajaani was. And, with only a little more thought, he knew who was likely to be writing him from the Kuusaman town, though the envelope bore no return address.

He almost tore that envelope open there in the lobby, but made himself wait till he'd gone upstairs to his flat. There he flung the useless sheets of paper on to the sofa and opened the one that mattered. Sure enough, the letter – written in excellent classical Kaunian – was on the stationery of Kajaani City College, and from the theoretical sorcerer named Pekka.

My dear colleague, she wrote, *I thank you for your interest in my work and your inquiries into my research. Unfortunately, I must tell you that much of my recent silence in the journals has sprung from nothing more than the demands on my time my son takes. I do eventually hope to publish more, but when that may be I cannot say. Meanwhile, my life is busy in many different ways. Hoping this finds you well and your own work flourishing, I remain – Pekka, Professor of Theoretical Sorcery.*

Fernao's excitement dissolved like a little ink in a lot of water, leaving his mood duller and darker than it had been before. He had to fight to keep from crumpling the letter and tossing it over with the rest of the mail he'd received. He'd got similar bland missives from other Kuusaman theoretical sorcerers to whom he'd written. Had the letters been identical and not merely similar, he would have known for a fact that the mages were acting in concert. As things were, he had to infer it, but it wasn't the subtlest inference he'd ever drawn.

"They know something, all right," he muttered. "They don't want anyone to know they know it, either. That means it's big, whatever it is." So much had been obvious since his meeting with Ilmarinen, the meeting that should have been with Siuntio. It was even more obvious now.

He wondered what the Kuusamans had found. Something that had to do with the relationship between the laws of contagion and similarity, plainly. But what? Lagoan mages, more often than not of a more practical bent than their Kuusaman counterparts, hadn't explored the question in depth.

"Maybe we should have," Fernao muttered under his breath. If the Guild of Lagoan Mages were to try to catch up with the Kuusamans, to discover whatever they were hiding, how best to go about it? The only answer that occurred to Fernao was getting some talented sorcerers together and having them proceed from the point where Siuntio and Pekka and the rest of the Kuusamans had, for whatever reason, fallen silent.

He laughed an unhappy laugh. Even Grandmaster Pinheiro would have a hard time getting a group of Lagoan mages to work on a project he proposed rather than on whatever they felt like doing themselves. Fernao was about to throw the notion into his mental trash bin when he suddenly stiffened. He wondered if, in Trapani or some other Algarvian town, another group of mages was already hard at work going down that same path. If so, how could Lagoas afford to ignore it?

He glanced at Pekka's note again. Maybe, just maybe, she was telling the truth and he'd been starting at shadows all along. With the note in his hand, he could – or maybe he could – make a fair stab at finding out. He set the note on the table and went to the cabinet of sorcerous gear that stood next to the stove in the kitchen. Had he been a better cook, he would have had a cabinet full of spices there instead. From the cabinet, he took a lens mounted in a polished brass ring and a dried lapwing's head: the lapwing, being a sharp-eyed bird, was to a mage a sovereign remedy against deception.

Holding the lapwing's head between a lamp and the lens that focused its power on the note, he chanted a cantrip in classical Kaunian. If the writing on the note was true, he would see the black ink as bright blue. If the writing was false, he would see it as burning red.

But he continued to see it simply as black. Frowning, he wondered if he'd somehow botched the charm. He didn't think so, but ran through it again, this time with special care. The ink continued to seem black to his eyes. It shouldn't have, not after that spell, not unless . . .

"Why, the tricksy minx!" Fernao exclaimed. "If she hasn't magicked the note against this very sorcery, I'm an addled apprentice."

Shaking his head at Pekka's forethought, he put away the lens and the bird's head. Now he couldn't be sure whether the Kuusaman theoretical sorcerer had been lying or telling the truth, not by any objective means. But he could still draw inferences. That Pekka hadn't wanted him to know whether or not she was telling the truth strongly suggested she wasn't. If she wasn't, the Kuusamans were indeed likely to be hiding something important.

He'd already believed that. "One more bit of evidence," he murmured, and then kicked at the carpet. Evidence of what? *Something*. That was as much as he knew. He wondered if some dapper, clever young mage in Trapani, a fellow with waxed mustachios and a hat worn at a jaunty angle, knew more.

For his sake, for his kingdom's sake, he hoped not. But when he looked north and west, toward the Algarvian capital, he knew he had fear in his eyes.

East of Cottbus, a half ring of dowsers did their best to detect Algarvian dragons so they could give the capital of Unkerlant some warning against attack from the air. Marshal Rathar swung off his horse at one such post, a crude hut in the middle of a forest of birch trees. Letting soldiers see him, letting them see he was still in the fight and still thought Unkerlant could win, was one reason he went out to the field as often as he could. Another reason was learning as much as he could about all aspects of the war.

Still another was escaping King Swemmel for a while. Soon enough, he'd have to go back to the palace and see what sort of advice the king would give. Sometimes, Rathar was convinced, Swemmel saw further than any other man living. Sometimes he could not see past the end of his pointed nose. Telling which was which on any given day, though, was anything but easy, and King Swemmel remained as convinced about the virtues of his bad ideas as he was about his good ones.

Rathar shook his head as a horse bedeviled by flies might flick its tail. He'd come out here to get away from Swemmel, and the king had come with him in his mind. Where was the relief in that? When the dowsers came tumbling out of their hut to salute him, he was glad to nod to them. As long as he talked with them, he could get away from the mental presence of his sovereign.

"Aye, lord Marshal," said one of the off-duty dowsers, a lieutenant named Morold, "we've had pretty good luck feeling out the redheads so far." He hefted his forked rod. "A dragon's wings *will* disturb the air, you know, and that's what we sense. But the Algarvians are getting better at masking what they're up to, curse 'em."

"I've read somewhat of this in the reports coming back to Cottbus," Rathar replied. "But, as you say, a dragon *must* flap its wings now and again. How do the Algarvians propose to prevent that?"

Morold's strong-nosed peasant face crinkled into a grin of reluctant admiration. "The sneaky buggers don't even try, sir, may the powers below swallow 'em down. What they do instead is, they have some of their dragons carry baskets full of folded-up strips of paper. When they get close enough that we're right on the edge of spotting 'em" – he held up the dowsing rod again — "they spill the baskets out into the air, and these thousands of strips of paper all start fluttering down. The rods pick up those flutters, too, so trying to tell what's dragons and what isn't is like trying to see a white horse in a blizzard. Do you follow what I'm saying?"

"Aye," Rathar said, "and I thank you. You've made it clearer than the reports ever did. You still can find the dragons, then?"

"We know something's up, sir," Morold told him, "but not exactly what or exactly where, the way we would have before."

"You must do better. Unkerlant must do better," Rathar said. "If you'd been into Cottbus lately and seen the burnt-out blocks, you would know Unkerlanter must do better." He did not want to blame the dowsers, who were trying as hard as they could — and whose work had led to a good many Algarvian dragons knocked out of the sky. Something else occurred to him: "Are our dragons using these strips of paper, too, to confuse the Algarvian dowsers?"

"Lord Marshal, you'd have to ask the dragonfliers, for I'm sure I can't say," Morold replied.

"I'll do that," Rathar said. *Maybe I'll do that. If I remember, I'll do that.* He scrawled a note. He'd scrawled a lot of notes on the little pad of paper he carried in his belt pouch. Eventually, he hoped to do something about each and every one of them. The way things had been going lately, he wrote new notes faster than he could deal with old ones.

The dowsers' spirits seemed high, which cheered the marshal of Unkerlant. As long as the soldiers thought the war could be won, it could. That was not to say it would be won, not with the Algarvians still advancing in the north, the south, and in the center — in the direction of Cottbus. But if the Unkerlanter army despaired of throwing back the redheads, the fight was lost without hope of recovery.

Morold said, "We need more crystals, lord, and more heavy sticks to blaze down the enemy's dragons. The Algarvians talk back and forth among themselves more than we do, and it shows in all the fighting."

"I know that." Rathar did not take out the little pad again. He'd scribbled that note before. "The mages are doing everything they can. We need too many things at the same time, and have not enough mages to make all of them at once."

Morold and the other dowsers looked unhappy to hear that. Rathar was none too happy to say it, either. But he did not want to lie to them, either. News sheets put out plenty of pleasing lies, and put the best face they could on the truth. That was fine for townsmen. Soldiers, Rathar thought, deserved the truth unvarnished.

He commandeered a fresh horse from among those tied near the dowser's hut and rode back toward Cottbus. A single bodyguard rode with him. He would have done without even the one retainer, but the idea scandalized every other general – and Rathar's adjutant. At least he'd made sure he had a solid veteran at his side, not a relative he was holding away from the fighting or some pretty boy.

Heading to Cottbus, he passed a troop of behemoths trotting east, toward the battle lines. They kicked up a great cloud of dust. Because they were still far from the fighting, they did not wear their heavy mail, but carried it in carts they pulled behind them. Whatever color their long, shaggy hair had been before, it was dust-brown now. A couple of the soldiers mounted on them waved to Rathar. Coughing, he waved back. His tunic was scarcely fancier than theirs; they more likely thought him just another soldier than the highest-ranking officer in the Unkerlanter army.

He rode past a dead Algarvian dragon. An old man – too old to go to the front – was stripping the harness from it. Rathar nodded. Anything his kingdom could steal from the redheads was one thing fewer its artisans would have to make.

Few people, and most of them women, were on the streets of Cottbus. As he trotted through a market square, he saw a long queue to buy pears and plums, and an even longer one in front of a stern-faced woman with a basket of eggs. There looked to be plenty of fruit; the eggs were going fast, and the people at the end of that line would have to do without.

When Rathar strode into his office, his adjutant hurried up to him with a worried look on his face. "Lord Marshal, his Majesty urgently requires your presence," Major Merovec told him.

"Of course the king shall have what he requires," Rathar replied. "Do you know why he requires me?" Merovec shook his head. Rathar let out a silent sigh. He wouldn't know whether King Swemmel intended merely to confer with him or to sack him or to take his head till he got to the audience chamber. "I shall go see him at once, then."

Swemmel's guardsmen in the antechamber were as meticulous as ever, but did not seem hostile to Rathar. The marshal took that as a good sign.

No more guards awaited him in the audience chamber. He took that as a better sign.

"Arise, arise," King Swemmel said after Rathar completed the ritual prostrations and acclamations before his sovereign. Swemmel sounded impatient and angry, but not angry at the marshal. "Do you know what that swaggering popinjay of a Mezentio has done?" he demanded.

King Mezentio had done any number of things to Unkerlant's detriment. Evidently, he'd just done one more. Rathar answered with simple truth: "No, your Majesty."

"Curse him, he has raised up a false King of Grelz down in Herborn," Swemmel snarled.

Ice ran through Rathar. That was one of the nastier things Mezentio might have done. A good many people in the Duchy of Grelz still resented the Union of Crowns that had bound them to Unkerlant even though it was almost three hundred years old. If Algarve restored the old Kingdom of Grelz under a pliant local noble, the Grelzers might well acquiesce in Algarvian control. "Which of the counts or dukes did the redheads pick as their pretender?" Rathar asked.

"Duke Raniero, who has the dishonor to be Mezentio's first cousin," King Swemmel answered.

Rathar stared. "King Mezentio named an Algarvian noble to be King of Grelz?"

"Aye, he did," Swemmel said. "None of the local lickspittles seemed to suit him."

"Powers above be praised," Rathar said softly. "He could have struck a harder blow against us with a Grelzer than with a man the folk down there will see as . . . a foreign usurper." He'd almost said *another foreign usurper.* Swemmel would not have been grateful for that, not even a little.

"You may be right." Swemmel sounded almost indifferent to what was in Rathar's eyes a blunder big as the world. A moment later, the king explained why: "But the insult is no less here. If anything, the insult is greater, for Mezentio to presume to set an Algarvian as king on Unkerlanter soil."

"He did the same thing in Jelgava, when he made his brother Mainardo king there," Rathar said. "The Algarvians have always been an arrogant lot."

"Aye," King Swemmel agreed. "If the Jelgavans are spineless enough to take Mezentio's worthless brother as their sovereign, they deserve him. Unkerlanters will never accept an Algarvian for a king." He looked sly; Rathar knew from long experience that he was never more dangerous – to his foes or sometimes to himself – than when he wore that expression. "We shall make certain that Unkerlanters do not accept an Algarvian for a king."

"May it be so, your Majesty." Rathar thought the course of the fighting itself more urgent than any political machinations. He pointed to a large map in the audience chamber. "We had better make sure Mezentio has no chance to proclaim a redheaded King of Unkerlant in Cottbus."

"Even if he does, we will fight on from the west," Swemmel said.

Would anyone follow orders from a king who'd fled to a provincial town one jump ahead of the Algarvians? Rathar had no idea. He didn't want to have to learn by experiment, either. He looked toward the map himself. The bites Gyongyos was taking in the far west were annoyances. In the north, Zuwayza hadn't gone far beyond the borders she'd had before her first clash with Unkerlanter. But the Algarvians aimed to tear the heart from the kingdom and keep it for themselves.

"We also have to hold Cottbus because of all the ley lines that converge here," Rathar said. "If the capital falls, we'll have a cursed hard time moving caravans from north to south."

"Aye," Swemmel said. "Aye." His nod was impatient, absent-minded; ley-line caravans weren't the topmost thing in his thoughts, or anywhere close to it. He walked over to the map. "We still have a corridor open to Glogau. The Lagoans have sent us some prime bull behemoths to improve our herds, and they came through."

"So they did." Rathar had heard that. It still left him faintly bemused. "The Zuwayzin could have pressed their attack on the port's defenses harder than they have."

"They love Mezentio little better than they love us," Swemmel said, which evidently seemed clear to him but did not to his marshal. The king went on, "Were the black men but a little wiser, they would love Mezentio less than they love us."

"Had we treated them a little better, that might also be true," Rathar remarked.

"We did not give them a tenth part of what they deserve," Swemmel said. "Nor have we yet given the Algarvians a tenth, nor even a hundredth, part of what *they* deserve. But we shall. Aye, we shall." Whatever else one said of Swemmel, he had no yielding in him. Maybe Unkerlant, or what remained of Unkerlant, would go right on obeying him even if the Algarvians ran him out of Cottbus. Marshal Rathar still hoped with all his heart he wouldn't have to find out.

Dressed in holiday finery – ordinary trousers worn under embroidered tunics – Skarnu, Merkela, and Raunu came into the village of Pavilosta to witness the installation of Simanu, the late Enkuru's son, as count over the local countryside. Neither Skarnu nor Raunu had a tunic that fit as well as it might; both theirs had formerly belonged to Gedominu. Merkela had altered them, but they remained tight.

"Waste of our time to come here," Raunu grumbled, as a true farmer might have. "Too much work to do to care who's over us. Whoever it is, he'll take too cursed much of what we make."

"Aye, that's so," Merkela agreed. "And Simanu's been squeezing as hard as Enkuru ever did. He sucks up to the Algarvians as hard as his father did, too. That's the only reason they finally decided to let him take over as count instead of putting in one of their own men."

She didn't bother keeping her voice down. People who heard her shied away. One of them hissed, "Powers above, you fool of a woman, put a shoe in it before Simanu's men or the redheads drag you up into the count's keep. Going in is easy. Coming out's a different story – aye, it is."

She lifted her chin. "It wouldn't be, if the men around here deserved the name."

Skarnu set a hand on her arm. "Easy, darling," he murmured. "The idea isn't to show how much we hate the redheads and the traitors who do their bidding. The idea is to hurt them without letting them know who did it."

Merkela looked at him as if he were one of the enemy, too. "The idea is also to make more people want to hurt them," she said in a voice like ice.

"But you're not doing that. You're just frightening folk and putting yourself in danger," Skarnu said. Merkela's glare grew harder and colder still. The next thing she said would be something they'd all regret for a long time. Seeing that coming, Skarnu quickly spoke first: "Simanu and the Algarvians do more in a day to make people want to hurt them than we could do in a year."

He watched Merkela weigh the words. To his great relief, she nodded. To his even greater relief, she kept quiet or talked of unimportant things as they made their way into Pavilosta's central square. Raunu muttered, "The Algarvians don't want anybody starting trouble today, do they?"

"Not even a drop," Skarnu muttered back. Redheads with sticks prowled the rooftops looking down into the square. More Algarvians guarded the double chair in which Simanu would be installed. "They aren't stupid. They wouldn't be so cursed dangerous if they were stupid."

A small band – bagpipe, tuba, trumpet, and thumping kettledrum – began to play: one sprightly Valmieran tune after another. Skarnu watched some of the Algarvian troopers make sour faces at the music. Their own tastes ran more toward plinkings and tinklings that were, to Valmieran ears, effete. And then he watched one of their officers growl something at them in their own language. The sour faces disappeared. The smiles that replaced them often looked like bad acting, but were unquestionably smiles. The redheads didn't offend except on purpose. No, they weren't stupid, not even slightly.

After a little while, the band struck up a particularly bouncy tune, the drummer pounding away with might and main. "That is the count's air," Merkela murmured to Skarnu and Raunu. Had they grown up around Pavilosta, as she had, they would have heard it on ceremonial occasions all their lives. As things were, it was new to both of them. Skarnu assumed an expression that suggested it wasn't.

"Here he comes," someone behind him said. People's heads turned toward the left: They knew from which direction Simanu would come. Skarnu didn't, but again couldn't have been more than half a heartbeat behind everyone else – not far enough (he hoped) for even the most alert Algarvian to notice.

Dressed in a tunic stiff with gold thread and trousers of silk with fur at the cuffs, the late Count Enkuru's son advanced toward the double chair in which he would formally succeed his father. Simanu was somewhere in his mid-twenties, with a face handsome and nasty at the same time: the face of a man who'd never had anyone tell him no in his whole life.

"I've served under officers who looked like that," Raunu muttered.

"Everybody loved 'em – oh, aye." He rolled his eyes to make sure no one took him seriously.

Simanu bestowed his sneer impartially on the Valmierans over whom he was being set and the Algarvians who were allowing him to be set over those townsmen and villagers. Just for a moment, the cast of his features reminded Skarnu of his sister Krasta's. He shook his head. That wasn't fair . . . was it? Had Krasta ever really worn such a snide smile? He hoped not.

After Simanu came more Algarvian bodyguards and a peasant obviously cleaned up for the occasion. The fellow led two cows, one fine and plump, the other a sad, scrawny, shambling beast. Raunu muttered again: "Have to find out who that bugger is and make sure something bad happens to him."

"Aye, we will," Skarnu agreed. "He's as much in bed with the redheads as Simanu is." He turned to Merkela. "Why the beasts?" He held his voice down – one more thing a proper peasant from around Pavilosta would have known from childhood.

"Only watch, and you'll see," Merkela answered. She might not have seen this ceremony before – Enkuru had been the local lord for a long time – but it was second nature to her. It probably figured in tales the peasants in this part of the kingdom told their children. For all Skarnu could tell, diligent folklorists back in Priekule had composed learned dissertations about it.

Simanu strode up to the double chair, one side of which faced east, the other west. "People of Pavilosta, people of my county," he called out in a voice as poisonously sweet as his face, "I now come into my inheritance." He sat down facing west toward Algarve. That was, no doubt, intended to symbolize his defense of the region against the kilted barbarians who had so often troubled the Kaunian Empire and the later Kaunian kingdoms. His facing west now, with Algarvians surrounding and upholding him, felt cruelly ironic.

The scrubbed peasant, still holding the lead ropes for the two cows, took his seat back-to-back with Simanu. Then he rose again, and led the beasts around the double chair to the new count. He held out both ropes, one in each hand.

"Now you'll see how it goes," Merkela murmured to Skarnu. "Simanu has to choose the skinny cow, and he has to let the peasant give him a box on the ear – just a little one, mind – to show he governs here not for his own sake but for the sake of his people."

But when Count Simanu got to his feet to face the peasant, his smile had grown nastier still. "People of Pavilosta, people of my county, the world has changed," he said. "Vile brigands slew my father, and still have not got their just deserts because their wicked fellows conceal them and keep them safe from harm. Very well, then. If you will not give, you will not get."

Speaking thus, he seized the fat cow's rope in his left hand and with his right dealt the peasant a buffet to the side of the head that sent the fellow sprawling with a cry of pain and surprise. Simanu threw back his own head and laughed loud and long.

For a moment, his laughter was almost the only sound in Pavilosta's central square. The peasants and townsfolk simply stared, having trouble believing anyone would pervert their ancient ceremony. Maybe the Algarvians had trouble believing it, too. Their officers gaped like the Valmieran peasants around them — gaped and then started to curse. In their shoes, Skarnu would also have cursed. Their chosen puppet had just chosen to outrage the people they wanted him to control.

Someone threw an apple at Simanu. It missed, and smashed against the double chair. The fat cow took a couple of steps forward and crunched it up. Then someone else threw a cobblestone. That one didn't miss: It caught Simanu in the ribs. He let out a yell louder than the cleaned-up peasant had.

More stones and fruits and vegetables whizzed past Simanu. Some of them didn't whiz past, but thumped against him. He yelled again. So did the Algarvian officer in charge of the Valmieran noble's kilted body-guards: "You cursed idiot! Why did you not do the ceremony as it should be done?"

"They did not deserve it," Simanu said, wiping blood from his face. "By the powers above, they still do not deserve it, not with how they treat me."

"Fool!" the Algarvian started. "Make them happy in the small things and you can rule them in the large ones. This way—" He raised his voice to a shout that filled the square: "You Valmierans! Stop this riotous nonsense at once and peacefully go back to your ho — *oof!*" That last came when a cleverly aimed stone hit him in the belly and he folded up like a concertina.

"Nicely thrown," Skarnu remarked.

"I thank you, sir," Raunu answered. "Nice to know the arm still works."

"Aye." Skarnu looked around. He stood near the front of the crowd, but not so near that any Algarvian could easily see who he was. Drawing in a deep breath, he let it out in a shout of his own: "Down with the vicious count and the Algarvian tyrants!"

No redhead could have identified him in the moments following that cry, for Merkela grabbed him, pulled his face down to hers, and gave him the most savage kiss he'd ever had, a kiss that left the taste of blood in his mouth. Because of that kiss, he hardly noticed the Valmierans surging past him toward the scapegrace Count Simanu and his Algarvian protectors.

"Back!" the Algarvian officer shouted in Valmieran. "Back, or you will be sorry for it!" He had mettle; no man without it would have found his voice so fast after making the acquaintance of Raunu's stone. But the townsfolk and peasants, roused by tradition flouted as perhaps by nothing else, did not go back. More stones flew – Skarnu flung one himself. It missed, which made him curse.

"Down with Simanu!" the Valmierans roared, a cry that echoed through the square. "Down with Simanu! Down with—"

"Blaze!" the Algarvian officer shouted, not about to let the outraged Valmierans overrun his men. "Blaze them down!"

Blaze them down the redheads did. A few men got in among the kilted soldiers, but they did not last long. Both the Algarvians around Simanu and those on the rooftops turned their sticks on the furious Valmierans. As men – and women – began to fall, the rest broke and fled.

Skarnu had to drag Merkela away by main force. "Let me go!" she kept shouting. "I want my crack at them!"

But he would not let her go. "Come on," he said. "I don't want you dead, curse it." As if to underscore his words, a man beside them fell with a groan. Skarnu went on, "The Algarvians and Simanu have just done us a favor. Before, people would put up with them. No more – now they've found out what they get when they do. We'll have five people willing to fight them for every one who would before. Do you see?"

Merkela must have, for she let him lead her out of Pavilosta. But she never admitted he was right, not out loud.

Five

Krasta rounded on her maidservant. "Curse you, Bauska, I ought to box your ears," she said furiously. "It's only the middle of the afternoon. If you think you can fall asleep on me, you had better think again."

"I am sorry, milady," Bauska said around a yawn. "I'm sure I don't know what's come over me the past few days." Wise in the way of servants, Krasta had no doubt she was lying, but couldn't tell why. Bauska yawned again, yawned and then gulped. Her complexion, always pale, went distinctly green. After another gulp, she made a strangled choking noise, turned, and dashed out of Krasta's bedchamber.

When she returned, she still looked wan but somewhat better, as if she'd got rid of what ailed her. "Are you ill?" Krasta demanded. "If you are, you had better not give it to me. Colonel Lurcanio and I are supposed to go to a banquet tomorrow night."

"Milady . . ." Bauska stopped. A faint – a very faint – flush darkened her white, white cheeks. She resumed, picking her words with obvious care: "What I have, it is not catching, not between me and you."

"What *are* you talking about?" Krasta asked. "If you're ill, have you seen a physician?"

"I am sick now and then, milady, but I am not ill," her servant said. "And I have no need to go to a physician. The moon has told me everything I need to know."

"The moon?" For a moment, the words meant nothing to Krasta. Then her eyes widened. *That* explained it. "You are with child!"

"Aye," Bauska said, and again blushed faintly. "I have been sure now for the past ten days or so."

"Who's the father?" Krasta said. If Bauska presumed to tell her it was none of her business, she promised herself the maidservant would regret it for the rest of her life.

But Bauska did nothing of the sort. Looking down at the carpet, she whispered, "Captain Mosco, milady."

"You are carrying an Algarvian's bastard? A cuckoo's egg?" Krasta said. Not raising her eyes, Bauska nodded. Anger shot through Krasta, anger oddly mixed with envy: She'd thought from the beginning that Mosco, who was years younger than Lurcanio, was also better-looking. "How did it happen?"

"How?" Now Bauska did look up. "In the usual way, of course."

Krasta hissed in exasperation. "That is not what I meant, and you know it perfectly well. Now, then – have you told this fellow what he's done to you?"

Bauska shook her head. "No, milady. I have not dared, not yet."

"Well, you are about to." Krasta seized her maidservant by the arm. Had she been just a little more provoked, she would have seized Bauska by the ear. As things were, she gripped Bauska tightly enough to make the servant whimper. Krasta ignored that; she was used to ignoring protests from her servants. Bauska whimpered again when Krasta marched her down the stairs and into the wing of the mansion the Algarvians occupied. Krasta ignored that, too.

A couple of the clerks who helped administer Priekule for King Mezentio looked up from their desks as the two Valmieran women went by. They eyed Krasta (and Bauska, too, though Krasta paid no attention to that) far more brazenly than Valmieran commoners would have dared to do. Their leers had infuriated Krasta at first. Now she accepted them, as she accepted so much of Algarvian rule.

"But there are limits," she muttered. "By the powers above, there *are* limits." Bauska made a questioning noise. Krasta went right on ignoring her.

She knew where Captain Mosco worked: in an antechamber outside the larger room that served these days as Colonel Lurcanio's office. Mosco was speaking into a crystal mounted on a desk undoubtedly plundered from a Valmieran cabinetmaker's shop. He murmured something in Algarvian. As the image in the crystal faded away, he rose and bowed and shifted into his accented Valmieran: "How lovely to see you, ladies – and twice as lovely to see you both together."

Oh, he was smooth. Bauska smiled and curtsied and started to say something sweet – exactly what the situation didn't call for, as far as Krasta was concerned. What the situation did call for seemed plain enough. "Seducer!" Krasta shouted at the top of her lungs. "Betrayer of innocence! Defiler of purity!"

That made all the officious Algarvian clerks – or at least the ones who understood Valmieran – stare through the doorway at her with something other than lust on their minds. It also brought Colonel Lurcanio out into the antechamber. It did not, however, much abash Captain Mosco. Like so many of his countrymen, he had crust. With another bow, he said, "I assure you, milady, you are mistaken. I am no defiler, no betrayer, no seducer. I assure you, also" – he looked insufferably male, insufferably smug – "no seduction was necessary, not with the lady your maidservant being at least as eager as I."

Krasta glared at Bauska. She was perfectly willing to believe the commoner wench a slut. With some effort, though, she remembered that was neither here nor there. She had considerable practice sneering, and put that practice to good use. "Lie however you please," she said, "but all your lies will not explain away the child this poor woman is carrying."

"What is this?" Lurcanio said sharply. Mosco stared, then kicked at the carpet. He still looked very male, but now like a sulky small boy caught after he'd broken a fancy vase he should have handled carefully.

"Speak up!" Krasta told Bauska, and squeezed the maidservant's upper arm – which she'd never let go of – harder than ever.

Bauska whimpered yet again, then did speak, in a very small voice: "Milady tells the truth. I will have a baby, and Captain Mosco is the father."

Mosco had wasted no time recovering his aplomb. With an extravagant Algarvian shrug, he said, "Well, what if I am? That's what comes of poking, every now and then, anyhow." He turned to Lurcanio. "It's not as if I'm the only one, my lord Count. These Valmieran women spread their legs at a wink and a wave."

"I know that," Lurcanio answered. He was looking at Krasta. Blood rushed to her face – the blood of outrage, not that of embarrassment. She squared her shoulders and drew in a deep breath, preparatory to scorching Lurcanio. But, a moment later, she exhaled, the scorching undelivered.

She did not care to admit it even to herself, but Lurcanio intimidated her as no one else ever had.

He spoke to Mosco now in Algarvian. Mosco kicked at the carpet again as he answered in the same language. Krasta had no idea what they were saying. Though she had an Algarvian for a lover, she had not bothered learning above half a dozen words of his language.

To her surprise, Bauska leaned over to her and whispered, "They say halfbreeds are the last thing they want. What are they going to do to me?" She looked as if she wanted to sink through the floor.

"You understand the funny noises they make?" Krasta said in some surprise. To her way of thinking, servants barely had the wit to speak Valmieran, let alone any other language. But Bauska nodded.

Lurcanio and Mosco went right on talking, taking no notice of the two women. Krasta squeezed Bauska's arm again to make the maidservant tell her what they were jabbering about. In due course, Bauska did: "Mosco says they'll have to make sure the baby weds an Algarvian, come the day. In a few generations, he says, the Kaunian taint will be gone."

"He says that, does he?" Krasta whispered back, outraged all over again. Everyone knew – everyone in her circles knew – Kaunian blood was infinitely superior to that of the swaggering barbarians from Algarve. But she did not have the nerve to throw that obvious truth in Lurcanio's face. Instead, she tried a different ploy: "How happy will Captain Mosco's wife be to learn of his little bastard?"

She wasn't sure Mosco had a wife. By the way he flinched, though, he did. Lurcanio spoke in a flat voice, the one he used to give orders: "You will not say a word to Captain Mosco's wife, milady."

After gathering herself, Krasta looked defiance at him. In trying to keep her from playing the game of scandal, he had, for once, overreached himself. "I will bargain with you," she said. "If Mosco acknowledges the bastard as his, if he supports the brat and Bauska as they deserve, his wife need not hear anything unfortunate. If he acts as so many men are in the habit of acting . . ."

Lurcanio and Mosco spoke back and forth in Algarvian. Again, Krasta had no idea what they were saying. Bauska did, and let out an angry squawk. Pointing at Mosco, she said, "You certainly *are* the father! *I* don't tomcat around, and you've proved you do." Krasta didn't know whether to believe her or not; she operated on the assumption that servants lied whenever they got the chance. But Bauska sounded convincing, and Mosco wouldn't have an easy time proving she lied – not for some months, anyhow.

He thought of that, too. "If the child has hair the color of straw, it can starve for all of me," he growled. But then, with a sour look at Krasta, he went on, "If I see signs I did in truth sire it, it shall not lack, nor shall its mother. This I would do for my own honor's sake, but—"

"Men speak of honor more often than they show it," Krasta said.

"You do not know Algarvians as well as you think," Mosco snapped.

"You do not know men as well as you think," Krasta retorted, which drew a startled gasp of laughter from Bauska and a couple of harsh chuckles from Lurcanio.

"I was trying to tell you – if that is so, the child and mother shall not lack," Captain Mosco said. "And, if they do not lack, not a word of this shall go back to Algarve. Is it a bargain?"

"It is a bargain," Krasta said at once. She did not ask Bauska's opinion; Bauska's opinion meant nothing to her. When her maidservant nodded, she scarcely noticed. Her contest was with the Algarvians – and she had done better against this pair than the Valmieran army had done against Mezentio's men. *If only we might have blackmailed the redheads instead of fighting them*, she thought.

Lurcanio sensed that he and Mosco had come off second best. Waggling a finger under Krasta's nose, he said, "Do you remember, you have made this bargain with my aide, who has his own reasons for agreeing to it. If you seek to play such games with me, you shall not be happier for it afterwards, I promise you."

Nothing could have been more nicely calculated to make Krasta want to try to punish him for his Algarvian arrogance . . . though having his child struck her as going too far. And Lurcanio had shown her he was not in the habit of bluffing. Disliking him for the steadfastness she was also compelled to respect, she made her head move up and down. "I understand," she said.

"Good." He was arrogant indeed. "You had better." And then his manner changed. He could take off and put on charm as readily as he took off and redonned his kilt up in Krasta's bedchamber. "Shall we go out this evening, milady, as well as tomorrow? Viscount Valnu, I hear, has promised one of his entertainments on the spur of the moment." He raised an eyebrow. "If you are irked at me, I can always go alone."

"And bring some ambitious little tart back here?" Krasta said. "Not on your life!"

Lurcanio laughed. "Would I do such a thing?"

"Of course you would," Krasta said. "Mosco may not know men, but I do." Lurcanio laughed again, and did not presume to contradict her.

Pekka hurried around the house, flicking at imaginary specks of dust. "Is everything ready?" she asked for the dozenth time.

"As ready as it can be," her husband answered. Leino looked around the parlor. "Of course, we haven't stuffed Uto into the rest crate yet."

"You told me I'd get in trouble if I went in the rest crate," Uto said indignantly. "That means you can't put me in there, either. It does, it does." He drew himself up straight, as if defying Leino to deny it.

"Big people can do all sorts of things children can't," Leino said. Pekka coughed; she didn't want this issue complicated. Leino coughed, too, in embarrassment, and yielded the point: "This time, you're right. I'm not supposed to put you in the rest crate." Under his breath, he added, "No matter how tempted I am." Pekka heard that, and coughed again; Uto, fortunately, didn't.

Before any new arguments could start – and arguments accreted around Uto as naturally as nacre around a bit of grit inside an oyster – someone knocked on the front door. Pekka jumped, then hurried to open it. There stood Ilmarinen and Siuntio. Pekka went down on one knee before them, as she would have before one of the Seven Princes of Kuusamo. "Enter," she said. "Your presence honors my home." It was a commonplace greeting, but here she meant it from the bottom of her heart.

As the two elderly theoretical sorcerers stepped over the threshold, Leino also bowed. So did Uto, a beat slower than he should have. He stared at the mages from under his thick mop of black hair.

Ilmarinen laughed at that covert inspection. "I know about you, young fellow," he said. "Aye, I do. And do you know how I know?" Uto shook his head. Ilmarinen told him: "Because I was just the same way when I was your size, that's how."

"I believe it," Siuntio said, "and you haven't changed much in all the years since, either." Ilmarinen beamed, though Pekka wasn't sure Siuntio had meant it as a compliment.

Gathering herself, she said, "Masters, I present to you my husband, Leino, and my son, Uto." She turned to her family. "Here we have the mages Siuntio and Ilmarinen."

Leino and Uto bowed again. Leino said, "It is indeed an honor to have two such distinguished men as my guests." He smiled wryly. "It would be an even greater honor were I privileged to hear what they discuss with my wife, but I understand why that cannot be. Come on, Uto – we're going next door to visit Aunt Elimaki and Uncle Olavin."

"Why?" Uto had his eye on Ilmarinen. "I'd rather stay and listen to *him*. I already know what Auntie and Uncle will do."

"We can't listen to these mages and your mother talk, because they'll be talking about secret things," Leino said. Pekka thought that only more likely to make Uto want to stay, but her husband retrieved the situation by adding, "These things are so secret, even I'm not supposed to hear about them."

Uto's eyes widened. He'd known his parents didn't – couldn't – tell each other about everything they did, but he'd never seen that brought home so dramatically. He went with Leino to Pekka's sister's house without another word of protest.

"A likely lad," Ilmarinen said. "Likely to make you want to pitch him into the sea a lot of the time, I shouldn't wonder, but likely the other way, too."

"I think you're right on both counts," Pekka said. "Sit. Make yourselves comfortable, I pray you. Let me bring refreshments." She hurried into the kitchen, then returned with bread, sliced smoked salmon and onions and pickled cucumbers, and a pot of ale from Kajaani's best brewer.

By the time she got back, Siuntio had spectacles on his nose and a Lagoan journal in his hand. He set it aside willingly enough to eat and to accept a mug of golden ale, but his eyes kept sliding over to it. Pekka noticed and said nothing. Ilmarinen noticed and twitted him: "The Lagoans watch us, and so you feel compelled to watch the Lagoans?"

"And what if I do?" Siuntio asked mildly. "This does, after all, touch upon our reason for coming to Kajaani."

Not even Ilmarinen could find a way to disagree with him. "The vultures gather," he said. "They clawed at the scraps of what we published. Now that we've stopped publishing, they claw at the scraps of what isn't there."

"How good a mage is this Fernao?" Pekka asked. "From the questions he asked me in his letter, he knows as much as I did a couple of years ago. The question is, can he ferret out the direction I've taken since then?"

"He is a first-rank mage, and he has Grandmaster Pinhiero's ear back in Setubal," Siuntio said, sipping at his ale.

"He is a sneaky dog, and would have stolen everything in Siuntio's belt pouch had the two of them met," Ilmarinen said. "He tried slitting mine, too, but I'm an old sinner myself, and not so easy to befool."

"He came to us openly and innocently," Siuntio said. Ilmarinen made a rude noise. Siuntio corrected himself: "Openly, at any rate. But how many mages from how many kingdoms are sniffing at the trail of what we have?"

"Even one could be too many, if he served King Swemmel or King Mezentio," Pekka said. "We don't know yet how much power lurks at the heart of this link between the two laws, or how to unleash whatever there is, but others with the same idea might pass us on the way, and that would be very bad."

Ilmarinen looked east. "Arpad of Gyongyos has able mages, too." He looked west. "And Fernao is not the only good one in the stable of Vitor of Lagoas. Gyongyos hates us because we block her way across the islands of the Bothnian Ocean."

"Lagoas does not hate us," Siuntio said.

"Lagoas doesn't need to hate us," Ilmarinen answered. "Lagoas is our neighbor, so she can covet what we have without bothering to get excited about it. And we and the Lagoans have fought our share of wars over the years."

"Lagoas would have to be mad to fight us at the same time as she wars with Algarve," Pekka said. "We outweigh her even more than Mezentio's kingdom does."

"If she were ahead of us on this path you mentioned, that might not matter so much," Siuntio said.

"And she is at war, and kingdoms at war do crazy things," Ilmarinen added. "And the Lagoans are cousins to the Algarvians, which gives them a good head start on craziness by itself, if anyone wants to know what I think."

"Kaunians are proud because they're an old folk, as we are," Siuntio said. "Algarvic peoples are proud because they're new. That doesn't make them crazy, but it does make them different from us."

"Anyone who's enough different from me is surely crazy – or surely sane, depending," Ilmarinen said.

Pekka declined to rise to that. She went on with Siuntio's thought: "And Unkerlanters are proud because they aren't Kaunian or Algarvic. And Gyongyosians, I think, are proud because they aren't like anyone else at all. When it comes to that, they're like us, but no other way I can think of."

"They're much uglier than we are," Ilmarinen said. Siuntio sent him a reproachful look. He bore up under it. "They cursed well are – those overmuscled bodies, that tawny yellow hair sprouting every which way like dried-out weeds." He paused. "Their women do look better than their men, I will say that."

And what do you know of Gyongyosian women? The question stood on the end of Pekka's tongue, but she didn't ask it. Something in Ilmarinen's expression warned her that he would tell her more than she wanted to hear. He had, after all, been attending mages' meetings longer than she'd been alive. Instead, she said, "We have to learn more ourselves, and we have to be careful while we're doing it."

"Oh, indeed," Siuntio said. "There you have in the compass of an acorn shell one of the reasons for our journey from Yliharma."

Ilmarinen glanced over to him. "Aside from gulping down Mistress Pekka's excellent food and guzzling her ale, I thought that was *the* reason we came to Kajaani."

"Not quite," Siuntio said. "I have been pondering the implications of your truly astonishing insight into the inverse nature of the relationship between the laws of similarity and contagion." He bowed in his seat. "I would never have thought of such a thing, not if I examined the results of Mistress Pekka's experiment for a hundred years. But, once furnished with the insight that sprang from a mind more clever than mine, I have tried to examine some of the avenues down which we may hope to follow it."

"Look out," Ilmarinen said to Pekka. "The more humble he sounds, the more dangerous he is."

Siuntio took no notice of Ilmarinen. Pekka got the idea that Siuntio had a lot of practice taking no notice of Ilmarinen. From his belt pouch, Siuntio drew out three sheets of paper. He kept one and gave one to each of his fellow theoretical sorcerers. "I hope you will not hesitate to point out any flaws you may find in the reasoning, Mistress Pekka," he said. "I do not give Ilmarinen the same warning, for I know he will not hesitate."

"Truth is truth," Ilmarinen said. "Everything else is fair game." He donned a pair of spectacles to help him read. After a little while, he grunted. After another little while, he grunted again, louder, and looked over the tops of the spectacles at Siuntio. "Why, you old fox."

Pekka made slower going of the lines of complex symbols Siuntio had given her. About a third of the way down the closely written sheet, she exclaimed, "But this would mean—" and broke off, for the conclusion to which Siuntio was leading her seemed one only a maniac could embrace.

But he nodded. "Aye, it would, or I think it would, could we but find a way to do it. Believe me, I was quite as surprised as you."

"You old fox," Ilmarinen repeated. "This is why you're the best in the business. Nobody pays attention to the details the way you do – nobody. If I had a hat on, I'd take it off to you."

Pekka worked her way down to the bottom of the sheet. "This is amazing," she said. "It's elegant, too, which argues that it ought to be true. I find no flaws in the logic, none whatever. But that I don't find them doesn't mean they aren't there. Experiment is an even better test of truth than elegance."

She hoped she hadn't offended the master mage, and breathed a sigh of relief when Siuntio grinned. "Truly you will go far in your craft," he told her, and she inclined her head in thanks. He went on, "Some of the required experiments may – will – be difficult to formulate."

"I shouldn't think so," Pekka said. "Why—" She explained an idea that had come to her while she was nearing the end of Siuntio's work.

Now Siuntio dipped his head to her. To her surprise, so did Ilmarinen, who said, "Well, well. I wouldn't have come up with that."

"Nor I," Siuntio agreed. "You deserve to be the one to try it, Mistress Pekka. In the meanwhile – for I can see that it will take some preparation – Ilmarinen and I will acquaint Raahe and Alkio and Piilis with our progress, for the three of us seem to have drawn somewhat ahead of them. Is that agreeable to you?"

"Aye." Pekka knew she sounded dazed. The two finest theoretical sorcerers in Kuusamo had just let her know they thought she belonged in their company. All things considered, she decided she'd earned the right to sound a little dazed.

Back in his study, Brivibas labored over yet another article on the bygone days of the Kaunian Empire. By immersing himself in the past, Vanai's grandfather did what he could to ignore the unpleasant present. Vanai wished she could find such an escape for herself.

She longed for escapes of all sorts, escape from Major Spinello chief among them. She glanced back toward the study. Brivibas would not come out till suppertime, and would do his best to ignore her while they ate. She had hours in which to try her spell, the casting of which would take only a few minutes. Her grandfather would be none the wiser, and what he did not know he could not tell.

As Vanai opened the book of classical Kaunian sorcerous lore, she laughed without much humour and bowed in the direction of the study. "You have not trained me in vain, my grandfather," she murmured, "even if I use my knowledge to ends different from yours."

Though she was no trained mage, the spell before her looked simple enough. She'd had no trouble getting daffodil root from Tamulis the druggist; to this day, the boiled root was a simple against bladder pains, and Brivibas had reached an age where it was easy to imagine him suffering from such. And Vanai's mother had owned a set of silver earrings, necklace, and bracelet set with sea-green beryls. Taking an earring from the dusty jewelry case without her grandfather noticing had been simplicity itself.

"Now," she said, gathering herself, "to hope this proves a true spell." There lay the rub, as she knew only too well. However loath Brivibas was to admit it, the ancient Kaunians had been a superstitious lot, believing in all manner of demons modern thaumaturgy proved nonexistent. Some of what they'd reckoned magic, too, was nothing but imagination run wild. Too many of their spells gave no results when worked by – or against – skeptical moderns.

Vanai shrugged. One way or another, she'd learn something. *I can write a paper afterwards*, she thought. But she did not want to write a paper. She only wanted Major Spinello gone.

As the classical text recommended, she'd made a crude straw image of her Algarvian tormentor. Soaking the top of the image's head in red ink showed its model came from Mezentio's kingdom. Now that the ink had dried, Vanai held the image in her left hand. With her right, she stirred a bowl of water in which she'd boiled the daffodil root. As she cast the image into the bowl, she called out the classical Kaunian invocation from the text: "Devil, begone from my house! Devil, begone from my door!"

Devil, begone from my bed, she thought. She wanted to say that aloud – she wanted to scream it. But the charm said, *Follow exactly what is written, and thou shalt surely gain thy desire: and this hath been proved in our time.* She would not deviate, not yet. If the charm failed her (which she knew to be only too likely), she would think about what to do next.

For now, she took the image out of the bowl of infused water and dried it on a rag. Some of the red ink had smeared, which made the straw man look badly wounded. Vanai's lips skinned back from her teeth in a predatory grin. She didn't mind that. No, she didn't mind that at all.

Once the image was dry enough to suit her, she laid the beryl on its ink-stained chest. "Beryl is the stone that driveth away enemies," she intoned. "Beryl is the stone that maketh them meek and mild and obedient to the operator's will." *And my will is that he go away and never trouble me again, or any other Kaunian either.*

When she was done, she threw the image and the rag on which she'd dried it into the cookfire. For one thing, she hoped that would hurt Spinello, too. For another, it got rid of the evidence. Like conquerors since the days of the Kaunian Empire, King Mezentio's men took a dim view of those they had defeated practicing sorcery against them. After the image had gone up in smoke, she poured down the privy the daffodil root and the water in which she had boiled it. The earring went back into the case from which it had come, the book of charms on to its shelf.

As she set about peeling and slicing parsnips to add to the pot of bean soup simmering above the fire, she wondered if she'd just wasted her time. Also like conquerors since the days of the Kaunian Empire, King Mezentio's men were warded against their enemies' magecraft. And she didn't know whether she'd truly practiced magecraft or simply tried to use one of her ancestors' outworn, mistaken beliefs.

But she hoped. Oh, how she hoped.

Brivibas, as usual these days, was taciturn over supper. He'd given up lecturing her and reproving her, and had no idea how to talk to her in any more nearly normal, more nearly equal way. Or maybe, she thought as she watched him spoon up the soup, he had so many nasty things he wanted to tell her, he simply couldn't decide which one to shout out first and so swallowed all of them. However that worked, his silence suited her.

Major Spinello did not visit her the next day. She hadn't expected that he would; she'd come to know the rhythms of his lust better than she wanted to. Knowing them at all, for that matter, was knowing them better than she wanted to. When he stayed away the day after that, she began to hope. When he stayed away the day after *that*, too, her heart sang a hymn of freedom inside her.

That made the peremptory, unmistakably Algarvian knock on the door the following morning all the more devastating. Brivibas, who had been examining one of the antiquities in the parlor, let out a disdainful sniff and retreated across the courtyard to his study. He slammed the door behind him as if taking refuge in a besieged fortress.

He would be long since dead, were I not doing this, Vanai reminded herself. But her steps dragged even more than usual as she made her way to the door. "Took you long enough," Spinello said. "You don't want to keep me waiting, you know, not if you want to keep your grandfather breathing."

"I am here," Vanai said dully. "Do what you will."

He took her back to her bedchamber and did exactly that. And then, because he hadn't done it for longer than usual, he wanted to do it again. When he didn't rise to the occasion quite so promptly as he'd hoped he would, Vanai had to help him. Of all the things he made her do, she despised that most of all. *If I bite down hard*, she thought, not for the first time — for far from the first time — *the redheads will slay me and my grandfather, and the powers above only know what they'll do to the rest of the Kaunians in Oyngestun*. And so she refrained, though the temptation got stronger every time.

At last, after what seemed like forever, Spinello gasped his way to a second completion. He preened and strutted as he got back into his kilt and tunic. "I know I'm spoiling you for every other man," he said, meaning it as a boast.

Vanai cast down her eyes. If Spinello wanted to think that maidenly modesty and not disgust, she would let him. "Aye, I think you are," she murmured. If he wanted to think that agreement rather than disgust . . . again, she would let him.

He left Brivibas' house whistling cheerfully, the picture of sated indolence. Vanai barred the door after him. She went back to the house's crowded bookshelves, to the text from which she'd taken the classical spell of repulsion. She'd hoped that, because it was so old, Spinello would not be warded against it. Maybe he was. Or maybe the spell, like so many from the days of the old Empire, had no real value. Either way, she wanted to throw the book into the fire or drop it down the privy.

As she had when pleasuring Spinello, she refrained. She'd made sure she put the text back exactly where she'd got it. If it went missing, Brivibas would know, and would hound her without mercy till it turned up or till she explained why it couldn't. Or he might think Spinello had stolen it. If anything could rouse her grandfather to violence, a purloined book might.

Spinello returned three days later – he probably needed extra rest after his unusual exertion during his previous visit – and then again two days after that. In his own way, he was nearly as regular and methodical as Brivibas. Vanai cursed the classical Kaunians under her breath, and some-times above it. Her grandfather remained convinced his ancient ancestors had been the fonts of all knowledge. Maybe so, but what they'd reckoned magecraft couldn't keep the Algarvian major out of her bed. As far as she was concerned, that made them useless – worse than useless, for she'd built up her hopes relying on their wisdom, only to see those hopes dashed.

Two days later, Spinello came back, and then two days after that. By then, Vanai had resigned herself to the failure of her ploy. She let him do what he wanted. He did leave more quickly these days than he had at first; he'd discovered she didn't care to listen to his tales of Algarvian triumphs in Unkerlant, and so had stopped regaling her with them. He allowed her all sorts of small courtesies, but not the larger one of deciding whether she wanted to give herself to him.

And, after another two days, he returned once more. This time, to her surprise, he had a couple of ordinary Algarvian troopers at his back. Horror blazed through her. Was he going to give her to them as a reward for good service? If he tried to do that, Vanai would . . .

She realized she didn't have to decide what she would do then. One of the troopers carried a crate holding four jars of wine; the other was festooned with sausage links and cradled a ham in his arms. Spinello spoke to them in Algarvian. They set the food and drink inside the front hall, then went away.

Spinello came in and closed the door behind himself. As he was barring it, Vanai found her voice: "What's all this?"

"Farewell gift," Spinello answered lightly. "My superiors, in their wisdom, have decided I am better suited to fighting the Unkerlanters than to administering a Forthwegian village. It will be boring, I expect – no antiquities, and mostly homely women – but I am the king's to command. You will have to take your chances with the constables who take over from me. But" – he slid a hand under her tunic – "I am not gone yet."

Vanai let him lead her back to her bedchamber. When he had her straddle him, she did it joyfully. It was not the joy of fulfilled desire, but it was the joy of *a* fulfilled desire, and surprisingly close to the other – closer than she'd ever come with Spinello, of that she was certain.

Had he wanted a second go then, she would have given it to him without much resentment, knowing it would be the last. But, after she'd brought him to his peak, he caressed her for a moment, then patted her bottom to show he wanted her to let him up. She did, and he began to dress.

"I'll miss you, curse me if I won't," he said, bending down to kiss her. An eyebrow quirked. "You won't miss me a bit, and curse me if I don't know that, but I brought the meat and wine to give you something to remember me by."

"I will always remember you," Vanai said truthfully as she got back into her own clothes. Now, perhaps, she might not remember him quite as she would have before his gift – or not to the same degree, at any rate. She might even hope he would live when he went into battle – though she might not, too.

To her relief, he didn't ask her anything about that. He kissed and fondled her at the doorway before going out. She closed the door and barred it. Then she stood in the entry hall for a couple of minutes, scratching her head as she stared down at the sausages. Had her spell got Spinello sent off to fight King Swemmel's men, or was this only a coincidence? If it was only a coincidence, had some coincidences like it convinced the ancient Kaunians they had an effective cantrip?

How could she be sure? Had she been her grandfather, she would have gone to the shelves of dusty journals to find out what historians and historical mages had written. But she was not Brivibas. Knowing how she'd got free of Spinello didn't matter to her. Knowing that she'd got free did. There in the crowded little hallway, she began to dance.

For once, Corporal Leudast looked at behemoths with admiration rather than dread. These behemoths belonged to his own side, and were trotting into action for King Swemmel and against the Algarvian invaders. "Stomp 'em flat!" he shouted at the Unkerlanter soldiers riding the big beasts.

"Poor tactics, Corporal," Captain Hawart said. "More efficient to blaze the redheads down or toss eggs on to their heads." But, having delivered that admonition, he grinned. "I hope they stomp the buggers flat, too."

"We've got fine big behemoths there to do it," Sergeant Magnulf remarked. "I think they're bigger than most of the ones the Algarvians breed."

Hawart nodded. "I think you're right. That's the far western strain, bigger and fiercer than any the redheads or the Kaunians ever tamed. I wish we had more of them." His grin faded. "I wish the size difference mattered more nowadays, too. With the weapons behemoths carry, it's not body against body and horn against horn as often as it used to be."

"Maybe not, sir," Leudast said, "but if I don't like medium-sized Algarvian behemoths coming at me, Mezentio's men sure won't like great big Unkerlanter behemoths coming at them."

"Here's hoping they don't," Hawart said. "Whatever we do, we've got to hold the corridor between Glogau and the rest of the kingdom. The Zuwayzin have stopped their push, but the Algarvians—" He broke off, his face grim.

Leudast wondered if anything could stop the Algarvians. Nothing had yet, or he and his comrades – those of them left alive – wouldn't have been pushed so far back into Unkerlant. But new recruits in rock-gray tunics kept coming out of the training camps farther west. King Mezentio's men occupied his own village along with countless others, but Unkerlant still held even more.

"Come on!" Captain Hawart shouted to the mix of veterans and new men making up his regiment. "Forward, and stick close to the behemoths. We need them to smash a hole in the enemy's line, but they need us, too. If the redheads pop up out of the grass and blaze the men off those beasts, they aren't any good to us by themselves."

"Algarvian tactics," Leudast remarked.

Sergeant Magnulf nodded. "The redheads had a long time to figure out how to put all the puzzle pieces together. We're having to learn on the fly, and I think we're doing a lot better than we were just after they hit us."

"Aye," Leudast said. "Nothing comes cheap for them these days." But trying to hold back the Algarvians didn't come cheap, either. As one who'd started fighting them in central Forthweg and was still fighting them here deep inside Unkerlant, Leudast understood that better than most.

"Forward!" Magnulf shouted, echoing Captain Hawart, and Leudast shouted, too, echoing his sergeant. And forward the Unkerlanter foot-soldiers went, on the heels of their behemoths. In a way, such willingness to keep on counterattacking was surprising, considering how often such blows either came to nothing or were frittered away; Leudast remembered the fight for Pfreimd only too well. In another way, though . . . A lot of the men who'd retaken Pfreimd only to have to yield it up again were by now dead or wounded. The fresh-faced young soldiers who'd replaced them didn't realize how easily their superiors could throw their lives away for no good reason.

They'll find out, Leudast thought. *The ones who live will find out.* The ones who died would find out, too, but the knowledge would do them no good. After another couple of strides, he wondered how much good it would do the ones who lived.

He pounded along, hunched forward at the waist to make himself as small a target as he could. Men who'd seen some fighting imitated him, and also imitated him in zigzagging frequently so as not to let any Algarvian footsoldiers grow too sure where they'd be in the next moment. Troopers newly pulled from their villages stood straight up and ran straight ahead. The ones who lived would soon learn better, and that lesson would actually do them some good.

Bursting eggs from the behemoths' tossers tore up the wheatfield ahead. The Algarvians were supposed to have come that far, though no one on the Unkerlanter side seemed sure of exactly where they were. That struck Leudast as inefficient. Quite a few things about the way his side was fighting the war struck him as inefficient. But mentioning them struck him as efficient only in the sense that it would be an efficient way to get himself into trouble.

Sure as sure, a behemoth-rider threw up his arms and slid out of his seat to lie crumpled and still among stalks of wheat now going from green to gold. Leudast hadn't seen whence the beam came. But a couple of Unkerlanters cried out "There!" and pointed to a spot in the field not far ahead of him.

A moment later, a beam blazed past his head, so close he could feel the heat on his cheek. He threw himself flat and scrambled forward through the grain. The rich smells of fertile soil and ripening wheat reminded him the harvest would be coming soon. Were he back in his village, were this a time of peace, he would follow the horse-drawn reaper, gathering up the grain it cut down. Now he wanted to cut down that Algarvian soldier who'd come so close to reaping him.

As he moved toward the spot where he thought the redhead hid, he tried to work out what the Algarvian would be doing. If he was a new man himself, he'd probably be running. But a veteran might well sit tight, knowing he was unlikely to escape and intent on doing all the damage he could before being hunted down and killed. The way this fellow had coolly blazed down the behemoth-rider argued that he knew what he was about.

Never had it crossed Leudast's mind that the redhead might come hunting him. But the stalks of wheat parted in front of him, and there was the Algarvian, waxed mustachios all awry. He shouted something in his language and swung the business end of his stick toward Leudast.

He was smart and dangerous and very fast. But so was Leudast, and Leudast blazed first. A neat hole appeared in the redhead's face, just below his right eye. The beam boiled his brains inside his skull; most of the back of his head blew out. He was dead before he crashed to the ground like a dropped sack of barley.

"Powers above," Leudast muttered. Cautiously, he got to his feet and looked around to find out what had happened in the bigger fight while he and the Algarvian carried on their own private war. The Unkerlanter behemoths and his comrades were still going forward. He too hurried ahead.

Algarvian dragons fell out of the sky on the behemoths. But a couple of those dragons smashed to earth; the Unkerlanters manning the heavy sticks some of the behemoths carried were not caught napping. And Unkerlanter dragons, their scales painted the rock-gray of Leudast's tunic, attacked the beasts gaudy in Algarve's red, green, and white. The red-heads hurt the troop of behemoths, but could not wreck it.

Here and there, little fires smoldered in the wheat. Had the wind been stronger, they would have grown and spread. A couple of them, one around the burning body of a dragon, were trying to spread anyhow. Leudast skirted them and ran on. He'd seen far worse things than fields afire.

More eggs began falling among his comrades, these not dropped from dragons but hurled by Algarvian egg-tossers behind the line. Leudast threw himself into a hole one of them had made in bursting. A moment later, after another burst close by, Sergeant Magnulf jumped into the same hole – and on to Leudast, who said, "Oof!"

"Sorry," Magnulf said, though he didn't sound very sorry. Leudast wasn't unduly put out; Magnulf worried about saving his own neck first and everything else afterwards, as any sensible soldier would have. The sergeant went on, "Stinking redheads hit back faster than you wish they would, don't they?"

"Aye," Leudast said. "I wish I could say you were wrong." He tried to look on the bright side: "We're getting better at that ourselves, too. Our dragons gave them more than they wanted a little while ago."

"I know, but they do it all the stinking time," Magnulf said. "The whoresons have more crystals than we do, and they keep on talking into them."

Shouts from ahead warned that the Algarvians were doing more than talking into their crystals. Leudast and Magnulf scrambled up to the edge of their hole and looked east. Behemoths and soldiers and eggs had flattened enough of the wheat to let them see troopers in tan kilts and tunics running toward them in loose order.

Leudast laughed out loud. "They didn't do enough talking this time. Look, Sergeant – they didn't bring any behemoths with 'em, and we've still got some of ours."

Magnulf's eyes glowed. "Ha! They'll pay for that." Gloating anticipation filled his voice.

Pay for it the Algarvians did. The Unkerlanter behemoths' heavy sticks blazed them down at a range from which the redheads could not hurt the beasts or their riders. Eggs from other behemoths' tossers burst among the Algarvians, tossing some aside like broken dolls and making most of the rest go to earth to keep from suffering a like fate.

"Forward!" Captain Hawart called. Leudast heaved himself out of the hole and made for the Algarvians. So did Sergeant Magnulf. Almost without noticing they were doing it, they spread apart from each other, making themselves into less inviting targets for the enemy.

But the Algarvians were as quick to correct their own mistakes as they were to punish the Unkerlanters'. Reinforcements came to the rescue of the men the Unkerlanter attack had been on the edge of crushing, and those reinforcements included behemoths with redheads aboard. One thing Leudast had seen before was that Algarvian behemoth-riders went after their Unkerlanter counterparts the instant they spied them. So it was in this fight, too, and, with fewer behemoths backing them, King Swemmel's footsoldiers faltered.

Shouting King Mezentio's name, the Algarvians came on again, hot to retake the stretch of ground the Unkerlanters had wrested from them. But a flight of dragons painted rock-gray swooped down on them, dropping eggs on their behemoths and flaming their footsoldiers. Leudast shouted himself hoarse, or rather hoarser, for the smoke in the air had left his throat raw now for quite a while.

When he looked back over his shoulder, he was surprised to see the sun dipping toward the western horizon. The fighting had gone on all day, and he'd hardly noticed. Now he felt how worn and hungry and thirsty he was.

Unkerlanter reinforcements came up during the night. So did a little food. Leudast had more than a little food on him; he knew supplies were liable to be erratic. During the night, the wind shifted, as it had a way of doing as summer swung toward fall. It blew from out of the south, a cool breeze with a warning of rain in it.

Sure enough, at dawn gray clouds covered most of the sky. Eyeing them, Sergeant Magnulf said, "It'll already be raining, I expect, down in the village I come from. Nothing wrong with that, you ask me."

"No," Leudast said. "Nothing wrong with that at all. Let's see how the redheads like slogging through the mud. If the powers above are giving us an early winter, maybe they'll give us a nasty winter, too." He stared up at one of the few patches of blue sky he could see, hoping the powers were listening to him.

Along with a dozen of his comrades, Tealdo sheltered in a half-wrecked barn somewhere in southern Unkerlant. It was raining almost as hard inside the barn as it was outside. Tealdo and Trasone held a cloak above Captain Galafrone to keep water from dripping down on to the map the company commander was examining to try to figure out just where they were.

"Curse me if I know why I'm bothering," Galafrone frowned. "This miserable thing lies more often than it tells the truth."

Trasone pointed to a line printed in red. "Sir, isn't that the highway?"

"That's what the *map* says," Galafrone answered. "I saw Unkerlanter roads during the Six Years' War, but I thought they might have gotten better since. They were supposed to have gotten better since. But the stinking 'highway' is just another dirt track. Huzzah for Swemmel's efficiency."

"Mud track now," Trasone said. His legs, like everyone else's, were mud to the knees and beyond.

Tealdo said, "Maybe Swemmel's efficient after all. Hard for us to go very far very fast if we bog down every step we take."

Galafrone gave him a sour look. "If that's a joke, it's not funny."

"I didn't mean it for a joke, sir," Tealdo said. "I meant it for the truth."

"They have as much trouble in this slop as we do," Trasone said.

"What if they do?" Tealdo answered. "They're not trying to go forward right now, or not so much. They're only trying to hold us back."

That produced a gloomy silence. At last, Captain Galafrone said, "We've got 'em by the ears and we've got 'em by the tail. Can't very well let go now, can we?" He bent closer to the map, then swore. "I'll be cursed if I don't need spectacles to read the fornicating letters when they're printed that fornicating small. Where in blazes is the town called Tannroda?"

Trasone and Tealdo both peered at the map – rather awkwardly, since they had to keep holding the cloak over it. Tealdo spotted the place first. He pointed with his free hand. "There, sir."

"Ah." Galafrone's grunt held more weariness than satisfaction. "My thanks. Northwest, is it? Well, that makes a deal of sense – it's in the direction of Cottbus. Once we take his capital away from him, King Swemmel won't be so much of a much." He folded up the map and put it back in his belt pouch. "Come on, boys. We've got to get moving. The Unkerlanters won't wait for us."

"Maybe they've all drowned in the mud," Trasone said.

"Don't I wish." Galafrone grunted again. For the first time since the veteran had taken command of the company, Tealdo thought he saw his years telling on him. Galafrone made himself rally. "It's too much to hope for, and you know it as well as I do. If we don't shift 'em, they won't get shifted."

"Maybe the Yaninans can do the job," Tealdo said slyly as Galafrone started toward the open barn door.

The captain stopped and gave him a baleful look. "I wouldn't pay you a counterfeit copper for a whole army of those chicken thieves. They think we're supposed to do the fighting while they steal anything that isn't spiked down. Only thing they're good for is holding down quiet stretches of the line – and they're not much good for that, either. Come on. We've wasted too much time here."

Out they went. The rain was still coming down hard; Tealdo felt as if he'd been slapped in the face with a wet towel. More bedraggled Algarvians emerged from the farmhouse, which had taken an even worse beating than the barn. Still others were resting in haystacks and under trees. Like Tealdo, they all squelched forward toward Tannroda and, beyond it, Cottbus.

Every step was an effort. Tealdo, like most of the company, stayed on what was called the highway for lack of a suitably malodorous word. Others insisted moving through the fields to either side was easier. It probably didn't make much difference, one way or the other. Mud was mud.

They slogged past a ley-line caravan whose forwardmost several cars no longer floated above the ground but lay on it, canted at drunken angles. The Algarvian soldiers who'd been riding in those cars now stood around in the mud – except for the ones who lay in it, hurt when the caravan went awry.

"Poor dears," Tealdo said. "They'll get wet."

Trasone's laughter had a nasty edge. "They look like new men – probably never saw an Unkerlanter in all their born days. They've been drinking wine and pinching pretty girls back in Algarve while we've had to go out and work for a living. Whoresons might as well find out what it's like over here." He spat into the muck. The drumming rain drowned his spittle.

They hadn't gone much farther before the reason the caravan had come to grief became obvious. Three or four Algarvian mages stood around and in a large hole in the ground that was rapidly turning into a pond. A colonel shouted at them: "Hurry up and fix the damage to this ley line, powers below eat you all! I have men to move, and how am I supposed to move them with the line broken?" He stamped his booted foot, which only made it sink into the soggy ground.

"Try walking," Tealdo called, confident the rain would cloak him. And, sure enough, the colonel whirled in his direction, but couldn't pick him out from among the other vague, dripping shapes.

In any case, the officer was more concerned with the mages, and they with him. One of them said, "My lord Colonel, the egg the cursed Unkerlanters buried and then burst did too good a job of wrecking the line for us to repair it right away. It wasn't meant to try to absorb so much energy all at once. And the Unkerlanters use different spells from ours to maintain the line – and they've done their best to obscure those, too. It'll be a while before you're gliding again."

"How long a while?" the colonel ground out.

Before answering, the mage put his head together with his colleagues. "A day, certainly," he said then. "Maybe two."

"Two?" the colonel yelped. He waved his arms and stamped his foot again and loosed some extravagant curses, as any Algarvian might have. None of that did him any good. Being under his command, the mages had to try to soothe him instead of telling him what they thought of him, which Tealdo knew he would have wanted to do had he been in their place.

"Come on," Galafrone said. "They may be stuck, but we're not – quite."

On the footsoldiers went, leaving the sabotaged ley line behind them. After another mile or so, the road became an even worse bog than it had been. Dragging himself out of the ooze, Tealdo discovered the going *was* better – not good, nowhere close to good, but better – in the field to one side.

"Something else is buggered up ahead," Trasone predicted. "You wait and see – we'll find out what it is."

They'd gone only a little farther when the wide-shouldered bruiser proved himself a good prophet. There ahead were half a dozen behemoths stuck belly-deep in the clinging mud. "Hurrah," Tealdo said. "First they ruined the road for us, then they went and ruined it for themselves, too."

"They're in so deep, they're liable to drown there," Trasone said. One of the trapped behemoths evidently thought the same, for it lifted its head and let out a loud, frightened bellow. It thrashed in the mud, trying to get free, but succeeded only in miring itself even worse.

"There, precious, there." One of the behemoth-riders was down in the mud with the beast, doing his best to keep it calm. Tealdo would not have wanted that fellow's job, not for anything. The behemoths' crews had already done everything they could to lighten their animals, stripping off not only egg-tossers and heavy sticks but also the chainmail coats the behemoths wore. As far as Tealdo could tell, none of that had done much good.

A troop of Algarvian horsemen rode up across the field. Not having been churned by the behemoths, the ground there held their weight better than the alleged road would have. The horsemen had ropes with them. The men who rode the lead behemoth began making lines fast to their beast. "Do they really think they'll be able to pull him out?" Tealdo asked.

"If they don't, they're going to a cursed lot of trouble for nothing," Trasone answered.

Tealdo hadn't the faintest idea how to go about putting ropes around a behemoth to get it out of the mud. Unlike him, though, the men who rode the great animals looked to have considered the problem before, for they went about the business as matter-of-factly as he would have built a fire.

"Go!" a behemoth-rider shouted to the horsemen. They urged their animals forward, but could not move the heavy behemoth. "Go!" the rider shouted again. The horses had no better luck the second time. The behemoth-rider threw up his arms in despair. Then his eye fell on the men of Captain Galafrone's company slogging past. "Lay hold of the ropes and lend a hand, will you?" he asked – begged, actually.

Had he tried to order Galafrone's soldiers to help, Tealdo was sure the company commander would have consigned him to the powers below. As things were, Galafrone said nothing but, "Aye – needs doing," and ordered his men to the ropes.

With a company of soldiers adding their strength to that of the horses, the behemoth came up, ever so slowly, out of the clinging mud. The men who rode him cheered themselves hoarse. Then they fastened the ropes to the next behemoth so that the footsoldiers and horses could pull him free, too.

Getting all six of the great beasts out of the ooze took all day. And, by the time the dripping sky began to darken, Tealdo was more worn than he had been after any battle in which he'd ever fought. Too weary to eat, he wrapped his blanket around himself, lay down not far from where he'd labored so hard, and slept like a dead man.

Someone kicked him awake, not unkindly, at dawn the next day. A field kitchen had found the company sometime in the night; he wolfed down a couple of bowls of hot barley porridge with bits of unidentified meat floating in it. In his civilized days, he would have turned up his nose at such coarse fare. Now it brought him back to life. He resumed the long tramp westward with more spirit than he would have thought possible before he ate.

"We're going to be late to Tannroda," Galafrone muttered discontentedly. "Powers above, we're already late to Tannroda."

When they got to the town, it didn't seem worth reaching. The Unkerlanters must have fought hard there; it looked as if a giant had set it afire and then stamped out the flames with his feet. A military constable asked Galafrone to which regiment his men belonged. The captain told him, looking apprehensive. But the fellow just nodded and said, "You're only the third company through – this wretched weather is playing hob with everyone. Use the northwest road – that one there. The Unkerlanters, curse 'em, are mounting another counterattack."

"I thought King Swemmel was supposed to be running short of men by now," Tealdo said as he and his comrades slogged on to try to throw the Unkerlanters back yet again.

"You've been in the army a while now," Trasone answered. "Don't you know better than to believe everything you hear yet?" Tealdo pondered, grunted, nodded, and kept marching.

Tired as usual after a long day's labor, Leofsig made his way through the streets of Gromheort back toward his home. He stepped carefully; the pavement was wet and slippery from a shower that had passed through earlier in the afternoon. He was wet from the shower, too, which meant he was a little less filthy than on most days. He thought about heading for the baths, but decided not to bother. The sooner he got home, the sooner he could eat and sleep. Nobody was as clean as in the days before the war.

He'd got more than halfway home before he noticed the new broadsheet pasted to walls and fences and trees. The Algarvians had put it up, of course – the penalty for a Forthwegian putting up a broadsheet was death, and the penalty for a Kaunian probably something worse. But, regardless of whether the Algarvians had put it up, it showed the tough, jowly image of King Plegmund, arguably Forthweg's greatest ruler, and a troop of hard-looking soldiers carrying spears and bows and dressed in the styles of four hundred years before.

PLEGMUND SMASHED THE UNKERLANTERS, read the legend below the illustration. YOU CAN, TOO! JOIN PLEGMUND'S BRIGADE. BEAT BACK BARBARISM. Smaller letters gave the address of the recruiting station and also warned, *No Kaunians will be accepted into this Brigade.*

With a snort, Leofsig walked on. He had a hard time imagining Kaunians wanting to join a brigade under the control of people intent on grinding their noses in the dirt. For that matter, he had a hard time imagining Forthwegians wanting to join a brigade under Algarvian control. Who would do such a daft thing? Somebody one jump ahead of the constables, maybe. He wished the Algarvians joy of trying to make such recruits into soldiers.

A blond woman about his own age stepped out from between a couple of buildings as he went by. "Sleep with me?" she called, doing her best to make her voice alluring. Her tunic and trousers clung so tightly, they might have been painted on to her.

Leofsig started to shake his head and walk on. Then, to his dismay, he realized he recognized her. "You're Doldasai," he blurted. "My father used to cast books for yours."

As soon as the words left his mouth, he wished he had them back. Better for both of them if he pretended he didn't know her and gone on his way. Too late for that now. She hung her head; she must have wished he'd kept his mouth shut, too. "You see my shame," she said. If she remembered Leofsig's name, she didn't want to use it. "You see my people's shame."

"I'm sorry," he said, which was true and useless at the same time.

"Do you know the worst of it?" Doldasai said. "The worst of it is, you can still have me if you pay me. I need the silver. My whole family needs the silver, and the Algarvians won't let any of us make it any other way." Nasty promises glowed in her blue-gray eyes, promises of things he hadn't done, perhaps of things he'd scarcely imagined.

And he was tempted, and hated himself for being tempted. When he still hoped Felgilde would let him slip his hand under her tunic – she hadn't yet – why wouldn't he have been tempted to find out what all he'd been missing? Of itself, his hand slid toward his belt pouch.

Doldasai made a peculiar noise, half bitter mirth, half . . . disappointment? Leofsig gave her a couple of coins. "Here. Take this," he said. "I wish I could afford to give you more. I don't want anything from you." That wasn't quite true, but it kept things simpler.

She stared down at the small silver coins, then abruptly turned her back on him. "Curse you," she said, her voice thick and muffled. "I didn't think anyone could make me cry any more, not after everything I've had to do. Go on, Leofsig" – she knew who he was, all right – "and if the powers above are kind, we'll never see each other again."

He wanted to help her with something more than a little money. For the life of him, though, he couldn't think of what he might do. And so, ingloriously, he left. He didn't look back over his shoulder, either, for fear he would see Doldasai propositioning some other Forthwegian who might part with cash for a few minutes' pleasure.

"You made good time coming home," Elfryth remarked as she unbarred the front door to let him in.

"Did I?" he said, not wanting to tell his mother he'd fled Doldasai as the Forthwegian army had ended up fleeing the Algarvians.

"Aye, you did." To his relief, his mother didn't seem to notice any false note in his voice. "You have time to wash a little" – which meant he remained rank in spite of the rain shower – "and drink a glass of wine before supper. Conberge even came up with some meat to mix in with the peas and beans and pulses."

"What kind of meat?" Leofsig asked suspiciously. "Roof rabbit?"

Elfryth shook her head. "The butcher called it mutton, but I think it's got to be goat. It's been in the pot for hours, and it isn't close to tender yet. But even tough meat is better than no meat at all."

Leofsig couldn't argue with her. He wondered how long it had been since Doldasai and her family had eaten meat. His family was going through hard times. Hers was going through catastrophe. He grabbed a towel off the rack and went off to use the pitcher and basin in his room. It wouldn't be a bath, but would be better than nothing.

Ealstan looked up from a page of work: not problems from their father, for once, but verses of a poem. "Why the grim face?" Leofsig's younger brother asked.

"I didn't know I had one," Leofsig answered as he started to wash.

"Well, you do," Ealstan said. "How come?"

"Do you want to know why?" Leofsig considered. Ealstan wasn't a baby any more. "I'll tell you why. I ran into Daukantis' daughter coming home – remember, the olive-oil merchant?" He told the tale in a few words.

Ealstan clicked his tongue between his teeth. "That's hard," he said. "I've heard other stories like it, but not anybody we know. You ought to tell Father – if anyone can do anything for them, he can."

"Aye, that's so," Leofsig said through the towel he was using to dry his face. He looked over it at his brother. "It's a good idea, in fact. You're getting a man's wits faster than I did, I think."

"Living under the redheads pushes everybody along faster – except for the people it pushes under, like the Kaunians," Ealstan said. "Did you see the broadsheet for what the Algarvians are calling Plegmund's Brigade?"

"Aye, I saw it. You'd have to be blind not to see it; they've slapped up enough copies," Leofsig answered. "Disgusting, if you ask me."

"Well, I think so, too, but Sidroc says he's dead keen on joining." Ealstan held up a hand before Leofsig could burst like an egg. "I don't think he loves Mezentio. I think he just wants to go out there and kill something, and this would give him the chance."

"What do Father and Uncle Hengist have to say about it?" Leofsig asked.

"Uncle Hengist was shouting at him just before you got here," Ealstan said. "He thinks Sidroc's flown out of his bush. Father hasn't said anything that I know of; maybe he figures Sidroc is Hengist's worry."

With practicality so cold-blooded it alarmed even him, Leofsig said, "Maybe he ought to join Plegmund's Brigade. If he's marching on Cottbus, he can't very well tell the Algarvian constables here that I broke out of the captives' camp."

His brother looked horrified. Before Ealstan could say anything, Conberge came by in the courtyard, calling, "Supper's ready." Ealstan hurried off to the dining room with transparent relief. As Leofsig followed, he decided he was just as well pleased not to have that conversation go any further, too.

Whatever the meat in the stew was, it wasn't mutton. He knew it at the first bite. It might have been goat. For all he could prove, it might have been mule or camel or behemoth. It didn't taste spoiled; he'd had to choke down spoiled meat in the army and in the captives' camp. He wouldn't have taken Felgilde to a fancy eatery to dine off this, but it helped fill the enormous hole in his belly.

He kept glancing over at Sidroc. His cousin seemed as intent on eating as he was himself. Leofsig wondered if he really wanted Sidroc to join the Algarvians' puppet force. If Sidroc joined of his own free will, what could be wrong with that?

After a sip of wine, Leofsig's father turned to Uncle Hengist and remarked, "The news sheets talk about heavy fighting in the west."

"Aye, Hestan, they do," Hengist said. Neither of them looked at Sidroc. Hestan was less ostentatious about not looking at him than Hengist was. Up until today, Hengist would probably have added some comment about how the Algarvians were still moving forward in spite of the hard fighting. Now he just nodded, still not looking at his son. He wanted Sidroc to think about what hard fighting meant. The trouble with that was, Sidroc had never experienced it. Leofsig, who had, hoped he never did again.

In a musing voice, Hestan went on, "Heavy fighting's bound to mean a lot of men dead, a lot of men hurt."

"Aye," Hengist said again. Again, he said no more. A couple of days before, things would have been different, sure enough.

Sidroc spoke up: "A lot of Unkerlanters stomped down into the mud, too. You'd best believe that." He glowered at Hestan, as if defying him to disagree.

But Leofsig's father only nodded. "Oh, no doubt. Still, would King Mezentio want Forthwegians to do his fighting for him if he weren't running low on redheads?"

"If we don't show we can fight, how will we ever get our kingdom back?" Sidroc said. "If you ask me, *that's* what Plegmund's Brigade is all about."

Now no one else at the table wanted to look toward Sidroc. "Fighting is all very well," Leofsig said at last, "but you have to remember for whom you're fighting, and against whom you ought to be fighting." He didn't see how he could put it any more plainly than that.

Ealstan found a way. Very quietly, he asked, "Cousin, who killed your mother? Was it Swemmel's men, or Mezentio's?"

Uncle Hengist drew in a sharp breath. Sidroc stared. In spite of everything he could do — and he fought hard — his face began to work. His eyes screwed shut. He let out a great sob. Tears poured down his cheeks. "Curse you, Ealstan!" he shouted in a grief-choked voice. "Powers below eat you, starting at the toes!" He sprang to his feet and ran blindly from the room. A moment later, the door to the bedchamber he shared with his father slammed. In the silence enveloping the table, Leofsig could hear his weeping even through the thick oak portal.

Leofsig leaned toward Ealstan and murmured, "That was well done."

"Aye, lad, it was," Uncle Hengist said. He shook himself. "Sometimes we lose track of what matters. You did right to remind Sidroc — and me, too, I'll own."

"Did I?" Ealstan sounded not at all convinced.

"Aye, son, you did," Hestan said. Elfryth and Conberge also nodded.

Not even his family's reassurance seemed to persuade Ealstan. "Well, it's done, and I can't change it," he said with a sigh. "I just hope Sidroc won't hate me in the morning the way he does now."

He was looking at Leofsig. Leofsig started to ask why it mattered what Sidroc thought. But that answered itself. If Sidroc decided he really hated Ealstan, he was liable to decide he really hated Leofsig, too. Even if he also hated the Algarvians, who could guess what he might do in such a state. "I hope he won't, too," Leofsig said.

Six

Ealstan ate his porridge and gulped down his morning cup of wine. He looked across the table at Sidroc as he might have looked at an egg that had fallen from below a dragon's belly but failed to burst. Sidroc ate stolidly, eyes down on his bowl. At last, Ealstan had to speak: "Come on. You know they'll thrash us if we're late."

Sidroc didn't say anything to that, not at first. Ealstan cursed under his breath. He stirred in his seat, ready to head for his first class without his cousin. *Maybe Sidroc doesn't care if they break a switch on his back. I do.* But, just as he was gathering himself to go, Sidroc said, "I'm ready," and got up himself.

They walked along in silence for a while. Every time Ealstan spied the broadsheet proclaiming Plegmund's Brigade, he pretended he hadn't. Sidroc must have seen the broadsheets, too, but he didn't say anything about them. He strode toward the school with a set expression on his face that Ealstan didn't like.

They had to pause to let a couple of companies of Algarvian soldiers march past along a cross street. "Remember how, the day the Duke of Bari died, we had to wait for our own cavalrymen?" Ealstan asked. "That spilled the chamber pot into the soup, all right."

"We did, didn't we?" Sidroc said. By the wondering look in his eye, he'd forgotten till Ealstan reminded him. Then he scowled again. "And a whole lot of good our cavalrymen did us, too. Fighting beside them" – he pointed to the Algarvians – "that'd be something. They're winners."

"Remember what my father said," Ealstan answered. "If they were doing as well as all that, they wouldn't need the likes of us to help them."

Sidroc had his sneer back. "If your father were half as smart as he thinks he is, he'd be twice as smart as he really is. He knows numbers, so he thinks he knows everything. He doesn't, you hear me?"

"I hear a lot of wind." Ealstan wanted to punch his cousin. If he did, though, what would Sidroc do? Getting into a brawl was one thing when all they could do was beat on each other. It was something else again when Sidroc could betray Leofsig to the Algarvians – and Ealstan's father with him. Ealstan's eyes slid toward Sidroc again. *If I ever get the chance, I'll knock out one of your teeth for every time I've had to hold back. Then you can spend the rest of your days sipping supper through a straw.*

They passed a couple of mushrooms pushing up through a gap between a couple of the slates of the sidewalk. As any Forthwegian – or, for that matter, any Kaunian who lived in Forthweg – would have done, Ealstan slowed to eye them. "They're just scrawny little worthless toadstools," Sidroc said. "Like you."

"If you are one, you know one," Ealstan retorted. Boys had probably been saying that to one another since the days of the Kaunian Empire. One glance at the mushrooms, though, told him that, but for the insult, Sidroc was right. He said, "Pretty soon, the ones worth having will start sprouting."

"That's so, and we'll all go off to the fields and the woods with baskets." Sidroc leered. "And maybe you'll come home with that Kaunian wench's basket again – or maybe you'll stick your mushroom in her basket." He guffawed.

One more tooth you'll lose some day, Sidroc, Ealstan thought. Aloud, he said, "She's not like that, so why don't you drag your mind out of the latrine?" He did hope he would see Vanai again. And if she turned out to be a little bit – *only the tiniest bit*, he assured himself – like that, he didn't think he'd mind.

By then, they were very close to the school. Ealstan braced himself for another day of meaningless lessons. Putting up with his masters, though, would be a pleasure next to putting up with Sidroc.

He endured the boredom. When called on to recite, he recited. He'd dutifully memorized all four assigned verses of the rather treacly poem from two hundred years before, and delivered the first one without a bobble. Sidroc got called on for the third verse, made a hash of it, and got his back striped. "Curse it," he said as they went on to their next class, "I knew the first verse. Why didn't I get chosen in your place?"

"Just luck," Ealstan answered. He'd known the third verse as well as the first, so he wouldn't have minded getting called in Sidroc's place. With his cousin feeling abused and put upon, he decided not to mention that.

Sidroc got through the rest of the day without any more beatings, which left him in a somewhat better mood as Ealstan and he headed home. Ealstan, on the other hand, felt gloomier than he had in a while. It must have shown on his face like a fire in the night, for Sidroc – hardly the most perceptive fellow ever born – asked him, "Somebody go and steal your last bite of bread?"

"No," Ealstan said, though the clichéd question for *What's wrong?* had taken on a new and literal meaning in these hungry times in Gromheort. His wave encompassed the whole battered city. "It's just that – I don't know – everything looks so shabby and broken and gray. I've been thinking about how things were that day when we saw the Forthwegian cavalry and how they are now, and I keep wondering how anybody stands it."

"What else can we do?" Sidroc said. They walked on a little farther. Sidroc kicked a small stone out of the way. As he watched it spin off, he went on, "Maybe that's one of the reasons Plegmund's Brigade doesn't look so bad to me. It would get me away from – this." His wave was as all-embracing as Ealstan's had been.

Ealstan found himself too surprised to answer. He hadn't imagined Sidroc could look so keenly at himself. He also hadn't imagined his cousin might have such a sensible-seeming reason for thinking about fighting on King Mezentio's side. As far as Ealstan was concerned, Plegmund's Brigade remained the wrong answer, but now, at least, he understood the question Sidroc was asking. *How can I escape?* had crossed his own mind, too, many times.

An Algarvian constable threw up his hands to stop pedestrians and carts and riders. "Halting!" he shouted in halting Forthwegian.

"We've got stuck going to and from today," Sidroc grumbled, sounding more like his usual self. Ealstan nodded. He hadn't been happy about waiting for his own kingdom's soldiers; he was far less happy about having to wait for the conqueror's troopers.

But this procession held only a few Algarvians: guards, sticks at the ready. Most of the men who flowed past the intersection where Ealstan and Sidroc stood were Unkerlanter captives. As far as looks went, there was little to distinguish them from Forthwegians: they were most of them dark and stocky and hook-nosed. And their beards were growing out, which made them look even more like Ealstan's people.

Sidroc shook his fist at them. "Now you know what it's like to have your kingdom overrun, you thieves!" he shouted. Some of the Unkerlanters looked at him as if they understood. They might have; the northeastern dialects of their language weren't far from Forthwegian.

Most of them, though, kept shambling on. Their stubbly cheeks were hollow, their eyes blank. They'd endured – how much? However much it was, they would have to endure more. "What do you suppose the redheads will do with them – to them?" Ealstan asked.

"Who cares, the stinking backstabbers?" his cousin answered. "As far as I'm concerned, the Algarvians can cut their throats to make sticks, or work whatever other magic with their life energy they care to." He shook his fist at the Unkerlanter captives.

"They won't do that," Ealstan said. "If they do, the Unkerlanters will start cutting the throats of their Algarvian captives, and then where will we be? Back in the red days after the Kaunian Empire fell, that's where."

"If you ask me, the Unkerlanters deserve it." Sidroc drew his thumb across his own throat. Ealstan started to say something. Before he could, Sidroc went on, "If you ask me, the redheads deserve it, too. Powers below eat both sides."

Ealstan pointed frantically toward the Algarvian constable. The redhead stood so close to them, he couldn't have helped hearing. But he didn't speak enough Forthwegian to understand what they were saying. The last few Unkerlanter captives tramped past, and the last couple of Algarvian guards. The constable gave a sweeping wave, as if he were a noble graciously granting peasants a boon. Along with the rest of the Forthwegians who'd been waiting for the procession to pass, Ealstan and Sidroc crossed the street.

"Why do you keep going on about Plegmund's Brigade if that's the way you feel about the redheads?" Ealstan asked his cousin.

Sidroc said, "I wouldn't be joining for the Algarvians. I'd be joining for me."

"I can't see the difference," Ealstan said. "I bet you King Mezentio wouldn't be able to see the difference, either."

"That's because you're a blockhead," Sidroc said. "If you want to tell me Mezentio's a blockhead, too, I won't argue with you."

"I know what I'll tell you," Ealstan said. "I'll tell you I'm not the biggest blockhead here, that's what."

Sidroc mimed throwing a punch. Ealstan mimed ducking. They both laughed. They were still insulting each other, but not the way they had been lately. This was just schoolboy's foolish talk, not the sort of business that could poison things between them for years to come. A little stretch of childishness felt good.

They hadn't stopped tossing insults around, or laughing about it, by the time they knocked on the door of Ealstan's house. Conberge unbarred it and stood in the entry hall looking from one of them to the other. "I think both of you stopped in a tavern on the way here," she said, and Ealstan couldn't tell whether she was joking or not.

Sidroc stepped up and breathed in her face. "No wine," he declared. "No ale, either."

Conberge mimed reeling away. "No, but when was the last time you cleaned your teeth?" she said. Considering how little love she bore for Sidroc, her voice should have had an edge. Had it borne one, it would have wrecked the moment like a bursting egg. Somehow, it didn't. Sidroc breathed in Ealstan's face. Not about to let his sister outdo him, Ealstan mimed falling over dead. He and Sidroc were laughing so hard, they had to hold each other up. Conberge could not more help laughing, too, than she could help breathing.

A door opened across the street. A neighbor stared at the three of them, wondering what could be so funny in grim, occupied Gromheort. Ealstan wondered, too, but not enough to stop laughing. Maybe part of him sensed that this little glowing stretch couldn't last long no matter what.

The neighbor closed the door, shaking her head. That was funny, too. But then Conberge, who hadn't been quite so immersed in giggles as Ealstan and Sidroc, said, "The two of you are later than you should be if you came straight home."

"We did," Ealstan said. "Really. We had to wait for a bunch of Unkerlanter captives to shuffle through the middle of town. I suppose they're on the way to a camp." As soon as he'd spoken, he knew he'd punctured the magic. Captives and camps didn't go with heedless laughter.

From out of the south, a cloud rolled across the sun, plunging the street into gloom. Ealstan wondered how he could have let himself be so silly, even if only for a little while. By Sidroc's expression, the same thought was in his mind. Ealstan sighed. "Come on, let's go in," he said. "It's getting chilly out here."

Bembo did not like marching along a road roughly paved with cobblestones and other bits of rubble, especially not when the cobbles and other bits of rubble were slick and wet with last night's rain. "If I slip and fall, I'm liable to break my ankle," the Algarvian constable complained.

"Maybe you'll break your neck instead," Oraste said helpfully. "That would make you shut up, anyhow."

"Both of you can shut up," Sergeant Pesaro growled. "We have a job to do, and we're going to do it, that's all. End of story." He tramped along, full of determination, his big belly bouncing ahead of him at every stride, and set a good pace for the squad of constables he led.

In a low voice, Bembo told Oraste, "I've got silver that says he'll be done in long before we get to this Oyngestun place."

"I know you're a fool," the other constable answered, "but I didn't know you thought I was one, too. I'm not stupid enough to throw my money away on a bet like that."

They tramped past fields and almond and olive groves and little stands of woods. Here and there, Bembo saw Forthwegians and Kaunians, sometimes in small groups but more often alone, examining the ground and occasionally digging. "What are they doing?" he asked.

"Gathering mushrooms." Pesaro rolled his eyes. "They eat them."

"That's disgusting." Bembo stuck out his tongue and made a horrible face. None of the other constables argued with him. After a moment, he added, "It's liable to be dangerous, too – to us, I mean. They could be sneaking around doing anything at all while they're pretending to go after mushrooms."

Pesaro nodded, then shrugged. "I know, but what can you do. The soldiers say these whoresons'd revolt if we tried to keep 'em inside their towns this time of year. We're stuck with a little trouble – I hope it's a little trouble – but we stay out of big trouble. And we can't afford big trouble here right now. We've got too much farther west."

"Ah." Trades like that made sense to Bembo. They were part of a constable's life. "Maybe we ought to make 'em pay to go out and hunt the cursed things, the way you get a free one from a floozy now and then so you won't haul her in."

Some sergeant would have pitched a fit to hear something like that. Pesaro only nodded again. "Not a half bad idea. Maybe we ought to pass it on up the line. Anything we can squeeze out of this miserable place puts us that much further ahead of the game." He walked on for another few paces, then took off his hat and wiped at his sweaty forehead with his sleeve. "Long, miserable march." Bembo gave Oraste an I-told-you-so look. Oraste ignored him. Pesaro went on, "This big, heavy stick doesn't make things any easier, either."

He was right about that. Bembo had long since got sick and tired of the army-style stick he'd been issued for this assignment. Carrying it made his hand tired and his shoulder ache. Carrying it also worried him. If his superiors didn't think a short, stubby constabulary stick would be enough to keep him safe in Oyngestun, how much trouble was he liable to find there?

Pesaro, who had been slumping like suet on a hot summer day as the constables neared the village, rallied just before they got into it. "Straighten up, there," he barked at his men. "We're not going to let these yokels catch us looking like something the cat dragged in. Show some spunk, or you'll be sorry."

Bembo was already sorry, from the feet up. Nevertheless, he and his comrades did their best to enter Oyngestun with proper Algarvian swagger, shoulders back, heads up, faces arrogant. If they weren't the masters of all they surveyed, they acted as if they were. As with any magic, appearance could easily be made into reality.

Oyngestun's Forthwegians did their best to pretend the newly arrived constables did not exist. Most of the village's Kaunians stayed behind closed doors. That would not do. Pesaro shouted for whatever Algarvian constables were already in Oyngestun. All three of them tumbled out. Pesaro handed the most senior one a scroll with his orders inscribed on it. After the fellow had read it and nodded, Pesaro said, "Turn out the Kaunians – all of 'em – in the village square. We'll help."

"Aye," the constable quartered in Oyngestun said. As he handed Pesaro's orders back to him, he added, "I see what you're doing, but I don't see why."

"You want to know the truth, I don't see why, either," Pesaro answered. "But they pay me on account of what I do, not on account of why I do it. Come on, let's get moving. The sooner we're done, the sooner we can get out of this place and leave it to you and the cobwebs."

"Heh," the seniormost constable in Oyngestun said. He couldn't very well quarrel with Pesaro, who outranked him and was following orders to boot. Instead, he yelled at his own men while Pesaro instructed the squad who'd come with him from Gromheort.

The instructions were simple. They went through Oyngestun, especially the Kaunian section on the west side of the village, shouting, "Kaunians, come forth!" in classical Kaunian, in Forthwegian, and in Algarvian, depending on what they knew. "Come forth to the village square!"

And some Kaunians did come forth. Some doors, though, remained closed. Bembo and Oraste had picked up a stout length of timber and were about to break down one of those doors when a local constable called, "Don't bother. I know those buggers went out first thing this morning with a basket. They're even madder for nasty mushrooms than most folk round these parts."

"Whoever wrote our orders had his head up his backside," Bembo said. "How are we supposed to round up the stinking Kaunians if they're all running through the woods with baskets?"

"Powers below eat me if I can tell you," Oraste said. "Maybe they'll cook up some bad mushrooms and keel over dead, the way King What's-his-name in the story did when he ate bad fish."

"Serve 'em right if they did, sure enough," Bembo agreed. He walked to the next house, pounded on the door, and shouted, "Kaunians, come forth!" in what he thought was Kaunian. He was about to pound again when the door opened. His eyebrows shot upwards. Behind him, Oraste let out a couple of short, emphatic coughs. "Hello, sweetheart!" Bembo said. The girl standing in the doorway was about eighteen, and very pretty.

She looked at him and Oraste as if they'd crawled off a dungheap. An older man appeared behind her – a much older man, his hair thinning and gone from gold to silver. Oraste laughed coarsely. "Why, the dog!" he said. He looked the girl up and down. "Aye, a young wife with an old husband can have a baby, as long as there's a handsome young fellow next door." He laughed again, and Bembo with him this time.

Then the old Kaunian startled them both by speaking slow but very precise Algarvian: "My granddaughter does not understand when you insult us, but I do. I do not know if this matters to you, of course. Now, what do you want with us?"

Bembo and Oraste looked at each other. Bembo tried not to offend except on purpose. Roughly, he said, "Get along to the village square, the both of you. Just do as you're told, and everything will be fine." The old man spoke in Kaunian to his granddaughter. She said something in the same language; Bembo couldn't make out what. Then they headed in the direction of the square.

On to the next house. "Kaunians, come forth!" This time, Oraste did the shouting.

After they had pounded on doors till they were good and sick of it, the two constables went back to the village square themselves. A couple of hundred Kaunians milled about there, talking in their own old, old language and in Forthwegian, no doubt trying to figure out why they'd been summoned. All at once, Bembo was glad to be carrying the full-sized, highly visible military stick about which he'd groused most of the way from Gromheort. The blonds he and his comrades had assembled badly outnumbered them. They needed to see they'd pay if they started anything.

Sergeant Pesaro was looking around the square, too. "Is that all of them?" he asked.

"All of them that weren't out chasing mushrooms," one of the constables said.

"Or hiding under the bed," another added. He pointed to a Kaunian couple. The woman was tying a rag around the man's bloodied head. "Those whoresons there tried that, but I caught 'em at it. They won't get gay again, I don't suppose."

"All right." Pesaro turned to another constable. "Translate for me, Evodio."

"Aye, Sergeant." Unlike his fellows, Evodio hadn't forgotten almost all the classical Kaunian he'd had rammed down his throat in school.

Pesaro took a deep breath, then spoke in a parade-ground bellow: "Kaunians of Oyngestun, the Kingdom of Algarve requires the services of forty of your number in the west, to aid with your labor our victorious campaign against vile Unkerlant. Laborers will be paid, and will be well fed and housed: so declares King Mezentio. Men and women may serve Algarve here; children accompanying them will be well cared for."

He waited for Evodio to finish translating. The Kaunians talked among themselves in low voices. A man came forward. After a moment, a couple followed him, a man and woman holding hands. Two or three more unaccompanied men came out.

Pesaro's frown was fearsome. "We require forty from this village. If we do not have forty volunteers, we will choose to make up the number." As if on cue, a ley-line caravan pulled into Oyngestun from the east. Pesaro pointed to it. "There is the caravan. See? – there are already Kaunians in some of the cars."

"A lot of Kaunians in some of those cars," Bembo murmured to Oraste. "They're packed as tight as sardines in olive oil."

"Sardines are cheaper than olive oil," Oraste answered. "The cursed blonds are cheaper than space in caravan cars, too." He spat on the cobblestones.

Three or four more Kaunians stepped out of the crowd. "This won't do," Pesaro said, shaking his head and setting hands on hips in theatrical dismay. "No, this won't do at all." In an aside to his own men, he added, "Hard to get this across when I can't do it in Algarvian."

Someone in the crowd of Kaunians asked a question. Evodio translated: "She wants to know if they can bring anything with them when they go west."

Pesaro shook his head. "Just the clothes on their backs. They won't need anything else. We'll take care of them once they're there."

Another question, this one from a man: "How long will we be there?"

"Till the war is won, of course," Pesaro said. Somebody shouted in his direction from the ley-line caravan. He scowled. "We haven't got all day. Any more volunteers?" Another pair of Kaunians stepped forward. Pesaro sighed. "This isn't good enough. We've got to have the full number." He pointed to a man. "You!" He jerked his thumb. A woman. "You!" Another man. "You!" He pointed to the pair Bembo and Oraste had summoned. "You – the old hound and his young doxy. Aye, both of you."

Bembo said, "She's his granddaughter, Sergeant."

"Is she?" Pesaro rubbed his chin. "All right, never mind. You two instead." He pointed at a pair of middle-aged men. "Probably a couple of quiffs." Before long, the selection was done. Under the sticks of the Algarvian constables and the guards already aboard, the chosen Kaunians squeezed into the ley-line caravan cars. "Go home!" Pesaro shouted to the rest of the blonds. Evodio translated, for the ones who were dense. The Kaunians left the square a few at a time, some of them sobbing for suddenly lost loves. The caravan glided away.

"There's a good day's work done," Oraste said.

"How much work do you think we'll get out of them, hauled off the street like that?" Bembo asked. Oraste gave him a pitying look, one Sergeant Pesaro might have envied. A lamp went on in Bembo's head. "Oh! It's like that, is it?"

"Got to be," Oraste said, and he was surely right; nothing else made sense.

Bembo was very quiet on the long tramp back to Gromheort. His conscience, normally a quiet beast, barked and snarled and whined at him. By the time he got back to the barracks, he'd fought it down. Somebody far above him had decided this was the right thing to do; who was he to argue? Tired as he was from marching, he slept well that night.

Autumn in Jelgava, except up in the mountains, was not a time of great swings in the weather, as it was in more southern lands. People went from wearing linen tunics and cotton trousers to cotton tunics and trousers of wool or wool and cotton mixed. Talsu's father had his business pick up a little, as men and women bought replacements for what had worn out during the last cool season.

"I need more cloth, though," Traku grumbled. "Thanks to the cursed Algarvians, I can't get as much as I could use. They're taking half of what we turn out for themselves."

"Everybody needs more of everything," Talsu said. "The redheads are stealing everything that isn't nailed down."

His father glowered. "This is what happens when a kingdom loses a war."

"Aye, it is," Talsu agreed. "But powers above, I wish you'd get over the notion that I lost it all by myself."

"I don't think that for a moment, son," Traku said. "You had help, lots of help, starting with the king and going straight on down through your officers." He did not bother to lower his voice. In the old Jelgava, that would have been insanely dangerous. But the Algarvians didn't mind if the common people reviled King Donalitu – on the contrary. They didn't even seem to mind too much if the common people reviled them. Talsu wouldn't have wanted to try such tolerance too far, though.

He was very pleased for a moment, thinking his father didn't blame him for the kingdom's defeat after all. Then he listened again in his mind to what Traku had said, and realized he hadn't said anything of the sort. All he'd said was that Traku hadn't been the only one who lost it.

Before Talsu could start the argument up again, Dustbunny trotted into the tailor's shop, tail held high and proud. The small gray cat, who had thus far managed not to become roof rabbit at the butcher's shop, carried in her mouth a large brown rat. She dropped it at Talsu's feet, then looked up at him with glowing green eyes, waiting for the praise she knew she deserved.

Talsu bent down and scratched her ears and told her what a brave puss she was. She purred, believing every word of it. Then she pushed the dead rat with her nose so it half covered one of his shoes. Traku laughed. "I think she expects it to go into the stew pot tonight."

"Maybe she does." Mischief kindled in Talsu's eyes. He called up the stairs to the living quarters over the shop: "Hey, Ausra, come down here a minute."

"What is it?" his sister called back.

"Present for you," Talsu answered. He winked at his father, and held a finger to his lips to keep Traku from giving him the lie. Traku rolled his eyes but kept quiet.

"A present? For me?" Ausra hurried down the stairs. "What is it? Who gave it to me? Where did he go?"

"So you think you have boys leaving you presents all the time, do you?" Talsu said, relishing his joke more than ever. "Well, I have to tell you, you're not quite right. A little lady delivered this one, and it's all yours." He brought his foot forward, shying the rat in Ausra's direction.

She disappointed him. Instead of screaming or running off, she picked up the rat by the tail, called Dustbunny, and told her what a fine kitty she was. Then she tossed the deceased rodent back to Talsu. "Here. If you liked it well enough to get it for me, you can be the one who gets rid of it, too."

Now Traku laughed loud and long. Talsu gave his father a dirty look, but could hardly deny Ausra had outdone him this time. He picked up the rat rather more gingerly than she had, carried it outside, and dropped it in the gutter. When he came back into the tailor's shop, he was wiping his hands on his trouser legs.

Dustbunny spoke up in feline reproach. Maybe she really had thought the rat would make the main course at supper that night. "Go catch me another one," Talsu told her. "We'll serve it up with onions and peas, or maybe with olives. I like olives a lot." The cat cocked its head to one side, as if contemplating the possible recipes. Then she meowed in approval and departed with purposeful stride.

"If you want rat with peas and onions, you can cook it yourself," Ausra told Talsu. She waved a finger at him. "And if you try doing this to Mother, she'll make you cook it and she'll make you eat it, too."

Since Talsu thought his sister was right, he didn't answer. He hoped Dustbunny wouldn't come back with another rat too soon. If she did, Ausra was liable to have some unfortunate ideas about what to do with it.

Before he could take that worrisome thought any further, someone came through the door. He started to put on the automatic smile of greeting he gave any customer. So did Traku. So did Ausra. The shop did not have so many customers as to let them omit any courtesy, no matter how small.

Even so, the smile froze half formed on Talsu's face. His father and sister also looked as much stunned as welcoming. The man standing before them wore tunic and kilt, not tunic and trousers. His coppery hair streamed out from under his hat. His mustache was waxed out to needle-sharp spikes; a little vertical strip of hair – not really a beard – ran up the center of his chin. He was, in short, an Algarvian.

"Hello. A good day to you all," he said in accented but understandable Jelgavan. He swept off that hat, bowed to Traku, bowed to Talsu, and bowed more deeply to Ausra.

Slower than he should have, Traku answered, "Good day." Talsu was content – more than content – relieved – to let his father do the talking.

"This is the shop of a tailor, is it not so?" the redhead said. He was, Talsu saw by his rank badges, a captain. That no doubt meant he was a noble. Coming out and telling him to take his business elsewhere was bound to cause trouble.

Traku must have reached the same unhappy conclusion. "Aye, it is," he admitted.

"Excellent!" The Algarvian sounded as delighted as if Talsu's father had told him he was about to win his weight in gold. His eyes, green as Dustbunny's, sparkled with glee. Algarvians, Talsu thought, were funny people. The fellow went on, "For I require the services of a tailor. I would not come here for a cabinetmaker, is it not so?" He thought he was the funniest fellow around.

"You want me . . . to make clothes . . . for you?" Traku sounded as if he didn't believe it, or even more as if he didn't want to believe it.

But the Algarvian nodded. "You understand!" he cried, and bowed again. "You are, you must be, a man of great understanding. You will make for me a set of clothes, I will pay, and all will be well."

Talsu doubted that last. So, evidently, did his father, who said, "What kind of clothes . . . sir? How much will you pay me . . . sir? When will you want them . . . sir?"

"You do not trust me?" The Algarvian sounded as if that had never crossed his mind. After a shrug suggesting the world was a crueler place than he'd imagined, he went on, "I want a good wool tunic and kilt, in civilian style, to wear for the coming winter. I will pay you silver, the price we agree by dickering, in the coin of either King Donalitu or King Mainardo – both circulate at par."

"They shouldn't," Traku said. "Mainardo's coins are lighter."

"By law, they are at par," the captain said. Talsu's father kept quiet. He was a formidable man in a haggle, as Talsu knew. Talsu also knew his father had never made a kilt in his life. Traku didn't let on about that, either. He just waited. At last, the Algarvian threw his hands in the air. "All right! All right! I will pay in Donalitu's coin, or in silver by weight to match the price in Donalitu's coin. There! Are you happy now?"

"Happy? No, sir. I haven't got a lot to be happy about." Traku shook his head. "But fair's fair. Now then, if we come to a price – and you'll pay me half beforehand and half when you get the clothes – when will you need this outfit?"

"Ten days," the Algarvian said, and Traku nodded. That much, at least, proved easy. The redhead went on, "Price will depend on the cloth, is it not so?"

Traku nodded again. "Wool, you said? I can show you some samples, if you care to take a look. You'll have to tell me how long you'll want the kilt, and how full, and how many pleats and how deep. That will let me know how much material I'll need."

"Aye. I understand." The Algarvian waggled a finger at Traku. "You are not to change for cheaper goods afterwards, mind."

Traku's father glared at him. "If you think I'd do that, you'd better find yourself another tailor. I'm not the only one in Skrunda." Talsu knew how much Traku needed the business, but Traku said not a word about what he needed. Talsu was proud of him.

"Let me see your samples," the Algarvian captain said. Presently, he pointed to one. "This weight and grade, in a forest green. Can you get it?"

"I think so," Traku answered. "If I can't, you get your half-payment back, of course." He turned to Talsu. "Measure him, son. Then we'll talk about the kilt' – he muttered something that might have been *barbarous garment* under his breath – "and then we'll talk price."

The Algarvian inclined his head. Talsu grabbed the tape measure. The redhead stood very still while he measured and took notes. Only after he'd finished did the fellow raise an eyebrow and remark, "I think you would sooner be measuring me for a coffin, is it not so?"

"I didn't say that, sir," Talsu answered, and gave the notes to his father.

Traku and the redhead talked about the kilt: its length, its drape, its pleating. Traku looked up at the ceiling and mumbled to himself. When he got done calculating, he named a price. The Algarvian screamed as if he'd been scalded – Talsu and Ausra both jumped, while the fur on Dustbunny's tail puffed up in alarm. Then the Algarvian named a price, too, one less than half as high.

"Nice talking with you," Traku said. "Close the door after you go out."

They haggled for the best part of an hour. Traku ended up getting what struck Talsu as a good price; despite noisy histrionics, the Algarvian yielded ground more readily than the tailor. The redhead was muttering to himself when he did leave.

"Forest green," Traku said. "I think I can get that. I ought to short him on the goods, though, just on account of that crack."

He did get the cloth in the right color and the proper weight, then set to work. The tunic was straightforward: it had a higher, tighter collar than Jelgavan fashion favored, but presented no new problems. For the kilt, Traku worked much more carefully. After he'd made the waistband and hemmed the garment, he sewed two pleats by hand. Then, sweating with concentration, he set thread along the kilt where the other pleats would go and used a tailoring spell based on the law of similarity. Talsu watched in fascination as the rest of the pleats formed, duplicating the first two in spacing and stitchery.

Traku held up the finished kilt with a somber sort of pride. "Ready-to-wear can't come close to a good tailor's work," he said. "The big makers use cheap originals and they stretch the spells too thin, so the clothes they make aren't even properly similar to the originals." He sighed. "But they're cheap, so what can you do?"

When the Algarvian captain came in to try on his outfit, he kissed his fingertips, he blew a kiss at Ausra, and for a horrid moment Talsu thought he and Traku were going to get kissed, too. But the redhead restrained himself, at least from that. He paid the second half of the price and left the shop a happy man.

"Good thing he liked it," Traku said after he'd gone. "If he didn't, what in blazes would I do with a cursed kilt?"

"Sell it to another Algarvian," Talsu said at once.

His father blinked; maybe that hadn't occurred to him. "Aye, I suppose so," he said. "I wouldn't get as much for it, though."

Talsu rang coins on the counter. The music was sweet. "You don't need to worry. We don't need to worry." He checked himself. "We don't need to worry for a little while, anyhow."

Vanai was glad to be out of the house she shared with her grandfather and even gladder to be out of Oyngestun. With so many Kaunians shipped off to the west to labor for the redheads in the war against Unkerlant, the village felt as if it had a hole in it, like a jaw with a newly pulled tooth. She and Brivibas might have been among those taken for labor. Remembering what a few days of work on the roads had done to her grandfather, Vanai knew she was lucky to escape.

She also remembered, all too well, the price she'd paid to get Brivibas back from the labor gang. She had no great love for the Unkerlanters – they struck her as being even more barbarous than their Forthwegian cousins – but she hoped with all her heart that they gave Major Spinello a thin time of it.

Meanwhile, she had mushrooms to find. With rain coming a little early this year, she thought the crop would be fine. And, at last, she'd persuaded her grandfather to let her search by herself. That had proved easier than she'd thought it would. He didn't cling to her as he had before she gave Spinello what he wanted.

And so, while Brivibas went south, Vanai headed east, in the direction of Gromheort. When they separated, her grandfather coughed a couple of times, as if to say he knew why she was going in that direction. She almost walloped him with the mushroom basket she was carrying. Before she swung it, though, she noticed it was the one that belonged to Ealstan, the Forthwegian from Gromheort. Brivibas would surely have noticed, too, and would have taken a certain satisfaction in being proved right in his suspicions.

"But he's not right," Vanai said – most emphatically, as if someone were about to contradict her. "He doesn't know what he's talking about. He never knows what he's talking about."

A troop of Algarvians on unicorns came trotting up the road from Gromheort toward Oyngestun. The redheaded riders leered at Vanai. They whooped as they passed her, and called out lewd suggestions, some of which she understood because of Spinello. She breathed a silent sigh of relief when they kept on riding. Had they decided to ravish her one after another and then cut her throat, who could have stopped them? She knew the answer to that: no one. They were the occupiers, the conquerors. They did as they pleased.

Along with sighing in relief, Vanai cut across fields instead of staying close by the road. The going was harder that way, and her shoes soon got wet and muddy. She didn't care. The next Algarvians who came along the highway – three crews mounted on their behemoths – could have seen her as nothing more than a blond-headed speck in the distance. Not one of them waved or called out to her. That suited her fine.

She came across a nice patch of meadow mushrooms, and put some in her basket – Ealstan's basket, actually – to make sure she wouldn't go back to Oyngestun empty-handed. A little later, she clapped her hands in glee when she found some chanterelles, yellow and vermilion growing together. She liked the yellow ones better – vermilion chanterelles tasted acrid to her – but gathered some of each.

And then, at the edge of an almond grove, she almost stepped on some bright orange imperial mushrooms. They were still small, but unmistakable because of their color. As she plucked them from the ground, she recited a snatch of ancient poetry: they'd been favorites back in the days of the Kaunian Empire.

But her pleasure at picking them evaporated a moment later. The mushrooms remained, but the Kaunian Empire was only rubble. Even the Kaunian kingdoms of the east had fallen into the Algarvians' hands these days, and as for Forthweg . . . The Forthwegian majority despised the Kaunians still living among them, and the Algarvians delighted in showing the Forthwegians the Kaunians were even worse off than they.

After Vanai discovered the imperial mushrooms, she had no luck for quite a while. She saw three or four Forthwegian men down on their hands and knees in the middle of a field, but did not go over to them. They were unlikely to be willing to share whatever they'd found, and not so unlikely to try to make sport with her as the Algarvians might have done. She put some bushes between herself and them and went on her way.

The sun was nearing its high point in the north when she came into the oak wood where she and Ealstan had accidentally exchanged baskets – and where they'd met the year before that, too. With her grandfather miles away, she could at last admit to herself that she hadn't come here altogether by accident. For one thing, she did want to give him his basket if she saw him again. And, for another, he'd been a sympathetic ear, and she hadn't had many of those lately.

She walked among the trees. Her muddy shoes scuffed through leaves and acorns. Some of the oaks' gnarled roots lay close to the surface. She wondered if she ought to try digging for truffles. In the days of the Kaunian Empire, rich nobles had trained swine to hunt the precious fungi by scent. Without such aid, though, finding them was a matter of blind luck. She shook her head – she didn't have time to waste, and not much in the way of luck had come her way lately.

She wandered through the wood, finding a couple of puffballs, which she picked, and quite a few stinkhorns, which she avoided with wrinkled nose. She saw no sign of Ealstan. She wondered if he was out hunting mushrooms at all. For all she knew, he could have been back in Gromheort or out searching in a different direction. It wasn't as if she could make him step out from behind a tree by wishing.

No sooner had that thought crossed her mind than Ealstan stepped out from behind a tree – not the one she'd been looking at, but a tree nonetheless. Her eyes widened. Had she turned into a mage after all?

If Ealstan had been conjured up, he didn't realize it. "Vanai!" he exclaimed, a grin stretching itself across his face. Instead of using Forthwegian, he went on in his slow, careful Kaunian: "I had hoped I would see you here. I am very glad to see you here. And look – I remembered your basket." He held it up.

Vanai laughed. She did that so seldom these days, each time stood out as an occasion. "I remembered yours, too," she said, and showed it to him.

"Now my family can wonder at me if I bring back my own basket, as they did when I brought back yours last year," Ealstan said with a chuckle. But the good humor quickly slipped from his face. "I am *very* glad to see you here again," he repeated. "The Algarvians took many Kaunians out of Gromheort and sent them west. I was afraid they had done the same in Oyngestun."

"They did," Vanai answered, "but my grandfather and I were not among them." She remembered how close they'd come to being chosen. "For his sake, I'm glad; he couldn't have done the work." She'd seen he couldn't do it. That made her think of Spinello again, and then wish she hadn't.

"In Gromheort, they did not seem to care," Ealstan said. "They scooped up young and old, men and women, till they had enough to satisfy them. Then they herded them into caravan cars and sent them west with only the clothes on their backs. How can they hope to get any proper work from anyone like that?"

"I don't know," Vanai answered in a small voice. "I've asked myself the same question, but I just don't know."

"I think they are lying about what they want. I think they are doing something . . ." Ealstan shook his head. "I do not know what. Something they do not want to talk about. Something that cannot be good."

He kept on using Kaunian. Because it was not his birthspeech, he paused every now and then to search for a word or an ending. To Vanai, that deliberation made him sound more impressive, not less. And he sounded more impressive still because he obviously did not care about what happened to the Kaunians in Gromheort and Oyngestun.

Vanai wasn't used to sympathy from Forthwegians. Vanai, lately, wasn't used to sympathy from anybody, though her own people were less harsh to her now than when Spinello had been visiting Brivibas rather than her. Tears stung her eyes. She looked away so Ealstan wouldn't see. "Thank you," she whispered.

"For what?" he said – she'd startled him into Forthwegian.

How was she supposed to answer that? "For worrying about my folk when you don't have to," she said at last. "Most people these days have all they can do to worry about themselves."

"If I do not worry about anyone else, who will worry about me?" Ealstan said, returning to Kaunian.

"When you speak my language, you sound like a philosopher," Vanai said; she meant his delivery as much as what he said. Whatever she meant, she made him laugh. She laughed, too, but persisted: "No, you truly do." To emphasize the point, she reached out with her free hand and took his.

Only after she'd done it did she realize she'd astonished herself. Since Spinello began taking advantage of her, she hadn't wanted anyone male, even her grandfather, to touch her. And now she'd touched Ealstan of her own accord.

His hand closed on hers. That was almost enough to make her pull away – almost, but not quite. Even if she didn't finish the motion, though she must have begun it, for he let go at once, saying, "You must have enough things to worry about without putting a Forthwegian you scarcely know on the list."

Vanai stared at him. They were much of a height, as was often true of Kaunian women and Forthwegian men. Slowly, she said, "You care what I think." By the way she said it, she might have been announcing some astonishing discovery in magecraft.

He heard her surprise. "Well, of course I do," he said, surprised in turn.

Plainly, he meant it. Having been used and scorned and condescended to so much, Vanai hardly knew what to make of caring. She astonished herself again, this time by leaning forward and brushing her lips across Ealstan's.

He wasn't too swarthy to keep her from watching him flush. Something sparked in his eyes. *He wants me*, she thought. Seeing that should have disgusted her. It always had with Spinello. Somehow, it didn't. At first, she thought that was because Ealstan didn't forthwith try to grope her, as Spinello would have. Then, belatedly, she realized the warmth inside her had nothing to do with the weather, which was on the chilly side. *I want him*, she thought, and that was most astonishing of all: she'd been sure Spinello had curdled desire within her forever.

"Vanai . . ." Ealstan said in a hoarse voice.

She nodded and, much later than she should have, set down her basket of mushrooms. "It will be all right," she said, not pretending she didn't know what he had in mind. Then she found something better to add: "We'll make it come out all right."

And, in spite of everything, they did. It was, clearly, Ealstan's first time. Had it been Vanai's, too, it probably would have ended up a clumsy botch. As things were, what Spinello had made her learn came in handy in ways she hoped the redhead would not have appreciated. She guided Ealstan without being too obvious about it.

But, after a while, she began to enjoy what they were doing for its own sake. Ealstan didn't come close to Spinello as far as technique went; maybe he never would. It turned out not to matter too much. The Algarvian's touch, no matter how knowing – perhaps because it was so knowing – had always made her want to cringe. Ealstan cared for her as Vanai, not as a nicely shaped piece of meat. That made all the difference. How much difference it made she discovered when she gasped and arched her back and squeezed Ealstan tight with arms and legs, Major Spinello utterly forgotten.

Ealstan stared down into Vanai's face, only a hand's breadth below his own. His heart thudded, as if he'd just run a long way. Next to the delight that filled him, the pleasure he'd got from touching himself hardly seemed worth remembering.

He started to lean down to taste the sweetness of her lips again, but she said, "You're not as light as you think you are. And we'd better get dressed before somebody who's looking for mushrooms comes along and finds us instead."

"Oh!" Ealstan exclaimed. He'd forgotten about that, and was glad Vanai hadn't. He scrambled to his feet, yanked up his drawers, and threw on his tunic. Vanai's clothes were more complicated, but she got into them about as fast as he did.

"Turn around," she told him, and brushed leaves off him. Then she nodded. "No stains on your tunic. That's good. Now you take care of me."

"Aye," Ealstan said. Despite what they'd just finished doing, he hardly dared touch her. Warily, he picked bits of dry leaf from her hair. Even more warily, he brushed some from her backside. Instead of slapping him, she smiled thanks over her shoulder. "Your clothes are all right," he told her.

"That's good," she said again. Slowly, her smile faded. "I didn't come here . . . expecting to do this." The expression her face took on alarmed Ealstan. It would have alarmed him more had he thought it aimed at him.

"I did not, either," he said, which was nothing but the truth. He might have imagined it once or twice, but he'd told himself he was being foolish. He felt foolish now, delightfully foolish, as if he'd had too much wine. Trying not to wear an idiotic grin, he went on, "I did hope I would see you, though." Speaking Kaunian helped. It made him sound serious, even if he wasn't.

Vanai's face softened. "I know. You brought my basket." She looked down at the dead leaves on the ground. "And I brought yours."

Ealstan felt like cutting capers. Instead, very much his practical father's son, he said, "Shall we trade some of what we have found?" As long as they were doing that, she wouldn't go away. He didn't want her to go away.

They sat down where they'd lain together, sat down and swapped mushrooms. They sat very close together. Their hands clung as they passed the mushrooms back and forth. Every so often, they paused to kiss. Ealstan discovered how quickly desire revived at his age. But when he reached for one of the toggles on her tunic, she set her hand on his and kept him from undoing it. "We were lucky once," she said. "I don't know if we would be again."

"All right," he said. It wasn't quite, but he would make the best of it. He took his hand away. Vanai's face showed he'd passed a test. "Shall we take back our old baskets?" he asked, and then answered his own question before Vanai could: "No, we had better not. That would tell people we had met. This way, no one has to know anything – no one except us."

"Aye, you're right: better if we don't," Vanai agreed. She studied him. "It's good you think of things like that."

He shrugged, pleased and embarrassed at the same time. "I do my best," he said, and again had no idea how much he sounded like Hestan. He looked at Vanai. Regardless of what they'd just done, they hardly knew each other. He coughed. "I do want to see you again, though, before next mushroom season." He hoped that didn't sound too much like, *I want to lie with you again, as soon as I can.* He did, but that wasn't what he meant, or wasn't all of what he meant, anyhow.

"I want to see you again, too," Vanai said, and once more Ealstan had all he could do to keep from jumping up and turning handsprings. She went on, "Tomorrow is market day, so I don't think I can get away, but I can come here the day after."

His heart leaped – and then fell. "My schoolmasters will beat me," he said glumly, "the ones not out gathering mushrooms themselves, at any rate." He could think the switchings he got worthwhile as long as he lay in Vanai's arms – but not, he feared, very long afterwards.

To his relief, he saw his unwillingness to drop everything for her sake hadn't offended her. Instead, she was nodding. "You have a head on your shoulders," she remarked. Anyone who knew him would have said the same. But she didn't, not yet, not with the mind as well as the body.

Out beyond the oak grove, someone called to someone else. It wasn't aimed at either Ealstan or Vanai, but both their heads came up in alarm. Nervously, Ealstan asked, "Did your grandfather come hunting mushrooms with you?" Brivibas, that was the old man's name. If Ealstan had to be polite in a hurry, he could.

But Vanai shook her head. "No. He's searching by himself." Her voice went cold and distant. She hadn't talked about her grandfather like that before. Something must have happened between them. Ealstan wondered what. He saw no way to ask. Vanai found a question of her own. "What about your cousin – Sidroc?" She'd remembered things about Ealstan, too. He felt outrageously flattered.

"He went off to the north a while ago. We are supposed to meet back at the city gate at sunset." Ealstan leaned over and kissed Vanai. She clung to him. The kiss went on and on. They started to lie back on the leaves again, but whoever was outside the little wood called out again, louder and closer this time. "We had better not take the chance," Ealstan said, and heard the regret in his own voice.

"You're right." Vanai slipped out of his embrace and got to her feet.

"You can send me letters, if you like. I live on the Street of Tinkers in Oyngestun."

Ealstan nodded eagerly. "And I live on the Avenue of Countess Hereswith, back in Gromheort. I *will* write to you."

"Good." Vanai nodded, too. "My grandfather will wonder when I start getting letters from Gromheort, but I don't much care what my grandfather wonders, not any more." Something had indeed happened between her and Brivibas. Maybe she would tell him what in a letter.

"I had better go," he said, though he didn't want to leave her.

But she nodded once more. "And I," she said, and then, as an afterthought, "I will address my letters to you in Forthwegian. I wouldn't want to put you in danger by letting anyone know you're friendly to Kaunians."

He was grateful, and ashamed of himself for being grateful. "If I can do anything for you – or for your grandfather," he remembered to add, "let me know. My father is not a man without influence."

"I thank you," Vanai said, "but would he use that influence for the cursed blonds?" She didn't try to hide her bitterness.

"Aye," Ealstan said, and nothing more.

He saw he'd startled her. "Well," she said, "if he's your father, perhaps he would."

"He will," Ealstan said, though he didn't know if Hestan's influence reached to Oyngestun. "And so will I." He had no influence at all, and did know that. But he would have promised Vanai anything just then. By the way her eyes shone, she believed him, too, or at least was glad he'd said what he had.

Ealstan kissed her one last time, then started back to Gromheort. He kept looking over his shoulder at Vanai, and almost walked into a goodsized oak. Feeling silly, he waved to her. She was looking over her shoulder, too, and waved to him. Only when they couldn't see each other anymore did Ealstan turn forward and walk straight.

As he walked, he wondered what to say to Sidroc. He laughed. The easiest thing might be to tell his cousin the truth; Sidroc would surely call him a liar. But what Sidroc would call Vanai didn't bear thinking of. He'd been making lewd jokes about her since the day Ealstan met her. Now . . .

She'd given herself to Ealstan without hesitation. By everything people in Forthweg – Forthwegians and Kaunians alike – said, that made her a slut, almost as much a slut as the Kaunian girl who'd tried to get Leofsig to go to bed with her for money.

"But it wasn't *like* that," Ealstan said, as if someone had declared it was. Whatever had brought Vanai into his arms, he got the idea that raw lust was only a small part of it. Loneliness and a desire to escape, if only for a little while, had probably played bigger parts. That didn't flatter him, but flattery wasn't so important to him. Seeing clearly counted for more.

And calling Daukantis' daughter a slut wasn't easy, either, not when the Algarvians had left her with the choice between whoring and starving. From the height of his seventeen years, Ealstan saw that the older he got, the less the world looked like the things everybody said.

He hoped the redheads hadn't swept up the oil merchant's daughter (he couldn't remember her name, though Leofsig had mentioned it) when they gathered laborers in Gromheort. Something was strange there, though he couldn't see what. But had the Algarvians only been after laborers, they would have chosen differently and let the Kaunians they did choose bring along more than they had.

He shrugged. He couldn't do anything about that. His features softened as his thoughts returned to what he and Vanai had done. He spent most of the walk back to Gromheort trying to fix in his memory every kiss, every murmured endearment, every caress, every incredible sensation. Remembering wasn't as good as lying down with her again, but it was all he could do now.

Gromheort's gray stone wall loomed higher and higher as he neared the city. Behind the wall, the sky was gray, too, gray as lead. It looked as if it would rain again soon. Autumn was shaping up as wet and nasty, which meant winter probably would be, too. He wondered if it would snow. That didn't happen every year, not this far north.

Someone standing by the wall waved. Ealstan squinted. Aye, that was Sidroc. Ealstan waved, too, and tried to bring his mind back from Vanai to mushrooms. Sidroc came toward him. He pointed to the basket Ealstan was carrying. "Ha!" he said. "That's the one you brought home last year, not yours. Didn't run into the little Kaunian bitch this time, eh? Too bad for you. You might have had a good time."

The only thing that let Ealstan get through was having been sure Sidroc would make some such crack. "No, I didn't see her," he answered, hoping he sounded casual. "Even if I had, we'd have just traded some mushrooms." That would have been true the year before. It wasn't any more.

Sidroc gestured derisively. "She's got to be sweet for you, Ealstan," he said. "Powers above, if I'd found her out there in the woods, I'd have got her trousers down faster than you could say King Offa."

"In your dreams," Ealstan said.

"Aye." Sidroc grabbed his own crotch. "In my wet dreams." Ealstan managed to laugh at that, which seemed to convince Sidroc nothing unusual had happened out in the oak grove. Sidroc chaffed him as they went into Gromheort, but not too hard. They both chaffed the Algarvian constable at the gate when the fellow looked disgusted at the baskets of mushrooms they showed him.

"More for us," Ealstan said to Sidroc. The constable must have spoken some Forthwegian, for he made as if to retch. Ealstan and his cousin both laughed. Ealstan kept laughing all the way through the city, all the way back to his house. If Sidroc wanted to think he was laughing at the Algarvian, he didn't mind a bit.

Rain beat into Colonel Sabrino's face as he led his wing east from the front toward the miserable excuse for a dragon farm at which they were based. His dragon didn't like the rain, not even a little. It flew heavily, laboring much more than it would have had the weather been good.

Sabrino didn't like the rain, either. He had a demon of a time keeping track of the dragonfliers under his command, and had to rely on his squadron leaders more than he wanted. He couldn't see far enough to do anything else. Nor could he see far enough to spy Unkerlanter dragons, and thanked the powers above the enemy couldn't see very far, either.

He had a demon of a time finding the dragon farm, too. Flying low to glimpse the ground through the curtain of rain, he almost flew his dragon into the side of a hill. The beast screeched protests when he made it pull up. It would have liked hitting the hillside even less, but was too stupid to know that.

He might not have found the dragon farm at all had he not flown over the victory camp that had gone up just north of it. Seeing the Kaunians huddled in dripping misery behind their palisade made him wonder what they thought of the name some clever clerk had come up with. He doubted the Algarvian guards on the palisade were any too happy, either. In this weather, their sticks wouldn't carry very far before raindrops attenuated their beams.

But that was their worry, not his. His worries shrank, because spotting the victory camp told him where he was. He swung his dragon into a sharp turn. The beast screamed at him, not wanting to obey. He whacked it with his goad, and shouted into the crystal he carried as he did so. The dragons he could see through the rain were conforming to his movements, but he wanted to make sure the rest of the wing didn't keep on flying back toward Forthweg and Algarve.

And there was the farm, too, with the dragon handlers waving and shouting to keep him from missing them. He brought his dragon down to a landing that splashed muck over the keepers who came running up to chain the beast to a stake. How they made stakes hold in this muddy morass was beyond him, but they did.

"What's it like at the front?" one of the keepers asked as Sabrino slid down from the base of the dragon's neck and into the mud.

"By everything I saw, we're stuck," Sabrino answered. "Hard for us to go forward – and harder than it might be, because the Unkerlanters are still wrecking bridges and ley lines and everything else they can. That gives them an edge of sorts, because they're bringing up their reinforcements on ground that's not quite so badly chewed up."

"Aye." The keeper wiped his eyes with a sleeve, an utterly useless gesture. "Cursed Unkerlanters are tougher than we figured they would be, too."

"So they are." Sabrino remembered General Chlodvald, then wished he hadn't. The retired soldier had been right when he said his countrymen would fight as hard as they could and would keep on fighting.

More dragons splashed down into the muck. Seeing to his fliers and their beasts gave Sabrino an excuse not to think about General Chlodvald. After a while, he splashed past the keeper with whom he'd been talking. The fellow jerked a thumb toward the north. "If all else fails, those Kaunian whoresons in there'll make sure we give King Swemmel what he deserves."

Sabrino's stomach lurched, as if his dragon had sideslipped and dove without warning. "I hope it doesn't come to that," he said. "If it does, though . . ." He shrugged uneasily.

At least with the whole wing down and safe – a minor miracle, in that ghastly weather – he could get under canvas. The ground was no drier inside his tent than outside, but the oiled canvas did keep water from pouring down on to his head. After he'd changed into a fresh tunic and kilt, he invited his squadron commanders to sup with him.

He had no idea what they'd get. It turned out to be fried trout, boiled beets, and a jar of clear spirits that kicked like a mule – more nearly Unkerlanter fare than Algarvian. "Phew!" Captain Orosio said after a pull at the spirits. "If Swemmel's boys drink this stuff all the time, no wonder they're mean."

After a swig of his own, Sabrino wheezed, "Aye. I think I'll send my gullet out for copper plating." But that didn't stop him from taking another swig a little later.

He'd never been fond of beets, especially plain boiled ones. He was still picking at them when a commotion outside penetrated the noise of the rain drumming on his tent. "Have the Unkerlanters managed to sneak raiders past our lines?" Captain Domiziano said, half rising from his seat.

But then one of the shouts out there in the night came clear: "Your Majesty!" A moment later, a dragon handler burst into Sabrino's tent. "Sir, the king honors us with his presence!" he exclaimed.

"Powers above," Sabrino said softly. "I wish I were better placed to honor him in turn than in this miserable bog. Well, it can't be helped. See if you can delay him long enough for the cooks to bring in another serving of supper, anyhow."

As things worked out, King Mezentio and the servitor bringing more fish and beets arrived at the same time. "Go on," Mezentio told the cook. "I can't very well eat that till you set it down, now can I?"

The wind had blown his umbrella inside out. He was almost as wet as the dragonfliers had been. Sabrino and his squadron commanders sprang to their feet and bowed. "Your Majesty!" they said in unison.

"Save the ceremony for later, can't you?" Mezentio said. "Let me eat, and if you'll pour me some of that, whatever it is, I'll thank you for it, too." He knocked back a slug of the spirits as if his gullet were already lined with metal.

After the king had demolished his supper – beets fazed him no more than the spirits had – Sabrino presumed to ask, "What brings you to the front, your Majesty? And why this particular part of the front?"

"Not just the pleasure of your company, my lord Count," Mezentio answered. He poured from the jar again, then drank. "Ah, that warms me, curse me if it doesn't. No, not the pleasure of your company. I probably wouldn't have come if the Unkerlanters hadn't stalled us." His lips pulled back from his teeth in what was more nearly snarl than smile. "But they have, and so I'm going to watch what we do with a victory camp."

"Ah." Orosio beamed. "That's fine, your Majesty. That's very fine."

Sabrino's stomach lurched again. "Has it truly come to that?"

"It has." King Mezentio's voice brooked no argument. "If we delay, we risk not taking Cottbus. And if we fail to take Cottbus, the war grows longer and harder than we ever thought it would be when we embarked on it. Is that true, or is it not?"

"Aye, your Majesty, it is," Sabrino answered, grimacing, "but—"

Mezentio made a sharp chopping gesture with his right hand. "But me no buts, my lord Count. I did not come to this miserable, cursed place to argue with you, and nothing you can say will change my mind. The mages are here, the soldiers are here, the stinking Kaunians are here, and I am here. I came here to see it done. We shall go forward, and we shall go forward to victory. Is that plain, sirrah?"

Sabrino's squadron commanders were staring with wide eyes, as if wondering how he presumed to argue with his sovereign. With King Mezentio glaring at him, he also wondered how he presumed. "Aye, your Majesty," he said. But then, being the descendant of a long line of freeborn Algarvian warriors, he added, "It had better do all we – you – hope it will, or we'd be better off never having tried it."

"You leave such worries to the mages and me," Mezentio growled. "Your duty to the kingdom is to fly your dragons, and I know you do it well. My duty to the kingdom is to win the war, and I aim to do exactly that. Need I make myself any plainer?"

"No, your Majesty," Sabrino said. He took another swig from his glass of spirits – he needed fortifying. As the spirits mounted to his head, he reflected that he'd done everything he could; more, probably, than he should have. King Mezentio had overruled him. He inclined his head. "I shall obey."

"Of course you shall." For a moment, Mezentio sounded very much the way King Swemmel was supposed to sound. But then he softened his words: "After we parade through Cottbus in triumph, I am going to say, 'I told you so.'" He grinned engagingly at Sabrino.

"I'll be glad to hear it then," Sabrino said, and grinned back.

Mezentio did his best to set his battered umbrella to rights. "And now I have to go find the tent they've got waiting for me – somewhere. Always a pleasure to see you, my lord Count, even if not always to argue with you." He nodded to Sabrino's squadron commanders. "Gentlemen." Without waiting for a reply, he went out into the wet, wet night.

"You don't live dangerously, sir," Captain Domiziano said to Sabrino. "Not half you don't."

"It's war, sir," Orosio added. "Anything we can do to kick the lousy Unkerlanters' teeth down their throats, we'd better do it."

"I suppose you're right," Sabrino said. "I have no choice but to suppose you're right. His Majesty made that clear enough, didn't he?" Discovering he could still laugh at himself came as something of a relief. All the same, he drank himself to sleep.

King Mezentio did not visit the dragon farm again. Sabrino told himself that was because his sovereign had come to Unkerlant for other reasons, which was no doubt true. But he knew he hadn't endeared himself to Mezentio. Men seldom found favor by questioning kings.

Whether or not Mezentio was there to watch it, Sabrino's wing kept on fighting the Unkerlanters. In that miserable weather, they did less than they might have earlier in the year, but the Unkerlanter dragons were similarly hampered. Sabrino began using the victory camp full of Kaunians as a landmark. It was far larger and easier to spy from the air than his own dragon farm.

And then, about the time he began wondering if decent weather were gone for good, the sun returned to the sky. Days remained chilly, but the ground began to dry. Behemoths were once more able to move at something more than a squashy, heavy-footed walk. The Algarvians wasted no time in going over to the attack.

But the Unkerlanters wasted no time counterattacking. They had been gathering men and beasts and dragons against the day of need, and threw them into the fight without seeming to worry about how many came out again, if only they stopped their foes. They didn't quite stop the Algarvians, but slowed their advance from gallop to crawl.

Sabrino and his wing spent as much time over the front as their dragons could stand to stay in the air. They attacked Unkerlanter soldiers and behemoths on the ground and fought hard to keep the Unkerlanter dragons from savaging their own countrymen.

One fine, bright, almost springlike morning, the dragonfliers were over the Unkerlanter lines when the world changed below them. The earth shook, a roar Sabrino could hear even high in the air. Trenches and holes closed on the Unkerlanter soldiers in them. Flames burst from the ground, consuming men and behemoths, unicorns and horses. Not all perished, but the greater part did, up and down the front as far as Sabrino could see. He shouted into his crystal: "Now we slaughter the ones who are left!"

As the dragons stooped on their horrified, bewildered foes, Algarvian footsoldiers and behemoths and cavalry erupted from their lines and joined in the assault. Their exultant shouts reached high into the sky; the disaster that smote the Unkerlanters had not hurt them in the least. They tore through the gutted enemy positions and swarmed westward.

When Sabrino flew over the victory camp, bringing the dragons back to their farm in triumph at the end of the day, he saw what he knew he would see: a camp full of corpses.

Seven

Cornelu pulled his socks up above his knees. He wished they were thicker wool, so they might keep his legs warmer. The wind that blew into the hills above Tirgoviste came from the southwest, off the Narrow Sea and the land of the Ice People, and carried the chill of the austral continent with it. Snow wouldn't have surprised him.

He stared down from the hills toward the harbor town. With three Algarvian officers quartered in her house – *my house, too, curse them*, Cornelu thought – Costache would assuredly be snug and warm, and so would Brindza. The Sibian naval officer consigned the Algarvians to the powers below all the same.

"Come on, you lazy bugger," shouted the boss of the woodcutting gang for which he'd been working the past few weeks. "Swing your axe or I'll throw you out on your cursed arse."

"Aye," Cornelu said, and then again, wearily, "Aye." The weariness was more of the spirit than of the body, though the work made a man sleep every night like one of the logs made from trees he cut down. But Cornelu had lived his whole life in polite company, and was used to politely phrased orders. He found few of those here.

He returned his attention to the pine he'd been attacking. When he swung the axe, he imagined it bit into the Algarvian's neck rather than the dark, scaly bark of the tree, and that blood spurted in place of dribbles of fragrant, resinous sap. The gang boss, a wide-shouldered bruiser named Giurgiu, grunted in something approaching satisfaction and went off to shout at another woodsman who wasn't working so hard as he might have.

To give Giurgiu his due, he did almost as much work as any two of the men in the gang. He handled the axe as if it were light as a schoolmaster's switch, and did far more than his share on a two-man saw.

His hands bore calluses half an inch thick, and looked and felt hard as rocks.

Cornelu's hands had bled the first several days after he'd joined the woodcutters. He'd never used them so roughly before. Rubbing them with turpentine made him want to shriek, but it had also helped him gain calluses that gave him some protection. By now, swinging the axe was just work, not torment.

Chips flew as he struck the tree again and again. "Come on, you whore!" he panted. Having been reviled, he in turn reviled something that could not argue back. He let out a snort. Maybe this work wasn't so much different from the Sibian Navy after all.

He heard a crackling deep inside the tree, a crackling and a groan. He struck harder than ever, looking up toward the crown of the pine as he did so. The tree stood straight for another couple of strokes. Then it began to lean.

"She falls!" he shouted. Woodcutters near him scattered. He hadn't known to let out a warning cry when he first joined the gang. The second tree he felled had almost driven Giurgiu into the ground like a sledge hitting a spike. He'd had trouble blaming the boss for cursing him then.

With a loud crackling, the pine went over. Cornelu stood on the balls of his feet, ready to leap out of the way if it looked like falling on him. He'd almost driven himself into the ground two or three times. Here, though, he put the trunk right where he wanted, a skill he'd acquired without quite knowing how. The pine thudded down into yellowing grass near the edge of the wood.

Giurgiu came over and examined it. He nodded. "I've seen worse jobs," he rumbled at last – from him, high praise. "Now we turn it into stovewood. They're going to get chilly down in the city before too long, and they have to cook even when they aren't chilly. As long as the hills still have woods on them, the likes of us won't go hungry."

"Aye," Cornelu said. He wondered how much longer the hills *would* have woods on them. In earlier times, forests had covered far more land than they did now. Before the days of iron ships that coursed the ley lines, great trees were essential for the timbers and masts of the merchantmen that had made Sibiu rich and the galleons that had made her strong. Great stretches of forest had been royal preserves then. Things were different nowadays. Cornelu doubted they were better – with the Algarvians occupying the kingdom, they couldn't very well be.

Giurgiu brought over a big two-man saw. "Come on," he said. "Act lively. We'll cut the trunk into wheels, and then you can split the wheels into wedges. Don't stand there gawping, curse it – it's not like you've got a lot of time to waste."

"Aye," Cornelu repeated. But for his foul mouth, Giurgiu did think like a naval officer. Cornelu grasped the handle of the saw and lowered it to the tree trunk.

Round after round of wood leaped off the trunk. Manning a saw with Giurgiu was like manning it with a demon – he never seemed to tire. Cornelu tried his best to keep the boss woodcutter from doing too much more than his share of the work. Giurgiu noticed, too. "You're not the handiest fellow I've ever seen," he remarked when even he had to pause for a blow, "but you can pull your weight when you set your mind to it." That left Cornelu absurdly pleased.

A boy of about fourteen scooped up sawdust – and a little dry grass and dirt with it – and stuffed it into a leather sack. It got sold for kindling. So did pine needles, after they were dry.

"There!" Giurgiu said after a surprisingly short time. "You can deal with the wheels yourself, like I said before. And lop the branches into short lengths, mind. Don't leave 'em as long as you did that one time." He didn't wait for Cornelu's agreement, but strode off to see how some of the other woodcutters were doing.

That one time had been weeks before. Giurgiu hadn't forgotten, and made sure Cornelu didn't forget, either. He was indeed very much like an officer in some ways.

By the time Cornelu finished turning the tree into wood, darkness was falling. This far south, days quickly got short as autumn wore on. Here in the woods, that made itself more obvious to Cornelu than it had back in Tirgoviste. There, light to hold night at bay had been easy to come by; Tirgoviste sat on a power point. Simple firelight couldn't come close to matching it.

Cooking over a simple fire didn't measure up, either, not to Cornelu. Meat came out burnt on the outside and raw in the middle when held over the flames on a stick. The porridge of beans and barley and peas would have been boring no matter how it was cooked. But appetite made a wonderful sauce.

And exhaustion made a wonderful sleeping draught. Cornelu had discovered that in the navy, and now was reminded of it again. Though the night was long, Giurgiu had to shake him awake at dawn. He was not the only one to be treated so, which spared him embarrassment. He gulped down more of the bland porridge.

Giurgiu said, "I'm going to send Barbu and Levaditi into town with the wagons today." He eyed Cornelu as he spoke.

Sure enough, Cornelu jerked as if stung by a wasp. "What?" he yelped. "You told me I'd get to drive one of those wagons."

"And now I'm telling you something different," the boss woodcutter answered. "Barbu's got a sister who's sick down in Tirgoviste town, and Levaditi's our best haggler unless I go myself. I didn't much care for the price you brought back on that last load you took in."

"But . . ." Cornelu said helplessly. He ached to see his wife. More than that, he ached to touch her. He didn't know whether he could have managed either of those things, especially the latter, but he wanted the chance to try. Thinking of Costache under siege from three lecherous Algarvian officers – and what other sort was there? – ate at him. Next to that, haggling seemed of small import. So did anyone else's troubles.

Giurgiu folded massive arms across his massive chest. "That's what I'm telling you now, and that's how it's going to be." He looked Cornelu up and down. "If you don't like it, you can leave, or else you can make me change my mind."

The rest of the woodcutters chuckled. Giurgiu wasn't the gang boss only because he knew the business inside and out. He was also stronger and tougher than any of the men he led. From what Cornelu heard, no one had challenged him for a long time. But Cornelu knew skill counted for as much as strength. He set down the bowl from which he'd been eating and got to his feet. "All right, I'll have a go at that," he said.

Giurgiu stared. So did the other woodsmen. Giurgiu walked out on to the meadow. "Come on, then," he said over his shoulder. "You've got stones in your bag, anyhow, but I don't think it'll do you much good. And you'll go out and work after they throw water in your face, too."

"No, I won't," Cornelu said. "I'll drive the wagon instead of Levaditi." He wondered how foolish he'd just been. Giurgiu moved more like a cat than a bear, and he was a lot bigger than Cornelu. The woodcutters gathered in a circle around the two men.

"Come on," Giurgiu said. "You want me, come and get me. Either that or pick up your axe and get back to work."

With a silent sigh, Cornelu approached. No, it wouldn't be easy. But he couldn't back down now, not unless he wanted to lose all his pride. He rushed at the boss woodcutter, deliberately making his attack look clumsy. Fooling Giurgiu into overconfidence seemed his best hope.

And it worked. Giurgiu let fly with a haymaker that would have knocked Cornelu through a boulder had it landed. But Cornelu seized the woodcutter's beefy arm, bent his own back, and threw Giurgiu over it and down to the dying grass. He started to leap on the bigger man. But Giurgiu didn't land like a falling tree, as he'd hoped. The boss woodcutter rolled away and bounced to his feet while the rest of the gang exclaimed in astonishment.

Giurgiu eyed Cornelu. "So you know what you're doing, eh? All right. We'll see who's left standing at the end." Now he advanced with grim concentration.

In the unpleasant minutes that followed, Cornelu hurt his opponent several times. He blacked one of Giurgiu's eyes and landed a couple of solid kicks in the ribs. But the head woodsman gave more than he got. Blood poured from Cornelu's nose, though he didn't think it was broken. His own ribs gave eloquent testimony of how Giurgiu's had to feel. Somewhere in the middle of the brawl, he spat out a small chunk of tooth, and counted himself lucky not to lose most of a mouthful.

At the last, Giurgiu got round behind him, seized his arm, and bent it back. "You won't be able to work if I break something in there," he remarked. "Had enough, or shall I go ahead and do it?" He bent the arm a little farther. Cornelu's shoulder screamed.

"Enough," Cornelu mumbled through swollen lips and even more swollen self-disgust.

Giurgiu let go of him, got up, and hauled him to the feet. Then he slapped him on the back and almost knocked him down. "Well, you do have stones," he said, and the other woodcutters nodded. "You made me sweat for it." The men nodded again. Giurgiu went on, "Now wash your face and get to it. You're not taking a wagon down to the city today, and that's flat."

"Aye," Cornelu said. Someone brought him a bucket. Before splashing away the blood, he looked at his reflection. He was not a pretty sight.

Maybe it was just as well Costache wouldn't get the chance to look at him.

"Your Majesty . . ." Marshal Rathar licked his lips, then said what he had to say: "They have broken through in the north. They have broken through in the south, too, though not so badly. The weather hampers them worse there."

King Swemmel's dark eyes burned in a face as pale as that of a Kaunian kept out of the sun his whole life long. "And how did this happen?" he asked in a deadly voice.

"It was magecraft, your Majesty," Rathar answered. "I am only a soldier; I can tell you no more than that. If you would have the details, you must have them from Archmage Addanz here."

Swemmel's burning gaze swung toward the chief sorcerer of Unkerlant. "Aye, we will have the details, Addanz," he said, even more harshly than he had spoken to Rathar. "Tell me how you and yours failed Unkerlant in her hour of need."

Addanz bowed his head. Like Rathar, he was in the flower of his middle years. Most of the old men who might have served Swemmel were dead. Some, the lucky ones, had died of natural causes. Others had chosen the wrong side in the Twinkings War or displeased Swemmel afterwards. Their ends, commonly, were harder.

"Your Majesty," Addanz said, still not looking up, "I did not expect the Algarvians to do as they did. None of us expected the cursed Algarvians to do as they did." He freighted the adjective with more than its usual mild weight of meaning. "When they did as they did, the world shuddered, for those with the wit and training to sense such things. By the powers above, your Majesty, the first time they did as they did, I almost fell over dead."

"Better if you had," Swemmel snarled. "Then we could appoint someone of some wit in your place." He turned back toward Rathar. "And yours."

"Mine?" Rathar said – yelped, rather. He'd hoped that, with the king's wrath turned on the archmage, he might escape unscathed. No such luck, he saw. He let out a muted protest, the only kind safe around King Swemmel: "What did I do?"

"Nothing – which is why you are in part to blame," the king answered. "You should have known the stinking redheads would try some such ploy when straightforward war began to fail 'em."

"Your Majesty, none of us dreamt they would do – this," Addanz said. Rathar nodded to him in grateful surprise. For the archmage to defend him took more courage than he'd known the other man to possess. Addanz went on, "You surely know, your Majesty, how life energy is a very potent source of power for magecraft – how soldiers whose sticks run low on blazes may recharge them with the death of a captive or of a brave comrade."

"Aye, we know this," Swemmel said. "How could we not know it? The soldiers in the far west, particularly, have used the life energy of some few of their number to help the rest hold back the louse-ridden, fuzzy-bearded Gongs."

Addanz nodded. "Even so. *Of some few of their number*, your Majesty, is the critical phrase. For life energy is the most potent, most concentrated form of sorcerous energy. And the Algarvians, you might say, went suddenly from the retail to the wholesale use of such energy. They gathered together a couple of thousand Kaunians in one place – in each of several places, actually – and slew them all together, all at once, and their mages turned the energy from those slaughters against our armies."

"That is the way of it," Rathar agreed. "The mages who aid our soldiers against the foe did everything they could to hold back the great storm of sorcery raised against 'em" – as Addanz had defended him, he returned the favor – "but they were overwhelmed."

"It is a great wickedness, the greatest of wickednesses," Addanz said in a voice filled with dread. "To take men and women who have done nothing, to use them so, to slay them so as to steal their life energy . . . I did not think even Algarvians could stoop to such a thing. They fought hard in the Six Years' War, but they used no more vileness than anyone else. Now . . ." He shook his head.

King Swemmel heard him out. Indeed, Swemmel listened intently. That relieved Rathar, who had feared the king would burst into one of his rages and start shouting for executioners. Then Swemmel's eyes swung back to him, and he wondered if relief had come too soon. "How do we stop 'em?" the king asked. Now his voice was calm, dangerously calm.

It was the right question. It was, at the moment, the only question. Still, Marshal Rathar wished his sovereign had not asked it. Though he knew it might cost him his head, he answered with the truth: "I do not know. If the Algarvians will massacre by the thousands those they've conquered, we facing them are like a man in a tunic with a knife facing another in chainmail with a broadsword."

"Why?" Swemmel asked in startled curiosity – so startled, it took Rathar by surprise.

"Because they have no scruples about doing what we will not," the marshal replied, setting forth what seemed obvious to him.

Swemmel threw back his head and laughed. No, more: he howled. A small drop of spittle flew across the table at which he and his subjects sat and struck Rathar in the cheek. Tears of mirth rolled down the king's face. "You fool!" he chortled when at last he could do anything but laugh. "Oh, you milk-fed fool! We never knew we had a virgin leading our armies."

"Your Majesty?" Rathar said stiffly. He hadn't the faintest notion what King Swemmel meant. He glanced over to Addanz. The archmage's face held horror of a different sort – to Rathar's amazement, horror of a worse sort – than it had while Addanz was explaining what the Algarvians had done. That deeper horror told Rathar everything he needed to know. He stared at Swemmel. "You would not—"

"Of course we would." Laughter dropped from the king like a discarded cloak. He leaned forward in his seat and brought the full weight of his presence to bear on Rathar. "Where else, how else, shall we get chainmail and a broadsword of our own?"

That was another question Rathar wished Swemmel had not asked. Having fallen into the abyss themselves, the Algarvians would now pull him in after them. He had never been a man to look away from trouble, but he looked away now, trying to distract King Swemmel from a large concern with small ones: "Where would we get the victims?" he asked. "We had but a handful of Kaunians on our soil, and even if you thought to use them for such purposes, they're in Algarvian hands now. And if we start slaying redheaded captives, they'll murder ours in place of the Kaunians."

Swemmel's shrug chilled the marshal with its indifference. "We have plenty of peasants. We care nothing – nothing at all – if only one of them is left alive when the fighting's over, so long as the very last Algarvian is dead."

"I don't know if we can quickly match them in their magecraft,"

Addanz said. "As with so much else, they have been readying themselves for long and long. Even if we are forced to this thing to survive" – he shuddered – "we have much learning to do."

"Why did you not begin learning before?" the king demanded.

His archmage looked back at him in harassed fury. "Because I never imagined – no one ever imagined – the Algarvians would be so vile. I never imagined anyone could be so vile. And I three times never imagined *I* could be forced to be so vile."

Rathar had seen that defiance sometimes got Swemmel's notice in a way nothing else could. Sometimes a defiant man found he didn't want Swemmel's notice once he had it, but that didn't happen here. In surprisingly mild tones, the king asked, "And would you rather go down to ruin because the redheads were vile and you couldn't stomach matching them?"

"No, your Majesty." Addanz had to know his head would answer for any other reply.

"Nor would we," King Swemmel said. "Go, then. You and your mages had better learn how to do as the Algarvians do, and you had better learn it soon. We promise you, Archmage: If we do fall before the redheads, you will not last long enough for Mezentio's men to finish off. We shall make certain of that. Do you understand us?"

"Aye, your Majesty," Addanz said. Swemmel made a peremptory gesture of dismissal. Addanz fled. Rathar did not blame him. The marshal would have liked to flee, too. But the king had not dismissed him.

Swemmel said, "Your task, Marshal, is to make sure the Algarvians cannot finish us before we find out how best to fight back. How do you aim to do that?"

Rathar had been thinking of little else since word of the disasters reached him. He began ticking points off on his fingers: "We are spreading our men thinner, so the Algarvians cannot catch so many of them with one sorcerous stroke. We are making our positions deeper, so we can attack the redheads even if they pierce our front."

"This will slow Mezentio's bandits. It will not stop them," Swemmel observed. He wasn't stupid. Often, he would have been easier to deal with had he been stupid. He was shrewd, just shrewd enough to think himself smarter than he really was.

Here, however, he was also right. Rathar said as much, and then continued, "The weather also works for us. Try as they will, the Algarvians cannot go forward as fast as they would like. We trade space for time."

"We have less space to trade than we did," the king growled.

And you were on fire for charging straight at King Mezentio, Rathar thought. He couldn't say that. He did say, "Winter is coming. Advancing will get no easier for them. And, your Majesty, we are also doing all we can to send parties behind the enemy's position to sabotage the ley lines coming out of Forthwegian. If the cursed redheads can't bring the Kaunians forward, they can't very well kill them."

Rathar seldom won out-and-out approval from Swemmel, but this was one of those times. "Now that is good," the king said. "That is quite good." He paused; his approval never lasted long. "Or is it? Can the redheads not slay them back in Forthweg and bring the power of the magic forward?"

"You would do better asking Addanz than me," Rathar said. "My answer is only a guess, but it would be no. If the Algarvians could do that, why would they put the Kaunians in camps near the front?"

Swemmel fingered his narrow chin. But for being dark of hair and eye, he *did* look like an Algarvian. He grunted. "It could be so. And if we overrun any of those camps, we can dispose of the Kaunians in them instead of using our own folk. That would be funny, having the redheads do our gathering work for us."

He had a rugged sense of humor. Rathar had seen as much over the course of many years. The marshal said, "We might do better to turn them loose and let them try to get back to Forthweg."

"Why would we want to do such a wasteful thing as that?" King Swemmel said.

"If any of them make it back to their own land and tell the truth about what the Algarvians are doing to them, don't you think Forthweg might rise against Mezentio?" Rathar asked.

"Maybe, but then again maybe not," the king replied. "Forthwegians love Kaunians hardly better than the redheads." Swemmel shrugged. "We suppose it might be worth a try. And it would embarrass Mezentio, which is all to the good. Aye, you have our leave to do it."

"Thank you, your Majesty." Something new occurred to Rathar. "If the Algarvians slaughter their thousands for the sake of sorcery and we slaughter as many to stop them, the war will come down to soldier against soldier once more. I wonder if Mezentio thought of that before he set this fire."

"We do not care," King Swemmel said. "Whatever fires he sets, we shall set bigger ones."

Try as she would, Pekka could not enjoy the Principality. She knew Master Siuntio had meant nothing but kindness when he booked her into Yliharma's finest hostel after calling her to the capital. But she would have come to the capital whether he'd summoned her or not. The cold fear and horror in her would have pushed her out of Kajaani.

She hadn't been the only mage riding the ley-line caravan north to Yliharma. She'd spotted three or four other women and men with set, worried faces. They'd nodded when they saw her and then gone back to their private woes, which were, no doubt, much like hers.

But Siuntio had arranged to have the Seven Princes of Kuusamo also gather in Yliharma. Pekka could not have done that on her own. She was glad the Seven Princes took the business as seriously as their mages did. She'd been far from sure they would.

A knock on the door sent her hurrying to open it. There in the hallway stood Siuntio. "A good day to you," he said, bowing. "I have a carriage waiting to take us to the princely palace. Ilmarinen will ride with us, too, unless he's gone off chasing a barmaid while I came up to get you."

"Master Siuntio, you didn't need to come here to bring me to the palace," Pekka said sternly. "I could have found my own way. I intended to find my own way."

"I wanted the three of us to come before the Seven Princes together," the elderly theoretical sorcerer answered. "Prince Joroinen, I know, has been keeping his colleagues apprised of our progress, when we have any. If we join together in a show of alarm, it will have weight for all of the Seven."

"You flatter me beyond my worth," Pekka said. His face as serious as she'd ever seen it, Siuntio shook his head. Flustered, she turned and took a thick wool cloak from the cabinet that stood in the little entry hall. As she settled it on her shoulders, she spoke in a rough voice to cover her own embarrassment: "Let's go, then."

When she got downstairs, she discovered Siuntio hadn't been joking. Ilmarinen was chatting up a pretty young woman whose slanted eyes, swarthy skin, and broad cheekbones were all Kuusaman, but who had auburn hair far more typical of a Lagoan. He blew her a kiss as he went off to join Siuntio and Pekka. "Just making certain she'd not a spy sent out from Setubal," he said airily.

"Of course you were," Siuntio answered. "I'm certain you intended to probe her very deeply."

Ilmarinen started to nod, but Pekka's giggle told him he'd missed something. After a heartbeat, he gave Siuntio a dirty look. "You think you're funny," he growled. "I think you're in your second childhood, is what I think."

"I almost wish I were," Siuntio said. "Then I could have gone on living my life instead of screaming like a man on the rack at the supper table a few days ago. I alarmed the whole eatery, but not so badly as I alarmed myself."

Ilmarinen grimaced. "Aye, it was bad," he said. Pekka nodded. The memory of that moment would stay with her all her days. Ilmarinen sighed and went on, "We'd best be at it. The wench will wait. This business won't."

Chill air smote Pekka as she and Siuntio and Ilmarinen left the warmth of the Principality. A little snow lay on the sidewalks and in the streets of Yliharma. It was half melted and gray with soot. Kajaani lay on the southern side of the Vaattojarvi Hills. It took the full brunt of the storms rolling up from the land of the Ice People. The snow there was unlikely to melt till spring.

Horses' hooves clopping, the carriage bore the three mages to the princely palace. It stood on the highest ground in Yliharma, having begun its history as a hill fort centuries before the Kaunians crossed the Strait of Valmiera farther west. Savants still dug below the far more splendid buildings gracing the hilltop these days, and sometimes came up with fascinating finds.

"What sort of man is Prince Rustolainen?" Pekka asked. "Living down in the south, I hear less of him than I'd like."

"He's not the sort to think the doings of the Prince of Yliharma belong in the news sheets, anyhow," Siuntio said, at which Ilmarinen nodded. Siuntio went on, "He's a solid sort, and far from a fool."

"Less forward-looking than Joroinen," Ilmarinen added. "He sees what is, not what he wants to be. But Siuntio's right – he's solid about what is."

The Seven Princes of Kuusamo went in for less in the way of gaudy ceremonial than did the kings on the mainland of Derlavai – or King Vitor of Lagoas, for that matter. The usher who brought the mages before the Seven announced them as matter-of-factly as if he were presenting them to seven prominent merchants. Pekka went to one knee for a moment; Siuntio and Ilmarinen bowed.

Prince Joroinen said, "We need stand on no special ceremony here this morning." He looked along the table behind which the Seven sat. No one contradicted him. The princes dressed more like prosperous merchants than rulers, too.

Prince Rustolainen sat in the center of the group, since they were gathered at his castle. Being the prince whose domain included Yliharma, he was the most powerful among the Seven no matter where he sat. He leaned forward, nodding to Siuntio. "Master mage, you have persuaded me to call my comrades together. I have explained the business as best I can, but I am no sorcerer. Tell it to them plain, as you told it to me."

"They will have also heard from mages in their own domains, I expect," Siuntio said, and some of the princes nodded. Siuntio went on, "In any case, it is less a matter of magecraft than of simple right and wrong. The Algarvians have turned to murder in their war against Unkerlant."

"War is about murder," Rustolainen said.

Siuntio shook his head. "So you said when I first brought this to your notice, your Highness. I told you then and I tell you now, war is about killing. A soldier's foe has a chance to slay him. The Algarvians took folk who could not possibly fight back and killed them for the sake of their life energy, which they then turned against King Swemmel's armies. They go forward once more because of it, where they had been stopped."

"How strong a magic can they make this way?" asked Prince Parainen, whose lands were in the far east, looking across the Bothnian Ocean toward Gyongyos.

"How many Kaunian captives do they care to kill?" Siuntio answered bluntly. "The greater the murder, the greater the magecraft."

"Killing is easier than it used to be in the old days, too," Ilmarinen added. "They don't have to go up to each captive and smite him with a sword or an axe. They can beam the victims down one after another with sticks. Ah, the modern age we live in!" His glee was savage and sardonic.

Prince Joroinen asked, "How does the power of this magic the Algarvians are using compare to the force of the new magecraft the three of you and your colleagues are investigating?"

To Pekka's surprise, both Siuntio and Ilmarinen looked toward her. She said, "Your Highness, no wood fire can burn hotter than a coal fire. We are looking at coal, or at something hotter than coal. But a large wood fire will do more harm than a small coal fire. The Algarvians have kindled the largest wood fire the world has ever seen, and the one with the foulest smoke."

"A good figure," Siuntio murmured. Pekka smiled her thanks.

"We summoned the Algarvian minister to Kuusamo before us yesterday," Rustolainen said, and the rest of the princes nodded. "He denied that his kingdom has done any such thing – says it's a lie put about by King Mezentio's enemies. How say you?"

"Your Highness, I say Algarve has a bad conscience," Siuntio replied. "The thing was done. They could not hide it, not from those with the senses and training to feel it. They can only pretend to innocence they no longer have."

"They say that, if anyone worked such a magic, it was the Unkerlanters, trying to hold them back," Rustolainen said.

Pekka, Ilmarinen, and Siuntio all laughed bitter laughs. "Oh, indeed," Ilmarinen said. "That's why Swemmel's troops go back in triumphant retreat, while the Algarvians advance in fear and chaos and disorder."

"Results speak louder – and truer – than words," Pekka agreed.

Joroinen asked, "How soon will you have your hotter fire ready to burn?"

That was more Pekka's to answer than either of her colleagues'. She said, "Your Highness, I was almost ready to make the experiment to see how the new fire would burn – or if it would burn at all – when the Algarvians . . . did what they did. We will know more after I finally do make it. How long we will need to control it, if there is anything to control, I can't say, not yet. I'm sorry." She looked down at the carpet. It was woven in a pattern of rushes, to imitate the rushes Kuusaman chieftains had strewn on their floors before they knew of carpets.

"The Algarvian minister may talk prettier than we do. He may talk fancier than we do," Ilmarinen said. "But there's one other difference you had better remember, you Seven of Kuusamo: we tell you the truth."

As usual, Prince Rustolainen spoke for the group: "And what would you have us do?"

Siuntio took a step forward. "It must be war, your Highness," he said. "If we let them do this without punishing them, the world will suffer because of it. Men must know they may not do such things. I say it sadly, but say it I must."

"What of our war with Gyongyos?" Prince Porainen exclaimed. That war concerned him more intimately than any of the other princes, for his ports looked out toward the islands on which it was fought.

"Your Highness, the war with Gyongyos is a war for Kuusamo's advantage," Siuntio said. "The war against Algarve will be a war for the world's advantage."

"With Unkerlant for our partner?" Parainen raised an eyebrow, for which Pekka had trouble blaming him. He put his objections into words: "King Swemmel, I think, would sooner wreck the world than save it."

"Doubtless he would," Ilmarinen agreed. "But what Swemmel would do, Mezentio is doing. What has the greater weight?"

Swemmel might have taken the mage's head for such lese majesty. Parainen bit his lips and, ever so reluctantly, nodded. Rustolainen said, "If we war against Algarve, we war without the new magic, is it not so?"

"It is so, your Highness, at least for now," Pekka said. "It may come. I don't know how soon it will, and I don't know how much good it will do when it does."

"A leap in the dark," Porainen muttered.

"No, your Highness – a leap into the light," Siuntio said.

"Is it?" Porainen remained unconvinced. "Swemmel will start slaughtering his own as soon as he thinks of it. Tell me I am wrong."

Pekka didn't think he was wrong. She feared he was right. But she said, "Two things, your Highness. What a man does to save himself is different from what he will do to hurt another. And Mezentio is leaving his own untouched. He has other victims, who can do nothing to make him stop."

The princes murmured to one another. Rustolainen said, "We thank you, Masters, Mistress. If we need to hear more of your views, we shall summon you." Pekka left the conference chamber downhearted. She had hoped for more – she had hoped for a promise. But the news of the Seven Princes' declaration of war on Algarve beat her carriage back to the Principality. She had never dreamt she could be so pleased about something that promised such sorrow.

Rumors swirled through Priekule. Some were frightened. Some were furious. Krasta had no idea which of them to believe, or whether to believe any. She wanted to ignore them, but could not do that, either.

If anyone would know the truth, Colonel Lurcanio would. He looked up from his paperwork when she pushed her way past Captain Mosco and stood in the doorway to the chamber he was using as his office – she didn't quite dare bursting in on him. "Come in, my dear," he said with his usual cruelly charming smile, setting down a steel pen. "What can I do for you?"

"Is it true?" Krasta demanded. "Tell me it is not true."

"Very well: it is not true," Lurcanio said agreeably. Krasta knew a moment's relief, a moment shattered when her Algarvian lover's smile grew broader and he inquired, "Now – what are we talking about?"

Krasta set her hands on her hips. Her temper flared, as it had a way of doing. "Why, what everyone says, of course."

"'Everyone says' all manner of things," Lurcanio replied with a shrug. "Most of them are stupid. Almost none are true. I think I stood on fairly safe ground when I denied yours, whatever it was." He made as if to go back to his papers.

Being brushed off, even by the formidable Lurcanio, was more than Krasta would tolerate. Voice whipcrack sharp, she said, "Then why did Kuusamo go to war against Algarve?"

She succeeded in getting her lover's attention. He set down the pen and looked her full in the face. His smile, now, was gone. The expression that replaced it made Krasta wish she hadn't sounded so prickly: she'd got more of Lurcanio's attention than she wanted. "You had better tell me just what you are saying, and where you heard it, and from whom," he said softly; unlike every other man she knew, the quieter he was, the more menacing he sounded.

"You know perfectly well, or you cursed well ought to." Krasta tried to hold on to her defiance. Against Lurcanio, that was next to impossible. He had the edge on her, just as Algarve's army had had the edge on Valmiera's a year and a half before.

And he knew it. "Suppose you tell me," he repeated. "Suppose you tell me in great detail. Come in and sit down; do make yourself comfortable. And close the door behind you."

Krasta obeyed. She was very conscious of obeying, of following his will rather than her own. It chafed at her, like trousers too tight in the crotch. Trying to get a little freedom, a little breathing space, she gave Lurcanio a saucy smile and said, "Your men will think I came here for another reason." She'd done that once, on a whim, and certainly had distracted Lurcanio from whatever he'd been working on.

She did not distract him today. "Let my men think whatever they please," he said. "You came down here to tell me you had heard . . . certain things. Now you do not seem to want to tell me what these things are. I need to know that." He waited, looking at her.

Again, Krasta felt herself obeying. Because she was obeying and not doing as she wanted – as she did whenever she was not around Colonel Lurcanio – she gave it to him full in the face: "Is it true that Algarve is taking Kaunians out of Valmiera or Jelgava or . . . or wherever" – she'd been shaky in geography, as she'd been shaky in a good many subjects at the academies she'd sometimes (often briefly) graced – "and doing horrible things to them off in barbarous Unkerlanter?"

"Oh. That." Lurcanio gestured dismissively, as if flicking a speck off his tunic. "I thought you were talking about something important, my sweet. No, it is not true that we are taking people out of Valmiera or Jelgava or doing anything to them anywhere. There. Is that plain enough?"

She didn't notice he hadn't answered quite all of her questions; had she paid closer attention at one of her academies or unfinished finishing schools, perhaps she might have. But his assertion didn't lay a fortnight's rumors to rest at a stroke, either. "Then why do people say you are?" she persisted.

"Why?" Lurcanio sighed. "Have you not seen for yourself that most people – especially most common people – are fools and will repeat anything they hear, as if they were so many trained jackdaws?"

That, aimed at Krasta, was a shrewder stroke. "I certainly have!" she exclaimed. "The commoners who aren't fools are commonly knaves. Commoners . . . commonly." She laughed. She made jokes mostly by accident, and didn't always recognize them even then. When she did, she felt uncommonly pleased with herself.

Lurcanio laughed, too, more than the feeble wordplay deserved. "There – you see? Out of your own mouth you convict these liars. Have any of your friends disappeared? Have any of your servants disappeared? Have any of *their* friends disappeared? Of course not. How could we hope to keep such a thing secret if it were so? It would be impossible."

"Aye, so it would," Krasta admitted. Had anything truly been going on in Valmiera, the rumors would have been juicier, full of more detail. Now that she thought about it, she saw that plain. Still . . . "Why does Kuusamo war on you, then?"

"Why?" Colonel Lurcanio raised an elegantly sardonic eyebrow. "I'll tell you why, my sweet: because the Seven Princes are jealous of our triumphs, and look for any excuse to tear us down."

"Ah." Again, that made sense to Krasta. She'd done the same thing to social rivals, and had it done to her. She nodded.

Now Lurcanio's smile was charming again. He pushed his chair back and away from his desk. The chair was Algarvian military issue; its brass wheels squeaked. "As long as you are here, do you care to give my men something to gossip about?"

This time, his voice held no command. He never tried to force Krasta in such matters: not overtly, anyhow. Had she chosen to walk out the door, he would never have said a word about it. Not least because she was free to refuse, she decided not to. Knowing the other Algarvian officers *would* be jealous of Lurcanio didn't hurt, either. She sank to her knees in front of him and flipped up his kilt.

Having eased her mind (and her body; Lurcanio was scrupulous about returning such favors), she went back to her bedchamber to choose a cloak for the day's journey through the shops of Priekule. Bauska was no help. With her, what people called morning sickness lasted all day long. She was liable to gulp and flee at any moment. If that was what carrying a child meant, Krasta wanted no part of it.

Her driver, also muffled against the chill of approaching winter, took the carriage to the Avenue of the Horsemen. As soon as he handed her down on to the street, he took a flask out of his pocket and swigged from it. That would help keep him warm, or at least make him stop caring he was cold.

Krasta was more intent on what she would do than on what her servitor was doing. The Avenue of Horsemen, which held Priekule's finest shops, was not what it had been before the Algarvians came. Far fewer people walked – paraded, really – along its splendid sidewalks. Many who did were redheaded soldiers in kilts. Shopkeepers did good business with them, at any rate; as often as not, packages filled their arms. Krasta's smile was nasty as she watched a couple of Algarvians emerge from a shop that sold lingerie. Would the silks and lace they'd bought adorn their Valmieran mistresses or go home to keep their wives happy and unsuspecting?

She wished Lurcanio would buy her presents there. If he didn't, though, the world wouldn't end. Several earlier lovers already had. The dainties rested in a drawer in her bedchamber, smelling of cedar to hold the moths at bay.

A few doors past the lingerie shop stood a clothier's Krasta enjoyed visiting. She peered past the peeling gold leaf in the window to see what new things he was displaying. If she didn't stay up with fashion, Lurcanio might decide to buy lingerie for someone else.

She stopped and stared. The nearly military cut of the new tunics and trousers on display wasn't what caught her eye. She had never imagined a Valmieran clothier would put kilts out for sale after Algarve beat her own kingdom in war. It struck her as indecent – no, worse, *un-Kaunian*.

But out of a dressing room stepped a young blond woman wearing a kilt that stopped a couple of inches above her knees and left the rest of her legs bare. "Indecent," Krasta muttered. She'd worn kilts before the war, but now? It seemed a far more public admission of defeat than taking an Algarvian lover. But the clothier's assistant clapped her hands in delight, while her customer reached into the pockets of the trousers she wasn't wearing any more and paid for the kilt.

I won't shop there again, Krasta thought, and walked on, discontented. She stepped into a jeweler's, looking for earrings, but he had nothing that suited her. She reduced the shop girl to tears before leaving. That restored most of the good humor she'd lost standing in front of the clothier's.

And then, walking up the street toward her, she saw Viscount Valnu. He waved gaily and went from a walk up to a trot. Krasta stiffened and turned away. Valnu was wearing a kilt.

"What's the trouble?" he asked, and leaned forward to kiss her on the cheek.

She turned away again, not playfully as she so often had but in grim earnest. "What's the trouble?" she echoed. "I'll tell you what's the trouble. *That's* the trouble." She pointed in the general direction of the kilt. On a man even more than on a woman, it seemed an admission – even a celebration – of defeat.

Valnu pretended not to understand. "What, my knees?" Wicked laughter filled his thin, handsome face. "My pet, you've seen a great deal more of me than my knees."

"Never on the street," Krasta ground out.

"Oh, you have so," Valnu said. "That time you ended up shoving me out of your carriage – we weren't just *on* the bloody street, we were *in* it."

"That's different," Krasta said, though she couldn't have told him how. Then she asked the question that was really on her mind: "How can you stand to wear it?"

"How can I stand it?" Ever the opportunist, Valnu rested a hand on her hip. "Sweetling, the way things are, I should hardly dare not to don the kilt, wouldn't you say? It's protective coloration."

Krasta might have heard the phrase once or twice, but it made no sense to her here. Impatiently, she said, "What *are* you talking about?"

"What I said," Valnu answered. "You know, the butterflies that look like dry leaves when they fold up their wings and the bugs that look like twigs, all so the birds can't eat 'em. If I look like an Algarvian . . ." His voice trailed away.

"Oh." Krasta wasn't the cleverest woman in Valmiera, but she saw what he meant. "They aren't really doing that. I don't think they're really doing that. Lurcanio says they aren't doing that. If they were, we'd have heard about people who went missing, don't you think?"

"Not if they didn't go missing from Valmiera," Valnu said.

"We'd have heard about Jelgava, too, or the Jelgavan nobility would have, and they would have started screaming their heads off. We'd have heard that," Krasta said. It was Lurcanio's argument, but it had convinced her, and she made it her own.

If it didn't convince Valnu, it made him thoughtful. "Maybe," he said at last. "Just maybe. By the powers above, how I wish it could be true. Still and all, though" – he ran the hand that wasn't on Krasta's hip down his kilt – "better not to take chances. Laws of similarity and all that. And don't I look splendid?"

"You look grotesque." Krasta exercised tact only around Colonel Lurcanio. "As grotesque as an Algarvian in trousers. It looks unnatural."

"You say the sweetest things. I'll tell you what it is, though." Valnu leaned toward her, almost close enough for his tongue to touch her ear as he whispered, "It's bloody drafty, that's what."

He startled a laugh out of Krasta, despite her best intentions. "Serves you right," she said. This time, when Valnu tried to kiss her on the cheek, she let him. He went on his way cheerfully enough, but she found she could get no more pleasure out of shopping, and rode back to her mansion in a glum and dour mood.

"Coming on!" an Algarvian soldier shouted in bad Unkerlanter. "More firewoods!"

"Aye, more firewood," Garivald said, and dumped his bundle at the redhead's feet. Every stick the Algarvians burned was one the villagers of Zossen couldn't, but anyone who complained got blazed. No one complained, then – not where the Algarvians could hear.

It could have been worse. Only a squad or so of Algarvians garrisoned the village. The men of Zossen could have risen and wiped them out. The men of a village a few miles away had risen and killed all of Mezentio's soldiers there. That village was gone now. The Algarvians had brought in more soldiers, behemoths, and dragons, and wiped it off the face of the earth. The peasant men were dead. The women . . . Garivald didn't want to think about the women.

His friend Dagulf thumped a load of firewood at the Algarvian's feet. The fellow nodded and gave a theatrical shiver. He might not speak much Unkerlanter, but, like a lot of redheads Garivald had seen, he had a gift for gestures. "Cold," he said. "Very cold."

Garivald nodded; disagreeing with the occupiers didn't pay. Dagulf nodded, too. They caught each other's eye. Neither laughed or even smiled, though Garivald knew he felt like it. It was only a little below freezing, and might even get about it by the middle of the day. If the Algarvian thought this was cold, he hadn't seen anything yet.

After they'd got out of earshot of the redhead, Dagulf said, "He hasn't got the clothes he needs for this kind of weather."

"No," Garivald said, and then, "Too bad." He and Dagulf did laugh now. Garivald scratched. His calf-length wool-tunic was twice as thick as the one the Algarvian wore. Beneath it, he had on a wool undertunic, wool drawers, and wool stockings. He was perfectly comfortable. When winter came on, he'd add a thick wool cloak and a fur hat. He wouldn't be perfectly comfortable then, but he'd manage.

"Wouldn't catch me wearing one of those little short kilts," Dagulf said.

"Curse me if I'll argue with you," Garivald said. "First blizzard comes, it'd freeze right off." He paused meditatively. "Might be the best thing that could happen to the whoresons, eh?"

"Aye." Dagulf pulled a sour face. "They're a lickerish lot, Mezentio's buggers. Looks like they'll swive anything that moves – and if it doesn't move, they'll shake it."

"That's so," Garivald said. "We've already had more scandal since they came than for years before. And afterwards, the women say the soldiers made 'em do it and they didn't have a choice, but a lot of 'em look pretty cursed contented while they say it. All this Algarvian swaggering and hand-kissing and what have you spoils 'em, you ask me."

Dagulf said something vaguely related to hand-kissing. He and Garivald let out loud, coarse laughs. Then he said, "You ought to make a song about it – a song that'd keep our women from lying down with the redheads, I mean."

"Nothing will keep them from lying down if it's that or be blazed," Garivald observed. "You can't blame 'em for that. But the other . . ." His voice trailed away. His expression went slack and distant. Dagulf had to nudge him to get him to keep walking. He murmured, "We'd have to be careful where we sung it."

Dagulf grunted. "So we would." He pointed toward Waddo the firstman, who was limping toward them across the village square. With the ground partly frozen, Waddo's stick got better purchase than it had when everything was knee-deep in mud. Dagulf went on, "Algarvians aren't the only reason we'd have to be careful, either."

"He wouldn't betray us to the redheads," Garivald said, but then softened that by adding, "I don't think."

"He might," Dagulf said darkly. "Selling us out is about the only way I can think of that he'd get himself in good with the Algarvians."

"He hasn't pulled anything like that yet, powers above be praised."

Garivald knew something else that might make King Mezentio's men happy with Waddo. If the firstman led them to the buried crystal, they might forgive him for having buried it. And if he wasn't sure they would, he might try to blame everything on Garivald, who'd helped him hide it.

"Hello, hello," Waddo said as he came up to them at last. "A very good day to you both, I am sure." He didn't sound so sure of anything as he had before the Algarvians seized Zossen. He remained firstman, and did their bidding when they gave him any bidding to do, but he'd lost most of the authority he'd had as the nearest approach to King Swemmel's representative in the village. As far as King Mezentio's men were concerned, he was just a dog slightly larger than the other dogs in Zossen – and much more likely to be kicked.

"Good day," Garivald and Dagulf said together. Dagulf pointed to Garivald and added, "Our friend here may be in the way of coming up with a new song."

Garivald wished he hadn't said even so much. Waddo, however, beamed. "I saw him looking all dreamy, so I hoped he might be. A new song would help make the long, cold winter nights pass quicker."

"I'll do what I can," Garivald said. Now he'd have to come up with an ordinary song as well as the one urging the village women not to give themselves to Algarvian soldiers. He hoped Waddo wouldn't hear that one, even if the firstman had a daughter of an age, if not of a beauty, to draw the redheads' notice.

"If it's half as good as a couple you've come up with, it'll be twice as good as a lot of the ones we've known for years," Waddo said. "A minstrel in our own village – a songsmith, no less. Who would have thought it?"

"I thank you," Garivald said shyly. The idea that he could make songs still astonished him.

"No, we thank you. You do us credit." Waddo was very effusive. *Is he laying it on too thick?* Garivald wondered. *Is he trying to lull me to sleep so he can sell me to Mezentio's men?* He wondered if he ought to dig up the crystal and hide it somewhere only he knew or throw it in a creek. If he could do it without being noticed, that might prove wise.

Of course, if the Algarvians caught him digging up the crystal, they'd blaze him, or maybe just hang him with a placard round his neck warning others not to do as he had done. Did Waddo want him to try something foolish? That way, he'd be punished, leaving the firstman in the clear. Garivald shook his head, as if to knock such notions out of it. He hated having to think that way.

"Aye, a new song would be fine," Waddo said. "Anything that takes our minds off our empty bellies would be fine."

"It would have been a good harvest," Dagulf said mournfully. "If we'd got to keep more of it, it would have."

"The redheads—" Waddo's head went back and forth in the automatic cautious gesture the rest of the villagers had always used to make sure he wasn't around before they spoke some of their minds. He didn't see anything untoward – Garivald knew because he looked around, too – but he didn't say much, either, contenting himself with a sigh and the remark, "That can't be helped."

"Neither can grasshoppers," Dagulf said. Garivald contrived to step on his foot; the other peasant wasn't thinking enough before he spoke today.

Waddo nodded. Garivald didn't trust him even so. The firstman might find favor with the Algarvians by betraying other villagers, too.

After as little small talk as he could get away with and still stay polite, Garivald went back to his house and told Annore, "I'm going out to the woods again. This time, if I'm lucky, I'll be able to cut some firewood for us, too, not just for the redheads."

"That would be good," his wife said. "If you could knock a squirrel out of a tree with a rock or club a rabbit or two, that would be even better."

"If I'm lucky, I will," Garivald answered. "Of course, if I were lucky, there wouldn't be an Algarvian within a hundred miles of Zossen."

"And isn't that the truth?" Annore said bitterly. "Well, go on, then. Maybe some small luck will help make up for the big."

"Here's hoping. Hand me the whetstone, will you?" He took the hatchet off his belt and got the edge as sharp as he could. While he was working for the Algarvians, he didn't care what state his tools were in; dull ones gave him an excuse for going slower and doing less. Working for himself, he wanted to do the job right.

He hurried out among the trees. Firewood and the chance to hunt weren't all that drew him. There in the quiet, words shaped themselves in his head more readily than back in the village. He'd had a whole verse vanish from his mind when Syrivald asked him a question at just the wrong time.

Waddo expected a song to make winter nights pass more pleasantly. Garivald knew that was the piece he should have been working on. Naturally, the other one he had in mind, the one that urged Unkerlanter women not to give their bodies to King Mezentio's soldiers, kept forcing its way forward.

He threw a stone at a gray squirrel on the gray bark of a birch. The stone slammed into the trunk a few inches to one side of the little animal. The squirrel scurried around to the far side of the tree, chattering reproachfully.

"Whore," Garivald muttered. He chopped at a sapling. Unlike the squirrel, it couldn't run away. He stuffed lengths of the trunk and the bigger branches into a leather sack he carried over his shoulder. As his body did the work, his mind roamed free. Two verses centered on the word *whore* shaped themselves before he quite knew what had happened.

He quietly sang them to himself, weighing the sounds, seeing if the rhythm was right, looking for ways to make the verses better. By the time he went back to Zossen, he'd have them just the way he wanted them.

After singing them, he changed a couple of words, then sang them again. He was about to change one of the words back when someone behind him clapped his hands. Garivald whirled in alarm, his hand tightening on the hatchet's handle. Some of the villagers thought the best way to get along with the Algarvians was to suck up to them. Anyone who tried taking this tale back to them would be sorry.

But the fellow who'd clapped didn't come from Zossen. Garivald had never seen him before. He was skinny and dirty and mean-looking. Once upon a time, his grimy tunic had been rock-gray. He carried a stick; Garivald's hatchet wasn't much against it. He wasn't pointing it at Garivald, though. Instead, he was nodding in slow approval.

"Good song," he remarked, and his accent proved he hadn't been born anywhere near the Duchy of Grelz. "Did you make it?"

"Aye," Garivald answered before realizing he should have lied.

"Thought so – hadn't heard it before," the stranger said. "Aye, a good song. Sing it over, friend, so I get it straight."

Garivald did, this time all the way through. The stranger listened, then made a peremptory gesture for him to do it again. Now, the stranger sang along. He had a good ear; he made few mistakes.

"My pals will like that," he said. "Aye, in a few months people will be singing that all over the countryside. Not everyone's given up against the

Algarvians, no indeed, not even after their behemoths ran over us. What's the name of your village yonder?"

"Zossen," Garivald answered.

"Zossen," the stranger – a soldier who hadn't surrendered? – repeated. "Zossen will hear from us one of these days." He sketched a salute, as if to an officer, before slipping away between the trees. He was far better in the woods than Garivald, and vanished almost at once.

Fernao didn't know why he'd been summoned to the royal palace in Setubal. The bored functionary who'd linked crystals hadn't explained, saying only, "All will be made clear upon your arrival, sir." In a way, Fernao supposed his caution made sense: A good mage could spy on the emanations passing between two crystals. But not knowing why he had to go to the palace irritated him.

As he got off the caravan car in front of the palace grounds, an unpleasant thought crossed his mind: what if it had to do with the exiled King Penda of Forthweg? That was worse than irritating. It was down-right frightening. He would have been perfectly happy – powers above, he would have been delighted – never to see Penda again.

He worried as he walked up the broad red-brick path toward the palace, worried so much that at first he paid little attention to the building itself. Having lived his whole life in Setubal played a part in that; he took the palace for granted, where a man who saw it but seldom would not have.

Even for him, it wasn't easy. The Lagoan royal palace cried out to be noticed – cried out in a loud, piercing voice. It was built in the ornate Algarvian style of the century before last: the Algarvian style carried to an extreme only the royal treasury could have supported. Everything leaped toward the heavens, and everything was carved in incredible, maniacal detail. The entire history of Lagoas up till that time appeared on the walls and buttresses and towers, all of it perfect, much of it swathed in gold leaf. Fernao wondered how many stonecutters had gone blind while the palace rose.

If anything, the great bronze doors that led into the royal residence were even more astonishing than the building. On them was the Second Battle of the Strait of Valmiera – in which, not long before the palace went up, Lagoas had won a smashing victory over Sibiu – all picked out in enamelwork whose brilliance had not diminished a bit over the course of two centuries.

Muttering under his breath, Fernao passed through those brazen doors and into the palace. A dozen secretaries sat behind desks in the antechamber there. He went up to one of them and gave his name.

"A moment, sorcerous sir, if you please," the fellow said. "Let me consult my list of appointments." He ran his finger down the sheet. "Ah, here you are – and right on time, too. Your appointment is with Colonel Peixoto, in the Ministry of War. That is in the south wing, sir – go through this hall and take the corridor to your left."

"Thank you very much," Fernao said. The secretary bowed in his chair, almost as ceremonious as an Algarvian. Fernao walked through the antechamber with a new bounce to his stride. Only the splendor of his surroundings kept him from whistling as he walked. Whatever this was about, it had nothing to do with Penda. *And if it has nothing to do with Penda*, he thought, *I don't care what it is.*

As he got farther from the parts of the palace where King Vitor actually lived, interior decoration grew less grandiose. By the time he reached the offices of the Ministry of War – a good ten minutes' walk from the antechamber – he'd come to surroundings in which he could actually imagine men doing serious work.

A uniformed clerk took charge of him. After making him touch his Guild card – had he been an impostor, the spot he touched would have glowed red – the clerk led him to Peixoto's office. The Lagoan colonel was younger and leaner than Fernao had expected: within a couple of years of the sorcerer's own age. He was also more enthusiastic than Fernao had looked for in a soldier.

"A pleasure to make your acquaintance, sir, a very great pleasure," Peixoto said, springing from his seat to clasp Fernao's hand. "Here, take a chair, make yourself comfortable. Will you drink a glass of wine with me?" Without waiting for an answer, he clapped his hands. The military clerk hurried in with a bottle and a couple of glasses.

The wine had the tang of oranges and lemons. "A Jelgavan vintage," Fernao remarked without bothering to look closely at the bottle.

"Aye, so it is," Colonel Peixoto answered. "The Algarvians make better, but I'll be cursed if I want any of theirs now. I'd think I were drinking blood." His face, which seemed sunny most of the time, clouded. "That's a filthy trick they've pulled in Unkerlant."

"You're not a mage, Colonel – you have no notion how filthy it feels to me," Fernao said. "If you've called me here to try to put a stop to it, I am your man, and with all my heart." He emptied his wineglass, then poured it full again.

"Well, in a manner of speaking, sir mage, in a manner of speaking," Peixoto said. "We aim to put a thorn under the wings of King Mezentio's dragons, so we do. And from all I can see" – he rustled papers on his desk – "you are the perfect man – the perfect man, I tell you – for the job."

"Say on," Fernao told him.

"I'll do just that," Colonel Peixoto replied. "Curse me if I won't. Now, then – I see you've served as a ship's mage. You were doing that when the war broke out, weren't you? Can't very well hit the Algarvians a proper lick unless we cross the sea to get at 'em, can we?"

"No, indeed," Fernao said. The wine lent his voice extra solemnity. "Although the research I'm working on now is important, if you think I could best serve the kingdom by going back to sea, I'll do it."

Peixoto beamed. "Spoken like a patriot, my dear sir. But that's not precisely what we have in mind for you, by your leave. You're not far off – don't get me wrong – but you're not quite on, either. Plenty of mages – plenty of Lagoan mages, anyhow – go to sea. But do you know – do you know, sir? – that only a handful of Lagoan mages, and fewer of the first rank, have ever set foot on the land of the Ice People?"

Fernao discovered he'd made a mistake, a dreadful mistake, when he'd decided he didn't care why he'd been called to the palace so long as it had nothing to do with King Penda. "Colonel," he said plaintively, "have you ever eaten boiled camel hump? Have you ever tried to gnaw through strips of dried and salted camel meat?"

"Never once, powers above be praised." Colonel Peixoto sounded pleased that that was true, too, for which Fernao could hardly blame him. The mage wished it were true for himself. Peixoto went on, "But since you have, that makes you all the more valuable for this expedition. You must see that, mustn't you?"

"What expedition?" demanded Fernao, who was not in the mood to see anything if he could help it.

"Why, the one we're planning to the austral continent, of course," Peixoto said. "With a little bit of luck – with only a little bit of luck, mind you – we'll throw out the Yaninans and however many Algarvians they've got down there to give them a hand, and then where will they be? Eh? Where then?"

"Somewhere warm and civilized," Fernao answered. Colonel Peixoto laughed heartily, as if he'd said something funny rather than speaking simple truth. The mage asked, "Why on earth are we mad enough to want to take the land of the Ice People away from the Yaninans? As far as I'm concerned, they did us a favor when they ran us out of it last year."

"What's on the earth there doesn't matter, not a bit – no, not a bit. It's what's in the earth that counts." Peixoto leaned forward and breathed a wine-smelling word into Fernao's face: "Cinnabar."

"Ah," the mage said. "Indeed. But still—"

"But me no buts, my dear sir," Peixoto said. "Without the austral continent, Algarve has not got a lot of cinnabar. Without cinnabar, her dragons cannot flame nearly so fiercely as they can with it. If we take it away, that makes fighting the war harder for them. Can you tell me I am mistaken in any particular there?"

"No," Fernao admitted. "But can you tell me that whatever we have to spend to take the cinnabar from the land of the Ice People away from Mezentio's men won't be twice – three times – five times – what it costs them to do without?"

Peixoto beamed at him. The colonel really was too cheerful to make a typical soldier. "Ah, a very nice point, a very nice point indeed! But you must recall, we can think differently now that Kuusamo has joined the fight on our side and we don't have to worry about being stabbed in the back. Algarvian folly there, nothing else but."

"I do recall that, aye," Fernao said. He'd hoped it would mean the Kuusamans would start sharing whatever they know of whatever they weren't talking about. So far, it hadn't; they kept blandly denying everything. Pointing to a map on the wall by the desk, he continued, "But I also recall that Sibiu sits over our route to the austral continent, and that there are a certain number of Algarvians and Algarvian ships and Algarvian leviathans and Algarvian scouting dragons in Sibiu."

"It's true. Every bit of it's true." Nothing fazed Peixoto. "I never said this would be easy, sir mage. I said we were going to undertake it. If we succeed in landing men and dragons on the austral continent, we will require sorcerers somewhat familiar with conditions there – and also with conditions in the waters thereabouts. Can you deny you are such a mage?"

After his journey by levianthanback from the land of the Ice People to Lagoas, Fernao was more familiar with those waters than he'd ever wanted to be. "I don't suppose I can deny it, no," he said, wishing he could. "Even so—"

Colonel Peixoto held up a hand. "My dear sir, your voluntary cooperation would be greatly appreciated – greatly appreciated indeed. It is not a requirement, however."

Fernao glared at him. That was plain enough – unpleasant, but plain. "You will dragoon me, then."

"If we must, we will," Peixoto agreed. "We need you. I promise you this: the rewards of success will not be small, neither for the kingdom nor for yourself."

"Nor will the penalties – for me, anyhow – be small if we fail," Fernao said. "The kingdom, I expect, will survive it." He sighed. "At least I'll have till spring to prepare for this . . . adventure."

"Oh, no." Peixoto shook his head. "It will not be at once, but we aim to move later in the winter. The bad weather in the south will make it harder for the Algarvians to spy out what we're doing, and we have more practice sailing in those waters during wintertime than they do."

"Practice dodging icebergs, you mean," Fernao said, and the colonel, curse him, nodded. The mage went on, "And I suppose you intend landing your army at the edge of the ice pack and letting everyone march to real ground."

He'd intended that for sarcasm. To his dismay, Colonel Peixoto nodded. "Aye. Nothing better than taking the foe by surprise."

"A blizzard at the wrong time would take *us* by surprise," Fernao remarked. Peixoto shrugged, as if to say such things couldn't be helped. Fernao tried again: "What do you propose that we eat once we get down there?"

"We'll manage," Peixoto said. "After all, the Ice People do."

"You're mad," Fernao said. "Your superiors are mad. And you want me to help save you from yourselves."

"If that's how you care to put it," Peixoto said. "I'm going along, when we go. I'm not asking anything of you I dare not do myself."

"Oh, don't turn Algarvian on me," Fernao said crossly. "I'll go." He wondered how big a fool he was being. No – he didn't wonder. He knew.

Eight

Leofsig turned to his younger brother and asked, "Who's your friend in Oyngestun? This is the third letter you've gotten from there in the last couple of weeks."

He hadn't meant anything in particular by the question. The last thing he expected was for Ealstan to blush and look embarrassed and stammer out, "Oh, just, uh, somebody I, uh, got to know, that's all."

It so patently wasn't all that Leofsig started to laugh. Ealstan glared at him. "Somebody you got to know, eh? Is she pretty?" he asked, and then went on, "She must be pretty, to get you all flustered like that."

And, sure enough, Ealstan's face lit up like a sunrise. "Aye, she's pretty," he said in a low voice. He glanced out toward the doorway of the bedroom they shared, to make sure nobody was standing out in the courtyard and listening. Leofsig thought he was being foolish; on a miserably chilly night like this one, nobody in his right mind would want to linger out there.

"Well, tell me more," Leofsig urged. "How'd you meet her? What's her name?" He had trouble thinking of his baby brother as being old enough to care about girls, but Ealstan's beard was getting on toward man-thick these days.

"I met her gathering mushrooms," Ealstan answered, still hardly above a whisper. Leofsig laughed again; if that wasn't the way a quarter of the Forthwegian writers ever born started their romances, he'd eat his shoes. "Well, I did, curse it," Ealstan said. But something more than silliness at being caught up in a cliché was on his face. Leofsig had trouble naming it, whatever it was.

"What's her name?" he asked again.

That other thing grew stronger on Ealstan's face. Now Leofsig recognized it: It was fear. For a moment, he didn't think his brother would answer him. When at last Ealstan did speak, he said, "I wouldn't tell anybody but you, not even Father, not yet anyhow. Her name's . . . Vanai." The whisper was so quiet, Leofsig had to lean forward to hear it.

"Why are you making such a secret out of . . ." he began, and then, before he'd finished the sentence, he understood exactly why. "Oh." He whistled softly. "Because she's a Kaunian."

"Aye." Ealstan's voice was bleak. When he chuckled, the sound might have come from the throat of a weary, cynical old man. "My sense of timing couldn't be better, could it?"

"Not if you tried for a year." Leofsig shook his head, as stunned as if an egg had burst close by. "That would be hard enough any time. Now . . ."

Ealstan nodded. "Now it's a disaster. But it happened anyhow. And do you know what?" He stuck out his chin, as if challenging not only Leofsig but the whole world to make him take it back. "I'm glad it happened."

"You're head over heels, is what you are." Leofsig knew a stab of jealousy. He'd been taking Felgilde out since before he got summoned into King Penda's levy, and he didn't think he'd ever felt about her the way Ealstan obviously felt about this Vanai. But his brother had his eyes open, too: his wariness made that plain.

So did his next question: "Leofsig, do you think it's true, what people are saying about what the redheads did to the Kaunians they shipped off to the west?"

Leofsig started to sigh. His breath caught in his throat; what emerged was more of a choking noise, which seemed to fit. "I don't know," he answered, but that wasn't what Ealstan had asked. With another sigh, a real one this time, he went on, "By the powers above, I hope not. I wouldn't like to think . . . that of anyone, even the Algarvians." What he'd like to think wasn't what Ealstan had asked, either. "I tell you this, though: it could be true. The way they treated Kaunians in the captives' camp, the way they're treating them here . . . Aye, it could be true."

"I thought the same thing – I was hoping you'd tell me I was wrong," Ealstan said. "If you're right – if we're right – King Mezentio's men could go into Oyngestun for some more Kaunians to send west, and they might take her." Fear was back on his face; it rubbed his voice raw. "And I wouldn't be able to do anything about it. I wouldn't even know about it till I stopped hearing from her."

Leofsig had never had such worries with Felgilde (for that matter, he suspected she wouldn't be brokenhearted to see every Kaunian vanish from Forthweg). He eyed his brother with mingled sympathy and surprise. "You've got a man's load of troubles there, sure enough. I don't know what to tell you. I don't suppose you could move her here to Gromheort, could you?"

Ealstan shook his head. "Not a chance. She lives with her grandfather. And even if I could, the redheads would be as likely to grab her here as they would there." He clenched his fists. "What am I going to do?"

"I don't know," Leofsig repeated, that being kinder than saying, *There's nothing you can do.* After some thought, he added, "You might tell Father. He won't get mad at you for being sweet on a Kaunian girl – you know better than that – and he may be able to do you some good."

"Maybe." Ealstan didn't sound convinced. "I didn't want to tell anybody, but you asked just the right questions." He looked grim. "If I keep getting letters from Oyngestun, I won't need to do much telling, will I? Not unless I want to do a lot of lying, I mean." From grim, his features went to grimmer. "Pretty soon, Sidroc's going to figure things out. That won't be so good. He already knows about her."

"How does he—?" Again, Leofsig stopped in the middle of a question and answered it himself: "This is the girl whose basket you brought home last year." He thumped his forehead with the heel of his hand, angry he hadn't made the connection sooner.

"Aye, it is," Ealstan said. "But we were just friends then, not—" Now he stopped abruptly.

"Not what?" Leofsig asked. Ealstan sat on his stool and didn't answer. By not answering, he said everything that needed saying. Leofsig shook his head in bemusement. He'd only thought he was jealous of his younger brother before. He had hopes he might enjoy Felgilde – probably the night after he asked for her hand, if he ever did. That Ealstan didn't have to live on hope struck him as most unfair. He found another question: "What *are* you going to do now?"

"That's what we've been talking about," Ealstan said impatiently – and Leofsig wasn't used to his little brother's being impatient with him, either. "I don't know what to do, I don't know if there's anything I can do, and I don't want anybody else to know I've got to do anything."

"I still think Father could help," Leofsig said. "He helped me, remember."

"Of course I remember," Ealstan said. "If I think of anything he might do, I'll ask him." He suddenly looked very fierce. "But don't you dare say anything to him till I do – if I ever do. Do you hear me?"

Leofsig had used that tone with Ealstan any number of times. Up till now, Ealstan had never used it with him. He started to bristle. The set look on his brother's face warned that bristling would do no good, and might do a lot of harm. When he did speak, his voice was still rough, but not in the way it would have been a moment before: "Just don't go and do anything stupid, do you hear me?"

"Oh, aye, I hear you," Ealstan answered. "The way things are going, though, who knows whether I'll be able to listen to you?"

"I wish I could argue with that." Leofsig got up and clapped his brother on the shoulder. "I hope it turns out as well as it can for you."

"Thanks." Now Ealstan sounded like the younger brother he'd always been. As he looked up at Leofsig, his smile seemed familiar, too – for a couple of heartbeats. But then his face hardened into that of a near-stranger again. "About as much as anybody can hope for these days, isn't it?"

"Seems that way." Leofsig thought about adding the hope that things would get better soon. He held his tongue. As far as he could see, that hope would just rouse Ealstan to bitter laughter. Contemplating it almost roused him to bitter laughter. Instead of laughing, he yawned. "I'm going to bed. Shoving rocks around takes more work than Algarvian irregular verbs."

"Good night," Ealstan said, and then used an Algarvian irregular verb that startled Leofsig.

"Where did you learn *that*?" he asked. "The guards in the captives' camp used to yell it at us."

"From the constables," his brother answered. "They call people that all the time. They usually laugh when they say it, though. They're whoresons, aye, but they aren't as mean as the soldiers were."

"Maybe not – some of them don't seem to be bad fellows, anyhow," Leofsig allowed. "But they're still redheads." Having said that, he thought he'd given them all the condemnation necessary. Then, discovering he was wrong, he added, "And they're the ones who loaded the Kaunians into the caravan cars."

"So they are." Ealstan grimaced. "I'd forgotten that. I wonder how they sleep at night."

"I don't know." Leofsig yawned again. "But I can tell you how I'm going to sleep tonight: like a brick." He soon proved himself right, too.

A couple of evenings later, while Ealstan was wrestling with Algarvian irregular verbs or his father's bookkeeping problems, Hestan took Leofsig out into the courtyard and quietly said, "Something is troubling your brother. Do you know what it is?"

"Aye," Leofsig answered. He shivered a little; the weather had got no warmer.

When he said no more than that, his father clicked his tongue between his teeth. "Is it anything where I could help him?"

"Maybe," Leofsig said.

Hestan waited to see if anything more was forthcoming. When he found it wasn't, he chuckled under his breath. "In a gamesome mood tonight, are you? All right, I'll come out and ask: what is it?"

"I don't think I ought to tell you," Leofsig said. "He asked me not to."

"Ah." Hestan exhaled. A lamp inside the kitchen and another in a bedroom showed the puff of fog that came from his mouth and nose. "Whatever it is, it has to do with those letters he's been getting from Oyngestun, doesn't it?"

Too late, Leofsig realized Ealstan would have wanted him to say something like, *What letters?* When he didn't say that right away, his father slowly nodded. Leofsig's sigh brought forth mist, too. "I don't think I'd better say anything at all, Father."

"Why not?" Hestan was still quiet – he almost always was – but now he was quietly angry. "I did you some good, you know. I might be able to do the same for your brother."

"If I thought you could, I'd tell you fast as a blaze," Leofsig said. "I wish I did, but I don't. Have you got the pull to keep the redheads from shipping Kaunians west?"

Hestan stood silent. Just for a moment, his eyes widened, glittering in the dim lamplight. "So," he said, a word that stood for a sentence, or maybe two or three. "No, I don't have that kind of pull. No one has that kind of pull, no one I know of." Ever so slightly, his shoulders sagged.

"I was afraid of that," Leofsig said. Without another word, he and his father went back inside.

Skarnu gave the sky a warning glance, as if telling the powers above what they might and might not do. In case they weren't listening, he spoke to his comrades, too: "If it snows, we've got trouble."

"Aye." Raunu's gaze also flicked up toward those ugly gray clouds. "Snow can make hiding your tracks a lot harder."

Standing behind a bare-branched chestnut, Merkela clung to the hunting stick that had been Gedominu's. "We'll try it anyway – we've come too far not to," she said. "And if it snows hard enough, it'll cover our tracks as fast as we make them."

A peasant whose farm lay on the far side of Pavilosta, a short, dour, middle-aged man named Dauktu, shook his head. "If it snows that hard, cursed Simanu'll just stay inside his castle where it's nice and warm instead of coming out a-coursing," he said.

All of the double handful of Valmierans who hated Count Simanu and the Algarvians propping him up enough to risk their lives to try to be rid of him looked toward the fortress of yellow limestone that crowned a hill halfway between Pavilosta and Adutiskis, the other leading village in the county. Enkuru, Simanu's father, had made the place strong. The way he'd treated the local peasants, he'd needed a strong place of refuge. This forlorn squad could not hope to go in there and get Simanu out. They had to hope the word they'd got was good, and that he would come forth today after deer and boar and pheasant.

Raunu said, "Back before the days of egg-tossers, nobody could have stormed a keep like that."

"Even with egg-tossers, even with dragons, a stubborn garrison in there could have made the Algarvians work for a living," Skarnu said.

Dauktu spat on the ground. "Not Enkuru," he said bitterly. "He knew which side of his bread had honey on it. As soon as the redheads looked like winning the war, he rolled over on his back and showed 'em his throat and his belly, the way any cowardly cur-dog would."

"He's dead," Merkela said. "Powers below eat him, he's dead. Simanu deserves to be dead. And" – her voice roughened – "all the redheads deserve to be dead, too. What they did to Gedominu . . ."

Her war with the Algarvians was and always would be personal.

Skarnu said, "What they're doing now, there in the west . . ."

As Merkela's had, his voice trailed away. None of the other Valmierans said anything. None of them wanted to meet his eye. Skarnu still didn't know how much faith to put in the rumors that swirled through his conquered kingdom. He didn't want to believe any of them, but with that much smoke, he feared a fire had to be burning somewhere down at the bottom of it.

"You wouldn't think even Algarvians could do such a thing," Raunu said. "They're whoresons, aye, but they fought clean enough, taking all in all, in the Six Years' War."

"Barbarians. Always have been. Always will be." Dauktu spat again.

"Aye." Merkela's voice was fierce. No one – not Skarnu, not Raunu, not the peasants who'd known her all her life – had had the nerve to tell her she might not come with the men on this raid. Had anyone tried, she would have been more dangerous to him than the redheads were likely to prove.

The Algarvians would say, "Even Kaunians do thus and so," Skarnu thought. *They have the whip hand, though, and they're using it, curse them.* He gave no outward sign of what was going through his mind. Seeing the enemy's point of view was sometimes useful for an officer. Soldiers fought better when they reckoned the foe nothing but a barbarian, a whoreson.

A horn call, thin in the distance, drove such thoughts from his mind. He peered toward Count Simanu's castle, squinting to try to make his vision sharper. "Is that the drawbridge coming down?"

"Aye," Raunu said. "I can't hardly read at all without spectacles on my nose, but I don't have any trouble with what's far away."

"Here he comes," Merkela breathed. "Oh, here comes the whole band of hunters." Her voice was soft, but the passion it held matched – outdid – even her wildest moanings when she lay joined to Skarnu in the bedchamber she had shared with Gedominu.

Skarnu had no trouble seeing that, either: Every one of the hunters' mounts was a brilliant, gleaming white, a white that glowed even under this dark, lowering sky. "Those aren't horses," he said. "They're unicorns, for swank."

"Aye," Dauktu said. "You didn't know about the herd the counts keep?" He shrugged. "Well, can't be helped, I suppose. You're not from here."

If Skarnu lived out all his remaining days in this stretch of the kingdom, people would, he knew, be saying *You're not from here* even when he was a doddering old man. He put that out of his mind. "It makes our job harder," he said. "Unicorns are faster than horses, and they're smarter than horses, too."

"Aye, and all of those riders will have sticks of their own, and they'll know what to do with them," Raunu said. "Don't know about Simanu, but Algarvian cowards are few and far between, whatever else you say about the redheads."

"If you haven't got the stomach for the game, you can still go back to the farm," Merkela told him.

"You know better." The veteran underofficer locked eyes with Merkela. She looked away first, with a grudged nod. Skarnu's respect for Raunu, already high, went up another notch. Very few people were able to make Merkela give ground. He'd had scant luck there himself, and he was her lover.

Another horn call sounded. Simanu and his cronies drew nearer. Some wore trousers, others kilts. They were all fine riders, handling their unicorns with effortless ease. The lead rider – Skarnu thought it was Simanu himself – pointed in the direction of the thicket where the raiders waited.

Raunu chuckled mirthlessly. "Now we find out who's sold whom."

"Aye," Skarnu agreed. "Did that groom tell us the count would come this way today because he couldn't stand his master, or was he taking Simanu's money to suck us into the redheads' web?"

One of the peasants nodded in the direction of the fortress. "I don't see any more soldiers coming forth there, and we'd know if the Algarvians had men in these woods. They'd already be at us." What he meant by that was, *We'd already be dead.* Since Skarnu thought the fellow was right, he didn't argue.

Simanu shouted something. The count was still too far away for Skarnu to make out his words, but he sounded carefree. Maybe that meant he was a good actor. Skarnu hoped it meant he suspected nothing.

"We don't start blazing too soon," he warned his comrades – Merkela in particular. "This is likely to be the best chance we'll ever have. If we waste it, we're stuck with the bugger forevermore."

He wondered if he ought to be talking like that. Simanu was a reprobate, but he was also a member of Skarnu's class. Nobles who maligned their fellows to commoners got themselves a bad name. But what of nobles who went to bed with the Algarvians? What did they get? *Not half what they deserve*, Skarnu thought. He'd do his best to fix that.

Simanu shouted something else. This time, Skarnu caught a phrase – "after wild boar" – though the breeze blew away the rest. One of the Algarvians answered in his own language. Then Simanu said something in Algarvian, too; the rhythms and trills were unmistakable. Skarnu didn't know why that should have surprised him, but it did, and infuriated him, too.

"Closer," Raunu said softly. "Let 'em come closer." He might have been watching a wary doe approaching a deadfall. "We don't want to spook 'em by—"

Before he could finish, one of the peasants at the far end of their little line started blazing. The Kaunian behind Simanu threw up his hands and slid bonelessly off his unicorn. It was a very fine blaze. Skarnu didn't think he could have matched it, not at that range.

"Oh, you cursed fool," he muttered under his breath. Because it was such a fine blaze, who else would have the chance to get an easier one? No help for it now; Simanu and his henchmen were already shouting in alarm. Skarnu shouted, too: "Let's get them!" He raised his stick to his shoulder, aimed at Simanu, and blazed.

The collaborationist count's unicorn reared, let out a horrid shriek, and then toppled. Skarnu and his friends cheered. Then they cried out again, this time in dismay. Simanu had managed to kick free. Now he lay behind the beast's thrashing body and started blazing toward the woods.

Most of his henchmen galloped back toward the safety of the keep. A couple of men, though – both Algarvians, Skarnu saw with mixed admiration for their courage and shame that they had no Valmierans with them – spurred their unicorns straight for the woods. They blazed as they came, buying time for their comrades to get away. They couldn't have known how many foes they faced, or just where among the trees those foes hid, but they attacked anyhow.

Several beams converged on them. Merkela used Gedominu's hunting stick for all it was worth. As each redhead fell, she grunted breathily, as she might have done while building toward her peak of pleasure with Skarnu atop her. When they both lay unmoving, she nodded to him.

"You were right," she said. "They are brave. Now these two are brave and dead, which is better yet."

"Aye," Skarnu said. A hole appeared in a branch too close to his head for comfort. "But Simanu's not dead, curse him, and he's got some cover."

"We'd best do something about him quick, too," Raunu said. "They've seen something's wrong, back there in the castle. We'll have all of Simanu's cursed retainers coming down on us if we hang around too long."

"Aye." Skarnu called quick orders to Dauktu and the other raiders at the far end of the line.

They didn't obey automatically, as true soldiers would have had to do. "And while we're up to that, what's your part of the game?" Dauktu demanded.

"You'll see," Skarnu said. "I won't shrink, I promise. Now – do you want Simanu dead, or don't you?" That decided the peasants. They started blazing at the count without taking so much trouble about their cover. One of them cried out in pain a moment later, too, for Simanu was alert and no bad blazer himself.

But, while he traded beams with the raiders, Skarnu burst from cover a good ways away and rushed toward him. As soon as the unicorn's body no longer shielded the count, Skarnu raised his stick and blazed. He was almost too late; Simanu had already started to swing back toward him. But his beam caught Simanu in the face. The count wailed and went limp. Skarnu waited to see no more, but dashed back toward the trees.

When he stood panting by Merkela again, she kissed him as ferociously as she had when he'd shouted against Simanu in Pavilosta's market square. "Let's get out of here," he said when, after some long and mostly enjoyable time, he broke free. She didn't argue with him. Neither did any of the other raiders – he'd won his spurs today. But, even as he fled, he wondered what the Algarvians would do tomorrow, or the day after that.

Officially, Leudast remained a corporal. No one had bothered with the paperwork that would have promoted him. Unkerlant had neither time nor energy to spare on paperwork these days. Unkerlant had neither time nor energy to spare for anything save survival, and even survival looked to be too much to hope for.

Unofficially, Leudast led a couple of squads in the company Sergeant Magnulf just as unofficially commanded. Captain Hawart headed the regiment of which that company was a part. None of them had the rank for his job. They were all still alive and still fighting back against the Algarvians – a less formal qualification, but good enough.

Cold, wet, filthy, and frightened, Leudast peered east out of the hole in the ground he shared with Magnulf. One thought was uppermost in his mind: "When are they going to do it again?"

"Curse me if I know," Magnulf answered wearily. He looked as worn and disheveled as Leudast felt. Spitting into the mud at the bottom of the hole, he went on, "I could fight the redheads. Aye, they kept coming forward, but they paid for every inch of ground they stole from us. But this . . ." He shook his head, a man caught in the grip of horror.

"This," Leudast echoed. He shook his head, too. "And what are we doing to fight back? We keep bringing up more men, but so what? The Algarvians murder another raft of poor whoresons who never did 'em any harm, and they smash right through us again." He looked over his shoulder, toward the southwest. "If they smash through us two or three times more, they're in Cottbus, and what do we do then?"

He only half heard Magnulf's reply; he'd spotted a soldier trudging through the pitted muck toward them. The fellow called, "Captain Hawart's coming up to the front, and he's got some big blaze with him."

Leudast glanced over at Magnulf, who still outranked him. With an angry gesture, Magnulf said, "Aye, tell 'em to come ahead. We'll give 'em pheasant under glass, just like we're having, and they can sleep on the same featherbeds we use."

With a couple of chunks of stale, moldy bread in his wallet and a grimy blanket for a mattress, Leudast couldn't help snickering. The soldier shrugged and trotted away. He'd delivered his message. Past that, he didn't care what happened.

In a lazy sort of way, the Algarvians started lobbing eggs at the line the Unkerlanters held. A couple landed close enough to the hole in which Leudast and Magnulf sheltered to splash fresh mud on to them. "The captain would come forward in this," Leudast said, "but any big blaze'd turn up his toes – or else pick 'em up and run away." He paused, considered, and corrected himself: "Any big blaze but Marshal Rathar. He was right there in the thick of it up in Zuwayza."

"He's not afraid to mix it," Magnulf agreed. Now he looked back toward the rear, and a moment later let out a low whistle of surprise. "Turns out you're wrong. Here comes the captain, and he's got somebody in a clean tunic with him."

Hawart got down into the hole with Leudast and Magnulf without hesitation; he knew it could keep him alive. The fellow with him, a clever-looking man of middle years, got into it with wrinkled lip, as if fearing his tunic wouldn't stay clean.

"Sir," Hawart said to him, "let me present to you Magnulf and Leudast. They've been in this fight from the start, and they want to stay in it to the finish. Boys, this is Archmage Addanz, the top wizard in the whole kingdom."

"King Swemmel has seen fit to honor me with the highest rank," Addanz said. "Whether I have the highest skill in all the land may perhaps be a different question."

Leudast wasn't inclined to quibble. "Then you can stop the Algarvians when they hurl their magics at us?" he asked eagerly.

"That'd be wonderful," Magnulf exclaimed. "Let us fight the redheads man against man, and we'll lick 'em." The Unkerlanters hadn't licked King Mezentio's men even before they started using their blood-soaked magecraft, but they'd fought hard enough to lend Magnulf's words some weight.

One look at Addanz's face told Leudast his first wild hope was indeed too wild. "You can't do it," he said. He didn't mean it to sound like an accusation, but that was how it came out.

"I cannot do it, not yet," the archmage said. "I do not know if I will ever be able to do such a thing. What I can do, what I hope to do now, is to drop an egg on them of the same sort as they have been dropping on us."

"What do you—?" Leudast broke off. He didn't need to have Addanz draw him a picture. Like anyone else who'd grown up in an Unkerlanter peasant village, he knew how hard life could be. He asked only one question: "Will it work?"

Sergeant Magnulf, who'd grown up close to the Duchy of Grelz – now again the Kingdom of Grelz under Mezentio's cousin – found another one: "Can you do that and not have the people rise up against King Swemmel and for the Algarvians?" People who knew Grelzers well always thought in terms of uprisings.

"I can do it," Addanz answered. "My mages and I, under the orders of the king, have already begun to do it. The Algarvians will make far harsher masters than King Swemmel, so of course the people will follow him."

That meant he didn't know, and no one else did, either. Another egg burst near the hole, splattering the soldiers and the mage with more mud. Unkerlanter egg-tossers, slow as usual, began balls of sorcerous energy back at the Algarvians. "About time," Leudast growled. "Sometimes I think we've forgotten about fighting back since the redheads started doing this to us." That wasn't fair, and he knew it, but he didn't much care about being fair. He'd come too close to dying too many times to care about being fair.

Addanz clucked reproachfully. Leudast remembered he had King Swemmel's ear. If he chose to remember a name, if he chose to mention that name to the king . . . if he chose to do that, Leudast would regret saying what he thought.

Perhaps the archmage of Unkerlant was about to reprove him. If he was, he never got the chance. He stiffened, his mouth hanging open. Then he groaned, as if a beam had burnt its way through his body. "They die," he croaked in a voice that suggested he might be dying himself. "Oh, they die."

"Mezentio's men at their butchery again?" Captain Hawart demanded.

Addanz managed to nod. "Aye," he gasped. "And we have not gathered enough men behind our line to try to block them altogether." He gasped again, as if he'd run a long way. "Didn't . . . expect them to smite again so soon."

Leudast knew what that had to mean, but didn't want to dwell on it. He didn't have time to dwell on it, either. He spoke urgently: "We'd better get out of this hole. When the Algarvians start their spells, places like this have a way of closing up all of a sudden."

"He's right," Magnulf said. He, Leudast, and Hawart started to scramble out. So did Addanz, but his effort was feeble and plainly hopeless. With a curse, Leudast jumped back into the mud at the bottom of the hole and heaved the archmage up to Magnulf and Hawart. Then he got out again himself.

"My thanks," Addanz said. He looked as if he'd just gone through a four-day battle. "You have no notion of what it is like for a mage to feel the tapped death throes of so many at once. How the Algarvian sorcerers do what they do without blazing out their minds is beyond me. Their hearts are surely colder than winter in Grelz."

However the Algarvian mages did what they did, they chose that moment to loose their latest sorcerous onslaught. The ground shuddered beneath Leudast like the body of a man shackled to the whipping post when the lash bites. He imagined he heard it groan like a man under the lash, too.

Flame sprang upward all around, as if fire mountains were erupting all over the field. Here and there, men caught in those flames screamed – but not for long. With a wet, sucking noise, the lips of the hole in the ground by Leudast's feet pulled together. They would have pulled together had he been down in the hole, too.

"You were right to get us out of there," Hawart said. "I hope we didn't have too many men trapped this time."

Addanz groaned once more, as he had a couple of minutes before. "Are they doing it again, sir mage?" Sergeant Magnulf asked. Leudast understood the alarm in his voice. The Algarvians had never struck two such sorcerous hammer blows back to back. Going through one was bad enough. Could flesh and blood – to say nothing of earth and stone – stand two?

But the archmage of Unkerlant shook his head. Speech, just then, seemed beyond him. His head was turned back toward the west, toward land Unkerlant still held, not toward the east and the Algarvians. "Oh, by the powers above," Leudast whispered.

"No," Addanz croaked – he could talk after all. "By the powers below. Murder piled on murder, and where shall it end?" Tears trickled through the dirt on his face: he was dirty by now, almost as dirty as the soldiers around him.

Captain Hawart spoke as gently as he could: "We're only doing it because the redheads did it first. We're doing it to try to defend ourselves. If Mezentio hadn't done it, we would never have taken it up."

All that was surely true. None of it seemed to console the archmage. He swayed back and forth, back and forth, as if mourning something he would never see again – a cleaner time, perhaps.

Leudast started to reach out, to set a hand on his shoulder. But he stopped with the motion stillborn. Sooner than it had under any of the

Algarvians' earlier sorcerous onslaughts, the ground steadied beneath him. The flames shrank. Most of them, though not all, vanished. "I think, sir mage, your comrades back there did us a good turn."

Only then did he think of the peasants – he supposed they were peasants – who must have perished in the Unkerlanter countermagic. He didn't suppose they thought Addanz's sorcerous comrades had done them a good turn.

"Here come the redheads," Magnulf said. Algarvian behemoths lumbered toward the battered Unkerlanter line. Footsoldiers trotted along to help protect them and to take advantage of the holes they tore. Horse and unicorn cavalry, swift but vulnerable, trailed after them. If the holes were big enough, the cavalry would tear through, too, and spread chaos in the Unkerlanter rear.

"Do you know, I think we may just give them a nasty surprise," Captain Hawart said. "This time, maybe they think they've kicked us harder than they really have."

Leudast wasn't thinking about that. He was scurrying toward the nearest hole he could find. Over his shoulder, he called, "Get the archmage out of here. This isn't his kind of fight."

It was Leudast's kind of fight. He started blazing at the advancing Algarvians. He wasn't the only one, either – far from it. The redheads started dropping. Even without their magic's working as well as they would have liked, they kept coming, though. Leudast had fought them for too long to think they were cowards. He wished they had been. Unkerlant would have suffered far less.

"Fall back!" Captain Hawart shouted, as he'd had to shout so many times. Unwillingly, Leudast obeyed lest the Algarvians get behind him. As clashes went these days, the Unkerlanters had done well. By the time nightfall brought fighting to an end, Leudast and his comrades had lost only about a mile of ground.

Every once in a while, a handful of Unkerlanter dragons would appear over Bishah, drop a few eggs, and then flee back toward the south. They did little damage. Hajjaj judged they didn't come intending to do much damage, but rather to remind the Zuwayzin that King Swemmel hadn't forgotten about them even if he was involved in bigger fights elsewhere.

After the third or fourth visit, the Zuwayzi foreign minister noticed something else: most of the eggs the Unkerlanters dropped fell near the Algarvian ministry. He remarked on that to Balastro when King Mezentio's minister to Zuwayza held a reception: "I think you are trying to gather all the diplomats in the city here together to be wiped out at one stroke. Are you sure you're not in King Swemmel's pay rather than that of your own sovereign?"

Count Balastro threw back his head and laughed uproariously. "Ah, your Excellency, you do both me and the Unkerlanter dragonfliers' aim too much credit," he said. Lamplight glittered off his badges of nobility and rank, and also off the silver threads that ran through his tunic. Far from being naked, as he'd come to Hajjaj's hillside estate, tonight he displayed full Algarvian plumage. That was literally true: in his hatband glowed three bright feathers from some bird or another out of tropical Siaulia.

Hajjaj minded clothes tonight less than usual. With the sun almost as low in the north as it ever went, the weather was cool by Zuwayzi standards, mild by those of Algarve. He didn't feel as if his own tunic and kilt – not nearly so splendid as Balastro's – were trying to smother him.

"Some date wine, your Excellency?" Balastro asked. "We have what the dealer assured me was an excellent vintage – if that's the word one uses for date wines – though I hope you will forgive me for admitting I have not sampled it myself."

"I may forgive you eventually, but not soon." Hajjaj smiled, and the Algarvian minister to Zuwayza laughed again. Balastro was a charming fellow: good-natured, clever, cultured. Hajjaj eyed him, wondering how he could be all he was and yet . . . But that would wait. It would have to wait.

For now, the Zuwayzi foreign minister ambled over to the bar. The Algarvian servitor behind it bowed and asked, "What may I get you, sir?" in fairly good Zuwayzi. That made him likelier to be a spy than a tapman by trade, but these days Hajjaj assumed everyone a spy till proved otherwise. Painful experience with his secretary had taught him that was safest.

Balastro was eyeing him, to see what he'd choose. As much to humor the redhead as to please his own palate, he did ask for date wine. When the servitor poured it from the jar, Hajjaj's eyes widened. "Pressed from the golden dates of Shamiyah!" he exclaimed, and the Algarvian nodded. Hajjaj bowed partly to him, partly to the wine. "You do me great honor indeed, and great harm to King Mezentio's purse."

He sipped the lovely, tawny stuff. Almost, he went over to grab Balastro by the scruff of the neck and force him to taste the wine himself. In the end, he refrained. Balastro would say all the right things, but he would not mean them. No man who came to dates after grapes could appreciate them as they deserved to be appreciated. Hajjaj could, and did.

Sipping, he eyed the gathering. It was not what it would have been in times of peace. Ansovald, the Unkerlanter minister, had been sent south over the border once more when war between his kingdom and Zuwayza resumed. The ministries of Forthweg and Sibiu and Valmiera and Jelgava stood empty, untenanted. Zuwayza was not formally at war with either Lagoas or Kuusamo, but Algarve was, and Balastro could hardly have been expected to invite his king's foes.

That left delegations from Algarve, from Yanina, from Gyongyos, from small, neutral Ortah (which no doubt thanked the powers above for the mountains and swamps that let her stay neutral), and, of course, from Zuwayza: Hajjaj was far from the only dark-skinned person making the best of clothes tonight.

The Yaninan minister to Zuwayza was a plump, bald little man named Iskakis. He had the hairiest ears of any man Hajjaj had ever seen. On his arm was his wife, who couldn't have had more than half his years, and whose elegant, sculpted features bore an expression of permanent discontent. Hajjaj knew – he wasn't sure whether she did, too – Iskakis had a taste for boys. For a man with that taste to be married to such a woman seemed a sad waste, but Hajjaj could do nothing about it.

Iskakis was telling a Gyongyosian almost twice his size about the triumphs Yaninan soldiers were running up in Unkerlant. Neither he nor the big, yellow-bearded man spoke Algarvian perfectly. Being from the other side of broad Derlavai, the Gyongyosian might not know most of the triumphs Iskakis was describing were as imaginary as the Yaninan's command of the perfect tense. The Yaninan minister did not brag of his kingdom's might to Algarvians.

Horthy, the Gyongyosian minister to Zuwayza, made his way over to Hajjaj. He was a big man, too, his beard streaked with gray. "You do not seem joyful, your Excellency," he said in classical Kaunian, the only tongue he and Hajjaj had in common.

Hearing Kaunian spoke inside the Algarvian ministry and using it himself made Hajjaj's mouth twist. Again, he put that aside, answering,

"I have been to too many of these gatherings to let one more overwhelm me. The wine is very good."

"Ah. Is it so? I understand that. I have not seen so many as you, sir — I honor your years — but I too have seen enough." Horthy pointed to the goblet. "And you say you esteem that wine?"

"I do." Hajjaj's smile held an edge of self-mockery. "But it is made from a fruit of my country" — to his annoyance, he couldn't come up with the classical Kaunian word for *dates* — "rather than grapes, and is not to everyone's taste."

"I shall try it," the Gyongyosian minister declared, as if Hajjaj had questioned his manhood. He marched over to the bar and returned with a goblet of Shamiyah wine. Raising it to his lips, he said, "May the stars grant you health and many more years." He sipped, paused thoughtfully, and sipped again. After another pause, he delivered his verdict: "I would not care to drink it and nothing else, but it goes well enough as a change from the usual."

"Most Zuwayzin say the same of grape wine," Hajjaj said. "As for myself, your Excellency, I agree with you."

"Count Balastro is a good host: he lays in something to please all of us." Horthy leaned forward, toward Hajjaj, and lowered his voice. "Now if only he had laid in victory, too."

"He did invite us here some little while ago," Hajjaj replied, also quietly. "Perhaps he expected to be celebrating victory tonight. And, in truth, Algarve has won great victories against Unkerlant — as has Gyongyos, of course, your Excellency." He bowed to Czaban, not wanting to slight his kingdom.

"Our war against Unkerlant is what our wars against Unkerlant have always been," the Gyongyosian minister replied with a massive shrug: "a slow, hard, halfhearted business. In that countryside, what else can it be?" He laughed, a rumble deep in his chest. "Do you see the irony, sir? We of Gyongyos pride ourselves — and with justice — on being a warrior race, yet the stars have decreed that we are, because of our placement in the uttermost west of Derlavai, hard pressed these days to fight a war worthy of our mettle."

Hajjaj raised an eyebrow. "I hope you will not take it amiss if I tell you that kingdoms may have troubles far worse than the one you name."

"I did not expect you to understand." Horthy sipped again at the date wine. "Few if any outside the dominions of Ekrekek Arpad do. The Algarvians sometimes come near to the thing, but even they . . ." He shook his big head.

"I believe they, at the moment, face a problem the opposite of yours," Hajjaj said. Now Horthy's eyebrows climbed toward his hairline. Hajjaj explained: "Do you not think Algarve may have undertaken a war beyond her mettle, however great that may be? – and I hasten to add I think it is very great indeed."

"I mean no offense when I say I believe you are mistaken," Horthy replied, "and is it not so that you may be speaking too soon? King Mezentio's armies still move westward."

"Aye, they do." Hajjaj let out a sigh far more wintry than even the coolest night in Zuwayza. "But do they move forward by virtue of their mettle, or through some other means? Consider the language we use, your Excellency. You spoke before of irony. Do you see no irony here?"

"Ahhh," Horthy said: a long, slow exhalation. "Now I take your meaning, where I did not before. Worse that the Unkerlanters slaughter their own, in my view."

"We differ," Hajjaj said politely. As soon as he could do so with propriety, he disengaged himself from the Gyongyosian minister.

"A toast!" Count Balastro called. He had to call several times to gain the attention of all the feasters. When at last he had it, he raised his glass on high. "To the grand and glorious triumph of those united against the vast barbarism that is Unkerlant!"

To refrain from drinking would have made Hajjaj stand out too much. *The things I do in the name of diplomacy*, he thought as he raised his goblet to his lips. He did not sip now, but tossed back the date wine. It was sweet and potent and mounted to his head. He found himself moving through the crowd toward Balastro.

"How now, your Excellency?" the Algarvian minister said with a wide, friendly smile. It faded as he got a good look at Hajjaj's face. "How now indeed, my friend?" Balastro asked. "What troubles you?"

He *was* Hajjaj's friend. That made what the Zuwayzi had to say harder. He spoke anyhow, though in a voice he hoped only Balastro would hear: "Shall we also drink a toast to the vast barbarism that is Algarve?"

Balastro did not pretend to be ignorant of what Hajjaj was talking about. For that, Hajjaj gave him reluctant credit. "We do what we must do to win the war," Balastro said. "And the Kaunians have long oppressed us. You've lived in Algarve; you know that for yourself. Why blame us and not them?"

"When your armies broke into the Marquisate of Rivaroli, which Valmiera took from you – unjustly, in my view – after the Six Years' War, did your foes massacre the Algarvians there to gain the sorcerous power that might have thrown you back?" Hajjaj asked. He answered his own question: "They did not. And they could have, as you must admit."

"What they did to us in the years before that was as bad as a massacre," Balastro said. "For long and long, we fought among ourselves, Kaunian cat's-paws. Let people wail and moan as they please, your Excellency. I feel not the least bit of guilt." He threw out his chest and looked fierce.

"I am sorry for you, then," Hajjaj said sadly, and turned away.

"We grow strong, and you grow strong with us, riding on our backs," Balastro said. "Are you not ungrateful to complain about the road when you wanted revenge on Unkerlant?"

Hajjaj turned back. That held enough truth to sting. "Who now will want revenge on Algarve, your Excellency, and for what good reasons?" he asked.

Balastro's shrug was a masterpiece of both indifference and Algarvian theatricality. "My dear fellow, it will matter very little once we are the masters of Derlavai. Whoever wants revenge on us will no more be able to have it than a dog howling at the moon can make it come down for him."

"Surely the lords of the Kaunian Empire, at the height of their glory, thought the same," Hajjaj replied, and had the doubtful pleasure of seeing Balastro look very indignant indeed.

Cornelu felt no small pride at finally making it down into Tirgoviste town. He even had Giurgiu's leave to spend an extra couple of days there before returning to the woodcutting gang. He hadn't had to offer to fight the gang boss again to get it, either. He'd lost their last encounter, but had won a measure of respect.

And so now, bundled up against the icy south wind, he walked along the edge of the harbor. He might look like a rustic in town to sell firewood, but he surveyed the quays with a practiced eye. The Algarvians didn't have so heavy a naval presence here as Sibiu had, but he wouldn't have wanted to try breaking into the harbor against what they did have.

He cursed under his breath: cursed the surprise that had let Mezentio's men overpower his kingdom, and cursed their cleverness, too. How he wished a storm had blown up while their sailing ships were on the sea! But wishes were useless things. No one could change what had been, not the greatest mage ever born.

He ambled along as if he hadn't a thought in his head, and presently paused by the leviathan pens. An Algarvian sailor was tossing fish from a bucket to a leviathan not a quarter so fine as Eforiel had been. Cornelu paused to watch the fellow at his work. He paused too long. The sailor noticed him and growled, "Get moving, you stinking Sib, before we find out how this fellow likes *your* taste."

Cornelu probably would have understood that without speaking Algarvian. Were he a woodcutter who'd understood it, what would he do? He did it: he nodded, looked frightened, and hurried away. Behind him, the Algarvian laughed. Cornelu knew what a leviathan's jaws could do to a man. He wished the beast in the pen would do that to the sailor: one more wish he wouldn't see fulfilled.

Why do I linger here? he wondered. He'd gathered a little intelligence. To whom could he report it? No one — not a Lagoan, not a Sibian. All he'd done was briefly become the ghost of what he'd once been.

After starting toward a dockside eatery, he checked himself. He'd eaten there too often back in the days when Sibiu was a free kingdom, and he an officer in King Burebistu's service. Someone might recognize him in spite of his poorly shaved chin and shabby clothes. Most Sibians loathed their Algarvian occupiers. A few, though . . . The posters calling for Sibians to join the fight against Unkerlant were still pasted to walls and fences. King Mezentio had to be drawing recruits from the five islands of Sibiu. That he was shamed Cornelu.

Farther inland, he could crumble twice-baked bread into pea soup at a place where he'd never gone while wearing Sibiu's uniform. The meal he got showed he'd known what he was doing when he stayed away, too. But it made his belly stop growling like an angry dog. He set silver on the table and stalked out.

Before long, he found himself walking along his own street. That was stupidly dangerous, and he knew it. Old neighbors were far likelier to know him for who and what he was than were waiters at a seaside eatery. He couldn't help himself, though.

There stood his house. It looked very much as it always had. The flowers in front of it were dead and the grass yellow and dying, but that happened every winter. Smoke rose from the chimney. Someone was at home. Costache? Just Costache? Well, just Costache and Brindza? Or was one of the Algarvian officers quartered there, or more than one, at the house, too?

If one of the Algarvians answered, he could beg and then shamble away. They'd be none the wiser. But if it was Costache, if it was Costache . . . He'd posted a note saying he was coming into town and suggesting they meet tomorrow. To protect her and himself, he'd signed it *Your country cousin* and used a false name. She would know his hand.

All at once, tomorrow seemed impossibly far away. He started up his own walk. Aye, a risk, but one he couldn't help taking.

He was about to set his foot on the first step leading up to the porch when a man spoke inside the house. Those trilling "r"s could only come from an Algarvian's mouth. Cornelu hesitated, hating himself for hesitating. But the risk had just gone up.

As he was about to go on despite that risk, Costache laughed. She'd always had an easy, friendly laugh. It had brightened Cornelu's day whenever he heard it. Now he heard her lightly giving it to one of King Mezentio's men. That wounded him almost as much as if he'd peeked in their bedroom window and seen her limbs entwined with the Algarvian's in the act of love.

He turned away, staggering a little, as if he'd taken a beam from a stick. But his stride firmed faster than it would have after a physical wound. He no longer worried about being recognized; who would know him with this black scowl distorting his features?

"Tomorrow," he muttered under his breath as he hurried away from his neighborhood. Tomorrow, if the powers above were kind, he'd see his wife. Maybe she would have an explanation that satisfied him.

For the life of him, he couldn't imagine what it would be.

With the remains of naval discipline, he walked past half a dozen taverns. If he started drinking, he would either drink himself blind or drink himself angry. He could easily see himself storming up to his own front door with ale or spirits coursing through him and trying to kill all the Algarvians in his house, or maybe trying to slap Costache around for not being distant enough to them. That he could also see the tragedy that would follow immediately thereafter made the picture only a little less tempting.

He bought a sack of crumbs at the edge of a park and tossed them to pigeons and sparrows till late autumn's early dusk came. A couple of Algarvian soldiers walked by, but they didn't bother him. He wasn't the only fellow passing time in the park feeding the birds.

As soon as the sun sank below the northwestern horizon, the wind picked up. It seemed to blow straight through him, and carried the bite of the land of the Ice People, where it had originated. It blew the park empty in short order. Cornelu hoped the others who were leaving had better places to go than he.

He ate fried clams and allowed himself one mug of ale at a tavern that also sold meals. The clams weren't bad, but the ale had been watered to the point where two or three mugs would have done little to him. Next door stood a rooming house where he bought a cubicle for the night. The tiny chamber barely had room for the bed and the cheap nightstand that held a cup, basin, and pitcher.

The mattress smelled sour when he lay down on it. He might have done better rolled in a blanket in the park. But he might not have, too; the Algarvians might have picked him up for being out after curfew. He didn't want to fall into their hands for any reason. Eventually, he slept.

It was still dark when he woke. The clouds in the northeast had gone from black to dull gray, though, so dawn wasn't far away. He scratched, hoping the nasty bed didn't have bugs in it, then got dressed, went downstairs, and walked out of the rooming house. A new clerk had come on duty sometime in the night, but he looked as sullen and indifferent as the fellow from whom Cornelu had rented his little room.

He went back to the tavern. It was already crowded with fishermen fortifying themselves for the day ahead. The fried bread Cornelu ordered sat like a boulder in his stomach. The only resemblance the murky brown liquid the tavern served bore to tea was that it was hot. He drank it without complaint. On a morning like this, heat sufficed.

After stretching breakfast till sunrise, Cornelu went back to the park. A Sibian constable strolling through looked at him as if he were crazy, even after he displayed the bag of crumbs, still half full. The birds appreciated him, though, and came close to feeding right from his hand.

He stretched out the bread crumbs, too, making them last till nearly noon. Then he got up, brushed his hands on his kilt, and left the park for the short walk to the bell tower at the edge of Tirgoviste's old market square. He'd asked Costache to meet him there. "She'd better," he said as he made his way through the square. "By the powers above, she'd better."

Clang! Clang! The bells blared out noon just as Cornelu got to the base of the tower. He looked around. The square wasn't crowded, not the way it would have been before the Algarvians came, but he didn't see his wife.

And then he did. His heart leaped. Here she came, striding with determination across the square. If he could be alone with her, even for a few minutes . . . But he wouldn't be, for she was pushing the baby carriage ahead of her. Brindza's head popped up as she looked out. Cornelu knew he shouldn't hate his daughter, but remembering that wasn't easy when she kept coming between him and Costache.

He knew better than to show what was going through his mind. He smiled and waved and stepped forward to embrace her. He squeezed her to him. She raised her mouth to his. After a long, breathless kiss, he murmured, "Oh, it's good to see you again." *See you* wasn't exactly what he meant. *Feel you* came closer.

"And you," Costache said, a quaver in her voice that sent tingles through Cornelu. She looked him over with an expression he recognized: comparing what she recalled to what she saw. After a moment, she clucked in distress. "You've got so thin and hard-looking."

"I can't help it," he answered. "I've been working hard."

"Mama," Brindza said, and then, "Up." King Burebistu could have given no more imperious command.

Costache picked up her daughter – *my daughter, too*, Cornelu reminded himself. His wife looked tired. He'd thought that the first time he saw her after coming back to Tirgoviste. He said, "I wish you could have found a way to leave her at home."

She shook her head. "Mezentio's men won't take care of her for me, curse them. I've asked."

"Aye, curse them," Cornelu agreed. He eyed his wife again. "But you were laughing with one of them yesterday."

"How do you know that?" Costache asked in surprise. When he told her, she went pale. "I'm so glad you didn't knock!" she exclaimed. "All three of them were there. You'd be in a captives' camp now."

"Every day I'm away from you, I feel like I'm in a captives' camp," Cornelu complained. "This whole island is a captives' camp. This whole kingdom is a captives' camp. What else would you call it?"

Costache gave back a pace before his fury. Brindza stared at him with wide green eyes, the same shade as her mother's. After a moment, Costache said, "Things are hard, aye, but they're worse in the camps. When the Algarvians let people out of them, they come back as skeletons. I think half the reason Mezentio's men turn them loose is to frighten other people."

She spoke calmly, reasonably, logically. She made good sense. She said not a word Cornelu cared to hear. "Have you any notion of how much I want you?" he burst out.

"Aye," his wife answered in a low voice, "but I don't know when we can. I don't know if we'll ever be able to, not till the war is over, if it ever is."

Cornelu started to slap her for saying such a thing. Before the motion was well begun, though, he turned it into a quick spin away from Costache. He'd never imagined he could wish he'd stayed up in the hills chopping wood, but he did.

Snow blew into Tealdo's face. It numbed his left side worse than his right, for he still marched northwest, in the direction of Cottbus, while the wind roared up from the southwest, from the austral continent and the ice-clogged Narrow Sea. He wasn't used to snow; growing up in the north of Algarve, he'd seen it but seldom before joining King Mezentio's army. His education in such matters was advancing faster than he'd ever wanted.

Beside him, Trasone let out a chuckle: either that or Tealdo's friend was starting to come down with pneumonia. "You look like a scarecrow," Trasone said, raising his voice to be heard over the endless ravening wind.

"Heh," Tealdo answered. "Aye, it's too true. What we both look like is a couple of madmen who bought out a rummage sale."

"Everybody in the whole regiment looks the same way," Trasone said.

"If we'd had some decent winter gear shipped out to us, we wouldn't have had to steal from every Unkerlanter village we went through, either."

An inspecting officer would have had trouble proving he was even in uniform. He had on a long Unkerlanter tunic over his short tunic and kilt, a horse blanket over that, and a rabbit fur cap on his head in place of the dapper but not nearly warm enough hat he'd been issued. Trasone's garb was similarly outlandish.

"Winter gear?" Trasone chuckled again, sounding even more ghastly than before. "They're having trouble shipping Kaunians forward to kill, and you're worrying about winter gear? Too stinking many Unkerlanters running around loose behind us, and with what they do to ley lines, it's like the powers below have been eating them."

"That's all so, no doubt about it." Tealdo paused to knock snow – and possibly frozen snot with it – out of his mustache. "But if I freeze to death, I'm not going to care about the miserable Kaunians."

"I don't know if we'd have gotten as far as we have without slaughtering them," Trasone said.

"You just said they're having trouble bringing the blond buggers forward, but we're still advancing," Tealdo said. "What does that tell you about how much difference they've made?"

Trasone shook his head, which made the earflaps of his own looted fur cap flop up and down. "You won't sneak that by me so easy. Now that it's snowing, the ground's frozen up, and our behemoths can get going again."

As if to prove his point, a couple of the big beasts trotted past the footsoldiers. The behemoths were draped in stolen blankets, too. Their riders had covered them in preference to covering themselves. If the behemoths froze to death, their crewmen turned into footsoldiers, and not very useful footsoldiers at that. One of the men waved a mittened hand to Tealdo and Trasone. Tealdo waved back. He wore mittens, too, which kept the fellow on the behemoth from seeing the gesture he shaped.

He went back to the argument with Trasone: "The footing's better for the Unkerlanter behemoths, too, you know."

"Ahh, that doesn't help them so much," Trasone said with a scornful wave. "The Unkerlanters mostly don't know what to do with behemoths even when the ground is all right. A good thing, too, or we'd both likely be dead by now."

Tealdo thought about rising to that even though he knew it was true. But he saw a couple of men standing by a series of low rises in the snow. He needed a moment to realize the men were mages; they looked as draggled as everyone else in the Algarvian army these days. "What's toward?" he called to them.

"See for yourself," one of them answered, though the wind almost blew his words away from Tealdo. Curious, Tealdo ambled over. The mage kicked at one of the ridges in the snow. It turned out to be the body of an Unkerlanter: not a soldier, but a peasant woman. Her throat had been cut. The mage said, "This is how they fight back against us – with their folk as victims."

"Me, I'd sooner kill Kaunians than Algarvians – I'll say that," Tealdo remarked. "But if we're doing it and now they're doing it, too, wouldn't it be better if both sides stopped, since it's pretty much evened out?"

"If one side stopped and not the other, that could mean – would mean – disaster," the mage said. "Sometimes climbing on to a wolf is easier than climbing off again."

"Maybe somebody should have thought of that before we went in and got into this lousy war with Unkerlant in the first place," Tealdo said. "This is a cursed big wolf, and I ought to know. I've walked every miserable inch of the way from the Yaninan border to here."

"It is the inches you have yet to walk that truly matter," the mage said. "What could be more important than taking Cottbus?"

Staying alive, Tealdo thought. He kept that to himself, judging he'd already pushed the mage about as far as he could. He started marching once more, trotting a little to catch up to Trasone. Snow kept swirling down. The stuff was very pretty to watch, but Tealdo wouldn't have been sorry never to see it again.

By the time evening came, he had to lift up his foot at every step, which made him slow and awkward despite the hard ground under his feet. Captain Galafrone chose a grove of firs as a halting place. Tealdo had hoped for a village, but this would do; the trees grew close enough together to make a good windbreak. He sat down on the leeward side of one of the first. "This isn't as easy as they thought it would be back home," he said.

Captain Galafrone looked like an old man now. He'd given everything his kingdom asked of him and more, but he had very little left to give. Wearily, he said, "Can somebody get a fire going before we all freeze to death?" With the fir trees breaking the force of the wind and keeping off a good bit of the snow, Tealdo used his stick to start a small blaze. It wasn't really enough to keep the soldiers warm, but it did make them feel a little better.

Somebody said, "After we take Cottbus and drive King Swemmel off into the wilderness, this will seem worthwhile."

"My arse," Trasone exclaimed. "This'll be fornicating dreadful if we look back on it a hundred years from now. And half of Unkerlant's a fornicating wilderness. What do you call this where we're at right now, a fornicating playground?"

"We still have to take Cottbus," Galafrone said, rallying a little at the sight of the flames. "I'd like to see Swemmel try and fight a war without the place."

"Maybe, just maybe," Tealdo said in speculative tones, "we could spend some time out of the line, let some other people take it on the chin for a while."

"Can't let our mates down," Galafrone said reproachfully.

"No, I suppose not," Tealdo agreed, and his comrades nodded. He went on, "Not letting my mates down is about the only reason I see for going forward any more. I don't care one pile of behemoth dung for the greater glory of Algarve, I'll tell you that." The rest of the redheaded soldiers nodded again.

Galafrone said, "Anybody who went through the Six Years' War knows what glory's worth – not even a pile of shit, like you said. But we lost that war, and all our neighbors made us pay. If we don't want to pay again, we'd better win this one."

"Oh, aye," Tealdo said. "I remember how glad they were when we marched into the Duchy of Bari. That started us getting our own back." He shook his head in slow, chilly wonder. "Two years ago now, two years and more. A lot's happened since."

"I wonder how glad the folk of Bari are now that we marched in then," Trasone said. "Now they get the joys of fighting in Unkerlant, too. That wasn't the first thing on their minds back then, I bet."

"First thing on their minds then was screwing us till we couldn't see straight." Fond reminiscence filled Sergeant Panfilo's voice. "I like the way they thought."

Captain Galafrone climbed to his feet. "Like Tealdo says, that was a while ago now. Us, we've still got a war to fight. Come on, let's go do it."

As soon as the Algarvians came out of the shelter of the wood, Unkerlanters started blazing at them from behind snow-covered bushes. Tealdo threw himself down on his belly in the snow. A beam made steam hiss up from the white powder a couple of feet away from him. When he blazed back, more steam rose from the cover King Swemmel's men were using.

He thought the troopers under Galafrone's command outnumbered their Unkerlanter foes. Galafrone evidently thought the same thing, for he sent out flanking parties to left and right to make the Unkerlanters give ground or risk being blazed from three sides at once. A couple of his men fell, but more gained the positions to which they'd been running.

And then a pair of Algarvian behemoths came up from the southeast. The ground was hard now, but so much snow had fallen that they had to plant their feet with care. One of them bore a heavy stick on its back. That beam had no trouble punching through either the snow still falling or the snow on the bushes that had helped shield the enemy soldiers. One Unkerlanter after another fell.

The other behemoth carried an egg-tosser. When bursts of sorcerous energy sent snow and frozen dirt flying, the Unkerlanters decided they'd had enough and fled for the next patch of woods. More eggs pursued them. So did beams from the Algarvians' sticks.

"Obliged!" Tealdo shouted back toward the behemoths and their crews. One of the soldiers on the behemoth with a heavy stick waved his fur hat in reply.

"I'd be even more obliged if they'd got here sooner," Trasone said as he and his comrades rose to go after the Unkerlanters.

"So would I, but they can't be having an easy time there," Tealdo said. "Look how much trouble it is for them to move in deep snow."

"This is Unkerlant. This is winter, or near enough as makes no difference," Trasone said. "The snow's not going to up and disappear, not for a cursed long time it's not. How much good are the behemoths going to be till then?"

"Not as much as we'd like, odds are," Tealdo replied. "But the Unkerlanters won't have it any easier than we do."

"I want them to have it harder than we do, curse 'em up one side and down the other," Trasone said. "I want to lick the whoresons out of Cottbus, I want to help make sure they can't give us any trouble for a long time afterwards, and then, by the powers above, I want to go home. A lot of places in Algarve, it hardly snows at all."

"I know – I'm from one of them," Tealdo said wistfully. "Come on. Before we lick them out of Cottbus, we've got to lick them out of those woods there."

Before the Algarvians went in after the Unkerlanters, the behemoth with the egg-tosser flung death in among the trees. But it was tossing blind, without any visible targets. King Swemmel's men still showed plenty of fight when the troopers who followed Galafrone came to close quarters with them. Some of the fighting in the shadow of the pines and birches was with knives and with sticks swung club-fashion; men came on enemies too close to let them swing up their sticks and blaze.

A few Unkerlanters surrendered. More, though, fought till they were killed or retreated northwest, to take yet another stab somewhere else at holding the Algarvians away from Cottbus. When Galafrone's men emerged to continue the pursuit, Unkerlanter egg-tossers made them dive for cover.

"I enjoy this so much, don't you?" Trasone said, lifting his mouth an inch or so off the snow to speak.

"Aye, of course," Tealdo answered. "But we're still moving ahead, powers above be praised. We'll get there yet."

Nine

Halfway along the road from Gromheort to the village of Hwinca, the paving gave out. Bembo discovered that the hard way, by going into the mud almost up to his boot tops. Cursing, the Algarvian constable slogged through the soggy patch and up on to drier – if no more paved – ground.

"Don't blaze my ears on account of it," advised Oraste, whose boots were also befouled. "Take it out on the Kaunians when we finally get to this miserable place."

"I will, by the powers above," Bembo growled. "If it weren't for them, I'd be sitting back in the barracks, all warm and cozy." He was always ready to feel sorry for himself. "As a matter of fact, if it weren't for those miserable buggers, we wouldn't have a war, and I'd be back in Tricarico, happy as a clam at the beach, and not stuck here in stinking Forthweg."

Sergeant Pesaro looked over at him. "Remember, while you're cursing the Kaunians, odds are they're cursing us, too. I don't expect they'll be as easy to round up here as they were in that Oyngestun place – too many stories going around about what happens after they go west."

"They deserve it," Oraste said. "Bembo's right, Sergeant – weren't for them, we wouldn't have a war."

Bembo wondered if Oraste was feeling well. The dour constable hardly ever agreed with him. Bembo also wondered if the Kaunians really deserved it. Most of the time, he tried not to wonder about that. It did no good. He'd been ordered to gather them together and send them off to the west. He couldn't do anything about what happened to them afterwards. What point, then, to puzzling over who deserved what?

The constables tramped through a hamlet of half a dozen houses. An old woman on her knees in an herb garden looked up as they went. Her nose was like a sickle blade. Her chin almost met it. Her face was a tight-woven net of wrinkles. Her smile . . . Her smile chilled Bembo's heart. He'd seen some raddled old procuresses in his day, but none who could match the ancient, exultant evil this Forthwegian crone showed.

"No blonds here," she called in bad Algarvian made worse by her being almost toothless. "Blonds *there*." She pointed north, up the road toward Hwinca.

"Aye, granny, we know," Pesaro answered. With a chortle and a nasty smirk, the peasant woman went back to her weeding.

Oraste chuckled. "She loves Kaunians, too, just as much as we do."

"I noticed," Bembo said dryly. "A lot of Forthwegians do, don't they?"

"Keep moving, there," Pesaro said. He was puffing and sweating himself; he'd done more marching since coming to Forthweg than in all the years since he'd made sergeant and comfortably ensconced himself behind the station-house desk back in Tricarico. But he kept on putting one big foot in front of the other, steady as a stream, inevitable as an avalanche. As for Bembo, he wanted a breather. Pesaro didn't give him one.

It was most of an hour later when Oraste pointed ahead and said, "There. That must be the place. Miserable-looking little dump, isn't it? How many are we supposed to take out of it, Sergeant?"

"Twenty." Pesaro grunted. "Hardly looks like it's got twenty people in it, does it, let alone twenty Kaunians? But if we don't bring back twenty, we get blamed." He kicked a clod of dirt. "Life's not fair."

"Sergeant?" That was a youngish constable named Almonio. Bembo looked at him in some surprise; he hardly ever said anything.

"What is it?" Pesaro sounded surprised, too.

"Sergeant . . ." Now that he had spoken, Almonio looked as if he wished he hadn't. He marched along for several paces before going on, "When we get into this Hwinca place, Sergeant, may I have your leave not to help round up these Kaunians?"

"What's this?" Sergeant Pesaro studied him as if he were a double rainbow or a golden unicorn or some other astonishing freak of nature. Pesaro's beefy face clouded. "You telling me you haven't got the stomach for it?"

Miserably, Almonio nodded. "Aye, I think that's what it is. I know what's going to happen to the whoresons once we take 'em, and I don't much want to be a part of it."

Bembo's eyes got wider and wider as he listened. "Powers above," he whispered to Oraste, "the sergeant'll tear him limb from limb."

"Aye, so he will." Oraste sounded as if he was looking forward to it.

Pesaro, though, seemed more curious than furious. "Suppose we're rounding up the blonds and they try to fight us? What are you going to do then, Almonio? You going to stand there and let the Kaunians kill your comrades?"

"Of course not, Sergeant," Almonio answered. "I just don't want to have to drag them out of their houses, that's all. It's a filthy business."

"War is a filthy business," Pesaro said, but he still didn't sound angry. He rubbed his chins as he thought. At last, he pointed toward the reluctant constable. "All right, Almonio, here's what you'll do for today: you'll stand guard while the rest of us winkle out the Kaunians. If they give you trouble – if they even look like they might give any trouble – you start blazing. Have you got that?"

"Aye, Sergeant." Almonio stopped marching for a moment so he could bow. "I thank you, Sergeant."

"Don't thank me too much," Pesaro answered. "And, by the powers above, keep your cursed mouth shut, or we're both in hot water." He shook his head. "Warm water would feel good right now, but not that hot."

Well, well – isn't that interesting? Bembo thought. *I've got a hold on Pesaro, if I ever want one.* He lifted off his hat so he could scratch his head. The way things were, he couldn't see wanting one. He'd spent years getting used to Pesaro – and getting Pesaro used to him. Any other sergeant was too likely to be harder on him. He laughed a sour laugh. Wasn't that the way of the world? – come up with something that looked good and then decide you couldn't use it.

Into Hwinca marched the constabulary squad. The village was smaller and dingier than Oyngestun; it didn't lie on a ley line, and so seemed more a product of a distant time than Oyngestun had. And Oyngestun, as far as Bembo was concerned, hadn't been anything to write home about, either.

He didn't write home very often, anyhow. He'd quarreled endlessly with his father before going out on his own; they still had little to do with each other. His sister had quarreled with the old man, too. But Lanfusa's escape had been to marry a furrier who was now on his way to being rich. She didn't like being reminded her brother was only a constable. If he sent a letter to Saffa, she might write back. She was likelier to fall over dead from shock, though.

A few Forthwegians nodded to the constables. One of them grinned and winked and clapped his hands, almost as if he were an Algarvian. The leer on his face made Bembo remember that what he was doing in Forthweg probably ought not to go down in writing to anyone.

"Kaunians, come forth!" Pesaro shouted in a great voice when he got to Hwinca's village square. Evodio turned his words from Algarvian into classical Kaunian. That was the tongue the blonds hereabouts still spoke, or near enough as to make no difference.

No matter what language the order came in, the Kaunians ignored it. Bembo turned to Oraste. "There – you see? They've got a notion of what's going to happen to them. They won't come out all by themselves, not any more. We're going to have to go in after 'em. It'll be a lot of extra work from now on."

Oraste hefted his stick. "Liable to be dangerous work, too. If they figure they're going to get shipped west anyhow, who's to say they won't decide they've got nothing to lose and try and take some of us with 'em?"

"Aye." That had occurred to Bembo, too. He wished it hadn't.

Pesaro shouted again. His voice echoed off the houses and shops facing the square. Again, Evodio translated his words into classical Kaunian. Again, none of the yellow-haired men and women in Hwinca came forth. "Well, we'll have to do it the hard way," Pesaro said. His chuckle had a nasty edge. "You know what, though? I don't think it'll be too hard." He beckoned to the Forthwegian who'd applauded the constables' arrival. "Come here, pal. Aye, you. You speak Algarvian?"

With a show of regret, the villager shook his head. Pesaro looked exasperated. Neither he nor any of his men spoke any Forthwegian past what little they'd picked up since coming from Tricarico. Evodio said, "I'll bet he speaks Kaunian, Sergeant."

"Find out," Pesaro said. Sure enough, intelligence lit upon the Forthwegian's face. Pesaro nodded. "Good. Tell him we'll pay him – doesn't have to be anything much, or I'm a Yaninan – if he'll show us which houses the Kaunians live in."

That fellow turned out not to be the only villager who spoke Kaunian; three or four others clamored for a share of the reward, too. Bembo and Oraste followed one of them to a house that didn't look any different from those to either side of it. The Forthwegian pointed at the door, as dramatically as if he were a hunting dog pointing at a woodcock.

"Kaunians, come forth!" the two constables shouted together. Nobody came forth. Bembo and Oraste looked at each other. They drew back a couple of paces, then slammed the door with their shoulders. It flew inward, the brackets in which its bar rested pulled out of the wall. Bembo sprawled on his hands and knees in the front hall: he'd expected to bounce off his first try. Oraste kept his feet, but barely.

"They'll pay for that, the scum," Bembo muttered as he got to his feet. "Come on, let's turn this place inside out."

Sticks at the ready, he and Oraste swept through the house. They didn't have to search long or hard: they found the Kaunians – a man and woman of about Bembo's age, with two little girls too young to be interesting – cowering in a pantry in the kitchen. Oraste gestured with his stick. "Come out, every cursed one of you!" he growled.

"Aye, sir," said the man, in decent Algarvian. He was, Bembo judged, frightened almost out of his wits, but doing his best not to show it for the sake of his family. In a low, urgent voice, he went on, "Whatever you want so you will say you could not find us, I will give it to you. I have money. I am not a poor man. All of it is yours – only let us live."

"Kaunian," Oraste said: an all-inclusive rejection. Bembo gave his comrade a dirty look. He'd wanted to see how much the blond would offer. But he couldn't get away with that if Oraste didn't go along.

The yellow-haired man whispered something to his wife. She bit her lip, but nodded. "Not money, then," the Kaunian man said rapidly, desperately. "But anything you want. Anything." He gestured to the woman. She undid the top toggle of her tunic. She wasn't bad-looking – she wasn't bad-looking at all – but. . . .

"Out in the street, all of you," Bembo barked. He was disgusted at himself, but more disgusted at the Kaunians for sinking so low and for reminding him how low he'd sunk. The blond man sighed. Now that he saw it was hopeless, he regained a measure of the dignity he'd thrown away. He put his arms around his daughters and shepherded them out. His wife set her tunic to rights before following.

"Good. You've got four," Pesaro said, seeing the Kaunians Bembo and Oraste had found. A double handful more already stood glumly in the square. Before long, the constables had their quota from Hwinca.

Pesaro paid the Forthwegians who'd helped his men round up the blonds. One of the villagers said something in Kaunian as he got his money. Evodio translated: "He wants to know why we're only taking this many, why we're not cleaning out all of them."

"Tell him this is what we got ordered to do, so this is what we're doing," Pesaro answered. "It's just our job." That was how he thought of it, too. Almonio's conscience needed more of a shield. It all came down to the same thing in the end, though. The constables marched the Kaunians off toward Gromheort, off toward the caravans that would take them west.

Traku shook his head back and forth, back and forth, a man seemingly caught in the grip of nightmare. Before throwing his hands in the air in despair, he stared toward his son. "I have more cursed orders than I know what to do with," he moaned.

They'd been facing different problems a few weeks before. "That one Algarvian liked the outfit you made for him, so he went and told his friends," Talsu answered. "By everything I've seen, the redheads do like to talk."

"I wouldn't mind if . . ." Traku corrected himself: "I wouldn't mind *so much* if I didn't think all the talk going through Skrunda had to have some truth behind it. But if I'm slaving for the Algarvians while they're doing horrible things to our folk, that's hard to stomach."

"Aye," Talsu said, "but you know how rumors are. One day everybody says this was bound to happen, the next day it's that, and then the day after it's something else. In the war, the Algarvians weren't any worse than we were, and that's the truth. They might have been better." He remembered Colonel Dzirnavu and the captive Algarvian woman he'd taken into his pavilion. Not a soul in the regiment had shed a tear when she cut Dzirnavu's fat throat.

"Here's hoping you're right," Traku said. "I don't know that I think you are, but here's hoping."

Before he or Talsu could say anything further, the door to the tailor's shop opened and an Algarvian officer came inside. Not just *an* Algarvian officer, Talsu saw, but *the* Algarvian officer: the one who'd made Traku popular among his countrymen garrisoned in Skrunda. "Good day, sir," Talsu said, and then, on taking a closer look, "Are you all right?"

"All right? Of course I am all right. Why shouldn't I be all right?" the redhead said in his accented Jelgavan. He staggered rather than walking, red tracked his eyes, and the stench of strong spirits came off him in waves. Pointing a peremptory finger at Traku, he said, "My good man, I require a cloak of the heaviest stuff you can buy, and I require it as soon as you can possibly turn it out, which had better be pretty cursed quick, do you hear me?"

"Aye, sir, I do," Traku said, "though if you'll forgive my saying so, a heavy cloak isn't the sort of garment you'll get much use from in Jelgava."

"Jelgava?" the Algarvian officer cried. "Jelgava?" He might never have heard of the kingdom before. "Who said anything about cursed Jelgava? They're shipping me to Unkerlant, is what they're doing. They haven't had enough men killed there to satisfy them yet, so they're going to try to put me on the list, too. Go ahead, tell me I won't need a cloak like that in Unkerlant."

"It's supposed to be a cold kingdom, for true." Traku turned brisk. "Now, then, sir, what will you pay me for such a cloak?"

"As if money matters, when I am going to Unkerlant!" the Algarvian exclaimed. As far as Talsu was concerned, that proved how drunk he was: money always mattered. The redhead fumbled about in his belt pouch and set two goldpieces on the counter in front of Traku. "There! Does that satisfy you?"

"Aye," Traku answered in a strangled voice. Talsu stared at the gold coins, both stamped with King Mezentio's beaky visage. He didn't blame his father for sounding astonished. He couldn't remember the last time he'd seen gold. Traku gathered himself and asked, "When will you require the cloak, sir?"

"Day after tomorrow – no later," the Algarvian answered. "The cursed ley-line caravan leaves the day after that. Unkerlant!" It was almost a howl of despair. "What did I do to make someone want to send me to Unkerlant?"

"Maybe Algarve is running short on soldiers," Talsu said. He didn't want to sound as if he was gloating, but had trouble doing anything else. His father hissed at him in alarm, lest he queer the bargain. Traku might not want to serve the Algarvians, but he didn't mind taking their money.

Fortunately, the officer paid Talsu's tone no mind. "*Someone* still has to garrison Jelgava," he said. "It might as well be me."

This time, Talsu had the sense to keep his mouth shut. Traku said, "A cloak is not a complicated garment. I can make one for you in two days, sir. The heaviest wool I can lay my hands on, is that right?"

"Just exactly right." The Algarvian officer snapped his fingers. "The heaviest light-colored wool you can lay your hands on. I don't care to stand out like a lump of coal against the stinking snowfields."

"Aye," Traku said tonelessly. When Talsu glanced his father's way, Traku wouldn't meet his eye. Had he planned on giving the Algarvian a black cloak in the hope that it would get him killed? Talsu couldn't prove it, and he couldn't ask, either, no matter how drunk the redhead was. The fellow might note what he said and might remember it after leaving.

For now, the Algarvian just stood there, swaying gently. "Unkerlant," he said again, his voice a mournful bleat. "What did I do to deserve being sent to Unkerlant?"

"I couldn't say, sir," Traku replied. "I'll have your cloak ready day after tomorrow. Thick wool, light-colored. A very good day to you."

He was, Talsu realized, trying to get the officer out of the shop. Rather to Talsu's surprise, the Algarvian took the hint, too. He lurched back out on to the street, slamming the door behind him. When he was gone, Talsu stared at the coins he'd set on the counter. "Gold, Father," he murmured.

"Aye, and enough to buy him half a dozen cloaks," Traku answered. "Well, I'll give him a good one. I could face it with fur – powers above, I could cursed near face it with ermine – but he didn't ask for that, so he'll have to do without."

"You ought to give him something shoddy," Talsu said. "Who cares if the whoreson freezes? He'll do it a long way from here."

"Maybe I ought to, but I won't," his father said. "My pride won't let me. I'll dicker hard on price, but not on the quality of the goods once I have a price, and besides, the lousy bugger may write to his friends back here, or he may even come back here himself one day. The Algarvians are still moving ahead, or that's what the news sheets say, anyhow."

"They say whatever the Algarvians want them to say," Talsu pointed out. "They say Mainardo's the best king Jelgava ever had, and everybody loves him."

"Oh. That." Traku shrugged. "Everybody knows that's a lie, so what's the use of getting upset about it? Most of the time, though, you can find out when they're stretching things if you ask around a little. I haven't heard anybody say the Algarvians aren't still advancing. Have you?"

"No, not when you put it so," Talsu admitted. "I wish I had."

"That's a different story." Traku paused in thought. "Now, have I got the material he'll need in stock, or am I going to have to scour Skrunda for it?" He went through what he did have, then called to Talsu: "Here, come feel this bolt of beige stuff. Do you think it would do?"

Talsu rubbed it between thumb and forefinger. "I think you could wear it instead of chainmail, matter of fact. You'd feel like you were carrying another man on your back with a cloak made from it."

"He asked for heavy," Traku said. "He can't very well complain if it turns out even heavier than he looked for." He reached under the counter and pulled out a stout pair of pinking shears. "Get me his measurements, will you, son? I want to make sure I have the length just right."

When the Algarvian captain came into the shop to pick up the cloak, he was sober. He still looked no happier at the prospect of going off to fight in Unkerlant. From everything Talsu had heard about the weather in the huge western kingdom, he couldn't blame the redhead for that.

Traku draped the cloak over the Algarvian's shoulders, as fussy to get it right as if he'd made it for King Donalitu. "I put a lot of handiwork into it, sir," he said. "Not as much room to use magic in a cloak as there would be in, say, one of your kilts."

Staggering a little under the weight of the garment, the redhead said, "Plain enough that you didn't stint on the cloth." Before the tailor could answer, the officer gave a shrug – an effort-filled shrug, with the cloak still heavy on his shoulders. "Fair enough. I will probably need all of this in Unkerlant."

"I hope it is what you had in mind," Traku said.

"Oh, aye, very much so." The Algarvian shrugged again. "Even if it weren't, I'd be stuck with it, because my ley-line caravan leaves before sunup tomorrow morning." He took off the cloak and folded it with the sure hands of a man who knew how to care for clothing. "My thanks. I won't be the only one, nor even the only one from Skrunda, heading down the ley lines, you know."

"We hadn't thought about it," Traku said, including Talsu in his answer. To show he intended to be included, Talsu nodded.

"I am sorry for you," the Algarvian said. "This gives your counts and dukes more power. From what I have seen of them, you would be better off if they had all fled with your coward of a king. You would be better off if we had decided to blaze all of them, too, but we didn't."

Talsu said, "They will still be taking orders from you."

"And you don't like that, either, do you?" the officer asked. Without waiting for an answer, he went on, "How often does anyone of rank care what the common people think?"

Not often enough, was the answer that sprang into Talsu's mind. He would have said as much to his mother or father or sister or to a close friend; he had said as much to men he trusted in the army. But, even in the army, he'd been careful about speaking his mind. He was not about to unburden himself to one of the occupiers, a man on whom he had no reason to rely.

Maybe the Algarvian understood as much. With a nod, he said, "I'm off, then. We may see each other again one day." He bowed to Traku and said, "You do good work." With a comic shrug, he carried the cloak away.

"He's not a bad fellow." Traku spoke as if he hated to admit anything of the sort.

"No, he's not," Talsu agreed. "I saw that in the field. One by one, the redheads aren't much different from us. But put a bunch of them together and they turn into Algarvians. I don't know how or why that works, but it does."

"Put a bunch of them together and they start knocking over monuments," Traku said. "Every time I go near the market square, I miss the old arch."

Talsu nodded. "Aye, me, too. Put a bunch of them together, let them go conquering, and—" He broke off. "—And who knows what they might do?" he finished, not really wanting to give the rumors substance after all.

His father knew what he meant. "I still don't care to believe that," he said. "Not even Algarvians would sink so low."

"I hope you're right," Talsu said, and then, in thoughtful tones, "I wonder just how many soldiers and officers they're taking out of Jelgava to send to Unkerlant. I wonder if the ones who stay behind will be enough to hold down the kingdom. Of course, the other thing I wonder is if anyone would rise up for our nobles."

"I don't much fancy a cursed Algarvian calling himself my king," Traku said. Talsu thought about that, then nodded again.

The wind howled and screamed like a mad ghost. Snow blew horizontally up from out of the south. Except in front of boulders and bushes, it had trouble staying on the ground. Istvan's squad moved forward, leaning into that shrieking gale.

"What beastly weather!" Kun shouted. The scrawny little mage's apprentice had tied his spectacles on with twine to keep them from blowing away.

"It's only weather," Istvan shouted back, into the teeth of the wind. "It's like this every winter in my valley."

"The stars must hate your valley, then," Kun said. "In the capital, we have halfway decent weather in the wintertime."

"It's made you soft," Istvan said. Kun gestured derisively. Istvan didn't take the argument any further, but he felt he could have. Gyongyosians were a warrior race, weren't they? What kind of warrior was a man who couldn't even stand a blizzard?

Then Szonyi said, "I come from a little valley that's as chilly as any the stars shine down on, and I'm stinking cold, too, and I'm not ashamed to admit it."

"I never said I wasn't cold." Istvan backed a little way up the ley line, but not very far. "I said it's only weather, and it is, and I said we have to deal with it, and we do." He slapped at his chest. "We've got the gear for it, eh?"

Snow flew from his long sheepskin coat. He wore a wool blouse under the coat, and a wool undertunic beneath that. The coat went down below his knees. His baggy leggings were wool, and so were his long drawers, which itched in places it was embarrassing to scratch. Fur lined his boots and his mittens; he wore a fox-fur cap with earflaps and had a wool muffler tied over his nose and mouth so that only his eyes showed. He carried slit goggles in his belt pouch, in case the sun came out. By the way the blizzard raged, he wondered if it would ever come out again.

Kun said, "I can get by in this." He was as well protected against the storm as Istvan. "Curse me if I know how anybody's supposed to fight in it, though, us or the Unkerlanters."

"They manage, and so do we," Istvan answered. "They know about cold, the miserable whoresons, same as we do." He peered ahead. All he could see was swirling whiteness. Discontentedly, he muttered, "I wish I knew exactly where we are. We could blunder on to them without knowing it till too late."

"Or some of them could be sneaking up on us, and we wouldn't know that till too late, either," Szonyi added.

"Aye, we would." Even in the howling blizzard, Kun sounded smug. "I have a bit of magecraft, I'll have you remember. It spotted Kuusamans and it spotted a mountain ape, so it should work even on brutes like Unkerlanters."

Kun was proud of his little bit of magecraft. Istvan hoped he wasn't prouder of it than it deserved. But it had worked, and more than once; no denying that. It wouldn't work, though, if he didn't use it. Istvan said, "Maybe you'd better check now, just on the off chance. Those goat-eating buggers could be half a blaze away, and we'd never know it, not through this."

"Aye, Sergeant. That's not the worst notion I ever heard." By the way Kun said it, he managed to imply that Istvan had come out with most of the worst notions he'd heard.

"Don't get clever with me," Istvan snapped. He paused, appalled at how much like Sergeant Jokai he sounded. After a moment, he shrugged: where else to learn how to be a sergeant than from a sergeant? He hoped the stars treasured Jokai's spirit. Whether they did or not, he had things to attend to here. "Squad halt!" he shouted over the howl of the wind. "All right, Kun – do what you need to do."

"Aye," Kun repeated, and set about it. Whatever passes he made, his mittens hid. The wind blew away the words of his spell. After a couple of minutes, he turned to Istvan and said, "Sergeant, no Unkerlanters are moving towards us."

"Well, that's something," Istvan said. "But you can't be sure we're not about to stumble over them?"

Kun shook his head. "The spell detects an enemy's motion toward us, and nothing else. I wish I knew more."

I wish you knew more, too, and not just about magic, Istvan thought. But Kun this time, had done nothing to deserve an insult. "You tried your best," Istvan said, "and we know more than we did, even if we don't know as much as we'd like. Come on, lads – forward again. If we find the foe by falling over him, then we do, that's all."

"How do we even know we're going in the right direction?" Szonyi asked. "With all this snow flying every which way, who can say where east is?"

"If we keep the wind almost at our backs, we won't go too far wrong," Istvan answered, but he didn't sound happy about the reply even to himself. Nothing easier than for the wind to shift. He turned to Kun. "Do you know any spells for finding out which way we're headed?"

"There is one, quite a good one, but it depends on a bit of lodestone, and I have none," the mage's apprentice answered regretfully.

"Anyone have any lodestone?" Istvan asked. No one admitted to it. He wasn't surprised. He hadn't seen lodestone more than a couple of times in his life, both when traveling mountebanks did astonishing things with it. He turned back to Kun. "Any other ways?"

"I'm sure there are, Sergeant, but I don't know how to use them," Kun replied.

Istvan sighed through the muffler over his mouth. "All right, then. We'll just have to keep on and see what happens. Stars be praised, we're through the worst of the really rugged country. Not so much risk of blowing off a cliff here."

"If we can hold where we are till spring, we'll be in a place where we can stab deep into Unkerlanter's vitals," Kun said.

"I thought you were a mage's apprentice, not a news-sheet scribbler's," Istvan said. Kun was too swaddled in fur and fabric for Istvan to see if he changed expression, but he turned away and kept quiet for a while.

And then, up ahead, someone called a challenge – in Unkerlanter. Istvan knew no more than a handful of words of the language. Neither did anyone else in the squad. The challenge came again, sharper and more peremptory. "What do we do, Sergeant?" somebody asked.

"Get down, you fools!" Istvan shouted, suiting action to word. As he thumped down into the snow himself, he added, "Balogh, back to the rest of the company. Tell 'em we've found the enemy!"

Actually, the Unkerlanters had found them. Beams hissed overhead, blasting snowflakes to steam. Istvan worried about them less than he would have in clearer weather; snow attenuated their force even faster than rain did. But how large an Unkerlanter position lay ahead there, shielded by the blizzard? If he'd uncovered a regiment of King Swemmel's soldiers, they'd wipe out his squad as casually as he swatted a fly . . . provided they knew he had only a squad.

He blazed at the Unkerlanters a couple of times, not so much in the hope of hurting them as to make them believe he led a good-sized force. "Kun!" he hissed. "Hey, Kun! You all right?"

"Aye, for the time being," the mage's apprentice answered from over to his left.

"Can you make the Unkerlanters think we've got more men here than we really do?" Istvan asked.

For a moment, he didn't think the mage's apprentice had heard him. Then a voice – Kun's voice, he realized, but bigger and deeper and more resonant than it had any business being – answered, "Aye, Colonel!" Istvan looked around to see where so exalted a figure as a colonel might have sprung from, but then started to laugh. Kun was doing his best to follow orders.

And his best turned out to be better than Istvan had expected. Other voices came out of the snow from different directions: nonexistent captains positioning equally nonexistent companies for a charge. Mythical sergeants who sounded much fiercer than Istvan ever had gave their mythical squads orders.

Off to the east, the Unkerlanters started shouting, nerving themselves for an attack: "Urra! Urra! Urra!" Istvan's shiver had nothing to do with the snow on which he lay. From the sound of those shouts, he hadn't stumbled over a regiment: That had to be at least a brigade. He wished Kun had given him an imaginary brigade of his own. He would have enjoyed being a brigadier, even an imaginary one, for the few brief moments till the Unkerlanters overran him.

Amid the calls and the shouts, Kun spoke in his own voice: "What next, Sergeant? This can't last – they're bound to test it, all the men they have over there."

He was right, curse him. Balogh must have got lost, or else Captain Tivadar would have brought up real reinforcements. But Istvan, having begun the game, did not want to give it up. He got to his feet, advanced on the Unkerlanter position, and shouted a couple of the Unkerlanter phrases he knew: "You surrender! Hands high!"

King Swemmel's men didn't blaze him down out of hand. The shouts of "Urra! Urra!" died away. Only the wind spoke, the wind and Kun's conjured-up officers and sergeants. And then, dejectedly, an Unkerlanter shouted back: "We surrender!"

Istvan gaped. He'd known how colossal a bluff he was running, and was astonished past words that the Unkerlanters had fallen for it. If he showed that, though, everything was ruined. "Hands high!" he yelled again, not caring if he rasped his throat raw so long as he made his voice pierce the gale.

He aimed his stick eastward. He could do no more than that; the snow was blowing too hard to let him find a sure target. Out of that swirling snow came Unkerlanters in long, thick wool tunics with leggings beneath and long, hooded cloaks over them. They carried no weapons; their hands were above their heads. Catching sight of Istvan, the first one in the line repeated, "We surrender."

Gesturing with his stick, Istvan sent them back toward his comrades. As they glumly tramped past him, he counted them. Only twenty men were marching into captivity. Had more stayed behind or . . .? Sudden suspicion flowered in him. "Kun!" he shouted. "You've got to have more of their language than I do."

"Maybe, Sergeant, though I haven't got much," the mage's apprentice answered, sounding more respectful than he usually did.

"Tell 'em you're a first-rank mage who'll know if they lie, then ask 'em if all those cursed 'Urra!s' were magic to scare us off," Istvan said.

"I'll try." Kun sounded doubtful, but he spoke to the Unkerlanters. Istvan listened to gutturals going back and forth and watched gestures till Kun returned to Gyongyosian: "That's what they were doing, all right. They knew the jig was up when they heard our regiment forming for the attack."

Istvan laughed till tears came. The tears promptly started freezing his eyelashes together. He swiped at his face with his mittens. Then he heard shouts from the west: Captain Tivadar at last, bringing reinforcements against the Unkerlanter host . . . the Unkerlanter host Istvan had just captured. He made his way over to Tivadar. Saluting, he said, "Sir, the enemy position is ours," and laughed again at the flabbergasted expression on his company commander's face.

No one came back from the west. That, to Vanai, was the central fact to life in Oyngestun these days. No one came back. No one sent money from the wages the Algarvians had promised to pay. No one sent so much as a scrawled note. That continuing, echoing silence made the worst rumors easier and easier to believe as day followed day.

One chilly afternoon, Vanai went to the apothecary's to get a decoction of willow bark for her grandfather, who'd come down with the grippe. As Tamulis handed her the small jar of green glass, he remarked, not quite out of the blue, "If you hear the Algarvian constables are on their way here again, you'd be smart to take to the woods before they start yelling, 'Kaunians, come forth!'"

"Do you think so?" Vanai asked, and Tamulis nodded vigorously. Then she asked another question: "Is that what you intend to do?"

"Aye, I expect I will," the apothecary answered. "I'm no woodsman – anyone who knows me knows that. I don't know whether I'd starve before I froze or the other way round. But whatever happens, it has to be better than getting into one of those caravan cars bound for Unkerlant."

Vanai bit her lip. "You may be right. And thank you for telling me that. You've been as kind as . . . as anyone in Oyngestun." It wasn't enormous praise, but she could give it without feeling like a hypocrite.

"Life's hard," Tamulis said gruffly. "Life's hard for everybody, and especially for everybody with yellow hair. Go on, get out of here. I hope your grandfather feels better, the old fool. If he gets well, maybe you won't have to come in here so often and listen to me complain."

"It's not as if there's nothing to complain about." Vanai bobbed her head and then turned and went out the door.

A couple of Forthwegian men two or three years older than she leaned against the wall of the apothecary's shop. Vanai wasn't too surprised to see them in the Kaunian part of Oyngestun; Tamulis knew three times as much as his Forthwegian counterpart, and had plenty of stocky, swarthy, dark-haired customers.

But one of the Forthwegians pointed at her and said, "So long, blondy!" He drew a thumb across his throat and made horrible gagging, gargling noises. While he was laughing, the other fellow grabbed his crotch and said, "Here, sweetheart. My meat's got more flavor than an Algarvian sausage any day."

That the earth did not swallow them proved the powers above were deaf. Vanai stalked past them, pretending they didn't exist. She'd had plenty of practice doing that with both Forthwegians and Kaunians. But now she had to hide more fear than usual. Since the Algarvians sent that shipment of Kaunians west, Oyngestun's Forthwegians had grown bolder toward their neighbors. Why not? Would the redheads punish them for it? Not likely!

If these two laid hands on her . . . *I'll fight*, Vanai thought. *I don't have to lie there and take it, the way I did with Spinello.* She chose not to dwell on what her odds would be against two men both stronger than she. To her vast relief, they did nothing worse than taunt her. After she slipped round a corner, she breathed easier.

She passed the postman on the way home. He was a Forthwegian, too, but decent enough. "Letter for you," he said. "Something for your granddad, too."

"I'll take it to him," Vanai said. She almost always took him whatever mail there was; these days, she made a point of getting it first. Holding up the little green bottle, she added, "He's down with the grippe."

"Aye, it's been going around; my sister and her husband have it," the postman said. "Hope he feels better soon." With a nod, he went on his way.

Vanai hurried the rest of the way to the house she shared with Brivibas. Her heart sang within her. A letter for her had to be a letter from Ealstan. No one else wrote to her. She'd feared Spinello would, but he must have realized any letter he sent her would only go into the fire. Ealstan's letters she cherished. Strange how a few minutes of fondling and grunting and thrashing could make two people open their souls to each other. She had no idea how that happened, but was ever so glad it did.

As far as her grandfather knew, no one sent her letters. That was why she made a point of picking up the mail before Brivibas could. It wasn't hard; even well, he usually stayed in his study, on the far side of the house from the doorway.

But when Vanai opened the door, no letters shoved in under it lay on the entry-hall floor. She wondered if the postman had delivered them to the house next door by mistake, though he didn't usually do things like that. Then she heard her grandfather moving about in the kitchen, and she realized she might have a problem.

She had to go into the kitchen anyhow, to mix the bitter willow-bark decoction with something sweet to make it more palatable for Brivibas. "I greet you, my grandfather," she said when she saw him. "I have your medicine. How are you feeling?"

"I have been better," he answered, his voice a rasping croak. "Aye, I have been better. I came out here to make myself a cup of herb tea, and heard that ignorant lout of a postman slide something under our door. I went to get it, and found – this." He'd taken Ealstan's letter out of the franked envelope in which it had come.

"You read it?" Anger pushed fear from Vanai's mind. "You *read* it? You had no business doing that. Whatever Ealstan says there, it's not meant for you. Give it to me this instant."

"Very well, my dearest sweet darling Vanai." Brivibas quoted Ealstan's greeting with savage relish. Two spots of color, from fever or outrage or both at once, burned on his cheeks. He crumpled the letter into a ball and flung it at Vanai. "As for its being none of my business, I would have to disagree. I would say, just as a guess from the style, that this is not the first such letter you've received."

"That's not your business, either," Vanai snapped, cursing his literary analysis. She bent and picked up the letter and unfolded it far more carefully than Brivibas had wadded it up. Why couldn't he have stayed in bed till she got back?

"I think it is." His eyes glittered. "You still live under my roof. How much more shame must I endure on account of you?"

He still thought of what Vanai did in terms of how it affected him, not in terms of what it meant to her. Her chin lifted haughtily, as if she were a noblewoman from the days of the Kaunian Empire. "I don't propose to discuss it."

"It's fortunate that we have no Zuwayzin or Kuusamans close by," Brivibas said, "or you might seek to slake your lust with them as well."

Vanai threw the bottle of willow-bark decoction at his head. Rage lent her strength, but not aim. The bottle flew past and shattered against the wall behind him. "If you think I was slaking my lust with the cursed

Algarvian, you're even blinder than I thought," she snarled. "The only reason I sucked his prong was to keep you alive, and now—" *And now I'm sorry I did it* was in her mind, but she burst into tears before she could say it.

Brivibas took her words in a different direction: "And now this Forthwegian barbarian satisfies you better still, is that it?" he demanded.

When Vanai found herself looking toward the cutlery to see which knife was longest and sharpest, she spun away with a groan and fled to her bedchamber. It was less a refuge than she might have wanted, less a refuge than it would have been a year before. Lying on the bed alone, she couldn't help thinking of the times when she'd had to lie there with Spinello. If her grandfather thought she'd wanted to lie with the Algarvian . . . If he thought that, he had even less notion of what went on around him than she'd imagined.

She didn't know what she would have done had Brivibas knocked on her door then, or come in without knocking. Luckily, she didn't have to find out. Her tears – tears of fury rather than sorrow – quickly dried. She sat up and did a better job of smoothing the letter from Ealstan.

"At least someone cares about me," she murmured as she began to read it. It was, as her grandfather had sneeringly shown, filled with endearments, as were the ones she sent to him. But it was also filled with his doings, and those of his father and mother and sister and his cousin and uncle. She wondered if he knew how lucky he was to have a good-sized family where everyone – except, she gathered, Sidroc and Hengist – got along. Probably not. To him, that would be like water to a fish.

I honor you for choosing to stay with your grandfather, even though it means we must be apart, Ealstan wrote. *Please believe me when I say that. Please also believe me when I say I wish we could be together.*

"Oh, I wish we could, too," Vanai whispered. For the first time, she really thought of leaving the house where she'd lived almost all her life and traveling to Gromheort. She had no idea of what she would do there, or how she would keep from starving, but the idea of being away from Brivibas glowed in her thoughts like a fire catching hold in dry grass.

She shook her head, then wondered why she pushed the idea aside. When she was a child, she and Brivibas had fit together well enough. He did not fit her now, any more than one of the small tunics she'd worn then would. Why not go her own way, then, and leave him behind to go his?

Because if I leave him behind, he'll die in short order. Because if I wanted him to die in short order, I never would have let Spinello have me. Because, since I did let Spinello have me, I've given up too much to let him die in short order. But oh! – how I wish I hadn't!

After a little while, grimacing, she got up and opened the door. She couldn't even stay and sulk, not if she wanted to – or felt she should, which came closer to the actual state of affairs – nurse her grandfather back to health. She had to go fix his supper and fetch it to him. It wouldn't be much – vegetable soup and a chunk of bread – but she didn't trust him to be able to do it for himself.

She'd known all along that he underestimated her. Now she discovered she'd underestimated him, too. Her nose told her as much as soon as she came out of the bedchamber: she smelled cooking soup. When she came into the kitchen, she found the pot over a low fire and a note on the table nearby.

Brivibas' spidery hand was as familiar to her as her own: far more familiar than Ealstan's. *My granddaughter*, he wrote in a Kaunian straight out of the glory days of the empire, *judging it wiser that we not impinge on each other for some little while, I have prepared my own repast, leaving enough behind to satisfy, I hope, those bodily wants of yours susceptible to satisfaction through food.*

Vanai stared in the direction of his study, where he was probably spooning up soup even now. She had to look at the note twice before she noticed the sting in its tail. "Bodily wants susceptible to food, eh?" she muttered, and the stare turned into a glare. "Why didn't you come right out and call me a whore?"

In the end, though, she ate the soup Brivibas had heated. She was unhappy doing it, just as, no doubt, her grandfather had been unhappy eating a great many meals she'd made. When she was finished, she washed and dried her bowl and spoon and the ladle she'd used. She went to her bedchamber and started a letter to Ealstan. That made her feel better.

Felgilde squeezed Leofsig's hand as they walked along the street together. "Oh, this will be fun!" she exclaimed.

"I hope so," he answered, and then smiled and said, "You look very pretty tonight."

She squeezed his hand again, perhaps – he hoped – a little less archly than she was in the habit of doing. "Thank you," she said. "That's a handsome cloak you have on."

"Thank *you*," Leofsig said. He'd borrowed it from his father, but Felgilde didn't need to know that.

She said, "Ethelhelm's band is one of the two or three best in Forthweg. I'm so excited! This is the first time since the war they've come here from Eoforwic. They're supposed to have all sorts of new tunes, too – that's what everybody says, anyway. You were so lucky to be able to get tickets."

"I know," Leofsig said. His father had helped there, too; Hestan cast accounts for the hall where Ethelhelm's band was going to perform. But that was also nothing Felgilde needed to know.

He slid his arm around her waist. She snuggled closer to him. He brought his hand up a bit, so that the top of his thumb and wrist brushed against the bottom of her breast. Most of the time, she slapped his hand away when he tried that. Tonight, she let it stay. His hopes, among other things, began to rise. Maybe he wouldn't have to keep on being jealous of his younger brother for so long as he'd thought.

The hall was in a part of town that had housed a good many Kaunians. Some of them still remained, looking shabby and frightened. An old man with fair hair stood on the street not far from the entrance to the hall, begging from the people who were coming to hear Ethelhelm's famous band.

Leofsig let go of Felgilde to rummage in his belt pouch and take out a couple of coins. He dropped them into the bowl at the scrawny old man's feet. "Powers above bless you, sir," the Kaunian said in Forthwegian. He'd had little luck till Leofsig came by; only a few other coins, most of them small coppers, lay in the bowl.

"That was a waste of money," Felgilde said as they walked on. She didn't bother to keep her voice down, though the old Kaunian had already shown he could speak Forthweg's majority tongue.

"I don't think so," Leofsig answered. "My father always says Kaunians are people, too. That fellow looked like he could use a hand."

"*My* father says that if we hadn't listened to the Kaunians in Forthweg, we wouldn't have gone to war against Algarve when the blond kingdoms in the east did," Felgilde said. "He says we'd be better off if we hadn't, too."

Even the Forthweg would have been better off if King Penda hadn't gone to war against Algarve – better off for a little while, anyhow. Leofsig said, "How long do you think it would have been before King Mezentio went to war with us if we didn't stand by our allies?"

"I'm sure I don't know," Felgilde said with a toss of her head, "and I'm just as sure you don't know, either."

Since that was true, Leofsig could hardly argue with it. He didn't feel like arguing, anyhow. He knew what he felt like, and hoped Felgilde felt like it, too. To try to put her back in the mood, he slipped his arm around her waist again. She let him do that, but brushed his hand away when he tried to bring it up again. He gave her a resentful look. Hers in response might have said, *So there*.

She did get friendlier when he took out the tickets and gave them to the tough-looking fellow standing in the doorway. The bruiser nodded, smiled a surprisingly warm smile, and stepped aside to let them pass. They both held out their hands to a woman with a stamp and an ink pad. She marked them with the word PAID, then she too stood aside and waved them into the hall.

Ethelhelm's band occupied a raised platform in the middle. The men on viol and double viol, lute and mandolin, were tuning their instruments. The trumpeter and flute-player made runs up and down the scale. So did the piper, with results that set Leofsig's teeth on edge. Ethelhelm himself manned the drums. He was taller and slimmer than most Forthwegians, enough to make Leofsig wonder if he had a quarter or an eighth part of Kaunian blood. If he did, he didn't advertise it, for which prudent silence Leofsig could hardly blame him.

Felgilde pointed. "Look – there are a couple in the first row that haven't been taken. Come on! Hurry!"

She and Leofsig got to the seats before anyone else could, and sat down with no small feeling of triumph. Rows of chairs had been placed around the whole inner perimeter of the hall, all facing inward toward the platform on which the band would perform. There was considerable space between the front row and the platform, though: room for people to dance as the mood took them.

The hall filled rapidly. Before the war, Leofsig wouldn't have seen many blonds at one of Ethelhelm's appearances; Kaunians' tastes in music were different from Forthwegians'. Now he saw no Kaunians at all. That didn't surprise him, but did leave him sad.

People began clapping their hands and stamping their feet on the floorboards, eager for the show to start. Leofsig stamped along with everyone else, but put his arm around Felgilde's shoulder instead of clapping. She was clapping but, her good humor restored, leaned toward him while she did it.

When all the lights in the hall faded except for those aimed at the band on the platform, she clapped louder than ever. Leofsig whooped. He turned toward Felgilde and gave her a quick kiss. Her eyes sparkled. He grinned as foolishly as if he'd had a glass of wine too many. It looked as if it might be a good night after all.

"It's grand to be in Gromheort," Ethelhelm called. The crowd cheered. The band leader went on, "The way things are, it's grand to be cursed anywhere, and that's the truth." Leofsig laughed. He'd had that feeling more than once himself, after some narrow escape or another. Ethelhelm waved to the people who'd come to hear him. "Since we are all here, we may as well enjoy ourselves, isn't that right?"

"Aye!" the crowd roared, Leofsig and Felgilde loud among them.

"Well, then!" Ethelhelm brought his stick crashing down on to the drums. The band struck up a sprightly tune. Forthwegian songs didn't rely on thudding rhythms the way the music of the Kaunian kingdoms did, nor was it a collection of tinkling notes going nowhere in particular, which was how Algarvian music struck Leofsig's ears. This was what he'd heard his whole life, and it felt right to him.

The first few tunes Ethelhelm and the band played were familiar, some of them old favorites Leofsig's father and grandfather would have known, others songs by which the drummer and his fellow musicians had made their reputation. Some people got up and started to dance from the very first note. Leofsig and Felgilde sat and listened for a while before heading out on to the floor.

Then, after basking in yet another passionate round of applause, the band swung into a number that made Leofsig and Felgilde turn to each other and exclaim, "That's new!" They both leaned forward to listen closely.

Ethelhelm sang in raspy, angry-sounding bursts:

> "Doesn't matter what you choose
> When you've got nothing left to lose.
> Doesn't matter what you say
> When they won't listen anyway."

Felgilde's brow furrowed. "What's he talking about?" she asked.

"I don't know." Leofsig lied without hesitation. As he spoke, he looked around. The band had nerve – maybe more nerve than sense. Somewhere in the audience was bound to be an Algarvian spy. Singing about what life in an occupied kingdom was like struck Leofsig as gloriously foolish: the same sort of foolishness that had led Forthwegians on unicorns to charge Algarvian behemoths. He got to his feet. "Come on. Let's dance."

"All right." Felgilde rose with alacrity. "I usually have to start you going." She swayed forward into his arms.

Dancing helped take his mind off his worries; he half expected Algarvian constables to come pushing through the crowd and haul Ethelhelm and his band off to gaol. After a moment, he realized he was being foolish. Seizing Ethelhelm now would touch off a riot. If the redheads wanted the musicians, they'd wait till after the performance. As long as Ethelhelm kept playing, he was likely safe.

Leofsig didn't take long to stop worrying about Ethelhelm. Felgilde molded herself to him as closely as if they weren't wearing tunics. When his hand closed on her backside, she didn't squawk. She just sighed and pushed tighter against him still. "It's safe here," she murmured in a voice he couldn't have heard if her mouth hadn't been next to his ear.

She was right. Nobody in the hall paid one couple clutching each other the least attention. Dozens, hundreds of couples clutching one another filled the dance floor. They'd escaped their parents, and they were going to have the best time they could in as many different ways as they could.

Some of them were doing more out there on the floor than he and Felgilde had ever done in private. His eyes widened a few times. Up there on the platform, Ethelhelm saw everything that was going on. "You'll get in trouble when you go home," he warned the dancers between songs.

Then he laughed raucously. "Good, by the powers above! If you're going to get in trouble, get in trouble for something worthwhile. They'll yell at you anyway – give 'em something to yell about."

At his waved command, the band swung into another new tune, one so lascivious that a few couples, altogether carried away, hurried outside. Ethelhelm laughed again, harder than ever. Leofsig tried to steer Felgilde toward the door. That didn't work. She might have kindled, but she wasn't blazing.

At last, after what seemed not nearly long enough despite repeated encores, the band put down their instruments, called their last good-nights, and escaped. Leofsig and Felgilde reclaimed their cloaks and joined the stream of music lovers pouring from the hall.

Outside, the stream divided. Many couples, instead of going straight home, ducked into doorways in dark side streets to continue what they'd started on the dance floor. Hopeful but not expectant, Leofsig started to swing down one of those alleyways himself. He thought Felgilde would steer him back toward their houses. Instead, with a throaty chuckle, she followed.

Heart pounding, Leofsig found a doorway no one else had. He wrapped his cloak around both of them, though nobody could have seen much in the darkness anyhow. Felgilde's mouth found his as his hands roamed over her. He slid one under her tunic; it closed on the smooth, soft flesh of her breast. She sighed and kissed him harder than ever.

He rubbed at her crotch with his other hand. He'd never tried that before; he'd never thought she would let him try. "Oh, Leofsig," she whispered, and spread her legs a little to make it easier for him. And then she was groping him, too, through his tunic and his drawers. He grunted in astonishment and delight. It was hard to remember to keep his hand busy.

Felgilde whimpered and quivered. Her hand squeezed him painfully tight. A moment later, groaning, he made a mess in his drawers. Everything down there was wet and sticky, and he didn't care at all. "I *like* Ethelhelm's music," Felgilde said seriously.

"So do I," Leofsig panted. Now he really did head home.

If he couldn't bring Vanai to Gromheort, Ealstan wanted to go to Oyngestun. He wondered if he wouldn't be able to see her again till the next mushroom season. He was sure he'd go mad long before then.

But if he did see her, the first thing he'd want to do would be to find someplace where they could be alone. He knew that. He wondered if it would make her angry. He hoped not, but he couldn't be sure.

Maybe letters are better after all, he thought one morning at breakfast. Vanai had opened her soul, or at least some of it, to him, and he'd tried to do the same with her. He really felt he knew her now, which he couldn't have said when they lay down together in the oak grove. He marveled that she kept living with her grandfather, who in her letters sounded even more difficult than he'd seemed when Ealstan briefly met him a couple of years before. Ealstan didn't quite understand why Vanai and Brivibas had fallen out – she never did make that clear – but he was sure he would have fallen out with the stiff-necked old scholar, too.

And maybe letters aren't better, he thought. He couldn't stroke a letter's hair or kiss its lips or caress it. He couldn't . . . Thinking about all the things he couldn't do with a letter made him forget his morning porridge altogether, and he'd only been picking at it before.

"Hurry up, Ealstan – you're going to make both of us late." Sidroc snorted. "There! For once I get to nag you, not the other way round."

"I think it's the first time ever," Elfryth said. Ealstan's mother sent him an anxious glance. "Are you all right?"

"I'm fine." Recalled to himself, Ealstan proved it by gulping his wine and inhaling the porridge left in his bowl. He still finished after Sidroc, but not by more than a couple of spoonsful. Elfryth looked happier. Ealstan got to his feet. "All right, cousin, I'm ready. Let's get going."

They both exclaimed when they went outside. Sidroc said, "My nose is going to freeze." He wrapped his cloak around himself in a dramatic gesture, but that did nothing to protect the organ in question.

"Look!" Ealstan pointed to windows. "Frost!" Frost didn't come to Gromheort very often; he admired its delicate traceries. Then he rubbed his nose. Like Sidroc's, it was turning frosty, too.

He spent the first couple of blocks on the way to school shivering and complaining. After that, he resigned himself to the weather and went back to thinking about Vanai. That warmed him at least as effectively as his cloak. It also made him oblivious to Sidroc. He'd long wished for something that could do that, but it irked his cousin. Sidroc gave him a shot in the ribs with his elbow and said, "Powers above, you haven't heard a word I've told you."

"Huh?" Ealstan proved Sidroc right. Feeling foolish, he said, "Try it again. I really am listening now."

"Well, why weren't you before?" Sidroc demanded. "Half the time these days, you go stumbling around like a moonstruck calf. What in blazes is wrong with you, anyhow?"

I'm in love, Ealstan thought. But, since he'd been rash enough to fall in love with a Kaunian girl, Sidroc was the last person he wanted to know it. If Sidroc knew, he could endanger Ealstan himself, he could endanger Vanai, and he could endanger Leofsig, too. Ealstan set his jaw and said nothing. He did try to pay more attention to what his cousin said, which struck him as more trouble than it was worth.

"I know what it is!" Sidroc said with a guffaw. "Saying moonstruck made me think of it. I bet you're mooning over that blond floozy in the tight trousers you keep meeting during mushroom season. Aye, that's what it's got to be. Powers above, why don't you find a girl closer to home?"

"Why don't you soak your head?" Ealstan suggested, which made Sidroc laugh without letting him know how close to right he was. *Why don't I find a girl closer to home?* Ealstan thought. *Because I've lain with Vanai and I'm not interested in anyone else.* He clamped his jaw tight on that answer, too.

School loomed ahead, both literally and metaphorically. As he went into the gray stone building, he tried not to think about the long stretch of mostly meaningless, useless time ahead. The Algarvians seemed more determined every day that their Forthwegian subjects should learn as little as possible, which meant classes taught less and less. The one good thing about it was that it gave him more time to daydream about Vanai.

He spent too much time daydreaming during his Forthwegian literature class; the master warmed the back of his jacket after he failed to recite when called on. Sidroc snickered. He was more used to having the switch fall on his own back than to seeing it land on his cousin's.

"Ha!" he said when they were walking home together. "That's what you get for sighing over your yellow-haired tart."

"Oh, shut up," Ealstan snapped. "I was so busy thinking about all the different ways you're an idiot, I didn't even hear the master call my name." He and Sidroc had a more or less enjoyable time insulting each other till they got to their front door.

When they went inside, Conberge came up to Ealstan with a smile and handed him an envelope. "Here's another letter from your friend in Oyngestun."

Ealstan had asked Leofsig not to tell anybody else about Vanai. Evidently, his brother had kept the promise he'd made. He hadn't told Conberge, anyhow. Now, all at once, Ealstan wished he hadn't forced the promise out of Leofsig. "Thanks," he told Conberge with a rather sickly smile.

"Oyngestun," Sidroc said, as if wondering where he'd heard the name before. Ealstan had never before hoped so hard his cousin would stay stupid. By the way Sidroc's gaze suddenly sharpened, he knew that was going to be one more blighted hope. Sidroc snapped his fingers. "Oyngestun! That's where that what's-her-name, that Vanai" – to Ealstan's horror, he even came up with her name – "lives. And somebody's writing you from there? *Another* letter, your sister said. If you aren't a lousy Kaunian-lover, I don't know who is."

Maybe he meant it as a joke. Ealstan thought of that only afterwards. At the moment, he handed Vanai's letter back to Conberge and hit Sidroc in the face as hard as he could.

Sidroc's head snapped back; he didn't get an arm up to block the blow. He staggered backwards, fetching up against the wall of the entry hall. But he was made of rugged stuff. After a muttered curse, he surged forward, fists churning. A solid right thudded into Ealstan's ribs.

But, however aggressive Sidroc was, he was also still dazed from that first punch. He moved a little slower than he might have otherwise. Ealstan punched him again, right on the point of the chin. The sudden sharp pain he felt in his own knuckles told how effective the blow was. Sidroc stood swaying a moment, then toppled. His head hit the floor with a dull thud.

"Powers above!" Conberge exclaimed. "The way you went after him, anyone would think he knew what he was talking about."

"He did," Ealstan said shortly. Conberge's eyes widened. Ealstan knelt beside his cousin. "Come on, Sidroc. Wake up, curse it." Sidroc didn't wake up. He was breathing steadily – snoring, in fact, but he just lay there, his eyes half open. Ealstan glanced up at Conberge. "Get some water. We'll flip it in his face and bring him around."

But the water didn't bring Sidroc to himself, either. Drawn by shouts and thumps, Elfryth came into the front hall hard on Conberge's heels. Ealstan's mother stared at Sidroc inert on the floor and let out a small shriek. "What happened?" she cried.

"I hit him." Ealstan's voice was toneless. "I hit him, and he hit his head." He'd always thought he might be able to lick Sidroc, but wished he hadn't been proved quite so thoroughly right.

"Is he dead?" Elfryth asked.

Sidroc's snores should have told her the answer to that, but Ealstan said, "No, he's not," anyhow. Sidroc showed no signs of coming to, either. Rubbing at a bruised knuckle. Ealstan went on, "If he doesn't wake up, what will Uncle Hengist do? For that matter, if he does wake up, what will Uncle Hengist do?"

"He'll go to the Algarvians." Now Elfryth's voice came out flat.

"And if Sidroc does wake up, *he'll* go to the Algarvians," Conberge added. "Either that, or he'll wait for you to come round a corner and then bash out your brains with a fire iron." Ealstan started to say Sidroc wouldn't do anything like that, but the words clogged in his throat. Sidroc took revenge seriously.

Elfryth stared down at her nephew, loathing on her face. "He's been nothing but trouble since he had to come here." Her gaze swung toward Ealstan. When she spoke again, she was as grimly practical as Hestan had ever dreamt of being: "You had better go. Leave the front door open after yourself. Conberge and I don't know a thing about whatever happened here. Maybe it was a footpad. That's what we'll say if he doesn't come to himself – the footpad killed Sidroc and knocked the wits out of you so you went wandering off. You'll be able to come back then, eventually. But if Sidroc does wake up—"

"Take all those letters with you before you go," Conberge broke in. "He may not remember where this one came from. People who get hit in the head can have trouble remembering things."

"Letters?" Ealstan's mother asked.

"Never mind," Ealstan and Conberge said together. Ealstan turned to his sister. "Aye, you're right – I'll do that. Thanks." He paused a little while in thought. "I'd better not stay in Gromheort. I'll need whatever money we have in the house to keep me eating till I find work."

"I'll get it," Conberge said, and left.

"But where will you go?" Elfryth asked.

"Conberge will know. So will Leofsig," Ealstan answered. "At first, anyhow. After that" – he shrugged a man's slow, sour shrug – "I'll just have to see how things work out."

"What will you do?" his mother said.

He shrugged again. "I can dig ditches. I can cast accounts. I'm not as good at it as Father, but I'm not bad. I'm better than most of the bookkeepers they'll have in little towns, the ones who can't count past ten without taking off their shoes."

Conberge came back and handed him a heavy, clinking leather purse. "Here," she said, and he fastened it to his belt. She went on, "You have to get those letters. I don't know where you keep them."

"Aye." Ealstan retrieved them from the bedchamber, then went out to the front hall again. Sidroc still lay unconscious. Ealstan hugged his mother and his sister. Elfryth was fighting back tears as she withdrew.

Conberge kissed Ealstan. "Be careful," she said.

"I will." He went to the door, leaving it ajar as his mother had suggested. As he headed from Gromheort's west gate – the gate on the road to Oyngestun – he opened Vanai's letter, the one that had led him to flee, and began to read.

Ten

Skarnu hiked past Pavilosta toward Dauktu's farm. He carried a headless chicken by the feet. If an Algarvian patrol questioned him, he'd say he owed it to the other farmer. He didn't expect to be stopped – the Algarvians were spread thin in Valmiera these days, with the war sucking soldiers to the west – but he didn't believe in taking chances.

He'd never tramped country roads in wintertime till coming to the farm that had been Gedominu's and now was Merkela's – and, in an odd way, his. The leather jacket he wore had been Gedominu's, too. It didn't fit very well, but kept warm those parts of him it did cover. He'd had to buy new boots; he couldn't squeeze his feet into Gedominu's. After a couple of walks along country roads, the boots had got muddy and battered enough not to look new any more.

But for the mud and the cold, the countryside had a certain austere beauty. His sister would have sneered at it, but his sister was in the habit of sneering at everything. Bare trees and empty fields were not so much in and of themselves, but they held the promise of future growth. Looking at them as they were, he could see them as they would be. He hadn't been able to do that before.

A squirrel with a nut in its mouth scurried up the trunk of an oak tree. It knew to keep the tree trunk between itself and Skarnu. Living in a mansion down in Priekule, he would have turned up his nose at the idea of squirrel stew. Merkela had taught him it could be surprisingly tasty.

"Not today, little fellow," he told the squirrel as he walked past the oak. The squirrel chattered indignantly; it had to think he'd prove a liar if he got the chance, and it was very likely right.

He'd skirted Pavilosta, and saw no one on the road before he got to Dauktu's farm. Winter for the peasantry, he'd found, was a time of

pulling back, of tending one's own, of preparing for the spring sowing. It
was not a time for dances and feasts, as it was among the nobles of
Valmiera. Skarnu kicked a pebble in a show of defiance. Count Simanu
would give no dances this winter, host no feasts for his Algarvian friends
and overlords. *I made sure of that*, Skarnu thought.

Triumph filled him, which meant he needed longer than he should
have to notice that no smoke curled up from the chimney of Dauktu's
farmhouse. When he did notice that, he frowned; on a day like this, he
would have wanted a good fire roaring in the fireplace. And Dauktu had
plenty of firewood: a big pile, covered by a canvas tarpaulin, stood by the
barn.

Still, Skarnu didn't think much of it. If Dauktu and his wife and their
daughter preferred bundling themselves to the eyebrows, that was their
business. Swinging the chicken as he walked, Skarnu drew near the
farmhouse.

Then he noticed the front door standing open. He stopped in his tracks.
"Something's wrong," he muttered, and stood irresolute, not knowing
whether to go forward or to flee. In the end, warily, he went forward.

When he got closer still, he saw the door had something written on it.
Scratching his head, he took step by cautious step till he could read it. It
was five words in all, daubed on with whitewash that had run: SIMANU'S
VENGEANCE – NIGHT AND FOG.

He scratched his head again. "What's that supposed to mean?" he asked
the winter air. He got no answer. He raised his voice and called Dauktu's
name. Again, no answer. Wondering if he should go back, he went
forward again.

All at once, the quiet seemed eerie. When Skarnu set foot on the
wooden steps leading up to the porch, the thunk of his boot heel made
him start in alarm. He called Dauktu's name once more. Not a sound came
from the house. He went inside, though half of him was warning that he
ought to turn tail. *Too late for that, anyway*, he thought.

Something in the front room moved. Skarnu froze. So did the red fox
that had been eating from the plate spilled on the floor. The fox darted
under a rough-hewn chair. Skarnu went into the kitchen. The oven was
as cold and dead as the fireplace. When he walked back into the front
room, the fox had scurried away.

"Dauktu?" he called up the stairway. Only silence answered him.

Normally, he would never have presumed to go up to the farmer's bed-chamber uninvited. Now . . . Now he didn't think it would matter.

The bedchamber was neat and empty. So was the smaller one across the hall, which had to belong to Dauktu's daughter. As far as Skarnu could see by anything up there, the other farmer and his family might just have stepped away for a moment. They'd stepped away, all right. The spilled plate of food downstairs argued that they weren't ever coming back.

"Night and fog," Skarnu murmured. He'd never seen the phrase before. He didn't know exactly what it meant, but it couldn't have meant anything good for Dauktu and his wife and daughter.

Skarnu went back downstairs, and then back out of the farmhouse. He stared at the words painted on the doorway. Ever so slowly, he shook his head. Still carrying the chicken, he started the long walk back to the farmhouse where he lived. It seemed much longer than the walk out to Dauktu's house had. He'd been bubbling with ideas on how to strike another blow against the Algarvian occupiers of Valmiera. Unless he was dreadfully wrong, they'd struck a blow of their own.

Again, the road might have been deserted but for him. Everyone else might have vanished – *vanished into night and fog*, he thought uneasily, and his shiver had nothing to do with the weather.

When he got back, he breathed a silent sigh of relief to see Merkela scattering chicken feed in front of the barn. If disaster had struck Dauktu's farm, it might have struck here, too. But no: there stood Raunu not far away, nailing a fence rail to a post. Skarnu waved to both of them.

They waved back. Raunu called, "What's the matter? Dauktu didn't want that scrawny old hen, so you had to bring it back?"

Merkela laughed. Skarnu knew he would have laughed, too, had he found things different at Dauktu's farm. But he said, "He wasn't there." His voice came out as flat as if he were reciting a lesson in a primer.

Merkela went on feeding the chickens. She didn't know what that flat tone meant. Raunu, who'd seen combat since before Skarnu was born, did. Instead of asking where the other peasant had gone, he found the right question on the first try: "What happened to him?"

That made Merkela stop scattering grain and come to alertness herself. Skarnu answered, "Night and fog." He explained how he'd found the words painted on Dauktu's door, and what he'd discovered when he went into the farmhouse.

"Simanu's vengeance, eh?" Raunu looked unhappy. "Did they pick him because he was one of us, or just because they pulled his name out of a hat? And if they wanted to avenge Simanu, why didn't they leave his body there, and his family dead with him?"

"I don't know the answer to either of those." Skarnu felt as unhappy as Raunu looked. "I'd like to, especially the first."

"If people get killed, everyone knows how it happened," Merkela said. "If they just disappear, everybody wonders. Did the redheads take them away and murder them somewhere else? Or are they still alive and suffering because the Algarvians don't want to let them die?"

"There's a pleasant thought," Skarnu said. After a bit of thought, he admitted, "It makes better sense than anything I came up with on the way back here."

"Aye." Raunu nodded. "It'd be like the Algarvians to try and put us in fear."

"If they are torturing Dauktu and his kin, they've put me in fear," Skarnu said. "Who knows what a man's liable to blab when they're pulling out his toenails or working over his daughter in front of him?"

"They won't take me alive," Merkela declared. Like any farm woman, she wore a knife on her belt. She caressed its hilt as she might have caressed Skarnu. "Powers below eat me if I'll give them any sport or let them squeeze anything out of me."

"We'd all be smart to go armed some way or another for a while," Raunu said. Skarnu nodded, wondering if he'd be able to find the courage to slay himself. To save himself from Algarvian torment, he thought he might.

He slept close by his stick that night. But the Algarvians did not come, as they – or perhaps Simanu's henchmen, acting with their leave – had come to Dauktu's farm. The next morning, Raunu went into Pavilosta to buy salt and nails and, with luck, sugar: things the farm couldn't make for itself. The veteran underofficer took along a blade of his own, long enough to reach his heart.

After he'd vanished around a bend in the road, Skarnu and Merkela, without a word spoken, set aside their chores, hurried upstairs to her bedchamber, and made love. This time, he was as desperately urgent as she usually was; he wondered if it might be the last, and did his best to give himself something to savor for however long he had. When pleasure drowned him, he groaned as he might have under an Algarvian torturer's whip.

Drained, emptied, numb, he and Merkela went back out to the endless farm work. He did it at about half speed, waiting for Raunu or King Mezentio's men: whoever chanced to come to the farm first.

It was Raunu, a little bent under the weight of the pack on his back but his face glowing with news. "There must be a dozen of those 'Simanu's vengeance – night and fog' signs in town," he said as he set down his burden. "Not a one that I could tell was on the door of anybody who's fighting the redheads. They just picked people, powers above knows how, and now nobody knows what's become of 'em."

"That's good to hear," Skarnu said. "Good for anybody except the folk who had it happen to them, I mean."

"Night and fog," Merkela repeated musingly. "They want people to wonder what's happened to whoever they took, all right. Are they dead? Are they under torture, like we said before? Or are the redheads doing . . . what the stories we hear talk about?"

Skarnu's lips pulled back from his teeth in a horrid grimace. "One more thing I hadn't thought of. One more thing I wish you hadn't thought of, either."

"There may not be any Kaunians left alive in the world if the Algarvians have their way," Merkela said.

"They haven't taken anyone from Valmiera or Jelgava," Skarnu said. "We'd have heard if they started doing anything like that."

"Would we?" That was Raunu, not Merkela. He added three words: "Night and fog."

"We're still fighting," Skarnu said. "I don't know what else we can do. They won't get anything cheap, not from this county they won't."

"Aye." Merkela's angry nod sent a lock of her pale hair flipping down over her eyes. Brushing it back with a hand, she went on, "They say Simanu's had his revenge. We haven't even started taking ours yet."

"Keeping ourselves alive, staying in the fight – that's a kind of victory all by itself," Skarnu said. He wouldn't have thought so, not when the war was new and his noble blood entitled him to don shiny captain's badges. He knew better now.

Bembo lifted a glass of wine in salute to Sergeant Pesaro. "Here's to some time well spent in Gromheort," the constable said.

"Aye." Pesaro tilted his head back to upend his own glass, giving Bembo a splendid view of several of his chins. He waved to the busy barmaid. "Two more glasses of red here, sweetheart." The Forthwegian woman nodded to show she'd heard him. He turned back to Bembo. "I'm glad not to spend all day on my feet marching, I'll tell you that."

"That's the truth, sure enough," Bembo agreed. The barmaid came by with an earthenware pitcher and refilled their glasses. Since Bembo had bought the last round, Pesaro set a small silver coin down on the table. The barmaid took it. As she went off to serve someone else, Pesaro reached out and pinched her backside.

She sprang in the air and gave him a dirty look. "You shouldn't have done that," Bembo said mournfully. "Now she'll spend the rest of the day pretending not to notice us."

"She'd better not," Pesaro growled. "Besides, it's not like I'm the only one in this tavern who's ever got his hands on that arse."

Looking around, Bembo had to nod. Because it was across the street from their barracks, the tavern was always full of Algarvian constables – and Algarvians had never been shy about putting their hands on women, their own or those of the kingdoms they'd overrun. "Will she sleep with you for silver?" Bembo asked.

"Curse me if I know," Pesaro answered. "I never thought she was pretty enough to try and find out. The blond wenches in the soldiers' brothels look a lot better to me."

"Well, I won't tell you you're wrong about that," Bembo said. "All these Forthwegian women are built like bricks." He started to say something more, but then pointed to another constable a couple of tables away. "Oh, powers above! Almonio's gone and drunk himself into another crying jag."

Pesaro cursed as he twisted on his stool. He had to push it back to get his belly past the front of the table. He too watched the young constable sitting there with tears streaming down his face. Almonio was very drunk; a pitcher like the one the barmaid carried lay on its side, empty, on the table in front of him. "Miserable bugger," Pesaro said, shaking his head. "I don't know why he ever thought he could be a constable."

"Sergeant, you never should have let him beg off hauling Kaunians out of their houses with the rest of us," Bembo said. "I don't like it, either –

that's another reason I'm glad I'm back in Gromheort, aside from all the marching I'm not doing – but I pull my weight." He looked down at himself. "And I've got a deal of weight to pull, too." If he hadn't said it, Pesaro would have, even though he carried even more weight than Bembo.

As things were, Pesaro emptied his new glass of wine before asking, "You think he'd be better if I made him do it?"

"You're the one who always says things like there's nothing like a boot in the arse to concentrate the brain," Bembo answered.

"I know, I know." Pesaro waved for the barmaid again. Sure enough, she pretended not to see him. Muttering, the constabulary sergeant said, "He hasn't got the stomach for the job as is. I just thought I'd make things worse if I held him to it, so I didn't."

"Me, I haven't got the stomach for hard work," Bembo said.

"Never would have noticed," Pesaro said in tones that made Bembo wince. Pesaro called out to Almonio: "Powers above, man, pull yourself together."

"I'm sorry, Sergeant," the young constable replied. "I can't help thinking about what happens to the Kaunians when we ship 'em west. You know it as well as I do. I know you know. Why doesn't it drive you mad, too?"

"They're the enemy," Pesaro said with assurance. "You always hit the enemy as hard as you can. That's the rules."

Almonio shook his head. "They're just people. Men and women and children with blond hair and a funny language out of old times. A few of 'em were soldiers, aye, but we don't do anything special to the Forthwegians who yielded, or not to most of 'em, anyway. The women and children sure never hurt us."

"All Kaunians are out to get us," Pesaro said. "The Kaunians in Jelgava almost took Tricarico away from us, in case you forgot. They've hated us ever since we knocked their dusty old Empire flat, all those years ago, and they've really hated us since the Six Years' War. That's what King Mezentio says, and I think he's dead right."

But Almonio only shook his head again. Then he folded his arms on the table, bent forward, and fell asleep. Bembo said, "He'll be better when he comes around – till the next time he gets drunk, anyhow."

"Take him back to the barracks and pour him into his cot," Pesaro said.

"What, by myself?" Bembo said.

Pesaro grunted. He knew Bembo put no more effort into anything than he had to. But, at the last minute, the sergeant relented. "Oh, all right. There's Evodio over there by the wall. Hey, Evodio! Aye, you – who'd you think I was talking to? Come on and give Bembo a hand."

Evodio gave Bembo two fingers, at any rate: an Algarvian obscene gesture at least as old as any Kaunian ruins. Bembo cheerfully returned it. They draped one of Almonio's limp arms across each of their shoulders and half dragged, half carried him across the street.

"We ought to leave him here," Bembo said while they were crossing the cobbles. "Maybe a wagon running over his head would pound some sense into him."

"It's a dirty business we're in," Evodio said. "Maybe even dirtier than soldiering, because soldiers have real enemies who can blaze back in front of 'em."

Bembo stared at him in some surprise. "How come you weren't crying your head off with him, if you feel like that?"

Evodio shrugged, almost dropping his half of Almonio. "I can take it. I don't think we've got anything to be proud of, though."

Since Bembo didn't think the Algarvian constables had anything to be proud of, either, he kept quiet. Between them, they got the sodden Almonio into his cot. One of the constables in a dice game on the floor of the barracks looked up with a grin. "He's going to be miserable when he wakes up, the poor, sorry son of a whore," he predicted.

"He was pretty miserable already, or he wouldn't have gotten this drunk," Bembo answered.

"Ah, one of those, eh?" the other constable said. "Well, let him spend a while longer in this business and he'll figure out you're wasting your time if you get upset over stuff you can't do anything about." The next roll of the dice went against him, and he cursed furiously.

With a laugh, Bembo began, "You're wasting your time if you get upset—"

"Oh, shut up," the other constable said.

When Bembo stuck his nose outside the barracks the next morning, he shivered. Most of the time, Gromheort wasn't that much cooler than Tricarico. But the wind that blew out of the southwest today had a nasty chill reminiscent of the broad plains of Unkerlant from which it had come.

"Just my luck," Bembo grumbled as he headed out on patrol. He was always ready to pity himself, since no one else seemed interested in the job.

He took some consolation in seeing that the Forthwegians and Kaunians on the street looked as unhappy and put upon as he felt. Some of them had mufflers wrapped around their necks and heavy cloaks over their tunics or trousers, but more, like Bembo, simply had to make do. When a particularly nasty gust blew in under his kilt, he envied the Kaunians their trousers.

By now, he'd found a number of places whose proprietors were good for a handout. He stopped in at one of them for a mug of tea sweetened with honey. He drank it so fast, it burned his mouth. He didn't much care. It put some warmth in his belly, too, which was what he'd had in mind.

As he started tramping the pavement again, a wagon full of laborers clattered past, its iron-tired wheels loud on the cobbles. Most of the laborers were Forthwegians, a few Kaunians. The blonds looked even scrawnier and more ragged than the Forthwegians. They didn't get paid as much for the same work. Bembo's sympathy was fleeting at best. Those Kaunians could have been a lot worse off, and he knew it.

"Good morning to you, Constable," one of the laborers called. He was a Forthwegian, but used classical Kaunian – a good thing, too, because Bembo still hadn't learned more than a handful of words in the Forthwegian language.

After a moment, he recognized the laborer as the fellow who'd helped him find the barracks when he was new to Gromheort and very lost. He didn't want to speak Kaunian where a lot of people could hear him doing it. He did take off his hat and wave it to the Forthwegian. That seemed to do the job; the black-bearded young man waved a hand in return.

A couple of blocks later, Bembo heard a man and a woman shouting at each other in Forthwegian. Setting a hand on the bludgeon he wore on his belt, he turned a corner and tramped down a muddy alley to find out what was going on. "What's all this about?" he said loudly, in Algarvian. Whether anybody would understand him was liable to be a different question, but he'd worry about that later.

Sudden silence fell. The man, Bembo saw, was a prosperous-looking Forthwegian, the woman a Kaunian who had strumpet written all over her. Strumpet or not, she turned out to speak Algarvian. Pointing to the man, she said, "He cheated me. I gave him what he wanted, and now he won't pay."

"This bitch lies," the Forthwegian said, also in Algarvian – maybe he'd done business across the border before the war broke out. "I ask you, Officer – do you think I'd want a drab like this?"

"Never can tell," Bembo said – he'd heard of plenty of rich Algarvians with peculiar tastes, so why not a Forthwegian, too? Turning to the woman, he asked, "What do you say he wanted from you?"

"My mouth," she answered at once. "I know him – he's too lazy to screw."

Ignoring the Forthwegian's bellow of fury, Bembo glanced at the knees of the Kaunian woman's trousers. They had fresh mud on them. He hefted the bludgeon. "Pay up," he told the Forthwegian.

The man cursed and fumed, but reached into his belt pouch and slapped silver into the Kaunian woman's hand. He stomped off, still muttering under his breath. The Kaunian woman eyed Bembo. "Now I suppose you'll take half of this – or maybe all of it," she said.

"No," he answered, and then wondered why. A small offering to make up for all the blonds he'd herded into caravan cars? He didn't know. Then he had a new thought. "There's something else you might do . . ."

"I wondered if you'd say that," she answered with weary cynicism. "Well, come here." When he walked out of the alley a few minutes later, he was whistling. This had all the makings of a fine morning.

Retreat again, retreat through heavy snow even this far north. Leudast shivered and cursed and tugged at the hem of his white smock as he stumbled along what might have been the road running back toward Cottbus. Algarvian dragons thought it was the road; eggs kept falling out of the sky along with the snow. Every so often, Unkerlanter soldiers would shriek as one of the eggs burst close enough to wound.

"Sir," Leudast called out Captain Hawart when the regimental commander came close enough to recognize, "sir, are we going to be able to hold them out of the capital?"

"They won't take Cottbus till every last man defending it is dead," Hawart said.

For a moment, that reassured Leudast. Then he realized that all those deaths might not be enough. He trudged past a small field littered with corpses: Unkerlanter peasants slain by Unkerlanter mages in a desperate effort to blunt the power of the murderous sorcery the redheads aimed at their kingdom.

What sort of funeral pyre would King Swemmel light to hold the Algarvians out of Cottbus? Thinking about it made Leudast's blood run colder than the miserable winter weather around him. He hoped it wouldn't come to that. If it didn't, he and his battered comrades would have to be the ones who kept it from happening.

Some great shapes came lumbering across a field toward him. He started to bring up his stick, an automatic – and mostly futile – reaction whenever he saw behemoths. From behind him, Sergeant Magnulf called, "Don't blaze at those buggers. They're ours."

The behemoths were indeed moving east, to oppose the advancing Algarvians. "We do keep sending 'em into the fight," Leudast allowed. "Now if only they'd last a little longer, we'd be better off."

He didn't realize a village lay ahead till he was marching through its outskirts. "Peel off!" Hawart shouted to his men. "Peel off! We're going to make a stand here. We're going to make a stand at every village we come to from now on. We're going to keep making stands till none of us is left standing."

Leudast went into a peasant hut much like the one in which he'd lived till King Swemmel's impressers dragged him into the army. Being out of the wind made him feel warmer. He peered through a window, then nodded. He had a good view to the east, though with the snow he didn't know how soon he'd seen the Algarvians. But they would see him no sooner.

He'd hardly found a spot he liked before the Algarvians started tossing eggs at the village. The flimsy walls of the hut shook around Leudast; he wondered if the roof beams were going to come down on his head. "Efficiency," he said, with no small bitterness. King Swemmel preached it. The Algarvians seemed to know what it really meant. All through the war, their egg-tossers had kept up with the fighting better than Unkerlant's. *One more reason we've got our backs to Cottbus*, Leudast thought.

He knew what was coming next. After they'd softened up the position with eggs, the Algarvians would probe it and try to outflank it. He didn't know what sort of defenses lay to either side. He did know the redheads would get a bloody nose if they tried pounding straight through.

"Here they come!" somebody shouted.

Leudast peered through the window. Sure enough, little dark shapes were moving toward him through the snow. The Algarvians hadn't thought to use white smocks and hoods of their own to make themselves less conspicuous against an equally white background. Knowing Mezentio's men could overlook something like that made Leudast feel oddly better.

He rested his stick on the bottom of the window frame and waited. Keeping it there would steady his aim. Before the Algarvians got close enough for him to start blazing, Captain Hawart's rear guard east of the village sent beams their way. A few redheads fell. The rest had to slow down and develop the Unkerlanter position, to see what sort of opposition they faced.

Eggs started falling again, this time in front of the village. Leudast cursed. The Algarvians also had far more crystals than did his countrymen, had them and used them. Leudast wished the Unkerlanter egg-tossers were so flexibly directed – far from the first time he'd made that wish.

And then, as if to prove even an Unkerlanter corporal could get lucky once in a while, a great torrent of eggs rained down on the advancing Algarvians. Snow and dirt flew. So did bodies. Leudast whooped. He yelled himself hoarse. Someone, for once, had done the right thing at the right time. "See how you like that, you stinking whoresons!" he shouted in delight. "You don't buy anything cheap today."

He wondered if the Algarvians would have to murder another few dozen or few hundred Kaunian captives to get the magical boost they needed to push forward. He wondered if his own kingdom's mages would have to murder more Unkerlanter peasants to withstand that magic and even to hurl it back on its creators. He wondered if anything would be left of Unkerlant by the time the two armies and the two sets of mages were done with the kingdom.

Instead of magic, the Algarvians chose behemoths. Half a dozen of the big beasts lumbered toward the village. An egg had to burst almost on top of one of them to do it much harm. Twice Leudast shouted when a behemoth was knocked off its feet. Each time, he moaned a moment later when the animal staggered up and came on once more. The behemoths' advance was all the more frightening for being so slow and deliberate; enough snow lay on the ground to hamper their movements.

Hawart's rear guard had no real chance to do anything against the behemoths. They were so heavily armored, the only way a footsoldier with an ordinary stick could hope to bring one down was with a blaze through the eye. That was possible. It was very far from likely.

As they usually did, the Algarvian behemoths paused well outside the village. Four of them carried egg-tossers, which they used to pound the place some more. The other two bore heavy sticks. When they blazed, the beams they sent forth were like swords of light. They quickly set a couple of houses afire. Had one of those beams pierced Leudast, he would have died without knowing what struck him. There were worse ways to go in war. He was convinced of that; he'd seen too many, seen them and listened to them, too.

But before a heavy stick could swing his way, the behemoths and their crews were distracted by something off to their left. Leudast couldn't tell what it was without sticking his head out the window, which struck him as a good way to get a hole blazed through it. He stayed where he was and waited. With peasant patience, he understood he'd find out sooner or later what was going on.

And he did. Several Unkerlanter behemoths advanced against their Algarvian counterparts. They started tossing eggs at the behemoths on which King Mezentio's men rode. The Algarvian crews knew they were a greater danger than whatever footsoldiers might be defending the village.

When artists illustrated battles among behemoths, and when people talked about them, they always depicted and described the beasts charging full tilt at one another so they could use their horns to deadly effect. That did happen – in mating skirmishes, when the bulls fought without crews and without man-made weapons mounted on their backs. In war, such charges were all but unknown. Eggs and sticks did the bulk of the fighting, not the animals themselves.

A beam from a heavy stick tore through the chainmail an Algarvian behemoth wore. Leudast could hear the beast's agonized bellow. He cheered as the behemoth tottered and fell. Then a great blast of noise announced that an egg had indeed landed right on top of an Unkerlanter behemoth, not only slaying the beast but also touching off the eggs it carried. Leudast groaned as loudly as he'd cheered a moment before.

As the long-range duel among the behemoths went on, Leudast noticed something strange. The Algarvian beasts and their crews fought as if they were the fingers on a single hand, while each Unkerlanter behemoth might have been the only one on the field. He didn't know whether the redheads had crystals aboard all their behemoths or whether they were simply better trained to work together than the Unkerlanters, but the difference told. They lost two more of their behemoths, but after a while none of the Unkerlanter beasts remained in the fight.

The surviving Algarvian behemoths went back to pounding the village. An egg burst just behind the house in which Leudast was sheltering. The sudden release of sorcerous energies knocked him to his knees. He scrambled up again, his ears ringing; the next Algarvian assault wouldn't wait long.

"Here they come!" That dreaded shout rang out again. This time, though, Leudast knew at least a little relief to go with the dread: Someone beside him had survived.

He cautiously peered out the window once more. Sure enough, the redheads were moving forward in loose open order. No beam, no egg, would slay more than one of them.

None of the rear guard Hawart had set was still fighting. The Algarvians' advance remained unhindered till they got within range of the Unkerlanter soldiers holed up and waiting for them. "Mezentio! Mezentio!" The yell raised Leudast's hackles.

"Urra!" he cried as he began to blaze. "King Swemmel! Urra!" He picked off one Algarvian after another. He seemed unable to miss. Every time he blazed, another redhead fell. He'd never had such a run of luck.

But he couldn't kill the whole Algarvian army by himself. The soldiers he didn't kill kept on toward the village. Idly, he wondered what the name of this place was. If he died, he would have liked to know where he was doing it.

A beam almost as thick as his thigh struck the hut from which he was fighting. He stared in astonishment at the hole it made. The edges of that hole began to burn merrily. Leudast swatted at the flames with a rag, but couldn't put them out. They licked hungrily at the old dry boards of the wall.

Smoke started to choke him. He realized he couldn't stay where he was, not unless he wanted to burn, too. Reluctantly, he ran out into the street.

"Over here!" Sergeant Magnulf shouted, and waved to show where he was. "Come on – this is a good hole."

Leudast needed no further invitation. He dove into the hole. He didn't know how good it was, but it was very welcome. "We're still here," he said, and Magnulf nodded.

But the Algarvians were still there, too, and still there in large numbers. And their behemoths kept sending powerful beams through the village and tossing eggs into it. One of those eggs burst right in front of the hole.

Magnulf's head had been up above the edge. He shrieked and clutched at his face. Blood poured around the edges of his mittens. After a moment of standing there swaying, he slowly crumpled. His hands fell away from the hideous wounds. His eyes were gone, as if he'd never had any. His nose was burned away, too, leaving only a gaping hole in the middle of his face. Leudast grimaced. He'd seen a lot of horrors since the fighting started, but few close to this.

Magnulf likely wouldn't live, not with those wounds. If by some chance – some mischance – he did, he likely wouldn't want to. Leudast pulled a knife from his belt and drew it across the sergeant's burned and blistered throat. More blood fountained, but not for long. Even before Magnulf drew his last bubbling breath, Leudast was peering out as his friend had done, hoping he wouldn't be unlucky as his friend had been, and getting ready once more to fight to hold the Algarvians out of the village.

Fernao was wishing he'd never been born. That failing, he was wishing he'd never studied magecraft. And, that failing, he was wishing he'd never, ever, set foot in the land of the Ice People. Had he escaped that, Colonel Peixoto wouldn't have thought to include him in the Lagoan expeditionary force cruising the ley lines toward the austral continent.

"A plague of boils on King Penda's pendulous belly," Fernao muttered as the *Implacable* bucked beneath his feet like a unicorn gone mad. Had he not set out to rescue Penda, he wouldn't have had to go to the land of the Ice People. Setubal could be a dreary place during the winter. Next to a cramped cabin in a ship implacably gliding farther south and east every moment, dreariness seemed most attractive.

The ley-line cruiser's bow pitched down into the trough. That pitched Fernao off his feet. Fortunately, he landed on his bunk, not on his head.

"Gliding," he said, packing the word with enough loathing to suit a major curse. On land, a caravan traveling along a ley line stayed a fixed distance above the ground, and the ground stayed fixed, too. But the surface of the sea wasn't fixed – was, in these southern waters, anything but fixed. The *Implacable*, like the rest of the ships in the Lagoan fleet, drew from the ley line the energy she used to travel. She couldn't possibly hope to draw enough energy to stay steady when the sea refused to do the same.

Rubbing his shin, which had banged off the bunk's iron frame, Fernao got up and left the cabin. He felt trapped in there. If anything happened to the *Implacable*, he'd die before he found out what was wrong. *And if you go up on deck, you'll die knowing exactly what's wrong*, his mind gibed. *Is that an improvement?*

In an odd sort of way, it was. The ship's corridors and stairs had handrails that helped in a fierce sea. Fernao used them. Had he not used them, he would have suffered far worse than a barked shin.

When he came out on deck, sleet blew into his face. Sailors ran about doing their jobs with no more concern than if the cruiser had been tied up at a quay in Setubal. Fernao envied them their effortless ease – and kept a hand on a rail or a rope at all times. The wind howled like a hungry wolf.

Captain Fragoso came up to Fernao, walking along the slanting deck as casually as the sailors did. "A fine morning, sir mage," he shouted cheerily. "Aye, a fine morning." If he noticed the sleet, he gave no sign of it.

"If you say so," Fernao answered, also raising his voice to make himself heard above the gale. "I must tell you, though, Captain, I have more than a little trouble discerning its charms."

"Do you? Do you indeed?" Fragoso's hat was secured by a chin strap. The wind almost blew it away anyhow. After settling it back on his head, he went on, "If you like, then, I will tell you why it is a fine morning."

"If you would be so kind," the mage said.

"Oh, I will, I will, never you fear," Fragoso said, cheerful still. "It's a fine morning because, during this past long, black night, we sailed by Sibiu – as close as we were ever going to come – and the Algarvians didn't spot us. If that doesn't make it a fine morning, curse me if I know what does."

"Ah," Fernao said, and then gravely nodded. "You're right, Captain; it *is* a fine morning. Of course, the Algarvians probably weren't looking for us very hard, either, being under the impression no sane men would sail in such a sea. I confess, I was under the same impression myself."

"Aye, well, such is life," Captain Fragoso said. "But they could have hurt us if they'd seen us. The one great disadvantage of ley-line ships is that they can only dodge where the lines cross. We wouldn't enjoy it if dragons started trying to drop eggs on us, not even a little we wouldn't."

Fernao shivered at the prospect. He was shivering anyhow, but this was something new and different. But then, looking up toward the dark, scudding clouds overhead, he remarked, "I don't think the dragonfliers would enjoy going up in weather like this, either."

"Something to that, I shouldn't wonder," Fragoso said. A wave smacked the *Implacable* broadside, sending spray and water over the rail and drenching the naval officer and Fernao. Fernao cursed and shuddered; Fragoso took it in stride. "Part of my business, sir – just part of my business."

"Along with chilblains and pneumonia, I suppose." Something else occurred to Fernao. "We may well be able to get through all right, Captain. We're a surprise." He was surprised the fleet had sailed in dead of winter, so he didn't wonder that the Algarvians were, too. "But we won't be able to keep it a secret once we've landed on the austral continent. If we need reinforcements, King Mezentio's men will be on the lookout for them."

"Ah, I see what you're saying." Fragoso shrugged. "They'll just have to do the best they can, that's all." No one had thought about anything past this first fleet, was what that meant. Fernao had hoped for better, but hadn't really expected it.

Up in the crow's nest atop the only mast the *Implacable* carried, the lookout let out a screech: "Ice! Ice off the port bow!"

Fernao had hoped for better than that, too, but hadn't really expected it. In sailing to the land of the Ice People, he would have been a fool not to expect ice drifting in the water. But the fleet still was farther north than drifting bergs commonly came so early in the season. *Aren't we lucky?* the mage thought.

Fragoso shouted into a speaking tube, ordering the mages who drew energy from the ley line to bring the *Implacable* to a halt and let the ice float past. Then he shouted into another tube, this one sending his voice to the crystallomancer: "Warn the other ships in the fleet what we've seen – and warn them not to ram us while we're stopped, too."

Fernao hurried toward the bow to get a good look at the iceberg. He'd seen them before, but the fascination remained. That great, silent mass, far larger than the ley-line cruiser, looked as if it had no business existing, let alone being dangerous. But it did and it was; it could smash in the *Implacable*'s sides as if they were made of eggshells rather than iron. As the ship slowed, Fernao remembered what Fragoso had said about ley-line ships' inability to dodge. He wished he hadn't.

Closer and closer drifted the mountain of ice, its surface rocking slightly in the surging sea. Fernao gripped the rail as hard as he could. The iceberg came close enough to let him see green grading into blue grading into white. It came close enough to let him see a gull – or perhaps it was a petrel – strolling about on the ice as casually as a man might stroll down the Boulevard of Kings in Setubal. If the iceberg hit the cruiser, the bird would fly away. The *Implacable*'s sailors wouldn't be so lucky. Neither would Fernao.

A sailor loosed a triumphant shout: "It's past!" Sure enough, Fernao had to look to his right – *to starboard*, he reminded himself – to see it. It couldn't have missed the ley-line cruiser by more than fifty yards. He wondered how many more bergs the fleet would have to evade before drawing up to the ice shelf that formed even on the northernmost fringes of the austral continent every winter. He hoped finding the answer to that question wouldn't be too expensive.

In the middle of the following night, an iceberg did hit another cruiser. The berg's weight and momentum carried the stricken ship off the ley line, leaving it helpless and the rest of the fleet unable to go after it for a rescue. The cruiser did have lifeboats. If by oars or sails or current they reached another ley line, the men who managed to board them might live. If not . . . Fernao grimaced.

"How long till we near the land of the Ice People?" he asked at breakfast the next morning. Tables and benches in the galley were mounted on gimbals, to minimize the chance of porridge and smoked pork and wine flying every which way.

Commander Diniz was in charge of the *Implacable*'s egg-tossers. "Tomorrow morning, if all goes well," he answered, spooning up porridge as if immune to the ship's motion. "If we strike ice first, we'll take a little longer."

Fernao admired his easygoing good humor. He also admired the way the officer ate. His own stomach seemed uncertain whether it was supposed to cower between his feet or crawl hand over hand up his throat.

The mage finished his own porridge and pork with grim determination. Food in the Royal Lagoan Navy was made to be tolerated, not relished. Compared to what lay ahead on the austral continent . . .

"Have you ever eaten boiled camel's flesh?" he asked Diniz.

"No, sir mage, can't say that I have," the officer replied. "Of course, I won't be going ashore, so it's a treat I'll just have to do without."

"Oh, that's right," Fernao said in a hollow voice. He'd forgotten that. Misery loved company, and here he had to be alone. His gloom didn't last long. Few others from the *Implacable* would be going ashore, but she and her fellow warships escorted freighters full of soldiers. They would soon discover the joys of cuisine in the land of the Ice People.

He wondered what the Ice People themselves would make of the Lagoan expeditionary force. From everything he'd seen, civilization meant little to them. But his brief contempt faded. No one would deny Algarve was a civilized kingdom, but the Ice People could never have done what King Mezentio's mages had used the tools and spells of civilization to accomplish.

He also wondered how Algarve would respond to the Lagoan thrust. Mezentio couldn't well afford to lose his main source of cinnabar, but could he well afford to send an army across the Narrow Sea to help Yanina fight the Lagoans? *If Cottbus falls, he can*, Fernao thought uneasily. But the capital of Unkerlant hadn't fallen yet. *Maybe it won't.* He wondered if he was whistling in the dark.

There was plenty of dark in which to whistle. This far south, just past the winter solstice, the sun hardly peeped above the northern horizon before setting again. Clouds turned what little light it sent into dusk.

And yet, the Lagoan fleet came up to the edge of the ice shelf jutting out from the austral continent on schedule and without further mishap. Fernao tipped his hat to Colonel Peixoto and the colonel's comrades back in Setubal. He wouldn't have believed such a thing had he not seen it with his own eyes.

"Over the side you go." Captain Fragoso seemed happy about the business. As Commander Diniz had said, he didn't have to climb down that rope ladder.

Fernao did. Once he got down on the ice, he promptly slipped and fell despite the spiked shoes he was wearing. The sight of a fair-sized army descending from the freighters — and of the soldiers there also stumbling on the ice – went further to console him than he'd expected. Sure enough, misery did love company.

He had plenty of company. He was plenty miserable, too. Night had already begun to fall by the time the Lagoan army began its slow, awkward slog across the ice in the direction of the Barrier Mountain. The army didn't reach land till dawn the next day. A couple of men of the Ice People sat mounted on their hairy, two-humped camels, watching the Lagoans approach. Fernao peered at them through a spyglass he borrowed from an officer. They were laughing. Fernao fell down on the ice for about the twentieth time. He decided he couldn't blame them.

Marshal Rathar was used to smelling wood smoke and coal smoke as he walked through the streets of Cottbus. For the past couple of days, he'd been smelling a new, sharper odor with them: paper smoke. Frightened clerks in the Unkerlanter capital were starting to burn their records lest they fall into Algarvian hands. They thought Cottbus would fall. Even if they proved right, Rathar doubted getting rid of their files would do them much good. King Mezentio's men would still have them, after all.

Some of the clerks – and some higher officials, too – seemed to have come to the same conclusion, and seemed determined not to let the Algarvians catch them. Every ley-line caravan heading west was full of important-looking people with official-looking orders urgently requiring their presence away from Cottbus. Some few of those orders might even have been genuine. Rathar wouldn't have bet more than a couple of coppers on it, though.

He kicked his way through a knee-high snowdrift as he neared the great open plaza around the royal palace. As far as he was concerned, Cottbus was better off without functionaries who skedaddled when trouble came near. He wanted people around him who could keep their heads. But if King Swemmel ever found out how many people were fleeing, a lot of them were liable not to keep their heads, in the most literal sense of the words imaginable.

A team of horses was dragging the body of a dragon painted in Algarvian colors across the square. Mezentio's dragonfliers kept trying to drop eggs on the palace. They had no easy time of it; heavy sticks all around made the immense building perhaps the toughest target in all of Unkerlant.

One of the men in charge of the horses waved to Rathar. He waved back. Seeing men going about their business as if the Algarvians were two hundred miles away – as if there were no war at all – cheered him.

"Good morning, Lord Marshal," his adjutant said when he strode into his office.

"Good morning, Major Merovec," Rathar answered, hanging his cloak on a hook. The colder it got outside, the warmer the palace was heated. That was the ancient Unkerlanter way of doing things. Doctors said it helped lead to apoplexy, but who listened to doctors? Glancing toward the map, Rathar asked, "What change in the situation since last night?"

Merovec often looked gloomy. Today he looked like midwinter midnight on the far side of the Barrier Mountain. Pointing, he said, "In the north, sir, the Algarvians have pushed us out of Lehesten. And in the south" – he pointed again – "they're threatening Thalfang." With a certain somber satisfaction, he added, "We do seem to be holding them in the center."

"That's not good enough," Rathar said. "Curse it, Lehesten should have held. I thought it would hold . . . longer than this, anyhow. And Thalfang? Powers above, you can see Thalfang from the tops of the palace spires! If they take it and sweep west from there, they can put a ring around Cottbus, the same way they put a ring around Herborn down in Grelz. We have to hold them out of Thalfang, no matter what. Draft orders to shift troops south."

"Lord Marshal, everything we have in the vicinity is already committed," Merovec answered worriedly. "I don't know where we're going to come up with more."

"If we don't come up with more in the next few days, we won't have the chance to do it later," Rathar said, and Merovec nodded; he understood the problem as well as the marshal of Unkerlant did. Rathar smacked a fist into the palm of his other hand. "We have a lot of things we're right on the edge of trying. If we can't buy a little time to finish getting them ready, we'll lose the war before we have the chance to use them."

"Aye." Merovec nodded again. "But we have so many men committed on other fronts, I don't know where we can find more for this one."

"King Swemmel won't turn enough men loose for this front. That's what you mean," Rathar said, and his adjutant nodded once more. The marshal sighed. "I'd better have a talk with him, hadn't I?"

"Lord Marshal, someone had better, anyhow," Merovec answered. He opened his mouth to say something more, then shut it again. Rathar knew what would have come out – something like, *He might listen to you, and he probably won't listen to anybody else.* That was true, and Rathar knew it as well as Merovec. But, with the war going as it was, Swemmel might also decide he wanted his marshal's head. Rathar had no way to know beforehand.

Even so, he said, "I'll do it. Anyone else would have to work up his nerve before he tried, and we don't have the time to wait. Better to do it now than before everybody has to run west for his life."

He walked out of that part of the sprawling palace where the high officers in the army worked and into the core of the building, the king's residence. "I don't know if he will see you, Lord Marshal," a servitor said doubtfully. "I don't know if he will see anyone."

Rathar fixed him with a stare that would have chilled the heart of every Unkerlanter breathing – except King Swemmel. "Well, go find out," he growled, and folded thick arms across his broad chest, as if to say he wouldn't move from where he stood till he got an answer. The servant eyed him, then fled.

He came back looking very unhappy. Rathar would have bet Swemmel had scorched him, too. But he said, "His Majesty will receive you in the audience chamber in a quarter of an hour." Rathar nodded, a single sharp jerk of his big head. He cared not a copper for the servitor's feelings. Getting to see King Swemmel . . . aye, he cared about that.

In the anteroom in front of the audience chamber, the marshal endured removing his sword and permitting the guards their intimate search of his person. He endured the prostrations and acclamations he had to make before Swemmel once admitted to the royal presence. At last, with security and ritual satisfied, the king rasped, "Get up and say whatever it is you have to say. We shall listen, though why we should, with the kingdom in such straits, is beyond us."

"Your Majesty, I ask you one question," Rathar said: "Would the kingdom be in better straits with another man commanding your armies? If you think so, give him my sword and my baton and give me a stick, so I can go out and fight the Algarvians as a common soldier."

Swemmel stared down at him from his high seat. The king's eyes glowed. His shoulders hunched forward, giving him the aspect of a vulture peering around for carrion. His embroidered robe, encrusted with pearls and jewels, seemed hastily thrown on for this audience. "Rest assured, Marshal: did we think that, you would long since have gone forward thus."

"Good," Rathar said. A sour odor came to him from Swemmel. Was the king drunk? Or, worse, was he hung over? Were his wits working at all, or would he blindly lash out at whatever displeased him? Rathar took a deep breath. He'd find out.

"What do you propose now?" the king demanded. "You could not defend the border, you could not hold Herborn – and now you must defend Cottbus. How will you go about it?"

"Your Majesty, the enemy has taken Lehesten. He threatens Thalfang. We must retake the one and keep the other from falling, or else we are ruined and Cottbus falls." There. Now it was said. How would Swemmel take it?

"Cowards," Swemmel muttered. "Cowards and traitors. They're everywhere – everywhere, curse it." His gaze paralyzed Rathar as readily as the marshal had overawed the servant. "How are we to overcome them?"

"We'd better beat Mezentio's men first," Rathar answered. "If we don't do that, nothing else matters. We need every soldier now – *every* soldier, your Majesty, and every dragon, and every behemoth, and our little surprise for the Algarvians as well. Such things are best saved for when they are needed most, and this is the time."

"Can our person be properly protected if these men and beasts are taken away?" Swemmel asked anxiously.

"Can your person be properly protected if you have to try to flee for your life from Cottbus with the redheads closing a ring around it after they push on from Thalfang and Lehesten?" Rathar returned.

King Swemmel grunted, a sound full of pain. "Traitors," he muttered again. "Who will save us from traitors?" He glared at Rathar.

"One way or another, my head will answer for this, your Majesty," the marshal said. "Whatever happens, I am not going west from Cottbus. If we have to fight here in the city, then here I will fight."

"If only this whole kingdom had but a single neck!" Swemmel cried. "Then I'd take its head and use its energy to build a magical fire that would burn Mezentio in his palace in Trapani – aye, and all his kingdom with him."

Rathar believed every word. Could Swemmel have done it, he would joyously have swung the sword. Rathar said, "Your Majesty, we have . . . reduced the power of their magecraft." He wondered how many Unkerlanter peasants had paid with their lives for that reduction. Better not to know. Aye, better by far. War of a more ordinary sort was his proper business, and he stuck to it: "It's more nearly man against man and beast against beast than it was for a time. But we need the men and beasts. We need all the men and beasts." He realized he was pleading. King Swemmel seldom listened to pleas.

After a long pause, the king said, "We have learned there were riots against the Algarvians in Eoforwic yesterday."

"That's good news!" exclaimed Rathar, who hadn't heard it. "Anything that keeps the redheads from using all they have against us is good news."

"Aye," Swemmel agreed, though he sounded almost indifferent. "Kaunians and Forthwegians went into the streets together, we have heard. Perhaps your notion of sending Kaunians back to Forthweg with their tales of woe bore fruit after all."

"I hope so, your Majesty." Rathar wondered if any Unkerlanter peasants had escaped the clutches of their own kingdom's mages and brought tales of woe back to their villages. He doubted it. Swemmel preached efficiency more readily than he practiced it, but he'd been most efficient about killing since the days of the Twinkings War.

Somewhere in the middle distance, eggs started bursting: Algarvian dragons over Cottbus again. Swemmel turned and stared east. "Curse you, Mezentio," he whispered. "You I trusted, and you betrayed me, too."

How had he trusted Mezentio? To be unready to fight when the time for fighting came? So it had seemed then. It also seemed, as it always had to Rathar, a dreadful miscalculation. The marshal said, "Give me the men, your Majesty. Give me the men and the dragons and the behemoths. We *can* throw them back." He didn't know if Unkerlant could, but he wanted the chance to try.

"Who will protect us?" the king said again. But then, jerkily, he nodded. "Take them. We give them to you. Throw them into the fire, and may they smother it with their bodies. And now, we dismiss you."

Rathar went through the ceremonial involved in leaving the chamber without a shadow of unhappiness. Swemmel had given him the chance. How could he make the most of it?

A blizzard howled around Istvan and his squadmates and all the other Gyongyosian soldiers trying to carry the war in the stars-forsaken mountains to Unkerlant. Wool and sheepskin went only so far in warding them. Flaps from Istvan's sheepskin cap protected his ears, but his beaky nose had long since gone numb. He hoped it wasn't frostbitten.

"Even my valley doesn't have weather like this," he said: no small admission, when Gyongyosians from the interior would sometimes come to blows over whose home valley suffered through the nastier winters.

"What's that, Sergeant?" Szonyi asked. He tramped along only a few feet from Istvan, but the shrieking wind blew words away.

"Never mind." Istvan's next complaint had more substance to it: "How are we supposed to fight a war in weather like this?"

"We're a warrior race," Szonyi answered.

"You're a warrior blockhead," Istvan said, but not too loud. He didn't want Szonyi to hear him. Even if the other soldier wasn't too bright, he was a good man to have along when a squad of Unkerlanters burst out from behind snow-covered rocks yelling "Urra!" at the top of their lungs.

The path – Istvan hoped it was the path, though he had trouble being sure – rose toward the outlet of yet another pass. Istvan wondered what lay beyond. Actually, he could make a pretty good guess: another valley not worth holding, with plenty of snow-covered rocks behind which Unkerlanters could hide. Every now and again, he wondered why Gyongyos wanted this miserable country. He shrugged inside his coat. That wasn't his concern. All he had to worry about was taking the mountains away from the Unkerlanters and staying alive while he was doing it.

Somewhere back behind him was the whole intricate structure even a warrior race like the Gyongyosians needed to wage war in this day and age: baggage train, supply dumps, roads, and ley-line caravans eventually reaching back to Gyongyos itself. Istvan seldom thought about that structure, not least because it *was* behind him. He and his comrades were the very tip of the Gyongyosian spearpoint piercing the kingdom of Unkerlant.

Downhill. He'd been walking downhill for some little while before he realized he was doing it. Either he'd found the top of the pass and was heading down into the next valley or . . . "Kun!" he shouted, breathing out almost as much smoke as if he were a dragon. "You frozen to death yet, Kun?"

"Aye, a couple of hours ago, Sergeant," Kun answered, appearing at his elbow.

"Heh," Istvan said. "All right, then. What I want to know is, are we still marching east, or have we gotten turned around in the snow? If we're heading back toward our own men, they'll cursed well blaze us for Unkerlanters."

"Wind's still blowing from behind us," replied the corporal who had been a mage's apprentice.

Istvan hadn't thought of that, but it didn't fully reassure him, either. "Here in the mountains, the wind blows all sorts of crazy ways."

"That's so." Kun plucked at his tawny beard. Like Istvan's, it was covered with rime. Unlike Istvan's full, shaggy one, it grew by patches and clumps, and so did less to keep Kun's cheeks and chin warm. "I can't do anything about the wind, you know."

"I don't want you to do anything about the accursed wind," Istvan snapped. "I told you, I want to know if I'm going east or west."

"Oh, aye. So you did." Kun plucked at his beard some more, as if hoping to find the answer there. After a few paces, he spoke again: "Have to see where the sun is."

"If I could see where the sun is, would I need to ask you stupid questions?" Istvan shouted. Kun could make him as ready to burst with fury as an egg was with sorcerous energy. But, having burst, he calmed again. "*I* can't see the sun. If you can, tell me where it's at."

Kun wore heavy wool mittens. He took them off so he could fumble in his belt pouch. He finally pulled out a piece of what looked to Istvan like murky, milky glass. He held it in front of his right eye and peered through it now at one part of the sky, now at another.

"What are you doing?" Istvan asked.

"Looking for the sun," Kun replied, as if to an idiot child. After a moment, he condescended to explain more: "The property of this spar, as it is called after a ship's pole, is to let in light of a certain sort only."

"What?" Istvan frowned. "Light is light, eh?"

"Not to a mage," Kun said loftily. Then he gnawed at his lower lip and admitted, "I do not understand the theory as well as I wish I did. But a man does not need to know how a knife cuts to know that it cuts. And so I can use this spar and tell you more light shows ahead of us, which means the sun lies in that direction. Since it is surely after noon, we are marching west."

"That's what I wanted to find out," Istvan said. "Thanks." The wind shifted, blowing snow into his face. He let out a couple of weary curses and went on, "Fine to know I'm liable to be blazed by the Unkerlanters and not by our own men."

"I'm glad to know I relieved your mind," Kun replied. Istvan made a crack about relieving some part of himself a long way removed from his mind.

He and Corporal Kun both laughed. So did Szonyi, who was close enough to hear. He said, "I wish the stars wouldn't let things like getting blazed by your own side happen. If they're as wise and strong and all-knowing as everybody says, why do they let things like that happen sometimes?"

"That's for them to know, not for the likes of us," Istvan said, which was what his family and other people in his home valley had told him when, as a boy, he'd asked such questions.

Kun said, "Why isn't it for us to know? We know a lot more than our grandparents, and even more than *their* grandparents. Why shouldn't we know things like that?"

"Because we aren't meant to," Istvan answered.

"Who told you that?" Kun asked. "How did he know? How do you know he knew?"

Istvan grappled with those unfamiliar questions for a little while. Not having any good answers for them, he said, "If you go on talking that way, you might as well not believe the stars have any power at all."

Kun shook his head; snow flew from his hat. "I have to believe, because I've seen spells that call on them work." He slogged on for another couple of paces. In thoughtful tones, he added, "But the Unkerlanters' spells work, too, and they're goat-eating savages who reverence the invisible powers above that aren't even there."

Now Istvan asked the hard question, not Kun: "What does that mean?"

"May I be accursed if I know," the former mage's apprentice answered.

"I'm going to have to think about that for a while."

"Think about Unkerlanters blazing you instead," Istvan said. "Think about mountain apes sneaking down and carrying you off before you even know they're there. Think about avalanches. Think about things you can do something about."

"What can I do about an avalanche?" Kun asked.

"You can walk soft and try not to start one. And you might be able to run to the side of one if it isn't too big and you see it soon enough," Istvan said. Kun trudged on for another few paces, then nodded, yielding the point. Istvan felt proud of himself. He knew Kun was smarter than he was, and knew Kun knew it, too. When they fenced with words, the sergeant seldom made his corporal back up. He had this time.

Sometimes, in clear, quiet weather, you could hear an egg sighing through the air toward you. In the middle of the snowstorm, the first Istvan knew that the Unkerlanters had started tossing was when the egg burst in front of his squad. Even then, the wind muffled the roar and the deep snow in which the egg landed helped muffle the blast of sorcerous energy that came from it. The snow the burst threw up masked the flash of that energy, too.

Before the second egg landed, Istvan was down on his belly in a snowdrift, crawling toward the nearest rocks he could find. "Stagger your cover if you can," he shouted to his men. "Those Unkerlanter goat-buggers'll be coming after us as soon as they think we're in enough trouble."

Between the bursting eggs and the shrieking wind, he didn't know how many soldiers in his squad heard him. He worried less than he would have with a squad of men seeing battle for the first time. His troopers were all blooded; they didn't need him to do their thinking for them. Some of them – Kun, for instance – resented it when he tried.

"Urra! Urra!" Through the wind, through the thunderstorm of bursting eggs, came the Unkerlanter battle cry. Istvan bared his teeth: now he was worried. It sounded as if King Swemmel's men outnumbered the Gyongyosians who faced them. Their hoarse, angry shouts grew louder.

Istvan shouted, too: "Here they come!"

He blazed at the first figure in rock-gray he saw through the swirling snow. He heard his beam hiss, and cursed the sound: every snowflake the beam seared weakened it before it got to its target, and there were a lot of snowflakes in the air. The Unkerlanter went down, but Istvan didn't think he was out of the fight.

A beam burned a furrow in the snow not far from him. That reminded him he needed to roll away, to make sure he didn't make a fat, juicy target by staying in one place too long. As he rolled, he also made sure his knife was loose in its sheath. With sticks so weakened, this little battle would be fought at close quarters.

Rolling did one more thing – it coated his long sheepskin jacket with snow, making him all but invisible. Sure enough, an Unkerlanter ran right past him, not having any idea he was there. Istvan rose from the snowy ground like one of the mountain apes he'd been talking about a little while before. But he had better weapons than a mountain ape's teeth and muscles, better even than the club the ape he'd killed might have been carrying.

He stabbed the Unkerlanter in the back. The fellow let out a scream that held almost as much surprise as pain. He threw out his arms. His stick flew from his hand. Red stained the snow as he fell. Istvan sprang on to him and slashed his throat, spilling more scarlet on to white.

"Arpad! Arpad! Arpad!" Those were Gyongyosians, coming to the rescue of their beleaguered comrades. Istvan feared the Unkerlanter egg-tossers would take a heavy toll on them, but King Swemmel's men back at the tossers had trouble spying them because of the blizzard, and they made short work of the Unkerlanter footsoldiers.

"Forward!" a Gyongyosian officer shouted.

"Stay spread out," Istvan added. "Don't bunch up and let one egg take out a lot of you." That proved good advice: The Unkerlanters finally realized their attacking party had failed, and started lobbing more eggs toward the mouth of the pass. By then, it was too late. Istvan's countrymen began the business of taking another valley away from Unkerlant. The only thing that could have made Istvan happier was thinking anybody would want the valley once Gyongyos had it.

Eleven

Rain splashed down outside the tailor's shop in Skrunda where Talsu helped his father. The bad weather pleased Traku, who said, "We'll have some wet people coming to buy cloaks today."

"Aye, but half of them will be Algarvians," Talsu answered.

His father made a sour face. "They're the ones with the money," he said. "If it weren't for them, we'd have had a lean time of it." He let out a long, slow exhalation. "I keep telling myself it's worth it – and telling myself, and telling myself."

"You keep telling yourself what?" Talsu's mother asked, coming down the stairs from the living quarters above the shop.

"That you're nosy, Laitsina," Traku replied.

Laitsina snorted. "Why do you keep saying that? If you have so much trouble remembering it, it can't be true." Before Traku could answer, his wife went on, "Out with it, now."

Talsu smiled. His mother *was* nosy. She knew it, too, but that didn't make her stop. After a couple of wordless grumbles, his father said, "Oh, all right, all right." He usually did. That was safer than really annoying Laitsina by not telling her what was going on.

When Traku was done, Laitsina said, "Well, we'll sit around getting lean tonight if you or Talsu doesn't go over to the grocer's and buy some dried chickpeas and some olives and some beans."

"I'll do it," Talsu replied at once.

His mother and father both laughed. "Are you sure you want to head out in the rain?" Traku said. "I can go a little later, if it lets up."

"That's all right," Talsu answered. "I don't mind. I don't mind a bit."

Traku and Laitsina laughed again, louder this time. Shaking a finger at

Talsu, his mother asked, "Would you be so keen about getting wet if the grocer didn't have a pretty daughter?"

That made Talsu's parents laugh harder than ever. His ears heated. "Just let me have the money and I'll go," he muttered.

Traku pulled coins from his pocket. "Here you are," he said. "I remember how much soap I used to buy, because the soapmaker had a pretty daughter." He grinned at Laitsina, who waved her hand as if to say she'd never imagined such a thing. Traku added, "I must've been the cleanest fellow in Skrunda in those days."

"Oh, there were some others buying plenty of soap, too," Laitsina said. "But I do think you got the most. Probably the reason I chose you – I can't think of any other, not after all these years."

Leaving his parents to their good-natured bickering, Talsu grabbed his own cloak from a peg near the door and headed down the street toward the grocery, which wasn't far from the market square. His fellow Jelgavans hurried wherever they were going, with hats pressed low on their foreheads or hoods drawn up from their cloaks. Rain didn't come to Skrunda all that often even in wintertime; save that it made the crops grow, they looked on it as a nuisance.

Four or five Algarvian soldiers came up the street toward Talsu. A couple of them looked as miserable to be out in the wet as any man of Skrunda. The rest, though, seemed perfectly content even though water dripped from the broad brims of their felt hats and ruined the jaunty feathers in their hatbands. Talsu had heard it rained all the time in the forest country of southern Algarve. Maybe those redheads had got used to bad weather there. On the other hand, since they were Algarvians, maybe they just didn't know any better.

He had to press himself against a stone wall to give them room to pass. That got him wetter. They took no notice – though they would have if he hadn't gotten out of the way. He glared at them over his shoulder. Fortunately for him, none of them looked back.

With a sigh of relief at escaping the rain, he flipped back his hood as he ducked into the grocer's shop. With even more relief, he saw that the fat old fellow who ran the place wasn't behind the counter, and his daughter was. "Hello, Gailisa," Talsu said, swiping at his hair with his hand in case the cloak had left it in disarray.

"Hello," Gailisa answered. She was a year or two younger than Talsu;

they'd known each other since they were both small. But Gailisa hadn't been so nicely rounded then, and her hair hadn't shone so golden – or if it had, Talsu hadn't noticed. He did now: he made a point of noticing. She went on, "I'm glad you're not an Algarvian."

"Powers above, so am I!" Talsu exclaimed.

She went on as if he hadn't spoken: "You don't always keep trying to handle the merchandise."

For a moment, he didn't understand exactly what she meant. When he did, he wanted to kill every lecherous Algarvian soldier in Skrunda. He couldn't, but he wanted to. "Those miserable . . ." he began, and then had to stop again. He couldn't say what he thought of the redheads, either. A soldier's ripe vocabulary was the only one that fit, and Gailisa wouldn't have cared to listen to it.

She shrugged. "They're Algarvians. What can you do?"

Talsu had already thought of one of the things he'd like to do. He would also have liked to handle the merchandise himself. If he tried, though, he was gloomily certain Gailisa would do her best to knock his head off. He wasn't a conquering soldier, just a fellow she'd known forever.

"What can I get you?" she asked. He told her what his mother wanted. She frowned. "How much of each? It makes a difference, you know."

"I know that, aye," he said, flustered. "I don't know how much, though."

"You chowderhead," she said. She'd called him worse than that when he got orders mixed up. "Well, how much money did you get to buy this stuff?"

He had to fish the coins his father had given him out of his pocket and look at them before he could tell her, which only made him feel more foolish. "As far as I'm concerned, you can give me mostly olives," he said. "I like 'em."

"And then tomorrow I can explain to your mother why she couldn't make the stew she wanted." Gailisa rolled her eyes. "No, thank you." She dipped up some salted olives from a jar: enough to fill a waxed-paper carton. Then she beckoned to him and gave him a couple of olives to eat. "Nobody has to know about these."

"Thanks." He popped them into his mouth, worked the soft, tasty pulp off the pits with his teeth, and spat the pits into the palms of his hand.

Gailisa pointed to a basket next to the counter. He tossed the pits into it. "More?" he asked hopefully.

Gailisa gave him another one. "When my father asks why we're not making any money, I'll tell him it's your fault," she said. She dipped beans and chickpeas out of barrels and into larger cartons. "There you are, Talsu. Now you've spent all your silver; I'll give you three coppers' change."

"Don't bother," he said. "Let me have three coppers' worth of dried apricots instead."

"I love those, but right after olives?" Gailisa made a face. She gave him the little handful of dried fruit, though.

He ate one apricot, just to see her make another face. Then he pushed the rest of them back across the counter. "Here, you take them. You enjoy them more than I do, anyhow."

"You don't need to do that," she said. "I can reach into the crate any time I please, and I know times are tight for everybody." Talsu looked out through the doorway at the rainy street, as if he hadn't heard a word she said. "You're impossible!" she told him, and he thought she'd got angry. But when he turned around, she was eating an apricot.

He took the groceries and hurried home through the rain. When he got back, he found his father arguing with an Algarvian military mage. He took the beans and olives and chickpeas up to his mother, then went back down to see if his father needed any help. The mage was gesturing violently. "No, no, no!" he exclaimed in excellent, excitable Jelgavan. "That is not what I said!"

"That's what it sounded like to me," Traku said stubbornly.

"What's going on?" Talsu asked. His father seldom got that worked up when talking with an Algarvian. For one thing, Traku didn't think it was worth the effort most of the time. For another, arguing with redheads was dangerous.

Bowing, the Algarvian military mage turned to Talsu. "Perhaps you, sir, can explain to your . . . father, is it? . . . that I am not saying he ought to do anything that would in any way violate his conscience. I only suggested—"

"Suggested?" Traku broke in. "Powers above, this fellow says I don't know how to run my own business, when I've been at it as long as he's been alive." That was an exaggeration, but not by much; the mage was somewhere in his thirties, about halfway between Traku and Talsu.

"I was seeking to buy a new tunic," the Algarvian told Talsu with dignity, "and I discovered the handwork your father proposed to put into it, and I was appalled – appalled!" He made as if to tear his hair to show how appalled he was.

Stiffly, Traku said, "That's what makes fine tailoring, by the powers above: handwork. You want ready-to-wear, you can get that, too, and it's just as ready to fall apart before very long. No, thank you. Not for me."

"Handwork, aye," the mage said. "But needless handwork? No, no, and no! I know you are a Kaunian, but must you work as folk did in the days of the Kaunian Empire? I will show you this is *not* needful."

Traku stuck out his chin and looked stubborn. "How?"

"Have you got a tunic – of any style – cut out and ready to be sewn and spelled together?" the Algarvian asked. "If I ruin it, two goldpieces to you." He took them out of his belt pouch and dropped them on the counter. They rang sweetly.

Talsu's eyes widened. He'd seen Algarvian arrogance before, but this went further than most. "Take him up on it, Father," he said. "You've got a couple of tunics under the counter."

"So I do," Traku said grimly. He took out the pieces for one and glared at the mage. "Now what?"

"Sew me a thumb's width of your finest seam, anywhere on the garment," the redhead told him. "Then lay out thread along all the seams, as you would before you use your own spells."

"That's not near enough handwork," Traku warned, but he did it.

The Algarvian praised his work, which made him no happier. Then the mage murmured his own spell. It had rhythms not far removed from those Jelgavan tailoring sorcery used, but quicker and more urgent. The thread writhed as if alive – and the tunic was done. "Examine it," the mage said. "Test it. Do as you will with it. Is it not as fine as any other?"

Traku did examine it. Talsu crowded up beside him to do the same. He held the seams close to his face to look at the work. He tugged at them. The mage was scribbling something on a scrap of paper. Reluctantly, Talsu turned to his father. "I don't quite know how it'll wear, but that's awfully good-looking work."

"Aye." The word came out of Traku's mouth with even greater

reluctance. His eyes were on those goldpieces, the ones he couldn't claim.

Even as he eyed them, the mage scooped them up again. He set down the paper instead. "Here is the spell, sir. It is in common use in Algarve. If that is not so here, you will have more profit from it than these two coins, far more. A pleasant day to you – and to you, young sir." He bowed to Talsu, then swept out of the shop.

Traku snatched up the spell and stared at it. Then he stared out the door, though the Algarvian was long gone. "No wonder they won the war," he muttered.

"Oh, they're always coming up with something new," Talsu said. "But they're still Algarvians, so a lot of the new is nasty, too. It'll bite 'em in the end, you wait and see."

"I hope so," his father said. "It's already bitten us."

After so long away, after so long at the leading edge of the war, where its teeth bit down on land previously peaceful, Sabrino found Trapani curiously unreal, almost as if it were a mage's illusion. Seeing people going about their business without a care in the world felt strange, unnatural. His eyes kept going to the cloudy sky, watching out for Unkerlanter dragons that would not come.

Oh, the war hadn't disappeared. It remained the biggest story in the news sheets. Commentators spoke learnedly on the crystal. Soldiers and occasional sailors showed off far more uniforms than would have been on the streets in peacetime. But you could ignore all that. Over in Unkerlant, the war was not to be ignored.

Sabrino didn't want to ignore it even though he'd got leave. He'd come to the capital to enjoy himself, aye, but he'd fought too hard to forget the fighting just because he wasn't at the front. "Big announcement expected!" a news-sheet vendor shouted. "Big news coming!" He waved his sheets so vigorously, the colonel of dragonfliers couldn't make out the headlines.

"What's the news?" Sabrino demanded.

"It's three coppers, that's what it is," the vendor answered cheekily. He checked himself. "No, two to you, sir, on account of you're in the king's service."

"Here you are." Sabrino paid him. He walked down the boulevard reading the news sheet. It was coy about giving details, but he gathered that King Mezentio was about to announce the fall of Cottbus. Sabrino let out a long sigh of relief. If the Unkerlanter capital fell, the Derlavaian War was a long step closer to being over. He could think of nothing he wanted more.

A small boy looked up at him, reading the badges on his uniform tunic. "Are you really a dragonflier, sir?" he asked.

"Aye," Sabrino admitted.

"Ohhh." The boy's hazel eyes grew enormous. "I want to do that when I grow up. I want to have a dragon for a friend, too."

"You've been listening to too many foolish stories," Sabrino said severely. "Nobody has a dragon for a friend. Dragons are too stupid and too mean to make friends with anybody. If you didn't teach them to be afraid, they'd eat you. They're even dumber – a lot dumber – than behemoths. If you want to serve the kingdom and ride animals you can make friends with, pick leviathans instead."

"Why do you ride dragons, then?" the kid asked him.

It was a good question. He'd asked it of himself a fair number of times, most often after emptying a bottle of wine. "I do it well," he said at last, "and Algarve needs dragonfliers." But that wasn't the whole answer, and he knew it. He went on, "And maybe I'm about as mean as the dragons are."

He watched the boy think that over. "Huh," he said at last, and went on his way. Sabrino never did find out what the effect of his telling the truth was.

He went into a jeweler's. "Ah, my lord Count," said the proprietor, a scrawny old man named Dosso. He started to bow, then cursed and straightened, one hand going to the small of his back. "Forgive me, sir, I pray you – my lumbago is very bad today. How may I serve you?"

"I have here a ring with a stone that has come loose from the setting." Sabrino took from his belt pouch a gold band and a good-sized emerald. "I wonder if you would be kind enough to restore it while I wait. And can you also size the ring so that it will fit on Fronesia's finger?"

"Let me see; let me see." Dosso took a loupe from a drawer under the counter and clipped it on to his spectacles. Sabrino gave him the ring and the emerald. The jeweler examined them. Without looking up, he said, "Unkerlanter work."

"Aye," Sabrino admitted, faintly embarrassed. "One way or another, I happened to get my hands on it."

"Good for you," Dosso said. "I've got a son and two grandsons out in the west. My boy is a second-rank mage, you know; he's repairing the ley lines when Swemmel's forces wreck them. His son rides a behemoth, and my daughter's boy is a footsoldier."

"Powers above keep them safe," Sabrino said.

"All hale so far," Dosso answered. He pointed to the ring. "You've got one good prong here—"

"I should hope I do, my dear fellow," Sabrino exclaimed.

He won a snort from the jeweler. Dosso continued, "That will help, for I can use the law of similarity to shape the others. Magecraft – my son would laugh to hear me call it that; he'd reckon it just a trick of the trade – is faster than handwork, and will serve just as well here. And your lady . . . let me see, she's a size six and a half, eh? Aye, I can do that. I'll size the ring first, and use the gold I take out to make up what's missing from the broken prongs. That way, I won't have to charge you for it, as I would if I used gold of my own."

"That's kind of you, very kind indeed." Sabrino's back didn't pain him; he bowed himself almost double. He'd been coming to Dosso for many years, not least because the jeweler thought of things like that.

"Have a seat, if you like," Dosso said. "Or you can go round the corner and drink a glass of wine, if you'd rather do that. Don't drink two, or I'll be done before you finish the second unless you really pour it down."

"I'll stay, by your leave," Sabrino answered. "The company is apt to be better here than any I'd find in that tavern." He perched on one of the wooden stools in front of the counter, almost as if he were at a bar.

Dosso snipped gold from the ring opposite the prongs that held the stone, then reshaped it in Fronesia's size, using a blowtorch to heat the ends and weld them together. After he'd finished shaping the metal and it had cooled, he held up the ring. "I defy you to tell me where the join is, my lord Count."

Sabrino looked at the gold circlet. He ran his fingers around it, touch often being more sensitive than sight in such matters. "I'd like to catch you out, but I can't do it."

"Now for the prongs." Dosso held out his hand. Sabrino gave him back the ring. Dosso set it down so that it lay on top of the gold he'd snipped. He used a thin gold wire to touch first the good prong, then the extra gold, and last one of the two damaged prongs. As he did that, he muttered to himself.

The little chant didn't sound like Algarvian. After a moment, Sabrino realized it wasn't: it was classical Kaunian, with some of the words turned into nonsense syllables from who could say how many generations of rote repetition. A chill ran through the dragonflier.

But those endless repetitions had made the charm extremely effective, even if some of the words were ground into meaninglessness. As Sabrino watched, the damaged prong reshaped itself. Dosso slid the emerald into place between what were now two good prongs. As he repeated his ritual, the third one grew out and embraced the stone. With a grunt of satisfaction, Dosso handed Sabrino the restored ring. "I hope it pleases your lady."

"I'm sure it will. She's fond of baubles." Sabrino paid the jeweler and went off well pleased with himself.

When he let himself in, Fronesia greeted him with a hug and a kiss that told without words how long it had been since they'd seen each other. Then she asked the question he'd known she would: "And what have you brought me?"

"Oh, a little something," he said, his voice light, and slipped the ring on to her finger.

Fronesia stared at him. The emerald was of an even deeper green than her eyes. Part of that stare was simple admiration; part of it was a calculated assessment of how much the piece was worth. "It's lovely. It's splendid," she whispered, both sides of her character evidently satisfied.

"You're lovely," he said. "You're splendid." He meant it. Her hair glittered in the lamplight like molten copper. Her nose had a little bend in it, just enough to make it interesting; her mouth was wide and generous. Her short tunic displayed perfectly turned legs. She was within a couple of years either way of thirty. That gave him more than a twenty-year head start of her, a truth he would sooner have forgotten. "I hoped you'd like it."

"I do, very much." One of her carefully plucked eyebrows rose. "And what did you bring your wife?"

"Oh, this and that," he said casually. The countess knew about

Fronesia, of course, but hadn't asked Sabrino what he'd got her. Maybe that was the restraint of noble blood. On the other hand, maybe she just didn't want to know.

"Have you seen her yet?" Fronesia asked.

That took it further and faster than she usually went. "Aye, I have," he replied. "It is good form, you know." Algarvian nobles ran on form hardly less than their Valmieran or Jelgavan counterparts.

Fronesia sighed. Form was harder on mistresses than it was on wives. Sabrino found that fair: mistresses were supposed to be having more fun than wives. Nobles married for money or for family alliances far more often than for love. If they wanted love – or, sometimes, even a physical approximation of it – they looked elsewhere.

Sabrino asked, "And what have you been doing while I've been . . . away?" *Trying not to get myself killed* didn't sound right, even if it was what he meant.

"Oh, this and that," Fronesia answered – casually. She wasn't a pretty fool. Sabrino wouldn't have been interested in her had she been. *Well, I wouldn't have been interested in her for long,* he thought. He wasn't blind to a pretty face or a pleasing figure: far from it. But gaining his interest was one thing. Holding it was another. "And with whom have you been doing it?" he asked. Her letters hadn't said much about her friends. Did that mean she didn't get out much, or that she knew when and what to keep quiet?

"Some of my set," she answered, her voice light and amused. "I don't think there's anyone you know." Sabrino had more practice than she might have thought at reading between the lines. That couldn't mean anything but, *Everyone else I know is younger than you.*

Was she doing more than going to feasts and parties with her set? Was she being unfaithful to him? If he found out she was, if she made him notice she was, he'd have to turn her out of this fancy flat, or at least make her find someone else to pay for it. He was glad he hadn't had to pay anything for the emerald ring but the cost of repair. The Unkerlanter noble from whose house he'd taken it wouldn't worry about rings – or anything else – ever again.

Fronesia turned it this way and that, admiring the emerald. Suddenly, she threw her arms around his neck. "You are the most generous man!" she exclaimed. Maybe she hadn't thought he might be bringing back loot rather than spending money on her. He didn't bother pointing that out. Instead, though his back groaned a little, he picked her up and carried her to the bedchamber. He'd come to Trapani to enjoy himself, after all, and enjoy himself he did. If Fronesia didn't, she was an artist at concealing it.

She made him breakfast the next morning. Fortified by sweet rolls and tea with milk, he went off to greet his wife. The countess would know where he'd spent the night, but she wouldn't let on. That was how the nobility played the game. The new day was bright, but very chilly. That didn't keep vendors on the street from shouting about a special announcement due at any time. They were still shouting it when Sabrino took his wife to dinner that night, and the next morning, and the day after that.

Pekka had helped bring Kuusamo into the Derlavaian War, but the war had not yet come home to Kajaani. Oh, not much shipping was down at the harbor, but not much shipping would have been down at the harbor in the middle of any year's winter. The sea hadn't frozen – that didn't happen every winter – but enough icebergs rode the ocean to the south to make travel by water risky.

And few additional men had yet been called into the services of the Seven Princes. That would happen; she knew it would. It would have to. So far, though, the war remained as theoretical as applications of the relationship between the laws of contagion and similarity.

War was its own experiment and gave its own results. It asked questions and answered them. Her experiment with the acorns had asked new questions of the sorcerous relationship. Ilmarinen's brilliant insight had suggested the direction in which the answer might lie. Now she needed more experiments to see how far she could push magecraft in that direction.

Examining her latest set of notes, she thought she knew what needed trying. She smiled as she rose from her squeaky office chair and headed for the laboratory. Professor Heikki would not come complaining about her spending too much time and too much of the department's budget there, not any more she wouldn't. Professor Heikki, these days, left Pekka severely alone.

"Which suits me fine," Pekka murmured as she went into the laboratory. Theoretical sorcery was most often a lonely business. Here, when it was linked so closely to Kuusaman defense, it grew lonelier still. She couldn't even talk about her work with Leino, though her husband was a talented mage in his own right. That did hurt.

Several cages of rats sat on tables by one wall of the laboratory. All the animals – some young and vigorous, others slower, creakier, their fur streaked with gray – crowded forward when the door opened. They knew that was a sign they might be fed.

Pekka did feed them, a little. Then she took out two of the old, gray-muzzled rats and ran them, one after the other, through the maze a college carpenter had knocked together out of scrap lumber. They both found the grain at the end of it with no trouble at all. She'd spent weeks training all the old rats to the maze. They knew it well.

She let the second one clean out the grain set in the little tin cup once he'd got to it. Then she gave him a honey drop as an extra reward. He was a happy old rat indeed when she put him back in his cage and carried it over to a table on which, once upon a time, an acorn had rested.

She made careful note of which rat he was, then searched among the cages housing young rodents. Finding his grandson didn't take long. The law of similarity strongly bound kin. The younger rat went on the other table that had once held an acorn.

Again, Pekka noted the rat she had chosen. When this experiment was over, she would either have insured her fame (which she didn't care about) and learned something important (which she cared about very much) or . . . She laughed. "Or else I'll have to start over again and try something else," she said. "Powers above know I've had to do that before."

Despite laughter, she remained nervous. She took a deep breath and recited the ritual words her people had long used: "Before the Kaunians came, we of Kuusamo were here. Before the Lagoans came, we of Kuusamo were here. After the Kaunians departed, we of Kuusamo were here. We of Kuusamo are here. After the Lagoans depart, we of Kuusamo shall be here."

As always, the ritual helped calm Pekka. Whether this experiment succeeded or failed, her people would endure. Confident in that, she could go on with more assurance. She raised her hands above her head and began to chant.

The spell she used was a variant of the one she'd employed with the two acorns, the spell that had made one of them grow at a furious pace while the other disappeared. Ilmarinen's inversion suggested an answer to what had happened to that acorn. After a good deal of thought, Pekka had – or hoped she had – come up with a way to find out if the inversion was merely clever mathematics (anything Ilmarinen did would be clever, regardless of whether it was true) or if it described something in the real world at which she could point.

She had to tell herself not to look at either of the cages while she was incanting. If something did happen, she wouldn't see it while she was shaping the spell, only afterwards. The old rat scrambled about in his cage, which sat on the table that had held the disappearing acorn. The young rat peered out through the bars of his cage, which sat on the table that had held the acorn that sprouted at preternatural speed.

Don't make a mistake, she told herself again and again. How many discoveries had been delayed because of chance errors in spells? On and on she went, watching herself perform as if she were an outsider. Everything was going as it should. Her tongue hadn't stumbled. She wouldn't let it stumble. *I won't*, she thought. *No matter what, I won't.*

"So may it be!" she exclaimed at the very end, and slumped forward, utterly spent. Performing magic was much harder work than considering how it might be performed. She wiped sweat from her forehead, though the laboratory was cool and the ground outside covered with snow.

So may it be, she thought, wondering what would be, what had become. Now she could examine the cages, and the rats inside them. *Make sure you see what's really there*, she thought. *Don't see what you wish were there.*

The first thing she saw was that both cages still held rats. That was a relief; she didn't know what she would have done if one of the little beasts had vanished, as one acorn had during her earlier experiment. She supposed she'd have gone back, weakened her spell some more, and tried again.

She examined the older rat first. The changes in him, if there were any, would be easier to spot than those in his grandson. He looked up at her, his little black eyes shining, his whiskers quivering. His muzzle, which had been flecked with gray, was as dark as that of any rat for which a housewife had ever set a trap.

Heart pounding, Pekka noted the changes in appearance she saw.

Then she went to the cage that housed the other rat. He'd had a sort of awkward gangliness about him, a sense of being not quite comfortable in a full-sized body, about him. Adolescent rats and people were similar, at least in that. Now . . .

Now he looked like a mature rat, a rat of about the same apparent age as his grandfather. "Powers above," Pekka said softly. "That *is* what it does." She checked herself. "I think that's what it does." But had the spell rejuvenated the older rat at the expense of the younger one, or had it sent both of them traveling through time in opposite directions? Ilmarinen's work suggested the first, but didn't rule out the second.

Pekka had a way to find out. She'd built one into the experiment. She took the grandfather rat out of his cage and took him over to the maze. If he had trouble running it, she would know he'd been carried back through time to a point in his persona lifeline before he'd learned which route led to the food. If he didn't, he would show he was essentially the same rat with a newer body.

"Tell me," she whispered. "Come on, rat, tell me." She set him down in the maze and waited to see what he would do.

For a moment, he did nothing at all. He sat there at the beginning of the path, his little black nose twitching, his tail wiggling. Had Pekka found him in her kitchen, she would have tried to land him with a frying pan. As things were, she gave him an indignant look. His indecision was liable to make her have to repeat the experiment.

She wondered if poking him to get him started would distort her results. As if the rat sensed what she was thinking, he started to move. He went through the maze with as much assurance as he had before she subjected him to magecraft. Pekka had forgotten to refill the grain cup that served as his reward. Now he looked indignantly at her. "I'm sorry," she said, and gave him what he wanted, and another honey drop to boot.

After he'd eaten, she picked him up and returned him to his cage. He was, at the moment, the most valuable rat in the world, though of course he didn't know it. She and her colleagues would have to repeat the experiment a good many times, but if the results held . . . *If they hold, we're going somewhere at last*, Pekka thought. Where that might be, she didn't know, but the research, whatever else one said about it, was stalled no more.

She went back to her office, carrying her notebooks with her. There she activated her crystal and attuned it to that of one of the men waiting to hear what she had done. A moment later, Siuntio's image, tiny but perfect, appeared in the depths of the sphere. "Ah," he said, smiling as he recognized her in the crystal. "What have you got to tell me?"

"Master, the famous Lagoan navigator has just landed on the tropical continent," she answered. Should some mage be tapping their emanations, that would confuse him.

Fortunately, it didn't confuse Siuntio. His smile got broader. "Is that so? Were the natives friendly?"

"Everyone landed safe and happy." Pekka cast about for a way to continue the improvised code, and found one: "He seems to have discovered the bigger part of the continent, not the smaller one." That would tell Siuntio Ilmarinen's more probable set of results looked to be true, not the less probable grouping.

In the crystal, Siuntio nodded. "And does the man who made the compass know what the navigator did with it?"

"Not yet," Pekka said. "I wanted to tell you first."

"You flatter me, but he should be the one to hear this news," Siuntio said. With a wave of farewell, he broke the attunement between their crystals.

Pekka did call Ilmarinen then. She used the same phrases to get the news across to him as she had with Siuntio. He also understood them; she'd expected nothing less. But, where Siuntio had seemed pleased with the news, Ilmarinen's mobile features twisted into a scowl. "We're so cursed good at finding answers these days," he said morosely. "If only we could find the questions to go with them."

"I don't follow you, Master," Pekka said.

Ilmarinen's scowl got deeper. "Suppose I'm your grandfather," he said, and put on a quavery old man's voice nothing like his real one as he pointed to her. "Sweetheart, I'm running out of years. Can I take five from you? You won't miss 'em; you've got plenty left." He resumed his natural tones to add, "We can do that now, you know. You've just shown us how. And will the rich start buying – or going out and stealing – years from the poor?"

Pekka stared in horror. All at once, she felt like burning her notebooks. But it was too late for that. What had been found once would be found again, sure as the sun would – briefly – rise tomorrow.

In the crystal, Ilmarinen pointed at her. "And I assume your spell used all convergent elements. It would have, with the setup you'd want to check things with your mice." Before Pekka could correct him about the animals, he went on, "Try it with a divergent series – but calculate some of the possible energy releases before you start incanting. Powers above keep you safe." He waved. His image disappeared from the crystal. Pekka began to wonder why she'd ever thirsted after abstract knowledge.

Cornelu was splitting lumber with an axe when he saw the Algarvian patrol trudging up the road from Tirgoviste town and its harbor. His grip tightened on the axe handle. What were King Mezentio's men doing, coming up into the hilly heart of Tirgoviste island? Till now, they'd mostly been content to hold the harbor and let the rest of the island take care of itself.

He wasn't the only one to have spotted them, either. "Algarvians!" Giurgiu called, and the rest of the woodcutters took up the warning.

"What do they want?" Cornelu demanded. "They can't be looking for rebels." He'd been looking for rebels ever since he splashed back up on to his home island. He'd found plenty of people who despised the Algarvian occupiers, but almost no one who despised them enough to want to pick up a stick and blaze at them.

King Mezentio's soldiers seemed to feel the same way about that as he did. They tramped along in easy open order. Had irregulars been lurking in the woods, the Algarvians wouldn't have lasted a heartbeat, but they had nothing to fear from woodcutters.

Their leader, a young lieutenant with mustaches waxed to sharp spikes, waved to Giurgiu. The big, burly lumberman took no notice of him. Cornelu snickered. Giurgiu didn't love Algarvians; Cornelu knew that.

"You, there!" the lieutenant called. Giurgiu pretended to be deaf as well as blind. That was a dangerous game; Algarvians were famous for their short tempers. The lieutenant went on, "Aye, you, you great ugly lout!"

"Better answer him," Cornelu said softly. "He'll use that stick if you push him too far."

Giurgiu looked up from his work. It was as if he were seeing and hearing the Algarvian officer for the first time. He made a better actor than Cornelu had thought he could. When he did answer, it was in upcountry dialect: "What do you want, eh?" Even Cornelu, who'd grown up on Tirgoviste, had trouble following him. To the lieutenant, his words were likely gibberish, though most Algarvians and Sibians could understand one another with a little work.

"We're looking for somebody," the lieutenant said, speaking slowly and clearly.

"What say?" Giurgiu kept right on acting like a moron – an outsize and possibly dangerous moron, for he leaned on the handle of an axe bigger and heavier than those of the other woodcutters.

"We're looking for someone," the Algarvian repeated. He sounded as if his patience was wearing thin. Staring from one woodcutter to another, he asked, "Does anybody here speak Algarvian, or even a civilized dialect of Sibian?"

No one admitted to that. Under other circumstances, Cornelu might have, but not now. He wondered which man in particular Mezentio's soldiers were looking for. He didn't think the Algarvians knew he was here, but . . .

"What say?" Giurgiu repeated, in dialect even broader than before. He didn't crack a smile. He didn't even come close. Cornelu admired his straight face.

"Bunch of bumpkins, sir," one of the Algarvian troopers said. "Bunch of ugly, stupid bumpkins."

Maybe he was just saying what he thought. Maybe he was trying to make the Sibians angry enough to show they understood Algarvian. Maybe he was doing both at once; Cornelu wouldn't have put it past him.

Whatever the trooper was doing, the officer shook his head. "No," he said in tones of cheerful unconcern. "They're just lying. They can follow me well enough, or some of them can. Well, we'll pay plenty of silver if they bring us this chap called Cornelu. And if they don't, we'll hunt him down sooner or later. Come on, boys." He gathered up the soldiers by eye and headed up the track past the woodcutters.

We'll hunt him down sooner or later. Cornelu fumed at the Algarvian's arrogance. But the fellow was a pretty good officer. He'd sown the seeds of betrayal. He was probably doing that everywhere he went. Now he would wait to see where they ripened.

The woodcutters returned to work. Cornelu kept on splitting rounds of lumber. He didn't look up from what he was doing. He seldom did, but now even less than usual. Whenever he straightened and looked around, he found other men's eyes on him. Cornelu wasn't the rarest Sibian name, but it was a long way from the most common.

At supper – a big bowl of oatmeal mush with a little salt pork stirred in – Giurgiu strode over and sat down beside him on a fallen pine. "You the fellow Mezentio's hounds are sniffing after?"

"I don't know." Stolidly, Cornelu spooned up some more oatmeal. "I could be, I suppose, but maybe not, too." He wished he'd given a false name when he joined this gang.

Giurgiu nodded. "Thought I'd ask. Fellow who fights like you likely learned how in the army or navy. Somebody who learned there might be somebody those loudmouthed fools'd want to work over."

"Aye, that's so." Cornelu still didn't look up from his oatmeal. He didn't want to meet Giurgiu's eyes – and he was hungry enough to make such bad manners seem nothing out of the ordinary. All the woodcutters ate like that; the work they did made them eat like that. Between a couple of mouthfuls, Cornelu added, "I'm not the only one who knows those tricks, though. There's you, for instance."

"Oh, aye, there's me, all right." Giurgiu's big head bobbed up and down, almost as if he were once more making himself out to be more rustic than he really was. "But that Algarvian didn't know my name. He knew yours."

Anger flared in Cornelu. "Turn me in, then. If I'm the one they want, they'll probably pay you plenty. They'd like us to be sweet. 'Sibians are an Algarvic folk, too.'" With savage sarcasm, he quoted the broadsheet he'd seen down in Tirgoviste town.

"Bugger that with an axe handle," Giurgiu said. "If they loved us so bloody much, they shouldn't have invaded us. That's how I see things, anyway. But there's liable to be some as see 'em different."

"Traitors," Cornelu said bitterly.

Giurgiu didn't argue with him. All he said was, "They're there. You try and pretend they aren't, it'll cost you." He got to his feet, towering over Cornelu. "Try to stay warm tonight. I've got a feeling the weather's going to turn nasty by sunup."

Cornelu had the same feeling. He wouldn't have expected it in a man who spent all his life on land. The weather was often bad at this season of the year; Tirgoviste lay far to the south, and they were well up in the hills. Even on rare clear days, the sun hardly seemed to have risen before it set again in the northwest. When clouds covered the sky, murk and night were hardly distinguishable.

Like everyone else, Cornelu had plenty of thick wool blankets. He swaddled himself in them, curling up close to the cookfire. On nights like this, it burned till daybreak, even if that meant throwing on timber the woodcutters might otherwise have sold.

Snow started falling a couple of hours after he fell asleep, borne on the wings of a wind doubtless whipping whitecaps on the seas surrounding Sibiu. Cornelu woke, pulled a length of blanket over his head, and went back to sleep.

When morning came, the world was white. Down in Tirgoviste town, Cornelu knew, it probably wouldn't be snow. It would be sleet or freezing rain: to his mind, even nastier. He wished he were down there, back in his own house, making love with Costache in front of a crackling fire – a fire made from wood he hadn't cut himself. As an afterthought, he remembered Brindza. Fitting her into all that, he wished her asleep in a cradle, or wherever toddlers of that size slept.

Did the cook give him an odd look while dishing out the morning oatmeal? He couldn't be sure, and didn't dwell on it. He did dwell on shoveling down the oatmeal as fast as he could so it would put a little extra warmth in his belly. He gulped two mugs of herb tea, too, for the same reason, even though the stuff tasted nasty.

"Get moving, dears," Giurgiu called to his men, voice full of false solicitude. "Down by the sea, they'll be wanting what we've got to sell, that they will. I know you don't care to get your fingers cold, but it can't be helped. Remember what brave fellows you are, that's all."

Instead of going back to work on the rounds of lumber he'd been chopping up the day before, Cornelu got called over to help bring down a big fir. Before long, he was sweating in spite of the snow and the wind that was blowing it. He let out a grunt of intense satisfaction when the tree crashed down, throwing up a brief, blinding cloud of snow when it did. Woodcutting had its points; he could actually see what he was accomplishing through the strength of his arms.

He walked along the trunk, methodically lopping off the big branches one after another. Work felt good in weather like this. If he hadn't been working, he would have been freezing. He swung the axe again and again, breathing in great gulps of resin- and sap-scented air, breathing out great clouds of steam and fog. Losing himself in the labor, he might have been mechanism, not man.

Losing himself in the labor, he forgot about what Vlaicu, the other man who'd felled the tree, might be doing. He was reminded when he heard a boot crunch in the snow in back of him. That was almost too late. He'd just raised his arms for another axe stroke . . . and the other woodcutter tackled him from behind.

Vlaicu had probably hoped to get Cornelu down and get him hogtied before he could do anything about it. He'd lost his fight with Giurgiu, after all. But Giurgiu knew all the tricks of the trade, and was bigger and stronger besides. Vlaicu didn't, and he wasn't far from Cornelu's size.

Cornelu went down on his knees, but not to his belly. Hanging on to his axe with his right hand, he used his left to break the other woodcutter's grip on him, then drove an elbow into Vlaicu's midsection. It wasn't perfectly placed, but it forced a grunt of pain from his foe. Cornelu threw another elbow, twisted, and scrambled to his feet.

Vlaicu leaped back, almost stumbling in his haste to recover his own axe. He could have killed Cornelu instead of jumping him, but the Algarvians had seemed to want him alive, and so he'd tried to make him a captive instead. But, since that hadn't worked, a head might do as well. Cornelu made an awkward leap away from a stroke that would have cut him in two.

Then he surged forward again, chopping at his foe. Dimly, he heard more woodcutters shouting as they came up. So did Vlaicu, who bored in, swinging wildly. He must have realized most of the others wouldn't favor him. Cornelu ducked, straightened, and slammed the side of his axehead against Vlaicu's temple. The other woodcutter tottered, then fell like the fir. Blood stained the snow.

Giurgiu bent beside him, but only briefly. "Dead. You caved in his skull," he told Cornelu.

"He jumped me. He was going to give me to the Algarvians," Cornelu answered.

But Vlaicu had friends on the crew, too. "Liar!" they cried. "Murderer!" Other woodcutters shouted at them. More axes were raised.

"Hold!" Giurgiu roared. Such was his might that they *did* hold, instead of leaping at one another. "I think Cornelu's telling the truth. Why else get in a fight now?" But Vlaicu's friends kept on shouting, and he had quite a few of them – more than the dismayed Cornelu had thought. Giurgiu jerked a thumb at the trail that led out of the hills and down to Tirgoviste. "You've always been wanting to go into town. You know what's good for you, you'd better get out of here now," he told Cornelu. "I'll make sure you have a start."

Looking at those furious faces, Cornelu wouldn't last a day – or, more to the point, a night – if he stayed. "Aye," he said bitterly. After an ironic salute, he shouldered his axe as if it were a stick and trudged north, toward the seashore.

Snow poured down on Thalfang. Fire and smoke rose up from the burning Unkerlanter town. Tealdo crouched in a doorway, ready to blaze anything that moved. His whole company had been thrown into the meat grinder here. He didn't know how many men were still alive, but he did know the company would never be the same again after it came out the other side of the town – if it ever did.

From the next doorway over, Trasone called, "Maybe we'll make it to Cottbus after all if we can take this stinking place first."

"How much do we have left to take it with?" Tealdo answered. "Not a whole lot of reinforcements behind us, that's for cursed sure. And where are our behemoths? I've hardly seen any the past few days."

"We came past some that were frozen to death, remember?" Trasone said.

Tealdo did remember, and wished he hadn't. He also wished his comrades wouldn't be quite so sardonic. He said, "I was hoping I'd see some that would do us some good."

"With this much snow on the ground, the powers below might as well be pulling at the beasts' feet," Trasone commented. "How are they supposed to go forward in weather like this? How are we, for that matter?" He risked a quick look around the corner to make sure no Unkerlanters were sneaking up, then turned back to Tealdo. "And I wouldn't mind a few more dead blonds helping the mages push us forward, either." He scowled at Tealdo, as if defying him to disagree.

With a shrug, Tealdo answered, "Hard getting 'em up here these days, what with the weather and with the Unkerlanters playing games with the ley lines. Besides, Swemmel keeps on killing his own, too."

He didn't know what Trasone would say to that. Before Trasone could say anything, the Unkerlanters started lobbing eggs at the forward-most Algarvians. Tealdo huddled in his doorway, making himself as small as he could. King Swemmel's men had a great swarm of egg-tossers north of Thalfang.

And the Algarvians did not respond so readily or so strongly as they would have a few weeks or even a few days before. Pulled by horses or mules or behemoths, egg-tossers had an ever harder time keeping up with footsoldiers as they pushed the front forward. Tealdo hoped for dragons, but the cold and the snow were hard on them, too.

After about a quarter of an hour, the eggs stopped falling as abruptly as they'd begun. In the sudden silence, Captain Galafrone raised a shout: "Forward, men! The Unkerlanters are still getting ready to hit us. We'll cursed well hit them before they *are* ready." He shouted again: "Mezentio!"

"Mezentio!" Tealdo yelled, and sprang up from his hiding place. Other officers were shouting their men forward, too; more than half a year of war had taught them how their foes fought. And, sure enough, they caught King Swemmel's soldiers out of their holes and gathering for their own attack. That made the white-smocked Unkerlanters easier targets than they would have been resting in the soot-streaked snow or scurrying from house to house.

Tealdo blazed a couple of enemy troopers. More fell to beams from his comrades' sticks. But the rest, instead of retreating, surged forward. Tealdo dove behind a snow-covered pile of bricks. He came up blazing, and knocked over another Unkerlanter. In an abstract way, he might have admired the courage King Swemmel's men showed. They'd shown it ever since the fighting started. They'd been forced back, but they hadn't given up on themselves the way the Valmierans and Jelgavans had. He wished they would have despaired. In that case, Algarve would be victorious, and he wouldn't have to worry about getting killed any more.

"Forward!" Captain Galafrone shouted again. "Once we break out of Thalfang, they won't have anything left to stop us."

Tealdo didn't know whether the Algarvians could break out of Thalfang, and kept thinking about all the eggs the Unkerlanters had thrown at them. But he scrambled to his feet. He sprinted for the next bit of cover he saw – an overturned wagon in the middle of the street. He crouched behind it, blazing at the Unkerlanters. Their attacking force melted as the snow hereabouts wouldn't do till spring.

Trasone ran past him. "Come on," Tealdo's burly friend called. "Do you want to be late for the party?"

"Can't have that." Tealdo got up and advanced again. As he ran, he realized something had changed. He needed a moment to know what it was. Then he exclaimed in glad surprise: "The snow's stopped!"

"Oh, happy day!" That wasn't Trasone; it was Sergeant Panfilo. "Any minute now, the sun will come out, and then you can go climb a fornicating palm tree, just like they've got in fornicating Siaulia."

A few minutes later, the sun did come out. Tealdo saw no palm trees, fornicating or otherwise. All he saw was a battered Unkerlanter town; sunshine made it dazzling without making it beautiful. Ahead lay a broad expanse of empty, snow-covered ground. "The market square!" Tealdo shouted. "We're halfway through this stinking place, anyway."

"Aye, so we are," Trasone answered. "And there's half as many of us as there were when we got here, too."

Tealdo nodded, but he wasn't really listening. He was staring northwest, across the market square, across the rest of the ruins of Thalfang, toward higher ground in the distance. He pointed, "Curse me if those aren't the towers or whatever they call them of King Swemmel's palace."

Trasone stopped and stared, too. "You're right," he said, his rough voice softened for once. "We've come all this cursed way, and there it is, close enough to reach out and touch." He stretched out a hand, then shook his head and laughed. "Of course, we've still got a few Unkerlanters to go through."

"Aye, a few." Tealdo nodded. "They know they can't afford to lose this town. And I'm not looking forward to crossing the square. They're bound to have snipers on the far side, and we're not decked out in white like they are. Makes us too easy to spot."

"Ought to cut the balls off whoever didn't think to lay in white smocks for us," Trasone growled. "Some bespectacled whoreson in a nice warm office back in Trapani probably figured we'd lick the Unkerlanters before we needed them, so he didn't bother having any made."

"Come on, boys! There's Cottbus ahead!" Captain Galafrone pointed in the direction of King Swemmel's palace. "It'll be as easy to grab as a whore's snatch now. Forward!" As if spying the towers had sorcerously restored his youth, he charged out into the market square. Every Algarvian within the sound of his voice followed.

Thalfang's square was bigger than the one an Algarvian town with about as many people would have had. Not being so crowded in their kingdom, the Unkerlanters could and did use space more lavishly. And slogging through deep snow made the market square seem bigger still.

Something moved, there in one of the streets leading into the market squire from the far side. Tealdo blazed at it, but couldn't be sure whether he'd hit it or not. Then eggs came whistling into the square out of the north and west. They burst all around the advancing Algarvians. Wounded men screamed and flopped in the snow like newly landed fish.

Tealdo threw himself down. "The captain's hit!" somebody yelled – Tealdo thought it was Trasone, but he couldn't be sure, not with his ears stunned from so many bursts close by. The Unkerlanters had more left than anyone had thought they did, and they were throwing in every bit of it to try to hold Thalfang.

That thought had hardly crossed his mind before fresh shouts of dismay rose from some of the Algarvians caught in the open. "Behemoths!" Raw terror edged those cries. "Unkerlanter behemoths!"

Into the market square they came. Tealdo lifted his head and blazed at them. Now he knew what he'd seen, there in the street across the square. He expected to have all the time in the world to pick off their crewmen, even if he couldn't do anything much to the beasts themselves. If Algarvian behemoths bogged down in snowdrifts, surely Unkerlanter behemoths would do the same.

But they didn't. They came forward almost as swiftly as they would have over dry ground in summer. Gaping, Tealdo saw that they had wide, net-laced contraptions strapped to their feet. *Snowshoes*, he thought numbly. *The Unkerlanters have tricked out their cursed behemoths in snowshoes. Why didn't we come up with something like that?*

He got no time to brood about it. The behemoth began tossing eggs with deadly accuracy. Beams from heavy sticks hissed like giant serpents when they struck snow, kicking great clouds of steam up into the frosty air. Some of that steam was tinged with red; those beams boiled a man's blood as readily as a snowbank.

Behind the behemoths came white-smocked Unkerlanter soldiers, also on snowshoes. Unlike the Algarvians, they didn't flounder through the drifts, but strode along atop them. And there were so cursed many of them! Captain Galafrone had said that, once the Algarvians got past Thalfang, not much stood between them and Cottbus. From somewhere or other, King Swemmel had found reserves Galafrone hadn't known about.

Well, Galafrone was already down. Tealdo didn't know how badly he was hurt, or whether he realized how wrong he'd been. Along with the behemoths, the Unkerlanters were throwing a couple of brigades at a banged-up battalion's worth of Algarvians. And how many more soldiers did they have flooding into Thalfang from the north?

Those behemoths were terrifyingly close now. They'd already passed – or run over – the forwardmost Algarvians. Did they intend to trample Mezentio's men as well as tossing eggs at them and blazing them with heavy sticks? Tealdo rose a little to blaze down an Unkerlanter behemoth-rider who was fitting an egg to his tosser. But other behemoths were already past him, with footsoldiers close behind them. Cries of "Urra!" and "Swemmel!" mingled and began to drown those of "King Mezentio!"

Tealdo didn't feel the beam that burned its way through his middle, not at first. All he knew was that his legs didn't want to work any more. Then he found himself face down in the snow. And then, a couple of heartbeats later, he began to scream.

"Tealdo!" Trasone cried. His voice seemed to come from very far away.

From even farther away, Sergeant Panfilo shouted in despair: "Back! We have to fall back!"

Dimly, Tealdo knew the sergeant was right. Despair filled him, too, despair and anguish. Thalfang wasn't going to fall. If it didn't, Cottbus wouldn't, either. If Cottbus didn't fall, what would the war look like then? *It'll look a lot harder, that's what*, Tealdo thought as he tried to use his arms to crawl back toward the edge of the square from which he'd set out. He left a trail of red behind him in the white.

He looked around for his stick. It was gone . . . somewhere. Color washed out of everything, leaving only gray fading toward black. However the war turned out, he wouldn't know about it. He lay in the square in burning Thalfang. Unkerlanters on snowshoes shuffled past him, and his countrymen retreated.

Rain pattered down on Bishah and on the surrounding hills. That happened every winter – several times in a wet winter – but always seemed to take the Zuwayzin by surprise. Hajjaj had been through winters in Algarve. He'd even seen winter in Unkerlant. He knew how lucky his kingdom was to enjoy a warm climate, and also knew it needed what rain it got. All the same, watching drops splash down on the flagstones of his courtyard, he wished the rain would go away.

Tewfik came up behind him. Hajjaj knew that without turning his head; no one else's sandals scraped across the floor the same way. The crusty old majordomo stopped, waiting to be noticed. Hajjaj was not so rude as to keep him waiting. "How now, Tewfik?" he asked, glad to turn away from the wet outside.

"Well, lad, they've found another leak in the roof." Tewfik spoke with a certain morose satisfaction. "I've sent a runner down to the city to lay hold of the roofers, provided he doesn't break his neck in the mud."

"My thanks," Hajjaj said. "The trouble is, everyone's roof leaks when it rains, because no one bothers fixing a roof when the sun shines. Powers above only know when our turn with the roofers will come."

"It had better come soon, or I'll have a thing or two to say about it," Tewfik declared. "Everyone's roof may leak, but not everyone is the foreign minister of Zuwayza."

"All the other clanfathers are just as grand as I am," Hajjaj answered. "And all the rich merchants in the city are closer to the roofers than we are."

Tewfik's first sniff said he cared little for the pretensions of Zuwayzi nobles not fortunate enough to have him serve them. His second sniff said he cared even less for any merchants' pretensions. "I know what's required, and the roofers had cursed well better, too," he growled.

Arguing with him was pointless, so Hajjaj yielded: "All right. How are the walls holding up?"

"Well enough," Tewfik said grudgingly. "The wind's not too bad, so the eaves keep the water away."

"They'd better," Hajjaj said. Like most Zuwayzi houses, his was made of thick bricks baked only by the sun. If they got soaked, they turned back into the mud from which they'd been made. In every rainstorm, people died when their houses fell in on them.

A serving woman came into the chamber where Hajjaj and Tewfik stood. "Excuse me, your Excellency," she said, bowing to Hajjaj, "but General Ikhshid awaits in the crystal. He would speak with you."

"Ikhshid himself? Not an aide-de-camp?" Hajjaj asked. The maid-servant nodded. One of Hajjaj's graying eyebrows rose. "Something's gone wrong somewhere, then. I'll speak with him; of course I will."

He hurried to the crystal's chamber, next to the library, and took care to shut the door behind him; he didn't want the servants listening in. Sure enough, there in the crystal was the reduced image of General Ikhshid. "Good day, your Excellency," the plump old soldier said when he saw the foreign minister. "Keeping dry?"

"As best I can," Hajjaj replied. "Harder now than when I saw you last down in the desert near the old border with Unkerlant. What's toward?" With crystals, as opposed to face-to-face meetings, coming straight to the point was good form.

Ikhshid said, "It might be best if you drove down to the palace. No matter how tight our control spells are, you never can tell who's liable to pick up the emanations from a crystal."

Hajjaj weighed that. "Is it really so bad?"

"If it weren't, would I ask you out in the rain?" Ikhshid returned.

You'd better not, Hajjaj thought. *If I come down there and it's not important, you'll be sorry.* Ikhshid came from a powerful clan; Hajjaj had known him for upwards of forty years, and judged him a pretty good officer. If the news wasn't important, he'd make him sorry even so. Meanwhile . . . The foreign minister sighed. "I'm on my way."

"Good." Ikhshid's image disappeared. Light flared, and then the crystal was merely a transparent globe once more.

Tewfik yowled like a scalded cat when he found out Hajjaj proposed leaving the house while it was still raining. "You'll catch your death, lad, from inflammation of the lungs," he said. When he found Hajjaj obdurate, he stood out in the rain, naked as any Zuwayzi, lecturing the driver on his responsibility to get Hajjaj to and from the palace safely. Though a good many years older than the foreign minister, he didn't worry about the possibility of coming down with pneumonia himself.

The driver took longer than Hajjaj would have liked. The roadway, usually rock solid, was full of gluey mud. And, once the carriage got into Bishah, it moved slowly even on paved roads. A couple of tangles on rain-slick cobbles had created snarls that would take hours to unknot.

At last, Hajjaj raised an umbrella – far more often used as a parasol – above his head and walked into the palace. Several servitors exclaimed in surprise at seeing him there. He didn't tell them why he'd come. Of course, they would start guessing, but he couldn't do anything about that.

He made his way through the winding corridors that led to General Ikhshid's office (and past a couple of pots with water dripping into them, proving not even the royal roof was exempt from leaks). Then he went through the inevitable ritual of tea and wine and cakes, until, finally, he could ask, "And what is it you would not speak of through the crystal?"

Ikhshid wasted few words: "The Algarvians have begun falling back from Cottbus."

"Have they?" Hajjaj murmured. For a moment, ice ran through him, as if an Unkerlanter winter lived in his belly. Then he rallied: "Is it very bad?"

"Well, your Excellency, it's not what you'd call good," the general answered. Like most Zuwayzi soldiers, he felt more passion for the alliance with Algarve than did Hajjaj, who saw the need for it but, these days, found little to love in King Mezentio's followers than in King Swemmel's. Ikhshid went on, "If Cottbus doesn't fall, Unkerlant doesn't fall, you know." He gave Hajjaj an anxious glance, as if uncertain whether the foreign minister really did know that.

"Oh, aye," Hajjaj said absently. "The fight just got harder, in other words." General Ikhshid nodded. He'd served in the Unkerlanter army in the Six Years' War; he knew about hard fighting. At the moment, he looked thoroughly grim. Hajjaj found another question: "How do we know this? Are you sure it's true?"

"How?" Ikhshid said. "The Unkerlanters are trumpeting it so loud, it's a bloody wonder you need a crystal to hear them, that's how."

"The Unkerlanters," Hajjaj observed with delicate understatement, "have been know to trifle with the truth."

"Not this time." Ikhshid sounded positive. "If they were lying, the Algarvians would be yelling even louder than they are. And the redheads aren't. Except for saying there's heavy fighting, they're keeping real quiet."

Hajjaj clicked his tongue between his teeth. "Quiet from the Algarvians is never a good sign. They boast even more than Unkerlanters."

"I wouldn't say that." Ikhshid checked himself; he was at bottom an honest man. "Well, maybe I would, but they aren't so obnoxious to listen to."

"Something to that," Hajjaj said. "They're more like us – they want to impress with how they say things, too. But never mind that. If we start talking about why foreigners are the way they are, we'll be at it for the next year. We have more important things to worry about. For instance, have you told his Majesty yet?"

Ikhshid shook his head. "No. I thought you'd better find out first."

Hajjaj made another clicking noise. "Not good, General. Not good. King Shazli needs to know these things."

"So do you, your Excellency," Ikhshid said. "It could even be that you need to know more than he does."

That had truth written all over it, no matter how impolitic it was. But truth, Hajjaj was convinced, held many layers. "Would your heart be gladdened if I undertook to tell him?"

"It would, I'll not deny," Ikhshid replied at once.

"I'll tend to it, then," Hajjaj said, trying not to sound too resigned. Getting him to tell the king of the Algarvians' misfortune was liable to be more than half the reason the general had summoned him down from his hillside home in the rain.

Being who he was, he had no trouble gaining audience with King Shazli. "Beastly weather, isn't it?" the king said after Hajjaj had bowed before him. He sent his foreign minister a curious look. "What brings you down from your nice, dry house on a day like this, your Excellency?"

"My house leaks, too, your Majesty," Hajjaj answered. "When duty called, I answered – which seems to be more than one can say of roofers."

"Heh," Shazli replied. The curious look hadn't gone away. "And what sort of duty was it?" He shook his head. "No, don't tell me now. Let's refresh ourselves with tea and wine and cakes before you get into it."

Being the king, Shazli had the right to interrupt the rituals of hospitality. The foreign minister wished he would have exercised it. Holding in such important news felt wrong.

But, as Hajjaj nibbled on a cake flavored with honey and pistachios, as he sipped first tea and then date wine, he decided it didn't matter so much after all. Shazli was no fool. He would realize the duty that had brought Hajjaj down from the hills didn't involve good news. Presently, the king repeated his earlier question.

"General Ikhshid summoned me on the crystal," Hajjaj told him. "He convinced me I ought to hear his news straight from his mouth to my ear."

"Did he?" King Shazli still had wine left in his goblet. He drank it off now. "Let me guess: Mezentio's men have fallen short of Cottbus."

"So it would seem, your Majesty." Hajjaj inclined his head to the king. No, Shazli was not a fool. "The Unkerlanters have declared it and the Algarvians haven't denied it, which means it's likely true."

Shazli let out a long sigh. "Things would have been so much simpler if they'd driven King Swemmel howling into the uttermost west of Unkerlant."

"That they would," Hajjaj said. "Things are seldom so simple as we would wish, though." He wondered if King Shazli really understood that. Not only was Shazli still a young man, he'd had whatever he wanted since he was very small. Who could be surprised if things looked simple to him?

But he said, "We have got as much as we could out of this war now — would you not agree? The best thing we can hope for now is to keep as much of it as we can."

That struck Hajjaj as a good, sensible attitude. It was, in fact, not so far removed from his own attitude. He said, "Your Majesty, I'll do everything I can to make sure we manage exactly that."

"Good," Shazli said. "I know I can rely on you."

Hajjaj inclined his head once more. "You do me too much honor," he murmured, and hoped he was being overmodest.

Twelve

Garivald wasn't drunk yet from this latest jar of spirits, but he wasn't far away, either. There just wasn't that much else to do, not with snowdrifts taller than a man on the ground in Zossen.

Oh, the livestock took up some time, but less than in summer; the pig and the chickens and Garivald's couple of sheep and the cow shared his thatch-roofed house with him, Annore, Syrivald, and Leuba. They would freeze if they tried to go through the winter outdoors. Here in the hut, they helped the hearth keep things warm.

They also made a dreadful mess, even if the floor was only of rammed earth. Annore did her best to clean up after them, but her best, though better than that of most village wives, wasn't nearly good enough. Garivald didn't mind the stink; he'd long since got used to that, as he did every winter. He didn't like stepping in freshly dropped dung, but a careful man didn't do that very often.

He lifted his mug and let another swig of spirits burn its way down his throat. "Well, it's not as bad as it could have been, I suppose," he said.

"What isn't?" Annore asked darkly. She was washing Leuba's feet. Leuba, at not quite three, didn't watch where she stepped, and didn't much care, either.

"Having the Algarvians in Zossen," Garivald answered.

"What? The redheads?" Annore's thick eyebrows shot upwards. "Powers above curse them, *I* say!" She set hands on hips to show how strongly she meant it. Her nostrils flared. She pointed at Garivald. "You say that when they've worked you like a slave chopping wood for them?"

"Aye, I do," he answered. "Think – in spite of everything, we have more to get us through the winter than we did in any other year I can remember. Aye, they work us like slaves sometimes. Aye, they robbed the harvest. But we still managed to store away more than usual. Go ahead. Tell me I'm wrong." He folded his thick arms across his chest and looked a challenge at Annore.

A lot of Unkerlanter husbands, especially after they'd started drinking, would have followed up that challenge by going over and smacking their wives around. Garivald didn't. What restrained him wasn't so much chivalry as the nagging fear that he'd wake up one morning with his throat slit if he got too rough with her.

She shrugged. "Maybe we did," she said in grudging tones.

"No maybes about it," Garivald exclaimed. "Aye, powers above curse the Algarvians, but they're lousy thieves. Inefficient, I say. King Swemmel's inspectors would have found a lot more of the hiding places where we squirreled things away."

"Maybe," Annore repeated.

"Maybe," Leuba said gaily. She didn't know what her mother and father were talking about – for which Garivald envied her – but she wanted to join in.

"No maybes," Garivald said again. "They're not up to a proper job of robbery, the way Unkerlanter inspectors would be."

Words formed inside his head. *They're lousy thieves*, he thought, *And who believes/ They're here to stay?/ For Swemmel's soldiers/ Grow ever bolder/ To drive them away*. It wasn't a great song. He knew that. But it was a beginning. Maybe he could turn it into something worth hearing. He hadn't known he could make songs till the summer before. Now they kept spring into his mind all unbidden.

Softly, he sang those first couple of scrappy verses to Annore, setting them to the tune of a sprightly dance. She nodded approval, but warned, "You'll have to be careful about letting people hear that one. Somebody's liable to go to the Algarvians with it, and then where would you be?"

"I know," Garivald said. "You'd best believe I know. But maybe our own soldiers will come back to Zossen before too long. The redheads are still retreating, they say." *They* were his fellow villagers, who know no more than he did, and roaming small bands of Unkerlanter soldiers still on the loose after being bypassed by the advancing redheads, who might.

"Here's hoping they're right," Annore said, "but be careful anyhow, until the rightful king's men take Zossen back."

"What?" Now Garivald raised an eyebrow. "You don't call Raniero your king?"

"This for Raniero," Annore said, and made a rude noise. Delighted, so did Leuba. And so did Syrivald, who, these days, was almost as tall as his mother. Garivald laughed. After the redheads overran southeastern Unkerlant, Mezentio had proclaimed him his cousin Raniero King of Grelz.

Once upon a time, Grelz had been a kingdom, before shrinking to a duchy in the Union of Crowns with Unkerlant. But Grelzers and Unkerlanters were closest kin; Grelz had never had an Algarvian king. As far as Garivald was concerned, it still didn't: only an Algarvian cat's-paw.

Leuba wasn't likely to talk enough to get Garivald into trouble. He did eye his son. "You have to remember, Syrivald, nobody needs to hear what we say inside the house."

"I know, Father," Syrivald said seriously. After eyeing him, his father nodded. Syrivald, by now, was used to keeping his mouth shut. Before the redheads swept through this part of the kingdom, people hadn't wanted Waddo to hear a lot of what they said. That became especially true after Zossen got a crystal of its own, a direct connection between the village and King Swemmel's vast corps of inspectors and impressers. Now different people might betray things to the redheads, but the principle remained the same. Garivald was glad Syrivald understood it.

Outside, boots crunched on snow. Garivald grew alert. Visitors in dead of winter weren't that common. People stayed indoors most of the time. He didn't care to leave the house, to go outside in the cold and wind. He wondered who among his fellow villagers would.

When he heard the knock, he knew. Unkerlanter knocks, even worthless Waddo's, were casual, friendly things. This one served notice: if he didn't come to the door right away, whoever was on the other side would break it down.

Annore's lips shaped a soundless word: "Algarvians."

"Aye," Garivald agreed. "But I've got to let them in." He regretted saying they weren't so bad. When they pounded on his door, they were very bad indeed.

Reluctantly, he went to the door. Even more reluctantly, he opened it. Sure as sure, three Algarvian soldiers stood there shivering and trying to look fierce. Their own kingdom hadn't given them proper cold-weather gear; they'd added hats and cloaks stolen from villagers to their short tunics and kilts. That made them look less uniform and, somehow, less ferocious. It didn't make them look much warmer.

"We coming in," one of them said in bad Unkerlanter. The other two pointed their sticks at Garivald, as if to tell him he'd better not complain.

He already knew that. "Well, come in if you're coming," he said gruffly. "Don't stand there letting all the heat out." Cold flowed over his feet and legs in waves. As soon as the tall redheaded soldiers were inside, he shut the door behind them.

One of them wrinkled his nose and spoke in his own language. The other two grinned. Garivald didn't know what they were grinning about, and didn't want to find out. These garrison soldiers had been in Zossen since the village was captured. Not all of them were bad fellows, not as people. He'd come to know them. That didn't mean he wanted them in his house.

They were looking around. He didn't like it when their eyes settled on Annore. The garrison troops lived up to the Algarvians' name for lechery. Regardless of whether they carried sticks, if they aimed to torment his wife they'd have to kill him first. But, after a couple of leers, their gaze showed what they really had in mind.

"You giving us a pig," said the one who spoke Unkerlanter. "You giving us a sheep, too. Or—" He gestured with his own weapon.

"Take them," Garivald said in disgust. Aye, he shouldn't have said anything about how the Algarvians weren't so good at robbing peasants as Unkerlanter inspectors were. The words came back to mock him. But, even if he had to eat peas and beans and pickled cabbage till spring, he wouldn't starve, and neither would his family. "Take them," he repeated. The sooner the Algarvians were out of the house, the smaller the chance they'd start looking toward Annore again.

They'd come prepared. One tied a rope around the sheep's neck. The other two had a harder time catching the pig, but they managed. Both animals let out piteous sounds of protest when the redheads took them out into the snow, but they went. Garivald closed and barred the door once the Algarvians were gone.

"Well," he said with pleasant fatalism, "the house isn't so crowded now." But fatalism went only so far. "Powers below eat the stinking thieves as they'll eat my beasts!" he burst out.

"Aye, and may their bellies gripe," Annore agreed.

A couple of days later, new Algarvian troops came stumbling into Zossen out of the west. They were leaner, tougher-looking men than the little squad of garrison soldiers: wolves rather than dogs. But they were sadly battered wolves, a couple of them wounded, all of them half frozen and weary unto death. After they'd paused to get warm and to eat – maybe some of Garivald's pork and mutton – they went on, heading east. The soldiers they'd left behind began looking like worried dogs.

Dagulf came to visit in a state of high excitement. "Maybe our own men'll be coming back in a few days," he said, sipping the mug of spirits Garivald gave him. That was a thought worthy of getting a man out of his own house – and Dagulf's wife nagged. He went on, "Maybe they'll chase these raggedy kilted buggers back to Algarve where they belong."

"That'd be good." Garivald was halfway to being drunk himself, and would have agreed to almost anything.

Dagulf had a scar on his cheek. It twisted his smile. "Aye, it would," he said. "And then we can let people know who played along with the redheads. You know names. So do I. Not as bad here as some places, they say. Some places, lots of people are willing to lick Raniero's Algarvian arse."

But the folk of Zossen did not get the chance to inform on their collaborationist neighbors. No Unkerlanter soldiers fought their way into the village to slaughter the garrison or drive King Mezentio's men back toward the border. Instead, struggling forward through the snow, half a dozen Algarvian behemoths and a company of footsoldiers camped in Zossen.

One of their officers, a young lieutenant, spoke Unkerlanter pretty well. At his order, the villagers had to assemble in the central square. "You wish we were gone, don't you?" he said with an unpleasant smile. "You wish Swemmel's men were here instead, don't you? If they do come, how glad will you be to see them after they cut your throats to power their magecraft against us? Eh? Think on it."

By the next morning, the Algarvians were gone, heading west to get into the fight. Garivald feared more would be coming, though. "He was lying, wasn't he?" Annore said. Garivald only shrugged. He remembered the convicts who'd been sacrificed for the sorcerous energy to power Zossen's crystal. He wished he didn't, but he did. Who could say what

Swemmel would or wouldn't do to drive the redheads back?

When Krasta walked through the west wing of her mansion, the wing given over to the Algarvians who helped rule occupied Priekule, she knew at once that things were not as they should have been. On any normal day, the clerks and spies and military constables who labored there would have leered and muttered among themselves as she walked past. They were redheads. Leering at good-looking women was in their blood. The only thing that kept them from reaching out and fondling her as she went by was her being Lurcanio's mistress. The count and colonel could punish anyone who got too gay with his hands.

Today, though, the Algarvians scarcely seemed to notice her, though she was wearing a pair of green velvet trousers cut like a second skin. Mezentio's men talked in low voices, but not about her. The looks on their faces put her in mind of those the servants had worn after her parents died. They'd had a shock, and they were wondering what would come next.

When she strode into the anteroom where Captain Mosco worked, she demanded, "Nothing's gone and happened to your precious king, has it?"

Colonel Lurcanio's aide looked up from his paperwork. "To Mezentio?" he said. "No indeed, milady – as far as I know, he's hale as can be." But his face had that pinched, pained expression on it, too, and his voice was full of things he wasn't saying. Setting his pen in the inkwell, he rose from his desk. "I'll tell the colonel you're here." He returned a moment later. "Aye, he'll see you."

Krasta went into Lurcanio's office. The Algarvian was, as always, courteous as a cat. He got to his feet, bowed over Krasta's hand, and gallantly raised it to his lips. He handed her into the chair across from his desk. But it all struck Krasta as a performance, and not a very good one at that. "What *is* the matter with you people today?" she fumed.

"Have you not heard?" Lurcanio asked. Even his accent seemed thicker than usual, as if he wasn't trying so hard to shape the sounds that went into Valmieran.

"If I'd heard – whatever there is to hear – would I be asking you?" Krasta said. "By all the long faces out there, I thought something was wrong with your king. Mosco said that wasn't it, but he didn't say what was."

"No, Mezentio is hale," Lurcanio said, echoing his aide. "But, against all expectations, we have been thrown back before Cottbus, which naturally pains us."

"Oh," Krasta said. "Is that all?"

Lurcanio stared at her from under gingery eyebrows going gray. "You may not think it so much of a much, milady, but there are those who will tell you it is no small thing. Indeed, I fear I am one of them."

"But why?" Krasta asked in genuine perplexity. "By the powers above, Lurcanio, it's on the other side of the world." Few things outside Priekule, and next to none outside Valmiera, carried much weight with her.

Lurcanio perplexed her by rising and giving her another bow. "Ah, milady, I almost envy you: you are invincibly provincial," he said. By his tone, it was a compliment, even if Krasta didn't quite understand it.

"As far as I'm concerned," she said with a sniff, "King Swemmel is welcome to Cottbus. A nasty place for a nasty man."

"He is a nasty man. It is a nasty place," Lurcanio agreed with a sniff of his own. "But Unkerlant has a great many nasty places, and none of them so strong or so strongly held as Cottbus. It should have fallen. That it did not fall will mean . . . complications in the war ahead."

To Krasta, tomorrow was a mystery, a week hence the far side of the moon. "You will beat the Unkerlanters," she said. "After all, if you beat us, you can beat anyone."

For a moment, what looked uncommonly like a smirk lit Lurcanio's face. It vanished before Krasta could be sure she'd seen it. He said, "Actually, the Unkerlanter army has given us a rather better fight than Valmiera's did."

"I can't imagine how that could be," Krasta said.

"I know you can't. I almost envy you that, too," Lurcanio said; he might have been speaking Gyongyosian for all the sense he made to her. "But whether you can imagine it or not, the thing is there, and we have to see what comes of it."

Krasta tossed her head. "I know what will come of it. No one will be having any parties worth going to until you people decide you can be happy again, and powers above only know how long that will take." Before Lurcanio could answer, she spun on her heel and stalked out of his office.

She swung her hips more than usual when she headed back toward the part of the mansion that still belonged to her. Even so, hardly any of the Algarvians looked up from their work as she went by. That only made her unhappier. If no one was watching her, she hardly felt she was alive.

"Bauska!" she shouted when she got back into her own section of the mansion. "Curse it, you lazy slut, where are you hiding?"

"Coming, milady," the maidservant said, hurrying down the stairway and up to her. She was very pale, and gulped as if hoping her stomach would stay quiet. As far as Krasta was concerned, she'd been next to useless since Captain Mosco put a loaf in her oven. Gulping again, she said, "How may I serve you?"

"Fetch me my wolfskin jacket," Krasta said, enjoying the prospect of sending Bauska back upstairs. "I am going to go for a walk on the grounds here."

"You *are*, milady?" Bauska sounded astonished. Walking the grounds was not Krasta's usual idea of amusement. The only good Krasta usually saw in having wide grounds, as a matter of fact, was in keeping neighbors at a nice, respectful distance. But she was feeling contrary today, all the more so after that unsatisfactory conversation with Lurcanio.

And so she snapped, "I certainly am. Now get moving." With a sigh, Bauska trudged up the stairs to get the jacket. She gave it to Krasta, and gave her a reproachful look with it. That was wasted; Krasta never noticed it.

Fastening the wooden toggles on the wolfskin jacket, Krasta went outside. She exclaimed as the cold bit at her cheeks and nose, but neither of the Algarvian sentries at the front door stirred an inch. She cursed their indifference under her breath.

The skins in the jacket came from Unkerlant; few wolves survived farther east in Derlavai. Krasta patted the soft gray sleeve. At the moment, she quite enjoyed wearing something from Swemmel's kingdom. She wished she could throw that in Lurcanio's face, but knew she didn't dare. He got quite stuffy where what he saw as Algarve's honor was concerned.

Snow crunched under her shoes. It was a couple of days old; soot from the countless coal and wood fires in Priekule had already streaked it with gray. Everything was cold and quiet, so quiet she could hear the scream of a dragon high overhead. The Algarvians kept a couple of them in the air above Priekule all the time, to give warning of Lagoan raiders. The

Lagoans didn't fly north very often. Krasta sniffed. She scorned Valmiera's former allies even more than she did its conquerors. The Algarvians, at least, had proved their strength.

She walked on, getting chillier with every step in spite of the wolfskin jacket. The Algarvians had to be mad to want to fight a war in Unkerlant in the wintertime. They should have settled down where they were and waited till spring. *Next time I meet a general at some feast or other, maybe I'll tell him so*, Krasta thought. *Some people just can't see what's in front of them.*

What was in front of her were more snow-covered grounds and bare-branched trees. In the summer, the trees screened Priekule from her sight. For the most part, that suited her fine; the city had altogether too many commoners in it for her to want to look at it very much.

Now, though, the spires of the royal palace and the taller, paler shaft of the Kaunian Column of Victory were plainly visible. Inside the palace, King Gainibu drowned his humiliation in spirits. Krasta didn't care to dwell on Gainibu. A king, as far as she was concerned, shouldn't be a sot.

That left the Column of Victory to draw her eye. There it stood, as it had since the days of the Kaunian Empire, proud and fair and beautifully carved . . . and Algarvian soldiers patrolled the park whose centerpiece it was, and all of Priekule, and all of the Kaunian kingdom of Valmiera.

Sudden unexpected tears stung her eyes. Her eyelashes started to freeze together. Angrily, she knuckled them. *Foolishness*, she thought. She was getting by. She was doing better than getting by. With an Algarvian protector, the hardships that had hold of the kingdom hardly touched her.

She nodded. She was looking at things the right way. The redheads had won the war, and nothing that happened in far-off Unkerlant could have anything to do with that. She was certain she was right there. Why, then, did the tears keep trying to come back?

Before she could find an answer – or, more likely, stop looking for one – a couple of Algarvians mounted on unicorns came trotting up the road from Priekule. One of the unicorns still bore some splotches of the dun-colored paint that had made it harder to spot during the fighting. The other was the white to which even clean snow could only aspire.

Both riders slowed to leer at Krasta. Most times, she would have withered them with a glance colder than the weather. Now, oddly, she welcomed their attention. She welcomed any attention. The smile she gave them was just this side of an invitation to a lewd act in the snow.

"Well, hello, sweetheart!" one of them said in accented Valmieran. "Whose girl you being? You being anybody's girl?"

"My companion is Colonel Lurcanio," Krasta answered before she thought. That would kill the unicorn riders' interest in her, and she didn't want it killed.

But it was. Both redheads grimaced. The one who'd spoken gave her a formal salute, as if she rather than Lurcanio were his superior officer. "Meaning no offense," he said, and spurred his unicorn toward the mansion. The other cavalryman followed close behind.

Krasta stooped and scooped up a snowball and threw it after them. It fell short. They had no idea she'd flung it. The snow stung her hands. She rubbed them on the fur of her jacket, opening and closing them to get the blood flowing and make them less icy.

The two Algarvians tied their unicorns in front of the mansion and went inside. *They don't even know it's my house*, Krasta thought. Oh, they might suspect, because Colonel Lurcanio's woman wouldn't be anyone ordinary, but they didn't know. They would have leered at Bauska, too.

"And I've come out of the war better than most," Krasta murmured. "Powers above!" She looked over toward the Kaunian Column of Victory once more. The triumphs it celebrated were vanished now. The Emperor who'd won them was only a name in history books, history books she hadn't read. Pretty soon, the Algarvians would write the history books, and then no one would ever hear his name again.

She headed back toward the mansion. Even after she went inside, she was a long time feeling warm.

Ice was forming in Count Sabrino's waxed mustachios. Snow lay on the plains of Unkerlant far below. The Algarvian colonel's dragon had carried him into air colder still.

He reached up with his right hand to knock the ice away. He used the goad in his left to whack the side of the dragon's long neck, swinging its course more nearly southwest. The dragon let out an immense, furious hiss. Stupid like all its kind, it wanted to do what it wanted to do, not to follow its dragonflier's commands.

Sabrino whacked it again, harder this time. "Obey, curse you!" he shouted, though the freezing wind blew his words away. The dragon didn't hiss this time; it screamed. He wondered if it would twist its head back and try to flame him off it. That was a dragon's ultimate sin. He waited, ready to whack it on the sensitive end of its nose if it so forgot its training.

But, screaming again, it took the course he wanted. He looked back over his shoulder to make sure the wing he commanded was following. Sure enough, thirty-seven dragons painted in stripes of green, white, and red – the Algarvian colors – matched his change of course. His mouth twisted; like any man of his kingdom, he showed what he thought. His wing should have numbered sixty-four. But fighting had been desperately heavy these past few weeks – men and dragons were dying faster than replacements could reach the front.

A burning peasant village sent smoke high into the air, almost as high as Sabrino flew. He eyed the column of smoke in mild surprise; he'd thought most of the Unkerlanter villages hereabouts had gone up in flames during the Algarvian advance on Cottbus. Now, down there on the ground, the Unkerlanters, at home in winter, were the ones moving forward.

No sooner had that thought crossed Sabrino's mind than he spied a group of Unkerlanter behemoths tramping east. They skirted the village, which might still have Algarvian defenders holed up in it. Over the drifts came the great beasts – literally. Some bright Unkerlanter had had the idea of fitting them with outsized snowshoes. Those let them cope with deep snow far better than Algarvian behemoths could. Sabrino grimaced – what an embarrassment, to be outthought by Unkerlanters!

When it came to cold-weather fighting, King Swemmel's men had outthought the Algarvians several different ways. Sabrino was nearly sure Unkerlanter footsoldiers accompanied those behemoths. He couldn't see them, though, not from this height. The Unkerlanters wore white smocks over the rest of their clothes, and were nearly invisible in the snow. That sort of need hadn't occurred to Sabrino's countrymen. With thick wool tunics and stockings, with heavy felt boots, with fur hats and fur-lined capes, the Unkerlanters had an easier time staying warm than the Algarvians, too.

The dragons flew over another village, this one wrecked in the earlier fighting. Lumps in the snow around it might have been dead behemoths. Sabrino flew too high to spot snow-covered human corpses. In any case, they were too common to attract much notice.

There ahead lay the shattered town of Lehesten, north and slightly east of Cottbus. Algarvian troops had briefly held it, just as they'd fought their way into Thalfang south of the Unkerlanter capital. Sabrino had heard they'd spied the spires of King Swemmel's palace from Thalfang. He didn't know whether that was true. If it was, they hadn't seen them for long. Fierce Unkerlanter counterattacks had shoved the Algarvians out of Thalfang, and out of Lehesten, too.

Now the Unkerlanters were pouring footsoldiers and behemoths and even horse and unicorn cavalry through Lehesten, using the town as a marshaling point for their counterattack. Sabrino whooped to spot a column of behemoths hauling heavy egg-tossers toward the fighting front. Even with snowshoes on the behemoths' feet, even with skids under the egg-tossers, that column wasn't going anywhere fast.

Activating the crystal attached to his harness took only a muttered word of command. The faces of his three surviving squadron leaders, tiny but perfect, appeared in the crystal. "We are going to tear up that column," Sabrino told them.

"Aye, Colonel!" Captain Domiziano exclaimed.

"Aye, Colonel," Captain Orosio agreed. "Let's hurt the whoresons." He was perhaps five years older than Domiziano in the flesh, thirty years older in the spirit.

Sabrino spoke to the newest squadron leader, Captain Olindro: "Your men and dragons will fly top cover for us. If the Unkerlanters come against us, you'll hold them off till we can get some height and join you." *You'll do that, or you'll die trying,* Sabrino thought. Olindro's predecessor had.

As Domiziano and Orosio had before him, Olindro said, "Aye, Colonel." If he thought about his predecessor's fate, he didn't let on. A good soldier couldn't let his fears and worries show, though Sabrino had never known a fighting man without them.

"Let's go!" he shouted, and whacked his dragon again, this time in the command to dive. For once, the dragon obeyed with alacrity. Even its tiny brain had come to associate diving with fighting, and it liked fighting better than feeding, perhaps even better than mating. Domiziano and Orosio's squadrons followed Sabrino down. The icy wind thrummed in his face. Had he not worn goggles, it would have blinded him.

Behemoths and egg-tossers swelled from specks to toys to real things in what seemed no time at all. Sabrino led the dragons against the column from the rear, hoping to put off for as long as he could the moment when the Unkerlanters realized they were under attack.

He always used that tactic. Sometimes, as today, it worked very well indeed. Secure in their possession of Lehesten, secure also in their possession of the initiative, the enemy soldiers paid the air no attention till Sabrino ordered his dragon to flame.

A sheet of flame, fueled by brimstone and quicksilver, burst from the dragon's mouth. It engulfed a behemoth, the men riding on the beast, and the egg-tosser perhaps ten feet in front of it. The behemoth never made a sound. It might have been inhaling when the fire rolled over it. It simply toppled, dead before its flank hit the snow.

A couple of men in white smocks trudging along beside the egg-tosser did shriek as flames devoured them. The egg-tosser's carriage, being made of more wood than metal, caught and began to burn. So did the casings of some of the eggs on the carriage. Mages made them to stand up to a good many things, but not to dragonfire. Bursts of sorcerous energy from the unleashed eggs finished the work of wrecking the tosser the flame had begun.

The rest of the dragons in the two squadrons Sabrino had ordered into action flamed the column with him. Only a handful of men and a couple of behemoths escaped their first onslaught.

No one had ever said the Unkerlanters lacked courage – or, if anyone had said it, he'd been a fool. The survivors of the Algarvian attack promptly started blazing at the men and dragons who'd tormented them so. Only luck would let a footsoldier bring down a dragon: the beasts' bellies were painted silver to reflect beams, and even a blaze through the eye might not pierce their small, bone-armored brains.

Dragonfliers were more vulnerable. A beam hissed past Sabrino. He used the goad to hit the dragon in the throat, urging it to climb. It didn't like that; it wanted to go back and use more flame. In the end, bad-tempered as usual, it obeyed him.

He was willing to go round and make another pass at the Unkerlanters. But before he could give the order, Olindro's tiny image appeared in his crystal. "Dragons!" the squadron leader said, face twisting in alarm. "Unkerlanter dragons – lots of them!"

Sabrino looked up. Sure enough, Olindro's squadron was under assault from perhaps twice its number of dragons, all painted the rock-gray of Unkerlanter military tunics.

His dragon saw the enemies, too. It didn't much care for the beasts on its own side, but had – slowly – learned not to quarrel with them. Screaming with fury, it flew hard toward the dragons the Unkerlanters rode. The great muscles that powered its wings pumped hard.

As Sabrino drew near, he unslung his stick and aimed it at an Unkerlanter flier. His forefinger went into the activating hole at the base of the stick. A beam blazed forth from the other end. It missed the Unkerlanter. Good blazing was hard from dragonback, with both target and blazer moving so swiftly.

Cursing even so, Sabrino forced his dragon up through and past the enemies attacking his men and beasts. Most of the two squadrons he led followed his example. They were, almost to a man, veteran dragonfliers; they knew what needed doing. Dragonfights were war in three dimensions. Height mattered.

By the way the Unkerlanters flew, a lot of them were new aboard their bad-tempered mounts. They didn't try to keep Sabrino's men from gaining altitude; they were intent on destroying Olindro's squadron. Under that waxed mustache – which was icing up again – Sabrino's lips skinned back from his teeth in a savage grin. Inexperience could and, he vowed, would be an expensive business.

He chose the enemy dragon he wanted, then urged his own beast into a dive. The Unkerlanter dragonflier had no notion he was there. Without the slightest twinge of conscience – the Unkerlanter would have exulted at doing it to him – he blazed the fellow in the back.

The Unkerlanter threw out his hands. His stick flew from one of them. He slumped down on to his dragon's neck. The beast, no longer under his control, showed its true nature: it struck out wildly at friend and foe alike, then flew off to prey on the frozen countryside below. The war had left it plenty of carrion on which to feed.

Sabrino blazed at another Unkerlanter dragonflier. He missed again, and cursed again. But his dragon was flying faster than the enemy's mount. Nearer and nearer he drew. This Unkerlanter was a little more wary than the other one had been, but not wary enough. He'd only started to swing his dragon around to face Sabrino when the count ordered his own dragon to flame.

Again, fire burst from the dragon's jaws. It caught the Unkerlanter beast in the flank and, more important, in the membranous wing. Bellowing horribly, flaming back with fire falling short, the Unkerlanter dragon fell out of the sky toward the ground far below. Sabrino thought he heard the dragonflier's fading scream.

More Unkerlanter dragons were plummeting to earth or flying off under no man's control. So were some of his own. He howled his fury at the losses. Algarve couldn't afford them – and the men were friends as well as comrades.

But, before long, the Unkerlanters had had enough and fled back toward the west, the direction from which they'd come. Sabrino didn't order a pursuit. He didn't care to face the fresh squadrons King Swemmel's men might send up with his own beasts tired. Instead, he waved back toward the east, toward the Algarvians' own chilly makeshift of a dragon farm.

When they flew over the front, he quietly thanked the powers above that he wasn't down there fighting on the ground. One reason he'd started flying dragons – and the best one he'd ever found – was that it beat the stuffing out of the footsoldier's life.

Bembo wished he were back in Tricarico. Walking a constable's beat in a provincial town in northeastern Algarve hadn't been the most exciting job in the world, but now he realized he hadn't appreciated it enough while he had it. Compared to some of the things he had to do here in Gromheort and in the surrounding villages, that beat seemed like paradise.

The plump constable didn't mind – well, he didn't mind too much – being plucked out of his comfortable home and sent west to help keep order in one of the kingdoms Algarve had conquered. Somebody had to do it. And besides, serving as a constable in occupied Forthweg, while harder than doing it in his own home town, was in most ways infinitely preferable to being issued a stick and sent off to the front in Unkerlant.

In most ways, but not in all. Along with the rest of a squad of constables from Tricarico, Bembo led several dozen trousered Kaunians through the streets of Gromheort toward the town's ley-line caravan depot. Some of the blonds walked along as if they had not a care in the world. But most had trouble hiding the fear they surely felt. Husbands comforted wives; mothers comforted children. Even as they did so, though, those husbands and mothers were biting their lips and fighting back tears themselves.

A man turned toward Bembo and stretched out his hands. "Why?" he asked in Algarvian; a fair number of people in Gromheort spoke some of the constable's language. "What did we do to deserve this?"

"Keep moving," was all Bembo said. "Keep moving, or you'll be sorry." He was always sorry to draw this duty, but the Kaunian didn't have to know. *The people over me know what they're doing*, Bembo thought. *If we're going to win the cursed war, we have to do what we have to do. It's only Kaunians, after all. Can't make an omelet without breaking eggs.* At the thought of an omelet, his stomach rumbled hungrily.

"Aye, you'd better keep moving, you buggers or you'll get what for," Sergeant Pesaro said, also in Algarvian. Pesaro was a good deal plumper than Bembo. Evodio translated the sergeant's warning into classical Kaunian for the blonds who couldn't follow Algarvian.

The Kaunians and their guards tramped past a young Forthwegian man in a long tunic coming the other way. Like most Forthwegians, the fellow was blocky and dark, with a big tuber of a nose right in the middle of his face. He would have looked just like his Unkerlanter cousins farther west had he not let his beard grow out. He shouted something in his own language at the Kaunians. Bembo didn't understand a word of it, but the way the Forthwegian drew a thumb across his throat could mean only one thing. So could his coarse laughter.

Oraste laughed, too. "The Forthwegians are happy as clams that we're cleaning the Kaunians out of their kingdom for them," he said, and spat on the cobblestones. "It's good riddance, as far as I'm concerned."

"Powers above know I don't especially love Kaunians, but . . ." Bembo's voice trailed away. He watched a pretty young mother – if he was going to watch Kaunians, he preferred to watch their women – keeping a boy of about six walking along. The child seemed happy enough. The mother's face was set tight against a scream. Bembo ground his teeth. No, parts of this duty weren't what he would have wanted.

Oraste had no doubts, for which Bembo envied him. Oraste seldom had doubts about anything. Like a hound, like a hawk, the veteran constable brought in whatever his superiors aimed him at. He said, "Weren't for the cursed Kaunians here and in Valmiera and Jelgava, we wouldn't have a war now. Far as I'm concerned, the whoresons deserve whatever happens to 'em. Sneaks and sluts, the lot of 'em.'"

"Aye," Bembo said abstractedly, but he was still watching that nice-looking blonde and her little boy.

Another Forthwegian passerby jeered at the Kaunians on the way to the caravan station. Maybe nine out of ten people in the shattered Kingdom of Forthweg were actually of Forthwegian blood, the tenth being the blonds who'd dwelt in this part of the world since the long-vanished days of the Kaunian Empire. As Oraste had said, most of the Forthwegians had scant use for their trousered neighbors.

"Keep moving," Sergeant Pesaro called again. "You'd better keep moving, if you know what's good for you. This isn't stinking Eoforwic, you know. Not a single bloody soul in these parts believes your lies." Again, Evodio translated his words into classical Kaunian: The Empire's language had changed very little here.

Like almost all Algarvians, like almost everyone in the west of Derlavai, Bembo had studied classical Kaunian in school. Like most people, he'd forgotten just about all of it as soon as he didn't need it any more. Evodio was an exception. He didn't look scholarly; he looked almost as much like a bruiser as Oraste did.

One of the Kaunians spoke in his own tongue. Evodio translated what he said for Pesaro: "He asks why you say they're lies. Everyone knows they're true. You must know it, too, he says."

"I don't care what he says," Pesaro growled. "Anybody who riots on account of a pack of lies is fair game, and *that*, by the powers above, goes for Kaunians and Forthwegians both."

Only rumors about the riots in Eoforwic had drifted east to Gromheort. Some Kaunians seemed to have escaped – or to have been released by Unkerlanter raiders; the rumors weren't clear on that – from the labor camps the Algarvians had set up for them near the western front. They claimed their folk were being used not for labor but for their life energy, with the Algarvians slaying them so mages could use that energy to power great sorceries against King Swemmel's soldiers.

Bembo was pretty sure those claims were true, but most of the time did his resolute best not to think about it. "Even Forthwegians went up in smoke when they heard what we were up to out in the west," he said – very quietly – to Oraste.

"Always a few hotheads," Oraste answered with a fine, indifferent Algarvian shrug. "We're back in the saddle in Eoforwic, and that's what counts." No, he didn't waste time on doubts. Instead, he pointed ahead. "Almost there."

Gromheort's ley-line caravan depot, a massive pile of gray stone not far from the count's palace, had taken considerable damage when the Algarvians seized the city. Nobody'd bothered repairing it since; so long as the ley lines themselves were clear of rubble, everything else could wait till victory finally came. Pesaro said, "Step it up." Evodio translated for the Kaunians' benefit – though that wasn't really the right word.

Inside the depot, Bembo's boots made echoes kick back from the walls as he strode across the marble floor. No lamps burned, leaving the depot a dank and gloomy place. The roof leaked. It had rained a couple of days before – Gromheort rarely got snow – and little puddles dotted the floor. A cold falling drop got Bembo in the back of the neck. He cursed and wiped it away with his hand.

An Algarvian military policeman carrying a clipboard came up to Pesaro. "How many of these blond whoresons have you got?" he asked.

"Fifty," the constabulary sergeant answered. "That was the quota they gave me, and I deliver." He puffed out his chest, but, however much he puffed, it would never reach out past his protruding belly.

"Fine," the other Algarvian said, obviously not impressed. He studied his clipboard, then scribbled something on it. "Fifty, eh? All right, take 'em over to platform twelve and load 'em on to the caravan there. Twelve, you hear?"

"I'm not deaf," Pesaro said with dignity. He would have scorched a constable who sassed him, but had to be more careful around soldiers. Since he couldn't tell the military policeman off, he shouted instead at the Kaunians the squad had rounded up: "Come on, you lousy buggers! Get moving! Platform twelve, the man said!"

"Likes to hear himself make noise, doesn't he?" Oraste said under his breath.

"You just noticed?" Bembo answered, and the other constable chuckled. But then, more charitably, Bembo added, "Well, who doesn't?" He knew he did, and knew very few Algarvians who didn't. The Forthwegians and Kaunians he'd met since coming to Gromheort seemed less given to display. Sometimes, he just thought that made them dull. Others, though, he got suspicious – what were they hiding?

No one could have hidden anything out on platform twelve, which stood open to a chilly breeze blowing out of the west. Once upon a time, the platform had had a wooden roof; the stumps of a few charred support pillars were all that remained of it.

There by the edge of the platform, the cars of the caravan floated a couple of feet above the ley line from which they drew their energy and along which they would travel. Looking at those cars, Bembo said, "Where are we going to fit this lot of blonds? I don't think there's room for 'em." He didn't think there was room for about a third – maybe even half – of the Kaunians already jammed in there.

"We'll shoehorn 'em in somehow," Oraste said. "Where there's a will, there's a lawyer." He chuckled nastily. "And we can feel up the broads as we shove 'em in."

The blond man who knew Algarvian turned to him and said, "I already knew better than to expect mercy from you. Is the smallest decency too much to ask for?"

"You Kaunians spent years and years and years grinding a foot down on Algarve's neck, and nobody ever heard a word about mercy or decency from you," Oraste said. He chuckled again. "Now you're going to get it in the neck, and see how you like it."

Guards opened doors on some of the cars. They and the constables herded the Kaunians into them. It did take a lot of pushing and shoving. The seat of the trousers was one obvious place to shove. Oraste enjoyed himself. Bembo confined his shovings to the back, though he couldn't have said why he bothered.

Even before the last of the Kaunians were inside the cars, workmen – Forthwegians with an Algarvian boss – began nailing over the windows wooden grates with only the narrowest of openings between the slats. "What's that all about?" Bembo asked.

At last, the job was done. The guards forced the caravan-door closed, then barred them from the outside. From within, Bembo could still hear the moans and cries of the Kaunians as they sought whatever comfort they could find. He doubted they would find much.

Oraste waved to the cars, though with those grates on the windows the men and women inside could hardly have seen him. "So long," he called. "You think it's bad now, it only gets worse later. Off to Unkerlant with the lot of you!" He threw back his head and laughed.

A couple of Forthwegian carpenters must have understood Algarvian, for they laughed, too. But Sergeant Pesaro rounded on Oraste, growling, "Shut up, curse you! They won't want trouble on the caravan while it's going west, so don't stir up the stinking Kaunians."

"He's right," said Bembo, who as usual on roundup duty wished he were doing anything but. Oraste nodded to Pesaro and gave Bembo a dirty look.

As soon as the carpenters had nailed a grate over the last window, the ley-line caravan silently glided away. For a moment, Bembo simply watched it. Then he gaped. "It's going east!" he exclaimed. "East, toward Algarve! Why are they sending Kaunians that way?" No one had a good answer for him; all the Algarvians on the platform looked as surprised as he was.

Skarnu laughed softly as he strode through Pavilosta toward the market square. Merkela, who walked beside him, sent him a curious look. "What's funny?" she asked. "The town hasn't changed much, not that I can see."

"No, the town hasn't changed," Skarnu agreed, "but I have. I've been on your farm so long now, and spent so much of my time there, that Pavilosta's starting to look like a big city to me."

"It looks big to me," she answered, matching him stride for stride. She wasn't far from his height or from his strength; she'd done farm work all her life, not just over the past year and a half. Looking first to one side of the street and then to the other, she murmured, "Buildings all around, and some of them three, four stories high. Aye, it looks plenty big enough."

"It does to me, too – now," Skarnu said. "I grew up in Priekule, though. Pavilosta didn't used to seem so much of a much, not after the capital. It's all what you get used to, I suppose."

An Algarvian soldier carrying several links of sausage looked Merkela up and down and gave her a saucy smile as he walked by. Her answering stare would have chilled live steam to ice on the instant. It didn't chill the soldier, who went on up the street laughing.

"Some things you never get used to," Merkela said. "Some things you keep on fighting, even if they slay you for it."

"Aye," Skarnu said. Unlike most of Valmiera, Merkela and he were still fighting.

"Vengeance," Merkela murmured softly. It was, these days, the most important thing she lived for. One reason she favored Skarnu these days was that he lived for it, too.

They walked past a broadsheet pasted on a wall. FOR THE KILLER OF COUNT SIMANU, 1,000 GOLDPIECES, it proclaimed. Merkela reached out and squeezed Skarnu's hand. He'd slain Simanu, after all. And if he hadn't, Merkela might have.

A greengrocer's was quiet, while the rest of the shops on the street bustled. Painted across the window were half a dozen words: REVENGE FOR SIMANU – NIGHT AND FOG. Skarnu's shiver had nothing to do with the weather. Whoever met night and fog vanished off the face of the earth. He'd found that out when he visited a comrade's farm. Dauktu was gone, and all his family with him.

Skarnu didn't want to think about that. As he and Merkela neared the square, he remarked, "Do you know what I miss from Priekule?" She shook her head. Her straight blond hair, even fairer than his, flew back and forth. Skarnu said, "I miss news sheets."

Merkela shrugged. "Pavilosta never had one of its own. It isn't big enough for that, I suppose. Sometimes they bring them in from other towns. These days, a news sheet would be full of Algarvian lies, anyhow."

"Aye, so it would," Skarnu agreed. "The biggest news is, the redheads have to keep on fighting in Unkerlant. If they'd taken Cottbus, we'd all be singing a sorry tune right now."

"Good they didn't," Merkela said fiercely. "The only thing wrong is, the Unkerlanters won't give Mezentio's men everything I would." Skarnu wasn't so sure of that; the soldiers who followed King Swemmel were anything but gentle. Then Skarnu glanced over to Merkela. On second thought, she was probably right. Whatever Swemmel's men did to the Algarvians, it wouldn't match what she'd do if only she could.

He didn't remark on that. Whatever he said, Merkela would come back with something like, *Well, of course.* One of the reasons she'd been drawn to him, even before the Algarvians killed her husband, was that he'd refused to quit fighting them. He didn't think it was the only reason – he hoped not – but he was a long way from sure it was the smallest one.

Instead of a daily or a weekly news sheet, Pavilosta had the market square. People gathered to gossip as much as they did to buy and sell. Algarvian soldiers walked through the square, but not so many as had walked it before fall turned into winter. That wasn't the cold keeping them indoors so much as it was the war in the distant west pulling them out of Valmiera. Skarnu wished it would pull them all out of his kingdom.

Merkela went off to buy pins and needles, which she couldn't make for herself on the farm. Skarnu cared nothing about pins and needles. He wandered over to the table from which an enterprising Pavilosta taverner sold ale. The taverner nodded to him as he came up. He would never be a proper local, not if he stayed on the farm near town till his hair went from gold to silver. But he'd been here long enough – and kept his mouth shut well enough – to win a little respect. He laid coins on the table. The taverner poured him ale from a big stoneware jug.

He sipped, then nodded. "Good," he said. His accent still announced that he came from the capital, not the provinces. Imitating the local dialect only made him sound like a bad actor. Imitating peasant taciturnity worked better.

"Aye, it is, though the weather's too cold for the proper tang to come through," the taverner answered. He was no peasant, and the hinges of his jaws worked fine. He looked around for the closest Algarvians. Not seeing any kilted soldiers within earshot, he leaned forward across the table and asked, "Have you heard the latest?"

"Don't think so." Skarnu leaned forward, too, till their heads almost touched. "Tell me, why don't you?"

"I'll do that. I will indeed." Had the taverner brought his mouth any closer, he could have given Skarnu a kiss. "They say – I can't prove it's true, but they do say it, and nobody says anything different, not that I've heard – they say the redheads have knocked over the Column of Victory down in Priekule."

"What?" Skarnu jerked as if stung by a wasp. "They can't do that!" His memories of the column went back to earliest childhood, back to the days before his parents had died in a ley-line caravan collision, orphaning him and Krasta.

"They can. They already have, matter of fact – that's what I'm telling you," the taverner said. "Pretty rotten piece of business, anybody wants to know what I think . . . which isn't too likely, especially if you listen to my wife go on."

Skarnu was only half listening. He picked up the mug of ale, gulped it down, and shoved it and coins across the table for a refill. He took a long pull at that, too, trying to imagine the capital's skyline without that pale stone needle thrusting up from the middle of the park. He couldn't do it; he had an easier time visualizing the royal palace gone. "Powers above," he said at last. "They're not just knocking down a monument. They're trying to make us forget who we are."

Now the taverner gave him a blank look. The fellow might be shrewd in business, but how much education did he have? Not much, probably. That wasn't so for Skarnu, who'd always been a better student than his sister. Valmiera's roots, like those of Jelgava to the north, were anchored in the soil of the long-ago Kaunian Empire. Monuments survived all over both kingdoms; the Column of Victory was just one of the more spectacular. If the Algarvians were trying to destroy them . . .

"They're trying to kill our Kaunianity," Skarnu said.

Intelligence kindled in the taverner's eyes. He understood what that meant, all right. "Hadn't thought of it so," he said, "but curse me if I'll tell you you're wrong. No, curse the redheads."

"Aye, curse the redheads," Skarnu agreed.

"Aye, curse the redheads," Merkela said, coming up beside him. "Buy me some ale and tell me why we're cursing them this time." She didn't bother keeping her voice down. Both Skarnu and the taverner looked around the square in alarm. Fortunately, none of the Algarvians seemed to have heard. Skarnu explained – in a voice hardly above a whisper – what Mezentio's men had done. Merkela nodded. "Powers below eat them," she snarled.

"May it be so," Skarnu said, and did his best to change the subject: "Have you got what you need?"

Such ploys failed more often than they worked. This time, he got lucky. "I do," Merkela answered, "and for a better price than I thought I would, too. Every copper counts these days." That set her cursing the Algarvians again, but in a more restrained way. "What about you?"

"Oh, I just came along to keep you company and get out of a morning's work," Skarnu answered. *And to keep you out of trouble*, he added to himself. As for the work, only in winter could a farmer – or even someone turning into a farmer – say such a thing and get away with it.

Even at this season of the year, Merkela reproachfully clicked her tongue between her teeth. "Work shouldn't wait," she said, which might have been a peasant's creed all over Derlavai. She drank the mug of ale Skarnu had got her, then slipped her arm into his. For a moment, he thought that was fond possessiveness. Then she declared, "Come on, let's go. You can finish most of the chores this afternoon, and not leave so much for tomorrow."

She was in deadly earnest. She usually was. Skarnu wanted to laugh it off, but didn't quite dare. Meek as any henpecked husband, he let her lead him out of the square, out of Pavilosta, and back toward the farm. He was chuckling inside, but made sure it didn't show.

Like most towns, Pavilosta had gone up at a power point, which let mages work there without fueling their sorcery with sacrifices. Pavilosta's power point was small and feeble, one reason the place remained no more than a village.

Another reason was that it did not lie on the ley line connecting two stronger local power points. That line lay between Pavilosta and Merkela's farm. Most times going to and from the village, Skarnu hardly noticed it. The Algarvians kept the brush down along it, as had the Valmierans before them; but in winter there was no brush to keep down.

Today, though, he and Merkela had to pause at the ley line because a long caravan was passing by; it was heading southeast, in the direction of Priekule and, beyond the capital, the Strait of Valmiera. Merkela stared at the cars as they silently slid past. "Why are all the windows covered with those wooden grates?" she asked.

"I don't know," Skarnu answered. "I've never seen anything like that, either." But, after the caravan had passed, a stench lingered in the cold, crisp air. It put him in mind of the smell of the trenches – unwashed men and undisposed-of waste – but it was stronger and even more sour. "Maybe it's a prison caravan," he suggested.

"Maybe." Merkela looked along the ley line. "If those are prisoners of the Algarvians, I hope they get away." Skarnu peered after the caravan, too. Slowly, he nodded.

When Ealstan fled Gromheort, he'd thought everything would turn out fine after he got to Oyngestun. Vanai lived there, after all. If he hadn't fallen for her, he wouldn't have fought with his cousin and had to flee the city. Falling for a Kaunian girl would have been hard enough for a

Forthwegian even in peacetime. With the redheads occupying the kingdom . . .

I wonder if I killed Sidroc, Ealstan thought for the hundredth, or maybe the thousandth, time. Sooner or later, he would hear from his family. Leofsig would know where he'd gone. Leofsig or their father would find a way to get in touch with him. Ealstan didn't dare write back to Gromheort; that would tell the local constables, and maybe the Algarvians, too, where he was staying.

Of course, if Sidroc wasn't dead and didn't have his wits scrambled when he hit his head after Ealstan punched him, he would likely know where Ealstan was, too. But if Sidroc wasn't dead and didn't have his wits scrambled, he and Uncle Hengist would have gone to the Algarvians because of the fight. That constable coming up the Street of Tinkers might have Ealstan's name and description. He might take out his stick and threaten Ealstan with death if he didn't come along quietly.

He did nothing of the sort. He walked past Ealstan without even noticing him. For all he knew, Ealstan's ancestors might have lived in Oyngestun for generations uncounted. The Forthwegians whose ancestors had lived in the village for generations uncounted knew better, of course. But a stranger here wasn't such a prodigy as he would have been before war stirred the countryside like a woman stirring soup in a pot above a kitchen hearthfire.

Ealstan walked the Street of Tinkers from one end to the other, as he had every day since coming to Oyngestun. Vanai lived in one of the houses along the street. Ealstan knew that from the letters they'd sent back and forth. But he didn't know which one. They all looked much alike, presenting only walls − some whitewashed, some painted − and doorways and tiny windows to the street. Most Forthwegian houses were like that: built around a central courtyard, and not showing the outside world whatever ostentation lay within.

He kicked at the cobblestones in frustration. He hadn't dared ask after Vanai. That might have involved her in his trouble − and it might have got back to the constables or the redheads. Even had he known which house was hers, she shared it with her grandfather. Ealstan had no doubt Brivibas was as appalled at the notion of his daughter's falling in love with a Forthwegian as most Forthwegians would have been at the idea of one of their kind's loving a Kaunian.

"Powers above," Ealstan muttered to himself. "Doesn't she ever come outside? Doesn't she even look outside?"

As best he could tell, Vanai didn't. He couldn't spend every waking moment pacing up and down the Street of Tinkers, however much he wanted to. That would get him noticed, the last thing he wanted.

"I ought to go away," he murmured. "I ought to go far away, go someplace where nobody's ever heard of me, and wait for things to blow over."

He'd said that before. Logically, intellectually, it made good sense. No matter how much sense it made, he couldn't do it. Vanai was here . . . somewhere. Of course she drew him now, as a lodestone drew bits of iron.

Shaking his head, he went back to the tavern where he was renting a nasty little chamber above the taproom. The drunken racket below made his nights hideous, but he couldn't very well complain. The taverner made more from the noisy drunks than he did from Ealstan.

A few doors up the street from the tavern was an apothecary's shop run by a plump Kaunian named Tamulis. Ealstan had been in there a couple of times, in search of a nostrum to knock down the headaches he got from not sleeping enough. He hadn't had much luck.

He was just coming up to the apothecary's door when it opened and someone came out of the shop. He had to step smartly to keep from running into her. "I'm sorry," he said in Forthwegian. Then he stopped in his tracks, his mouth falling open. "Vanai!"

She hadn't recognized him, either, not for a moment. Her jaw dropped, too; her blue-gray eyes opened enormously wide. "Ealstan!" she exclaimed, and flung herself into his arms.

They separated almost at once, as if each found the other burning hot. To be seen embracing was to court danger from Algarvians, Forthwegians, and likely Kaunians as well. But the memory of Vanai pressing against him warmed Ealstan better – deeper – than his long, heavy tunic and the wool cloak he wore over it.

"What are you doing here?" Vanai demanded. She spoke Forthwegian as readily as Kaunian; Ealstan could use Kaunian, but only more slowly. She held a green glass bottle in her hand. Ealstan had an identical bottle of willow-bark decoction up in his room. It might have helped fight fever from the grippe; he couldn't tell that it did any good against a headache.

In a few terse sentences, he explained what he was doing in Oyngestun, finishing, "After Sidroc wouldn't wake up, I knew I had to get out of Gromheort. There was only one place I wanted to come, and here I am."

Vanai flushed; with her fair skin, far paler than Ealstan's, the progress of the blush was easy – and fascinating – to watch. She knew why he wanted to come to Oyngestun. "But what will you do now?" she asked. "You can't have a lot of money."

"More than you think," he answered. "But I've been doing odd jobs, too: anything I can to get my hands on some extra cash so I don't go through what I've got so fast." As a bookkeeper's son, he understood he needed income to balance his expenses.

"All right. Good." Vanai nodded; she had a briskly practical streak. Then she repeated the question she'd asked before: "What will you do now?"

Ealstan knew what he wanted to do. Holding Vanai would have put the thought in his mind had it not been there already. But that wasn't what she meant. And he'd had time to think, pacing along the Street of Tinkers. He said, "If you want, we could go to Eoforwic together. From all I've heard, there are more mixed couples there than in the rest of Forthweg put together."

Vanai flushed again. "Maybe there were, back before the war – in fact, I know there were, back before the war," she said. "But now, under the Algarvians . . . Do you want to put yourself through that?"

"Why else would I have come to Oyngestun?" Ealstan asked. Vanai murmured something too low to hear and looked down at her shoes. Ealstan said, "You aren't talking about your grandfather, the way you always did before."

"No, I'm not talking about my grandfather," Vanai agreed wearily. "I think I may have said everything there is to say about him, and done everything there was to do for him. And he's certainly said everything there was to say about me." Her jaw set. Ealstan thought she was a year or so older than he. Suddenly, she looked a good deal older than that, and harder than he'd dreamt she could.

He started to ask what her grandfather had said about her. A second glance at her face convinced him that wouldn't be a good idea. Instead, he said, "Will you come with me?"

Her laugh had a raw edge to it. "This is only the fourth time we've ever set eyes on each other. We haven't spent more than a few hours together, and we've sent a few letters back and forth. And because of that, you want me to leave behind everything and everybody I've ever known and go off with you to a place neither one of us has ever seen?"

Dull embarrassment filled Ealstan. He'd let his hopes run away with him. Life as you lived it wasn't really much like what it was once the writers of romances got through with it. Kicking at the cobbles once more, he began, "Well, I—"

"Of course I'll come with you," Vanai broke in. "By the powers above – the powers above who are deaf and blind to everything we Kaunians have suffered – how could whatever happens to me there be worse than what's happened to me here?"

He knew he didn't know everything that had happened to her here in Oyngestun. Once more, he realized asking wouldn't be smart. In any case, joy and astonishment left him little room to worry about such things. "I don't want anything bad to happen to you," he said. "Not ever."

To his astonishment, her face worked. She bit her lip, plainly fighting back tears. "Nobody but you has ever said anything like that to me," she whispered.

"No?" Ealstan shook his head in bewilderment. "A lot of people have wasted a lot of chances, then." He saw he'd flustered her again. Since he didn't want that, he asked, "Will your grandfather be all right if you leave him alone?"

"I hope so. In spite of everything, I hope so," Vanai answered. "But the redheads are as likely to scoop me up on the way to Eoforwic as they are to grab him here. I can't do anything about that. I managed to keep him from going out and having to work himself to death on the road, but those days are gone now."

"How did you stop the Algarvians from sending him out to do road work?" Ealstan asked.

"I managed," Vanai repeated, and said no more. Her face went hard and closed again. None of the pictures that flooded into Ealstan's mind was any he wanted to see. He asked no more questions, which seemed to relieve Vanai.

Now she tried to break the tension: "How can we go to Eoforwic? I don't think they'll let us ride together in a caravan car, and I wouldn't feel safe in one, anyhow. Too easy for the Algarvians to stop the caravan and haul away everybody with yellow hair."

Ealstan nodded. "I think caravans are dangerous, too. That leaves walking, unless we find someone to give us a wagon ride for part of the way." He grimaced. "With the two of us, I don't know how likely that is."

"Not very," Vanai said succinctly, and Ealstan nodded again. She went on, "Let me take this to my grandfather and get a heavier cloak and some stouter shoes." She sighed. "I'll leave him a note to tell him some of what I'm doing, so he won't think the Algarvians got me. He'll have some learning to do, but I think he can. He's not stupid, even if he is a fool. Wait for me here. I'll be back soon." She hurried away.

Instead of waiting, he went up to his room and gathered his own meager belongings, then returned to the apothecary's shop. Good as her word, Vanai came up a few minutes later. She was wearing the heavier cloak, and had a cloth bag slung over her shoulder. "Let's go," Ealstan said. Side by side, they started out of Oyngestun, heading east.

As soon as a grove of pale-leaved olive trees hid the village behind them, they began holding hands. They leaped apart when a Forthwegian on a mule came past them, but then resumed. Not long after that, they were kissing. Not too much longer after that, they went off the road into another, thicker grove. It wasn't perfect privacy, but it was good enough. When they started walking again, they both wore foolish smiles. Ealstan knew he was in trouble, but had a hard time worrying about it. He was, after all, only seventeen.

Thirteen

Priekule was a gray, unhappy town after more than a year and a half of Algarvian occupation. Krasta still frequently left her mansion to visit the shops and cafes in the heart of the city, but what she found there satisfied her less and less often.

The food in the cafes seemed to get nastier every week. Sometimes a mere sniff after she went inside one was enough to send her stalking out again, elegantly straight nose high in the air. Jewelers hardly ever showed anything new. And the clothes . . . She'd occasionally worn kilts back in the days when Valmiera and Algarve were at peace, but only trousers – proper, traditional Kaunian garments – ever since. These days, though, more and more clothiers were showing kilts for both men and women. She knew people who wore them. She couldn't make herself do it.

After walking out of one such display, she angrily strode along the Avenue of Horsemen: tall, lean, arrogant. A news-sheet vendor called, "Fierce Algarvian counterattack in Unkerlant! Read all about it!"

Krasta stomped past him. She didn't care two figs about Unkerlant. Out there in the distant west, it might have been on the far side of the moon as far as she was concerned (the same held true for virtually the entire world outside of Priekule). She did know mild surprise that the Algarvians hadn't conquered it yet, as they had every other kingdom they'd assailed. But the details of the fighting mattered not at all to her.

A few days farther on, she paused, staring at three words whitewashed on to the window of a confectioner's shop: NIGHT AND FOG. The shop was closed. It looked to have been closed for some little while. She wondered when, or if, it would open again.

Another vendor, peddling a different news sheet, waved it in her face.

Krasta impatiently pushed past him and strode on down the sidewalk. She decided she wished after all that the Algarvians had taken Cottbus. Then the war would have been over, or as near as made no difference. After that, maybe the world could have started coming back to normal.

A couple of Algarvian soldiers, cloaked against the chill of Priekule's winter, strode up the street toward her. They both leered shamelessly; as far as the occupiers were concerned, any woman was fair game. Krasta stared straight through them, as if they didn't exist. They doubtless didn't know she was a noblewoman, and wouldn't have cared had they known – what were the ranks of the conquered to the conquerors?

One of them proved as much: still undressing Krasta with his eyes, he spoke in bad Valmieran: "Sleeping with me, sweetheart?" He reached under his cloak and shook his belt pouch. Coins jingled and clinked.

Krasta's temper kindled, as it had a way of doing. "Powers below eat you, you son of a whore," she said, slowly and distinctly – she wanted to make sure he understood. "May it rot. May it fall off. May it never stand again."

She started by the soldiers. The one who hadn't spoken grabbed her by the arm – maybe he understood some Valmieran, too. He did; he said, "Not talking like that, bitch." His trilling accent grated on her ears.

"Take your hands off me," she told him, ice in her voice.

"I don't thinking so," he said with a nasty smile. "You insulting us. You paying for that."

He was one of the conquerors, all right, used to doing whatever he wanted with and to Valmieran women. Later, Krasta realized she should have been afraid. At the time, only fury filled her. "Take your hands off me," she repeated. She had a trump to play, and played it without hesitation: "I am the woman of Colonel Lurcanio, the count of Albenga, and not for the likes of you."

That did the trick. She'd been sure it would. The Algarvian soldier let go of her arm as if magecraft had suddenly turned it red-hot. He and his comrade both hurried away, babbling ungrammatical apologies.

Nose in the air again, Krasta went on down the Avenue of Horsemen. Triumph filled her narrow soul – hadn't she just given those boors a lesson in whom they might annoy? Had she been more introspective, she might have realized that defending herself by proclaiming she was a prominent occupier's mistress only showed how low Valmiera had fallen.

Such insight, though, was beyond her, and probably would be for all her days to come.

She kept on walking to the end of the boulevard full of expensive shops: farther than she'd intended, but she needed to burn off the rage with which the arrogant Algarvians had filled her. Arrogant herself, she recognized no one else's right to be that way – except Lurcanio's, and he intimidated her far more than she was willing to admit.

At the end of the Avenue of Horsemen was one of Priekule's many parks, the grass dead and yellow now, with muddy ground showing through here and there. Trees sent bare branches reaching toward the cloudy sky, as if they were so many skeletons supplicating the powers above. Pigeons and sparrows begged for crumbs from the few people who sat on benches by the brick walkways, probably because they had nowhere better to go.

In the center of the park towered the Kaunian Column of Victory. The marble column had stood there for more than a thousand years, since the days of the Kaunian Empire. How many years more than a thousand it had stood there, Krasta couldn't have said. She hadn't done well in history – or in many other subjects – at the series of finishing schools and academies she'd attended till everyone gave up on her education. She did know the victory it celebrated was of civilized imperials over the Algarvian barbarians who even in those ancient days had swarmed out of their forests to attack the Empire. Algarvian eggs had damaged the column during the Six Years' War, but it had been restored since.

Now, a good many kilted Algarvians stood at the base of the Column of Victory. They gestured with the theatrical enthusiasm of their kind. Life, to Algarvians, was melodrama. A couple of Valmierans looked to be arguing with them. A tan-clad soldier knocked down one of Krasta's countrymen.

Because she gave herself to Colonel Lurcanio, no redhead of lower rank could cause her much trouble. Conscious of that near-immunity, she strode down the sidewalk toward the column. "What on earth is going on here?" she demanded in a loud, harsh voice.

The Valmieran who'd been knocked down got to his feet. One trouser knee was torn, though he seemed not to notice. He had a pinched, intelligent face – not the sort of man Krasta would normally have looked at twice, or even once. He was intelligent enough to recognize her rank, saying, "Milady, these men mean to topple the column."

"What?" Krasta stared not at the Algarvians but at her fellow Valmieran. "You must be out of your mind."

"Ask them." The man pointed to the redheads. Some were ordinary soldiers, like the one who'd pushed him to the bricks. Some were officers, including, Krasta saw, a brigadier. She wondered if she was as immune from trouble as she'd thought. And a couple had the indefinable air of mages about them, the air of seeing and knowing things ordinary people didn't see and couldn't know. They set Krasta's teeth on edge.

She turned to the Algarvians. "You can't be thinking of doing what he says."

"Who are you, to say we can't?" That was the brigadier, a big-bellied fellow in his mid-fifties – twice her age, more or less – with graying red mustachios and a chin beard all waxed to spikelike points. He spoke Valmieran well – almost as well as Lurcanio did.

She drew herself up to her full height, which came close to matching his. "I am the Marchioness Krasta, and this is my city." She sounded as if she were King Gedominu's queen – although, as she'd seen herself, Priekule wasn't really even Gedominu's city any more.

No sooner had that thought crossed her mind than the Algarvian proceeded to rub it in. Turning back to the Column of Victory, he said, "These cursed carvings tell lies. They make my ancestors, my heroic ancestors" – he drew himself up, too, though with his bulging belly it wasn't so impressive – "out to be cowards and robbers, which every honest man knows to be a base and vile lie. Now we have the chance to correct this, and correct it we shall."

"But it's a monument!" Krasta exclaimed.

"A monument of lies, a monument of curses, a monument of humiliation," the fat brigadier said. "It does not deserve to stand. Now we are the victors, and it shall not stand. Two days from now, my lads here" – he pointed to the mages – "will set eggs by the base, burst them, and topple it like an old pine."

"You can't do that," Krasta said. The Algarvian brigadier laughed in her face. She started to slap him, but then remembered the unfortunate things that had happened after she was rash enough to slap Lurcanio. This redhead outranked her lover. She spun on her heel and hurried away.

"Do what you can, milady," the clever-looking Valmieran man called after her. Then he cried out in pain – the Algarvian soldiers had set on him again.

Krasta found her carriage waiting on a side street. Seeing her approach, the driver corked a small flask and stuck it in his pocket. Krasta ignored that. "Take me back to the mansion," she snapped. "This instant, do you hear me?"

"Aye, milady," the driver answered, and prudently said no more.

The mansion lay on the outskirts of Priekule; it had been a country estate when it was built almost four centuries before. These days, Algarvian administrators of Valmiera's conquered capital used and dwelt in the west wing, leaving the rest for Krasta. Her brother would have shared it with her, but Skarnu had never come home from the war. She occasionally missed him.

Now, though, he didn't enter her mind. She stormed through offices that had been drawing rooms and salons, taking no notice of the Algarvian clerks who filled them. Only when she neared the smaller chamber where Lurcanio worked did she slow. She had to snarl her way past Captain Mosco before she could see him. Snarl she did, and see Lurcanio she did, too.

He looked up from his paperwork – sometimes he reminded Krasta more of a clerk than of a colonel – and smiled. That made his wrinkles shift without removing them; he wasn't too much younger than the Algarvian brigadier in the park. "Hello, my dear," he said in his excellent Valmieran. "What is it? It must be something, by your face."

Bluntly, Krasta answered, "I want you to keep them from wrecking the Column of Victory."

"I wondered when you would learn of that." Lurcanio shrugged an extravagant Algarvian shrug. "I can do nothing about it. And" – his voice hardened – "I would not if I could. That column affronts Algarve's honor."

"What about Valmiera's honor?" Krasta demanded.

"Well, what about it?" Lurcanio said. "If Valmiera had honor, you would have held the Algarvian army in check. That we have this conversation here in the heart of a conquered kingdom, that you welcome me to your bed rather than my wife welcoming a Valmieran conqueror to hers, proves whose honor has more weight. Now do please let me work. I have too much to do, and not enough time in which to do it. Close the door when you go out."

Furious, Krasta slammed the door so hard, the whole mansion shook. Unable to do anything more than that to take out her wrath on Lurcanio, she screamed at her servants instead. That did no good. Two days later, the Kaunian Column of Victory came crashing down. She heard the roar of the bursting eggs and the falling stone and cursed with a fluency a teamster might have envied.

When Lurcanio sought her bed that night, she welcomed him with a barred bedchamber door. She kept the door barred for another week. But then she relented, partly because she craved pleasure and partly because she feared that, if she kept on rejecting Lurcanio, he would simply find someone else. She didn't care to be without an Algarvian protector, not with Priekule as it was these days. What that had to say about honor never once crossed her mind.

Garivald was well on the way to being drunk when someone pounded on the door to his house. "Who's that?" he growled irritably. Like most of the peasants in Zossen, he'd managed to hide plenty of spirits from the Algarvians who occupied the village. When winter came, what else was there to do but drink?

The pounding came again, louder than before. "Opening up or we breaking down!" an Algarvian shouted.

"Open it, Annore," Garivald said. He was sitting on a bench closer to the door than his wife, but he was also drunker than she. He didn't feel like getting up and moving just then.

Annore sent him a dark look, but rose and unbarred the door. After a few heartbeats, Garivald did get up after all and stand behind her – you never could tell what an Algarvian might be after. The redheads glaring at him looked miserably cold; their capes weren't up to the weather here. One of them said, "You coming to the village square."

"Why?" Garivald asked.

Both Algarvians were carrying sticks. With a chill that had nothing to do with winter, Garivald realized they weren't men who garrisoned Zossen, but real combat soldiers, mean as wild boars. He wished he hadn't given them any backtalk. The one who'd spoken aimed his stick at Garivald's face. "Why? Because I saying so."

"Aye," Garivald said hastily, ducking his head in submission as he would have to an Unkerlanter inspector. He took out his fear by shouting at Annore: "Come on, curse it! Don't just stand there. Grab our cloaks."

Annore did as he asked without arguing. They threw on the thick wool garments; Garivald hoped the Algarvians wouldn't steal them. "Syrivald, watch the baby," Annore said. Syrivald nodded, eyes wide. Leuba, playing happily on the floor, was the only one who didn't know anything was wrong.

When Garivald and Annore got to the square, it had already started filling. Under the sticks of more Algarvian combat soldiers, several villagers were putting up an odd-looking wooden frame. After a moment, Garivald realized what it was: a gibbet. Another icy pang of fright ran through him.

A couple of Unkerlanter men he'd never seen before stood near the gibbet, their hands tied behind them. They were scrawny and ill-shaven and looked to have seen hard use – blood covered the face of one of them, while the other had an eye swollen shut. More redheads kept watch on them.

Waddo the firstman limped into the village square. Close behind him came the Algarvians stationed in Zossen. They looked almost as alarmed at what was going on as the villagers did.

One of the newly come Algarvians proved to speak pretty good Unkerlanter. Pointing to the captives, he growled, "Are these miserable whoresons from this stinking hole of a village? We caught them in the woods. Anybody know them? Anybody know their names?"

For a moment, nobody spoke. Then all the men and women in Zossen started talking at once. With a single voice, they denied ever setting eyes on the men before. They know what happened to a village that harbored men who kept fighting against the Algarvians.

So did the redhead who'd asked the questions. With a sneer, he demanded, "Why should I believe you? You'd lie and say your mothers weren't whores. We ought to wreck this place just for the sport of it." By his tone, he wasn't more than a finger's breadth away from ordering his troopers to do just that.

Everyone's eyes swung toward Waddo. The firstman looked about ready to burst into tears. But he did what he had to do – in the most abject tones Garivald had heard even from his lips, he cried, "Have mercy, sir!"

"Mercy?" The Algarvian threw back his head and laughed. He spoke one word in his own language – probably translating for his men. They laughed, too, and their laughter was like the baying of wolves. "Mercy?" the redhead repeated. "What have any Unkerlanters ever done to deserve mercy?"

"These are not men of our village." Waddo pointed at the captives as the Algarvian had. "By the powers above, they aren't! If you don't believe me, ask your own men who have been here for months. They will know."

"He's selling those two poor buggers to the Algarvians," Garivald whispered to his wife.

"If he didn't, he'd be selling all of us," Annore whispered back. Reluctantly, Garivald nodded. He wouldn't have wanted to stand in Waddo's felt boots, not for all the money in the world.

And he wondered if Waddo's betrayal of the Unkerlanter irregulars caught in the forest would go for naught. The Algarvian still seemed poised to order his men to start blazing. But the soldiers stationed in Zossen spoke up. They spoke up, naturally, in Algarvian, which Garivald didn't understand. But his hopes rose when he saw how unhappy the leader of the combat troops looked. Algarvians always seemed to show just what was in their minds – one more reason they struck Garivald as strange, hardly human.

At last, the bad-tempered redhead who spoke Unkerlanter threw his hands in the air. He shouted something in his own language at the garrison troops. They all grinned. Garivald knew they'd helped save Zossen not least because they wanted to go on living here, but *why* didn't matter. What they'd done did.

"We'll still hang these lousy bandits," the combat leader said. He jerked a thumb toward Waddo. "You! Aye, you, fat and ugly – you with the big mouth. Fetch me a coil of rope, and be quick about it."

Waddo gulped. He had no choice, not if he wanted Zossen to stay standing. "Aye," he whispered, and limped away as fast as he could go. If he'd said he had no rope, the Algarvian would have blazed him on the spot – him and who could say how many others? He came back in a hurry, clutching a coil.

The hangings were worse than Garivald had imagined they could be. The Algarvians simply fastened nooses around their captives' necks and tossed the ropes up over the top beam of the gibbet. Then they hauled the captives up off the ground to kick their lives away.

"This is what comes to anyone who tries to fight against Algarve," the combat leader shouted while the Unkerlanters were still thrashing. "These swine deserved it. You'd better not deserve it. Now get out of here!"

Several people – not all women, by any means – had fainted in the snow. Garivald and Annore didn't wait to see them revived. They fled back to their own hut as fast as they could. "What was it?" Syrivald asked. "What did they do?" Fear and curiosity warred on his face.

"Nothing," Garivald mumbled. "They didn't do anything." His son would find out it was a lie as soon as he went outside; the Algarvians had been wrapping the ropes around and around the top beam of the gibbet, to keep the corpses hanging on display. But Garivald couldn't bring himself to talk about what had happened, not yet.

Syrivald turned to his mother. "What did they do? You can tell me!"

"They killed two men," Annore answered bleakly. "Now don't ask me any more questions, do you hear?" Her voice warned what would happen if Syrivald did. He nodded. He understood that tone.

Annore found the jar of spirits and took a long pull at it. "Leave some for me," Garivald warned. He wanted to drink himself into oblivion, too. After another swig, Annore passed him the jar. They kept passing it back and forth till they fell asleep side by side.

When Garivald woke, he almost wished the Algarvians had hanged him. His head pounded like a hammer on the smith's anvil. His mouth tasted the way it would have if the livestock had fouled it. When he took a sip from the jar, his stomach loudly told him what a bad idea that was.

And, as soon as he was conscious, visions of the dead irregulars came flooding back. He couldn't find a better reason for drinking himself blind again. He wanted to stay blind drunk till spring came, and maybe after that, too.

Annore looked no happier than he felt when she opened her eyes. She reached for the jar. He handed it to her. She drank as desperately as he had. With a grimace, she wiped her mouth on the sleeve of her tunic. "It really happened," she said.

"Aye, it did." Garivald didn't care for the sound of his own voice. He didn't care for the answer he had to give her, either.

"I knew we didn't want them here, but I didn't think they'd do – that," his wife said.

"Neither did I," Garivald answered. "Now we don't have to listen to the tales people older than we are tell of the Twinkings War. Now we know, too."

Another song began to form in his mind, a song of how the two Unkerlanter irregulars had met their deaths without a word. Even more than most of the songs he shaped, he would have to be careful where he sang that one. But those two men had had friends in the woods, friends the Algarvians hadn't caught. They would want to hear such songs – the dead men were their comrades. And thinking of rhymes and rhythms distracted him from his hangover.

Later that day, when he had to go out, he found more details to add to the song. Having hanged their captives, the Algarvian troop of combat soldiers had pulled out of Zossen. They'd left the gibbet behind. The bodies on it still swayed in the breeze. No one had dared cut them down.

Each corpse had a new placard tied round its neck. The characters were those of the Unkerlanter language. Garivald knew that much, even if he couldn't read them. They probably told about the dead men, and said what fools they were to fight the Algarvians. He couldn't think what else Mezentio's soldiers would have had to say.

He hurried back to his hut, words spinning in his head. Once inside, he barred the door and started drinking again. By her slack features, Annore had hardly stopped. Staying indoors through the winter shielded people from the worst the weather could do, just as staying in the village had shielded them from knowing the worst war could do. But the war had come home to them now. The Algarvians had brought it home.

"Curse them," he muttered.

His wife didn't need to ask whom he meant. "Aye, curse them," she said. "Powers below eat them."

"Curse!" Leuba said cheerfully. She didn't know what the word meant, only that her parents stressed it when they spoke.

Tears – the easy tears of drunkenness – sprang out in Garivald's eyes. He seized his daughter and fiercely hugged her to him. She squealed, then wriggled to get free. Such shows of affection didn't come her way very often. But Garivald had looked death in the face, and knew how afraid he was.

More than half of Pekka wished she could have performed this experiment down in Kajaani, her home town, rather than coming to Yliharma. Failure in the capital of Kuusamo, failure with all the Seven Princes hoping for success, would be far more humiliating than all the failures she'd known back home.

Both the senior mages who'd invited – for all practical purposes, ordered – her to Yliharma met her at the caravan depot. They laughed when she spoke of her fears. "Nonsense, my dead," Siuntio said. His smile lit up his wide, high-cheekboned face. With his hair graying toward white, he looked far more like a kindly grandfather than the leading theoretical sorcerer of his generation. "I'm sure everything will go splendidly."

Pekka brushed back a few strands of straight black hair that the frigid breeze kept blowing into her eyes. Yliharma had a milder climate than Kajaani, but no one would ever mistake it for the nearly tropical beaches of northern Jelgava. She said, "This is the first time we'll have tried a divergent series. Too many things can go wrong."

That set Ilmarinen laughing. Where Siuntio looked like a kindly grandfather, he put Pekka in mind of a disreputable great uncle. But his record was second only to Siuntio's, and a fair number of people – himself emphatically included – would have argued about that.

Leering at Pekka, he asked, "Which are you more afraid of, having nothing happen, or having too much?"

He had a knack for unpleasantly pointed questions. "Having nothing happen would mortify me," Pekka said after a little thought. "If too much happens, it's liable to kill me."

"Don't think small," Ilmarinen said cheerfully. "If too much happens, you're liable to take out half of Yliharma – maybe even all of it, if you get lucky." Pekka didn't think she would call that luck, but contradicting Ilmarinen only encouraged him.

Siuntio gave his longtime colleague a severe look. "That is most unlikely, as you know full well. We do have some notion of the parameters involved. It's not as if we were back in the days of the Kaunian Empire, when mages were ignorant of the theoretical underpinnings of their craft."

"We're ignorant of these underpinnings," Ilmarinen said with unfortunate accuracy. "If we weren't, we'd be using them; we wouldn't be experimenting."

Pekka thought he was right and hoped he was wrong. Siuntio simply declined to be drawn into the argument, saying, "Let's get Mistress Pekka settled at the Principality – you needn't fret, my dear: the Seven Princes are footing the bill – and make her as comfortable as we can, so she'll be well rested for tomorrow's conjurations."

They insisted on carrying her bags, though she was less than half the age of either one of them. A hired carriage waited just outside the depot. Had the driver looked any more bored, he would have been dead. The horse didn't seem very excited about the business, either. With slow and reluctant steps, it started for the hostel, the finest one Yliharma boasted.

Sitting at a window, Pekka stared out at the town. Though dwarfing Kajaani, Yliharma didn't compare to Setubal or to Trapani. Still, Yliharma had started as a hill fort before either of the other capitals was settled.

Most of the people on the streets looked like Pekka and her sorcerous companions. Some, though, were taller and fairer. A few sported beaky noses or auburn hair – marks of Lagoan blood. Some few of the folk in Setubal were short and black-haired rather than rangy and redheaded, too.

At the Principality, Pekka unpacked, then indulged in the steam room and cold plunge attached to her chamber. Invigorated, she sent down a supper order by the dumbwaiter and demolished the poached salmon in dill sauce when it arrived. If she was staying at the Seven Princes' expense, she would eat well.

She wished she could activate the crystal in the room and talk with her husband. But a talented mage could pick emanations out of the air, and Kuusamo was at war with Algarve. Leino would understand why she didn't try to reach him. He knew secrets needed keeping.

Instead of calling him, she studied. Most of the mathematics behind what she would attempt tomorrow was Ilmarinen's; anything he did demanded careful study. Siuntio, after whom Pekka tried to model herself, was clear and straightforward. Ilmarinen's thoughts writhed like an adder with a broken back – and, like an adder, could bite to deadly effect when least expected.

She checked and rechecked, examined and reexamined. A mage who attempted any conjuration unprepared was a fool. A mage who attempted a conjuration aimed at drawing energy from the place where the two laws of similarity and contagion met would be a dead fool if she tried it unprepared. Pekka knew she might die anyhow; that was what exploring the unknown entailed. But she intended to know as much as she could.

Because she studied so long and so hard, she got less sleep than she wanted. A breakfast of rolls and hot tea with plenty of honey helped make up for that. As ready as she'd ever be, she went downstairs and found another carriage waiting for her. "The university, isn't it?" the driver asked.

"Aye," Pekka said. She didn't want to try this magic in the Seven Princes' palace. If it got away from her at the university, it wouldn't slay all of Kuusamo's lords, or as many were in town. She hoped it wouldn't, anyhow.

Again, Siuntio and Ilmarinen greeted her when she arrived. "Welcome to my lair," Ilmarinen said with a grin displaying irregular teeth. "Now we'll see what we'll see – if we see anything."

"We will." Siuntio sounded perfectly confident. "With your brilliant theorizing and Mistress Pekka's inspired experiments, how can we do anything but wring the truth from nature?"

Pekka said, "As if you had nothing to do with this, Master Siuntio. You've done more work, and more important work, on the two laws and the relationship between them than anyone else. You deserve the bulk of the credit."

Ilmarinen looked as if he might be inclined to argue that, but said only, "Or the bulk of the blame."

"Aye, that is so," Siuntio agreed imperturbably. "Power, any power, is not evil in itself, but surely may be used to evil ends."

That soft answer also seemed to irk Ilmarinen. He said, "That's why we do the experiment: to see how we can keep from wringing the truth from nature, I mean."

Busy checking cages of rats, Pekka did her best to ignore the bickering. It wasn't easy; Ilmarinen craved as much attention as her little son Uto, and had as few scruples as Uto about going after it. She chose a pair of cages showing that the rat in one was the grandson of the animal in the other. If all went well, these rats would become as famous as the ones with which she'd experimented down in Kajaani. She shook her head. They'd become as important as those other rats. They'd be in no position to appreciate their fame. Pekka hoped she would be. If things went wrong . . .

Resolutely, she shoved that thought out of her mind, or at least down to its basement. She'd been working toward this moment her whole professional career. If she could draw useful sorcerous energy from the fusion of the laws of similarity and contagion, she would prove theoretical sorcery had some eminently practical uses. And, if she did get into difficulties, Siuntio and Ilmarinen would get her out of them if anyone could.

What if no one can? She forced that thought into the basement of her mind, too.

Turning to the senior mages, she asked, "Are we ready?" Siuntio nodded. Ilmarinen leered. She took that for an affirmative. Dipping her head to each of them in turn, she said, "I begin, then."

Don't make a mistake. She thought that whenever she went from her desk to the laboratory. No matter what Siuntio said about her experimental technique, she knew she was theoretician first, practical mage a distant second. Perhaps that made her more careful than a more practical mage would have been. She hoped so.

As she chanted the carefully crafted spell, as she made pass after intricate pass, confidence began to rise in her. She saw Siuntio smiling approval, silently cheering her on. Maybe she was borrowing the confidence from him. She didn't care where it came from. She was glad to have it.

And then everything went wrong.

At first, as the chamber began to sway around her, Pekka thought she'd made a mistake after all. Even while she wondered whether she'd die in the next instant, she reviewed all she'd done. For the life of her – literally, for the life of her – she couldn't see what she'd done wrong.

A heartbeat later, she realized the disaster had come from without, not from within. At the same moment, Siuntio gasped, "The Algarvians!" and Ilmarinen howled, "Murderers!" like a wolf in ultimate anguish.

When the Algarvians murdered Kaunians by the hundreds, perhaps by the thousands, to fuel their military sorcery against Unkerlant, Pekka had felt it, as had sorcerers throughout the world. She'd felt it, too, when the

Unkerlanters fought back by murdering their own. But those slaughters, however horrific, had been far to the west. The massacre she felt now was close, close. It was like the difference between feeling an earthquake far away and one right under her feet.

She *was* feeling an earthquake right under her feet. Even as the building groaned, as cages flew through the air and shelves toppled, her mind leaped. "The Algarvians!" she cried, as Siuntio had before her. She could hardly hear herself through the din. "The Algarvians are turning their death-powered magic against us!"

The war against King Mezentio hadn't come home to Kuusamo till now. Oh, a handful of Algarvian dragons flying from southern Valmiera had dropped a few eggs on the coast, and ships clashed in the Strait of Valmiera that severed Kuusamo and Lagoas from the mainland of Derlavai. But the Seven Princes had thought – as what Kuusaman had not? – they could prepare behind the Strait and strike at Algarve when they were ready. Algarve, unfortunately, had other ideas.

As earthquakes will, this one seemed to last forever. How long it really went on, Pekka couldn't have said. At last, it stopped. Rather to her surprise, it hadn't shaken the building down around her ears. The lamps had gone out, though. Everything in the chamber lay on the floor. Some cages had broken open; rats were scurrying for hiding places. The tremor had knocked Siuntio and Ilmarinen off their feet. Pekka had no idea how or why she was still standing.

Ilmarinen got up without help. He and Pekka pulled some shelves off Siuntio so he could rise. Siuntio was bleeding from a cut above one eye, but that wasn't why anguish filled his face. "Our city!" he cried. "What the Algarvians have done to our city!"

"We had better find out what they've done to our city," Ilmarinen said grimly. "We had better get out of here, too, before the building falls down on us."

"I don't think it will, not if it hasn't already," Pekka said. "This isn't like a natural earthquake – I've been through some. There are no after-shocks." But she hurried out with Ilmarinen and Siuntio.

When she was standing on the snow-dappled dead grass in front of the thaumaturgical laboratory, Pekka gasped. She could see a great deal of Yliharma, and much of what she could see had fallen down. Pillars of smoke rose here and there from rapidly spreading fires. And, when she looked toward the high ground at the heart of the city, she let out an agonized wail: "Not the palace, too!"

"They have struck us a heavy blow," Siuntio said, wiping blood from his face as if he'd just realized it was there: "heavier than I ever dreamt they could."

"That they have." Ilmarinen still sounded like a wolf, a hungry wolf. "Now it's our turn."

"Aye," Pekka said fiercely.

King Swemmel paced back and forth, back and forth, in Marshal Rathar's office. With his body hunched forward and his jewel-encrusted robe swirling out behind him, the king of Unkerlant put his marshal in mind of a hawk soaring over a field, waiting for a rabbit to show itself.

The difference was that, unlike a hawk, King Swemmel wasn't inclined to wait. He stabbed out a long, thin finger at the map tacked to the wall. "We've got the redheads on the run now!" he gloated. "All we have to do is hit them hard everywhere, and they'll shatter like a dropped plate."

Swemmel's moods swung wildly; he could despair – or grow furious – as readily as he exulted. One of the things Rathar had to do, along with the small task of commanding Unkerlant's armies, was to try to keep the king on something close to an even keel. "Aye, we have forced them back some, your Majesty," he said, "but they're still fighting hard, and they're still too close to Cottbus."

Now he pointed toward the map. Gray-headed pins showed Unkerlanter positions, green-headed ones Algarvian forces. He hardly looked at the pins; he knew where the armies were at the moment. He looked at the pinholes west of the present positions, the pinholes that showed how far the Algarvians had come. There was a hole in the middle of the dot labeled *Thalfang*, terrifyingly near the capital of Unkerlant. On a clear day, you could see Thalfang from the spires of Swemmel's castle. The redheads had fought their way into the town, but they hadn't fought their way through it.

"Aye, they are still too close to Cottbus," the king agreed. "They were too close the instant they crossed the border. That is why we have to hammer them hard all along the line, to drive them from our kingdom."

Rathar chose his words with great care: "Hammering them all along the line may not be – I do not think it is – the best way to beat them back."

"Say on." Suspicion gleamed in Swemmel's dark eyes. Had he not had those eyes and dark hair, he would have looked more like an Algarvian than an Unkerlanter. But, in his ability to smell plots whether they were there or not, he was very much a man of his kingdom. And, like every king of Unkerlant since its earliest days, he didn't fancy contradiction.

Knowing that, Marshal Rathar kept on speaking carefully: "Look how the Algarvians attacked us, your Majesty. They didn't just swarm across the border from south to north."

"No?" Swemmel growled. "Then why does the fighting run all the way from the icy Narrow Sea up to the desert the treacherous Zuwayzin infest?"

Rathar vividly remembered the sorts of things King Swemmel did to those who displeased him. But, more than any other courtier who served Swemmel, he also remembered what Unkerlant needed. He spoke more frankly to the king than did anyone else in the palace. One day, that would probably cost him his head. Meanwhile . . . "Don't look only at what the Algarvians did, your Majesty. Look at how they did it."

"Vile, treacherous dogs," Swemmel muttered. "Traitors everywhere. They will pay. How they will pay! How everyone will pay!"

Pretending not to hear, Rathar went on, "They used behemoths and dragons massed together to tear holes in our lines, then met behind the front and cleaned out the pockets they made. If they'd attacked all along the line, they wouldn't have been able to find or make so many weak places."

"And you want us to imitate them." By King Swemmel's tone, he wanted to do anything but.

"If we aim to beat them back, we'd better," Rathar said. "Whatever else they are, man for man they're the best warriors in Derlavai."

Whatever else they are. The Algarvians had also turned out to be the most accomplished murderers in Derlavai. They wouldn't have come so far so fast without their murders, either. That sickened Rathar. Swemmel hadn't been shy about imitating them there – not a bit. That sickened his marshal, too.

"Are they?" Swemmel said. "We doubt it. If they were, how could our armies have beaten them back?" He sniffed contemptuously.

"Because we have more men than they do. Because we put snowshoes on our behemoths, where they didn't think of that. Because we had the sense to give our soldiers white smocks. Because we understand winter better than they do." Rathar ticked off the points on his fingers one by one. He went on, "But you must recall, your Majesty, they're learning, too. Unless we can hurt them badly while they're still off balance, our job gets harder."

He wished King Swemmel would trust him to command Unkerlant's armies and would stay out of his way. While he was at it, he wished for the moon. He had about as much chance of getting one as the other. Swemmel stayed strong not least because he allowed no subjects too much strength. Rathar was, without a doubt, the second most powerful man in Unkerlant. To those looking up, that made him great and mighty. But, if the king crooked a finger, the kingdom would have a new marshal the next instant. Rathar understood that all too well.

"Oh, we want to hurt them, too." Swemmel's voice was a low, hungry croon. "We want to see their armies fall apart and fall to ruin. We want to see Algarvian soldiers frozen in the snow. We want to see our borders restored before spring comes."

"Unless they fall to pieces, I don't think we can do so much," Rathar warned. Because Swemmel could get anything he wanted in the palace just by crooking his finger, he too often thought he could do the same in the wider world. His inspectors and impressers made him all-powerful in those parts of the kingdom he still ruled. King Mezentio's men, though, put up a stiffer fight than did Unkerlanter peasants. Swemmel needed to grasp that.

He looked petulant. "Why do we have armies, if we cannot get the best use from them?" he demanded.

"Your Majesty, you *are* getting the best use from them," Rathar answered. "If you expect more than men and beasts can give, you are doomed to disappointment."

"We are always doomed to disappointment." Swemmel wasn't deaf to the bittersweet songs self-pity sang. "Even our own twin betrayed us. But we had revenge on Kyot – aye, we did."

King Guntram, Swemmel and Kyot's father, had died just after the end of the Six Years' War. Neither twin would admit he was the younger, and the other thus the rightful heir. The Six Years' War had cost

Unkerlant a dreadful price. But the Twinkings' War that followed made its toll seem light by comparison. In the end, Swemmel had boiled Kyot alive.

Coming back to the here-and-now, the king said, "Very well, Marshal. If you think we must fight like the Algarvians, fight like the Algarvians we shall. You have our leave to make it so. But our arms had best meet with success, or you will be judged for your failures." Robes flapping behind him, he swept out of Rathar's office.

Momentarily alone, the marshal allowed himself the luxury of a long, loud sigh of relief. He'd just finished it when his adjutant came into the office. Major Merovec's strong-boned face bore an anxious expression, as any officer's might have after a visit from the king.

"We go on, Major," Rathar said, understanding him completely.

"Powers above be praised," Merovec said, and said no more. Suddenly, he looked anxious in a different way, as if realizing even that little might have been too much. Only Rathar had heard him, but the comment gave the marshal a hold on him he hadn't had before. Such was life in the Unkerlanter royal palace.

"His Majesty wants us to keep pressing the Algarvians hard," Rathar said. "He is not the only one who wants that, of course. The discussion was about the means, not the end."

"And?" Major Merovec asked. He knew as well as Rathar that sometimes Swemmel *would* give orders and *would* insist they be obeyed. Unkerlant had had its share of disasters over the years because of that.

"And we are to continue as we have been doing," Marshal Rathar replied. Merovec didn't let out a noisy sigh of relief, but the urge to do so was written all over his face.

"Any more word out of Kuusamo?" Rathar asked, glad to talk about anything, even bad news, that had nothing to do with Swemmel.

"Two princes dead, they say, and half the capital wrecked," Merovec told him. "I wonder how many Kaunians the redheads had to kill to bring that off. Powers above be praised they didn't try to do it to Cottbus."

"No promises they won't," Rathar said, and his adjutant, looking sour, nodded. The marshal of Unkerlant went on, "Of course, when they're fighting us, they have to worry about our soldiers. There aren't any Kuusaman soldiers in the fight yet, not to speak of."

"Aye, though I wish there were." Merovec sounded sour, too. "After this, it'll take longer for the Kuusamans to get into the fight, too."

"You're likely right," Rathar said. "But they're liable to fight harder once they are finally in. Now they know what sort of foe they're up against. I hope Mezentio's men don't decide to do the same to Setubal. That would hurt us."

"Aye, Lagoas truly is in the fight, even if it's only in the land of the Ice People," Merovec said.

"And on the sea," Rathar added. His adjutant grunted dismissively. "We don't pay the sea enough attention," Rathar insisted. "We didn't start worrying about losing Glogau, up in the north, till almost too late, but where would we be without it? In a cursed mess, that's where."

"That's so." Merovec's admission was grudging but real. "Still and all, though, you win wars or you lose them on land."

"*I* think so," Rathar said. "If you asked Mezentio's marshals, odds are they'd think so, too. But if you asked in Sibiu or Lagoas or Kuusamo, you'd hear some different answers."

"Foreigners," Merovec muttered under his breath. Far and away the largest kingdom on Derlavai, Unkerlant was and always had been to some degree a world unto itself. Like Rathar's adjutant, a lot of Unkerlanters had little use for anyone from outside that world.

But the Algarvians had stormed into it and were doing their best to tear it to pieces – and their best had proved terribly, terrifyingly good. "His Majesty hopes we can win the war this winter," he said, wanting to learn what Merovec thought of that.

As a marshal's chief aide, Merovec was at least as much a political animal, a courtier, as he was a soldier. Whatever he thought, he wasn't about to show much of it. All he said was, "I hope his Majesty is right."

Rathar sighed. He hoped King Swemmel was right, too, but he wouldn't have bet a broken tunic toggle on it. Sighing again, he said, "Well, we'll just have to do our best to make sure he is right."

"Aye, so we will." Merovec could agree with that, and he did, enthusiastically.

"First things first." Rathar started to pace in Merovec's office, then stopped in his tracks: what was he doing but imitating the king? He needed a moment to recover his caravan of thought: "We have to push the redheads as far back from Cottbus as we can. That will make it harder for them to do to us what they did to Kuusamo. And we have to keep the corridor to Glogau open, and we have to take back as much of the Duchy of Grelz as we can. We have to do that if we intend to keep eating next year, anyhow."

"All true," Major Merovec said. Then, thinking like a political animal, he added, "The more of Grelz we take back, the bigger the black eye we give Mezentio and his puppet king, too."

"That's so," Rathar agreed. "He could have hurt us much more if he'd named one of the local nobles King of Grelz instead of his own cousin. The peasants won't want to do anything for an Algarvian with a fancy crown on his noggin."

After the Twinkings War, after Swemmel's years of harsh rule, he'd feared the peasants and townsfolk of Unkerlant would welcome the Algarvians as liberators. Some had. More would have, he suspected, had the redheads not made it so very plain they came as conquerors.

"If the foe makes mistakes, we had better take advantage of them," he said. "He hasn't made enough, curse him. And we've made too many of our own."

No one else at Swemmel's court would have said such a thing. Merovec looked horrified that Rathar had. "Be careful, lord Marshal," he said. "If word of that got back to the king, either he would blame you for what goes wrong or he would think you were blaming him."

Either of those, from Rathar's point of view, would be equally disastrous. Nodding brusquely to acknowledge the point, the marshal of Unkerlant strode back into his own office and studied the map. An attack into Grelz was already under way. He examined the disposition of his forces. He could also attack to the northeast of Cottbus, which would keep the Algarvians from shifting troops to the south. Nodding again, he called in Merovec and began giving orders.

Rank, or at least some rank, had finally caught up with Leudast. He was, at last, officially a sergeant. He was also commanding a company: a handful of veterans like himself, fleshed out with recruits who no longer deserved to be called fresh-faced — a few days in the line and they were as grimy and disreputable looking as anybody else.

He wondered how many other sergeants in King Swemmel's army were commanding companies. A lot of them, or else he was a black Zuwayzi in disguise. He also wondered when the extra pay that went with his new rank would start catching up with him. He didn't intend to hold his breath.

Thinking about money made him laugh, anyhow. What could he do with it, up here at the front, but gamble? He couldn't buy much – there wasn't much to buy. And he wouldn't hold his breath waiting for leave, either. Every man who could carry a stick was in the line these days, or so it seemed.

But, for the first time in the fight against Algarve, the Unkerlanter armies were moving forward. Leudast was almost inclined to cheer every time snow or freezing rain came pelting down, even if he had to endure them out in the open. He knew Marshal Winter had done as much to stop the redheads as Marshal Rathar had.

Somewhere not far away, eggs began bursting. The Algarvians holed up in the village northeast of the trench in which he huddled weren't about to give up without a fight. They had plenty of egg-tossers and, no doubt, plenty of stubborn soldiers, too. A wounded man started scream-ing not far away. Leudast clicked his tongue between his teeth. The Algarvians might be retreating, but they weren't making life easy for their foes.

Captain Hawart came up to Leudast, leaving tracks behind him in the snow. Hawart had started out commanding the company Leudast now led. These days, the captain was in charge of a brigade's worth of men. He hadn't been promoted at all, and was doing a senior officer's work on a junior officer's pay.

He'd also grown forgetful like a senior officer, for he called, "A good day to you, Magnulf."

"Magnulf's dead," Leudast said. Had he been looking out of the hole he'd shared with his sergeant when the egg burst in front of it, he would have been the one who didn't come out. *Luck*, he thought. *Nothing but luck.* "I'm Leudast."

"Well, so you are." Hawart took off his fur hat and whacked himself in the side of the head. "And I'm Marvefa, the fairy who makes new leaves grow every spring."

"Wouldn't surprise me a bit, sir – you look just like her," Leudast said, and Captain Hawart rocked back on his heels and laughed. He was a pretty good officer, and didn't slip very often. Leudast went on, "What now?"

Hawart pointed ahead, toward the village from which the Algarvians were still tossing occasional eggs. "Tomorrow morning, we're going to throw them out of that Midlum place," he answered. "We're supposed to have behemoths coming up to give us a hand, but we'll take a whack at it whether they do or not."

"Aye, sir," Leudast said resignedly, and then, because he couldn't help himself, "If they don't show up, we're going to leave a lot of dead men in the snow in front of Midlum."

"I know." Captain Hawart sounded resigned, too. "But those are the orders I got, so that's what I'm going to do. Even if we get slaughtered, we help the kingdom."

"Huzzah," Leudast said in tones that sounded like anything but celebration.

More often than not, Hawart would have laughed again and agreed with him. Today, the captain said, "Like it or not, it's true. We're doing our best to shove our way back into Grelz. This attack – and we're just part of it – is supposed to keep the Algarvians from moving reinforcements down there."

"All right, sir," Leudast said. "Once I'm dead, I'm sure I'll be glad to know it was for some good reason."

"Probably because I hit you over the head with a rock." But Captain Hawart was laughing again. He slapped Leudast on the back. "Have your men ready. We move before sunup, with the behemoths or without 'em."

"Aye, Captain." Leudast didn't expect the behemoths. The whole course of the war had taught him not to expect them. There were rarely enough to go around; more stretches of line needed the great beasts than could have them. He got his company ready to attack Midlum without them. For once, he was glad he had only a handful of veterans. The new troops would go forward without knowing how unlikely they were ever to get into the village.

And then, in the middle of the chilly night, the behemoths did come up to the front, chainmail clinking below the heavy blankets that helped their shaggy fur keep them warm. Starlight glittered off their long, sharp, iron-shod horns. Thanks to the great snowshoes attached to their feet, they had little trouble making their way over the drifts.

Real hope – a strange feeling – began to rise in Leudast. "We're going to do this," he told his men. "We're going to kick the redheads out of that village, we're going to chase them across the fields, and we're going to slaughter them. This is what they bought for coming into Unkerlant and trying to take away our homes. Now they'll pay full price – every last copper."

His own home village, not too far from what had been Unkerlant's border with Forthweg, lay far to the east of where he squatted now. He wondered how his kinsfolk fared under Algarvian occupation. The only thing he could do to help them was hurt Mezentio's men as much as he could.

In the darkness, his men's heads bobbed up and down. They listened earnestly. Most of them lacked the experience to know what they were getting into. After the coming day's fighting, though, they'd be veterans, too – the ones who wouldn't be corpses strewn across the frozen ground.

Almost on time, Unkerlanter egg-tossers started pounding Midlum. "Get ready, boys," Leudast said. "It won't be long now." He peered across the fields toward the bursts of sorcerous energy ahead. Now the Algarvians would know something was coming their way. With luck, the bursting eggs would keep them from doing too much about it. With luck . . .

They were alert, there in Midlum. Leudast had never known the Algarvians when they weren't alert. He wished this might be one of those times, but it wasn't. Eggs began flying back toward his own position. Fortunately, the Algarvians were tossing a little long, so they didn't hurt too badly the men gathered to attack them.

Whistles blew, all along the Unkerlanter line: officers ordering their men forward. Leudast was doing an officer's job, but he didn't have the formal rank, so he didn't have a whistle, either. A shout had to do: "Let's go!"

The behemoths went forward, too. They paused outside of Midlum. Some, the ones that mounted egg-tossers on their backs, joined in pounding the village and the Algarvians inside. Others sent beams from their heavy sticks against the houses to the east. Fires began to burn, lighting up the eastern sky as if dawn were coming too soon.

Leudast flopped down behind what he thought was a snow-covered boulder. But boulders didn't have hair: it was a dead behemoth – a long-dead behemoth, which meant it had probably belonged to the Algarvians. "Blaze and move!" he shouted. "Blaze and move!"

His men knew what they were supposed to do: Some were to blaze to make the Algarvians keep their heads down while others advanced into new cover. Then the two groups would reverse roles. But knowing what to do and doing it right the first time you tried it were two different things. Leudast had expected no better than he got.

He wondered if the Algarvians had any behemoths in Midlum. If they did, the beasts needed to come out and fight: the only thing with much hope of stopping one behemoth was another. But no behemoths came forth from the village. Maybe they'd all frozen to death. Leudast hoped so.

When it was his turn, he ran forward, toward the burning village. He pounded past a young man lying in the snow clutching both hands to his belly. Those hands couldn't keep the Unkerlanter soldier's lifeblood from pouring out. Steam rose from the pool it formed. Leudast shook his head and ran on.

He'd fought to hold the Algarvians out of a good many villages. He knew how the job was done. So did they, worse luck, and they proved as stubborn in defense as they ever had on the attack. But they couldn't simply stay in Midlum and fight it out to the last man there, for the Unkerlanters were not only assailing the strongly held village but also sending men around it to either side to cut it off from other territory the redheads held.

You taught us that trick, you whoresons, Leudast thought. *How do you like having it pulled on you?*

He didn't know what he would have done in the Algarvian commander's predicament. The redhead sent some of his men east toward their comrades and used the rest to make a stand. Unkerlanter behemoths lumbered after the Algarvians struggling through the snow. With the eastern sky now going gray with true dawn, the retreating Algarvians made easy targets.

Inside Midlum, though, the enemy kept on fighting hard. A beam zipped past Leudast's head. He threw himself flat and blazed back. A scream answered him. He grunted in satisfaction, but didn't rise too soon. Any Algarvians who'd come this far were likely veterans, and full of the tricks veterans knew.

Well, Leudast had a few tricks, too. "Surrender!" he shouted in his own language and then in what he thought was Algarvian. Returning to

Unkerlanter – he had no choice – he went on, "You can't get away."

Maybe some of Mezentio's men understood Unkerlanter. Maybe they didn't need to understand it – maybe they could see what was so for themselves. Little by little, the blazing died away. Algarvians started coming out of battered huts and holes in the grounds. They carried no sticks. Their hands were high. Fear filled their faces.

"Powers above," Leudast whispered in something approaching awe. He'd never seen so many redheads surrender, not all at once. After staring, he rushed forward with the rest of his men to plunder the Algarvians.

As Trasone stumbled south and east through the snow, he thought about what might have been. "Hey, Sergeant!" he called, his breath making a bank of mist around his head. "Did we really see the towers of stinking Swemmel's stinking palace?"

"Don't know about you, but I sure as blazes did," Sergeant Panfilo answered, his voice coming muffled through the wool scarf he'd wrapped around the lower part of his face. "You were there in the market square at Thalfang, same as me. If we could have made it across to the other side . . ."

"Aye. If." Trasone shrugged his broad shoulders; he was almost as thickly built as an Unkerlanter. He was hard to faze, too, or else too stubborn to admit that any trouble could be so very bad. "I'll tell you something, Sergeant: A lot of good lads went into that cursed square. A lot fewer came out again."

"That's the truth." Panfilo's big head went up and down, up and down. "Captain Galafrone was maybe the best officer I've ever known, and I've seen plenty. I'd say as much to the king's face, even if Galafrone hadn't a drop of noble blood in him."

"You ought to say it, on account of it's true." Trasone tramped past the stiff carcass of a unicorn that had frozen to death. Its coat was whiter than the snow in which it lay. He jerked a thumb at it. "Somebody ought to butcher that beast. Plenty of good meat on it, if we ever get to a place where we can make a fire and cook it."

"Aye." Panfilo liked to eat, but that wasn't what was on his mind. "I had this company – powers above, I had this whole fornicating battalion – for a few days, but will they make *me* an officer? Not bloody likely, not when my old man made shoes for a living."

"I don't know about that, Sergeant," Trasone said. "The way they're using up nobles these days, before long there won't be enough of 'em to fill all the slots that need filling. Stay alive and you may get your chance yet."

"Won't have one if I'm dead, that's certain." Panfilo twisted his head this way and that. Trasone knew what he was doing: looking for Unkerlanter behemoths with snowshoes or Unkerlanter footsoldiers wearing them. In this cursed weather, Swemmel's soldiers were more mobile than the Algarvians they pursued. Trasone kept his eyes open all the time, too.

He didn't see any foes now, for which he thanked the powers above. When he trudged past the frozen corpse of an Algarvian soldier, he started to laugh.

"What's funny about him?" Panfilo asked.

"Poor whoreson's in the same pose as that unicorn we went by a little while ago," Trasone answered.

"Heh," Panfilo said, and then, "Heh, heh." Trasone shrugged and kept on walking. That was about as much credit as the comment deserved.

From up ahead came the sharp crack of bursting eggs. A moment later, Trasone heard a dragon screaming high in the air. "Got to be an Unkerlanter beast," he said wearily. "Where are our own dragons, curse the lazy buggers who fly 'em?"

Panfilo tried to look on the bright side: "They come over now and again. But they're stretched thin along so much front."

"The Unkerlanters have dragons to drop eggs on us," Trasone said resentfully. "The front's no shorter for them." He waved before Panfilo could speak. "I know, I know – somewhere along the line, we're dropping eggs on them, too. But they're doing it here, curse them, and one of those stinking eggs is liable to come down on my head."

"They weren't worrying about us – we're small fry." Panfilo pointed ahead, to a burning town. "Unless we're even more lost than I think we are, that's Aspang. A ley line runs through it. How are we going to get men and supplies forward if it's going up in flames around us?"

For an Algarvian, Trasone was a stolid man. Still, his shrug would have been extravagant for someone from any other kingdom. He said, "Who knows? Odds are, we won't. Powers below have been eating at our supply system ever since the snow started coming down."

When the battered company got into Aspang, Trasone discovered he would have made a good prophet. Several of the eggs the Unkerlanter dragons dropped had landed squarely on the ley-line caravan depot. It was burning merrily. So was a caravan that had stopped there. And so were mountains of supplies that had just come off the caravan and hadn't yet been loaded on to wagons for the trip to the front – not that wagons had an easy time moving through the snow, either.

His stomach didn't care about troubles with wagons. But it growled like a starving wolf – an all too apt figure – to see food burning. The bursting eggs had knocked one car off the ley line and down to the ground on its side. It was, for the moment, safe from the flames. A crowd of Algarvian soldiers had gathered around it.

Trasone hurried toward the caravan car. "That's got to be something to eat," he called over his shoulder to his comrades. "I'm going to get some, and you'd better do the same." He waited for Sergeant Panfilo to curse and bully him back into the line. Instead, without a word, the sergeant followed him. More than anything else Trasone had seen, that told of the troubles the Algarvian army had known since winter came to Unkerlant.

One of the soldiers already at the caravan car looked up with a laugh. "More starving rats, eh? Well, come on and get your share."

"What's to get?" Trasone asked.

By way of reply, the other soldier tossed him a square block of orange stuff that had to weigh a couple of pounds. Automatically, Trasone caught it. "Cheese!" said the fellow who'd thrown it. "If you're going to be a rat, you may as well be a fat rat, eh?"

"Aye." Trasone broke a corner off the block and stuffed the cheese into his mouth. With it still full, he went on, "Toss me a couple more of those, pal, will you? It's not the greatest stuff in the world, but it'll keep a man going for a while."

"Help yourself – stuff your pack full," the other Algarvian said. "If we don't haul it away with us, it's not going anywhere." Trasone took him up on that. So did Sergeant Panfilo. They both ate as they loaded up, too. Trasone guessed a lot of the soldiers at the caravan car had been garrisoning Aspang. They didn't have the abraded look of men who'd been fighting and marching and fighting again for much too long.

Eggs began bursting once more, this time west of Aspang. Trasone looked up, but saw no dragons. That meant the Unkerlanters had brought their egg-tossers almost far enough forward to start hitting the town. Trasone cursed under his breath. He'd hoped the rear guard would have done a better job of holding back King Swemmel's men than that.

"To me!" shouted the officer who'd taken over the battalion, or what was left of it, after Sergeant Panfilo brought it out of Thalfang. "Come on – we have to hold this place. Can't let the Unkerlanters have it, come what may."

Trasone was more than willing to ignore the dapper little nobleman, but Panfilo, after stuffing a last brick of cheese into his pack, turned away from the caravan car. "Come on," he told Trasone. "Major Spinello's not so bad, as officers go."

"Not *so* bad," Trasone agreed grudgingly. "But I'd got used to being commanded by commoners – first Galafrone, then you. Nobles just aren't the same after that. Harder to take 'em seriously, if you know what I mean."

"Oh, aye," Panfilo said. "Don't worry, though I'm still commanding you. Now get moving."

Get moving Trasone did. Major Spinello was still flitting every which way at once, and talking like a man possessed: "Come on, my dears. If the Unkerlanters are going to pay us a call, we must be ready to receive them in the style they deserve. After all, we wouldn't want to disappoint them, now would we?"

He sounded like a bad caricature of every noble officer Trasone had ever known. Even the dour veteran couldn't help snickering. Up till very recently, Spinello hadn't been a combat soldier; he kept going on and on about the Forthwegian village whose garrison he'd headed till the war here in the west yanked him out of it. Not all of his orders made the best sense in the world. But Trasone had already seen that he was recklessly brave. As long as he listened to Panfilo and others who actually knew what they were doing, he'd shape pretty well.

What needed doing here was obvious, and Major Spinello saw it. He posted his battalion in among the ruins at the western edge of Aspang. "Find yourselves some good holes," he urged the soldiers. "Make sure they're as tight and as deep as a trollop's twat." He sighed. "Ah, the one I was laying before duty called me here." He sighed again, and kissed his fingertips.

Trasone would sooner have been laying a pretty blonde than lying in wait for some ugly Unkerlanters, too. Nobody'd given Spinello a choice, and nobody was giving him one, either. He found cover behind a waist-high wall that was all that remained of a house or shop and settled in. Looking around, he spied a couple of other places to which he could withdraw in a hurry if he had to.

Unkerlanter eggs marched closer and closer to the town, then began bursting around him and his comrades. He kept his head down and huddled close to the wall. Before long, the storm of sorcerous energy moved deeper into Aspang. Trasone knew what Swemmel's men were doing: They were going after the Algarvian egg-tossers. He also knew that meant the attack was on its way.

He looked out over the ruined wall and steadied his stick on it. Sure enough, the Unkerlanters were forming up just out of stick range: row upon close-ranked row of blocky men in white smocks over rock-gray tunics. It was, in its way, an awe-inspiring sight.

To his surprise, he could hear the command the Unkerlanter officer shouted. The enemy soldiers stormed forward, some of them arm in arm. "Urra!" they shouted: a deafening roar. "Urra! Swemmel! Urra!"

Almost at once, eggs began bursting among them, tearing holes in their neat ranks – they hadn't succeeded in knocking out the Algarvian tossers after all. Still shouting, more Unkerlanters hurried up to fill the gaps. Along with his comrades, Trasone started blazing at them. Soldiers went down as if scythed. The ones who didn't go down, though, kept on coming, roaring like demons.

Trasone's mouth went dry. If that human wave broke over his battalion . . . He looked around at his lines of retreat again. Would he have time to use them? He wished Algarvian mages back of the front would slaughter some Kaunians to get the sorcerous energy for a spell to stop the Unkerlanters in their tracks.

No spell came. But King Swemmel's men didn't break into Aspang, either. Some prices were higher than flesh and blood could bear. Just outside the edge of town, the Unkerlanters broke and fled back across the snowy fields, leaving even more dead behind. Major Spinello did not order a pursuit. Trasone nodded somber approval. The major might be raw, but he wasn't stupid.

Fourteen

Fernao had seen the land of the Ice People in summer, when the sun shone in the sky nearly the whole day through and the weather, sometimes, got warmer than cool. The Lagoan mage had seen it in fall, which put him in mind of a hard winter in Setubal. Now he was seeing it in winter. He'd expected it would be appalling. He was finding out he hadn't known what *appalling* meant.

Outside the tent he shared with a second-rank mage named Affonso, the wind howled like a live thing, a malevolent wild thing. The tent fabric was waterproofed and windproofed, but the gale sucked heat out of the tent in spite of the brazier by which the two sorcerers huddled.

"I won't believe it," Affonso said. "Nobody could want to live in this miserable country the whole year round."

"It's no accident the Ice People are hairy all over, men and women both," Fernao answered. "And they like the austral continent fine. They think we're the crazy ones for wanting to live anywhere else."

"They're mad, every cursed one of them." Affonso picked up another chunk of dried camel dung – the most common fuel hereabouts – and put it on the brazier. Then he wiped his hands on his kilt. Under the kilt, he wore thick woolen leggings that came up far enough to meet his thick woolen drawers coming down. He might as well have had on trousers, but no kingdom of Algarvic stock took kindly to those Kaunian-style garments.

"No doubt, but they do live here, and we're having a miserable time managing that for ourselves," Fernao said.

The camel dung hissed and popped as it burned, and shed only a sullen red light. Across the brazier from Fernao, his colleague might have been a polished bronze statue, tall and skinny. Affonso had the long face typical of Lagoans, Sibians, and Algarvians, but a wide, flat nose told of Kuusamans somewhere down toward the roots of his family tree. In the same way, Fernao himself had narrow eyes set on a slant.

Only a minority of Lagoans thought such things worth fussing about. They were a mixed lot, and knew it. Some few of his countrymen took pride in pure Algarvic blood, but Fernao thought they were fooling themselves.

Even with the brazier, Affonso's breath smoked inside the tent. He must have seen it, too, for he said, "When I went out last night to make water, the wind had died down. It was so calm and quiet, I could hear my breath freeze around me every time I let it out."

"I've never heard that, but I've heard of it." Fernao didn't know if the convulsive movement of his shoulders was shiver or shudder or something of both. "The Ice People call it 'the whisper of stars.'"

"They would have a name for it," Affonso said darkly. He moved away from the brazier, but only to wrap himself in blankets and furs. "How far away from Mizpah are we?"

"A couple of days, unless we have another blizzard," Fernao told him. "I've seen Mizpah, you know. If you had, too, you wouldn't be so cursed eager to get there, believe you me you wouldn't."

Only a snore answered him. Affonso had a knack for falling asleep at once. That wasn't a trick the Guild of Sorcerers had ever investigated, or Fernao, himself a first-rank mage, would have known how to do it. He swaddled himself, too, and eventually dropped off.

He woke in darkness. The brazier had gone out. He fed it more camel dung and got the fire going with flint and steel. Most places, sorcery would have been easier. On the austral continent, sorcery imported from Derlavai or Lagoas or Kuusamo failed more often than it worked. The rules were different here, and few not born to them ever learned them.

Affonso also woke quickly and completely, something else for which Fernao envied him. "Another day's slog," he said.

"Aye," Fernao agreed in a hollow voice. He got up and wrapped a heavy hooded cloak over his tunic. "If we march hard enough, I'll almost be able to imagine I'm warm. Almost."

"That's a powerful imagination you have," Affonso remarked.

"Comes with my rank," Fernao said, and snorted to show he didn't intend to be taken seriously. After the snort, he had to inhale. Burning camel dung wasn't the only stink in the tent. "If I had a really powerful imagination, I could imagine myself bathing. Of course, then I'd have to imagine myself freezing to death the next instant."

"They say the Ice People never, ever bathe," Affonso said.

"They say it because it's true." Fernao held his nose. "Powers above, they stink. And we're on our way to matching them." He crawled toward the opening of the tent, a complicated arrangement with double flaps, designed to hold in as much heat as possible. "As for me, I'm on my way to breakfast." Affonso nodded and followed him out.

The sun hadn't climbed above the northeastern horizon yet, but wasn't too far below it; there was enough light by which to see. The cold struck savagely at Fernao as he got to his feet. Every inhalation felt like breathing knives. Every exhalation brought forth a new fogbank. He cocked his head to one side, listening, but couldn't hear the whisper of stars. That horrified him all over again, for it meant the weather could get colder still.

Snow didn't cover every inch of the local landscape. Parts of it were bare rock and frozen ground. That had perplexed Fernao till he realized the air down here was so cold, it held less moisture than it could farther north, and the endless ravening wind helped sweep the landscape clear.

Lagoan soldiers were emerging from their tents, all of them as muffled against the chill as Fernao and Affonso. Like Fernao, the fog from their breath hung around their heads. They stumbled toward the smoking cookfires, shivering and loudly cursing their fate.

Off in the distance, Ice People on shaggy, two-humped camels watched the Lagoan army. They'd been shadowing the force ever since it landed at the edge of the ice shelf that formed around the edge of the austral continent every winter. The nomads of the frozen waste had laughed then, to see King Vitor's men struggling over the ice. They weren't laughing any more. Fernao hoped they weren't passing the army movements on to the Yaninans. If they were, the Lagoans couldn't do anything about it; the Ice People could have run rings around them.

Man by man, the lines at the cookfires moved forward. A cook who looked not only cold but also bored slapped a glob of mush and a strip of fried camel meat – mostly fat – into Fernao's tin. "Eat fast," the fellow advised. "Otherwise you'll break teeth on it after it freezes up again."

He wasn't joking. Fernao had seen that. The mage was also ravenous. In this weather, a man needed far more food than he would have in a better climate. Affonso ate with the same dedication. Only after their tins were empty did Affonso remark, "I wish this cursed country didn't hold any cinnabar. Then we could let the Yaninans have it."

"Then King Tsavellas wouldn't want it," Fernao answered. "Nobody would ever come to visit the Ice People, except once in a while to buy pelts from them."

"Dragons." Affonso turned the word into a curse. Fernao nodded. Quicksilver came from cinnabar. Without it, dragons couldn't flame so hot or so far. Algarve, Yanina's ally (*Yanina's master* was nearer the truth these days), had only small stocks of the vital mineral. If Lagoas could take the land of the Ice People away from King Tsavellas' men, King Mezentio's dragons would have to do without. That would make Algarve's war harder.

Taking the cinnabar away from Algarve was making Fernao's life harder. The army trudged toward Mizpah. The town had been a Lagoan outpost till the Yaninans seized it after Lagoas went to war with Algarve. Fernao had been in it then. He counted himself lucky to have escaped, and something less than lucky to have returned to the austral continent.

Grudgingly, as if resenting the necessity, the sun rose. Fernao's shadow, far longer than he was tall, stretched off to his left. Because the sun couldn't get far above the horizon, its light remained red as blood. It was about to set when a couple of Ice People rode toward the Lagoan column on camelback, shouting at the tops of their lungs.

Lieutenant General Junqueiro, who commanded the Lagoan force, hurried over to Fernao. He was a big, bluff fellow with a bushy red mustache streaked with white. "What in blazes are they saying?" he asked the mage. "You speak their language."

"Not a word of it," Fernao answered, which made Junqueiro's eyes open very wide. "If you listen closely, though, you'll discover they're speaking Lagoan, after a fashion."

Junqueiro cocked his head to one side. "Why, so they are." He sounded astonished. Then his expression changed. "Is what they're saying true? Are the Yaninans really moving against us?"

Fernao eyed him in some exasperation. "I don't know – this country isn't friendly to magecraft, except the sort the shamans of the Ice People use. But don't you think you'd better get ready to receive them, on the chance those nomads aren't lying?"

"It's almost night again," Junqueiro said. "Not even the Yaninans would be mad enough to attack in the darkness . . . I don't think." But he began shouting orders, and the army shook itself out from column into line of battle.

And, sure enough, the enemy did attack. Eggs started bursting not far from the Lagoan forces – releasing energy like that was sorcery so basic, it worked all over the world. The Yaninans swarmed forward, howling like mountain apes. Beams from their sticks pierced the darkness. Junqueiro held back response as long as he could. Then all the light egg-tossers the Lagoans had brought with them began flinging eggs back at the Yaninans. The Lagoan footsoldiers, waiting behind cover, blazed away at the men who followed King Tsavellas.

To Fernao's delighted astonishment, the Yaninans broke in wild disorder. They must have thought they would be able to steal the battle by night, catching the Lagoans by surprise. When that didn't happen, some fled, some threw down their sticks and surrendered, and only a stubborn rear guard kept Junqueiro's army from bagging them all.

Even before twilight began to gray the northern horizon the next morning, the Lagoan commander declared, "The way to Mizpah is open!"

"You wouldn't sound so happy if you'd ever seen the place," Fernao said, yawning. Junqueiro paid him no attention. He hadn't really expected anything different.

Talsu had got used to Algarvians swaggering through the streets of Skrunda. He felt less embittered toward the redheads than did a lot of Jelgavans, not least because he'd done more against them in the war than had most of his countrymen. His regiment had invaded Algarve, even if it never had succeeded in breaking out of the foothills of the Bratanu Mountains and seizing Tricarico. And he hadn't thrown down his stick till Jelgava was truly beaten. Beaten his kingdom remained, but he didn't blame himself for it.

His father had other ideas. Looking up from the tunic he was sewing for an Algarvian officer, Traku sighed and said, "If only we'd fought harder, I wouldn't have to be doing this kind of work."

By that, Talsu knew he meant, *If only you'd fought harder.* His father felt guilty about not seeing battle. Because he did, he had a low opinion of those who had seen it and hadn't prevailed – like Talsu.

With a sigh of his own, Talsu answered, "No. Instead you'd be sewing jewels on to some noblewoman's cloak, and you'd be grumbling about that."

Traku grunted and ran his fingers through his hair. He was going gray but, like his son and most of his countrymen, was so blond it hardly showed. "Well, what if I would?" he said. "At least she'd be one of our own noblewomen, not a cursed redhead."

Before Talsu answered, he looked out into the street. No one there looked like coming into the tailor's shop above which Traku and Talsu and his mother and sister lived. Satisfied he could speak frankly, Talsu said, "If it weren't for all our idiot noblemen clogging up the officer corps, maybe we wouldn't have a cursed redhead calling himself King of Jelgava these days. I had to follow their orders, remember – I know what kind of soldiers they made."

Traku opened the cash box, took out a small silver coin with King Mainardo's beaky portrait stamped on it, and ground it under his heel. "That's what I think of having *any* Algarvian, let alone King Mezentio's worthless brother, set up as the ruler of a decent Kaunian kingdom."

"Oh, aye, I have no love for him, either," Talsu said. "Who does? But if King Donalitu hadn't run away to Lagoas after the redheads broke in here, we wouldn't have an Algarvian calling himself king now. You ask me, Father, Donalitu was as useless as his nobles."

"That's what the Algarvians want you to say," his father answered. "A king doesn't have a use, except to *be* king. He stands for his kingdom, or else he's no use at all. And how can an Algarvian king stand for a Kaunian kingdom? It's against nature, that's what it is."

Talsu had no good comeback for that. By everything he knew of magecraft – which wasn't much – Traku was right. But Traku thought of the Jelgavan nobility in terms of luxuries used up and money wasted. That was how Traku had thought of the nobles before the war. Now he thought of dukes and counts in terms of lives wasted, which were far more expensive.

"I'll see you later," he said, starting out of the shop. "Mother asked me earlier this morning to get her some olive oil and some garlic, and I haven't done it yet."

"Go on, then." Traku was willing to let the argument lie. "You'd better, if you expect to eat supper tonight."

Laughing – though his father hadn't been joking – Talsu headed for a grocer's a couple of blocks away. The weather was mild. Winter in Skrunda only rarely got chilly; the beaches on Jelgava's northeastern coast, the ones that looked across the Garelian Ocean toward equatorial Siaulia, were subtropical themselves. In happier times, they were a popular holiday resort for folk fleeing nasty weather farther south.

The grocer's lay in the direction of the market square. As always, Talsu looked toward the square on the off chance he might spy something interesting. He didn't, but gave a small double take anyhow. That was foolish; the Algarvians had wrecked the triumphal arch from the days of the Kaunian Empire months before. But he still wasn't used to its being gone.

One reason Talsu didn't mind going to the grocer's was his pretty daughter, Gailisa. She was behind the counter when he walked in, and smiled to see him. "Hello, Talsu," she said. "What can I get you today?"

"A pint of the middle-grade olive oil and some fresh garlic," he answered.

Gailisa said, "There's plenty of garlic, but we're out of the middle-grade oil. Do you want the cheap stuff or the extra-virgin?" Before he could answer, she held up a warning hand. "If you make jokes about that the way the miserable Algarvians do, I'll clout you with the jar, do you hear me?"

"Did I say anything?" Talsu asked, as innocently as if such thoughts had never entered his mind. The grocer's daughter snorted; she knew better. Talsu went on, "Let me have the good oil, if you please."

"All right – since you asked for it so pretty." Gailisa reached behind her, pulled an earthenware jar off the shelf, and set it on the counter. "Do you want to choose your own garlic, or shall I grab one for you?"

"Go ahead," Talsu told her. "You'd do a better job than I would."

"I knew that," Gailisa said. "I wondered if you did." She pulled a good-sized head off a string and handed it to him, then said something in classical Kaunian.

Talsu hadn't spent enough time in school to learn much of the old language, and modern Jelgavan had drifted too far from it to let him understand the phrase. He had to ask, "What was that?"

"'The stinking rose,'" Gailisa translated. "I don't know why they called it that back in the days of the Empire – it doesn't look anything like a rose – but they did."

"It doesn't stink, either," Talsu said. "I don't know anybody who doesn't like garlic. Powers above, even the redheads eat it."

"They eat everything," Gailisa said with a fine curl of the lip. "They're eating my father out of food, and they only pay half what it's worth. If he complained, they wouldn't pay anything at all – they'd just take. They're the occupiers, so they can do as they please."

"They've always paid my father – so far, anyhow," Talsu said. "I don't know what he'd do if one of them didn't; he gets a lot of business from them these days."

"They're thieves." Gailisa's voice was flat. "They're worse thieves than our own nobles, and they give us back less. I never thought I'd say that about anybody, but it's true."

"Aye." Talsu nodded. "They could have made a lot of people like them if they'd put down the nobles and walked small themselves, but they haven't bothered. King Mainardo! As if an Algarvian has any business being king here!"

"We lost the war. That means they can do whatever they want, like I said," Gailisa answered. "They beat us, and now they're beating us."

Talsu paid her for the garlic and the oil and left the grocer's shop in a hurry. Gailisa sounded almost like his father, blaming him for losing the fight. Maybe she didn't mean it that way, but that was how it sounded. *If I'd been in charge of things . . .*, Talsu thought, and then laughed at himself. If he'd been in charge of things, the Jelgavan army would still have lost. He didn't know how to run an army or a war. But the nobles who'd run the army were supposed to.

He stopped in a tavern and bought a glass of red wine flavored with orange and lime juice. The wine was rough and raw and cheap, but better than the thin, sour beer army rations had served up with breakfast every morning. Somebody'd probably promised better, then pocketed half of what he should have spent. That was how things had gone during the war.

As Talsu was leaving the tavern, a couple of Algarvian soldiers strode in. If he hadn't stepped back in a hurry, they would have walked right over him. He wanted to smash them for their arrogance, but didn't dare. Two against one was bad odds, and all the occupiers in Skrunda would come after him even if he won.

Hating the Algarvians, hating himself, he went home. His father, having sewn one half of the Algarvian officer's tunic, was muttering the charm that would finish the stitching. It wasn't quite a straight application of the law of similarity, because the left half was a mirror image of the right. Talsu wouldn't have wanted to try it himself; he knew he didn't have the skill. But his father was the best tailor in Skrunda and for several towns around, not only for his handwork but also for the craft spells that meant he didn't have to do everything by hand.

As soon as Traku spoke the final word of command, the thread he'd laid on the left side of the tunic writhed as if alive, then stitched itself through the fabric, duplicating his careful sewing on the right side. He watched anxiously, trusting even long-familiar magic less than his needlework. But everything turned out as it should have.

"That's a nice piece of work, Father," Talsu said, setting the oil and the garlic on the counter by the newly finished tunic.

"Aye, it is, if I say so myself," Traku agreed. "Cursed pity I'm wasting it on the redheads." Talsu grimaced and had to nod.

Eoforwic was like no place Vanai had ever known. Of course, she hadn't known many places in her young life: only Oyngestun and a few visits to Gromheort. She'd thought Gromheort a great city. Next to Oyngestun, it surely was. But measured against the capital of Forthweg – *the former capital of former Forthweg*, she thought – Gromheort sank down to what it was: a provincial town like two dozen others in the kingdom.

Gromheort had at its heart the local count's palace. Eoforwic had at its heart the royal palace. The palace was badly battered. Forthwegian soldiers had defended it against invading Unkerlanters, and then, less than two years later, the Unkerlanters had defended it against invading Algarvians. Even battered, though, it was far larger, far grander, and far more elegant than the count of Gromheort's residence. And the rest of Eoforwic was in proportion to its heart.

"Aye, it's a big place," Ealstan said one morning, doing his resolute best not to show how impressed he was. "More chances for us not to get noticed." His wave took in the cramped little flat they were sharing. "Like this, for instance."

Vanai nodded. "Aye. Like this." After the comfortable house in which she'd lived with her grandfather, the flat, in a rundown part of town, seemed especially small and especially dingy.

But living with Ealstan rather than Brivibas made a lot of difference. Her grandfather had neither known nor much cared about what she was thinking. Ealstan, by contrast, thought along with her: "I know it's not much. I'm used to better, too. But nobody who's not really looking for us would ever find us here. And the company's good."

She went around the rickety kitchen table and gave him a hug. After serving as an Algarvian officer's plaything, she'd thought she would never want another man to touch her, let alone that she would want to touch a man herself. Finding she'd been wrong was a wonder and a delight.

Ealstan pulled her down on to his lap – which made his chair, as decrepit as the table, creak – and kissed her. Then he let her go, something Major Spinello hadn't been in the habit of doing. "I'm off," he said matter-of-factly. "The last fellow I worked for has a friend who's also glad to find a bookkeeper who can count past ten without taking off his shoes."

"He couldn't possibly pay you what you're worth," Vanai said. This time, she kissed him. Why not? The door was closed, the window shuttered against late-winter chill. No one would know. No one would care.

"He'll pay me enough to keep us eating a while longer and keep a roof over our heads," Ealstan answered with a bleak pragmatism she found very appealing. He headed out the door as if he'd been going off to work every day for the past twenty years.

Vanai washed the breakfast dishes. She'd been doing that ever since she was able to handle plates without dropping them; her grandfather, while a splendid historical scholar, was not made for the real world. Then she went back into the bedroom and sprawled across the bed she and Ealstan shared at night.

Looking at the bare, roughly plastered wall only a couple of feet from her face made her sigh. She missed the books she'd left behind in Oyngestun. Until she met Ealstan books were almost the only friends she'd had. She missed the books more than she missed Brivibas. That should have shamed her, but it didn't. Her grandfather had been perfectly hateful toward her since she started giving herself to the Algarvian to get him out of the labor gang.

The only book in the flat was a cheap, badly printed volume the previous tenant had forgotten when he moved out. At the moment, it lay on the nightstand. Vanai picked it up, sighed, and shook her head. It was a Forthwegian translation of an Algarvian historical romance called *The Wicked Empire Aflame*.

Because it was the only book she had, she'd read it. It was laughably bad in any number of different ways. She had trouble deciding whether it took liberties with history or simply ignored it. All the Algarvian mercenaries were virile heroes. The men of the Kaunian Empire were cowards and villains. Their wives and daughters fairly panted to find out what the Algarvians had under their kilts – and find out they did, in great detail.

But Vanai didn't laugh at the romance, not any more, though she had when she first started reading. Being her grandfather's granddaughter, she saw through all the lies the writer was telling. But what would some ignorant Algarvian or Forthwegian think after reading *The Wicked Empire Aflame*? He'd think Kaunians were cowards and villains, that's what, and their women sluts. He'd think they deserved the massacre so lovingly described in the last chapter.

And if he thought that about the ancient Kaunians, what would he think about their modern descendants? Wouldn't he be more likely to think they deserved whatever happened to them, too, than if he hadn't read the romance?

Vanai wondered how many copies of *The Wicked Empire Aflame* were floating around in Algarve and, now, in Forthweg. She wondered how many similar romances Algarvian writers had churned out, and how many copies of them were floating around. She wondered what else the redheads had done to convince their own people and those they'd subjected that Kaunians weren't quite human.

Her mouth twisted. A lot of Forthwegians wouldn't need much convincing about that. A lot of Algarvians probably didn't need much convincing, either. Were things otherwise, how could they put Kaunians on caravan cars heading toward the miserable end awaiting them in the west?

She shivered. That had nothing to do with the weather; the flat, whatever its other shortcomings, was warm enough. But she and her grandfather had come within a hair's breadth of being herded aboard one of those caravan cars themselves. One Algarvian constable had persuaded another to pick a couple of different Kaunians from Oyngestun. They were surely dead now, while Vanai and Brivibas lived.

"If you call this living," Vanai muttered. She went out of the flat as seldom as she could. If the Algarvians saw her on the street, they were liable to seize her. She knew that. But staying cooped up with nothing to do had no appeal, either. The flat probably hadn't been so clean since the week after it was built.

Opening the shutters and looking out the window gave her some relief. It would have given her more had she been able to see anything but a narrow, winding street and, across from it, another block of flats as grimy and neglected as the one in which she was living.

Almost all the people on the street were Forthwegian. From everything she'd heard, Eoforwic was home to a large number of Kaunians. Either most of them were hiding as she was or a lot had already been shipped away. One of those prospects was bad, the other worse.

Three Algarvian constables strode up the street, sticks in hand. Vanai shrank back from the window. She didn't know they were trolling for Kaunians, but she didn't know they weren't, either. She didn't want to find out. The constables kept walking. Everyone who saw them scrambled out of their way. That no doubt appealed to their vanity. But, if they were such heroes as their strides made them out to be, why did they always travel in groups of at least three?

Time crawled on. A pigeon landed on the window sill and peered in at Vanai with its beady little red eyes. She knew several recipes that dated back to the days of the Kaunian Empire for roast squab, squab seethed in honey, baked squab stuffed with mushrooms and figs. . . . Thinking about them made her hungry enough to start to open the window. At the noise and the motion, the pigeon flew off.

Darkness had already fallen before Ealstan came upstairs with a couple of days' worth of groceries. The flat had no rest crate with spells to keep food from going bad, so he couldn't shop very far ahead. "I've got a nice soup bone here," he said. "A good bit of meat on it, and plenty of marrow inside. And I bought some ham. That'll keep till tomorrow."

"I'll get the fire going in the stove and chop some vegetables for the soup," Vanai said. "That does look like a good bone."

"Don't go yet." Ealstan was rummaging at the bottom of the cloth sack in which he'd brought home the food. "Here – I found these for you." He held up three Forthwegian romances – one, *The Deaf Mute's*

Song, a great classic. Apologetically, he went on, "I couldn't find you anything in Kaunian. I looked, I really did, but the redheads have made it against the law to print anything in your language, and I didn't dare ask too many questions."

"I know they've done that," Vanai answered. "I remember how furious my grandfather was when he had to try to compose in Forthwegian. Thank you so much! I was just thinking earlier today that I needed something to do, and now you've given me something."

"I was thinking the same thing – about you, I mean," Ealstan said. "Sitting up here by yourself all the time can't be easy."

Vanai's eyes opened very wide. Tears stung them, and she had to turn away. As best he could, Ealstan did look out for her and try to make her happy. That still astonished her; she was altogether unused to it. She'd gone away with him partly for his own sake, true, but also because she'd thought he couldn't be worse than her grandfather and because she'd felt guilty that he'd got into trouble in Gromheort on account of her.

She hadn't really expected she'd be so much happier in spite of everything. But she was.

Ealstan said, "And this fellow pays pretty well. We'll be able to salt plenty away. If things were different, we could think about moving to a nicer place, but they aren't – I think we're better off with ready cash."

Meeting Ealstan gathering mushrooms hadn't shown Vanai his solid core of good sense. Neither had lying with him, however much she'd enjoyed that – and however astonished she'd been that she could enjoy such things after Major Spinello. She quoted an adage in classical Kaunian: "Passion fades; wisdom endures."

"I hope passion does not fade so soon as that," Ealstan said in his slow, careful Kaunian. Hearing him speak the language with which she was most familiar always pleased her. Though she was more fluent in Forthwegian than he was in Kaunian, he made the effort for her. She wasn't used to that, either. Still in Kaunian, he went on, "And do you know what else?"

"No," she said. "Tell me."

"The man whose accounts I cast today knows Ethelhelm the band leader and singer, and he says Ethelhelm needs someone to keep books for him, too." Ealstan spoke as if a star were shining in broad daylight.

But the name meant little to Vanai. "Is that good?" she asked.

Forthwegians and Kaunians had different tastes in music; what pleased one group seldom delighted the other.

"It's the best!" Ealstan exclaimed, irked back into Forthwegian.

"All right." Vanai was willing to believe him even if she didn't share his enthusiasm. As she started into the kitchen to make soup, she realized that was at least a good start on love.

Night and fog. In winter – and, for that matter, at other seasons of the year, too – fog rolled off the ocean into Tirgoviste town, as it did into every other seaside city on the five major islands of Sibiu. Cornelu was out long after the curfew the Algarvian occupiers had imposed on his kingdom. He hoped, and had reason to hope, the Algarvian patrols that prowled his home town would never set eyes on him. He didn't want them to; they'd been looking for him up in the hills of central Tirgoviste, and no doubt they were looking for him down here, too.

But even if they did, he was pretty sure he could get away from them. He'd lived in Tirgoviste almost all his life; he knew its neighborhoods and alleys without having to see them. Mezentio's men might get lucky and blaze him before he could slide round a corner or into a doorway, but he didn't think so.

He exhaled, breathing out still more fog. He could hardly see that fog: No street lights burned, lest they guide Lagoan dragons to their targets. Cornelu knew the houses and shop fronts past which he walked were made from mortared blocks of the rough gray limestone. He knew they had steep roofs of red slate slabs to shed rain and snow. He knew all that, because he'd seen it. He couldn't see it now.

Shivering, he drew his ragged sheepskin jacket more tightly around him. He'd been a commander in the Sibian navy, as good a leviathan-rider as any officer who served King Burebistu. He'd had a fine wardrobe of tunics and kilts and cloaks of all weights. Now, as a woodcutter down from the hills, he wore the same clothes day in and day out, and counted himself lucky not to be colder than he was.

Carefully, he stepped forward. Aye, there was the curb. He started to step off the cobbles when he heard several men in heavy boots coming up the street toward him. He drew back. Somebody among those booted men stumbled and let out a couple of loud, vile curses. They were in Algarvian. He was fluent in the language, but likely would have understood most of them even if he hadn't been: Sibian and Algarvian were as close as brothers to each other.

He did understand those curses could mean trouble. Moving as quietly as he could, he drew back again, ready to flee if the Algarvians heard him. They didn't. They passed him by with no notion he was there. The fellow who'd stumbled was still grumbling: "—aren't going to be any stinking Sibs out on a night like this. It's a waste of time, that's what it is. Anybody who'd come out tonight would break his fool neck five minutes later, and serve him right, too."

"You almost broke yours, that's cursed sure," one of his comrades said. The others laughed. The grumbler cursed some more, and kept cursing till the patrol passed out of earshot.

By then, Cornelu had already crossed the street – quite safely. Had the Algarvians been able to see his smile through the darkness and murk, they would not have enjoyed it. The streets got steep in the direction they were going. Maybe one of them really would break his neck. Cornelu hoped so.

He went on another couple of blocks, then turned left on to his own street and hurried toward his own house, the house in which he hadn't lived, in which he hadn't even set foot, since the Algarvian invasion. Costache and Brindza lived there still. So did the three Algarvian officers quartered on them.

All the houses on his block, like the houses and shops and taverns in the rest of Tirgoviste, were dark, for the same reason street lamps were: dragons from Lagoas could reach Sibiu. Cornelu understood why the Algarvians wanted to make it hard for them to drop their eggs accurately. Here as elsewhere, understanding failed to bring sympathy.

Here was his walk, leading up to his front porch. As he strode along the walk, he reached under his jacket and pulled out a short stick, one of the sort a constable might carry. The stick had cost him most of the silver he'd brought down from the hills, but he didn't care. Even if it wasn't such a powerful weapon as a footsoldier's stick, it ought to be good enough to dispose of the officers who'd settled down here. Then Cornelu could take Costache and Brindza away to the southern side of the island, or maybe back up into the hills.

"And then," Cornelu muttered under his breath, "then, by the powers above, I can be alone with my wife." He ached for her, sometimes literally.

As quietly as he could, he stepped up on to the porch. He must have been quiet enough; no one inside called out in alarm. Once up there, he could tell lamps were lit within, though black curtains – new since he'd last seen the house – swallowed almost all the glare.

Cornelu paused a moment, pondering his next step. Did he knock? Would he do better to sneak in through a window? Could he break down the door, slay all of Mezentio's men, and get Costache and Brindza away before the commotion drew neighbors or more Algarvians? That was what he most wanted to do, but he knew the risks.

While he pondered, Costache's voice, bright and cheerful, came out through the window undimmed by the curtains: "Wait there, darling. I'll be with you in a moment."

Rather than Brindza's childish prattle, which Cornelu had expected, an Algarvian doing his best to speak Sibian answered, "All right, sweetheart, but you'd better not keep me waiting long."

"Don't worry," Costache said archly. "I won't be long, I promise. And you'll be glad when I get there." The Algarvian laughed.

Sick at heart, Cornelu turned away. He looked at his stick. If he blazed himself through the head, if he left his body lying on the walk, would Costache shed a tear? Or would she just laugh?

"I should have known," Cornelu said to himself in a sort of whispered groan. "Oh, by the powers above, I should have known." She hadn't wanted to see him, not really; she hadn't wanted to be alone with him. He'd wondered, he'd worried, but he hadn't believed, not deep in his heart. He hadn't wanted to believe.

He stared back toward his house – no, toward the house that had been his. He stared back toward the life that had been his, too. Things would never be the same now.

Looking at the stick, he shook his head. Costache had betrayed him. Why should he give her the satisfaction of finding him dead? What he really wanted was revenge. He started to swing back toward the house. If he killed not only the Algarvians but his wife, his faithless wife, as well . . .

What would he do with Brindza then? Kill her, too? She hadn't done anything to him. She hadn't even kept him from sleeping with Costache, as he'd thought before – Costache hadn't wanted to sleep with him anyhow. Take Brindza with him? He had no idea how to care for a toddler; he'd never had a chance to learn.

He slammed his forehead, hard, with the heel of his hand. He'd just found the last thing he wanted: a reason to let his wife live.

With a muffled curse, he hurried down the street, running as much from his fury as from his former home. He let his feet carry him; his mind was empty of anything even resembling thought. He'd gone several blocks before realizing he was heading down toward the harbor, not back up into the hills. He'd worked as a woodcutter in the hope of rejoining Costache and Brindza. His feet had realized before his head that that wouldn't happen, now. And if it wouldn't, what point to going back to the hills and to work he despised anyhow? Mezentio's men would still be looking for him there, too.

The smell of the sea was always strong in Tirgoviste town. But once Cornelu drew near the piers, he caught the reek of old fish from the boats the Algarvians still permitted to sail, an odor that didn't travel so far inland as the salt tang pervading all the Sibian islands, the main five and their smaller outliers. Through the damp, deadening fog, he caught the familiar slap of waves against the wooden pilings that supported the harbor piers.

He knew exactly where he was by the way the waves sounded. Discovering where his feet had brought him, he also discovered they'd had a better notion of where they were going than he'd imagined: he was within a stone's throw of the great wire pens where the Sibian navy had held its leviathans – and where the Algarvian occupiers held theirs these days.

Cornelu had come to look at the leviathans in an earlier visit to Tirgoviste. An Algarvian guard had cursed him and sent him away in a hurry. He snorted. What would the guard have done if he'd come up in his sea-green Sibian commander's uniform? Nothing so pleasant as cursing and running him off – of that Cornelu was sure.

Somewhere not far away, an Algarvian guard – maybe even the same Algarvian guard – was pacing through the fog. If he was like every other guard Cornelu had ever known, he would be cursing his luck at drawing duty on a night when the only way he could find a foe would be to trip over his feet.

As if thinking of the guard had conjured him into being, his footsteps sounded on the walk not far away. Like frost forming on a window, decision crystallized within Cornelu. The Algarvian didn't even bother trying to move quietly. He seemed sure he was the only man up and walking for miles around. Had the fellow been a Sibian, Cornelu would have reported him to his superior officer. As things were, he killed him instead.

It was almost absurdly easy. All he had to do was keep from stomping his feet on the stone of the walkway as he followed the Algarvian's footfalls. Mezentio's man hadn't the faintest notion Cornelu was coming up behind him. As soon as the guard became something more than the sound of booted feet, as soon as he became a dim shape ahead, Cornelu raised his stick and blazed him down.

His beam was a brief, bright line of light in the mist. That mist attenuated the beam, which was not all that strong to begin with. But, at a range of three or four feet, it was strong enough. It caught the Algarvian in the back of the head. He let out a startled grunt, as if Cornelu had tapped him on the shoulder. Then he quietly toppled. His own stick clattered as it slipped from his nerveless fingers.

Cornelu dragged the body off the walk, so it wouldn't be found at once. He picked up the stick and dropped it into the water in one of the leviathan pens. It made only a tiny splash.

But that splash, as he'd hoped, was enough to draw the leviathan to the surface to find out what had made it. Leviathans were even more curious than their squat cousins, the whales. Because of the fog, Cornelu couldn't see this one, but it was plain in his mind's eye: lean and long, about six times a man's length, with a beaky mouth full of sharp teeth. Wild leviathans were wolves of the sea. Tamed and trained, they turned into hunting dogs.

Moving quickly, Cornelu got out of his jacket and tunic, his kilt and his shoes. Naked, he jumped into the water of the leviathan pen. It was cold, but the chill did not pierce him to the core. He let out a long exhalation of relief: His sorcerous protection against the ice waters of the southern seas still held good. Had that not been so, he would have frozen to death before long.

He swam toward the leviathan. By everything Sibian spies knew, Mezentio's men guided their leviathans with pokes and prods almost identical to those Sibian riders used. He was betting his life the spies had it right. A man made a good mouthful for a leviathan, no more.

The great beast let him climb on to its back. His hand found the harness secured by its fins. The leviathan quivered expectantly, as if waiting for him to show what he was. He tapped it with the signal that, in the Sibian navy, would have ordered it to leap out of the pen. If the spies were wrong, he wouldn't last long, and would pass his final movements most unpleasantly.

The leviathan gathered itself. After a dizzying rush, it hurled itself through the air, then splashed down again. Cornelu let out a whoop of joy drowned in that titanic splash. He could go to Lagoas, which, while not home – he had no home, not any more – was not Mezentio's to do with as he would.

And, if he decided to drown himself halfway there, Costache would never know.

"We are a warrior race," Sergeant Istvan declared, and all the Gyongyosians in his squad solemnly nodded.

"Aye, indeed we are a warrior race," said Kun, who was less inclined to argue with his sergeant now that he had reached the exalted rank of corporal.

Istvan kept his face straight, though it wasn't easy. Kun looked about as little like a warrior as anything under the stars. He was skinny – weedy, when you got down to it – bespectacled, and had been a mage's apprentice before finding himself joined to the host of Ekrekek Arpad, the sovereign of Gyongyos. Even his tawny beard came in by clumps and patches, as if he needed some nostrum for mange.

Being thick-shouldered and furry himself, Istvan tended to look down his beaky nose at anyone who wasn't. But Kun, even if he did complain and split hairs whenever he got the chance, had fought well on Obuda out in the Bothnian Ocean, and he'd fought well here in the frozen, mountainous wasteland of western Unkerlant, too. And the little bits of magic he'd learned from his master had served his squadmates well.

"There is a village up ahead," Istvan said. "It is supposed to have Unkerlanter soldiers in it. Captain Tivadar says there aren't supposed to be too many of the goat-eating buggers in there. Stars grant he's right. However many there are, though, the company is going to clean them out."

"Unless we don't," Szonyi said. Istvan remembered when the hulking private had been as raw a recruit as Kun. It hadn't been so long before. Now Szonyi might have been an old veteran. He wasn't old, but he certainly was a veteran.

"We are a warrior race," Istvan repeated. "If the captain orders us to take this village, take it we shall, and he will lead us while we do it." Szonyi's big head bobbed up and down in agreement. Tivadar was an officer fit to command warriors, for he never asked his men to do anything he would not do and did not do himself.

"Onward!" Kun said. As a private, he would have been better pleased to hang back. Rank made hanging back embarrassing for him. It worked the same magic on Istvan. He wondered if it worked the same magic on Tivadar, too.

That didn't matter, and he had no time to worry about it, anyway. Other sergeants were haranguing their squads. Back when Istvan had been a simple soldier, he'd listened to sergeants as little as he could get away with. His own men listened to him that way, except when they listened closely so they could argue afterwards. But he heard his fellow sergeants, and even officers, with new ears these days. He had to get the troopers in his squad to do as he said. Any tricks he could pick up, he would.

Here came Captain Tivadar, who was only a few years older than Istvan. "Is your squad ready?" the company commander asked, glaring as if he intended to tear Istvan limb from limb if the answer was no.

But Istvan nodded and said, "Aye, sir."

"The Unkerlanters aren't supposed to have more than a section holding this miserable little place," Tivadar said. "They can't afford to fight out here in the middle of nowhere any better than we can – worse, in fact, because they're fighting the Algarvians, too, a quarter of the way around the world east of here."

"Aye, sir," Istvan repeated, and then added, "A quarter of the way around the world is too far for me to think about. All I know is, I'm too cursed far from my home valley."

Tivadar nodded. "A man can't be farther away than too far from home. But I'm glad we've got you with us, Sergeant. Even if the Unkerlanters have a regiment in there, you'll make 'em think we've got a brigade, and out they'll come with their hands up high."

Despite the flaps on his fur cap, Istvan's ears had been chilly. Now they heated in embarrassment; he wasn't used to praise from officers. "Sir," he said, "if my bluff – and Kun's little magic – hadn't worked back there, we'd have had to yield ourselves to the Unkerlanters instead of the other way round. The stars shone kindly on me that day."

"They shine on those who deserve it." Tivadar slapped him on the back with a mittened hand. "Kun got promoted. Can't very well promote you – you haven't the blood for it, of course – but the bravery bonus *will* be added to your pay once all the clerks are done playing with their counting boards."

"Unless I die of old age first," Istvan said with a wry chuckle he quickly choked off. He could die of a lot of other things besides old age. The Unkerlanters were going to get the chance to find some of them, too.

Reading his thoughts, Captain Tivadar said, "If the stars wink, your clan still gets the bonus; it won't be lost. And remember, your squad is on the left flank. If you can, lead them around behind the village while the main attack goes in from the front. Then, when the cursed Unkerlanters are all hot and bothered, you can hit 'em from the rear – easy as buggering a goat."

Istvan's lip curled. "Sir, that's disgusting." After a moment, though, he laughed. "It's pretty funny, too, isn't it?"

"Of all my sergeants, you're the one I want in back of the Unkerlanters." Tivadar slapped him again, a good, solid blow. "Let's get going."

"Did you hear that, boys?" Istvan said to his squad. He felt about to burst with pride. "We're the best, and the captain knows it. We'll wreck the Unkerlanters good and proper, won't we?"

"Aye," the soldiers chorused. They took their places on the left of Captain Tivadar's little line of battle, and started east with the rest of the company. The wind blew snow from the ground and lashed their backs. It blew snow through the bare branches of stunted birch trees that clung to the sides of the valley in which the village lay. Istvan and his squad scurried through the trees. They were the only cover the freezing landscape offered.

Eggs began bursting farther south. "May the stars go dark for the Unkerlanters!" Istvan said angrily. "They weren't supposed to have a tosser in there." What that meant was, Captain Tivadar hadn't warned him to expect one.

Kun said, "Their officers are probably saying we aren't supposed to be coming after them. We need to be more like mages and deal with what is, not with what's supposed to be." He went into a snow-covered hole in the ground that was where it wasn't supposed to be, and rose coated with white. Istvan was unkind enough to laugh.

Not three minutes later, he spied movement ahead, the distinctive movement only a human body can make. All the Gyongyosians in this part of the world were with him. That made the stooped figure ahead an enemy. Istvan threw his stick up to his shoulder and blazed.

The Unkerlanter shrieked and fell. "It's a woman!" Szonyi exclaimed as she kept on shrieking. "What's a woman doing out here?"

"We'll never know," Istvan said as he ran toward her through the snow. He pulled a knife from its sheath. "Wrong place at the wrong time, that's all. Have to shut her up." Nervously, he glanced south, hoping the noise of combat there would keep anyone in the village from hearing her cries.

She found a rock in the snow and threw it at him as he drew near. It missed. She was groping for another one when he cut her throat. Her blood splashed red across the winter white.

"That was a waste, Sergeant," one of his troopers said from behind him.

"We haven't got time for fun," Istvan answered with another shrug. "Too cursed cold to go whipping it out, anyhow. Come on. Keep moving."

He tried to gauge how the fighting was going by where the Unkerlanters' eggs were bursting. The rest of the company wasn't moving as fast as Captain Tivadar had hoped. Istvan scowled. Instead of just following orders, he'd have to start thinking for himself. He didn't care for that. It was, properly, an officer's job.

As if to reassure him, Szonyi pointed down in the direction of the village and said, "We've set it afire."

"Aye." Istvan considered that, then slowly nodded. "That'll help. The Unkerlanters will have a harder time aiming their tosser." He thought a little more. His mind didn't move very fast, but had a way of getting where it was going. "And with the wind blowing at our backs, the smoke'll help hide us when we get into place to come at 'em from behind. We'd better do that. The rest of the company is going to need us even more than the captain thought they would."

But for that luckless woman (what had she been doing? – gathering firewood, most likely), no one in the village had any notion his squad was moving around it toward the rear. Once in position, Istvan peered toward the place from behind a rock. Through blowing smoke, he saw Unkerlanter soldiers running here and there. The wind carried their guttural shouts to his ears.

One of them set an egg on the tosser's hurling arm. Another launched the egg toward Istvan's countrymen. Catching sight of the egg-tosser told him what he had to do next. He pointed toward it. "We're going to take that miserable thing. The rest of the boys will have an easier time then. Forward – and don't shout till you're sure they've spied us."

He was the first one to break cover and run toward the village. His men followed. If he went, they would go. The crunch of their boots on crusted snow seemed dreadfully loud in his ears. So did his own coughing after he sucked in too thick a lungful of smoky air.

But the tunic-clad Unkerlanters, intent on serving their egg-tosser and beating back the threat from the west, paid no attention to their rear till too late. Because of the smoke in the air, Istvan had to get closer than usual to them before he started blazing. First one of the enemy soldiers fell, then the other. The second Unkerlanter was grabbing for his own stick to blaze back when another Gyongyosian's beam finished him.

"Gyongyos!" Istvan did shout then, as loud as he could. "Ekrekek Arpad! Gyongyos!" The rest of the squad echoed the cry. To the Unkerlanters' frightened ears, they must have sounded like a regiment. They fought almost like a regiment, too, for the Unkerlanters, well concealed against Tivadar's attackers, were hardly hidden at all from men coming the other way.

King Swemmel's soldiers howled in dismay. Some tried to turn and face Istvan's squad, but they couldn't do that and hold off the rest of the attackers, too – they lacked the numbers. Some of them died in place. Others began throwing down their sticks, throwing up their hands, and surrendering.

Before long, the only Unkerlanters left in the ruined village were captives and a handful of the trappers and hunters and their womenfolk and children who'd lived there and hadn't fled east. Captain Tivadar sent them all back toward land Gyongyos held more securely. Then, in front of the whole company, he spoke loudly to Istvan: "Well done, Sergeant."

"Thank you, sir," Istvan said. Another few years of tiny victories like this, and the armies of Gyongyos might be in position for something larger. Istvan wondered if he'd live to see it.

As the sun sank below the western horizon, the Algarvian strawboss shouted, "Going home!" Along with the rest of his labor gang, Leofsig laid down his sledgehammer with a weary sigh of relief. The Algarvian strode through the gang handing out the day's pay: a small silver bit for Forthwegian laborers, half that much in copper for the handful of Kaunians.

A wagon came rattling up to take the gang back to Gromheort over the road they'd been paving; they were too far from the city to walk without adding unduly to their exhaustion. The blonds got the job of rounding up all the tools before the gang boss let them climb into the wagon, too. Like the Forthwegians, they sprawled limply over the wagon bed.

"Here, get off me," a Forthwegian growled at one of them. "Ought to send the whole lot of you whoresons west. Then we'd be rid of you."

"Oh, don't go unbuttoning your tunic, Oslac," Leofsig said. "We're all too tired to see straight."

Oslac glared at him, eyes glittering in the twilight. But Leofsig was bigger, stronger, and younger than the other laborer, whose dark beard was streaked with gray. Leofsig had been conscripted into King Penda's levy not long before Forthweg began her disastrous war against Algarve, and still thought of a man of thirty as one bearing respectable years. Knowing himself outmatched, Oslac did no more than mutter, "Stinking Kaunians."

"We all stink, too," Leofsig said, and Oslac could hardly argue with him there. He went on, "Let it alone, why don't you?"

Had some of Oslac's comrades backed him, he might have taken it further. Even the laborers who hated Kaunians worse than he did, though, seemed too worn to care. A couple of men had already started snoring. Leofsig rather envied them; no matter how much he'd done during the day, he couldn't hope to sleep on bare boards in an unsprung wagon jouncing over cobblestones.

An hour or so later – just enough time for him to start to go stiff – the wagon clattered into Gromheort. He helped shake the sleepers awake, then creakily descended from the wagon and started home.

The Kaunian he'd defended, a fellow named Peitavas, fell into step beside him. "My thanks," he said in his own language, which Leofsig spoke fairly well.

"It's all right," Leofsig answered in Forthwegian; he was too spent to look for words in another tongue. "Go home. Stay there. Stay safe."

"I'm as safe as any Kaunian in Forthweg," Peitavas said. "As long as I build roads for the Algarvians, I'm more useful to them alive than dead. With most of my people, it's the other way round." He turned down a side street before Leofsig could answer.

Leofsig cast a longing look toward the public baths. He sighed, shook his head, and walked on toward his home. His mother or sister would have a basin of water and some rags waiting for him. That wasn't as good as a warm plunge and a showerbath, but it would have to do. Anyway, with fuel scarce and expensive in Gromheort these days, the plunge more often than not wasn't warm. And getting into the baths cost a copper, a good part of what he'd spent the day slaving to earn.

Home, then, through the dark streets of the city. Curfew hadn't come yet, but wasn't far away. Once, an Algarvian constable stopped him and started asking questions in bad Kaunian and worse Forthwegian. He wondered if he'd land in trouble, and whether he ought to kick the chubby fellow in the balls and run. But then they recognized each other. Leofsig had helped the constable find his way back to his barracks when he got lost just after arriving in Gromheort. "Going on," the Algarvian said, tipping his hat, and went on himself.

And so, instead of returning to the captives' camp from which he'd escaped or having something worse happen to him, Leofsig knocked on his own front door a few minutes later. He waited for the bar to be lifted, then worked the latch and went inside. Conberge waited in the short entry hall. "You're late tonight," she said.

"Redheads worked us hard, curse 'em," he answered.

His sister wrinkled her nose. "I believe that." To leave no possible doubt about what she believed, she added, "The basin's waiting for you in the kitchen. It'll be mostly cold by now, but I can put in some more hot water from the kettle over the fire."

"Would you?" Leofsig said. "It's chilly out there, and I don't want to end up with chest fever."

"Come along, then," Conberge said briskly. She was between him and Ealstan in age, but insisted on mothering him in much the same style as their true mother. As Leofsig went past her and turned left toward the kitchen, she lowered her voice, murmuring, "We've heard from him."

Leofsig stopped. "Have you?" he said, also softly. "Where is he? Is he all right?"

His sister nodded. "Aye, he is," she whispered. "He's in Eoforwic."

"Not in Oyngestun?" Leofsig asked, and Conberge shook her head. "Is the Kaunian girl with him?"

She shrugged. "He doesn't say. He says he's happy, though, so I think she is. Now come on. People will have heard you come in, and they'll be wondering why you're dawdling in the hallway."

Fondly, Leofsig patted her on the shoulder. "You'd have made a terrific spy." Conberge snorted and stopped acting motherly; she elbowed him harder than Oslac could have done. Thus propelled, into the kitchen he went. His mother was stirring a pot hanging over the fire next to the kettle. By the way Elfryth nodded, by the secretly delighted look in her eye, he knew she knew the news. All she said was, "Clean yourself off, son. Supper will be ready soon."

"I'm going to give him some fresh hot water," Conberge said, and used a dipper to draw some from the kettle. As Leofsig scrubbed dirt and sweat from his arms and legs and face, she went on, "I think he ought to put on a clean tunic, too, before he comes to the supper table." That was also motherly: she didn't seem to think he had sense enough to change clothes unless she told him to.

"Let me have a cup of wine first," Leofsig said. Conberge poured him one. Before he drank, he raised the cup in salute. His sister and mother both smiled; they understood what he meant.

After putting on a fresh wool tunic and fresh drawers, he went across the courtyard to the dining room, which lay just to the right of the entry hall so as to make it convenient to the kitchen. As he'd expected, he found his father and uncle already there. Uncle Hengist was reading the news sheet: reading it aloud, and loudly. "No Unkerlanter gains reported on any front," he said. "What do you think of that, Hestan?"

Leofsig's father shrugged. "The Unkerlanters have already gained a lot of ground," he said in mild tones; his brother enjoyed hearing himself talk more than he did.

"But the Algarvians haven't fallen to pieces, the way you said they would a few weeks ago," Hengist insisted.

"I didn't say they would. I said they might," Hestan answered with a bookkeeper's precision. "Pretty plainly, they haven't. You're right about that." He nodded to Leofsig, looking to change the subject. "Hello, son. How did it go today?"

"I'm tired," Leofsig answered. He could have said that any day and been telling the truth. He raised an eyebrow at his father. Hestan nodded, ever so slightly. He knew about Ealstan, too, then. Neither of them said anything where Uncle Hengist could hear. After what had happened to Sidroc, if he knew where Ealstan was, he might let the Algarvians know, too. Nobody wanted to find out whether he would.

"If you want to work with me, you may," Hestan said. "Numbers are as stubborn as cobblestones, but not so backbreaking to wallop into place."

"You'd make more money, too," Uncle Hengist pointed out. His mind always ran in that direction.

"I still don't think it's safe," Leofsig said. "Nobody pays attention to one laborer in a gang. But the fellow who casts accounts for you, you notice him. You want to be sure he knows what he's doing. If he saves you money, you tell people about him. After a while, talk goes to the wrong ears."

"I suppose that's wise," his father said. "Still, when I see you come dragging in the way you do sometimes, I wouldn't mind throwing wisdom out the window."

"I'll get by," Leofsig said. Hestan grimaced, but nodded.

Conberge came in and set stoneware bowls and bone-handled spoons on the table. "Supper in a minute," she said.

"It smells good," Leofsig said. His stomach growled agreement. The bread and olive oil he'd eaten at noon seemed a million miles away. Any sort of food would have smelled wonderful just then.

"Same old stew: barley and lentils and turnips and cabbage," Conberge said. "Mother chopped a little smoked sausage into it, but only a little. You'll taste it more than it will do you any good, if you know what I mean. It's probably what you smell."

Elfryth brought in the pot and ladled the bowls full. As she was sitting down, she asked, "Where's Sidroc?" Uncle Hengist called his son, loudly.

After another couple of minutes, Sidroc came in, sat down, and silently began to eat.

He was burly as Leofsig had become despite not doing hard physical labor. He looked like Leofsig, too, though his nose was blobbier than their sharply hooked ones. It took after that of his mother; she'd been killed when an Algarvian egg wrecked their house, and he and Uncle Hengist had lived, not always comfortably, with Leofsig's family ever since.

After finishing his first bowl of stew, Sidroc helped himself to another, which he also devoured. Only then did he speak: "That . . . wasn't so bad." He rubbed his temples. "My head hurts."

He'd had headaches ever since he'd hit his head in the brawl with Ealstan. He still didn't remember what the brawl had been about, for which Leofsig and his father and mother and sister thanked the powers above. Ealstan's disappearance afterwards, though, had left both him and Uncle Hengist suspicious, most suspicious indeed. Leofsig wished his brother hadn't had to run off. But Ealstan couldn't have known Sidroc would wake up without remembering. He couldn't have known Sidroc would wake up at all.

"Have you finished your schoolwork?" Hengist asked Sidroc.

"Oh, aye – as much of it as I could do," Sidroc replied. He'd been an indifferent scholar before the knock on the head, and hadn't got better since. After taking a big swig from his wine cup, he went on, "Maybe I'll sign up for Plegmund's Brigade after all. I wouldn't have to worry about poems and irregular verbs there."

Everyone else at the table, even Uncle Hengist, winced. The Algarvians had set up Plegmund's Brigade to get Forthwegians to fight for them in Unkerlant. Leofsig had fought the Algarvians. He would sooner have jumped off a tall building than fought for them. But Sidroc had been talking about the Brigade even before the fight with Ealstan. *Maybe he needs another shot to the head,* Leofsig thought, *and a harder one this time.*

Fifteen

Officially, Hajjaj was far in the north, up in Bishah. Any number of witnesses would swear at need that the Zuwayzi foreign minister was hard at work in the capital, right where he should be. Hajjaj didn't want any of them to have to take such an oath. That would mean something had gone wrong, something had made the Algarvians suspicious. Better by far they never, ever learned he'd come down to Jurdhan.

He strolled along the main street, such as it was, of the little no-account town: one elderly black man wearing only a straw hat and sandals among many black men and women and children, all dressed, or not dressed, much as he was.

Nudity had its advantages. By leaving off the bracelets and anklets and gold rings and chains he would normally have worn, Hajjaj turned himself into a person of no particular importance. He would have had a harder time doing that with shabby clothes. When he walked into Jurdhan's chief – by virtue of being Jurdhan's only – hostel, no one gave him a second glance. That was just what he wanted.

He went upstairs (the hostel was one of a handful of buildings in town to boast a second story) and walked down the hall to the chamber where, he'd been told, the man he was to meet awaited him. He knocked once, twice, then once again. After a moment, the latch clicked. The door swung open.

A short, squat, swarthy man – swarthy, but far from black – wearing a knee-length cotton tunic looked him up and down. "Powers above, you're a scrawny old bugger," he remarked in Algarvian.

"Thank you so much, my lord Ansovald. I am so glad to see you again, your Excellency," Hajjaj answered in the same language. Speaking Algarvian to the former – and perhaps future – Unkerlanter minister to

Zuwayza tickled his sense of irony, which needed little tickling. But it was the one speech they truly had in common. His own Unkerlanter was halting, Ansovald's Zuwayzi as near nonexistent as made no difference.

If Ansovald noticed the irony, he didn't let on. "Well, come in," he said, and stood aside. "If you want to put on a tunic and hide that bag of bones you call a carcass, I've got one here for you."

That was the usual practice for Zuwayzi diplomats. Hajjaj had grown resigned to wearing a long tunic when calling on envoys from Unkerlant and Forthweg, a short tunic and kilt when seeing a minister from an Algarvic kingdom, a tunic and trousers when meeting with Kaunians, and clothes of some sort, at any rate, when dealing with lands like Kuusamo and Gyongyos, where style of apparel carried less political weight. But growing resigned to it didn't mean he loved it. He shook his head and answered, "No, thank you. This is unofficial, which means I can be comfortable if I please, and I do."

He'd thought about wearing a tunic to this meeting, too, thought about it and rejected the notion. Nothing would have drawn stares like a clothed Zuwayzi strolling through Jurdhan – nothing except a naked Unkerlanter strolling through Cottbus. And maybe his nudity would disconcert Ansovald.

If it did, the Unkerlanter diplomat didn't show that, either. "Come in, then," he said. "I told you that already. I'd sooner you were a woman half your age, but I don't suppose King Shazli would."

"No, in a word." Hajjaj walked into the chamber. Ansovald closed the door behind him, closed it and barred it. From any other kingdom's minister, Ansovald's words would have been monstrously rude. From the Unkerlanter, they were something of a prodigy. This was the first time Hajjaj could remember him caring in the slightest for what King Shazli thought.

The room was furnished Zuwayzi-style, with carpet piled on carpet and with cushions large and small a guest could arrange to suit his own comfort. Hajjaj wasted no time doing that. Ansovald followed suit rather more clumsily. He did not offer Hajjaj wine and cakes and tea, as any Zuwayzi host would have done. Instead, very much an Unkerlanter again, he bulled straight ahead: "We aren't going to settle the war between us this afternoon."

"I never expected we would," Hajjaj replied.

"And you can't tell me you're able to make the cursed Algarvians pack up and go home, either," Ansovald growled. "Aye, you and the redheads are in bed with each other, but I know which one's the tail and which one's the dog."

Despite the mixed metaphor, Hajjaj followed him. The Zuwayzi foreign minister said, "If Unkerlant hadn't come up and ravaged us by force, we would likely be neutral now, not allied to King Mezentio."

"Oh, aye – tell me another one," Ansovald jeered. "You'd kick us when we were down, just like everyone else."

That held a grain of truth, or more than a grain. But what was true and what was diplomatic often had only a nodding relationship, or sometimes none at all. Hajjaj said, "Wouldn't you be better off if you had fewer foes to fight?"

"What's your price?" Ansovald was an Unkerlanter, all right: no subtlety to him, no style, no grace. Hajjaj vastly preferred dealing with Marquis Balastro, Algarve's minister to Zuwayza.

On the other hand, the urbane and dashing Algarvians had been the ones who'd started murdering Kaunians for the sake of advantage in the war. By all accounts, King Swemmel of Unkerlant had wasted not a moment in imitating them, but Algarve went first. Try as he would, Hajjaj couldn't forget that.

"Your Excellency, Unkerlant went to war with us because the Treaty of Bludenz no longer suited your sovereign," he said.

"Kyot the traitor signed the Treaty of Bludenz," Ansovald said, which was true: Like Forthweg, Zuwayza had used the chaos reigning in Unkerlant after the Six Years' War to regain her freedom.

But Hajjaj said, "And King Swemmel always adhered to it afterwards. He got good results when he did, and bad results when he decided not to any longer and invaded us. Isn't it efficient to do what works well and inefficient to do the opposite?" Swemmel and, because of him, his countrymen prated endlessly of efficiency, but the talk came easier for them than the thing itself.

Ansovald's heavy features were made for scowling, and he scowled now. "You black thieves have stolen more land now than the Treaty of Bludenz ever gave you, and you know it cursed well, too."

Hajjaj breathed heavily through his arched nose. "One reason we have is that you tannish thieves stole so much of what you'd honestly yielded in the treaty. Give us the border we had before, give us guarantees that you mean to give what you say you're giving, and I may persuade King Shazli to be satisfied." Since the slaughters to power sorcery had started, the Zuwayzi foreign minister kept casting about for ways to get out of the war. He had some hopes for this one, the more so as Unkerlant had requested the meeting.

Ansovald proceeded to dash them, saying, "King Swemmel will give you the borders you agreed to in Cottbus, and not another inch of ground."

"I agreed to those because Unkerlant invaded my kingdom," Hajjaj exclaimed indignantly. "I agreed to them because we stood alone, without a friend in the world. Things are different now, and King Swemmel had better recognize it."

"Oh, he does," Ansovald said. "By even offering so much, he admits – unofficially, of course – Zuwayza has a right to exist. That is more than you have had from him before. Take it and be thankful."

The worst of it was, he had a point of sorts. But only of sorts. In tones far more frigid than Zuwayzi weather ever got, Hajjaj said, "It cannot be. Unkerlant got that border after beating us in war. We are not beaten now, as you yourself have said. And if King Swemmel did not recognize that Zuwayza has a right to exist, why were you his minister in Bishah for so long?"

"He treated with you. You Zuwayzin are *here*, after all." Ansovald sounded like a man admitting something he didn't care for but couldn't deny. "But being *here* is not the same as being a kingdom."

"This is the bargain for which I spirited myself out of Bishah? This, and nothing more?" Hajjaj asked. When Ansovald nodded, the Zuwayzi foreign minister felt betrayed. He said, "I cannot take it back to my own sovereign – who *is* King of Zuwayza, whether Swemmel recognizes him or not. I had hoped you might have some room to dicker, considering how much of Unkerlant Algarve holds these days."

"Less today than yesterday," Ansovald said, drawing himself up with touchy pride. "Less tomorrow than today. We will whip them out of our kingdom altogether before spring – and when we do, your turn comes next."

Hajjaj did not think that would happen. "It was only weeks ago that Cottbus was on the point of falling," he pointed out.

"It's not on the point of falling now," Ansovald growled. "By this time next year, Trapani will be on the point of falling to our brave Unkerlanter soldiers. You and your chief who calls himself a king had best bear it in mind and behave yourselves accordingly."

With dignity undamaged by creaking knees, Hajjaj got to his feet. Bowing to Ansovald, he said, "I had hoped to be dealing with a reasonable man." Since the Unkerlanter came as King Swemmel's envoy, that was probably optimistic, but he had hoped. He went on, "If you truly believe what you just told me, I can only conclude some malignant mage has stolen your wits."

"King Mezentio's armies are falling to pieces on the snow-covered plains of Unkerlant," Ansovald insisted.

"We shall see," Hajjaj said politely. "But I cannot tell you that I believe you are right, and I cannot see much point to any further discussions between us so long as we differ so widely." He bowed again. "Your safe-conduct will carry you back through our lines to your own kingdom." As a parting jab, he added, "You must remember, though, that it will not protect you from any Algarvic soldiers you may meet on your way back to Cottbus."

Ansovald gave him a dirty look. It was also, Hajjaj judged, an alarmed look; Ansovald knew where the lines ran. Gruffly, the Unkerlanter put the best face on it he could: "Less snow up here than in the rest of the kingdom. But we'll root the whoresons out of these parts, too; see if we don't."

"Good day, sir," Hajjaj said, and left Ansovald's chamber. He thought Ansovald said something after he closed the door, but didn't bother going back to find out; the Unkerlanter sounded unhappy with the world.

Sighing, Hajjaj went downstairs and out of the hostel. He was unhappy with the world, too. Zuwayza wouldn't be able to get out of the Derlavaian War so easily as he'd hoped. He sighed once more. That, all too often, was the way things worked: easier to get into trouble of any sort than to get free of it afterwards.

He made his way back to the ley-line caravan depot. Lying on a ley line was Jurdhan's reason for being. The next northbound caravan wouldn't be heading back to Bishah for several hours. He didn't have a special caravan laid on; the Algarvians might have noticed, and he – and his king – didn't want them to find out he'd been talking with the

Unkerlanters. The redheads would seek to become even more over-bearing allies than they were already.

He wished Zuwayza could have gone on without any allies at all. Then he sighed one more time. That *wasn't* the way things worked, worse luck.

Along with the rest of the Lagoan force on the austral continent, Fernao trudged west toward Heshbon, the easternmost colony the Yaninans had carved out for themselves on the northern coast of the land of the Ice People. He'd visited Heshbon before, after spiriting King Penda of Forthweg out of Yanina. He would willingly – eagerly – have forgone visiting the place again, but nobody'd asked his opinion.

"Well, you were right about one thing," Affonso said as the two mages kicked their way through the snow.

Fernao eyed his colleague and tentmate. "I'm right about any number of things," he said with a sorcerer's almost unconscious arrogance. "Which one have you got in mind?"

"I wouldn't eat camel meat if I had any choice," Affonso answered, "and neither would anyone else in his right mind."

"The Ice People like it." Fernao paused meditatively. "Of course, that proves your point, doesn't it?"

"Aye." The younger mage's sigh sent a foggy cloud out in front of him. "Cinnabar." He made the word into a curse. "No one would ever come here if it weren't for that. I wish I never had, I'll tell you that."

"There are furs, too," Fernao said, as the Lagoans did whenever discussions of why anyone bothered coming to the land of the Ice People began. Affonso proceeded to tell him, in great detail, what he could do with the austral continent's furs. His argument made up in intensity what it lacked in coherence. Fernao laughed loud and long.

After Affonso regained some of his temper, he said, "Do you suppose the Yaninans will come out and fight us this side of Heshbon?"

"Trying to figure out what the Yaninans will do is always foolish, because half the time they don't know themselves till they do it," Fernao answered. That was how Lagoans usually thought of Yaninans. Having been in Patras, the capital of Yanina, Fernao understood how much truth the cliché held.

"Can they hire enough Ice People to give us a hard time?" Affonso asked.

That was a better question, and one with a less certain answer. Fernao only shrugged and kept walking. The idea worried him. By what he'd seen in Heshbon, King Tsavellas' men hadn't gone out of the way to endear themselves to the natives of the austral continent. On the other hand, gold could be endearing all by itself. And the Yaninans hadn't had much luck attacking the Lagoan army on their own.

Two evenings later, just as the Lagoans were making camp, half a dozen Ice People rode up to them on camels plainly a cut above the common stock. One of them proved to speak Yaninan. Not many Lagoans did, so Lieutenant General Junqueiro summoned Fernao to interpret for him. Fernao's Yaninan was also less than perfect, but he thought he could make himself understood in the language.

The man of the Ice People who spoke Yaninan said, "Tell your chief I am Elishamma the son of Ammihud, who was the son of Helori, who was the son of Shedeur, who was the son of Izhar, who was the son of . . ." The genealogy went on for some time, till Elishamma finished, ". . . who was the son of a god."

He necessarily used a word from his own language for that last. Instead of abstract powers, the Ice People believed in men writ large on the face of the universe. Fernao found the notion ludicrous, to say nothing of barbarous. He hadn't come to argue such notions with Elishamma, though, but to translate for Junqueiro. Having done so, he added in Lagoan, "Give him all your forefathers, too." He started to say, *Whether they're real or not,* but refrained. No telling if some of Elishamma's companions understood Lagoan.

Junqueiro did him proud, naming a dozen generations of ancestry. If any of them was fictitious, Fernao couldn't have proved it. The lieutenant general said, "Ask him what he wants from us."

Fernao did. Elishamma told him, complete with histrionics centuries out of fashion anywhere but the austral continent: not even the Algarvians indulged in so much boasting and bragging. Fernao couldn't try to hurry it along, not without mortally insulting the chieftain.

At last, Elishamma ran down. That let Junqueiro ask once more, "And what do you want with us?"

"The mangy ones" — so Ice People spoke of men less hairy than themselves — "of Yanina will pay us gold to fight you. How much gold will you pay us to stay calm?"

"Before I answer, you will allow me to speak with my wise man here," the Lagoan commander said, pointing to Fernao. Junqueiro had chosen just the right lordly tone; Elishamma inclined his head in acquiescence. "You may remain here," Junqueiro told him. "My mage and I shall leave the tent to confer." After Junqueiro had turned that into Yaninan, he got up and went outside with the general. Junqueiro muttered, "Powers above! Don't they ever wash?"

"From all I've seen – and smelled – no, Your Excellency," Fernao said. Junqueiro rolled his eyes. The mage went on, "In justice, this is a cold country. Washing in a stream here, even when the streams aren't frozen, fairly begs for chest fever."

"Feh." Junqueiro dismissed the subject with a wave of his hand which proved that Lagoans, though at war with Algarve, were of Algarvic stock themselves. It also proved he couldn't smell himself any more. His hazel eyes sharpened. "To business. Have the Yaninans really made this offer? If they have, how much have they offered? Is it worth our while to pay the Ice People more? How much harm can they do us?"

"As for the first, I'd say it's likely," Fernao answered. "The Yaninans haven't had much luck fighting us by themselves, so why shouldn't they pay somebody to do the job for them?"

"You'd say it's likely." Lieutenant General Junqueiro clicked his tongue between his teeth. "Can't you use your sorcery to know for sure?"

Fernao's sigh brought forth a large cloud of fog. "In this country, sir, the spells of mages not born here have a way of going awry. They have a way of going dangerously awry, in fact."

Junqueiro gave him a dirty look. "Then why did we bring you hither?"

"Because Colonel Peixoto, back in Setubal, has more enthusiasm than brains," Fernao answered. "Sir."

By the expression on Junqueiro's face, that was mutiny, or as close to mutiny as made no difference. The commanding general visibly contained himself. "Very well," he said, though Fernao knew it wasn't even close to very well. "By your best estimate, sir mage, however you arrive at them, what do you think the answers to my other questions are?"

"However much the Yaninans paid Elishamma, it will be less than he claims," Fernao answered. "He will try to cheat us. No doubt he will try to cheat King Tsavellas, too. Aye, I think it's worth our while to pay him more than the Yaninans do, if we can. And I pray your pardon, sir, for I've forgotten your last question."

"If we don't pay them, how bad can they hurt us?" Junqueiro said.

"On those cursed camels of theirs, they move faster than we do – faster than we can," Fernao answered. "I wouldn't want them harrying our supply route by land, not with the Algarvians already harrying the sea route from Lagoas to the austral continent."

Junqueiro paced back and forth, kicking up snow at every step. He stopped so abruptly, he caught Fernao by surprise. "All right, then," he growled. "Let's go on in and dicker with the stinking – and I do mean that – son of a whore."

Elishamma's face helped him: It was almost impossible to read. His beard grew up to just under his eyes; his thick, grizzled mustache covered his lips. His hairline started low on his forehead, so low that his eyebrows were only thicker tufts at the bottom of it. That left next to no bare skin from which Fernao and Junqueiro could gauge his expression.

But he was not a great bargainer. And he made a mistake: he got greedy. When he solemnly declared the Yaninans had offered him a hundred thousand goldpieces to assail the Lagoan army, both that army's commander and its highest-ranking mage laughed in his face. "All of Yanina put together isn't worth a hundred thousand goldpieces," Junqueiro said. Fernao enjoyed translating that. It wasn't true, not literally, but it matched his feeling about the kingdom.

Elishamma yielded ground without visible embarrassment. Even had he been bare-faced, Fernao doubted he would have shown embarrassment. He had as much effrontery as any Yaninan ever born. "Maybe I was wrong. Maybe it was but fifty thousand."

Fernao responded to that without wasting time translating for Junqueiro: "All of Yanina put together isn't worth fifty thousand goldpieces, either."

When Elishamma lowered the proposed bribe again without loudly declaring he'd been telling the truth all along, Fernao smiled to himself and brought his commander back into the discussion. Junqueiro knew how much the army could afford to pay out, which Fernao didn't. He beat the chieftain from the Ice People down to just over a tenth of what he'd originally tried to get.

"Is it agreed, then?" Elishamma said at last.

Junqueiro nodded and started to speak. Before he could, Fernao said, "Aye, with one exception: what hostages will you give us? These fellows you brought here with you may do." He turned the words into Lagoan so his superior could understand. Junqueiro looked startled, and probably had to work hard not to look horrified, for taking hostages had gone out of style in civilized countries – though rumor said the Algarvians were reviving it in the lands they occupied.

But Elishamma only sat still and then slowly nodded. "I did not know if you would think of this," he said. "You mangy ones are often absent-minded when it comes to such things. Had you not spoken, I would not have reminded you."

"I believe that," Fernao said. "But I have come to this land before, and I know something – not everything, but something – of its ways. What is your fetish animal?"

Again, Elishamma paused. Finally, he said, "I do not think I will tell you. You are a shaman, after all. Foreign magic is not strong here, but I do not care to take a chance with you."

"You flatter me," Fernao said. In fact, odds were Elishamma did flatter him. But his tone suggested he might be able to harm Elishamma if he learned to which animal the chieftain was mystically bound.

"What are you two saying?" Junqueiro asked. Fernao explained. Junqueiro surprised him by finding exactly the right thing to do: he leaned over and patted Fernao on the back, as if to say he was certain the mage could indeed put paid to Elishamma if he found out what his fetish animal was. The chieftain noted that, too. He looked unhappy enough for Fernao to recognize the expression.

Now Junqueiro asked, "Is it agreed?"

"It is agreed," Elishamma said. "You have here Machir and Hepher and Abinadab and Eliphelet and Gereb." He proceeded to give all their genealogies, too. "Their heads shall answer for my good faith." He spoke to his followers in their own guttural language. They bowed to him in acquiescence.

"Do any of you speak the Yaninans' language?" Fernao asked in that tongue. None of the men of the Ice People answered. Fernao shifted to Lagoan: "Do any of you speak this language?" Again, the hostages kept silent. Were they concealing what they knew? How much would it cost to find out? Fernao knew no sorcerous way of learning. He headed into the future as blind as any other man.

Bembo paced through the streets of Gromheort. He was glad to be walking a regular constable's beat today, not going after Kaunians to ship them west – or even east, though he still didn't understand why that one caravanload of blonds had headed off in the wrong direction.

When he remarked on that, Oraste grunted and gave him three words' worth of what was undoubtedly good advice: "Don't ask questions."

Not asking was easier – Bembo had no trouble seeing that. He had nothing against doing things the easy way; he'd always preferred it. And so, instead of asking another question, the plump constable said, "Don't hardly see any Kaunians on the streets these days."

"I don't miss 'em, either," Oraste answered. Like a lot of what he said, that not only didn't need a reply but practically precluded one.

"Here we go." Bembo strode into an eatery. The Forthwegian proprietor greeted Oraste and him with a broad smile that was bound to be false but was welcome anyhow. Then he handed them lengths of spicy sausage and cups of wine. They tossed back the wine and left the eatery tearing bites off the sausage.

"Not too bad." Oraste finished the last of the meat, licked his fingers, and wiped them on his kilt.

"No," Bembo agreed. "They know they have to keep their constables happy, or else the constables will keep them unhappy." That was how things worked back in Tricarico. And the Forthwegians were a conquered people. If they didn't keep Bembo and his comrades happy, the Algarvians could be a lot tougher on them than ever they could back in their own kingdom.

Oraste jerked a thumb at a broadsheet as he and Bembo marched past it. "What do you think of that?" he asked.

The broadsheet showed bearded Forthwegians in long tunics marching side by side with uniformed Algarvians sporting imperials or waxed mustaches or side whiskers or no facial hair at all. Bembo couldn't read Forthwegian to save his life, but he knew about Plegmund's Brigade. With a shrug, he answered, "If these buggers want to blaze Unkerlanter, that's fine by me. And if the Unkerlanters blaze them instead of hurting our boys, that's fine by me, too."

"Suppose the Forthwegians decide to up and blaze us instead?" Oraste said: practically a speech, from him.

"Then we smash 'em," Bembo answered; he liked problems with simple answers. After a moment, he added, "Not too much risk of that, I don't think. The Forthwegians don't love us, but they don't love Swemmel, either. Of course, I can't think of anybody who does love Swemmel – can you?"

"Nobody in his right mind, anyhow," Oraste said, and laughed, more likely at his own joke than at Bembo's. They marched on for another couple of strides. Then Oraste grunted. "Besides, we're cleaning out the Kaunians here. Aye, that'll keep these whoresons happy."

A troop of unicorn cavalry trotted west past the two constables, heading toward the distant front. Some, though not all, of the Algarvians on the unicorns wore white smocks over their tan tunics. Back when the fight against Unkerlant began, no one in Algarve had dreamt it would last into the winter, let alone almost through it. The unicorns' white coats – whiter by far than the concealing smocks – were splotched with gray and brown paint, to make the animals stand out less against a background of melting snow.

One of the cavalry troopers jeered at Bembo and Oraste: "You boys have the soft jobs. Want to trade with me?"

Bembo shook his head. "Not me," he said. "I may be a horse's arse, but I know better than to be a unicorn's, by the powers above." That won a snort from Oraste and another from the Algarvian cavalrymen, who went on riding, his unicorn's harness jingling at every stride.

Oraste said, "I wouldn't mind getting rid of the Unkerlanters." Bembo shrugged again. The trouble with going off to fight in the west was that the Unkerlanters were altogether too likely to get rid of him. He didn't point that out; if Oraste couldn't see it for himself, the burly constable was a lot dumber than Bembo thought he was.

Besides which . . . "Be careful what you wish for, because you may get it," Bembo said. "They're sending a whole great whacking lot of men off to the west." That most likely meant a whole great whacking lot of men off to the west were getting killed or maimed, something on which Bembo would have preferred not to dwell.

And he didn't have to dwell on it, either, for a plump, middle-aged Forthwegian woman burst out the front door of a block of flats and ran toward him and Oraste, shouting, "Constables! Constables!" The Forthwegian word was similar to its Algarvian equivalent; the Forthwegians had never heard of constables till the Algarvians introduced them to the western part of Forthweg, which had been ruled from Trapani for a century and a half before the Six Years' War.

"What's this?" Oraste asked suspiciously. Bembo didn't know, either, and was just as suspicious. His experience had been that Forthwegians didn't look for constables – they looked out for them. The woman spewed forth a stream of gibberish: the handful of Forthwegian words Bembo knew were vile.

"Wait!" he said, and threw up his hands as if stopping an oncoming wagon. "Do you speak any Algarvian?" The woman shook her head. Her massive bosom shook, too. Bembo found the spectacle anything but entrancing. He sighed, then shifted languages and asked a question that obscurely embarrassed him: "You speaking Kaunian?"

"Yes, I speak some Kaunian," the woman answered – she had more of the tongue than he did, which wasn't saying much. "Live next to those nasty people long enough and some rubs off."

Bembo tried to follow her, and at the same time to dredge up vocabulary he hadn't had to worry about since the last time a schoolmaster beat it into his back with a switch. "You wanting to telling me what?" he asked. He gave up on grammar and syntax; if he could make himself understood, he was ahead of the game.

And the woman did understand him. Pointing back toward her building, she said, "A wicked wizard has cheated me out of a week's pay. I wait on tables. I am not rich. I will never be rich. I cannot afford to have a miserable mage take away my money."

"What's she yattering about?" asked Oraste, who either had never learned Kaunian or didn't remember so much as a word. Bembo explained. Oraste's long face got longer. "A wizard? Oh, aye, that's just what you love to do when you're a constable: go after a wizard. Have to blaze the whoreson if he tries to give you trouble. Otherwise, he doesn't just try – he cursed well does it."

"I know, I know. Don't remind me." Bembo turned back to the Forthwegian woman. "Wizard doing was what?"

"What was he doing?" Her bosom heaved once more. Sparks flashed in her dark eyes. "He was cheating me. I told you that. Did you not listen?"

Constabulary work could be exasperating in Tricarico, too. Every kingdom had its share of fools. Bembo remained convinced he met more than his share. He pointed at the woman. "You taking toward he we."

Into the block of flats they went. It was more battered and more crowded than any equivalent back in Algarve. The stairway stank of stale olive oil and staler piss. Bembo wrinkled his nose. The Forthwegian woman took the smell for granted, which suggested it had been there before the Algarvians overran Gromheort.

On the third floor, the woman pointed to the doorway farthest from the stairs. "There!" she said loudly. "The thief lives there."

"Kick it in?" Oraste asked.

"Not yet," Bembo answered. "We've only got this gal's side of it. For all we know, this fellow in there may be right. For all we know, he may not be a wizard at all. Powers above, he may never have set eyes on her before." The woman listened to him in impatient incomprehension. With an unhappy mutter, he started toward the door. "Cover me," he told Oraste.

"Oh, aye," his comrade said, and drew his stick. "Just in case the dingleberry *is* a mage."

Bembo was thinking the same thing. The thought made him carefully calibrate his knock. He was aiming for being firm without being overbearing. He didn't draw his stick, but had his hand on it. When he heard someone moving inside the flat, he didn't know whether to be relieved or alarmed.

After a click of the latch, the door swung open. The fellow who stood in the doorway staring at Bembo through thick spectacles might have been a mage. As easily, he might have been an out-of-work clerk. Comprehension filled his face when he saw the heavy woman behind the constables. He muttered something in Forthwegian that had to mean, "I might have known."

"You speak Algarvian?" Bembo barked at him.

To his relief, the fellow answered, "Aye, somewhat. I should have guessed Eanfled would summon the constables." He looked past Bembo and Oraste and said something to the woman. Bembo didn't know what she answered, but it sounded hotter than anything he'd learned.

He pointed to the woman. "Did you work magic for her?"

"Aye, I did," the man answered.

"What does he say?" the woman – Eanfled – demanded in Kaunian. Bembo, feeling harassed, did his best to answer. The man took over; he spoke Kaunian, too.

"Ask him what sort of magic he did," Oraste suggested – in Algarvian, of course. Again, Bembo tried to translate.

"She wanted to lose weight," the man said – in Kaunian. "I made a spell to take the edge off her appetite. I had to be careful. Too much and she would starve herself to death. No great loss," he added, "but people would talk."

Eanfled let out a furious screech that made doors open all along the hallway. "You cheated me, you whoreson!" she shouted. "Look at me!" There was certainly plenty of her at which to look.

"You were fatter before," the fellow with the spectacles answered calmly.

"Liar!" she yelled at him.

Oraste nudged Bembo. "All right, smart boy, what are they saying?" he asked. After Bembo told him, he grunted, "That's about what I thought. What are we going to do about it?"

"Shake 'em both down," Bembo answered. He turned to the low-ranking, or more likely amateur, mage, with whom he could converse more readily. "Tell this walking pork chop here that we're going to haul the both of you up in front of the military governor, and we'll see if there's anything left of either one of you when he's through."

Looking very unhappy, the bespectacled man translated that into Forthwegian. The fat woman looked even more appalled. Bembo wondered if she was part Kaunian and feared that would come out. She didn't look it, but you never could tell.

"Ahh . . . Do we really have to do that?" the Forthwegian man asked. Bembo didn't say anything. The fellow said, "Couldn't we come to some sort of understanding?"

"What have you got in mind?" Bembo countered. By the time he and Oraste left the block of flats, their belt pouches were full and jingling. If the would-be mage and his dissatisfied customer found themselves unhappy with Algarvian notions of constabulary work, Bembo cared very little. After all, he'd made money on the deal.

Shouldering his axe, Garivald trudged across fields still covered in snow toward the woods out beyond the village of Zossen. Pretty soon, the snow would start to melt. Then the fields would go from frozen to soupy, after which they would dry enough for plowing and sowing. Meanwhile, he still needed firewood.

As he tramped along, he glanced toward a spot in a vegetable plot not far from the house of Waddo the firstman. Zossen's crystal lay buried there. Garivald had helped bury it. If Zossen's Algarvian occupiers ever found out about that, they would bury him. He couldn't dig up the crystal now, either, because he'd have to do it secretly, and that was impossible. He just had to keep on worrying about it.

"As if I haven't got enough other things to worry about," he muttered.

It wasn't as if the crystal would work now. It wouldn't, not here in this magic-starved backwater of the Duchy of Grelz, not without blood sacrifices to power it. But it had connected Zossen to Cottbus – which meant it would connect Garivald to Cottbus, and to King Swemmel. He knew what the Algarvians would make of such a connection: They would make an end of it, and of him.

Once he got in among the trees, he breathed easier. He couldn't see the spot where the crystal lay buried any more, which took a weight off his mind. And none of the redheads could see him any more, either, even if they were looking for him. That was also a relief.

For a while, he didn't have to use the axe much. A lot of big branches had simply fallen off their trees, torn from them by the weight of ice they'd had to bear through the winter. Garivald just needed to trim them and stuff them into the leather sack he was carrying. He found some fine lengths of oak and ash that would burn long and hot in the hearth.

He was trimming the smaller branches from one of those lengths when, all at once, he whirled around, the axe ready to swing. He couldn't have said what had warned him he wasn't alone any more, but something had, and, whatever it was, it was right.

Bandits and brigands prowled the woods. That was what the Algarvians called them, anyhow: Unkerlanter soldiers who hadn't surrendered after Mezentio's men overran them. Some of them were nothing but bandits; others kept up the fight against the redheads. At first, Garivald thought this fellow came from that latter group. But the soldier – he was plainly a soldier – was too neat and clean for one of those men. And Garivald had never seen a hooded white smock like the one he wore. It was too thin to give any warmth; its only possible purpose was concealment.

Realization smote. "You're a *real* soldier!" Garivald blurted.

The fellow in the white smock chuckled. "Well, so I am," he said. "And what are you, friend? For that matter, what village are you from?"

"Zossen," Garivald answered, pointing back through the trees. Eagerly, he went on, "Are we going to be running the Algarvians out of here soon?"

To his disappointment, the Unkerlanter soldier shook his head. "No such luck, pal. I squeezed through the redheads' lines for a look around, that's all. How big a garrison have they got in your village?"

"Just a squad that's been there since they took the place," Garivald said. "But they've had other men coming through – a lot of 'em moving west lately."

"I wish you hadn't told me that," the soldier said with a grimace. "The hope was that they'd run out of men, and that we'd be able to roll 'em up and clean 'em out before the good weather comes back."

"Powers above make it so!" Garivald exclaimed. "Powers above make our powers grow. Powers above make the redheads go." More and more these days, he thought in doggerel. Sometimes it came out of his mouth, too.

"Well, I have to tell you I don't think it's going to happen," the Unkerlanter in the white smock said. "The cursed Algarvians didn't quite shatter the way we hoped they would. We've got a lot more fighting to do before we're finally rid of 'em."

"Too bad," Garivald said, though that sounded likely to him, too.

"And you're the fellow who makes songs, aren't you?" the soldier said. "I've heard about you."

"Have you?" Garivald didn't know what to think of that. His whole life in a peasant village had taught him that drawing notice was dangerous. But, if no one ever heard his songs, if no one ever played them, what good were they?

"Aye, I have," the soldier said. "That's one of the reasons I came this far east – because I've heard of you, I mean. Keep writing them, that's what the officers say. They're worth a regiment of men against the Algarvians."

Garivald's heart thudded in his chest. He didn't think he'd ever felt prouder. "A regiment of men," he murmured. "*My* songs, worth a regiment of men?" He wanted to make a song about that, even if he'd only be able to sing it to himself. Anyone else, even Annore, would laugh.

"Well, I'm on my way now," the soldier said, turning his face back toward the east. "Have to see if I can make it past the redheads going the other way. Shouldn't be too hard; they still don't know what to do in snow." Off he went, as used to the snowshoes on his feet as if he'd been born wearing them.

"Worth a regiment of men," Garivald repeated once more. But then, all of a sudden, he wasn't so glad the Unkerlanter in white had come looking for him. If that fellow knew where to find the peasant who made songs, how long would it be before the Algarvians figured it out, too?

He finished filling the leather sack with wood. Then, bent almost double under its weight, he staggered back toward Zossen. As he neared the village, he saw the man he least wanted to see. And, worse luck, Waddo saw him, too, saw him and waved and limped toward him, putting a lot of weight on his stick.

"Hello, Garivald!" the village firstman exclaimed, as if he hadn't seen the other peasant for the past ten years.

"Hello," Garivald answered warily. He and Waddo were bound together because of the buried crystal. He wished with all his heart they weren't. He didn't trust Waddo; the firstman had been King Swemmel's hand in Zossen, and had always sucked up to inspectors and impressers when they came to the village.

Of course, the Algarvians despised and harassed Waddo for that very reason. Here and there in the Duchy of Grelz, they'd hanged firstmen who did things that didn't suit them. Garivald didn't suppose he wanted to see Waddo dancing at the end of a rope. On the other hand, Garivald had just thought about how Waddo had maintained his tiny authority by aiding those who had more power. If he decided to bend the knee to the redheads' puppet King Raniero rather than to King Swemmel, how could he best ingratiate himself with the Algarvian garrison?

By throwing me to the wolves, Garivald thought. As if he were a mage, a wolf began to howl, somewhere off in the distance. Every few winters, Zossen or some nearby village would lose somebody to a hungry pack that came prowling close. It hadn't happened this year. *No,* Garivald thought. *This year, we have Algarvians instead. That's worse.*

Waddo heard the wolf, too, and grimaced. "I hope he finds a whole company of frozen redheads to eat."

"Aye," Garivald said. He agreed with Waddo – he hoped the wolves found a whole regiment of frozen redheads – but wished he didn't have to answer the firstman at all. Anything he said gave the other man a greater hold on him.

He needed a moment to realize he now had a greater hold on Waddo, too. Realizing it brought him little joy. To use that hold, he would have to betray Waddo to the Algarvians. He couldn't imagine anything that would make him want to do that. No matter how much he despised the firstman, he loathed the invaders far more.

"May next spring and summer be better," Waddo said.

"Aye," Garivald repeated. He started to look back toward the woods in which he'd met the Unkerlanter soldier, but checked himself before the motion was well begun. He didn't want Waddo wondering why his eyes went that way. He revealed as little to the firstman as a fellow cheating on his wife told her.

Waddo limped closer. He spoke in a hoarse whisper: "When the ground gets soft, we'll dig up that crystal and get it out of here."

"Aye," Garivald said for the third time, now with real enthusiasm. "The further, the better, as far as I'm concerned." Getting the crystal away from Zossen would reduce the danger that he'd wind up on the end of a rope.

"Maybe," Waddo said softly, "just maybe, we can even activate it again and get word back to Cottbus of what's going on in these parts."

Now Garivald stared at him as if he'd gone crazy. "Whose throat will you slit to power it?" he demanded. "Not mine, by the powers above."

"No, of course not yours," the firstman said, twisting his fingers into the gesture people used to turn aside words of evil omen.

"Whose, then?" Garivald persisted with peasant common sense. "It'd have to be someone's. We're not close to a ley line. We're not close to a power point, either. They're few and far between in these parts."

"I know. I know." Waddo sighed. "Maybe we could draw enough life energy from sacrificing animals. They used to do that in the old days, if you believe the stories the grannies tell."

"We might, I suppose." But Garivald remained unconvinced. "If Cottbus thought we could power a crystal with animal sacrifices, why did they send us captives to kill and guards to kill 'em to keep the thing going?"

The firstman sighed. "I hadn't thought of that," he admitted. "All right, maybe we can't make it work. But we can get it out of here and bury it in the woods somewhere so the Algarvians don't stumble over it."

"That would be good," Garivald said. "I already told you that would be good. I don't want the cursed thing around here any more than you do." Unlike Waddo, he'd never wanted the crystal in Zossen. He'd liked living in the middle of nowhere. That let him pass his life with only minimal interference from the grasping hands of everyone who served his king.

But the Algarvians had grasping hands, too. And they weren't just trying to seize his crops. They wanted his land and his village and everything he and everybody else had. They wanted Unkerlant, all of it. He could see that. Anyone who couldn't . . . Anyone who couldn't had to believe Raniero was the rightful King of Grelz.

Once the crystal got out to the woods, if it did, he might be able to let some of the men the Algarvians called brigands know it was there. They could likely find a way to use it. Maybe they would cut a few redheads' throats. Or maybe they would cut the throats of a few Unkerlanter traitors instead.

He nodded. One way or another, he judged, they could do the job. "Aye," he said to Waddo. "When the ground turns soft, we'll dig it up and get it into the woods. Then we won't have to worry about it any more." *But the Algarvians will*, he thought.

Raunu swung the hoe, lopped the stalk off a weed in Merkela's herb garden, and chuckled. "I'm getting good at this business," the veteran sergeant said. "Never thought I would. I was a town boy. My mother made sausages, and my father hawked 'em through the streets. So did I, before I got sucked into the army in the middle of the Six Years' War."

Skarnu was also weeding. "And you stayed in."

"That's right." Raunu nodded. He was more than twenty years older than Skarnu, but probably stronger and certainly tougher. "Once the fighting got done, it was easier work for better pay than I'd had before."

"Easier than farm work?" Skarnu asked, beheading a weed himself.

"In between wars, sure," Raunu answered. "And I was good at it, too, by the powers above. It took me a while, but I got as high up as a fellow like me was ever going to get in the army."

As a commoner was ever going to get, he meant. He'd spent thirty years serving Valmiera, and had risen to sergeant and no higher. Skarnu had joined the army with no experience, and immediately became a captain. But then, he was a marquis. As he wouldn't have before the war, he wondered if the rank and file of the Valmieran army would have fought harder against Algarve had a very few able men – his mind reached no further than that – had the chance to become officers.

Merkela came out of the slate-roofed farmhouse. She surveyed the weeding efforts of the two soldiers-turned-farmers with something less than full approval. Taking the hoe from Skarnu, she slaughtered a couple of weeds he and Raunu had both missed. Then she returned it with a flourish, like a drill sergeant showing a couple of raw recruits how a stick ought to be handled.

Raunu snickered. Skarnu felt faintly embarrassed. "I'll never get the hang of farm work," he muttered.

"You're better than you were when you first came here," Merkela said: an endorsement of sorts, but not a ringing one. Then her whole manner changed. Leaning forward, she asked, "Are we going to do it tonight?"

Raunu snickered again, in a different way. Skarnu knew Merkela didn't mean taking her up to her bedchamber and making love to her. He might do that, too, but only afterwards. "Aye," he said. "We are. People have to know that collaborating with the Algarvians has a price."

"Anyone who has anything to do with the Algarvians ought to pay the price," Merkela declared.

Skarnu wondered about that. Where did you draw the line between simply going on with your daily life and collaborating with the redheads? Was a tailor a collaborator if he made the occupiers tunics and kilts? Was the chap who steered a ley-line caravan a collaborator if he took Algarvians around Priekule? Maybe not. But what if he took them in the direction of fighting? What then? Questions were easy, answers less so.

Merkela didn't care to look so hard. She had her answers. Sometimes Skarnu envied her certainty. Seeing the world in black and white – or redhead and blond – was simple, and required next to no thought. He shrugged. In broad outline, they agreed. He knew who the enemy was, sure enough.

As if to echo that, Raunu said, "This Negyu's a bad egg, no doubt about it. He tells the Algarvians everything he hears, and everything his wife hears, too."

"And his daughter's carrying a redhead's bastard, the little slut," Merkela added. "And she doesn't even have the decency to be ashamed. I heard her bragging in the market square at Pavilosta about all the presents her man gives her. I bet she gave him one, too – the clap." No, she didn't need to look hard to hate.

"We'll take care of 'em," Raunu said.

"We ought to make it look as much like an accident as we can," Skarnu said. Blazing Negyu didn't bother him. Blazing Negyu's wife and his pregnant daughter felt different, even if they were as much hand in glove with the Algarvians as Negyu.

"Why?" Merkela shook her head, making her golden hair fly back and forth. "We ought to paint something like DAY AND SUNSHINE on their door, to give the redheads something new to think about."

"If we do, they'll take hostages and they'll blaze them," Skarnu said. That was why her husband Gedominu was no longer among the living.

But she said, "The more hostages they blaze, the more the people will hate them." Anything that made Valmierans hate the occupiers was fine by her. She looked to Raunu for support, since it didn't seem forthcoming from her lover.

But the veteran shook his head. "The more hostages they blaze, the more people will fear them, too." The glare Merkela gave him said he'd betrayed her. Raunu stood up under it without flinching; as a longtime sergeant, he'd stood up under more than his share of sour looks. Seeing that she couldn't sway him, she flounced off. Raunu glanced at Skarnu and muttered something under his breath. Skarnu could not quite make it out, but thought it was, *Better you than me.*

Sometimes farm work made the day pass swiftly. Sometimes, the sun seemed nailed to one place in the sky. This was one of those latter days. Skarnu felt he'd been working for a week before he went in to a supper of ale and cheese and a porridge of beans and sour cabbage and parsnips. Merkela was a good cook, but not even her skill could make the bland supper very lively.

Once it was done, once she'd washed the bowls and mugs and

silverware, she took Gedominu's hunting stick from its hiding place by the hearth. "Let's go," she said.

Skarnu kept their sticks – infantry weapons that blazed heavier beams farther than the one Merkela carried – hidden in the barn. After reclaiming them, they started south down the road toward Negyu's farm. They were all ready to dive off the road and into the undergrowth to either side at the least hint of trouble. The Algarvians had declared a curfew after the murder of Count Simanu, and did sometimes patrol the roads to enforce it.

About halfway to Negyu's farm, the road passed through a wood of mixed elms and chestnuts. They weren't in leaf yet, but they would be soon. Out of the darkness came a soft challenge: "King Gainibu!"

"The Column of Victory," Skarnu replied – not the most original challenge and answer for Valmieran patriots, but easy for them to remember. Getting the right response, four more men stepped out into the roadway. After handclaps, Skarnu said, "Single file down the road. Raunu, you're the best of us – you walk point. Let's go do what needs doing."

They obeyed without argument. To the farmers, Skarnu deserved to be obeyed because he'd been an officer in King Gainibu's army. They assumed he knew what he was doing. Raunu, who'd taught him everything he did know about fighting, understood how ignorant he remained. But he'd given the right order this time, and so the sergeant kept quiet.

The night was crisp, but not so cold as it had been earlier in the winter. It said spring would come, even if not quite yet. Skarnu was warm enough and to spare in the sheepskin jacket that had been Gedominu's, even if that jacket fit him worse than it might have.

As they drew near Negyu's farm, Raunu halted them. "All I can do is take us straight up the road," he said. "One of you fellows who've lived here forever will know of some little deer track that'll lead us straight to the whoreson's back door without the Algarvians ever being the wiser about how we got there."

That produced a low-voiced argument between two of the locals, each convinced he knew the best shortcut. Finally, resentfully, one of them yielded and let the other take Raunu's place at the head of the little column. "Leave it to me," the farmer said proudly. "Curse me if I don't get you there all right."

Maybe the powers above were listening harder than they were in the habit of doing. In the middle of another dark stretch of wood, a new challenge rang out – this one in Algarvian. Skarnu and his men froze, doing their best not even to breathe. Could he have done so in perfect silence, he would have throttled their know-it-all guide.

"Who going there?" This time, the challenge came in bad, trillingly accented Valmieran. Again, Skarnu and his comrades stayed perfectly still. Maybe the Algarvians would decide they'd imagined whatever they'd heard, and would go on their way.

No such luck. After a muttered colloquy, the men from the redheads' patrol began moving toward the Valmierans who'd come to hurt their pet collaborator. Closer and closer came the footsteps, though Skarnu wasn't sure he could see the enemy soldiers.

"Who going there?" another redhead called. *No one*, Skarnu thought loudly. *Go away*. But the Algarvians kept coming. With a moan of fright, one of the farmers who'd joined Raunu and Merkela and him – the very fellow who'd wanted and won the privilege of leading them to Negyu's farm – broke and ran. Naturally, the Algarvians started blazing at him. As naturally, the flash from their beams revealed to them that he wasn't the only Valmieran out breaking the curfew.

Those beams also revealed where some of the Algarvians were. Merkela was the first to blaze at them. A redhead fell with a groan. "Take cover!" Skarnu shouted to his followers, and was proud that his yell came out a split second before Raunu's.

Then Raunu yelled something else: "Reinforcements, come in from the left!" For a moment, that made no sense to Skarnu, who knew too well that he had no reinforcements. Then he realized the redheads didn't know he had none.

Fighting by night was a terrifying, deadly dangerous business. Every time anyone blazed, he gave away his position. That meant blazing and then rolling away at once, before an enemy looking for your beam could send one of his own at you. Skarnu had done it at the front against Algarve, back in the days – how distant they seemed now! – when Valmiera could hold a front against Algarve.

He wished he knew about how many Algarvians he was facing now. Not a company, or anything of the sort, or they would have rolled over his little band of raiders without a second thought. His comrades and he had probably been unlucky enough to stumble across a patrol with about as many in it as they had. But the Algarvians, curse them, would be carrying a crystal. They'd have more men here all too soon.

"We've got to break away," he shouted. But he couldn't slide off into the woods by himself, not without Merkela and Raunu. Keeping low, keeping to what cover he could, he scuttled toward where he thought they were, softly calling, "King Gainibu!"

After a moment, Merkela answered, "Column of Victory." Then, in no small anger, she added, "You idiot – I almost blazed you."

"Well, it's not as if you're the only one trying to," he answered. "We'd better find Raunu and slide away. We won't get to Negyu's tonight, or any time soon."

"No." Merkela's whisper held both ice and fire. "And how did they come upon us just when we were getting so close? Who let them know we were going to visit the traitor?"

That hadn't occurred to Skarnu. On the battlefield, he'd worried about incompetence and cowardice, not betrayal. But Merkela was right. This was – or could be – a different sort of war.

"King Gainibu!" From the darkness came Raunu's voice.

This time, Skarnu answered, "Column of Victory." He went on, "We won't have a victory this time, though. We'd better disappear – if the redheads let us."

"No arguments from me," Raunu said. Had he argued, Skarnu would have thought hard about staying and fighting. But Raunu only let out a glum sigh. "Cursed bad luck we ran into that patrol."

"Bad luck – or treason?" Merkela asked, as she had with Skarnu. Raunu grunted, almost as if he'd been blazed. Like Skarnu, he'd thought of war as a business where the sides were easy to tell apart. Skarnu realized he'd have to do some new thinking.

After the dreadful weather and hard fighting he'd gone through in Unkerlant, Colonel Sabrino found the mild air and bright sunshine above Trapani a great relief. An even greater relief was knowing that Algarve's enemies were all hundreds of miles away from the kingdom's borders, pushed back by the might of King Mezentio's soldiers – and by the might of his mages, though Sabrino did not like thinking about that so well.

He waved to the dragonfliers of his wing, who'd flown back to

Trapani with him, then pointed down toward the dragon farm on the outskirts of the capital. In good weather, with no enemies close by, he didn't bother using the crystal he carried. Hand signals were plenty good, as they had been back in his great-grandfather's days when men first began to master the art of flying dragons.

Down spiraled the wing. One after another, the dragons settled to earth. Groundcrew men ran up to chain the fierce and stupid beasts to their mooring stakes. That would keep them from fighting one another for food (foolish, for they all got plenty) or for no reason at all (even more foolish, but then they were dragons).

Sabrino undid his harness and dismounted. His dragon was too busy screaming at the groundcrew men to pay him any attention. Ground felt good under his feet. Being home felt good, too, even if only for a little while. The sunlight, the color of the sky, the green of the new grass that was beginning to sprout – all seemed right to him at a level far below thought. So did the smell of the air, even if one part of the smell was the rank reek of dragonshit.

Captain Domiziano came up to Sabrino. Saluting, the squadron commander said, "Good to get away from the front for a little while, and I'd be the last to deny it. Still and all, I wish we were going back soon. Powers above know the footsoldiers need the help of every dragon they can get in the sky above 'em."

"We have different orders," Sabrino said, and said no more about that: he liked those orders no better than Domiziano did. Instead, he went on, "Almost two and a half years since we flew our dragons out of here to fight the Forthwegians. I stood in the square below the palace balcony listening to the king declare war, then hurried down here fast as I could go. Some way, things have hardly changed since then. Others . . ."

"Aye." Domiziano's head bobbed up and down. Pride lit his handsome features. "Then we were the oppressed, the victims of the greed of the Kaunian kingdoms. Now we're the masters of Derlavai."

That wasn't what Sabrino had meant, but it wasn't wrong, either. He didn't explain what he had meant; he didn't feel like wasting time talking about it. "I'm going into the city," he said. "I want to freshen up – I smell like a stinking dragon – and pay some calls. We don't fly out of here till three days from now. Things shouldn't fall apart without me around till then."

"Oh, no, sir," said Domiziano, who, as senior surviving squadron leader, would command the wing till Sabrino returned.

"Good." Sabrino slapped him on the back, then headed for the stables to commandeer a carriage to take him to a ley-line caravan stop: the dragon farm didn't lie on a ley line. That could occasionally be a nuisance. Now, though, Sabrino enjoyed the chance to relax as he headed toward town.

He was tempted to go to his mistress's flat and freshen up there. Fronesia would be glad to see him. Since he paid for the flat and gave her lavish presents besides, it was her duty to be glad to see him. But he had duties of his own. If he called on Fronesia before he saw his wife, Gismonda would be furious when she found out, and how could he blame her? She would know he'd go see Fronesia later, but that would be later. He didn't want to hurt her pride, and so, with an inward sigh, decided to keep up appearances after all.

Trapani, set as it was on a broad, swampy plain in central Algarve, had never belonged to the Kaunian Empire. No one could have guessed that by the public buildings, though. Many of them were in the classical style, most with the marble painted, some left cool and white in the more modern mode. In days gone by, the Algarvians had envied and imitated their Kaunian neighbors. No more. The sharp verticals and extravagant ornamentation of native Algarvian architecture seemed far more natural to Sabrino than anything the blonds had ever built.

He hadn't sent a message ahead to let his household know he was coming. He hadn't known he was coming till he got the order to bring his wing east, and had had as few stops as he could manage since then. He chuckled as he walked up to his own front door. If the household couldn't stand a surprise every now and then, too bad. He grabbed the bell pull and yanked with all his might.

"My lord Count!" exclaimed the maidservant who let him in. "My lord Count!" exclaimed one of the kitchen wenches, who, fortunately, didn't drop the tray she was carrying toward the stairs. "My lord Count!" exclaimed the butler, who, with Gismonda, ran the household when Sabrino was away. Over and over, Sabrino kept agreeing that he was who he was.

"My lord Count!" Gismonda said when he went upstairs with the kitchen wench. "This is an unexpected pleasure."

Sabrino bowed and kissed her hand. "Good of you to say so, my dear," he replied. His wife was a handsome, determined-looking woman not far from his own age. He respected her and liked her well enough. As Algarvian nobles went, they had a tranquil marriage, not least because neither pretended to be in love with the other.

"With things as they are in the west, I truly didn't expect to have you back in Trapani any time soon," Gismonda said. No, she was anything but a fool.

"I have new orders. They take me out of Unkerlant," Sabrino said. His wife asked no more questions. That was only partly because she understood that, as a soldier, he couldn't tell her everything. More had to do with the polite pretenses and silences noble husbands and wives used to keep their lives tolerable.

Gismonda turned to the kitchen wench. "Fetch us a bottle of sparkling wine and two crystal flutes." After the girl had gone, Sabrino's wife looked back at him. "And when did you come to Trapani?"

Have you already gone to your mistress, to shame me? was what she meant. She knew how he thought. He'd been wise to come here first: indeed he had. "Not an hour and a half ago," he replied. "If you sniff, you can smell the brimstone reek of dragon on me yet. I want to make myself presentable before going to the palace."

Gismonda did sniff – and nodded, satisfied. "Will you take me to the palace?"

With another bow, Sabrino shook his head. "Would that I could, but I may not. I shall not wait on the king for pleasure, but in connection with these orders I have got."

"Will he change them for you?" his wife asked.

"I doubt it," Sabrino answered. "He trusts his generals – and he'd better, for if they aren't to be trusted, powers above preserve the kingdom. But I hope he will let me see some of the sense behind them, if any there be." Gismonda raised an eyebrow; that let her know what he thought of things.

Better for a hot soak, Sabrino changed into a fresh uniform, one that didn't bear the effluvium of dragon. Then, after a last nod to his wife, he caught a ley-line caravan for Palace Square, the power point – in more ways than one – at the heart of Trapani.

Walking into the palace, he felt a curious sense of diminution.

Anywhere else in the kingdom and he, a count and a colonel, was a presence of considerable consequence. In the building that housed the king, though . . . The servitors gave him precisely measured bows, less than they would have given were he a marquis, much less than they would have given were he a duke.

"His Majesty is not receiving at present," a gorgeously dressed fellow informed Sabrino. "A reception is planned for later this evening, however. Is your name on the list of invited guests, your Excellency?"

"Not likely, since I was in combat in Unkerlant till day before yesterday, but I'll be there anyway," Sabrino answered.

Had the palace official argued with him, Sabrino would have drawn the sword that was for the most part only a ceremonial weapon. But the man nodded, saying, "His Majesty is always pleased to greet members of the nobility who have distinguished themselves in action. If you will please give me your name . . ."

Sabrino did, wondering how pleased King Mezentio would be to greet him. He'd roused the king's ire by trying to talk him out of slaughtering Kaunian captives to power sorcery against the Unkerlanters. Mezentio had been sure that would win the war. It hadn't. No king was fond of meeting subjects who could say, "I told you so."

But there were other things Sabrino wanted to tell Mezentio. And so he nodded his thanks to the splendid flunkey and then left the palace to sup and drink a couple of glasses of wine before returning. When he came back, he wondered if the servitor had just been getting rid of him. But no: Now his name was on the list of Mezentio's guests. A serving woman whose kilt barely covered her buttocks led him to the chamber where the king was receiving. He enjoyed following her more than he expected to enjoy talking with his sovereign.

Flutes and viols and a tinkling clavichord wove an intricate net of sound as background to the gathering. Sabrino nodded approval as he headed over to get a glass of wine. No strident thumpings here. However civilized the Kaunians claimed to be, he couldn't stand their music.

Goblet in hand, he circulated through the building crowd, bowing to and being bowed to by the other men, bowing to and receiving curtsies from the women. He wouldn't have minded receiving more than a curtsy from some of the, but that would have to wait on events: and besides, he hadn't called on Fronesia yet.

King Mezentio seemed in good spirits. His smile didn't falter as Sabrino bowed low before him. "I greet you, my lord Count," he said with nothing but courtesy in his voice. But then, he was Sabrino's age or older; he'd had plenty of time to learn to hide what he thought behind a mask of policy.

"I am very pleased to meet you, your Majesty, though only briefly and in passing, as it were," Sabrino replied, bowing again.

"Briefly, eh?" Mezentio said. He planned Algarve's grand strategy; he didn't keep in mind where every colonel commanding a wing of dragons was going.

"Aye," Sabrino said. "My men and I are ordered across the Narrow Sea, to help the Yaninans in their fight with Lagoas. If your Majesty will pardon my frankness, I think we could do better fighting the Unkerlanters."

"I have pardoned your frankness before," Mezentio said, now with an edge to his voice – no, he hadn't forgotten their disagreement in Unkerlant. "But I will also say that, unless we keep the cinnabar that comes from the land of the Ice People, your dragons will have a harder time fighting anyone."

Stubbornly, Sabrino said, "There's also cinnabar in the south of Unkerlant, across the Narrow Sea from the austral continent."

"And I intend to go after it this summer, too," the king answered. "But I also intend to keep what I already have, and to do that I have to prop up the Yaninans on the other side of the sea." He sighed. "Since I see none in attendance here this very evening, I can tell you the truth: being allied to them is like being shackled to a corpse."

Any joke a king made was funny by virtue of his rank. This one actually amused Sabrino. Bowing once more, he said, "Very well, your Majesty. My men and I will do what we can to keep the corpse breathing a little longer." That, in turn, made Mezentio laugh – and when the king laughed, everyone around him laughed, too.

Sixteen

Marshal Rathar gnawed on chewy barley bread and knocked back a slug of raw spirits that made his hair try to stand on end under his fur cap. The campfire by which he sat sent a plume of black smoke up into the air. The Unkerlanter soldiers with whom he ate had dug several holes close by, in case that plume attracted a marauding Algarvian dragon.

He swigged again from the tin canteen of spirits. "Ah, by the powers above, that takes me back a few years," he said to the men in rock-gray sitting around the fire. "Does me good to get back in the field, it truly does. I swilled this rotgut all through the Twinkings War. The breath it gives you, you think you're a dragon yourself."

None of the youngsters said anything, though a couple did risk smiles. They saw the big stars on his collar tabs, and couldn't imagine him as anything but a marshal. They had no idea what getting older meant, or how it could change a man – they hadn't done that yet. He'd been young, and remembered what it was like.

He emptied the canteen, then belched and thumped himself on the chest with a clenched fist. That made a couple of more soldiers grin. He could feel the spirits snarling inside his head. Getting back into the field felt so good! Getting away from Cottbus, getting away from the palace, getting away from King Swemmel, felt even better.

"Are we going to lick these Algarvian whoresons right out of their boots?" he asked.

Now the soldiers spoke: "Aye!" It was as much a growl, a fierce hungry growl, as a word.

"Are we going to run 'em out of Unkerlant, out of the Duchy of Grelz here, with their tails between their legs?"

"Aye!" the soldiers repeated, as fiercely as before. They'd been pouring down spirits, too. Asking Unkerlanters not to drink was like asking roosters not to crow at daybreak. Officers did have some chance of not letting them drink too much.

"Are we going to show this so-called King Raniero that King Mezentio stuck on the throne that wasn't his to give away to begin with that we'd sooner hang him – or better yet, boil him alive – than go down on our bellies before him?" Rathar did his best to keep his tone light, but worried even so. Some Grelzers were perfectly content obeying a foreign oppressor, no doubt because, in the person of King Swemmel, they had been compelled to obey a domestic oppressor.

But the soldiers – several of them Grelzers – shouted, "Aye!" once more. They were dirty and ill-shaven, but they'd been moving forward ever since the weather got bad, and there was nothing like advancing to put a soldier's pecker up.

Rathar looked for the officer in charge of the unit – looked for him and didn't find him. Then he looked for a fellow wearing a sergeant's three brass triangles on each collar tab. Sergeants had had to command companies during the Six Years' War, and sergeants had been worth their weight in gold in the desperate fight between Swemmel and Kyot. Some who'd started as sergeants had risen high, Rathar highest of all.

Finding his man, the marshal said, "Tell me your name, Sergeant."

"Lord Marshal, I'm called Wimar," the fellow answered. By his accent, he was out of some village in the Duchy of Grelz.

"Well, Wimar, step aside with me," Rathar said, rising to his feet. "I want to know what you think about things, and I hope you'll give me straight answers."

"I'll do my best, sir," Wimar said as he also got up. He followed Rathar away from the fire. The eyes of the men he commanded followed them both. Rathar hid a smile. No one would give the sergeant any back talk for a while, not after the marshal of Unkerlant asked for his opinions.

Pointing east toward the front not too far away, Rathar asked, "What sort of shape are the Algarvians in right now?"

"Cold, frostbitten, miserable," Wimar answered at once. "They never once expected to have to do this kind of fighting. You'll know about that better than I do, sir. But they don't break to pieces, powers below eat them. You make the least little mistake against 'em and they'll cut off your dick and hand it to you with a ribbon tied around it. Uh, sir." By his expression, he didn't think he should have been that frank. By his breath, he'd had enough spirits to talk before he did a whole lot of thinking.

"I'm not angry," Rathar said. "They've come too cursed close to cutting off the kingdom's dick, Sergeant, and they may do it yet unless we figure out how to stop them once for all. Any notions you have, I'll gladly listen to."

Wimar needed a moment to believe what he was hearing. At last, he said, "I don't know how we'll fare when spring comes."

"All the more reason to push hard now, while we still hold the advantage, don't you think?" Rathar asked.

"Oh, aye," Wimar answered. "We push them back now, then see how far they push us back later."

King Swemmel had demanded that the Algarvians be pushed out of Unkerlant altogether by the coming of spring. That hadn't happened. It wouldn't happen. Not a quarter of it would happen. In the palace, Swemmel could demand whatever he pleased, and it would be his at once. Here in the real world, unfortunately, the redheads also had a good deal to say about the business.

Made bold by Rathar's forbearance, Wimar said, "Ask you something, sir?" Forbearing still, Rathar nodded. The sergeant licked his lips, then continued, "Sir, can we really beat 'em?"

"Aye, we can." The marshal spoke with great conviction. "We *can*. But we have no promise from the powers above that we *will*. The Algarvians may have been too confident when the fighting started." The dismal way some Unkerlanter armies had performed would have gone a long way toward making them overconfident, but he didn't mention that. "I think I can guarantee that the redheads won't be too confident this spring. We'd better not be, either."

"Anybody who thinks anything against Mezentio's buggers will ever be easy is a cursed fool, anybody wants to know the way it looks to me," Wimar said. When he was expressing strong emotion, his Grelzer accent got thicker.

Before Rathar could answer, the Algarvians started tossing eggs into the area, as if they'd decided to underscore the sergeant's words. Rathar had huddled behind burning rocks when he went up to Zuwayza to get that bungled campaign moving forward once more. Now he dove into a hole with a dusting of snow on the mud at the bottom. He knew a certain amount of pride that he got in there before Wimar could.

The sergeant cursed in disgust. "Their tossers have been short of eggs lately. They must have gotten a couple of caravans through."

An egg burst close enough to make the ground shudder under Rathar. "Be glad it was eggs and not Kaunian captives," he said as dirt rained down on the sergeant and him.

"Oh, aye, there is that," Wimar answered. "Of course, they might have brought eggs and Kaunians both. Have we got any old folks and convicts ready to slaughter in case they did bring up some of those poor whoresons – or even if they didn't, come to that? Every little bit helps, is what folks say."

"Every little bit helps," Rathar repeated in a hollow voice. Wimar thought of his countrymen the same way Swemmel did: as weapons, or perhaps tools, in the struggle against Algarve, nothing more. Rathar wondered what the people the king's inspectors routed from their villages thought. Whatever it was, it did them no good. Unkerlanter mages used their life energy as readily as the redheads stole that of the Kaunians.

More eggs fell, a heavier plastering than before. Wimar cursed again. "If I didn't know better, I'd say the stinking redheads were getting their ducks in a row for a counterattack," he said.

"Why do you know better?" Rathar asked, genuinely puzzled. "They've done plenty of counterattacking this winter."

"If they were going to counterattack, I expect they'd already be killing Kaunians," the sergeant answered. "We'd have to get out of this hole, too. It'd be a death trap."

"Ah." The marshal inclined his head. "I should have thought of that. But you have more experience in the field against them than I do."

"More than I want, sir – I'll tell you that," Wimar said.

Before the marshal could reply, cries rang out from the front: "The redheads!" "The Algarvians!" And another shout, more alarmed and more alarming than the rest: "Behemoths!"

Maybe Mezentio's men hadn't been able to bring any Kaunians to this part of the line. No matter what Wimar had expected, they were throwing themselves into the fight without much magic to back them up. And – Rathar looked around – there were no Unkerlanter behemoths anywhere close by.

All through the long, hard winter in Unkerlant, the Algarvians had lost a great many behemoths. Without snowshoes, the beasts had trouble in deep snow. Some the redheads had killed when they couldn't keep up with the retreating footsoldiers, to keep the Unkerlanters from capturing them. Others had frozen. Still others had been lost in action. Mezentio's men couldn't have very many more left down here in Grelz.

Because of all that, Rathar would have thought the Algarvians would use the behemoths they had left with caution. But doing things by halves was not the Algarvian way. When the redheads attacked, they still came at their foes with as much panache as they had when the war was new.

Peering out of the hole, Rathar saw half a dozen behemoths – animals that must have already broken through the Unkerlanters' first line – bearing down on the company Sergeant Wimar commanded. In the style they'd perfected, Algarvian footsoldiers followed the great beasts, advancing through the hole they'd created. "Mezentio!" the Algarvians yelled, as cheerful as if they were breaking into Cottbus after all. Most of them wore white; they were learning.

And Algarvian dragons dove out of the sky, dropping eggs ahead of the behemoths and spreading more chaos among the Unkerlanters. Wimar turned to Rathar. "Sir, if we don't fall back, they're going to trample us."

One of the things of which coming into the field reminded Rathar was how fast everything could turn upside down. "You have my leave, Sergeant," he said. "And if you think I'm ashamed to retreat with you, you're daft."

He scrambled back from one hole in the snow to another. Several times, spurts of steam rose from the snow not far away: the Algarvians were blazing at him. He blazed back whenever he got the chance. He thought he knocked down a redhead or two, but he wasn't the only Unkerlanter with a stick.

Just when he was wondering whether the powers below were going to eat this whole stretch of line, Unkerlanter dragons came flying up in force. They drove away the Algarvian dragons and began to drop eggs on the enemy's behemoths. Where nothing else had, that made the big beasts slow down and let the Unkerlanters bring up enough men to stop Mezentio's soldiers.

"Well, we only lost a couple of miles here," Wimar said as twilight deepened. "Could have been worse, but it could have been better, too, if our dragons had got here sooner."

"Aye," Rathar agreed mournfully. Over and over, he'd seen how much more flexible and responsive than his own forces the Algarvians were. "We need more crystals. We need more of everything. And we need it all yesterday, too." He'd been saying that since the beginning of the war against Algarve. He wondered how long he'd have to keep saying it, and how much finding out would cost.

"Come on," Ealstan urged Vanai. "If you wear a hooded tunic instead of your Kaunian clothes, no one at the performance will pay you any mind."

"I don't want to wear Forthwegian clothes," she said, and he could tell she was getting angry. "They're fine for you, but I'm not a Forthwegian." She stuck out her chin and looked stubborn.

I'm not a barbarian, lingered under the surface of the words. Ealstan felt irritated, too. There were, he was discovering, all sorts of reasons why matches between Forthwegians and Kaunians had trouble. But he was stubborn, too, and he had some notion why her thoughts traveled the ley line they did. Switching from his own language to Kaunian, he said, "I am certain your grandfather would agree with you."

"That's not fair," Vanai snapped, also speaking Kaunian. But then she paused, as if trying to figure out how to put into words why it wasn't fair.

Sensing his advantage, Ealstan pressed ahead: "Besides, you will enjoy yourself. My brother would hold his breath till he turned blue to get into one of Ethelhelm's performances, and this one will not even cost us anything."

Vanai's shrug told him he not only hadn't gained any ground, he'd lost some. "Forthwegian music isn't really to my taste," she answered. He thought she was trying to sound polite, but condescending came closer.

"He's very good, and he's sharp, too," Ealstan said, returning to Forthwegian. "He'd been casting his own accounts for a while till he hired me, and he could have kept on doing it, too – he has the skill. He just couldn't find enough hours in the day."

"I'd be about as interested in watching him do that as I would in listening to his band play music," Vanai said.

Ealstan really did want her to come along. He had one card left to play.

He'd hoped he wouldn't have to play it, but he did: "Did you know Ethelhelm is supposed to have a Kaunian grandmother?"

He'd done some fishing in the Mereflod, the river that ran past Gromheort, and he could tell when he got a nibble. He had one now. "No," Vanai answered. "Does he really?"

"Aye, I think he does," Ealstan said with a solemn nod. "You can't tell it by his coloring, but he's put together more the way a Kaunian would be: he's a little taller, a little skinnier, than most Forthwegians."

He watched Vanai. She was intrigued, all right. "Do you think I could get out every once in a while if I wore Forthwegian clothes?"

"'Every once in a while' is probably about right," Ealstan answered, "but people will be paying more attention to the music at Ethelhelm's performance than to anything else. I can get you a tunic, if you like." He didn't have to worry about precise size; Forthwegian women's tunics were always cut on the baggy side. That was one reason Forthwegian men leered at Kaunian women in their close-fitting trousers.

"All right, then," Vanai said abruptly. "I'll go. I'm so sick of staring at these walls. And" – her eyes twinkled – "my grandfather *would* fall over dead if he ever heard I'd got out of my trousers – and no, I don't mean like *that*." Having headed him off – she was learning how his mind worked, too – she added, "I still don't think I'll like the music very much."

"You may be surprised," Ealstan told her. Then he had to speak quickly, before she could tell him it wasn't likely: "And you'll be out and about in Eoforwic." She couldn't help but nod there.

On the way home the next evening, he bought a plain green hooded tunic of medium weight. Vanai tried it on in the bedchamber. When she came out into the front room, she asked, "What do I look like? We don't have a mirror big enough to let me get a good look at myself."

Ealstan studied her. Even with her bright hair pulled back inside the hood and her face shadowed, she didn't really look too much like a Forthwegian woman. But she wasn't so obviously a Kaunian as she was in her own people's clothing. Ealstan said, "I like your shape more when I can see it better."

"Of course you do – you're a man," Vanai said with a snort. "But will I do?"

"Aye, I think so," he answered. "We'll be out at night, after all, and that will help." Just for a moment, he let himself think about the dreadful things that could happen if someone recognized Vanai for what she was. Were those things worth, could they be worth, risking all on an evening of music? He wondered how foolish he'd been in suggesting it to her.

Even as he was worrying, Vanai said, "All right, then, I'll go. I'd do anything to get out of here for a while, even wear this drafty tunic." The second thoughts Ealstan might have voiced flew out the window. Vanai went on, "And if going to a concert of Forthwegian music doesn't count as *anything*, I don't know what does."

They left for the performance later than Ealstan would have done had Ethelhelm not assured him of a couple of good seats. *The advantages of connections*, he thought. Back in Gromheort, his father had a lifetime's worth. But he used them only sparingly, so they'd be more reliable when he really needed them.

Ealstan was glad to find the night cool. Lots of people wore their hoods up, so Vanai didn't stand out because of that. She kept looking around; she hadn't seen much of Eoforwic before she started hiding in their flat. There wasn't much to see. No street lamps glowed. No buildings had light streaming out through their windows. Unkerlanter dragons sometimes sneaked this far west. The redheads didn't care to offer them nighttime targets.

At the hall – only an angular shape in the darkness – he and Vanai had to pass through two black curtains before coming into the light. When he finally did, what seemed a sudden harsh glare made his eyes momentarily fill with tears. He gave his name at the entrance, Vanai hanging back while he talked to the fellow there.

After checking a list, the gatekeeper shouted for a flunky. "Take these people down front," he said. "They're friends of the band." Ealstan preened. He wished he could let the whole world see what a pretty girl he had with him. Unfortunately, that would have let the whole world see Vanai was a Kaunian. He took her hand and hurried after the impatient youth who led them to where they were supposed to sit.

"Here you go, buddy," the kid said to him, and waited expectantly. As soon as Ealstan tipped him, he hustled away.

"The seats couldn't be better," Vanai said. Ealstan nodded. Two steps and they could have scrambled up on to the stage. Some of the halls where Ethelhelm played allowed dancing; this one, with permanent seats fixed to the floor, didn't. Ealstan waited for Vanai to add something like, *Now if only I wanted to see the show*, but she didn't.

A lot of people filling up the first row had more money than Ealstan had dreamt of even when he was living back in Gromheort, where his family had been prosperous. Men wore fur-trimmed cloaks; jewels glittered on women. Some of those people gave him and Vanai curious looks, as if wondering how they'd managed to get the seats they had. Vanai kept tugging at her hood, to show as little of her features as she could.

And then, to Ealstan's relief, the house lamps faded, leaving only the stage awash in light. The roar of the crowd packing the hall behind him washed forward. When Ethelhelm and his band stepped into the light, the noise redoubled again.

One by one, the men on trumpet and flute, on viol and double viol, began tuning up. When the piper added his instrument's whining drone, Vanai nodded; bagpipes were part of the classical Kaunian tradition, too. Crouched behind his drums, Ethelhelm seemed shorter and more solid than he had striding out on to the stage.

But then he stood up again, and used to good advantage the height his Kaunian ancestry gave him. Stretching out his hands to the crowd, he asked, "Are you ready?"

"Aye!" The shout – in which Ealstan joined – was deafening. But Ealstan noticed that Vanai sat quiet beside him.

Ethelhelm nodded to the rest of the band, once, twice, three times. He brought his drumsticks down hard as they went into their first song. Forthwegian music didn't have the thumping beat that characterized Kaunian tunes. Neither was it one aimless tootling and tinkling noise after another, which was how Algarvian music struck Ealstan's ears. Strong and sinuous, it had a power all its own – at least, as far as he was concerned.

He couldn't see much of Vanai's face: she still kept the hood pulled forward. But the way she sat told him she was anything but entranced with the music. He sighed. He wanted her to enjoy what he enjoyed.

The first several songs the band played were old favorites. One of them, King Plegmund's Quickstep, went back four hundred years, back to the days when Forthweg was mightier than either Unkerlant or Algarve. Hearing it made Ealstan proud and worried at the same time: This was the Plegmund after whom the Algarvians had named their puppet brigade. Now Ealstan didn't want to know what Vanai was thinking.

But after the Quickstep was done, Ethelhelm grinned and called, "Enough of the stuff they put your granddad to sleep with. Do you want to hear something new now?"

"Aye!" This time, the crowd roared even louder than it had when asking the band to begin. Again, though, Vanai sat on her hands.

She stayed indifferent through the first couple of new tunes, even though they were the ones that had put the band on the map. But then, as Ethelhelm flailed away at his drums, his voice went low and raspy as he broke into a brand-new song, one so new Ealstan had never heard it before:

> "Doesn't matter, the color of your hair.
> Doesn't matter, the kind of clothes you wear.
> Doesn't matter – believe me, they don't care.
> They're gonna grab you, and they'll send you over there."

The beat was strong and insistent, about as close to a Kaunian style as Forthwegian music came. People who wanted to could lose themselves in that beat and pay no attention to the words Ethelhelm was singing. Ealstan almost did, but only almost. And Vanai . . . Vanai leaned forward as if drawn by a lodestone.

She turned to Ealstan. "He can't say that!" she exclaimed. "What's going to happen to him if he says things like that? Doesn't he think the Algarvians are listening? Doesn't he think some of the people in here will tell them every word he sings? He's mad!" But she was smiling. For the first time in the performance, she was smiling. "He's mad, aye, but, oh, he's brave."

"I hadn't thought of it like that," Ealstan said. But then, he wasn't a Kaunian, or even part Kaunian. To Vanai, a song that said whether you were blond or dark didn't matter had to hit with the force of a bursting egg. And such a song had to hit hard in Eoforwic, too: Forthwegians and Kaunians had both rioted against the redheads here.

When the song ended, Vanai cheered louder than anyone, though she stayed careful of her hood. She turned and gave Ealstan a quick kiss, saying, "You were right after all. I'm very glad I came."

★

Setubal felt different from the way it had during Cornelu's last time of exile there. Then Lagoas had been at war with Algarve, aye, but hadn't seemed to take the fight seriously. Her navy and the Strait of Valmiera protected her from invasion, and she'd been looking east as well as toward Sibiu and the mainland of Derlavai, fearful lest Kuusamo spring on her back if she committed herself to the fight against Mezentio. It had been enough to drive Cornelu and his fellow Sibian refugees wild.

No more. If Lagoas didn't have an army fighting on the mainland, she did have one fighting in the land of the Ice People. And she and Kuusamo were assuredly on the same side now – and what had happened to Yliharma made everyone in Setubal shudder. The Algarvians could have attacked the capital of Lagoas instead. For that matter, they could attack Setubal yet. Maybe they were just pausing to gather more Kaunians to kill.

"It is good to see the Lagoans worried," Cornelu said to Vasiliu, another exile, as they sat together in the barracks assigned to Sibian naval men who'd managed to escape their kingdom.

"It is always good to see Lagoans worried," his countrymen answered. They both chuckled, neither with much humor. Lagoas had stayed neutral in the Derlavaian War till the Algarvians overran Sibiu. That rankled. And, though Lagoas and Sibiu had fought on the same side in the Six Years' War, they were old enemies and rivals, being too much alike to make good friends. Lagoas, however, had for the past couple of hundred years been bigger and stronger.

"To be just, we should be worried here, too," Cornelu said. "If these Algarvians unleash their sorcery against Setubal, do you think it will spare us because we were born in Sibiu?"

"Nothing Mezentio does is meant to spare Sibians," Vasiliu snarled. Like Cornelu, like most from the five islands off the southern coast of Algarve, he had a long, dour face, a face on which anger and worry fit more readily than good cheer. He was scowling now. "What I wonder is whether the happy-go-lucky Lagoans are doing anything to stop Mezentio from serving them as he served Yliharma."

"I wonder if they *can* do anything – short of slaughtering people, I mean," Cornelu said. "And if they start slaughtering people, how are they different from Mezentio's cursed mages?"

"How? I'll tell you how, by the powers above: they're on our side," Vasiliu answered. "Swemmel won't let the Algarvians kick him without kicking back. Why should anyone else?"

"We'll all be monsters by the time this war ends, if it ever does." Cornelu rose from his cot. With training that had been enforced with switches during his cadet days, he smoothed the blanket so no one could see the wrinkles his backside had made. "And the Lagoans won't kill Kaunians like Mezentio, and they won't kill their own like Swemmel. So what does that leave them?"

"A kingdom in trouble," Vasiliu said at once.

Cornelu paced back and forth, back and forth. "They ought to be able to do *something*," he said, though he knew that wasn't necessarily so: sometimes – too often – there was no help for a situation. The image of Costache burned through his mind. He wondered which of the Algarvian officers quartered on her she was sleeping with. He wondered if she was sleeping with all of them. He wondered if he would have to greet a bastard or two when he came back to Tirgoviste, if he ever did.

Vasiliu pulled him back to the here-and-now by bluntly asking, "What?"

"Curse me if I know. I'm no mage," Cornelu replied. "And if I were a mage with an answer, I'd go to King Vitor, not to you." He paused. "I knew a Lagoan mage who might give me answers, though, if he's got any. I brought him back from the land of the Ice People on levianthanback."

"If he doesn't give you anything you want after that, visiting the austral continent has frozen his heart," Vasiliu exclaimed. "A ghastly place, by everything I've ever heard and read."

"What I saw of it doesn't make me want to argue with you," Cornelu agreed. "I'll see if I can hunt up this Fernao."

Cornelu remained a puzzle piece that didn't fit after his long-delayed and unexpected return from Tirgoviste. Till the Lagoans figured out how they were going to try to get him killed next, his time was his own. He sighed as he left the barracks where the Sibian exiles were quartered. Inside, he had his own language, his own countrymen. Outside was another world, one where he didn't feel he belonged.

Even the signs were strange. Aye, Lagoan was an Algarvic language like Sibian and Algarvian, but unlike its cousins it had borrowed heavily from both Kaunian and Kuusaman and swallowed most of the declensions and conjugations the other two languages used. That meant Cornelu could pick out words here and there, but had trouble deciphering whole sentences.

He went up to a constable, waited to be noticed, and asked, "Guild of Mages?" He would have had no trouble putting the question in Algarvian, but that probably would have got him arrested as a spy. Whenever he tried speaking Lagoan, he had to hope he was making himself understood.

The kilted constable frowned, then brightened. "Oh, the Guild of *Mages*," he said. To Cornelu, the Lagoan's words sounded the same as his own. Evidently, they didn't to the constable. The fellow launched into a long explanation, of which Cornelu got perhaps one word in five.

"Slowly!" he said, in more than a little desperation.

For a wonder, the Lagoan did slow down. In fact, he began speaking as if to an idiot child. No doubt that was patronizing. Cornelu didn't mind. After two or three repetitions, he learned which caravan line he needed to take to get to the Guild's headquarters. He bowed his thanks and went off to the corner – three blocks up, one block over, as the constable had said, and said, and said – at which the ley-line caravan would stop.

More ley lines came together in and around Setubal than anywhere else in the world. That was one reason why Setubal was the commercial capital of the world. But Setubal had been the greatest trading city in the world even back in the days of sailing ships and horse-drawn wains. It boasted a grand harbor, the Mondego River offered communication inland, and the Lagoans were not in the habit of disrupting their kingdom with internecine strife.

Too bad, Cornelu thought. *Sibiu would have been stronger if they were.* It was a relief when the caravan car came gliding up; he didn't have to go on with such gloomy reflections. He stepped up into the car, threw a copper in the fare box – the conductor's watchful eye made sure he did – and sat down on one of the hard, not particularly comfortable seats.

Ten minutes later, he got off the caravan car and crossed the street to the Grand Hall of the Lagoan Guild of Mages. It was a splendid white marble building in uncompromising neoclassical style, as were the statues in front of it. Had they and the hall been painted instead of remaining pristine, they might have come straight from the heyday of the Kaunian Empire.

The splendor inside the Grand Hall proclaimed louder than words that the Guild of Mages had been very successful for a very long time. When Cornelu asked the first mage he saw in what he thought was Lagoan how to find Fernao, the fellow stared at him in incomprehension, then put a return question to him: "Sir, do you speak Kaunian?"

"Badly," Cornelu answered. Scholars kept it alive to use among themselves, but he was a navy man, and had forgotten most of what he'd learned. Frowning in concentration, he tried to ask the question in the classical tongue.

He was sure he'd made a hash of the grammar, but the mage didn't criticize him. Instead, still speaking Kaunian, the Lagoan said, "I think you had better come with me." Cornelu wasn't sure he'd got that, but then the fellow turned and gestured, a language more universal even than Kaunian.

Instead of getting his question answered, Cornelu found himself conducted to a very impressive office with an even more impressive door, at the moment closed. Sitting in front of it, behind a desk wide as a ship's desk, was a clever-looking man going through papers. He looked up and exchanged words in Lagoan with Cornelu's guide. The Lagoan mage turned back and spoke in Kaunian: "Sir, this is Brinco, secretary to Grandmaster Pinhiero. He will help you."

Cornelu bowed. "My thanks."

He'd spoken only a couple of words, but Brinco looked alert. "Sibian?" he asked, and Cornelu nodded. Brinco switched languages, saying, "You will speak Algarvian, then," and Cornelu nodded again. This time, so did the secretary. "Good. We can talk. I read your tongue, but can't claim to speak it, and you have trouble with mine. What is it that you want with Fernao?"

"It does not have to be him, your Excellency—" Cornelu began.

"I am not an Excellency," Brinco answered. "Grandmaster Pinhiero is an Excellency."

"However you like," Cornelu answered. "But Fernao and I have met each other, so I thought I could ask him how you Lagoans will keep Algarve from doing to Setubal what she did to Yliharma."

"It is a good question," Brinco agreed. "But Fernao is not here to answer it; he is with his Majesty's forces on the austral continent."

"Ah," Cornelu said. "He was there, and came off, and now is back. I pity him. All right, sir, since I have been brought before you, I will ask you the question I would have asked him, and hope to learn from your answer."

"My answer is, we are doing everything we can, and we think it will help," Brinco said. "And my further answer is that I have no further answer. I pray you will forgive me, sir, for pointing out that, until my distinguished colleague brought you hither, I had not had the honor of making your acquaintance, even if Fernao did mention you in the report he prepared on his return to Lagoas."

"You do not trust me, you mean," Cornelu said slowly.

Brinco inclined his head. "It grieves me to say that is exactly what I mean. I intend no disrespect, but I will not put my kingdom's secrets in the hands of those whose trustworthiness I know less well than I might like. Such is life in these troubled times, I fear."

By his expression, he half expected Cornelu to take the matter further, perhaps through seconds. But the exiled Sibian officer gave back the same sort of seated bow he had received. "You make good sense, sir," he said, to Brinco's obvious relief. "Lagoans have a name among us for loose talk." Lagoan women had a name for looseness, too – but, after Costache, Cornelu preferred not to dwell on that. He went on, "I am glad to see this name is not altogether deserved."

"No, not altogether." Brinco's voice was dry. "We do the best we can."

"May it be good enough," Cornelu said. His best back home hadn't been good enough. Now he was back in the war. For that, at least, he'd been trained.

Back in Kajaani, Pekka wished she'd never gone north to Yliharma. It wouldn't have made any difference, of course: the Algarvians would have sorcerously assailed the capital of Kuusamo even if she hadn't been there to try her experiment. When she thought logically, she understood that. But logic went only so far. She still had the prickles-on-the-back-of-the-neck feeling that King Mezentio's mages had known what she was doing and timed their attack to foil her.

"That's nonsense," her husband said. "If they'd been after you then, they'd still be after you. They haven't been, so they weren't."

Leino was calm and logical, excellent traits in a mage – and an excellent mage he was, too, of a far more practical bent than Pekka. Most of the time, his solid good sense would have reassured Pekka, as it was meant to do. Now, though, it irritated her. "I know that," she snapped. "Up here, I know it." She tapped her forehead. "Down here, though" – she rubbed her belly – "it's a different business."

Wisely, Leino changed the subject. "When do you think you'll be ready to run your experiment again?"

"I don't know," she answered. "I just don't know. I'll need Siuntio and Ilmarinen to back me up, and powers above only knows when they'll both be able to get down here. And even if they do . . ." Her voice trailed away. She looked unhappy.

"Things would be better if the fall of the palace up there hadn't caught Prince Joroinen, wouldn't they?" Leino asked gently.

Pekka nodded. That was part of what ate at her, sure enough. "He was the one who really brought us all together," she said. "He was the one who believed we could do it, and who made other people believe it, too. Without him, our funds are liable to dry up." She rolled her eyes. "Without him, I'm already starting to have trouble with the distinguished Professor Heikki again."

The mage who presided over thaumaturgical studies at Kajaani City College was a specialist in veterinary sorcery. The next new idea she had would be her first. Irked that she couldn't learn more about the work Pekka was doing, she'd tried to cut off the theoretical sorcerer's experimental budget. Prince Joroinen had put a stop to that, and made Heikki remember for a moment that there was more to being a mage than attending departmental meetings. With him gone, the department head was already starting to reexert her petty authority.

Before Pekka could say anything more, a crash from the other end of the house sent her and Leino running to see what had made it. They almost ran over their son – Uto was coming their way as fast as they were going his. He barely had the chance to assume his usual look of almost supernatural innocence before his father snapped, "What was that noise?"

"I don't know," he answered, sounding as self-righteous as only a six-year-old could.

Pekka took up the challenge: "Well, what were you doing in the kitchen?"

"Nothing," Uto replied.

Leino took him by the shoulder and turned him around, saying, "That's what you always tell us, and it's never true. Let's go have a look."

Everything looked fine . . . till Pekka opened the pantry door. Somehow or other, a whole shelf had fallen down there, with all the groceries on it, and made quite a mess. "How did this happen?" she asked in tones of mingled horror and admiration.

"I don't know," Uto repeated in tones like a silver bell.

"You've been climbing again," Leino said. "You knew what would happen if you went climbing again."

Of course, Uto knew. Of course, he'd never thought it would matter. He'd no doubt managed to convince himself he'd never get caught no matter how often he did what he wasn't supposed to do. *Amazing how much like grownups children are some ways*, Pekka thought.

And, now that he had been caught, Uto reacted just as an adult would have. "Don't do it, Father!" he wailed, recalling all too well the promised punishment. "I'll be good. I promise I will."

"You've already promised," Leino told him. "You broke your promise after you made it. That's not something Kuusamans should ever do. And so your stuffed leviathan will go up on the mantel for a week." He started for his son's bedchamber.

"No!" Uto howled, and burst into tears. "It's not fair!"

"Aye, it is," Pekka said. "You didn't keep your word. How can we trust you if you don't keep your word?"

Uto was paying no attention to her or anything but his catastrophic loss. "I can't sleep without my tiny leviathan under my chin!" he cried. "How can I go to sleep without my leviathan?" He stamped his foot.

"You'll have to find out, won't you?" Pekka said evenly. She dreaded putting him to bed without his special toy, too, but she didn't want him to see that. "Maybe next time you'll think a little more before you do something we've told you not to."

"I'll be good!" Uto sounded as desperate as a bureaucrat caught with his hand in the till. Leino's footsteps coming up the hall announced the imminence of the tragedy ahead. Uto ran off to try to tackle him. "My leviathan!"

Following her son, Pekka wished her sister's husband had never bought Uto the stuffed toy. But if Olavin hadn't given him that one, he would have grown attached to some other stuffed animal: he had a good many. "It's over. It's done," Leino told him. "Go back to your room till you can go around without snot and tears dribbling down your face."

"I won't ever stop crying! Not ever!" Uto shouted, but off he went. A silence, as of a battlefield after the fighting has moved on, filled the front room.

"Whew!" Leino said, and made as if to wipe sweat from his forehead. "I'm going to get myself a thimble of brandy. I've earned it. That could have been him crashing down as easily as the shelf, you know."

"I certainly do," Pekka said. "As long as you're heading back toward the kitchen, pour me one, too, will you? Sooner or later, I'll think about putting the pantry to rights, but not just yet."

Noisy grief still came from Uto's room. Some of it was real, some sent forth at the top of the little boy's lungs to make his parents as unhappy as he was. Leino and Pekka both ignored him. Her sister and brother-in-law lived next door; if they heard Uto making a horrible racket, they would figure he had it coming, not that his parents were thrashing him to within an inch of his life.

Leino came back with two shots of pear brandy. He handed one to Pekka, then raised the other high. "Here's to all of us living through another one."

"I'll gladly drink to that," Pekka said. The pear brandy ran down her throat like sweet fire. She glanced over toward the stuffed leviathan, now lying dejected above the hearth, and started to laugh. But the laughter didn't want to come: She was thinking not only of Uto's outburst but also of the disaster the Algarvians had visited upon Yliharma. She'd come through that, and so had her sorcerous colleagues, but far too many in the capital hadn't.

Something of what was going through her mind must have shown on her face, for Leino said, "I'm glad you lived through that one," and gave her a hug.

"You're not the only one," she said fervently. She held Leino for a moment, just doing that, not thinking about anything else. But then, even with his arms around her, she shook her head. "So much work wasted. If only they'd chosen to wait another day. But they didn't, and so . . ." She shrugged.

Leino squeezed her again, then let her go. He still didn't know exactly what she was working on, but had no trouble figuring out that it was something important. He did his best to reassure her, saying, "I still don't believe the Algarvians know or care what you're about."

"Why?" she demanded. "How can you know, any more than I can?"

"Oh, I don't know," he admitted, "but I still don't believe it. And I'll tell you why: Look how many talented mages they must be using to forge the spells that use the life energy they release when they kill Kaunians. And their very best mages must be busy devising those spells. How could they have anything much left to try to travel along other ley lines?"

Pekka pondered that. Slowly, she nodded. "It makes sense," she said, but then checked herself. "It makes sense to me. Whether it makes sense in Trapani, I couldn't begin to say."

"If the Algarvians cared about what makes sense, they never would have started slaughtering Kaunians in the first place," her husband said. Pekka nodded again. But Leino, like a lot of Kuusamans, had the knack of seeing the other fellow's point of view. "I suppose they thought they'd only have to do it a couple of times, and then the war would be as good as won. But it didn't work out that way."

"No. Things too often don't work out the way you think they will." Pekka pointed down the hall. "That's what Uto found out just now."

"He's quieted down some," Leino said in no small relief.

"He couldn't stay that loud for very long, not even for his leviathan," Pekka said. "A good thing, too, or he'd drive us all mad." She cocked her head to one side, listening. "He's *very* quiet. I wonder if he's fallen asleep in there."

"Either that or he's getting ready to burn the house down and doesn't want us bothering him till after the fire starts." Leino sounded as if he were joking, but also as if he wouldn't necessarily put it past his son.

Pekka found herself sniffing. When she realized what she was doing, she made a face at her husband. "Uto!" she called. "What are you doing in there?"

"Nothing," he answered, as sweetly as he always did when he didn't feel like admitting what he was up to. He wasn't asleep, anyhow. And he couldn't get into too much mischief in his own room, or Pekka hoped not. She sniffed again. No, she didn't smell smoke.

Someone knocked on the door. As she wouldn't have done if she and Leino hadn't been talking about the Algarvians, Pekka looked out the window before she worked the latch. No redheaded assassins stood out there on the snowy walk: only her sister Elimaki and Olavin, the giver of the stuffed leviathan. They went back and forth with Pekka and Leino all the time. Elimaki took care of Uto when the two mages worked, too.

Olavin had sharp eyes. He spotted the leviathan on the mantel and said, "Oh, dear. What's my nephew gone and done now?"

"Tried to destroy the pantry," Leino answered. "He almost did it, too."

"Can't have that," Olavin agreed. "You'd need to borrow from me to put things right if he really did do the job." He was one of Kajaani's leading bankers.

"Maybe we could put Uto up as collateral," Leino said. Pekka gave him a severe look. That was going too far – and Pekka happened to know he'd been a terror when he was a little boy, too.

"Anyhow," Olavin said, "can you turn him loose long enough to let me say goodbye?"

"Goodbye?" Pekka and Leino exclaimed in the same breath. "Where are you going?" Pekka added.

"Into the service of the Seven Princes," her brother-in-law answered. "They're going to put a uniform on me, fools that they are." He shrugged. "I'd just get men killed if I tried to lead them in the field, but I ought to make a decent paymaster. I hope so, anyhow."

"Don't listen to him when he goes on like that," Elimaki said. "He's so proud, it's a wonder his tunics still fit him." She sounded proud, too, proud and worried at the same time.

"A lot of people are serving the Seven these days," Pekka said. "Algarve might have done better to leave Yliharma alone. We would have got ready to fight slower than we are now."

Leino set a hand on her shoulder. "The two of us have been in the service of the Seven for a while now." She nodded. Leino raised his voice: "Uto! Come out and say goodbye to Uncle Olavin."

Out Uto came, as sunny as if he'd never been in trouble. "Where are you going, Uncle?" he asked.

"Into the army," Olavin answered.

"Wow!" Uto's eyes glowed. "You have to kill lots of Algarvians for me, because I'm still too little."

"I'll do what I can," Olavin said solemnly. Elimaki squeezed his hand and didn't seem to want to let go. Pekka sighed. She wished war – she wished everything – were as simple as it looked through the eyes of a six-year-old child.

Krasta was in a vile temper this morning. Krasta was in a vile temper a good many mornings. Had she tried to justify herself – unlikely, since she was convinced she had a perfect right to her moods – the Valmieran noblewoman would have denied the peevish fury with which she faced the world was her fault. Other people's failings inflamed her. Had those around her done better – which is to say, done exactly what she wanted – she was convinced she would have been mild as milk. She'd always been good at fooling herself.

At the moment, the failings exercising her were her maidservant's. The woman had had the presumption not to appear the instant Krasta called. "Bauska!" she shouted again, louder and more sharply this time. "Confound it, where are you hiding? Get in here this instant, or you'll be sorry."

The door to her bedchamber opened. In came the serving woman, moving as fast as she could with a bulging belly that warned she would be having the baby inside before long. "Here I am, milady," she said with an ungainly curtsy. "How may I serve you?"

"Took you long enough," Krasta grumbled. Bauska's belly cut no ice with her, not when a half-Algarvian bastard was growing in there. Said bastard's father was Captain Mosco, Colonel Lurcanio's aide. That left Krasta half scornful, half jealous: Bauska's Algarvian lover was younger and handsomer than her own, even if of lower rank.

"I *am* sorry, milady." Bauska dipped her head. She'd suffered through a great many of her mistress' moods. "I was on the pot, you see." She put her hands on her swollen abdomen; her smile had a wry edge to it. "Seems like I'm on the pot all the time these days."

"It certainly does," Krasta snapped. She suspected Bauska of camping on the pot so she wouldn't have to work. She knew all about servants' tricks. Well, the wench was here now, so Krasta could get some use out of her. "I'm going to wear these dark green trousers today. Pick out a tunic that goes with them for me."

"Aye, milady," Bauska said, and waddled to the closet where Krasta kept her tunics (she had another one for trousers). After pawing through them, she held out two. "Would you rather have the cinnamon or the gold?"

Left to her own devices, Krasta would have dithered for an hour, maybe more, fuming all the while. Faced with a simple, clearcut choice, though, she was all decision. "The gold," she said at once. "It plays up my hair." She stepped out of the thin silk tunic and trousers in which she'd slept – leaving them on the carpet for Bauska to pick up – and got into the more substantial daywear. That done, she let her maidservant brush out her shining blond locks. After studying her reflection in a gilt-edged mirror, she nodded. She was ready to face the morning.

Bauska hurried downstairs ahead of her, to let the cook know she would want a cheese-and-mushroom omelet with which to break her fast. She wasn't wild about mushrooms. She wanted them as much to annoy Lurcanio as for any other reason; like most Algarvians, he had no use for them at all. She intended to dwell lovingly on them when she saw him, almost as if she were a mushroom-mad Forthwegian.

After the omelet and a slice of sweet roll stuffed with apples and a cup of tea, she went into the west wing of the mansion. She might as well have entered another world. Kilted Algarvians dominated – messengers bringing word of doings all over Priekule, clerks making sure those words went to the right official or file, and soldiers and military police who turned words into action.

The redheads eyed her as she went by – she would have been dis-appointed, or more likely insulted, if they hadn't – but kept their hands to themselves. Unlike those Algarvian louts on the Avenue of Horsemen, they knew without having to be told whose woman she was.

But when she got to the antechamber in front of Colonel Lurcanio's office, the officer there was not Captain Mosco but a stranger. "You are the marchioness, is it not so?" he said in slow, careful classical Kaunian, and rose from his seat to bow. "I do not speak Valmieran, I am sorry to say. Do you understand me?"

"Aye," Krasta answered, though her own command of the classical tongue was considerably worse than this redhead's. "Where are, uh, *is* Mosco?"

The Algarvian bowed again. "He is not here." Krasta could see that for herself; her temper kindled. Before she could say anything, though, the officer added, "I am replacing him. He is not returning."

"What?" Krasta exclaimed – in Valmieran, for she was startled out of classical Kaunian.

With yet another bow, the Algarvian said, "Colonel Lurcanio will be making it plain to you. I am to tell you you are to go in to him." He waved her through the antechamber, bowing one last time as he did so.

Even before Lurcanio looked up from the memorandum he was drafting, Krasta demanded, "Where's Captain Mosco?"

Lurcanio set down his pen. As the stranger in Mosco's place had before him, he got to his feet and bowed. "Come in, my dear, and sit down. You are here, and I am here, and that is more than we can say for the unfortunate captain."

"What do you mean?" Krasta asked as she sat in the chair in front of his desk. "Has something happened to him? Is he dead? Is that what that fellow out there meant?"

"Ah, good – you made some sense of Captain Gradasso's Kaunian," Lurcanio said. "I wasn't sure how much you would be able to follow. No, Mosco is not dead, but aye, something has happened to him. He won't be here again, I fear, not unless he is luckier than seems likely."

"Did he have an accident? Did footpads set on him?" Krasta scowled. "I hate it when you beat around the bush."

"And, if it suits you, you hate it when I don't," Lurcanio replied. "Still, I will answer your questions: no and no, respectively. Although I suppose you might call what happened to him an accident, a most unfortunate accident. He has been ordered to the west, you see, to Unkerlant."

"What will he do about the baby when it comes?" Krasta asked: as always, what affected her sprang most readily to her mind.

One of Lurcanio's eyebrows twitched sardonically. "I doubt that is the first thing on his mind right now," the Algarvian colonel said. "I only guess, mind you, but I would say he is most worried about not getting killed and next most worried about not freezing to death. In all the time he has left over from that, he may possibly give a thought to the little bastard yet to come. On the other hand, he may not, too."

"He promised to support that baby, or we would let his wife know about the games he was playing," Krasta snapped. "If you think we won't do that . . ."

Lurcanio's shrug was a masterpiece of its kind. "He will do as he will do, and you and your wench will do as you will do," he answered. "I don't know what else to say – except that, should you find yourself with child, do not seek to play these games with me."

Krasta's head came up. "Are you saying you have no honor? Honest of you to admit it."

Lurcanio got to his feet and set his hands on the desk, leaning across it toward her. He wasn't much taller than she, but somehow made it seem as if she were looking up at him from out of a valley. In spite of herself, she shivered. No one else she had ever met could put her in fear like that. Very quietly, the Algarvian said, "If you are foolish enough to speak such words again, you will regret them to your dying day. Do you understand me?"

He is *a barbarian*, Krasta thought. That brought with it another shiver of fright. With the fright, not for the first time, came a surge of desire. The bedchamber was the only place where she had any control over Lurcanio, though even there she had less than she would have liked, less than she would have had with most men. Luckily for the way she thought of herself, the idea that she amused her Algarvian lover never once entered her mind.

"Do you understand me?" Lurcanio asked, more softly still.

"Aye," she said with an impatient nod, and turned away. Lurcanio had a wife; Krasta knew that. The woman probably amused herself back in Algarve the same way as her husband was doing here in Priekule. *Algarvian slut*, Krasta thought, and did not dwell on what others might call her for lying with Lurcanio.

"Well, then, is there anything else?" Lurcanio said, now in the tones he used when he wanted to get back to his work.

Instead of answering, Krasta walked out of his office. He didn't laugh to speed her going, as he'd been known to do. Instead, he seemed to forget about her as soon as she started to leave, an even more daunting dismissal. She strode past Captain Gradasso. He tried to put some compliments into classical Kaunian; she didn't stay to listen to them.

With a sigh of relief, she returned to the part of the mansion that still belonged to her and her retainers. When she saw Bauska, she frowned. But the frown didn't last long. Here, after all, was another chance to pay back the maidservant for bedding the redhead she would have preferred to the one she had. Of course, now she would have to maintain the brat after it was born, but still. . . . "Come here," she called. "I have news for you."

"What is it, milady?" Bauska asked.

"Your precious captain is off getting chilblains in Unkerlant," Krasta answered.

Bauska had always been very fair. Since getting pregnant, she'd become paler yet; she was not one of those women who glowed because of the new life within them. Now she went white as the wall behind her. "No," she whispered.

"Oh, aye," Krasta said. "Don't you dare faint on me, either; there's too much of you to catch. I have it straight from Lurcanio, and he has himself a new aide, a fiddle-faced son of a whore who mumbles in the ancient language. If you plan on taking this fellow to bed, too, you'll need to bring along a lexicon."

That did make Bauska turn red. "Milady!" she cried reproachfully. "They've sent Mosco off to be killed, and that's all you can say?"

Krasta disliked any histrionics but her own. "Maybe he'll come back after the Algarvians finally beat Unkerlant," she said, trying to calm the servant or at least make her shut up.

Bauska astonished her by laughing in her face. "If the Algarvians were going to beat Unkerlant just like that" – the serving woman snapped her fingers – "why do they all dread being sent west so much?"

"Why, because they aren't lucky to stay in Priekule any more, of course," Krasta answered. Bauska rolled her eyes. If she hadn't been carrying a baby, Krasta would have hauled off and belted her for her insolence. As things were, it was a near-run thing. "Get out of my sight," the noblewoman snarled, and Bauska lumbered away.

Staring after her, Krasta muttered a curse. What a ridiculous notion, that the Algarvians might not win the Derlavaian War! If they'd beaten Valmiera, they would surely smash the Unkerlanter savages . . . wouldn't they? To hold sudden confusion and worry away, Krasta shouted for her driver and headed off to the Avenue of Horsemen to shop.

Spring came early, up in Bishah. The only real mark of it was that the rain that came occasionally during fall and winter stopped altogether. The weather would have done for high summer in more southerly lands. But the breezes that blew down off the hills and on to the capital of Zuwayza promised far more heat ahead. Hajjaj knew the promise would be kept, too.

He had, at the moment, other sorts of heat with which to contend. He had eaten sweet cakes with King Shazli, drunk date wine, and sipped delicately fragrant tea. That meant that, by Zuwayzi custom old as time, the king could at last begin talking business. And Shazli did, demanding, "What are we to do now?"

The Zuwayzi foreign minister wished his sovereign would have chosen almost any other question. But Shazli was still a young man – only about half Hajjaj's age – and sought certainty where his minister had long since abandoned it. With a sigh, Hajjaj answered, "Your Majesty, our safest course still appears to be the one we are following."

King Shazli reached up and tugged at the golden circlet he wore to mark his rank. It was his only mark of rank; it was, but for some other jewelry and his sandals, his only apparel. Shifting among the cushions on which he lolled, he said, "This leaves us still shackled to Algarve."

"Aye, your Majesty, it does." Hajjaj's mouth twisted; he liked that no better than did the king. "But our only choice is to be shackled to Unkerlant, and King Mezentio's chains are longer and looser than the ones King Swemmel would have us wear."

"Curse it, we are Zuwayzin – free men!" Shazli burst out. "Our ancestors did not suffer themselves to be tied to other kingdoms. Why must we?"

That was the heroic version of Zuwayzi history. Hajjaj too had grown up hearing minstrels and bards sing of it . . . but, when he had grown up, Zuwayza was a province – a disaffected province, aye, but a province nonetheless – of Unkerlant. Later, he'd gone to an excellent university in Trapani, and had got a different view of how and why things had gone as they had for his people.

"Your Majesty, our clan chiefs love freedom so well, even now they grudge bending the knee to you," he said. "They would sooner fight among themselves than listen to anyone who tells them they must not. That, of course, is how Unkerlant was able to conquer us: when one clan's holdings fell, the other chiefs did not join together against the foe, but often laughed and cheered to see their neighbor and old enemy beaten."

"I am not sure I see your point," Shazli said.

"It is very simple, your Majesty," the foreign minister said. "By trying to hold on to too much freedom, our ancestors lost all they had. They were so free, they ended up enslaved. We, now, have less freedom than we might like, but less freedom than we might like is better than no freedom at all."

"Ah." The king smiled. "You are at your most dangerous, I think, when you speak in paradoxes."

"Am I?" Hajjaj shrugged. "We are still free enough to make choices about who our friends should be. Things could indeed be worse, as you say; we might have no choices left to call our own. And we have taken back all the land the Unkerlanters stole from us when they conveniently forgot about the Treaty of Blundez – and more besides, to make the revenge sweeter still."

"Aye, for the time being we are victorious." Shazli stretched out a long, slim forefinger to point at his foreign minister. "But if you were so proud of our victories as all that, would you have tried to pull us out of the war?"

"Our victories depend on Algarve's victory," Hajjaj replied. "True, Algarve makes us a better ally than Unkerlant – were farther from Trapani than we are from Cottbus, after all. If I had a choice, though, I would sooner not be bound to a pack of murderers. That is why I tried to escape."

Shazli's laugh was bitter as the beans Zuwayzin sometimes chewed to stay awake. "We've picked the wrong war for principle, haven't we? King Mezentio slaughters his neighbors; King Swemmel slaughters his own. Hardly a pretty choice facing us, it is?"

"No, and I rejoice that you understand as much, your Majesty," Hajjaj said, respectfully inclining his head toward his sovereign. "Since principle is dead – since principle was murdered to power magecraft – all we can do is look out for ourselves. That we have done, as well as we are able."

King Shazli nodded. "The kingdom is in your debt, your Excellency. Without your diplomacy, Unkerlant would still be occupying much that is ours – and would have taken more in the fighting."

"You are gracious to me beyond my deserts," Hajjaj said, modest as any sensible man would be at praise from his king.

"And you, Hajjaj, you are one of the largest pillows lying beneath the monarchy," Shazli said. "I know it, as my father knew it before me."

Other Derlavaians would have spoken of pillars, not pillows. Hajjaj, far more cosmopolitan than most of his countrymen, understood as much. His years at the university in Algarve and his travels since sometimes made him look on Zuwayza's customs as an outsider. He could see foibles other Zuwayzin took for granted. *But so what?* he thought. It wasn't as if foreigners had no foibles of their own.

Shazli said, "We continue, then, and hope Algarve triumphs so that our own advances are not written on sand?"

An Algarvian or a man from the Kaunian kingdoms – likely an Unkerlanter, too – would have said *written on water*. But water, in Zuwayza, was scarce and precious, while the sun-blasted desert kingdom had an enormous superabundance of sand.

Hajjaj shook his head. He was woolgathering again. He did it more and more as he got older, and hated it. Was it the first sign of drifting into senility? He dreaded that more than the physical aches and pains of old age. To be trapped inside a body that would not die, while he forgot himself one piece at a time . . . He shuddered. And he was woolgathering again, this time about woolgathering.

Vexed, he gave the answer that should have come sooner. "If the powers above were kind, we would watch from the north until the last Algarvian and the last Unkerlanter beat in each other's heads with clubs." His shrug was mournful. "Life is seldom so convenient as we would wish."

"There, your Excellency, you touch on a great and mysterious truth, one that holds even for kings," Shazli said. He got to his feet, a sign he had given Hajjaj all the time he intended to spare today.

Grunting, his knees clicking, the foreign minister also rose, and bowed to the king. As kings went these days, Shazli was a good sort: not a sharp-tempered martinet like Mezentio, much less a tyrant fearful of his own shadow like Swemmel. But then, the clan chiefs of Zuwayza ceded fewer powers to their kings than did the Algarvian nobles, while the old Unkerlanter nobility, these days, was largely deceased, replaced by upstarts. Swemmel had so much power because no one around him had any.

After formal farewells that used up another quarter of an hour, Hajjaj made his way through the corridors of the palace to the foreign ministry.

The building was as cool a place as any in Bishah: its thick walls of sun-dried brick could challenge even the Zuwayzi climate.

"Nothing new to report to you, your Excellency," Hajjaj's secretary Qutuz said when the foreign minister poked his head into his office.

"I thank you," Hajjaj replied. He eyed Qutuz, a solid professional, with a wariness he hoped he kept covert. He'd trusted the man's predecessor, who'd proved to be in the pay of Unkerlant. No matter how well his new secretary performed, Hajjaj knew he would be far slower in warming to him, if he ever did. He said, "So long as things are quiet, I think I shall knock off early for the afternoon. Would you be so good as to summon my driver?"

"Of course, your Excellency," Qutuz said. Before long, Hajjaj's carriage was rolling up a narrow, twisting road into the hills above Bishah. Houses perched here were young fortresses, dating back to the days when any clan's hand was likely to be raised against its neighbor.

Hajjaj's home was no exception to the rule. Back in the days before mages learned to liberate great blasts of sorcerous energy, it could have stood siege for months. Even now, his large household included gate guards; no telling when some local lord might try to settle a score that had simmered, unavenged but forgotten, for half a dozen generations.

After the guards let the carriage roll through the entranceway, Hajjaj's majordomo Tewfik came waddling up to meet him. "Hello there, young fellow," Tewfik said, bowing to Hajjaj. He was the only man alive entitled to greet the foreign minister thus. He had been in the household longer than Hajjaj had been alive. Hajjaj thought he was about eighty-five, but he might have been older. As surely as Hajjaj ran Zuwayza's foreign affairs, Tewfik ran Hajjaj's domestic ones.

Returning the majordomo's bow, Hajjaj asked, "And how are things here?"

"Well enough, lord," Tewfik answered with another creaking bow of his own; his back didn't bend very far these days. "Peaceful, one might even say, now that that woman is no longer here."

That woman, Lalla, had until recently been Hajjaj's juniormost wife: a pretty amusement with whom to while away some time every now and then. She'd become an increasingly willful and expensive amusement. Finally, to the relief of everyone else in the household, she'd become too expensive and willful for Hajjaj to stand any more, and he'd sent her back to her own clanfather. Formerly respected for her position, she'd become *that woman* in the blink of an eye.

Tewfik said, "The lady Kolthoum will be glad to see you, your Excellency."

"And I, of course, am always glad to see my senior wife," Hajjaj answered. "Why don't you run along ahead and let her know I will attend her shortly?"

"Aye." And off Tewfik went, not running but plenty spry for a man of his years. Hajjaj followed more slowly through the buildings and courtyards and gardens that filled the space within the household's outer wall. Kolthoum would be irked if he didn't give her enough time to prepare herself and to ready refreshments for him.

When he did step into her chamber, she was waiting with tea and wine and cakes, as he'd known she would be. He embraced her and gave her a peck on the lips. They rarely slept together these days, the scrawny diplomat and his large, comfortable wife, but they were unfailingly fond of each other. Kolthoum understood him better than anyone else alive, save possibly Tewfik.

"Is it well?" she asked him, as usual cutting straight to the heart of things.

"It is as well as it can be," he answered.

His senior wife raised an eyebrow. "And how well is that?"

Hajjaj considered. "I simply don't know right now. Ask me again in a few months, and I may have a better notion."

"*You* don't know?" Kolthoum said. Hajjaj shook his head. Kolthoum raised both eyebrows. "Powers above help us!" This time, Hajjaj nodded.

Seventeen

"Home?" Vanai shook her head. "This isn't home, Ealstan. It's halfway between a trap and a cage."

She watched in dismay as Ealstan's face closed. She was sick and tired of being cooped up, and he was getting sick and tired of listening to her complain about it. He said, "You didn't have to come with me, you know."

"Oh, but I did," she answered. "My grandfather's house was a cage. Oyngestun was a trap. I still do feel trapped" – she was too proud to pretend not to have the feelings she had – "but at least the company is better when you're here with me."

That won a smile from her Forthwegian lover. "Only reason I'm not here more is because I'm working all the cursed time," he answered. "My father would always say the best bookkeepers were mostly here in Eoforwic, because the capital is where the money is. He usually knows what he's talking about, but I think he was wrong this time. If the bookkeepers here were so fine, there wouldn't be so many people who wanted to hire me."

"I don't know about that," Vanai said. "Maybe you're better than you think."

He looked very young then, and very confused, as if he wanted to believe that but didn't quite dare. "My father is that good," he said. "Me?" He shrugged and shook his head. "I know how much I don't know."

Vanai laughed at him. "But do you know how much the other bookkeepers in Eoforwic don't know?"

She watched him work his way through that. "It would be nice to believe that, but I really don't," he said.

"Then why does Ethelhelm want you to keep his books for him?"

Vanai countered, using the singer's name because Ealstan set such stock in him. She set more stock in Ethelhelm than she'd expected, not because of the Kaunian blood he might have but for the Forthwegian songs he wrote and sang.

But her question didn't have quite the impact for which she'd hoped. "Why? I'll tell you why," Ealstan answered. "Because the fellow who used to cast accounts for him walked in front of a ley-line caravan and got himself squashed, that's why. That's why Ethelhelm was doing his own bookkeeping for a bit, too, but he just didn't have the time to keep on." He got up from the table and stretched; something crackled in his back. "Ahh, that's better," he said. "I spend all my time on a stool, bending over ledgers."

Vanai was about to offer him the chance to spend some time in an altogether different position when she saw movement down on the street. She went to the window for a better look. "Algarvian constables," she said over her shoulder to Ealstan.

"What are they doing?" he asked, and then, coming up behind her, set a hand on her shoulder and drew her away from the grimy panes of glass. "Let me look – it won't matter if they see me here."

She nodded and stepped back. Ealstan did his best to take care of her. He stood there, his wide back to her, looking down. "Well?" she asked at last.

"They're putting up broadsheets," he said. "I can't make out what the sheets say, not from up here. Once they've gone on, I'll go downstairs and have a look."

"All right." Vanai nodded. All at once, with the constables passing through, the flat was a refuge once more. "Maybe they're just more recruiting sheets for Plegmund's Brigade." Those, at least, didn't have anything directly to do with her.

But Ealstan shook his head. "They don't look like them," he said. "The sheets for Plegmund's Brigade always have pictures on them, so the people who are too stupid to read can figure out what they're about. These are nothing but words. I can see that much." He turned away from the window, toward her. "Don't worry about it, sweetheart. Everything will be fine."

He didn't really believe that. She could see as much by the lines, deep past his years, that were carved into the skin by the corners of his mouth.

She could also see he didn't really expect her to believe it, either. But he said it anyhow, in the hope, however forlorn, it would make her feel better. And his caring for her feelings did make her feel better, even if she didn't think everything would be all right.

She stepped up and gave him a hug. He hugged her, too, and kissed her. One of his hands closed on her breast. When Major Spinello had done that, all Vanai had wanted to do was tear herself away. Now, though Ealstan was doing the same thing, her heart beat fast and she molded herself against him. It was, if you looked at it the right way, pretty funny.

Warmth flowed through her. But when she started to go back toward the bedchamber, Ealstan didn't come along. Instead, he returned to the window. "They've gone down the street," he said. "I can go down and look at the broadsheets without drawing any notice – plenty of people coming out to see what the latest nonsense is."

"Go on, then," Vanai answered. Putting business ahead of pleasure was like Ealstan. Right at the moment, she wasn't sure she liked that so well.

"I'll be back in a minute," he said. "And then—" Something sparked in his eyes. He hadn't forgotten her, not at all. Good . . . well, better. She waved toward the door.

But when he did come back, his face was as grim as Vanai had ever seen it. Any thoughts of making love right then flew out of her head. "What have the Algarvians gone and done?" she asked, dreading the answer.

"They're ordering all Kaunians to report to the Kaunian quarter here in Eoforwic," Ealstan answered. "They're all supposed to live there and nowhere else in town. Anybody who brings in word of one who hasn't reported to the Kaunian quarter gets a reward – the broadsheet doesn't say how much."

Vanai's voice went shrill with alarm: "You know why they're doing that."

"Of course I do," Ealstan replied. "With all the Kaunians in one place, the redheads won't have to work so hard to round your people up and ship you west whenever they need some more."

"Some more to kill," Vanai said, and Ealstan nodded. She turned away from him. "What am I going to do?" She wasn't asking Ealstan. She was asking the world at large, and the world had long since shown that it didn't care.

Whether she'd asked him or not, Ealstan answered: "Well, you're not going into the Kaunian quarter, and that's flat. Out here, you've got a chance. In there? Forget it."

"A price on my head," Vanai said wonderingly. She giggled, though it wasn't funny – perhaps *because* it wasn't funny. "What am I, a famous highwayman?"

"You're an enemy of the Kingdom of Forthweg," Ealstan told her. "That's what the broadsheet says, anyhow."

Vanai laughed louder, because that was even less funny than the other. "*I'm* an enemy of the kingdom?" she exclaimed. "*I* am? Who beat the Forthwegian army? Last I looked, it was the Algarvians, not us Kaunians."

"A lot of Forthwegians will forget all about that, though," Ealstan said bleakly. "Cousin Sidroc would, I think; maybe Uncle Hengist, too. Kaunians have always been easy to blame."

"Of course we are." Vanai didn't try to hide her bitterness. She might almost have been speaking to another Kaunian as she went on, "There are ten times as many Forthwegians as there are of us. That makes us pretty easy to blame all by itself."

"Aye, it does, though not all of us" – Ealstan didn't forget he was a Forthwegian – "feel that way about Kaunians."

Slowly, Vanai nodded. She knew how Ealstan felt about her. But, from everything he'd said, his father and brother would never have done anything to harm Kaunians – and neither of them had fallen in love with one. Following that thought along its ley line brought fresh alarm to Vanai. "What will the redheads do to anyone who helps hide Kaunians outside the quarter?"

Ealstan looked unhappy. Maybe he'd hoped that wouldn't occur to her. The hope was foolish; the Algarvian edict would surely be plastered all over the news sheets, too. Reluctantly, he answered, "There is a penalty for harboring fugitives – that's what they call it. The broadsheet doesn't say what it is."

"Whatever the Algarvians want it to be, that's what," Vanai predicted, and Ealstan had to nod. She pointed at him, as if the broadsheet were his fault. "And now you're going to be in danger on account of me." That seemed even worse than her being in danger herself.

Ealstan shrugged. "Not many people know you're here. I'm not sure the landlord does, and that's a good thing – landlords are a pack of conniving, double-dealing whoresons, and they'd do anything to put another three coppers in their belt pouches."

In their pockets, Vanai would have said, but the long tunics Forthwegians wore didn't come with pockets. She wondered how he spoke with such assurance about landlords, having lived at home all his life till fleeing after the fight with his cousin. She was about to twit him on that when she remembered he was a bookkeeper, and the son of a bookkeeper for good measure. He would know more about landlords and their habits than she might have guessed.

He went on, "I don't know if we'll be able to get you to any more of Ethelhelm's performances, or anything like that."

When he said he didn't know if she'd be able to go out, he meant he knew perfectly well she wouldn't. Vanai could see that. Even so, she was grateful for the way he phrased it. It left her hope, and she had little else. She looked around the imperfectly plastered walls of the dingy flat. Aye, they might have been the bars of a cage in the zoological garden.

"You'll have to bring me more books," she said. "A lot more books." Brivibas had given her one thing for which to remember him kindly, at any rate: as long as her eyes were going back and forth across a printed page, she could forget where she was. That was not the smallest of sorceries, not when this was the place she had to try to forget.

"I will," Ealstan said. "I'd already thought of that. I'll scour the secondhand stores. I can get more for the same money in places like that."

She nodded and looked around again. Aye, this would be a cage, sure enough. She wouldn't even dare look out on the street so much as she had been doing, lest someone looking up spy her golden hair. "Get me some cookbooks," she said. "If I'm going to spend all my time cooped up in here, cooking will help make the days go by." She pointed at Ealstan. "You'll get fat, you wait and see."

"I don't mind trying," he said. "Fattening me up won't be easy, though, not on what passes for rations these days."

Something unspoken hung in the air between them. *If Algarve wins the war, none of this matters.* Mezentio's men wouldn't need their savage sorceries any more after that, but by then they would have got into the habit of killing Kaunians. And that, as the history of her people in Forthweg attested, was a habit easier to acquire than to break.

There was one other thing she could think of to make time go by here in this little flat. She went over to Ealstan and put her arms around him.

"Come on," she said, doing her best to recapture the excitement that had been growing in her before the redheads ran up their broadsheets. "Let's go back to the bedchamber . . ."

Trasone tramped through the battered streets of Aspang. The burly Algarvian soldier looked on the devastation around him with a certain amount of satisfaction. The Unkerlanters had done everything they could to throw his comrades and him out of the place, but they'd failed. Algarve's banner of red and green and white still flew from flagpoles all over Aspang.

So did another flag, the gold and green of the revived Kingdom of Grelz. Trasone rumbled laughter deep in his chest when he saw a Grelzer flag. He knew the kingdom was a joke. Every Algarvian soldier in Aspang knew the same thing. And if the Grelzers didn't, they were even stupider than he thought.

He snorted. As far as he was concerned, Grelzers were just another bunch of stinking Unkerlanters. If you turned your back on them, they'd stab you. Every couple of paces, he looked around. No, you couldn't trust these whoresons, not even in a town full of Algarvian soldiers.

He strode out into the market square. Along with the rest of Aspang, it had taken a beating. Still, merchants from the town and peasants in from the countryside had set up tables on which to display their wares. If they didn't sell, they'd starve. And, no doubt, some of them took word of what they saw back to their Unkerlanter raiders who never stopped harassing the Algarvians behind their lines.

"Sausage?" a woman called to Trasone, holding up several grayish brown links. "Good sausage!" He would have bet every copper he owned that she hadn't known a word of Algarvian before the war.

"How much?" he asked. Algarvian soldiers were under orders not to plunder in the market square, though the rest of Aspang was fair game. The links looked better than what he was likely to get back at the barracks.

"One silver, four links," the sausage seller answered.

"Thief," Trasone growled, to start the haggling off on the right note. He got his four links of sausage, and paid less than half what the Grelzer peasant woman had first demanded. He strolled away happy. That the woman hadn't dared dicker hard against an occupying soldier with a stick slung on his back didn't cross his mind. Had it, he wouldn't have cared.

The bargain was all that mattered.

He hadn't gone far before he saw Major Spinello heading his way. As best he could with sausages in his free hand, he came to attention and saluted. "As you were," Spinello said. The battalion commander eyed his purchase. "You're supposed to give these Unkerlanter wenches your sausage, soldier. You're not supposed to take theirs."

"Heh," Trasone said, and nodded. "That's funny, sir." Even if the officer did go on and on about the Kaunian girl he'd been screwing before he got sent west, he'd done a good job with the battalion.

Now he took off his hat, waved it around to emphasize what he was about to say, and then set it back on his head at a jaunty angle. "You ask me, though, these broads are too ugly to deserve any Algarvian's sausage."

That just made Trasone shrug. "Even ugly broads are better than no broads at all," he said. He'd lined up for a go at a soldiers' brothel a few times. That wasn't the best sport in the world – far from it – but it was better than nothing.

Spinello didn't have to worry about standing in line. Officers' brothels were a cut above what the regular troopers got. Even so, he rolled his eyes. "Ugly," he repeated. "Every cursed one of 'em is ugly. When I was doing garrison duty back in that Forthwegian town, now . . ." And he was off on another story about the blond girl back in Oyngestun.

Trasone grinned as he listened. Spinello did spin a pretty good yarn. If half what he said was true, he'd trained that Kaunian bitch the way a hunter trained his hound. Of course, everybody lied about women except women, and they lied about men instead.

A few eggs started landing on the outskirts of Aspang, none of them very close to the market square. "Swemmel's boys are right on time," Spinello remarked. Other than that, he didn't react to the eggs at all. He had nerve.

"Think the Unkerlanters are going to have another try at running us out of here, sir?" Trasone asked.

"They're welcome to try, as far as I'm concerned," Spinello answered. "The way we've fortified Aspang since we got driven back here, they could send every soldier they have against us, and we'd kill 'em all before they broke in."

Maybe that was true. Aspang had held out against everything King Swemmel's men had thrown at it so far. But an awful lot of Algarvian soldiers had died holding the Unkerlanters out.

"Besides," Spinello went on, waving an arm, "the snow is starting to melt. For the next few weeks, nobody's going to move very far very fast – except to sink into the mud, I mean."

"Aye, something to that," Trasone agreed. "If Unkerlant doesn't hold the record for mud, I'm buggered if I know what does. Saw that last fall. Powers above, if it hadn't been for the mud, we'd have made it into Cottbus without even breathing hard."

Spinello waggled a finger under Trasone's nose. Trasone scowled. What did the officer know that would make him contradict? He hadn't been in Unkerlant then. He'd been back in Forthweg, happily boffing that Kaunian slut. But Spinello turned out to know more than Trasone expected. Lecturing like a professor, the major said, "Consider, my friend. The fall mud comes from the fall rains alone. The spring mud comes not only from the rain but also from the melting of all the snow on the ground. Which do you expect to be worse?"

As ordered, Trasone considered. His lips shaped a soundless whistle. "We'll be in mud up to our ballocks!" he exclaimed.

"Deeper," Major Spinello said. "But so will the Unkerlanters. Till that mud dries out, nobody will do much. When it does, we'll see who moves first, and where. And won't that be interesting?"

Again, he sounded more like a professor than a soldier. All Trasone said was, "I'm bloody well sick of going backwards. I want to be heading west again." He cared little for the big picture, much more for his own small piece of it. If he was retreating, Algarve was losing. If he was advancing, his kingdom was winning.

"Head west we shall." Spinello didn't lack for confidence. And he had his reasons, too: "If you don't think our mages are more clever than the Unkerlanters', you need to think again."

"Aye." Trasone nodded, then chuckled. "By the time this fornicating war is done, there won't be a Kaunian left alive." And if that included the wench with whom the major had been fornicating, Trasone wouldn't shed a tear.

"Or an Unkerlanter, either," Spinello said. "The ones we don't slay, King Swemmel's mages will. I, for one, won't miss them. Nasty people. Homely people, too, when you get right down to it." He drew himself up very straight. "We deserve to win, for we are better looking."

Did he mean that, or was it one of the absurd conceits he liked to come out with every now and then? Trasone couldn't tell. He didn't much care, either. Spinello had proved he knew what he was doing on the battlefield. So long as that held true, he could be as crazy as he liked away from it.

He thumped Trasone on the back. "Go on. Enjoy your sausages." Off he strutted across the market square, a cocky little rooster of a man. Trasone stared after him with almost paternal affection.

Then, with a shrug, the veteran headed back toward the theater where his company was quartered these days. The name of the play it had been showing before the Algarvians overran Aspang was still up on the marquee. That was what somebody had told Trasone the words were, anyhow. He couldn't speak Unkerlanter, and he couldn't read it, either; the characters were different from the ones Algarvians used.

Sergeant Panfilo had some onions. Even more to the point, he had a frying pan. The company had stolen a little iron stove from a house near the theater. Issued rations had often got erratic during the winter. When the soldiers came on food, they wanted to be able to cook it. Before long, a savory aroma rose from the pan.

One of the other troopers in Trasone's squad, a skinny fellow named Clovisio, came over and stood by the stove, watching with spaniel eyes as the sausages sizzled. Trasone's rumbling stomach made him less than polite. "You think you're going to scrounge scraps off us, you can bloody well think again," he growled.

Clovisio looked affronted as readily as he'd looked cuddly and endearing a moment before. "My dear fellow, I can pay my way," he said. He took a flask from his belt and gently shook it. Its suggestive gurgle brought a smile to Trasone's face – and to Sergeant Panfilo's.

"Now you're talking," the sergeant said. He turned the sausages with his knife, eyed them, and lifted the pan off the stove. "I think we're in business here." The three of them ate sausage and onions and shared nips of the fiery Unkerlanter spirits in Clovisio's flask.

"That's not so bad," Trasone said, chasing a couple of strings of fried onion around the pan with his own knife. He slapped his belly. "Blazes the stuffing out of meat hacked off the carcass of a behemoth that froze to death."

"Or meat hacked off the carcass of a behemoth that didn't freeze right away, but had time to start going bad first," Clovisio said. Trasone grimaced and nodded; he knew the sickly-sweet taste of spoiled meat as well as any other Algarvian soldier in Unkerlant.

Not to be outdone by his companions, Sergeant Panfilo added, "And it sure blazes the stuffing out of going empty."

"Aye," Trasone said. All three soldiers solemnly nodded. Like so many Algarvians in Unkerlant, they'd known emptiness, too. Trasone turned to Clovisio. "Anything left in that flask?"

Clovisio shook it again. It still gurgled. He passed it to Trasone. Trasone sipped, but didn't empty it. Instead, he handed it to Panfilo. The sergeant took a sergeant's privilege and tilted it up to get the last few drops.

For a moment, the three men squatted there, looking at the now empty frying pan. Trasone nodded, as if in agreement to something nobody had actually come out with and said. "That's not so bad," he repeated. "A full belly, a little something to drink—"

"Nobody trying to kill us right this minute," Clovisio put in.

"Aye, it could be worse," Panfilo agreed. "We've all seen that." Trasone and Clovisio nodded. They had indeed seen that.

"Even when it's been as bad as it can be, we get to fight back," Trasone said. "I'd rather be us than a pack of stinking Kaunians in what they call a labor camp waiting to be turned into fuel for magecraft."

"I'd rather be us than a pack of stinking Kaunians any which way," Clovisio declared. "The more of 'em we get rid of, the sooner we lick the Unkerlanters and the sooner we can go home."

"Home." Trasone spoke the word with dreamy longing. He shook himself like a man reluctantly awakening. "I don't even remember what it's like any more, or only just barely. I've been doing this too long. I know it's real. Everything else—" He shook his head. After a moment, so did Panfilo and Clovisio.

Leofsig didn't like the way his father was looking at him. Hestan drew in a long breath and then slowly let it out: a patient exhalation that wasn't quite a sigh. "But why, son?" he asked. "Our family and Felgilde's have been talking about this match for quite a while now, as you know full well. Her father is a merchant who's done well even in these sorry times. Joining Elfsig's house to ours would benefit both." He raised an eyebrow. "And Felgilde dotes on you. You must know that, too."

"Oh, I do, Father," Leofsig answered. They sat alone together in the dining room. Leofsig kept glancing at the doorways and the courtyard to make sure Sidroc and Uncle Hengist weren't snooping. For that matter, he didn't want his mother or sister listening, either. He didn't want to be having this conversation at all.

His father, though, had put his foot down. Hestan seldom did that; when he did, he usually got what he wanted. He said, "And I thought you were fond of the girl, too."

"Oh, I was, Father. I am," Leofsig said. *Fond* wasn't exactly the word he would have used, but it served about as well as the cruder equivalents that sprang into his mind.

"Well, then?" Hestan asked in what was for him a considerable show of annoyance. "Why won't you wed the girl? Then you could—" He broke off, but Leofsig had a good notion of what he'd been about to say. *Then you could do whatever you want with her.*

"No," Leofsig said, though he knew just what he wanted to do with Felgilde, and knew she wanted to do it, too.

"Why *not?*" His father raised his voice, something he did even more rarely than putting his foot down.

"Because I don't think it's a good idea for me to marry anybody I can't trust not to go to the Algarvians with word of where Ealstan is and who he's with," Leofsig answered. "That's why. And I can't, curse it."

Hestan didn't show surprise very often, either. "Oh," he said now, and then, a breath later, "Oh," again. "It's like that, is it?"

"Aye, it is." Leofsig's nod was somber. "She's got no use for Kaunians, and she's got no use for anybody who has a use for them. She's a sweet girl a lot of ways, powers above know" – he remembered the wonderful feel of her hand on him – "but we already have too many in our family we don't trust with our secrets."

"Not everyone would put his brother ahead of the girl who might become his wife." Hestan inclined his head. "You pay me a compliment by making me think I may possibly have done something right in raising you."

"I don't know about that," Leofsig answered with a shrug. "I do know there are plenty of girls out there, and I've only got one brother." He wondered where the girls he talked about were. Forthwegian girls of good family in Gromheort were mostly spoken for, as Felgilde had been for all practical purposes. Some Kaunian girls of good family were selling themselves on the streets these days, the Algarvians having prevented them from feeding themselves any other way. Leofsig sometimes found himself horrified and tempted at the same time.

His father sighed. "Now I'm going to have to tell Elfsig we can't proclaim a formal engagement, and I'm going to have to make up some kind of reason to explain why we can't."

"I'm sorry, Father," Leofsig said. "Believe me, I didn't want things to turn out this way." If he could have married Felgilde, he could have taken her to bed with no scandal attaching to either one of them. He envied his younger brother, who hadn't let scandal – double scandal, since his lover was a Kaunian – get in his way.

"I do believe you. I remember what I was like when I was your age," Hestan said with a reminiscent chuckle. Leofsig tried to imagine his father as a randy young man. He had little luck. Hestan went on, "But you have nothing to be sorry for – nothing that has anything to do with me, anyhow. I already told you, I'm proud of you."

He stroked his beard, his eyes far away as he thought. Leofsig noted with a small start how gray his father's beard was getting, even if Hestan's hair stayed mostly dark. That graying had all come since the war: one more evil to blame on it.

"Well, what will we do?" Hestan murmured.

"I'll come up with something," Leofsig said.

His father shook his head. "No, don't you worry about a thing. Your mother and I will take care of it, one way or another. We'll keep Elfsig sweet, or not too sour, one way or another, too."

"Tell him I picked up a disease in a soldiers' brothel," Leofsig suggested.

"That's what the Algarvians spend a lot of time complaining about," Hestan replied with a snort. "Of course, since they're the only ones who use their brothels, they never ask who gave the girls the diseases in the first place." With another snort, he added, "No, I think we'll find something else to say to the man who won't end up being your father-in-law."

"But what?" Leofsig was less inclined to worry or brood than his father or his brother, but saying goodbye to the girl he'd thought himself likely to marry wasn't going to be easy.

"Your mother and I will come up with something that will serve," his father said firmly, "so don't you trouble yourself about it. If you see Felgilde on the street, don't let on that anything is wrong."

"All right." Leofsig didn't know how good an actor he was, either. He hoped he wouldn't have to find out. Then he yawned. He wouldn't worry about it, not till he got up in the morning. "Thank you, Father," he said as he pushed back his chair and got up from the table.

"Don't thank me yet, not when I haven't done anything," Hestan answered. "But I do think we'll be able to take care of this without too much trouble."

When Leofsig stumbled out to the kitchen the next morning to eat porridge for breakfast and take along the bread and oil and onions and cheese his mother and sister had packed for his midday meal, he found his mother kneading dough for the day's baking. Making bread from scratch was cheaper than buying it ready-baked; Elfryth and Conberge had been doing more and more of it since the redheads occupied Gromheort. The dough wasn't quite the right color – it would have barley flour in it as well as wheat. At least it didn't have peas or lentils ground up with it, as it would have when things were hungriest the winter before.

"I think your father and I have found something to keep Felgilde's family from being too disappointed when we break off our arrangement," Elfryth said. "It will probably cost a little cash, but what is cash for except greasing the wheels every now and then?"

"You've already spent a lot on me," Leofsig said around a mouthful of barley porridge. He gulped the rough wine his mother had poured for him. "How many palms did you have to grease after I broke out of the captives' camp?"

"That doesn't matter," his mother said. "Besides, almost all the people we paid off then are gone now. As far as the Algarvian constables here these days know, you're right as rain."

He didn't argue; he didn't have time to argue. He grabbed the cloth sack that held his lunch and a tin flask with more cheap wine in it, then hurried out the door. In the early morning light, Gromheort seemed almost as sleepy as he felt. Only a handful of people were out and about to hear the great burst of song with which the birds greeted the sun in springtime.

Hardly any of that handful were Kaunians. Except for a few skulkers, the blonds were all packed into a neighborhood about a quarter the size of that in which they'd formerly lived. Algarvian constables patrolled the edges of that neighborhood, and let out only the few Kaunians who had to leave to labor elsewhere. Road workers fell into that group (so did streetwalkers).

Leofsig waved to Peitavas, who was arguing his way past the constables. The blond laborer waved back. After the constables finally let him go, he walked with Leofsig toward the west gate. "You shouldn't treat me as if I were a human being," Peitavas said in his own language. "It will give you a bad character among your own people and with the redheads."

As if I were a human being. Kaunian could be a remorselessly precise tongue; it was certainly better than Forthwegian for putting across fine shades of meaning. "I do not call that contrary to fact," Leofsig said, also in Kaunian.

"I know you don't," Peitavas answered. "That proves my point." He said very little after that, no matter how hard Leofsig tried to draw him out. And he made a point of climbing into a wagon different from the one Leofsig chose. Leofsig muttered to himself. What was he supposed to do if Peitavas didn't want to be treated like a human being? That the Kaunian might have been trying to protect him never entered his mind.

By the time he got out to the work, and especially by the time he'd put in a full day breaking rocks and making a roadbed, he was too worn to care. He didn't go back to Gromheort in a wagon with Peitavas or any other Kaunian, and he was too worn to care about that, either. He came as close to falling asleep on the way home as he'd ever done.

Not only because he wanted to be clean but also in the hope that a warm plunge followed by cold water would revive him, he did pay a copper and stop at the public baths not far from the count's castle. He knew how tired he truly was when he realized he was standing under a showerbath from a perforated bucket without imagining the naked women doing the same thing on the other side of the brick wall dividing the building in two.

But one of those women, he discovered when he left the baths, was Felgilde: she was coming out of the women's exit, still running a comb through her damp hair, at the same time as he was going out through the men's door. He pretended he didn't notice her. That gave him a couple of heartbeats' worth of relief, no more, for she called out, "Leofsig!" as soon as she saw him.

"Oh. Hello, Felgilde," he said, doing his best to sound surprised. He hadn't been so frightened since the battle when the Algarvians smashed the army of which he'd been a part not long after it began its invasion of Mezentio's kingdom. "Uh, how are you?" He had the bad feeling he would find out in great detail.

And he did. "I never want to see you again," Felgilde said. "I never want to talk to you again. I never want to have anything to do with you again. After all we did . . ." Had she a knife, she might have pulled it out and used it on him. "The nerve of your father!"

Since Leofsig didn't know just what his father had done, he kept quiet. Whatever it was, it seemed to have broken the not-quite-engagement. He stood there doing his best to look innocent, hoping Felgilde would tell him why he ought to look that way and why she thought he wasn't.

She didn't disappoint him. "The nerve of your father!" she repeated. "The dowry he asked for, a duchess' father couldn't afford to pay. And your family has more money than mine, anyhow." She sniffed. "I can . certainly see why; your father would dive into a dung heap to bring out a copper in his teeth."

That should have infuriated Leofsig. It did infuriate him, in fact, but he wanted to seem contrite. "I'm sorry, Felgilde," he said, and some small part of him was: by most Forthwegian standards, her views were normal and his strange. "When it comes to money, no one else in the family can argue with him."

Felgilde tossed her head. "Well, you can't have tried very hard. Since you didn't, goodbye." Nose in the air, she stalked off. Leofsig felt a pang, watching her go. But he also felt he'd just had a narrow escape. Trying to hold that feeling uppermost in his mind, he headed for home himself.

Leave. The word sang within Istvan. He'd spent far too long either at the front or on garrison duty, with never the chance to go back to his home valley and spend a little time there. Now, at last, he had it. He vowed to the stars to make the most of it, too.

He'd been walking for hours, at the ground-eating pace he'd acquired in the Gyongyosian army, from the depot at which the ley-line caravan had left him. No ley line came any closer to his valley than that. Now, looking down from the pass, he could see spread out before him the place where he'd spent his whole life till Gyongyos' wars pulled him away.

He stopped, more in surprise than from weariness. *How small and cramped it looks*, he thought. The valley had seemed plenty big enough while he was growing to manhood in it. He shrugged broad shoulders and started walking again. His village lay closest to the mouth of the pass. He'd be there well before nightfall.

The mountains that ringed the valley still wore snow halfway down from their peaks. That snow would retreat up the slopes as summer advanced on spring, but not too far, not too far. Even now, Istvan's breath smoked as he trudged along.

Snow still lay on the ground here and there in the valley, too, in places shaded from the northern sky. Elsewhere, mud replaced it, mud streaked with last year's dead, yellow grass and just beginning to be speckled with the green of new growth.

An old man, his tawny beard gone gray, was setting stones in a wall that marked the boundary between two fields: a boundary no doubt also marked in spilled blood a few generations before. He looked up from his work and eyed Istvan, then called, "Who are you, lad?" – a natural enough question, when Istvan's green-brown uniform tunic and leggings hid his clan affiliation and made him look different, too.

"I am Istvan son of Alpri," Istvan answered. "Kunhegyes is my village."

"Ah," the old man said, and nodded. "Be welcome, then, clansmate. May the stars always shine on you."

Istvan bowed. "May you always know their light, kinsman." He walked on.

But even as he walked, he realized he spoke differently from the old man. The accent of the valley – which had been his accent till he joined the army – now struck his ear as rustic and uncouth. His own way of speaking, these days, was smoother and softer. In the army, he still sounded like someone from the back country. Here in his old home, though, he would seem almost like a city man whenever he opened his mouth.

Like any village in Gyongyos, Kunhegyes sheltered behind a stout palisade. So far as Istvan knew, his home town remained at peace with the other two villages in the valley, nor was the valley as a whole at feud with any of its neighbors. Still, such things could change in the blink of an eye. The lookout up on the palisade was in grim earnest when he demanded Istvan's name.

He gave it again, and added, "You let me in this instant, Csokonai, or I'll thrash you till you can't even see."

The lookout, who was also Istvan's cousin, laughed and said, "You and what army?" But he didn't try to keep Istvan out; instead, he ran down off the palisade and opened the gate so his kinsman could enter. As soon as Istvan came inside, the two young men embraced. "By the stars, it's good to see you," Csokonai exclaimed.

"By the stars, it's good to be seen," Istvan answered, which made Csokonai laugh. Istvan laughed, too, but he hadn't been joking; plenty of times, he'd thought he would never be seen again, not in his home village.

Inside the palisade, Kunhegyes' houses were as he remembered them: solid structures of stone and brick, with steep slate roofs to shed rain and snow and to make sure no stick could set them afire. The houses stood well apart from one another, too, to make each more defensible. Despite that, the place seemed crowded to Istvan in a way it hadn't before he saw the wider world. *First the valley felt crowded, and now the village looks too small,* he thought. *What's wrong with me?*

"You must be glad to be back," Csokonai said.

"Oh, aye, so I must," Istvan agreed vaguely, though that had been the furthest thing from his mind.

"Well, don't just stand there, then," his cousin said. "I'll take you along to your house – not likely anybody else'll come along till I get back up on the palisade. We don't get one traveler most days, let alone two." His laugh said he was happy to dwell in such perfect isolation.

Istvan had been, too. He kept looking into shops and taverns. Was everything here really on such a small scale? Had it always been this way? If it had, why hadn't he noticed before? It had been air under the wings of a bird – that was why. He'd never imagined things could be any different. Now that he knew better, Kunhegyes shrank in his mind like a wool tunic washed in hot water.

Up the street toward him came a fellow ten years older than he, a bruiser named Korosi. Every so often, he'd made Istvan's life in Kunhegyes miserable. He still walked with a swagger. But, like everything else in the village, he seemed to have shrunk. Istvan walked straight toward him, not looking for trouble but not about to give way, either. In days gone by, he would have yielded. Now Korosi was the one who stepped aside.

He didn't even growl about it. Instead, he said, "Welcome home, Istvan. May the stars shine on you."

"And on you," Istvan answered, half a heartbeat slower than he should have. He glanced over toward Csokonai. His cousin seemed as surprised that he'd got a friendly greeting from Korosi as he was. *It must be the uniform*, Istvan thought, not realizing that he looked like what he was: a combat veteran who'd seen a lot of fights and wouldn't shy from one more.

Csokonai pointed. "There's the house, in case you've forgotten where you live. Now I am going to get back up on the palisade, before somebody notices I'm not where I'm supposed to be and pitches a fit."

"Not know my own house? Not likely," Istvan said. "If you think I'm that stupid, maybe I ought to knock some sense into your head." Csokonai beat a hasty retreat.

Istvan's own house, strangely, seemed as it should have to him. After a moment, he realized it has been shrinking for him as long as he could remember. What had seemed immense to a toddler was just the right size once he had some size of his own. Being away hadn't pushed that process any further; it had already gone as far as it could.

As with most houses in Kunhegyes, his had only little slits for windows, but out of them floated the delicious smell of his mother's pepper stew. Spit poured into his mouth. Where so much seemed less than it once had, the stew smelled even better than he'd expected. He hadn't had anything like it in a long time. He hurried forward to knock on the door.

He heard shouts within. A moment later, he found himself staring at an older, shorter version of himself. "Father!" he exclaimed.

His father had been holding a boot and a length of leather lacing with which he'd been repairing it. Now he dropped them both. "Istvan!" he said joyfully. Istvan's name produced more shouts farther back inside the house. His father embraced him. "Ah, by the stars, they've gone and made a man of you."

"Have they?" Istvan shrugged as he came inside. "I'm just me." Alpri, his father had the same backwoods accent as everyone else in the valley. Istvan didn't know why that surprised him so much, but it did.

People boiled forward to hug him and pound him on the back and tell him what a wonderful fellow he was: his mother, uncles and aunts, his sisters, cousins of both sexes, a great-uncle leaning on a stick. Somebody – he didn't know who – pressed a beaker of mead into his hand. He poured it down. As soon as he did, somebody else took it away and gave him another one. He drank that one straightaway, too. Mead wasn't the raw spirit for which he'd acquired a taste in the army, but it wasn't milk, either. After two beakers, sweat broke out on his face. He stopped worrying about people's accents. Everything anyone said seemed funny.

But not even a couple of beakers of mead could keep him from noticing how dark the inside of the house was after his father shut the door against the chilly drafts outside. And, with so many men just in from long days on the farms around Kunhegyes, the air got thick fast. But that didn't bother Istvan so much. Barracks weren't much better, and the field was commonly worse.

As if conjured up, yet another horn of mead appeared in his hand. "Come on." His mother took him by the arm. "I was about to put supper on the table."

"Let him stand a while and talk, Gizella," his father said. "He's just got back, after all, and he hasn't even said how long he can stay. Of course he'll want to hear everything that's happened since he's been gone."

"As a matter of fact, I am pretty hungry — and I haven't had proper pepper stew in a long time," Istvan said. Gizella beamed. Alpri looked surprised and disappointed, but put the best face on it he could. Istvan hurried to the table. To his large and noisy family, things that had happened in this end of their little valley were more important than the Derlavaian War that raged across the continent. The war wasn't real to them. And the valley hardly seemed real to Istvan any more.

The pepper stew tasted as good as it smelled, as good as he remembered. Istvan said so, over and over, which made his mother flush with pleasure. But sitting down to supper didn't keep — never had kept — his close kin from going on and on about weather and livestock and the local scandals and the iniquities of the folk who lived in Szombathely, the nearer village down the valley, and the even greater iniquities of the barely human wretches who lived in the next valley over. He wanted to make them quiet down, and he couldn't.

After what seemed a very long time, Istvan's great-uncle, whose name was Batthyany, asked, "What's it like out there, lad? Do the stars still remember you by your right name when you're so far from home?"

It was, at last, the right question. An expectant hush fell over the table as Istvan's clanfolk waited to hear what he would say. He looked around. A few of the men, he knew, had been out of the valley, but none had gone too far. They hadn't seen what he'd seen. They hadn't done what he'd done.

"Answer your grandfather's brother, boy," Alpri said, as peremptory as if Istvan were a child of ten or so.

"Aye, Father," Istvan said, and turned to Batthyany. "There's more world out there than I ever imagined, and it's a harder world, too. But the stars . . . the stars look down on all of it, Great-uncle. I'm sure of that."

"Well said," his father boomed, and everybody else nodded. "And before long we'll win this war, and everything will be fine."

Another expectant hush. "Of course we will," Istvan said. Then he went and got very drunk indeed. Everyone said what a hero he surely had to be.

Springtime in Jelgava carried with it the promise of summer – not the threat of summer, as was so in desert Zuwayza, but a definite assurance that, where the weather was warm now, it would be warmer later. Talsu reveled in the clear skies and the lengthening days. So did some of the Algarvian occupiers in Skrunda; northern Algarve's climate wasn't much different from this.

But more of the redheads in his home town sweated and fumed and fussed as winter ebbed away. The Algarvian heartland lay in the forests of the distant south, where it was always cool and damp. Talsu didn't understand why anyone would want to live in such weather, but a lot of King Mezentio's men pined for it. He listened to them grumbling whenever they came into the family shop to have Traku sew their tunics and kilts.

"If they don't care for the way things are here, they can go back where they came from," Traku said one evening at supper, spitting an olive pit down into his plate.

Talsu paused with a spoonful of barley mush dusted with powdered cheese halfway to his mouth. "They may not like it here, Father, but they like it a lot less in Unkerlant." His chuckle was deliberately nasty.

"I wouldn't want to go to Unkerlant, either," his younger sister Ausra said, and shivered. "It's probably still snowing there, and it hasn't snowed in Skrunda at all for years and years."

"There's a difference, though," Talsu said. "If you did go to Unkerlant, King Swemmel's men wouldn't want to blaze you on sight."

"Let's not talk about any of us going to Unkerlant," his mother said in a firmer tone than she usually used. "When folk of Kaunian blood go to

Unkerlant these days, it's not of their own free will. And they don't come back."

"Now, Laitsina, let's not borrow trouble, either," Traku said. "Nobody knows for sure whether those rumors are true or not." His words fell flat; he didn't sound as if he believed them himself.

"The news sheets say they're all a pack of lies," Talsu observed. "But everything in the news sheets is a lie, because the redheads won't let them tell the truth. If a liar says something is a lie, doesn't that mean it really isn't?"

"Well, the news sheets say we all love King Mainardo, and that's not true," Ausra said. "After you read that, you know you can't trust anything else you read." She got up from the table. "May I be excused?"

"Aye," Laitsina said, "but aren't you going to finish?" She pointed to Ausra's bowl, which was still almost half full.

"No, I've had enough," Ausra answered. "You can put it in the rest crate. Maybe I'll eat it for dinner tomorrow at noontime."

"I'll put it away," Talsu said, rising, too. His bowl of mush was empty; the only things on his plate were the rind from a slab of white cheese and a dozen olive pits. He might easily have finished Ausra's portion, too, but, while he might have wanted it, he knew he didn't need it.

"Thank you," Laitsina said, and, in an aside to Traku, "He really has grown up."

"It's the time he spent in the army," Talsu's father answered, also in a low voice.

Traku had more faith in the Jelgavan army than Talsu did, no doubt because he'd never serve in it. Talsu was convinced he would have become reasonably neat without sergeants screaming at him whenever they felt like it. He plucked Ausra's bowl off the table and carried it into the kitchen, where the rest crate lay beside the door to the pantry.

The sorcery that made the crate work was based on a charm from the days of the Kaunian Empire: A paralysis spell the imperial armies had used against their foes with great success till those foes found counterspells that rendered it useless. Then, for more than a hundred years, it had been only a curiosity . . . till, with the advent of systematic magecraft, wizards discovered it worked by drastically slowing the rate at which life went on. That made variations on it handy not only in keeping food fresh but also in medicine.

As soon as Talsu undid the latch and took the lid off the rest crate, he put the spell out of action. The food his mother had stored inside began to age at its normal rate once more. He set the half full bowl of barley mush on top of a coil of sausage links, then returned the lid to its proper place, reactivating the crate. He was just snapping the latch again when Laitsina called, "Make sure you put the cover on good and tight."

"Aye, Mother," Talsu said patiently. She might make noises about his having grown up, but she didn't believe it, not down deep inside. She probably never would.

Afterwards, he played robbers with his father till they were both yawning. He won three games, Traku two. As the tailor put away the board, the men, and the dice, he said, "You're better at the game than you were before you went into King Donalitu's service."

"I don't know why," Talsu answered. "I don't think I played it more than a couple of times. Mostly, we just rolled dice when we felt like swapping money around."

The next morning, after Talsu finished cutting the pieces for an Algarvian's summer-weight linen tunic, his mother came downstairs and pressed some coins into his hand. "Go over to the grocer's and bring me back half a dozen apples," she said. "I want to make tarts tonight."

"All right, Mother," Talsu said, and set down the shears with alacrity.

Laitsina smiled. "And don't take too long passing the time of day with Gailisa, either."

"Who, me?" Talsu said. His mother laughed at him. In some ways, she was ready to believe him grown up after all.

Whistling, he hurried over to the grocer's shop. Sure enough, Gailisa was taking care of the place: she was artistically arranging onions in a crate when he walked inside. "Hello, Talsu," she said. "What do you want today?"

"You don't sell that," he said with a grin, and she made a face at him. "But my mother sent me over here for some apples."

"Well, we've got some," Gailisa answered, pointing to a basket on the counter. "If they're for eating, though, I've got to tell you they're on the mushy side. The winter was just too mild for them to get as firm as they might."

"No, she wants them for tarts," Talsu said.

"They'll be fine for that." Gailisa went over to the basket. Talsu watched her hips work inside her trousers. "How many does she want?"

"About half a dozen, she said."

"All right." Gailisa bent over the basket and started picking them up one by one. "I'll give you the best ones we've got."

She was still going through them when a couple of Algarvian troopers in kilts strode into the shop. One of them pointed at her and said something in his own language. Laughing, the other one nodded and rocked his hips forward and back. Talsu didn't understand a word of what they said, but that didn't stop him from getting angry.

He turned toward them, not saying anything himself but not trying to hide what he thought of them, either. He wasn't afraid of Algarvians because they were Algarvians, not when he'd faced them over the sights of a stick. True, his army had lost to theirs, but that didn't mean they couldn't hurt and bleed just like Jelgavans.

They noticed his expression, too, noticed it and didn't like it. One of them jerked a thumb back toward the door through which they'd come and spoke in bad Jelgavan: "You – going out. Getting lost."

"No," Talsu answered evenly. "I'm waiting for the lady to choose some apples for me."

"Futtering apples," the Algarvian said. "Going out now. Going out now and – uh, or – being sorry."

"No," Talsu repeated.

"Talsu, maybe you'd better . . ." Gailisa began.

But it was already too late. The redheads understood what no meant. They were as young and headstrong as he was, and they were the conquerors, and there were two of them. Smiling most unpleasantly, they advanced on him. Gailisa darted around the counter and into the back of the shop, loudly calling for her father. Talsu noticed only out of the corner of his eye; almost all of his attention stayed on the Algarvians.

The fight, such as it was, didn't last long. One of the redheads swung at him, a looping haymaker that would have knocked him sprawling had it landed. It didn't. He blocked it with his left forearm and delivered a sharp, straight right. The Algarvian's nose flattened under his fist. With a howl, the soldier staggered back into shelves piled high with produce. He knocked them over. Vegetables spilled across the floor.

Talsu spun toward the other Algarvians. This fellow didn't waste time on fisticuffs. He yanked a knife from his belt, stabbed Talsu in the side, and then helped his friend get up. They both ran out of the grocer's shop.

When Talsu started to run after them, he got only a couple of paces before crumpling to his knees and then to his belly. He stared in dull surprise at the blood that darkened his tunic and spread over the floor. He heard Gailisa's shriek as if from very far away. The inside of the shop went gray and then black.

He woke puzzled, wondering why he wasn't seeing the grocer's shop. Instead, his eyes took in the iron rails of a bed, and a whitewashed wall beyond it. A man in a pale gray tunic peered down at him. "How do you feel?" the fellow asked.

Before Talsu could answer, he became aware of a snarling pain in his flank. He bit back a scream, as he might have done were he wounded in battle. "Hurts," he got out through clenched teeth.

"I believe it," said the man in the gray tunic – a healing mage, Talsu realized. "We had to do a lot of work on you while your body was slowed down. Even with the sorcery, it was touch and go for a while there. You lost a lot of blood. But I think you'll come through pretty well, if fever doesn't take you."

"Hurts," Talsu repeated. He was going to start screaming in a minute, whether he wanted to or not. The pain felt as big as the world.

"Here," the mage said. "Drink this." Talsu didn't ask what it was. He seized the cup and gulped it down. It tasted overpoweringly of poppies. He panted like a dog, waiting for the pain to go away. It didn't, not really. He did: he seemed to be floating to one side of his body, so that, while he still felt everything, it didn't seem to matter any more. It might almost have been happening to someone else.

The mage lifted his tunic and examined the stitched-up wound in his side. Talsu looked at it, too, with curiosity far more abstract than he could have managed undrugged. "He put quite a hole in me," he remarked, and the mage nodded. "Did they catch him?" Talsu asked, and this time the healer shook his head. Talsu shrugged. The drug didn't let him get excited about anything. "I might have known."

"You're lucky to be alive," the healer said. "You've got more stitches holding you together inside. If we'd come a little later . . ." He shook his head again. "But your lady friend made sure we didn't."

"My lady friend?" Talsu said vaguely, and then, "Oh. Gailisa." He knew he ought to be feeling something more than he was, but the drug blocked and blurred it. *Too bad*, he thought, still vague.

Having been nearly idle through the winter, Garivald was making up for it now that the ground had finally got firm enough to hold a furrow. Along with the rest of the peasants of Zossen, he plowed and sowed as fast as he could, to give the crops as long to grow as possible. He rose before sunset and went to bed after nightfall; only harvest time was more wearing than the planting season.

Along with everything else he had to do, he still had to go into the forest to cut wood for Zossen's Algarvian occupiers. How he'd hoped the Unkerlanter advance would sweep them out of his village! But it hadn't happened, and it didn't look as if it would, either.

He hacked at a tree trunk, wishing it were a redhead's body. When the Unkerlanters in grimy rock-gray tunics let him see them, he kept right on chopping wood. One of his countrymen said, "You're the singer, aren't you?"

"What if I am?" Garivald asked, pausing at last. "What difference does it make?"

"If you aren't, we might decide not to let you live," the ragged soldier answered, and made as if to turn his stick in Garivald's direction.

"You've already spent a while killing my hopes," Garivald said. "I thought the Algarvians would be gone from here by now." *Thought* probably took it too far; *hoped* came closer. But the men who skulked through the woods had taken his songs, had promised great victories, and then hadn't delivered. If they were unhappy with him, he was unhappy with them, too.

"Soon," said the soldier who hadn't surrendered to the redheads. "Very soon. The fight still goes on. It does not always go just as we would have it. But the king will strike another blow against the invaders soon. And when he does, we need you." Now he pointed at Garivald with his finger, not his stick.

"Need me for what?" Garivald asked in some alarm. If they wanted him to raise the village against the Algarvian occupiers, he was going to tell them they were out of their minds. As far as he could see, that would only get his friends and relatives – and maybe him, too – killed without accomplishing much. Zossen wasn't on a ley line; a rising here wouldn't keep the redheads from moving reinforcements wherever they pleased.

Zossen, in fact, wasn't even near a power point, which was why King Swemmel's men had had to keep sacrificing condemned criminals to gain sorcerous energy to make their crystal function.

The crystal . . . Garivald's hand tightened on the handle of his axe. Even before the ragged soldier spoke, Garivald guessed what he would say. And say it he did: "You have something we want, something buried in the ground."

Garivald had thought about digging up the crystal and passing it on to the Unkerlanters who kept resisting behind Algarvian lines. He'd thought about it, but he hadn't done it yet in spite of Waddo's urgings. Even trying to do it was risky. But having so many people know about it was also risky. He hadn't said a word to anyone. Somebody else in the village must have. And what got to the irregulars' ears also got to the Algarvians'.

"I'll get it for you," he said quickly. The irregulars could probably arrange to whisper into the redheads' ears if he proved recalcitrant.

"Good." All the ragged soldiers nodded. The fellow who was doing the talking for them went on, "*When* will you get it for us?"

"When I find it," Garivald snarled. "Powers above, dogs can't find the bones they bury half the time. I didn't leave any special marks to point the way to the cursed thing. If I would have, the Algarvians'd have it by now. I'm going to have to find it."

"Don't waste too much time," one of the other Unkerlanters warned him. "We need it, and no mistake."

"If you think you can get it faster than I can, go ahead and dig for yourselves," Garivald said. "Good luck go with you."

"Don't play games with us," the irregulars' leader said.

"Don't be an idiot," Garivald retorted.

He wondered if he'd pushed his countrymen too far. He tensed, ready to rush them with his axe if they tried to blaze him. He might be able to take one of them with him before he fell. But, after glancing back and forth among themselves, they slipped away deeper into the protecting woods without another word.

Garivald lugged his load of firewood back to the Algarvians. The only thanks he got were a grunt and a tick against his name so he wouldn't have to do it again for a while. Had the redheads worked to make people like them, they would have had no small following in the Duchy of Grelz. Garivald knew as much; the peasants hadn't had an easy time of it during

Swemmel's reign. Some folk clove to the Algarvians because of that, regardless of how they were treated. Most, like Garivald, saw they were getting no better bargain and stayed aloof.

"Took you long enough," Annore said when he came into their hut.

"Don't you start on me," Garivald growled. He looked around. Syrivald was outside doing something or other, while Leuba was occupied with a cloth doll stuffed with buckwheat husks. Lowering his voice, Garivald went on, "They want it."

His wife's eyes widened. "Can you get it?"

"I'm going to have to try."

"Can you get it without getting caught?" Annore persisted. "Do you even know exactly where it is?"

"I'm going to have to try," Garivald repeated. "I think I can, and maybe I'll be able to find out where it is."

"How?" Annore asked. "You're no mage."

"And I don't need to be one, either," Garivald said. "Everybody knows a lodestone will draw iron, and rubbed amber will draw feathers or straw. Haven't you ever heard that limestone will draw glass the same way?"

His wife snapped her fingers in annoyance at herself. "I have, by the powers above, but it slipped my mind. Lodestone and amber are toys to make children laugh, but how often does anyone need to draw glass to him?"

"Not very," Garivald replied. "And there's not much glass in Zossen *to* draw – the stuff's too expensive for the likes of us. But if that crystal isn't glass, I don't know what it is." If that crystal wasn't glass, the limestone wouldn't work. In that case, he'd have to start probing the plot where the crystal lay buried. He'd have to be lucky to find it so, and it would surely take a long time. Somebody was bound to find him first, to find him and to ask a great many questions he couldn't answer.

"All right," Annore said. "Limestone won't be hard to find, not when we spread it crushed on the fields to mellow the soil."

Garivald nodded. "I'll just need a chunk a little bigger than most, and a string to tie around it so it swings free – oh, and aye, a dark night."

"You'll have those the next few nights," Annore said. "After that, the moon will be getting bigger and setting later."

"I need one other thing," Garivald said after a moment's thought. His wife raised a questioning eyebrow. He explained: "I can't find the cursed crystal if it isn't there. If Waddo's already gone and dug it up, I'm wasting my time."

Waddo had talked about the two of them digging it up together, but who could tell what all went through the firstman's mind? Garivald wondered what he'd tell the Unkerlanter irregulars if Waddo had decided to take it on his own. Whatever he told them, they wouldn't want to listen. He didn't think Waddo had told the Algarvians about the crystal; had the firstman blabbed to the redheads, they would have come down on Garivald and his family like a falling tree. But Waddo might well have taken the crystal out of the ground himself and hidden it somewhere else to keep Garivald or one of the villagers who'd seen Garivald and him burying it from betraying him.

"Have to hope," Garivald muttered, and tramped back out to the fields. Finding a chunk of limestone the size of a finger joint didn't take long. He unraveled some of the hem of his tunic, using the thread for a string. Annore wouldn't be happy with him for that, but he had bigger things to worry about.

With the stone and the string in his belt pouch, he took care of endless chores till sundown. Supper was blood sausage and pickled cabbage, washed down with a mug of ale. After supper, Annore let the fire die to embers that shed only a faint red glow over the inside of the hut. She spread out blankets and quilts on the benches that lined the walls. Syrivald and Leuba curled up in them and went to sleep. Before long, Annore was snoring, too.

Garivald had to stay awake, though exhaustion tugged at him. He watched a stripe of moonlight crawl across the floor and up the wall. After the moonlight disappeared, after the inside of the house got darker than ever, he sat up, swallowing yet another yawn, and put back on the boots that were all he'd taken off.

Did Annore's breathing change as he went out the door? Had she only been pretending to be asleep? He'd find out later. He couldn't worry about it now.

Most of the village lay quiet. Farm work bludgeoned people into slumber when night came. That made the raucous singing from the house the Algarvians had taken as their own all the more irksome. But if they were in there carousing, they weren't out patrolling. Beyond wishing them ugly hangovers in the morning, Garivald had no fault to find with their way of whiling away the hours, not tonight.

He stepped as quietly as he could. If anyone did spy him, he'd say he was out to ease himself. That wouldn't work in the middle of the garden, though. Once he got there, he couldn't afford to waste a moment.

The two-story bulk of Waddo's house, looming dark against the sky, helped guide him to the plot he needed: Waddo's was the only two-story house in Zossen. As far as Garivald was concerned, it was also a monument to wretched excess. But that, like the redheads' racket, was beside the point right now.

Garivald took out the little chunk of limestone and swung it gently at the end of the length of thread tied to it. "Show me where the crystal went," he whispered as it swung back and forth. "Show me, as was truly meant." He didn't know if it was truly meant or not, but figured the assumption would do no harm.

And the limestone began gliding back and forth, as if he were swinging it. But he wasn't, not now; his hand and wrist were still. He went in the direction it led him, and it swung faster and faster, higher and higher. Then, after he'd gone on for a while, it began to slow. He stopped and reversed his field. The swings grew stronger and higher once more.

He stopped where the limestone swung most vigorously: stopped and squatted. That was where he began to dig with his knife belt. He didn't know how deep he'd have to dig or how big a hole he'd have to make. The only way to find out was to do it.

The tip of the knife grated off something hard and smooth. "Powers above!" Garivald whispered, and reached down into the hole. After guddling about for a moment, his hands closed on the cool sphere of the crystal. With a soft exclamation of triumph, he drew it out.

Then, as best he could, he filled in the hole, trying to make it seem as if no one had ever been there. He hurried away, back toward his own house. Clouds slid across the stars, swallowing them one after another. The air smelled damp. Maybe it would rain before morning. That would help hide what he'd been doing, and hide his tracks, too. It would also be good for the newly planted crops.

"Rain," he murmured, clutching the crystal tight.

Eighteen

Not even snowshoes helped behemoths make their way through the bottomless mud of the spring thaw. Leudast wished the thaw would have come later than it did – exactly the opposite of what he would have wished back in his village. An early thaw meant an early planting and a long growing season. But a late thaw meant the Unkerlanter army could have kept pushing the Algarvians eastward across solid ground. Solid ground, for the next few weeks, would be hard tq come by.

His company was still moving eastward, one laborious step at a time. Paved roads in Unkerlant being few and far between, the highways down which they advanced were as muddy as the fields to either side. Sometimes, because so many men and horses and unicorns and behemoths and wagons moved along them and tore up the dirt, they were muddier than the fields.

During the thaw, ordinary wagons were useless. No matter how many horses pulled them, they bogged down. But every village had a wagon or two useful in the mud or in deep snow; one with tall wheels and a curving bottom almost like that of a boat. Mud wagons could bring supplies to soldiers at the front line where everything else got stuck.

The Unkerlanter army had its own fleet of mud wagons, and confiscated any it found in reconquered villages. Such confiscations were few and far between, though, because the Algarvians stole the wagons, too.

Looking back over his shoulder, Leudast saw a couple of mud wagons making their way back toward the company he led. He waved to the driver of the lead wagon. The fellow waved back, calling, "You part of Captain Hawart's outfit?"

"That's right," Leudast answered. He would have said the same thing had the driver asked him if he were part of some regiment he'd never heard of. Supplies didn't come forward so often that he could afford to let them slip through his fingers. Lying to get his hands on them seemed no sin at all.

These, which were actually meant for his unit, didn't come forward in a hurry. Mud wagons didn't move quickly; what set them apart from every other vehicle was that they could move at all during the thaw. Leudast had plenty of time to shout for soldiers to help unload them before they actually arrived.

"What have you got for us?" he asked as his men swarmed over the wagons.

"Oh, some of this, some of that," the lead driver answered. "Bandages, potted meat, charges for your sticks so you won't have to cut a captain's throat to keep blazing, all sorts of good things."

"I should say so," Leudast exclaimed. Such bounty hadn't come his way in quite a while. "Powers above, we've been living hand-to-mouth for so long, I don't know what we'll do with all this stuff."

"Well, pal, if you don't want it, I figure there's plenty who do," the driver said. He laughed to show he didn't intend to be taken seriously. A good thing for him, too: Several of Leudast's soldiers were about to turn their sticks in his direction. They weren't going to let him and his fellow drivers get away before they'd gone through the wagons, either.

Captain Hawart himself squelched up before the plundering was quite complete. "You can't keep all the goodies for your own company, you know," he told Leudast. He wasn't laughing as he said it.

"Sir, I wouldn't do that," Leudast assured him.

"Of course you wouldn't," Hawart answered. "I've got my eye on you. Amazing how well people behave when somebody's watching, isn't it?"

"I don't know what you're talking about." Leudast did laugh. So did Hawart, now. They understood each other pretty well.

Hawart said, "You *are* going to share this stuff, Leudast, because we're ordered forward against the redheads in Lautertal up ahead past the woods there." He pointed.

"Are we?" Leudast said tonelessly. "They'll have had a deal of time to get ready for us, won't they? And we won't be able to come at 'em quick and flank 'em out, like we did so often in the snow."

"That's all true, every word of it," his superior agreed. "But we're ordered in anyhow, and so we'll go. They aren't supposed to have that many men holed up in the place. That's the word coming back to us, anyhow."

He didn't sound as if he believed it. He didn't look as if he believed it, either. Casting about for ways to ask how big a fiasco the ordered assault was likely to be, Leudast found one: "How hard are you going to push the attack, sir?"

"We're going forward till we can't go forward any more," Hawart answered. Spoken one way, that meant one thing; spoken another way, it meant something altogether different.

Leudast had no great trouble figuring out Captain Hawart's tone. "Aye, sir," he said. "You don't need to worry about my company. We always do our best."

"I know you do," Hawart said. "If they haven't killed us yet, they probably can't kill us at all, don't you think?"

"Aye," Leudast said, knowing he was lying, knowing Hawart knew he was lying. But if he lied to the captain, maybe he could lie to himself, too. He went on, "What help can we count on when we go at this Lautertal place? Egg-tossers? Behemoths? Magecraft?" *Magecraft* was a euphemism for slaughtered Unkerlanters, but he might be able to lie to himself about that, too.

In any case, Hawart shook his head. "Tossers are mostly stuck in the mud ten miles behind us. Same with the behemoths. And this isn't a big enough attack to deserve magecraft. Can't say I'm too sorry about that." He was probably lying to himself, too.

"Now we hope the Algarvians feel the same way about holding the place," Leudast said, and Hawart nodded. Leudast went on, "I'll let my men know what they'll be doing. No wonder the powers above" – by which he meant the Unkerlanter quartermasters, not the abstract powers beyond the sky – "decided to let us have enough supplies for a change."

After Hawart left, Leudast broke the news to the company he commanded. His veterans nodded in resignation. The new recruits exclaimed and grinned excitedly. They knew no better. They would, those who didn't pay an irredeemable price for the instruction the Algarvians were about to give them.

As soon as Leudast advanced out of the trees and on toward Lautertal, he knew the attack was in trouble. The town had a couple of buildings with tall spires that hadn't been knocked down. That meant the Algarvians would have lookouts in those spires, men who could see a long way.

They also proved to have egg-tossers in the town. Eggs began bursting among the Unkerlanters slogging across the liquid fields toward the town. The mud absorbed some of the sorcerous energy those eggs released – some, but far from all. Men shrieked as they were burned, or as bits of the egg casings scythed into them.

"Keep going!" Leudast shouted. "We can do it!" He didn't know whether the Unkerlanters could do it or not, but he did know they couldn't if they didn't think they could. "Urra!" he yelled. "Swemmel! Urra!"

"Urra!" the Unkerlanters shouted. They were game. They'd stayed game all through the dreadful summer and fall, when the Algarvians pushed them back almost at will. Leudast still marveled at that. Throwing down his stick and throwing up his hands would have been so easy. But he'd kept fighting, and so had his countrymen. Ever since fall gave way to winter, they'd been the ones advancing. That was enough to keep a man going all by itself.

But it wasn't enough to let the Unkerlanters take Lautertal. The Algarvians had indeed had some time in which to get ready and they'd used it well. They'd dug and then cleverly concealed blazing pits all around the town. They must have reinforced them, too, or the pits would have turned to muck during the thaw. The pits hadn't; King Mezentio's men took a steady toll on the Unkerlanters from them. And the egg-tossers kept dropping death on Leudast and his comrades.

He saw an egg spinning through the air toward him, saw it and flung himself face down in the muck before it burst. Fragments of the casing hissed malignantly over his head. The soggy ground under him shuddered as if in torment. But he'd known worse than that when the Algarvians started slaughtering Kaunian captives. Then the ground didn't merely shudder: trenches and holes closed on the soldiers unlucky enough to shelter in them, and flames burst up to catch men scrambling free. Algarvian magecraft was nothing to despise.

Since they had so many other defenses cunningly prepared, Leudast feared King Mezentio's men would also be ready to use Kaunians' life energy against the Unkerlanter attack. If they were ready, they didn't bother killing the captives. They had no need for anything so drastic.

Leudast and the other Unkerlanters had no chance to break into Lautertal, let alone to run the Algarvians out of it.

Wiping mud from his eyes, Leudast looked around. During the winter, King Swemmel's soldiers had taken to using the Algarvian tactic of flanking the enemy out of his position rather than smashing straight into it. With behemoths on snowshoes adding punch and speed to Unkerlanter attacks, the ploy had worked well. Now . . .

Leudast shook his head. Soldiers half drowned in muck were not going to produce a powerful flanking maneuver, not around Lautertal, not even if the Algarvians had no further unpleasant surprises waiting for them. The Unkerlanters couldn't go around, they couldn't go forward, and they were having an even harder time staying where they were.

"What do we do, sir?" one of Leudast's men cried, as if certain he would have the answer. "What *can* we do?"

Nothing, was the first thought that sprang into Leudast's mind. *Stay where we are and keep getting pounded*, was the second. He liked it no better, though doing it would have meant obeying orders to the letter.

He looked around again, trying to find a way in which the attack on Lautertal might succeed. Had he seen one, he would have ordered his men to keep trying: no war ever got won without casualties. But no war ever got won by throwing men into a meat grinder to no purpose, either. As far as he could see, that was all the Unkerlanters were doing here.

"Fall back!" he shouted. "Back to our own lines! We'll take another blaze at these buggers later on." He didn't know whether the Unkerlanters would or not. He did know this attack had failed.

Getting away from Lautertal proved almost as expensive as assailing the place had been. The Algarvians, fortunately, could no more pursue than the Unkerlanters had been able to attack, but their egg-tossers punished the retreating soldiers all over again. Back at the soggy trenches from which they'd begun the assault on Lautertal, King Swemmel's men reckoned up their losses. Leudast had seen worse, which was the most he could say.

"Who ordered the withdrawal?" Captain Hawart demanded.

"I did, sir," Leudast answered, and wondered if an avalanche of official wrath would fall on his head.

But Hawart only nodded and said, "Good. You waited long enough." Leudast let out a long, weary sigh of relief.

★

In all his years as a dragonflier, Count Sabrino had never faced such determined enemies in the air as the ones he met here in the land of the Ice People. Try as he would, he could not escape them. And all the wing he led suffered from their ferocious onslaughts.

He turned to Colonel Broumidis, who commanded the handful of Yaninan dragons on the austral continent. "Can we do nothing against them?" he cried out in torment. "Are we powerless?"

Broumidis' shrug had none of the panache an Algarvian would have given it. The Yaninan officer, a short, skinny man with an enormous black mustache that didn't suit his narrow face, seemed rather to be suggesting that fate had more to do with it than he did. All he said was, "What can we do but endure?"

"Go mad?" Sabrino suggested, no more than a quarter in jest. He slapped, then cried out in triumph. "There's one mosquito dead. That leaves only forty-eight billion, as near as I can reckon. The cursed things are eating me alive."

Colonel Broumidis shrugged again. "It is spring on the austral continent," he said, sounding even more doleful in his accented Algarvian than he would have in his own language. "All the bugs hatch out at once, and they are all hungry. What can we do but slap and light stinking candles and suffer?"

"I'd like to drop enough eggs on all the swamps to kill the wrigglers before they grow up, that's what," Sabrino said savagely. Broumidis raised a bushy black eyebrow and said nothing. Sabrino felt himself flush. He knew he'd been absurd. When the ice down here finally melted, half the countryside turned into a bog. And, as the Yaninan colonel had said, the bugs swarmed forth, intent on packing a year's worth of life into the few weeks of mild weather the austral continent gave them.

Sabrino looked back over his shoulder at Heshbon, the Yaninan outpost he and his dragonfliers had to help protect. *Miserable little place*, he thought. *I've flown over plenty of Unkerlanter peasant villages where I'd rather settle down, and I wouldn't be caught dead in an Unkerlanter peasant village.*

"Cinnabar," he muttered under his breath, making it into a curse.

"Aye, cinnabar," Broumidis agreed, mournful still. "It draws warriors as amber draws feathers. Us, the Lagoans – may the powers below swallow those wide-arsed whoresons – and now you."

"I would have been just as well pleased to stay on the other side of the Narrow Sea, I assure you," Sabrino said.

Colonel Broumidis sent him a hurt look. The Yaninan's large, dark, liquid eyes were made for such expressions. Sabrino sighed. He could have said a good deal more, but he didn't want to offend his ally. Shouting, *If you buggers had done any fighting on your own, I could have stayed on the other side of the Narrow Sea*, struck him as impolitic.

"Well, we shall have to carry on the war as best we can." Broumidis sighed, too. The Yaninans were hardly happier with the Algarvians than the other way round. They were a proud and touchy folk, and all the more touchy because of their failures in the field. Broumidis pointed. "Here comes the food for our dragons."

Several camels bore panniers full of chunks of meat. The meat came from other camels; cutting them up struck Sabrino as the best thing that could happen to them. They were almost as disagreeable as dragons. Sabrino knew no higher dispraise.

Mosquitoes didn't care about cut-up meat. They wanted theirs live. Flies and gnats and midgets weren't so fussy. They swarmed round the panniers in buzzing, swirling clouds. They were perfectly willing to torment the camels carrying the panniers, too. And, because the camels had started shedding their heavy winter coats, they suffered badly.

Not so the Ice People who led them. The natives of the austral continent remained swaddled in furs and robes, and offered the bugs few targets. Sabrino rather wished he were wearing something that covered more than a kilt; his legs looked hardly better than the meat the dragons were getting. And . . . "Before I came here, I thought the Ice People were hairy because that helped keep them warm. Now I wonder whether their being so hairy helps keep the mosquitoes away, too."

"It does," Broumidis said with assurance. "I have seen as much, in my service here." He inhaled, choked on a gnat, and spent the next minute or so coughing. When he could speak again, he went on, "Even so, I would not care to be among their number."

"No indeed, my dear fellow!" Sabrino exclaimed. His own groundcrew men took the camel meat from the Ice People. They dusted it with brimstone and lavishly with cinnabar before feeding it to the dragons. Sabrino said, "We need not stint here, at any rate. That's all to the good."

"Aye, dragons down here burn hot and flame far," his Yaninan counterpart agreed. "Not for nothing do we need what the Ice People trade us."

Before Sabrino could answer, an insect bit him on the back of the neck. It wasn't a mere mosquito; it felt as if it had driven a red-hot nail an inch into his flesh. He yelled and leaped in the air and slapped at himself, all at the same time. Something squashed under the palm of his hand. When he looked, he saw blood and bug guts. He scrubbed his palm on the new green grass shooting up now that the snow had melted. Like the bugs, like everything on the austral continent, the grass was speeding through its life as if it knew it had not a moment to waste.

Another camel approached from out of the east. This one was a riding beast, with a man of the Ice People perched atop the curious padded bench that served it for a saddle. Seeing Broumidis, the fellow steered the camel toward him. As soon as he came into earshot, he began shouting in his own throaty language, pointing back over his shoulder as he did so.

"You understand what he's saying?" Sabrino asked. His neck still throbbed.

"Aye," Broumidis replied, "or I do when I don't have to try to understand you, too." Sabrino shut up. The Yaninan spoke in the language of the Ice People, listened, and spoke again. After he got another set of answers, he turned back to Sabrino. "The Lagoans are coming. Pathrusim here spied them fording the Jabbok River, about forty miles east of here. They'll be across it now, of course, but not so far across it – they're mostly footsoldiers, and couriers camels ride like the wind. We can strike them. We can smite them."

He sounded quiveringly eager. Had all the Yaninans been so eager to go into action against King Vitor's men, Sabrino could have stayed in Unkerlant, in a fight he was convinced mattered more to his kingdom than this sideshow. The best way to escape the sideshow, though, was to smash the Lagoans. If they were beaten off the austral continent, he could go back to Derlavai.

He shouted for his bugler. The fellow came running up, horn in hand. "Blow the call to combat," Sabrino told him. "We fly against the Lagoans!"

Familiar martial music rang out. His dragonfliers burst from their tents and ran for their beasts, which screamed in fury at having their meals interrupted. They were going off to a fight, which they liked as well as eating, but they hadn't the brains to figure that out.

A couple of minutes later, a Yaninan trumpeter also started blaring away. Broumidis' men moved more slowly than the Algarvians' despite their commandant's shouts and curses. *Poor bugger*, Sabrino thought – *a good officer trapped in a bad service.* Sabrino's whole wing was in the air and speeding east before the first Yaninan dragons left the ground. Sabrino sighed: This was why King Mezentio's men had had to come give them a hand. With Yaninans for allies, Algarve hardly needed enemies.

Peering down from his perch at the base of his dragon's neck, Sabrino spied a couple of Lagoan behemoths lumbering ahead of the enemy's army. The Lagoans spotted his wing, too, and started blazing at the dragons with the heavy stick mounted on one behemoth. The wing, fortunately, was flying high, and even that powerful beam couldn't knock any dragons out of the sky. It did keep Sabrino from ordering his dragons to swoop down on the Lagoan behemoths, though. They would pay a high price if they tried that.

A few of the Algarvian dragonfliers did drop eggs on the behemoths. Down here on the austral continent, the wing had to carry eggs as well as fighting with flame and the fliers' sticks. Sabrino didn't see whether they knocked the Lagoan beasts down. He was looking ahead, trying to spot the Lagoans' main force.

He was also worrying. He'd flown against Lagoan dragons over the Strait of Valmiera; their fliers knew what they were doing. And the Lagoans, unlike the Unkerlanters, used crystals as freely as did his own kingdom. Those behemoths would let the rest of the Lagoan army know the dragons were coming.

And they did. The Lagoans might not have brought along many dragons, but they had lots of behemoths. Some of those beasts carried egg-tossers, but the ones with heavy sticks all started blazing at the wing of Algarvian dragons.

Captain Domiziano's face appeared in Sabrino's crystal. "Sir, shall we dive on them?" the squadron commander asked. By his tone, he would have liked nothing better.

But Sabrino shook his head. "No – it would hurt us too much. We can't afford to throw ourselves away – no telling if any more dragons will be able to come here if we do, and dragons can't stop a whole army on the march by themselves anyhow."

"The Yaninans won't be able to stop them, either," Domiziano predicted. "Are we going to have to send soldiers here, too?"

"I don't know. Do I look like King Mezentio? You'd better not say aye, by the powers above." Sabrino added the warning before Domiziano could say anything at all. "What I do know is, we're not going to give the Lagoans anything easy."

Eggs rained down on King Vitor's men at a height beyond that at which the foe's heavy sticks could harm the dragons. The only trouble was, it was also a height beyond that at which the dragonfliers could aim accurately. Here and there, a bursting egg flung Lagoans in all directions. More often than not, though, the eggs only cratered the ground.

After a while, there were no more eggs left to drop. "Back to the dragon farm, boys," Sabrino ordered. "We'll load up again and then hit these miserable whoresons another good lick."

The rest of the dragonfliers obeyed his command. As he spiraled down to a landing outside of Heshbon, the mosquitoes and flies and gnats he'd escaped in the upper air began to plague him once more. He cursed and slapped, neither of which did much good. Colonel Broumidis' few dragons were landing alongside their Algarvian allies. They'd done well enough, or so Sabrino supposed. He cursed them anyhow, for not stopping the Lagoans by themselves. If they'd managed that, he wouldn't have had to come to the austral continent and get nibbled to death by gnats.

Now that the land of the Ice People was no longer frozen hard as stone, Fernao could dig a hole for himself when eggs began dropping all around him. He got filthy when he dove into the muddy hole, but he vastly preferred getting filthy to getting killed.

Overhead, the Algarvian dragons wheeled unchallenged. They stayed high above the Lagoan army, not daring to swoop down and flame soldiers or behemoths. Fernao supposed that represented a moral victory of sorts. Moral victories, though, went only so far when measured against the real article. The Algarvians could hurt his comrades – and him, though he tried not to think about that – while the men on the ground could do little to the dragons as long as they stayed high.

As if to underscore that, a Lagoan soldier not far away started shrieking.

With a curse – he wasn't thrilled about exposing himself to danger – Fernao scrambled out of the hold where he sheltered and hurried to the wounded man's side. The soldier writhed, clutching at his belly. Blood rivered out from between his fingers. Either a fragment of egg shell or a sharp stone propelled by a nearby blast of sorcerous energy had laid him open as neatly as a butcher might have done.

Even as Fernao readied the spell that would slow the man down and give the physicians a chance to work on him, the fellow groaned one last time. He shuddered and went limp; his eyes rolled up in his head. When Fernao felt for his pulse, he found none. That might have been a mercy. The soldiers would have known nothing but torment after coming out from under the shadow of the magic, and fever, against which even mages had little power, might well have carried him off anyhow. Fernao jumped back into his hole again.

The Algarvian dragons seemed to stay in the air over the army forever. Part of that feeling came from being under attack; Fernao knew as much. And part sprang from the nature of daylight on the austral continent. When he'd first come, in winter, the sun had hardly peeked above the horizon. Not so very much farther south, it would never have risen at all. Now that spring had come, though, days grew longer with astonishing speed. Before long, the sun would spend almost all day in the sky. On the far side of the Barrier Mountains, it would never set.

At last, no doubt because they were out of eggs, the Algarvian dragons flew off toward Heshbon. Fernao shook his head to get rid of the echoing roar of bursting eggs. Mosquitoes buzzed malignantly; he could still hear those. When he inhaled, a tickling in his nose warned him he'd breathed in a couple of midges. He exhaled sharply, and got rid of them before he started to choke.

All over the field, Lagoans were emerging from the holes they'd dug for themselves. Like Fernao, his countrymen were worn and muddy. A lot of them had a look in their eyes that he didn't like: the look of men who'd had to take a beating without being able to hit back. A few officers were calling for them to push on toward the west, but Fernao could see at a glance that the soldiers were in no shape to advance.

Someone waved to him: Affonso. "You're still alive," the other mage called.

"Aye, I think so," Fernao said. "And you as well – congratulations."

Affonso bowed. "Thanks. I wish I could take credit for it, but it had more to do with luck or the powers above – your choice – than with me." He slapped at the back of his leg, just above the top of his wool stocking. "Stinking bugs."

"When I was here before, they'd already passed their peak," Fernao said. "Now it's a miracle they don't suck the blood out of everything."

"If they don't, the Algarvians are liable to," Affonso said gloomily.

To that, Fernao could only nod. Algarve had a much easier time sending men and supplies across the Narrow Sea to the austral continent than did Lagoas. The same held true for Yanina, but King Mezentio's men, unlike King Tsavellas', took war seriously. Fernao said, "If they ship over footsoldiers and behemoths, we're liable to be in a bad way."

"Aye," Affonso agreed, more gloomily still. "The dragons are bad enough. Even when they aren't dropping eggs on our heads, they're looking down to see just where we're going. Even Yaninan footsoldiers can put up a fight when they have an edge like that. Algarvians . . . I don't want to think about the bloody Algarvians."

"We have to have dragons of our own – that's all there is to it," Fernao said. He turned away.

"Where are you going?" Affonso asked.

"To tell Lieutenant General Junqueiro what I just told you," Fernao answered. "Maybe he hasn't figured it out for himself yet. The more I see of soldiers, the worse I think they are at trying to deal with things they've never met before."

He found Junqueiro in the middle of a heated argument with the hostages the chieftain of the Ice People named Elishamma had left with the Lagoan army. Since the general and the hostages had no language in common, the exchange of ideas was necessarily limited, but both sides seemed most sincere.

One of the hostages, a fuzzy fellow named Abinadab, spoke some Yaninan, even if he hadn't admitted it when Elishamma handed him over to the Lagoans. Seeing Fernao, he rounded on him. "You tell your big man to let us go," he cried. "Our chief not know mangy Yaninans have strong mangy friends when he gives us."

"Too bad," Fernao said. "We are not without power ourselves. We have marched a long way. Now we are almost in sight of Heshbon. Soon we will take it. Then the Algarvians will have a harder time fighting us."

"You dream," Abinadab said, and scornfully turned his back.

"What is he havering about?" Junqueiro demanded. "What are they all havering about? Powers above, they're ugly – and smelly, too." Fernao translated for him. The Lagoan general clapped a hand to his forehead. "Tell them that, if they don't like being hostages, they can be victims. I doubt their worthless lives have much energy, but they might keep a few sticks charged."

No matter what Fernao thought of Junqueiro, that was exactly the right line to take with the Ice People. If the mage enjoyed putting it into Yaninan so Abinadab could translate it for the rest of the nomads, no one but he had to know that. The men of the Ice People cried out in furious indignation, but when Fernao and Junqueiro both ignored them, they went off shaking their heads and muttering.

"Teach them the fear of the powers above," Junqueiro muttered, glaring at their backs.

"They don't believe in the powers above – only their foolish gods," Fernao said, the last word necessarily being in the language of the Ice People. " "But they do know strength, and they know weakness, too. If we don't get some dragons here, strength will not lie on our side."

He waited for Junqueiro to burst like an egg. No dragon could fly all the way from Lagoas even to the eastern edge of the land of the Ice People, let alone all the way to the neighborhood of Heshbon. But, to his surprise, the commanding general only nodded and said, "It's being taken care of."

"It is?" Fernao blinked. "How?"

Junqueiro chuckled. "Ah, so you mages don't know everything there is to know, eh?" Fernao gave him a dirty look: while talking with Affonso, he'd accused the general of being none too bright, and didn't enjoy having the charge flung back in his face. Junqueiro went on, "While you weren't looking, sorcerous sir, the Kuusaman navy built ley-line transports to haul dragons out to where they needed them. They used them against the Gongs out in the Bothnian Ocean. Now we have some, too, and a couple of them are on their way to the Narrow Sea, to give us a hand against Mezentio's dragons."

"We have? They are?" Not for the first time, Fernao found he really didn't know everything. The discovery never failed to annoy him. "When will they get here? Have they made it past Sibiu safe?"

"Aye, they have, or so my crystallomancer tells me," Junqueiro answered. "Now that a good deal of the ice has melted, they could follow ley lines farther south than any we dared use in dead of winter. No Algarvian dragons or leviathans out of Sibiu spied them. They'll be here in a couple of days, and then we'll have dragons of our own, powers above be praised."

"Powers above be praised indeed," Fernao agreed. "Nothing like giving Mezentio's men a nasty surprise the next time they come calling."

"Aye." Looking pleased with himself, the Lagoan general whuffled out air through his white-streaked mustachios. "They may have made us stop for a little while, but we're not down for good." He puffed out his chest and looked strong and brave. Fernao had always thought he was strong and brave. What the mage had wondered was whether Fernao had any brains. Now Fernao began to hope he did.

But the Lagoan dragons didn't get there to give the Algarvians a nasty surprise the next time the Algarvians flew overhead, for Mezentio's dragonfliers returned later that evening, not long before sunset would usher in the brief spring night. This time, they had more eggs than on their first visit. Huddled in a hole in the ground, Fernao hurled curses at them that he knew would not bite. He also cursed the mosquitoes that kept harassing him. The mosquitoes bit. Again, the curses didn't.

This time, a couple of dragons did swoop low to flame the Lagoan soldiers. A heavy stick on a behemoth's back blazed one of them out of the sky. Fernao cheered himself hoarse, even though the dragon's thrashing death throes did as much damage to the Lagoans on the ground as had its fiery breath.

After the Algarvians flew off again, a runner came shouting Fernao's name. On following the man, he discovered that three of the hostages had taken advantage of the chaos to flee. The ones who hadn't got away looked as if they expected to be blazed for their comrades' transgressions. Fernao wondered whether they were grateful to be spared or despised the Lagoans for their mercy.

When morning returned, so did the Algarvian dragonfliers. Going forward while eggs fell was impossible for the Lagoans. Scattering to minimize the damage from the enemy's eggs was a better ploy. It wouldn't have been had Junqueiro feared an attack from Yanina's footsoldiers, but the Yaninans had shown they had no stomach for such assaults.

The Algarvians came back twice more that day, keeping the Lagoans from advancing against Heshbon. The scouts Talsu did send forward showed that the Yaninans, despite their unwillingness to attack, were strengthening positions that covered the approaches to their coastal base. The commanding general cursed when he got the news, though he could hardly have expected anything different.

And then, that evening, Lagoan dragons did come flying into the army's unhappy camp – eleven of them, no more, and all in the last stages of exhaustion. The men who flew them were hardly in better shape. "Leviathan," one of them said, gulping at the flask of spirits a soldier pressed into his hand. "Cursed leviathan, or more likely a pool of them. We never knew we were in any trouble, either dragon transport, till the eggs they planted against our sides burst. By then they were long gone underwater. And not long after that, both our ships went under the water, too. Most of the dragons, most of the fliers, never made it out." He swigged again, tilting the flask so he could drain it dry.

"What will we do without enough dragons to fight the Algarvians?" someone asked. The question hadn't been aimed at Fernao, but he saw only one thing the Lagoans could do: they would have to retreat.

"We are not satisfied," King Swemmel told Marshal Rathar. "By the powers above, how can we be satisfied, with the cursed redheads still infesting so much of the richest part of our kingdom?"

Rathar bowed his head. Had he been in Swemmel's audience chamber, he would have gone down on his belly, but the king had come to his office, and so that indignity was spared him. He said, "Your Majesty, we may not have done so much as you'd hoped, but we have done a great deal. Even after the mud fully dries, the Algarvians will be hard pressed to mount another assault on Cottbus. The last one cost them dear, and we have new fortifications protecting the way west toward the capital."

He'd hoped his words would please the king, but Swemmel's eyes blazed angrily. "We care little for what the Algarvians may seek to do to us," he growled. "We care far more for what we can do to the Algarvians."

Within limits, that was a good attitude for a soldier to have. King Swemmel had never recognized limits, not for himself, not for those he commanded. Rathar said, "We will hit back at Mezentio's men in the south. But we must also make sure the capital is safe. When the ground lets the redheads move, they won't stand idle, waiting to be attacked."

The marshal of Unkerlant wondered how big an understatement that was. The previous summer and fall's campaign had proved the Algarvians had taken too big a bite to swallow at once. It hadn't proved they couldn't swallow it in several gulps rather than one. And Rathar remained uneasily aware that, man for man, Mezentio's soldiers were better than Swemmel's. He thanked the powers above that Unkerlant had more men.

Swemmel said, "We had better not rest idle, either. As soon as the ground dries, we want us to move first, before the Algarvians can." He walked over to the map on the wall by Rathar's desk. "You are always talking about flanking attacks. If we can flank them out of Aspang here, their whole position in Grelz crumbles."

Rathar nodded. The king had been furious for some time because the Unkerlanters hadn't driven King Mezentio's men out of Aspang. Having the redheads there didn't thrill Rathar, either. He'd managed to talk Swemmel out of a headlong assault on the city; Unkerlant had already tried that and bloodily failed. The marshal had no compunction about spending lives, but wanted to buy something with what he spent.

And if he'd managed to get the king thinking about flanking maneuvers, he'd accomplished something as important as winning a major battle. "I believe you're right, your Majesty. I would like to go south and prepare that attack myself. . . ."

But King Swemmel shook his head. "From your own mouth came the words: the Algarvians will not stand idle when the ground dries. What *will* they do, Marshal? What would *you* do, did you wear Mezentio's kilt?"

Swemmel *was* having a good day. He couldn't have found a more pertinent question to ask. Rathar did his best to think his way into King Mezentio's mind. One answer emerged: "I would strike again for Cottbus, here in the center. It's still as important as it ever was. No matter how well we've fortified the ground in front of it, the Algarvians will still want it."

"We agree," Swemmel said. "And, because we agree, we are going to keep you here in front of the capital, to defend it against the redheads."

"I obey, your Majesty," Rathar said glumly. He wished he could fault Swemmel's logic. But if he was the best general Unkerlant had and Cottbus the vital place likeliest to be endangered, where better to station him than here?

"Of course you obey us," Swemmel said. "Did you not, we should have got ourselves a new marshal some time ago. Now – ready this assault against the Algarvians around Aspang, pick a general who will run it well, and set it in motion as soon as may be." The king swept out of the office.

Major Merovec looked inside. When Rathar nodded, his adjutant came in. "What now?" Merovec asked cautiously.

Rathar told him what now. The marshal did not try to hide his frustration. Even if Merovec reported him to the king, Swemmel would have a hard time blaming him for wanting to go out and fight. That wasn't to say Swemmel couldn't blame him, but the king would have to work at it.

"Whom will you choose to command in the south, since you may not go yourself?" Merovec asked.

"General Vatran has fought as well as anyone could reasonably expect down there," Rathar answered, which was true: not even King Swemmel had complained of Vatran. "I'll leave him there till he proves he can't do the job – or till a more important one comes along and I promote him into it."

Merovec thought that over, then nodded. "He seems capable enough. Not like the early days of the fight with the redheads, when generals got the sack about once a week."

"They got what they deserved," Rathar said. "One thing war does in a hurry that peace can't do at all: It sorts out the officers who know how to fight from the ones who don't. And now, since I can't go south to lead the attack there, I am going to go to the lines in front of Cottbus, to see what we can do to help Vatran when the attack goes in."

The lines were a good deal in front of Cottbus these days. A finger's breadth between two pinholes on the map translated into three hours' travel in a ley-line caravan car through some of the most ravaged countryside Rathar had ever seen. Neither the Unkerlanters nor their Algarvian foes had asked for or given quarter. Every town and village had been fought over twice, first when the Algarvians advanced towards Cottbus and then when they fell back from it. A wall that hadn't been knocked down was unusual, a building unburnt and intact a prodigy.

About two-thirds of the way to the front, the caravan halted. "I'm afraid you'll have to get out now, Marshal," the apologetic mage said. "We haven't cleared all the Algarvian sabotage from the ley line east of here. We can't afford to lose you."

"You'd better have a horse waiting for me, then," Rathar growled.

"Oh, aye, sir, we do," the mage said. Sure enough, a groom held a peppy-looking stallion not far from where the caravan car had halted. Rathar, no splendid equestrian, would have preferred a gelding, but expected he could manage a more headstrong beast. He was a pretty headstrong beast himself.

The stallion must have been at the front for a while. It shied neither at the sharp stink of wood smoke as it trotted past one more burned-out village nor at the reek of dead meat, which seemed to be everywhere, sometimes faint, sometimes sickeningly strong.

One reason the horse was able to trot, as opposed to sinking hock-deep in mud, was that it stuck to a roughly corduroyed path leading east. Rathar rode past a gang of Algarvian captives laying boards in the roadway under the sticks of a squad of Unkerlanter guards. He wished every one of the soldiers who served King Swemmel could have looked at these filthy, scrawny, thoroughly cowed Algarvians. The redheads sometimes seemed to go forward for no better reason than that both they and the Unkerlanters they fought were convinced they could. This gang of Algarvians would never raise that particular awe in their enemies again.

At last, as the sun set behind him and evening twilight began to gather, the marshal heard the rumble of bursting eggs ahead. When he entered the next village, a couple of Unkerlanter sentries popped out of the ruins and barked, "Halt! Who goes there?"

"I am Marshal Rathar," Rathar said mildly. "Before you blaze me for not knowing the password, take me to your commander. He will vouch for me." He wondered just which colonel or brigadier was in charge in these parts. If it was a man whose career he'd blighted, the fellow might deny any knowledge of him and have him blazed for a spy. It wasn't likely, but stranger things had happened in Unkerlanter history.

In the event, Rathar wasted some perfectly good worries. The officer to whom the wide-eyed sentries led him, Colonel Euric, saluted so crisply, Rathar thought his arm would fall off. He gave Rathar his own battered chair, fed him a big bowl of boiled buckwheat groats, onions, and what was probably horsemeat, and poured him a heroic nip of spirits.

"I may live," Rathar said when he'd got outside of the meal and the drink. "All of me but my backside hopes I will, anyhow."

"They don't pay you to be a cavalryman, lord Marshal," Euric answered with a grin. "They pay you to tell cavalrymen what to do."

"I can't very well do that if I don't know what's going on myself," Rathar said. "That's why I like to come up to the front when I get the chance." He pointed at Euric, much as King Swemmel was in the habit of pointing at him. "What *is* going on up here, Colonel?"

"Not a whole lot, to tell you the truth, not right this minute," Euric answered. "We're waiting for things to dry out, and so are the stinking redheads. Meanwhile, we toss some eggs at them, they toss some at us, a few soldiers on both sides get killed, and it won't change the way the war turns out one lousy bit." He stuck out his chin, as if defying Rathar to come down on him for his frankness.

Rathar instead got up, walked over to him, and folded him into a bear hug. "I always praise the powers above when I run into a man who speaks his mind," he said. "It doesn't happen all that often, believe you me."

Euric laughed. He was young to be a colonel – not far past thirty. Rathar wondered how many men above him had been killed or disgraced to let him get where he was. Outspoken captains were common enough. Most of them never advanced past captain. Euric was likely to be good at what he did, and had surely been in the right place at the right time.

The colonel said, "I tell you this, too: we'll lick the buggers unless we do something stupid. And we're liable to." He raised an eyebrow and grinned at Rathar. "Nothing personal, of course."

"Of course." Rathar grinned back. He slapped Euric's shoulder. "You'll go far. No telling who'll chase you while you're going, but you'll go far."

Both men laughed. They shared a bond, the same bond that joined so many Unkerlanter officers: so far, they'd survived the worst both King Swemmel and the Algarvians could do to their kingdom. Rathar felt he was ready for anything now. By Euric's jaunty expression, they had that in common, too.

Algarvian dragons started dropping eggs on the village. Both Euric and Rathar jumped down into a hole in the ground behind the battered hut where Euric made his headquarters. "What will they think of you in Cottbus when you come back all covered with mud?" Euric asked.

"They'll think I'm earning my keep," Rathar replied. "Either that or they'll think I'm a cursed fool for taking chances I don't have to."

"As opposed to the rest of us poor sods, who do have to take chances," Euric said. Rathar shrugged. That had no answer, nor had it since the beginning of time. But Euric laughed and added, "You took your share before – I know that for a fact." An egg burst close by, showering Rathar with mud that stank of corpses. Even so, he felt . . . *forgiven* was the word he finally found.

"You do good work," Ethelhelm said to Ealstan as they sat in the band leader's flat sipping wine. "If I'd had you casting accounts for me since the days before the war, I'd've had a lot more money for the Algarvians to take away from me."

"Heh," Ealstan said. Ethelhelm's wit always had a bite to it. Rubbing his chin, Ealstan went on in musing tones: "Before the war . . . It was only two and a half years ago, but it seems like forever."

"Oh, longer than that." Ethelhelm cocked his head to one side, waiting to see how Ealstan took his reply. Ealstan laughed. A lot of people, he supposed – his cousin Sidroc assuredly among them – would have stared in blank incomprehension. Ethelhelm nodded, as if he'd passed an obscure test. "You're hardly old enough to piss without wetting yourself, but you've got an old head on your shoulders, don't you?"

"People say so," Ealstan answered. "I'm cursed if I know. I take after my father, is what I think it is."

"I took after my father, too, once upon a time," Ethelhelm said. "Took after him with a carving knife, as a matter of fact. Didn't catch him, though."

Ealstan couldn't imagine going after his father with a knife. Uncle Hengist? That was a different story. Ealstan wondered how Sidroc was doing, if he was hale, whether he'd gone off to fight for the Algarvians yet. He rather hoped Sidroc had. That would be the easiest on everyone – except perhaps Sidroc.

"I'd better get back," Ealstan said, rising to his feet. He couldn't suppress a pang of disappointment at leaving Ethelhelm's large, airy, elegantly decorated flat and having to go back to his own, which was none of these things. Ethelhelm was a wealthy young man; Ealstan knew to the copper just how wealthy the musician was. He'd made a fortune before the war broke out, and had managed to hold on to most of it despite Eoforwic's occupation first by the Unkerlanters and then by the Algarvians.

What with the business Ealstan had, not only from Ethelhelm but also from his other clients, he could have afforded better than the nasty little flat in which he and Vanai were living. He could have afforded better, but he didn't dare move. If he went to a better neighborhood, Vanai would draw more attention. That was the last thing he wanted, especially now that the redheads had herded all the Kaunians into one cramped bit of Eoforwic.

Ethelhelm came with him to the door and set a hand on his arm. "You're a good fellow, Ealstan. I wouldn't mind seeing more or you – or meeting your lady, either."

"Thank you," Ealstan said, and meant it. Not all his father's clients – probably not even half his father's clients – dealt with Hestan socially, as opposed to on business matters. And for Ethelhelm to say that about Vanai . . . Ealstan bowed. "We'd like that, too. But with things the way they are, I don't know how we'd manage it."

Ethelhelm had never seen Vanai in person, and Ealstan made a point of not referring to her by name. But the musician had shown, as much by what he didn't say and didn't ask as by what he did, that he had a good notion she was a Kaunian. "With things the way they are," he echoed. "Well, here's hoping they don't stay that way forever, my friend. You be careful, do you hear me?"

Ealstan laughed; it might have been his father's laugh coming out of his mouth. "You're talking to a bookkeeper, remember? If I weren't careful, what would I be?"

"Who knows what you'd be?" Ethelhelm answered. He hesitated; maybe he was wondering how much he ought to say, or whether to say anything. At last, he decided to: "You aren't careful all the time, or you'd be somebody with a different lady, or with no lady at all."

"I suppose so," Ealstan said. "But I'm careful now, by the powers above. I have to be." He didn't wait for Ethelhelm to reply, but stepped out into the hallway and closed the door behind him. Then he hurried downstairs. These stairs were carpeted, not bare, battered boards. They didn't smell of cabbage and beans and occasionally of urine. Ealstan sighed. He liked comfort. He'd grown up in comfort. He'd thrown it aside for love – and if that wasn't the hoariest cliché in bad romances, he didn't know what was. Vanai made him happy – made him joyful – in ways he'd never imagined before, but that didn't mean he was immune to missing his comforts.

Out on the streets, Eoforwic had the pallid, threadbare look of every other Forthwegian town in the third year of a war long lost. But Eoforwic's was a more genteel, more splendid shabbiness than, say, Gromheort's. The white-bearded man who strode past Ealstan wore a herringbone wool tunic shiny with age at the elbows and seat and with a frayed collar, but a garment that would have cost a lot new.

All the capital was like that. Buildings ruined in one round of fighting or another still showed fine bones. Buildings that hadn't been ruined also hadn't been kept up. Brickwork was filthy; weeds pushed their way into the sunlight between paving slabs. But the memory of what had been persisted. If Ealstan let his eyes drift a little out of focus, he could imagine Eoforwic with King Penda ruling it, not an Algarvian governor general.

When he got back to his own neighborhood, he didn't need to let his eyes go unfocused. This part of town had been grimy and unkempt during King Penda's reign. Of that he had no doubt whatever. Even the stray dogs on the narrow, winding streets moved warily, as if afraid of having their belt pouches slit.

Sure enough, the stairwell in his block of flats stank of piss. He wondered which neighbor had got drunk and been unable to hold it in. It was curiosity of the most abstract sort; he didn't really want to find out.

He knocked on the door to the flat he shared with Vanai in the rhythm of a Forthwegian children's verse. She unbarred the door, which she wouldn't have done had he knocked in an ordinary way. An ordinary knock meant a stranger, and strangers, these days, were deadly dangerous to Kaunians.

"Hello, sweetheart," Ealstan said, and quickly slipped inside. He barred the door again before Vanai could. The bar was reinforced with iron. The brackets on which it rested and the screws that secured those brackets to the wall were the strongest Ealstan could find, far stronger than the ones the landlord had used in the flat. Anyone who wanted to come in after Vanai wouldn't have an easy time of it.

"Tell me everything you did," Vanai said after they'd kissed. "Everything, from the moment you went out the door." Cooped up in here, she relied on him to be her eyes and ears on the outside world, as a blind man might rely on a cleverly trained dog to take him through streets he could not see.

His arms still around her, Ealstan obliged. Not only did he have a good memory for detail, he also had a most appreciative audience. And, as he talked, his hands wandered, now to the small of Vanai's back, now farther down, now straying upward to cup her breast. Touching her got him as drunk as wine did, with never a hangover afterwards.

She snuggled against him, too. He'd discovered she didn't like being surprised by touch. Her face would go hard and tight, and she would stand as stiff as if carved from wood. Something bad must have happened to her back in Oyngestun, but she'd never said what it was, and he didn't have the nerve to ask. But when she wasn't taken aback, he pleased her as much as she pleased him.

And what he had to say pleased her this evening. "Ethelhelm said that about me?" she demanded, and made Ealstan repeat it. "He said that? Really? He *is* a good fellow, isn't he?" She paused and lost a little of her glow. "Of course, he's also supposed to be part Kaunian himself."

"Aye – but I think he would have said the same thing even if he weren't," Ealstan answered. "You don't have to be part Kaunian to like Kaunians – I ought to know." He stroked her hair. She tilted her face up. They kissed for a long time.

At last, Vanai broke away. "Let me go take the pot off the fire so supper doesn't scorch," she said. She was gone only a moment. Then they went into the bedchamber together.

When they'd finished, they lay side by side for a while, one of her legs hooked over his. He leaned over, taking his weight on an elbow, so he could caress her with his free hand. He knew he would rise again pretty soon; at seventeen, he could make love about as often as he wanted to. But his stomach had other things on its mind, and growled loud enough for Vanai to hear.

She giggled. Ealstan's ears heated. She said, "Shall we eat now? We can always come back." With so little else to do and with both of them so young, they spent a lot of time in the bedchamber.

As if to leave no possible doubt about its opinion, Ealstan's stomach rumbled again. He laughed, which was the easiest way to hide his embarrassment. "All right," he said. "I'd better, or my belly will shake the building down."

He spooned up barley and onions and chopped almonds and a few tiny bits of smoked pork, thoughtfully smacking his lips. "You did something different this time."

Vanai nodded. "You got me that fennel I asked for, so I used it."

"Is that what it is?" Ealstan said. For Forthwegians, fennel was medicine, especially useful in hemorrhoid preparations. Kaunians did more cooking with it, a tradition that went back to the days of the Empire. Ealstan smacked his lips again. "Tastes better than I thought it would." Listening to himself, he admired his own calm. He hoped Vanai did, too.

By the way the corners of her mouth twitched, she was trying not to smile, or maybe not to laugh out loud. "You shouldn't have bought it if you didn't expect me to put it in the food, you know."

"I suppose not." Valiantly, Ealstan kept eating. People did cook with fennel, and they didn't perish as a result. He *had* bought this particular batch, and it *hadn't* gone into a hemorrhoid cream. And, when you got down to it, it wasn't so bad. "Interesting flavor," he admitted. This time, Vanai did laugh.

They'd just finished supper when shouts down on the street made them both hurry to the window to find out what was going on. Night had already fallen, and the street was poorly lit, but Ealstan didn't need long to make sense out of what was happening: a couple of men in kilts were forcing a fellow in trousers along the sidewalk. One of them took a bludgeon off his belt and walloped the luckless Kaunian, who cried out again. No one came to his rescue.

Gently, Ealstan pushed Vanai away from the window. "We have to be careful, sweetheart," he said. "We don't want them looking up here and seeing you."

Two tears slid down her cheeks. By her expression, they were tears of rage. "No, of course we don't," she said, her voice quivering. "As long as I stay inside my trap here, I'm perfectly safe."

Ealstan didn't know how to answer her. He didn't think there was any way to answer all the meanings she'd put into that. He did the best he could: "I love you."

"I know you do," Vanai said. "That just leaves the rest of the world out of the bargain."

Once again, Ealstan found himself without a good reply.

Skarnu felt a certain amount of pride at going into Pavilosta by himself. He'd been staying on the farm once Gedominu's for going on two years now: long enough for the locals to conclude he'd be around for a while, even if they'd call him things like *the new fellow* the rest of his days.

Silver jingled in the pockets of the homespun trousers Merkela had made for him. He needed a couple of drill bits. He knew more about them than Merkela did, and at least as much as Raunu, so he was the logical one to come and buy them. Even so, he felt small-boy enthusiasm for an outing of a sort he hadn't enjoyed before.

Down in Priekule, he would have gone into an ironmonger's, bought what he needed, and left with as much dispatch as he could. In a village like Pavilosta, he'd discovered, that was bad manners. A customer was supposed to pass the time of day rather than brusquely laying down his money. Skarnu found that peculiar, since the country folk were usually much more sparing of words than his old set back in the capital, but it was so.

After gossip about the weather, the way the crops were shaping, and a couple of juicy local scandals, Skarnu managed to make his escape. His time in and around Pavilosta had changed him more than he would have guessed, though, for instead of heading straight back to the farm, he ambled into the market square to see what he could see and hear what he could hear.

Maybe I'll learn something to help in the fight against the redheads, he thought. But he was too honest with himself to let that stand for long. *Maybe I'll pick up something to make Merkela laugh or cluck.* That came closer to the truth, and he knew it.

Somehow or other, he found himself gravitating toward the enterprising taverner who was in the habit of setting out a table at the edge of the square. If he stood around and soaked up a mug of ale, or even a couple of mugs of ale, he wouldn't look the least bit out of place. So he told himself, at any rate.

As a lure to the men who were both thirsty and curious, the taverner had set out a couple of copies of a news sheet that had come in from some larger town – from Ignalina in the east, Skarnu saw by the masthead. "Full of nonsense and drivel," the taverner said as the noble picked up the sheet.

"Well, why do you have it, then?" Skarnu asked.

"To give people something to complain about, more than anything else," the taverner answered. Skarnu laughed. The other fellow held out his hands. "What? D'you think I'm joking? See for yourself – you'll find out."

"I don't need to read it to know it'll be full of all the things the Algarvians want us to hear and empty of the ones they don't," Skarnu said.

"Right the first time," the taverner said. "Some people believe the manure the news sheets print, if *you* can believe that, pal." Skarnu nodded but said nothing. He would have bet that, while talking to people who got on well with the redheads, the taverner praised the news sheet to the skies. With him, the fellow went on, "Take a look at this here, for instance. Go on, just take a look at it."

BALL IN THE CAPITAL CELEBRATES ALGARVIAN-VALMIERAN AMITY, the headline read. The subscription fees for the ball had gone to pay for relief for wounded Algarvian soldiers. Skarnu hoped the redheads needed to collect lots and lots of money for such a worthy cause.

The list of those who attended the ball showed what the Algarvians meant by amity, too. Pointing to it, Skarnu said, "It's all their officers and our women."

"Oh, aye – did you expect anything different?" the taverner said with a scornful sneer. "These noblewomen, they're all whores, every cursed one of 'em."

Skarnu started to bristle at that slur against his class. He had to remind himself that he wasn't, at the moment, a member of his class. His eyes kept sliding down the list. It was always Brigadier and Viscount So-and-so, a redhead, coupled with Countess What's-her-name, a Valmieran. He had no doubt that most of the pairs named were coupled literally as well as metaphorically.

Colonel and Count Lurcanio and Marchioness Krasta. Skarnu almost missed that one pairing among so many. He stared and stared, wishing his eyes had gone on past without catching his sister's name. What was she doing? What could she be doing? But that had an all too obvious answer.

He stared so hard, the taverner noticed. "What's the matter, pal?" he asked. "See somebody you know?" He threw back his head and laughed uproariously at his own wit.

What would he do if Skarnu said aye? *Call me a liar, I hope*, Skarnu thought; every other possibility struck him as worse. "Likely tell," was all he answered, which made the taverner chuckle, but not chortle again.

Worst was that Skarnu couldn't just up and leave. He had to hang around and finish his ale and keep on chatting while he was doing it. Anything else would have been out of character and drawn notice.

Concealing his anguish was as hard as hiding a physical wound would have been. He'd always known Krasta was headstrong and willful, but what could have possessed her to take up with an Algarvian officer? He wondered if she knew; she'd never been long on self-examination.

After he could finally start back to the farm with propriety, he heaved a long sigh. His sister had made, or more likely unmade, her bed; now she would have to lie in it . . . with this Colonel Lurcanio. Skarnu sighed again. Whatever Krasta had done, he couldn't do anything about it.

He walked on for a while before realizing that wasn't true. If he and his comrades did somehow manage to expel the Algarvians from Valmiera, Lurcanio would go and Krasta, presumably, would stay. What would happen then? He couldn't imagine. Nothing pleasant – he was sure of that.

"My own sister," he muttered as he trampled along the road. It was safe enough; he could see a good long blaze in every direction. "My own *sister!*" He'd never dreamt of being on opposite sides of a civil war with Krasta.

When he got back to the farm, he told Raunu and Merkela the news straightaway. He knew he didn't have to; no one else was likely to associate his name and that of a noblewoman in Priekule. But he preferred not to take the chance: better they should hear it from him than from anybody else.

Raunu had been repairing the steps that led up to the farmhouse porch. He paused to pound in a couple of nails, using what struck Skarnu as needless force. Then he said, "That's hard, sir. Aye, that's about as hard to choke down as anything I can think of."

Merkela took Skarnu by the hand. "Come upstairs with me," she said. Raunu's ears went red. He drove one more nail in a tearing hurry, then almost ran out of earshot of the farmhouse; Skarnu listened to the veteran's footfalls fade as he himself followed Merkela up the stairs to her bedchamber. If this was how she wanted to make him feel better, he had no doubt she'd succeed.

In the bedchamber, she turned his way. He held out his arms to her. She stepped toward him – and slapped him in the face almost hard enough to knock him off his feet.

He staggered back, one hand coming up to his cheek, the other grabbing for the door frame to help him stay upright. "Powers above!" he exclaimed, tasting blood in his mouth. "What was that for?"

Merkela's eyes blazed. "I'll tell you what that's for," she snarled. "It's for caring about your sister now that she's an Algarvian's whore."

"She's still my sister," Skarnu mumbled. His cheek felt as if it were on fire. He probed the inside of his mouth with his tongue, trying to find out whether Merkela had loosened any of his teeth for him.

"You haven't got a sister, not any more." Merkela spoke with great certainty – in that, at least, she was a lot like Krasta. "If she knew what you were doing, don't you think she'd blab to this redheaded colonel and count, whatever his name was? Powers below eat him and eat his name, too."

Skarnu started to say, *Of course she wouldn't*. But the words clogged in his throat. He had no idea what Krasta would do if she found out he was one of the small, stubborn band of men – and women – keeping the war against Algarve sputteringly alive in the countryside. Maybe she would keep silent. But maybe she wouldn't, too.

Merkela saw the doubt on his face. She nodded. "You aren't trying to lie to me, anyhow. That's something."

"Lurcanio," Skarnu said. "His name's Lurcanio."

"I told you, I don't care what his name is," Merkela answered. "He's an Algarvian. That's enough to know. Your sister gave herself to him, and now you have no sister."

"Aye," Skarnu said dully. Merkela viewed the world in very simple terms. He'd known that all along. This time, though, try as he would, he couldn't find any way to believe she was wrong.

She eyed him. She nodded once more, in what looked like grudging approval. And then, in a swift, sudden motion, she pulled her tunic up over her head and threw it on the floor. She kicked off her sandals, yanked down her trousers and drawers, and took the couple of steps that brought her over to the bed. She lay down on it. Now she held out her arms to him. "You have no sister," she repeated. "But you have me."

Getting out of his own clothes was a matter of a moment. He lay down beside her, clutching at her flesh as fiercely as she grabbed for him. Very often, their lovemaking reminded him more of combat than of anything he'd ever known with other women. This was one of those times. She sank her teeth into his shoulder as if she meant to draw blood; her nails scored his back and flanks. He squeezed and pinched and prodded her. She pressed his hands to her, urging him to be rougher yet.

And when, not much later, he drove into her, he hardly cared whether he hurt her as well as pleasing her. By the way she moaned and bucked beneath him, she hardly cared, either, or knew the difference. His lips and teeth, jammed against hers, muffled her final cry. A couple of fierce thrusts later, he spent himself deep inside her.

Sweat made their bodies stick and slide against each other. Merkela pushed at him, to remind him to take a little weight on his elbows. He didn't want to pull away; he hoped he'd get hard again inside her, so they could start again. Now that he was past thirty, though, such things didn't happen very often. Sure enough, in a minute or two he flopped out.

Merkela reached for him. She wasn't trying to make him rise; it seemed almost a gesture of respect for an admired foe. "Later," she said. "There's always later."

"Aye," Skarnu said, though he thought she was talking more to part of him than to all of him.

And indeed, Merkela started slightly, as if his voice reminded her all of him lay in this bed with her. Maybe she needed reminding; even more than a year after they'd started lying down together, she often called out her dead husband's name at the moment of climax.

Her expression sharpened. She reached out and tapped Skarnu's chest with a fingernail. "You have no sister," she said once more, and he nodded again, admitting as much. She turned her head south, in the direction of Priekule. Her voice sank to a throaty whisper. "But oh, the vengeance you can take on her who was once your kin after the kingdom is free once again."

Skarnu thought about it. What *would* he do, if he ever saw Krasta face to face again? *Colonel and Count Lurcanio and Marchioness Krasta.* The words in the news sheet seared like vitriol. He nodded. "Aye."

Nineteen

Hajjaj's secretary – his new secretary, his loyal secretary, his secretary who was not an Unkerlanter spy – stuck his head into the Zuwayzi foreign minister's office and said, "Your Excellency, Marquis Balastro has arrived."

"Very well, Qutuz. I am ready to receive him." Hajjaj rose to display the Algarvian-style tunic and kilt he had donned for the occasion. They were making him sweat unreasonably, but that was one of the prices he had to pay for conforming to the diplomatic usages of the rest of Derlavai. "You may bring him in."

"Aye, your Excellency," Qutuz said, and went off to get the Algarvian minister.

A moment later, Hajjaj and Balastro were clasping hands. "Good day, good day," Balastro said. He was stocky, middle-aged, vigorous, and much smarter than he looked. Reaching out to pat Hajjaj's tunic, he said, "If you were a pretty young wench, I'd be disappointed you were wearing this. As is" – he shrugged a grandiloquent Algarvian shrug – "I can live with it."

"Your reassurances do so ease my mind," Hajjaj said dryly, and the redheaded Algarvian noble threw back his head and laughed out loud. Balastro would have laughed out of the other side of his mouth had Hajjaj told him Ansovald of Unkerlant had said something similar not so long before. Foreigners always thought of Zuwayzi nudity in terms of pretty young wenches. In one sense, Hajjaj understood that. In another, the ways it missed the point never failed to amuse him.

Balastro made himself comfortable with the cushions that did duty for chairs in Hajjaj's office. So did the Zuwayzi foreign minister. Unlike most of his countrymen, he had a desk, but a low, wide one, one he could use while sitting on the carpet: another compromise between Zuwayzi usages and those of the rest of Derlavai.

The secretary came in with a silver tray that held the ritual tea and cakes and wine. Unlike Ansovald, Balastro appreciated the ritual. As long as he and Hajjaj nibbled and sipped, he stuck to small talk. He had an abundant store of it; Hajjaj enjoyed listening to him and fencing with him. He said as much – tea and cakes and wine were also a time for frank praise.

Balastro gave back a seated bow. "I rejoice at pleasing you, your Excellency," he replied. "I do my best to 'treat my friend as if he might become an enemy,' and I hope that precludes inflicting boredom."

When he quoted the proverb, he did so in the original classical Kaunian. Hajjaj sipped at his cup of wine to keep from showing what he thought of that. Balastro was, and was proud to be, a man of culture. But he was also a man of Algarve, a man whose kingdom was tormenting the Kaunians who had shaped so much of the culture he displayed. Somehow, Balastro and his countrymen saw no contradiction there. Algarvians always wanted everything at once.

While partaking of tea and cakes and wine, Hajjaj could not say anything so serious without, by his own lights, becoming a boor. That he would not do. Presently, Qutuz took the tray away. Balastro smiled and said, "Well, shall we get on with it?"

"I am at your service, my lord Marquis," Hajjaj replied. "As you must know, I am always pleased to see you, and I am always curious to learn what is in your mind."

"Even when you don't like it," Balastro said, without much malice.

Hajjaj gravely inclined his head. "Just so, your Excellency. Even when I don't care for what you say, how you say it never fails to fascinate me." The Kaunian proverb crossed his mind again.

He won a chuckle from Balastro, but the Algarvian minister quickly sobered. "I can only speak simply here, for my message is of the plainest – Algarve needs your help."

"*My* help?" The Zuwayzi foreign minister raised an eyebrow. "Truly your kingdom is in desperate straits if you expect a skinny old man to shoulder a stick for you."

"Heh," Balastro said. "I thought we were coming to grip with things. I mean Zuwayza's help, of course."

"Very well, though my reply changes little," Hajjaj said. "Your realm is also in difficulties if you expect a skinny young kingdom to shoulder many sticks for you."

"Of course we are in difficulties," Balastro said – he could, sometimes, be refreshingly frank. "If we weren't, we would have taken Cottbus before winter froze us in our tracks."

He could, sometimes, also be disingenuous. "Winter did rather more than freeze you in your tracks," Hajjaj pointed out.

"Well, so it did," Balastro said. "We had misfortunes; I can hardly deny it. But we have the Unkerlanters checked now, all along the line. And this year . . . this year, by the powers above, we'll beat them once for all." He sat up very straight, as if making his bearing serve as proof for his claims.

From what the Zuwayzi generals said to Hajjaj, and from what he could gather for himself, Balastro was telling the truth about what had happened: the Unkerlanters were no longer advancing against Mezentio's men. How much the spring thaw had to do with that, Hajjaj wasn't sure. He suspected no one else was, either. As for the future . . . "You said last summer that you would beat Unkerlant then. Since you were wrong once, why should I not think you're wrong twice?"

"Because of everything we did to Unkerlant last year," Balastro answered – he had answers for everything, as most Algarvians did. "If you hit a man once, he may not fall right away. But if you hit him again and keep hitting him one blow after another, he *will* go down."

Unkerlant had hit Algarve one blow after another, too. Who would fall, as far as Hajjaj could see, remained anyone's guess. But Balastro would doubtless have some compelling explanations as to why it wouldn't be Algarve. Mentally stipulating as much, Hajjaj asked what he judged the more important question: "What sort of help do you need from us?"

"Our main effort this year will fall in the south," Balastro replied. "We aim to finish taking away Unkerlant's breadbasket, to lay our hands on the herds of horses and unicorns and behemoths she raises there, and to seize the cinnabar mines in the far southwest. With all that gone, King Swemmel can hardly hope to keep standing."

He was, Hajjaj judged, likely to be right; if Algarve could seize so much, Unkerlant *would* fall. Whether King Mezentio's men could do what they had in mind to do, though, was another question. Hajjaj said, "I will not ask my sovereign to send Zuwayzi warriors to the far south. He would say no, and I would agree with him. If you need more men than Algarve can provide, you have Yaninan allies there."

"So we do, and we'll use them." Balastro's expression said exactly what he thought of Algarve's Yaninan allies, but Hajjaj already knew that. The Algarvian minister went on, "Nor would I ask King Shazli to send brave Zuwayzin to a land in which bare skin is hardly a fitting uniform, however well it may fit." He laughed.

"What then?" Hajjaj asked, though by now he thought he knew. Balastro had glided down this ley line before.

Sure enough, the Algarvian marquis said, "King Mezentio would have you strike hard at the Unkerlanters here in the north, to tie down as many of their men as you can and to keep them from sending reinforcements to put in the line against us."

"I understand why you say this," Hajjaj answered slowly. "But I would remind you, your Excellency, that Zuwayza has already done everything in this war that she set out to do. We have taken back the line set up in the Treaty of Bludenz, and more land beyond it. That suffices. The clanfathers would not rejoice to hear that they needed to send their men into new battles."

"Would they rejoice to hear that everything they've won might be lost again through dithering?" Balastro returned.

Hajjaj had to work to hold his face impassive. Balastro had unerringly found the best argument he could use. But Hajjaj said, "I think we understand the notion of 'enough' better than you Algarvians. Some of the things you've done in your fight against Unkerlant—" He broke off. He'd long since made his feelings about massacring Kaunians plain to Balastro.

The Algarvian minister quoted another proverb in the original Kaunian: "'For a good cause, wrongdoing is virtuous.'"

Hajjaj didn't know whether to admire Balastro's gall or to be horrified by it. After a moment's struggle, horror won. "Your Excellency, considering what your kingdom is doing, how can you in good conscience let that language flow from your lips?"

"They would have done it to us, if only they'd thought of it," Balastro said. Hajjaj shook his head. The Kaunian kingdoms had had a good many

Algarvians under their rule when the Derlavaian War began. They hadn't slaughtered them. Maybe, as Balastro said, they hadn't thought of it. Hajjaj's guess was that they never would have thought of such an appalling thing.

He poured himself another cup of wine and tossed it down. That showed more of what he thought than he was in the habit of doing, but he couldn't help it. "We are your cobelligerents, your Excellency, not your servants," he said at last.

Balastro said, "This will serve your own interest as well as Algarve's. If we are beaten, will you be better for it?"

That would depend on how badly you hurt Unkerlant before Swemmel's men took you down, Hajjaj thought. Saying as much aloud struck him as undiplomatic. What he did say was, "This is a proposition I can take to his Majesty. The final choice lies in his hands."

"Oh, aye, likely tell," Balastro said. "Anyone who's neither blind nor deaf knows where Zuwayza comes by her dealings with other kingdoms." He pointed straight at Hajjaj.

"You are mistaken," said the foreign minister, who knew perfectly well Balastro wasn't. "King Shazli is his own man. Mine is but the privilege of advising him."

Balastro's laugh was loud and long and merry. "I haven't heard anything so funny since the story about the girl who trapped the eel, and I was only twelve years old then, so I doubt that one would hold up. Yours will."

"You do me too much credit," Hajjaj said.

"In a pig's arse," Balastro said cheerfully. "But all right: We'll play it your way. Since you know King Shazli so well, what do you suppose he's likely to say about what you'll ask of him?"

"I think he would be likely to ask the generals and the clanfathers for their views," Hajjaj replied.

Balastro sighed. "I was hoping you – ah, that is, of course, King Shazli – might make up . . . his mind more quickly, but I suppose it can't be helped. All right, your Excellency, I don't suppose I can complain. But tell your generals and clanfathers not to take too long deciding, because this dragon is going to fly with you or without you . . . and Algarve will remember which."

"I understand," Hajjaj said. Unkerlant would not let Zuwayza out of the war; Algarve insisted Zuwayza go in deeper. *Trapped*, Hajjaj thought, not for the first time. *Like all the rest of the world, we're trapped.*

Bembo and Oraste walked warily along the paths that meandered through the biggest park in Gromheort. The moon had set an hour before; they had nothing but starlight by which to see. No braver than he had to be, Bembo carried his stick in his hand, not on his belt. "Anything could be lurking in here," the Algarvian constable complained. "Anything at all."

"I'm not worried about *anything*," Oraste answered. "*Anybody*, now – that's a different business." His head kept turning now this way, now that.

So did Bembo's. The bushes by the edges of the path were shaggy and untrimmed; dead grass from the winter before remained tall enough for people to hide in it. "You'd think they'd do a better job of keeping this place up," Bembo said.

Oraste laughed. "If they haven't got the silver to repair most of their miserable buildings, what are the odds they're going to cut the grass?"

That made an unpleasant amount of sense to Bembo. Even so, he said, "How are we supposed to catch anybody in this miserable place if they don't?"

With a shrug, Oraste answered, "As if anybody cares whether we catch these worthless buggers, unless they bother Algarvians. But if the bad actors know we walk through the park, they won't be so likely to roost in it."

"Huzzah," Bembo said petulantly, and then, as he heard a rustle from the dead grass, "What's that?" Startlement made his voice go high and shrill.

"I don't know." Oraste, by contrast, sounded quiet and determined. He didn't have a lot of brains, he had no imagination at all, but he was a terrific fellow to have at your back in a brawl. He stepped off the path and moved purposefully toward the sound. "But we'd better find out, eh?"

"Aye," Bembo agreed in hollow tones. As much to keep up his own courage as for any other reason, he went on, "Any whoreson out to ambush us wouldn't make so much noise, would he?"

"Here's hoping," Oraste answered, which did little to reassure Bembo. The other constable added, "Now shut up."

However rude that was, it was good advice. Like Oraste, Bembo tried to step as lightly as he could, though he could hardly help making some noise while walking through thick, dry grass. The rustling ahead grew louder as the constables drew nearer. The breeze picked up. It made the grass rustle, too. With luck, it helped mask the sounds Bembo and Oraste were making.

Bembo sniffed. He was no bloodhound, but any constable would have recognized that smell. Fear ebbed. "Just some cursed drunkard who's gone and puked himself," he said.

"Aye." Almost invisible in the darkness, Oraste nodded. "Ought to beat the son of a whore to within an inch of his life for the turn he gave us. Stinking old Forthwegian bum."

After another couple of steps, Bembo smelled spilled wine as well as puke. He thought about putting away his stick and taking his bludgeon off his belt instead. Sergeant Pesaro wouldn't mind if he and Oraste did work out their alarm on a noisy drunk. Pesaro would just regret not being here to share the fun. Bembo pointed. "There he is."

"I see him," Oraste said. "Miserable white-haired bugger – why didn't he die twenty years ago?"

Along with Oraste, Bembo stood over the drunk. He sniffed again, then let out a theatrical sigh of relief. "Powers above be praised, at least he hasn't gone and shit his trousers." He had to listen to his own words to realize what he was saying. "He's not a white-haired old Forthwegian. He's a blond!"

"Well, curse me if you aren't right," Oraste exclaimed. He laughed out loud, the most joyous sound Bembo had ever heard from him. "Now nobody'll care at all if we kick him to death. Let's do it."

"I don't know . . ." Bembo had no great appetite for mayhem. All he wanted to do was get out of the park, finish his beat, and go back to the barracks so he could climb on to his cot again. "Let's just leave him here. He's so far gone, he won't even know we're stomping him, and the head he'll have in the morning'll hurt worse than a boot in the ribs."

"No," Oraste growled. "He's not where he's supposed to be, is he? You bet your arse he's not – all these Kaunians are supposed to be in their own district. And if we catch 'em outside when they aren't working, they're fair game, right? He looks like he's working hard, don't he?" He laughed.

But the Kaunian, however unsanitary he was, wasn't so far gone as Bembo had thought. As Oraste drew back his foot for the first kick, the blond opened his eyes and sat up. He spoke in Kaunian, a line of poetry Bembo recognized and understood because he'd had to memorize it: "'The barbarians are at the gates.'"

"Shut up, fool," Oraste said, and did kick him. An instant later – Bembo didn't see how – his partner was lying in the grass. With a curse, Oraste scrambled to his feet. He hauled off and kicked the Kaunian again. Again, he went sprawling, too, this time with a howl of pain.

The Kaunian, who was having trouble staying in a seated position, spoke again, this time in understandable if slurred Algarvian: "Leave me alone and I will extend you the same privilege."

"Leave you alone?" Oraste got up once more. "Powers below eat me if I will, you louse-ridden . . ."

"Wait!" Bembo grabbed Oraste before his partner could try to kick the drunk again. A light had gone on in his mind, however dark his surroundings remained. "I think he's a mage."

"A mage, a stage, an age, an outrage," the drunken Kaunian said, still in Algarvian. "If I were sober, I could do great things. If I were sober, I could . . . could . . ." He brought his hands up to his face and began to weep. Through his sobs, he went on, "But it is not enough. It could not be enough. Nothing could be enough." He looked up at the constables. "For you, *nothing* is enough. Do you wonder that I am not sober?"

"Let's get out of here," Bembo whispered urgently. "I don't want to tangle with a mage, even a drunk one, even a lousy one. Tangling with mages uses up a lot of constables."

Oraste let Bembo lead him a few paces away, but then shrugged off his comrade. "That Kaunian sorcerously assaulted me," he declared, as if before a panel of judges. "He has to pay the price." He whirled around and pointed his stick at the drunken blond sorcerer.

But the Kaunian wasn't there. Bembo stared. It wasn't as if the fellow were hiding in the dead grass; it was as if he'd never been there. Only the lingering stink of vomit and Bembo's memory said anything different.

Oraste said, "Nothing's enough for us Algarvians, eh? I'll show that blond what nothing's all about." And he blazed at the place where the Kaunian had been – the place where, Bembo realized, the Kaunian still had to be.

A shriek said his beam had found the mark. An instant later, the Kaunian reappeared – wounded, he couldn't keep holding the masking spell. Oraste blazed him again. The blond jerked as if struck by lightning when the beam hit him.

With what was plainly dying effort, the mage pointed toward the two constables and began intoning a spell in Kaunian. Bembo understood only a couple of words of it, but knew it had to be a curse. Now he blazed at the drunken mage, too, and his beam caught the Kaunian in the face. With a last groan, the mage sank back and lay very still.

"That's the way," Oraste said, and thumped him on the back. "See? You are good for something after all."

"Oh, shut up," Bembo answered. "You think I want to go around with a wizard's last curse on me, you're daft. But it never would have happened if you'd let him alone in the first place."

"He deserved what he got," Oraste said. "Powers above, he deserved more than he got."

"We'll have to tell Pesaro about it when we get back to the barracks," Bembo said. His stomach was lurching unpleasantly. He'd never killed a man before.

Oraste let out a couple of grunts probably meant for laughter. "Pesaro'll give us each a shot of brandy, tell us we did good, and put us to bed – and you know it as well as I do, too."

He was probably right. But Bembo's stomach did another few lurches. Now that he thought about it – something he tried not to do – he'd sent plenty of Kaunians off to certain death. Blazing the drunken mage still felt different. He couldn't pretend here, as he did there, that he really hadn't had anything to do with their deaths. Blazing a man in the face left no room for doubt about what happened.

On the other hand, the Kaunian mage might – would – have harmed Bembo and Oraste if Bembo hadn't blazed him. The Kaunians he hauled out of villages or off the streets of Gromheort hadn't done anything to him or to anybody else.

Bembo shook his head. Thinking about it was much too complicated – and too unpleasant, too. "Let's go," he said. "We'll get out of here, we'll finish our beat, and then we'll go back to the barracks. The carrion there won't be going anywhere till somebody comes and picks it up after we report in."

"Now you're talking sense," Oraste said. "Come on. Shake a leg."

The rest of the park was quiet. Even so, Bembo was glad to escape it. He didn't know whether he'd been talking sense or not. Like any constable with an ounce of brains or more than two weeks' experience, he craved quiet shifts. He'd hoped for one tonight, hoped and been disappointed.

Other constables patrolled the perimeter of the quarter where Gromheort's Kaunians had to live, but Bembo and Oraste came near that perimeter as they neared the end of their beat. "Won't be long," Oraste said. "I aim to do some serious sleeping once we get in."

Yawning, Bembo nodded. Morning twilight was beginning to paint the eastern sky gray and pink. He yawned again. He didn't like the late-night shift. And then he grew alert once more. "Powers above," he said softly. "Here comes another Kaunian – a woman, looks like." Even in twilight, that pale gold hair was hard to miss.

"Aye," Oraste said, and then, raising his voice: "What are you doing out of your district, sister?"

As the woman got closer, Bembo saw that her trousers were very tight indeed, her tunic of transparent silk. She was on the skinny side, but worth looking at. In slow, clear Algarvian, she answered, "I am going home. My name is Doldasai. I have leave to be out: I was sent for to screw one of your officers. You may check this. It is true."

Oraste and Bembo looked at each other. Unlike almost any other Kaunian, an officer's whore might be able to make trouble for them if they bothered her. Bembo said, "Well, go on, then." Doldasai strode past him as if he didn't exist. He turned to watch her backside, but she wasn't working now, and put nothing extra into her walk. He shrugged and sighed. You couldn't have everything.

As soon as the ley-line caravan stopped moving, Sergeant Leudast stood up in the straw of the car in which part of his company had traveled. The car was better suited to hauling livestock than soldiers; by the lingering stench that filled it, it had carried a lot of livestock. But Unkerlant, these days, used anything it could.

Leudast undogged the door and slid it open. The fresh air that poured into the car made him notice the livestock smell more than he had for a while; he'd got used to it as the caravan came down into the Duchy of

Grelz. "Come on, boys – out we go," he said. "Now we're here, and we'll have work to do."

His men held in their enthusiasm, if they'd ever known any. After the botched attack on Lautertal, they had to be wondering again about the orders they were getting. But, wondering or not, they had to obey. So did Leudast. He knew that, too.

He jumped down out of the car and waved to Captain Hawart, who waved back and came up to him with a grin. "Well, what did you think of Cottbus when we went through it?" Hawart asked.

"If you hadn't told me we were going that way, sir, I never would have known it," Leudast answered. "And in a closed car like that one, I didn't get a chance to see it at all. As far as I'm concerned, Cottbus smells like cows."

"As far as you're concerned, everything smells like cows right now," the regimental commander said, and Leudast could hardly disagree. Hawart went on, "But you should have known we'd be going through Cottbus even if I hadn't told you. It's the biggest ley-line center in the kingdom; that's one of the reasons we had to hold on to it no matter what."

Hawart was a man not just of wit but also of education. He paid Leudast a compliment by assuming the sergeant shared his background. Leudast knew only too well that he didn't. Trying to hold his own, he said, "You mean hanging on to Cottbus makes us more efficient." King Swemmel was wild for efficiency, which meant his subjects had to be, too.

To Leudast's relief and pride, Captain Hawart nodded. "That's right. If we'd lost Cottbus, we'd be going around three sides of a rectangle to get soldiers from the north down here to Grelz."

If they'd lost Cottbus, they would have lost the war. Hawart didn't dwell on that. Neither did Leudast. He said, "Well, we're here now, and we got here the short way. As long as we are here, we'd better make the redheads sorry about it."

"Aye, that'd be efficient, sure enough," Hawart agreed. He didn't dare sound anything but serious about King Swemmel's favorite word, either. He slapped Leudast on the shoulder. "Get 'em moving. Head 'em east." He might have been talking about cattle himself. "As soon as the whole army's in place, we'll show the Algarvians what we can do."

With shouts and waves and occasional curses, Leudast did get his men moving. The encampment into which Hawart's regiment went was one of the biggest ones he'd ever seen: rock-gray tents that stretched and clumped for a couple of miles. Here and there, heavy sticks thrust their noses up into the air.

Pointing to one of them, Leudast said, "Almost makes me hope the cursed Algarvians do send some dragons over. Those little toys will blaze them right out of the sky."

"So they will – if the weather stays clear so their crews can see where to aim, and so clouds don't make the beams spread too much to do any good," Captain Hawart told him. "Don't go wishing for any more trouble than you've got, Leudast. You'll generally have plenty."

Leudast knew good advice when he heard it. He saluted. "Aye, sir." After he made sure the soldiers in his charge were settled, he paced here and there through the encampment, trying to figure out what sort of orders the regiment would get when it went into action.

He returned to his company's tents certain of but one thing: whatever was coming would be big. The encampment held not only footsoldiers beyond counting but also units of horses and union cavalry – Leudast liked the bugling cries unicorns let out – and a good many behemoths, though he would have liked to see even more of the great beasts. There was also a large dragon farm.

"Oh, aye, Sergeant, we're as ready as can be for the stinking Algarvians," one of his troopers said. "What we get to find out next is how ready the redheads are for us."

Leudast wished he hadn't put it like that. The Algarvians were rarely anything but ready. They could be beaten – Leudast knew that now, where he hadn't been so sure the summer before – but they always put up every ounce of fight they had. Anybody who thought that would be different this time had to be drunk, either on spirits or, perhaps more dangerous, on hope.

Two days later, Hawart's regiment, along with a great many others, was ordered to the front. Leudast had got used to marching through land over which the Algarvians and Unkerlanters had already fought. This was another such battered landscape, one that looked as if a couple of petulant giants had vented their wrath on it: not so far wrong, if you looked at things the right way.

"All the egg-tossers!" said one of Leudast's troopers, a big-nosed kid named Alboin. "We're going to be dropping plenty on the redheads, we are."

"Aye," Leudast agreed. "We'll hit 'em a good first lick, that's for sure." What would happen after the first lick was anything but sure, as he knew too well. Egg-tossers had trouble keeping up with the rest of the army when that army was moving fast. He'd seen as much. He'd also seen that Unkerlanter egg-tossers had more trouble keeping up than their Algarvian counterparts.

Alboin had seen no such thing. He was one of the reinforcements who'd joined the company during the winter. By now, he'd had enough action to be well on the way toward making a veteran, but it had all been since the Unkerlanter counterattack began. "We'll lick 'em," he said, sounding absurdly confident.

"Aye, I think we will," Leudast said, more from policy than from conviction. From conviction, he went on, "Remember how they handled us at Lautertal. They can do worse than that. I'm not saying they will, but they can."

"Sure, Sergeant." But Alboin sounded as if he was talking from policy, too. He hadn't seen the Algarvians at their best, when the footing was good and they had the chance to maneuver.

Leudast said, "Listen to me. If the redheads weren't tough, nasty buggers, would we be fighting them in the middle of the Duchy of Grelz?"

Maybe that got through, maybe it didn't. Either which way, Alboin shut up and kept marching. That suited Leudast well enough.

Here and there up at the front, the Algarvians lobbed eggs at the Unkerlanters' positions. Leudast was glad when soldiers waved his company into the shallow trenches from which they would soon attack. The earthworks shielded his men and him from bursting eggs. Then, once in the trenches, he wasn't so glad any more. If the redheads started slaughtering Kaunians and making magic, the holes grubbed in the ground could turn into death traps.

He wondered if King Swemmel's mages would start slaughtering Unkerlanter peasants or old women or whomever it was they killed. On the one hand, he wanted magecraft to help the army move forward – and, more urgently, to help him stay alive. On the other, he couldn't help but think about the price his kingdom was paying to try to beat back the Algarvians.

Captain Hawart came along the line. "The attack goes in tomorrow morning before sunrise," he said, and walked on to keep spreading the word.

Leudast spread it, too. His troopers talked among themselves in low voices. They were ready. They were more than ready – they were eager. Leudast wondered how many of them would be eager after the attack, even if it succeeded. Not many, if his own experience was any guide.

Well before sunrise, the Unkerlanter egg-tossers started pounding at the Algarvian positions farther east. Leudast hoped they did lots of damage, because they were surely alerting King Mezentio's men to the coming assault. And the Algarvians responded, flinging eggs of their own at the Unkerlanters. But, as best Leudast could judge, his side had the better of the exchange. He huddled in his blanket and tried to sleep.

As black night gave way to gray twilight, the ground shook beneath him. He leaped up, ready to scramble out of the trench for his life if the shaking got worse. It didn't. Peering over the lip of the trench, he saw purplish flames spurting up from the ground he and his comrades would have to cross. These were Unkerlanter mages plying their trade, not Algarvians. Leudast muttered under his breath, hoping the sacrifice from his countrymen would help the army win victory.

Whistles shrilled, all along the line. Still not officially an officer, Leudast couldn't add another strident note. Instead, he shouted, "Come on, you buggers! They wanted to quarrel with us, and now they're going to pay the price."

"Urra!" his troopers roared as they burst from the sheltering trenches. "Urra! King Swemmel! Swemmel! Urra!"

Yelling himself, Leudast ran forward, too, one tiny drop in a rock-gray wave. However many of their own they'd killed to make the magic against Mezentio's men, the Unkerlanter mages hadn't got rid of all Algarvian resistance. Eggs fell among the advancing Unkerlanter troopers, making holes in their lines that reserves had to fill. Redheaded soldiers blazed down Unkerlanters, too.

But, try as they would, they couldn't stop or even seriously slow King Swemmel's men. Here and there along the shattered line, an Algarvian trooper would throw up his hands and try to surrender. Sometimes, the redheads managed to do it. Rather more often, they got blazed down.

"Forward!" Leudast shouted to his men, echoing Captain Hawart, who was doing his best to be everywhere at once for his regiment.

Unkerlanter magic had done dreadful things to the Algarvian trenches, so dreadful that Leudast and his countrymen had trouble pushing across the shattered ground. Flames still sullenly flickered every few feet. Resistance from the redheads stayed light.

"This is almost too easy," Leudast called to Hawart the next time he saw him.

"I like it," said Alboin, who chanced to be close by.

But Hawart looked worried. "Aye, it is," he said. "I haven't seen enough dead Algarvians to satisfy me, nor anything close. Where are they, curse them?"

"Buried when their trenches all caved in?" Leudast suggested.

"I hope so," the officer answered. "If they aren't, we're going to run into them pretty soon, and they won't be glad to see us."

"Powers below eat them, we weren't glad to see them, either," Leudast said. He ran and scrambled on, wondering how deeply the Algarvians had fortified their positions: there seemed to be no end to trenches and foxholes and barricades.

And then, as Hawart had worried about, the Algarvians started popping up out of holes beyond the reach of the Unkerlanters' magecraft. After that, nothing was easy any more.

Along with the rest of his company, Trasone stood at stiff attention in front of the barracks in Aspang. Major Spinello strode down the line with a box of medals. He paused in front of each man to pin one on to him, kiss him on the cheek, and murmur a few words before moving on.

When he got to Trasone, he said, "For making it through this cursed winter," and presented the decoration. After the ritual kiss that accompanied it, he pinned an identical decoration on Clovisio.

At last, everybody had his medal. Spinello strutted away. Trasone looked down at the decoration. It was stamped with a map of eastern Unkerlant and two words: WINTER WAR. He tapped Sergeant Panfilo on the shoulder. "Isn't that grand? We've all got frozen-meat medals to call our own."

Panfilo laughed, but not for long. "There's a lot of dead men only thawing out now," he said. "If you want to trade places with one of 'em, I doubt he'd complain."

"I like being alive just fine, thanks, Sergeant," Trasone said. "But twenty years from now I'm going to look at this cursed chunk of polished brass, and my feet'll start to freeze, and I'll taste behemoth that's starting to go bad. Once I get home, that's the stuff I want to forget, not remember."

"Now you do, aye," Panfilo agreed. "But how many times have you listened to veterans of the Six Years' War going on and on about everything they went through?"

Trasone grunted. That had the unpleasant feel of probability to it. "Good," he said. "My old man always bored me. Now I'll have an excuse to bore my kids, if I ever have any." He glanced west, in the direction of the Unkerlanters who still tossed eggs at Aspang. They wanted to make sure he wouldn't. So far, they'd had no luck.

When he woke up before dawn the next morning, he thought they'd smuggled more egg-tossers up close enough to strike at Aspang. But the rumbling roar, he discovered, came from the south, not from the west, and, while there were a great many bursts, none seemed close to the city.

"What's going on?" he asked around a yawn as he got up from his cot. "Are the Unkerlanters kicking up their heels, or have we got something laid on down south?"

"Nobody told me anything about an attack down south," Sergeant Panfilo said, "not yet, anyhow. I know we're shifting men down there, but we aren't set to move this soon."

"It's the Unkerlanters, then," Trasone said. "If they can't get us out of Aspang from the front, they're going to try and do it from the back. Fits the buggers, doesn't it?"

Panfilo laughed. "So it does. Now we have to find out if they get anywhere. If they don't, we can sit tight here. But if they do, we're liable to have to go out and work for a living again."

"Oh, aye, this is a rest cure, this is." Trasone snorted. "Come to beautiful Aspang for your health. The garden spot of southern Unkerlant, only eight months of winter a year. Don't fancy the weather? Wait a bit. It'll get worse."

"If you got any worse, they'd fling you in the bloody guardhouse," Panfilo said. "Too cursed early to be carrying on like that."

All the rest of the day, Trasone kept an ear on the racket from the south. It didn't fade; if anything, it got louder. He drew his own conclusions. Quietly and without any fuss, he made sure his kit was ready to sling on to his back at a moment's notice. He wasn't the only veteran doing the same thing, either.

Major Spinello burst into the barracks the next morning. "Let's go, let's go, let's go!" he shouted, full of energy as usual. "Swemmel's boys are getting rowdy, and it's up to us to show 'em that's our job."

He screamed at the men who weren't ready to move on the instant, and cursed the ones who were because they hadn't made sure their comrades were, too. That meant all the other officers and sergeants started screaming, too. If they'd wanted the battalion ready to move at a moment's notice, they could have started screaming earlier. For one thing, they weren't screaming at him, because he was ready. For another, he'd heard a lot of screaming in his time. It didn't faze him.

Under the lash of Spinello's tongue, the soldiers in the battalion tramped to the ley-line caravan depot and filed aboard cars that looked to have had better lifetimes. "We're going down to hit the Unkerlanters in the flank," Spinello said as they boarded. "Swemmel's boys are as nervous about their flanks as so many virgins, and we're going to screw 'em."

As they glided south out of Aspang, they passed the wreckage of several caravans lying by the side of the ley line. "Cursed Unkerlanters are a pack of *nervous* virgins," Trasone remarked, and got a laugh. If the Unkerlanters had managed to plant one more egg along the ley line, he and his comrades wouldn't have the chance to do much in the way of seduction.

But the ley-line caravan stopped where its operator wanted it to, not at the whim of some Unkerlanter irregulars. Trasone and his fellow troopers tumbled out. Again, Major Spinello was shouting, "Let's go! What are you waiting for? We have to move, curse it."

Maybe the major had been talking by crystal while on the caravan, because he seemed to know just where he was going. After Spinello led the battalion out of a stretch of woods, Trasone exclaimed in delight: "Behemoths!"

"*Our* behemoths," Clovisio said. "Where did they come from?"

"I don't know, and I don't care," Trasone said. "They're here, and the ground is nice and solid, so they can move. And when we've got behemoths that can do what they're supposed to do, the Unkerlanters had better watch out."

As if to underscore that, the behemoths trotted forward. Spinello shouted, "Come on, you lazy buggers, give 'em a hand. You know what to do." Not that many months off garrison duty, he didn't have any experience of what to do himself. But he was right, not only in his tactics but in being sure the veterans he commanded knew what to do. They hurried along with and behind the behemoths, ready both to protect them and to swarm through any holes they punched in the enemy's lines.

Unkerlanter egg-tossers kept pounding away at the Algarvian positions to the south and now to the southeast; by the sound of the fighting, King Swemmel's men had pushed the Algarvians back. That worried Trasone. But Sergeant Panfilo heard the same thing and grinned from ear to ear. "Those whoresons'll be so busy looking straight ahead of 'em, they won't even think about peering sideways till it's too late."

Trasone thought about that. "Here's hoping you're right, Sergeant."

By the affronted pose he struck, Panfilo might have been standing on the street of some Algarvian town rather than trotting across a wheatfield that was coming up rank with weeds. "Of course I'm right. Have you ever heard me wrong?"

"Only when you talk," Trasone assured him. Panfilo's glare deserved to go up on the stage. After a moment, though, the sergeant chuckled and got going again.

And Panfilo did turn out to be right. Half an hour later, the crews on the backs of the behemoths started lobbing eggs at swarthy soldiers in rock-gray. "Mezentio!" Major Spinello shouted, and all the troops echoed him: "Mezentio!"

The Unkerlanters had been moving forward, against the Algarvians to the east of them. When doing what they were ordered to do, whether that was making an attack or defending a position, they were among the stubbornest warriors in the world; along with so many other Algarvian soldiers, Trasone had found that out the hard way. When taken by surprise . . .

Taken by surprise, the Unkerlanters broke and fled in wild disorder. Some of them threw away their sticks so they could run faster. To complete their demoralization, a squadron of Algarvian dragons swooped out of the sky to drop eggs on some of them, flame down others, and start fires even in the green, damp fields.

After that, some of the Unkerlanters stopped running and threw up their hands in surrender. The Algarvians blazed them down a few of them in the heat of the moment, but only a few. Most got relieved of whatever they had worth stealing and sent up in the direction of Aspang.

"Keep moving!" Major Spinello shouted, not just to his own troopers but also to the behemoths' crews and to anyone else who would listen. "If we just keep moving, by the powers above, maybe we can get 'em all in a sack, cut 'em off from their pals, and pound 'em to pieces. How does that sound?"

"Sounds good to me," Trasone said, more to himself than to anyone else. He wondered how many other Algarvian officers were shouting the same thing on every stretch of this counterattack. Ruthless speed and drive had taken Algarve deep into Unkerlant. Now the Algarvians could use them again – and the Unkerlanters, Trasone vowed, were going to be sorry.

He also wondered what the Unkerlanter officers were shouting right now. The ones whose orders mattered, the ones with the higher ranks, wouldn't even know things had gone wrong yet. The Unkerlanters were too cheap or too lazy or too ignorant to give their soldiers as many crystals as they needed. That had cost them before. He hoped it would cost them again.

Because Swemmel's men didn't have a lot of crystals, they made elaborate plans ahead of time. Junior officers who changed plans without orders got into trouble. Here, that meant the Unkerlanters kept trying to go east even after the Algarvian counterattack against their northern flank. It also meant the counterattack got a lot farther than it would have otherwise. Not until midafternoon did Swemmel's soldiers realize the Algarvians had thrown a lot of men into the fight and really needed to be stopped.

By then, it was too late. Behemoths crushed the first few Unkerlanter regiments that turned from east to north. The Unkerlanters' strokes came in one after another instead of all at once, which made them easier to break up. The enemy even flung unicorn cavalry into the fight.

Trasone enjoyed blazing down cavalrymen. He enjoyed it even more when they rode unicorns than when they were on horseback. For centuries, unicorns with iron-shod horns had been the dreadful queens of the battlefield, terrorizing footsoldiers with their unstoppable charges.

Memories of them lingered in soldiers' minds to this day, even if sticks had made cavalry charges more dangerous to riders than to the men they attacked.

These days, behemoths ruled the field. They were ugly, but strong enough to carry not just soldiers but also egg-tossers and armor. The eggs they flung at the charging unicorns knocked down the splendid, beautiful beasts, sometimes three and four at a time. Wounded unicorns screamed like women in torment. Wounded riders screamed, too. Trasone blazed them once they were off their unicorns with as much relish as while they still rode.

The Unkerlanters were brave. Trasone had seen that ever since the fighting started. Here and now, it did them little good. A scratch force of cavalry couldn't hope to stop superior numbers of footsoldiers supported by behemoths. King Swemmel's men fell back in confusion. Trasone slogged after them. He and his fellow Algarvians were going forward again. All was right with the world.

Pekka went down on one knee, first to Siuntio, then to Ilmarinen, as if they were two of the Seven Princes of Kuusamo. Ilmarinen's chuckle and the leer that went with it said he knew the ancient significance of that particular gesture of obeisance from a woman to a man. Siuntio surely knew it, too, but was too much a gentleman to show he knew.

And Pekka, by this time, was used to ignoring Ilmarinen at need. "Thank you both, from the bottom of my heart," she said. "Without you, I don't think I could have persuaded the illustrious Professor Heikki" – she laced the words with as much sardonic venom as she could; Heikki was a nobody even in veterinary sorcery – "to release the funds to go on with the experiment."

"Always a pleasure to make a fool look foolish," Ilmarinen said, rolling his eyes. "Oh, and she is, too."

Siuntio said, "My dear, I only wish our intervention had been unnecessary. Were Prince Joroinen among the living, you would have had everything you needed in this laboratory here at the crook of a finger."

"Aye," Ilmarinen said. "You ask me, it's amazing you could get any work done at all in this miserable little hole of a laboratory."

Before she'd seen the elegant facilities at the university up in Yliharma,

Pekka would have bristled at that. Till then, she hadn't thought Kajaani City College was a bad place to do research. She knew better now, even if the Algarvian attack that had killed Joroinen had also kept her from performing her long-planned experiment.

"We do most of our work inside our heads, and can do it anywhere," Siuntio said with a chuckle: "the advantage of theory over practice. We only need the laboratory to see that we've done our sums correctly."

"Or, more often, that we've done 'em wrong," Ilmarinen put in. Siuntio chuckled again, this time on a note of wry agreement.

Pekka was too nervous to chuckle. Like any theoretical sorcerer, she knew her limits in the laboratory, and knew she was going to have to transcend them. "Let's see what happens when we use the divergent series," she said, her voice harsh. Bowing to her senior colleagues, she went on, "You both know what I'm going to do – and you both know what you'll have to do if things go wrong."

"We do," Siuntio said firmly.

"Oh, aye, indeed we do." Ilmarinen nodded. "The only thing we don't know is whether we'll be able to do it before things get too far out of control for anybody to do anything." His smile showed stained, snaggly teeth. "Of course, like I said, we do the experiment to find out what else we've done wrong."

"That isn't the only reason," Siuntio said with a touch of reproof.

Before the two distinguished old men could start snapping and barking again, Pekka repeated, "Let's see what happens. Take your places, if you please. And no more talking unless it's life or death. If you distract me, that's just what it's liable to be."

She wished Leino were down here with her instead of working on his own projects somewhere else in this rambling, sprawling building. Her husband was all business when he went into the laboratory. But, being all business, he cared little for theory, and theory was what counted here. One more thing to worry about: if the theory was wrong and the experiment went disastrously awry, she might take him with her in her own failure.

If she did, though, she'd never know it.

Looking from Siuntio to Ilmarinen, she asked, "Are you ready?" It was an oddly formal question: she knew they were, but until they acknowledged as much, she would do nothing. Siuntio's response was also formal; he dipped his head, a gesture halfway between a nod and a bow. Ilmarinen simply nodded, but his expression held no mockery now. He was as alive with curiosity as either of his colleagues.

Pekka went to the cage of one of the rats she'd selected. She carried the cage over to one of the white tables in the laboratory. After she stepped away, Siuntio came up and, peering through his spectacles, read the rat's name and identification number. Pekka solemnly repeated them and wrote them down, then pulled another cage off the shelf. She carried this one to an identical table and set it there. Now Ilmarinen stepped forward to read the beast's name and number.

Again Pekka repeated them and set them in her journal. She said, "For the record, be it noted that the specimens are grandfather and grandson." She wrote that down, too.

Siuntio said, "Be it also noted that this experiment, unlike others we have attempted before, uses a spell with divergent elements to explore the inverse relationship between the laws of similarity and contagion." Pekka also set that down in the journal.

Ilmarinen said, "Be it further noted that we don't know what in blazes we're doing, that we're liable to find out the hard way, and that, if we do, they won't find enough pieces of us to put on the pyre, let alone the precious experimental diary Mistress Pekka is keeping there."

"And be it noted that I'm not writing a word of that," Pekka said. Ilmarinen blazed her an impudent grin. She felt like blazing him, too, with the heaviest stick she could find.

"Enough," Siuntio said. Sometimes – not always – he was able to abash Ilmarinen, not the least of his sorcerous abilities. The other senior theoretical sorcerer quieted down now, even if Pekka doubted he was abashed.

"I begin," Pekka said. Then she spoke the ritual words any Kuusaman mage used before commencing a spell. They helped calm her. Kuusamo would go on even if she didn't, just as it had gone on for the millennia before she was born. Reminding herself helped take the edge off her nerves.

She started to incant, her voice rising and falling, speeding and slowing, in the intricate rhythms of the spell she and her fellow theoreticians had crafted. It wasn't the same version of the spell as she had begun to use in Yliharma when the Algarvians struck. Since then, she and

Ilmarinen and Siuntio had gone over it line by line, pruning here, strengthening there, doing their best to see that no error remained in either the words of the spell or the passes she made while chanting.

Spring in Kajaani was none too warm, but sweat sprang out on Pekka's face. She could feel the energies she was trying to summon and control. They were strong, strong. Every calculation had said they would be, but the distance between knowing and understanding had never felt greater.

"Powers above, aid us." Siuntio's voice was soft but very clear. He sensed it, too, then. Ilmarinen muttered something. Pekka didn't think it was anything like a prayer.

Even the rats started scurrying around in their cages. They worked at the doors with clever paws: clever, but not clever enough. The older one squeaked in fright. The younger one burrowed down into the straw at the bottom of his cage and tried to hide.

Pekka didn't blame him. She wanted to hide, too. The conjuration she'd made before, the one that had started her down this ley line, had been nothing like this. She wondered if some mage in the Kaunian Empire, or during the long, confused time after its fall, had tried a conjuration like this. If so, he hadn't lived through it – which the ancients would no doubt have termed summoning up a demon too strong to control. That old-fashioned terminology had always made Pekka smile . . . till now. What went through her mind now was, *I must be mad even for attempting this*. But she shook her head. The world around her had gone mad. She hadn't. She hoped she hadn't, anyhow.

She kept on with the spell. She had, by now, gone much too far into it to back out without consequences almost as bad as the ones she was trying to create – and with none of the safeguards her two colleagues could (she hoped) provide if everything went according to plan.

Don't do anything foolish. She always told herself that when she went to work magic instead of just working on it. She knew her limits as a practical mage. Because she knew them, and because she knew she was so close to them, she was doubly careful. She could afford a mistake no more than she could afford to try to abandon the conjuration.

"Ahh," Ilmarinen murmured. For a moment, Pekka, intent on spell and passes, didn't understand what had pulled that low-voiced exclamation from him. Then she too saw the thin, pale line of light running between the cages that held the two rats. She didn't smile – she was too busy to smile – but inside she exulted. Theory had predicted that discharge of energies, and theory, so far, was proved right.

As theory had also predicted, the line of light grew brighter with startling speed. Pekka had to squint through narrowed eyes to tolerate the glare. One of the rats – she never knew which one – squeaked in alarm.

If the conjuration didn't end soon, that light itself might prove enough to wreck the laboratory. Now Pekka worked with her eyes squeezed shut as tight as she could force them, but the brilliance swelled and swelled. She couldn't turn away, not unless she wanted to turn straight toward ruin. She smelled thunderstorms, as she might have if the beam from a stick passed close to her head. She wished the forces she was challenging were as trivial as that.

For a terrifying instant, she felt heat, heat that made the inside of a furnace seem like the land of the Ice People. The thunderclap that followed almost knocked her off her feet. All the windows in the laboratory broke, spraying shards of glass out on to the lawns.

Silence. Stillness. *I'm alive*, Pekka thought. *I hope the glass didn't hurt anyone*. And then, *Professor Heikki will be angry at me for putting all those windows on the department's budget*. The absurdity of that last thought made her snicker, but didn't make it any less likely to be true.

The odors of growing grass and of flowers bursting into blooms wafted into the laboratory chamber through the newly unglazed windows. Along with them, Pekka's nose caught a harsh reek of corruption. One way or another, the experiment had come to completion.

"Let's see what we've got," Ilmarinen said, echoing her thoughts.

Pekka went to the cage that had housed the older rat. He was still there – after a fashion. She nodded at seeing his moldering remains. Then she walked over to the other cage, the one that held – or rather, had held – his grandson. But for straw and a few seeds, it was empty now.

"Congratulations, my dear," Siuntio said. "This confirms your experiment with the two acorns, confirms and amplifies it. And, thanks to the refined conjuration and the life energy of the rats, it also confirms we can use this means to release sorcerous energy. And more will come."

Ilmarinen grunted. "Divergent series. They diverged, all right."

"Aye," Pekka said, still looking from one cage to another. "The one went on past the end of his span, the other back before the beginning of his time." She pointed to the empty cage. "Where is he now? Was he ever truly here? Did he ever truly exist? What would it be like, to be pushed out of the continuum so?"

"Do you want to find out?" Ilmarinen asked. "Experimentally, I mean?"

Pekka shuddered. "Powers above, no!"

One more long day like so many long days. Climbing down from the wagon that had brought him back to Gromheort from labor on the roads, Leofsig wondered if he shouldn't have picked a different line of work after all. He thought about going to the baths to revive himself, but lacked the energy to walk the couple of blocks out of his way he would have needed to get there.

"Home," he muttered. "Food. Sleep." As far as he was concerned, nothing else mattered tonight. Sleep loomed largest of all. If he hadn't known the Algarvian constables were liable to take him for a drunk and beat him up, he could easily have lain down on the sidewalk and fallen asleep there.

He put one foot in front of the other till he made it to his own front door. But even as he knocked, he heard a commotion inside. He came to alertness. Commotion was liable to mean danger for him or his whole family. If, for instance, Sidroc had got his memory back . . .

Someone in there heard his knock and lifted the bar off its brackets. Leofsig worked the latch and opened the door. And there stood Sidroc, a large, uncharacteristic grin spread over his heavy features. "I've finally gone and done it," he declared.

"Well, good for you," Leofsig answered. "Done what, now? If it's what it sounds like, I hope she was pretty."

His cousin guffawed, but then shook his head. "No, not that, though I won't have any trouble getting that, too, whenever I want it. I've gone and signed up for Plegmund's Brigade, that's what I've done."

"Oh," Leofsig said. "No wonder everybody in there is screaming his head off, then. You can hear the racket out here. Powers above, you can probably hear the racket over in the count's castle."

"Wouldn't surprise me one bit," Sidroc said. "I don't care. I made up my mind, and I'm going to do it. Powers below eat the Unkerlanters, and the cursed Kaunians, too."

"But fighting for Algarve?" Leofsig shook his head. He was too tired to argue as hard as he would have at another time. "Let me by, would you? I want to get some wine and I want to get some supper."

Now Sidroc said, "Oh," and stood aside. As Leofsig went past him, he continued, "Not so much fighting for Algarve as fighting for me. I want to go do this. I want to go see what the war is all about."

"That's only because you haven't done it," Leofsig said, remembering the smell of entrails laid open – and remembering the smell of fear, too.

"You sound like my father," Sidroc said scornfully.

"He hasn't done it, either, so he doesn't know what he's talking about," Leofsig answered, relishing the chance to say that about Uncle Hengist. "But I have, and I do, and I'm telling you you're crazy, too."

"You can tell me whatever you want. It doesn't matter worth a sack of beans, because I signed the papers this afternoon," Sidroc said. "Anybody who doesn't like it can cursed well lump it."

Leofsig wanted to lump Sidroc. But he also still wanted supper and sleep. And a house without Sidroc in it was liable to be a more peaceable place. So all he said was, "Have it your way," and walked down the entry hall and turned left into the kitchen.

His mother and sister were in there. "I heard you talking with him," Elfryth said in a stage whisper. "Fighting for Mezentio after what the redheads have done to our kingdom! The very idea! Did you persuade him not to?"

"No, Mother," Leofsig answered, and poured himself some wine. "And do you know what else? I didn't try very hard."

"Good." Conberge didn't bother holding her voice down. "I won't be sorry to see him out of this house, and nobody can make me say I will. Having him here has been nothing but trouble. If the Algarvians want him, they're welcome to him, as far as I'm concerned."

Sidroc must have gone back into the dining room after letting Leofsig in, for more shouts erupted from there: he and Uncle Hengist were going at each other hammer and tongs. Leofsig cocked his head to one side, wanting to catch some of the choicer names they were throwing back and forth. He almost missed his mother saying, "Here – I had a kettle of hot water over the fire waiting for you. You can wash now."

Reluctantly, he came back to the real world. "Oh. Thank you," he said, and hoped he didn't sound too vague.

Conberge set a basin on the floor for him. She and Elfryth headed out of the kitchen to give him privacy in which to wash. Over her shoulder, Conberge said, "Take the pork stew off the fire, if it starts to smell like it's burning."

"All right." Leofsig worked the pump handle in the sink to get cold water to mix with what his mother had heated for him. Then he scrubbed away at the dirt and sweat that clung to him. A washrag and a basin didn't let him do the job he could have at the baths, but he hadn't had to go out of his way to get here.

His father came into the kitchen while he was drying off. Leofsig didn't know whether Hestan had been home for a while or just stepped in. His father quickly made that plain: "You'll have heard the news, I expect."

"Oh, aye," Leofsig answered with a nod. "The whole neighborhood will have heard it by now, except for that old deaf man three doors down."

Hestan chuckled, then sighed. "That would be funny, if only it were funny, if you know what I mean. Sidroc doesn't want to listen to anybody, though I wish he would."

"You and Uncle Hengist are the only ones who do," Leofsig said as another blast of shouts came out of the dining room. "And I thought you'd be glad to see Sidroc gone, from most of the things you've said."

His father sighed again. "I would have been. Powers above, I was, till he said he was really going. After that . . . it's hard to watch your own kin walk into what can't be anything but a big mistake."

"If he goes, Ealstan's safer," Leofsig pointed out.

"That's so," Hestan said, "but Sidroc hasn't shown any sign of recalling just what happened there. I never felt safe enough about it to tell Ealstan he could come home, and he probably wouldn't want to now, not when he'd have to try to bring that girl with him."

"Vanai," Leofsig said, remembering how startled he'd been when Ealstan told him her name. "Aye. Now that the redheads are shutting so many of the Kaunians away, how could he bring her back to Gromheort?"

Before Hestan could answer, Sidroc shouted. "Curse you, you old shitter! Powers below eat you! I'm going where I *am* wanted!" A moment later, the door opened and then slammed shut. The whole house shook.

"That seems to settle that," Leofsig said, and his father nodded. He continued, "I'm sorry, but I'm not sorry, if that makes any sense. I won't miss him very much, and I'm safer with him gone, too, even if he hasn't made little sly cracks about turning me in to the Algarvians for a while."

"I don't think he ever meant them," Hestan said. "I hope he never did, I'll tell you that."

Leofsig was convinced his cousin *had* thought hard about betraying him to the Algarvian authorities, but held his tongue. Sidroc hadn't actually done it, and pretty soon he'd get shipped off to Unkerlant. He'd have plenty of more urgent things to worry about there.

Uncle Hengist came into the kitchen. He was Hestan's younger brother, and the handsomer and more dapper of the two. Now he looked older than Leofsig's father, and worn to a nub. "He's gone," he said, as if he couldn't believe it. "He walked out of here. He's gone."

"Aye," Hestan said. Leofsig busied himself with putting away the basin. That way, Uncle Hengist wouldn't be able to see the look on his face. As he'd said to his father, the whole block knew Sidroc was gone.

"Who would have thought he'd want to go fight for the Algarvians?" Hengist said, though Sidroc had been talking about doing that for months.

And Hengist had had some things to say about the redheads that didn't sit well with Leofsig, either. "Don't you think they're the coming thing any more, Uncle?" he asked.

His father gave him a look that told him to keep his mouth shut. Uncle Hengist scowled, but answered, "Even if they are, that's no reason to take up arms for them. They've got plenty of soldiers of their own."

You can't have it both ways, was what Leofsig wanted to say. One thing that stopped him was his father's warning glance, which had got more urgent than ever. The other was remembering that Hengist, like Sidroc, knew he'd escaped from an Algarvian captives' camp. He didn't dare push his uncle too far, not when he couldn't fully trust him.

Hestan said, "Powers above keep the boy safe, Hengist."

"*Boy* is right!" Hengist burst out. "But he's so cursed sure he's a man, and how can anyone tell him anything different?"

"He'll learn," Hestan said. "You did. I did. Leofsig has. We just hope he doesn't pay too high a price for his lessons."

"Easy for you to say," Uncle Hengist said.

"No, it's not," Leofsig's father answered. "I had a son in the army, the

Forthwegian army" – he couldn't resist the dig, and Hengist's mouth tightened – "and my other boy's gone, and who can say what happened to him? No one in Gromheort knows where Ealstan is. He might have fallen off the face of the earth."

"I never have understood what happened the day he disappeared, Hestan, the day Sidroc got hurt," Hengist said. "If I did understand it, I think I might have something more to say to you." He turned on his heel and walked away.

"He's liable to be more dangerous than Sidroc," Leofsig said in dismay after his uncle had gone.

"I don't think so," Hestan answered, and then, with one more sigh, "I hope not. He has other things than us on his mind right now, anyhow."

"Now that he won't have Sidroc staying with him, he ought to move out of here and find a place of his own," Leofsig said.

"Do you think so?" His father sounded genuinely curious. "My notion has always been that it's better to have him where we can keep an eye on him than to let him go off on his own and brood. Am I wrong?"

Leofsig considered. "No, I don't suppose you are. I wish you were, but I don't think you are."

From the hallway, Conberge called, "Are you decent in there? If you are, Mother and I would like to finish cooking."

"Come ahead," Leofsig said. "I have a better appetite for pork stew than I do for quarreling right now." His father raised an eyebrow, then solemnly nodded.

Twenty

For the first time since an egg from an Algarvian dragon killed Eforiel, Cornelu was back in his element: riding a leviathan in search of the most harm he could do to King Mezentio's followers. The leviathan, a Lagoan beast, wasn't trained up to the standards of the Sibian navy, but she was still young, and she could learn. He'd already seen as much.

True, these days, Cornelu patrolled the Strait of Valmiera, not the narrower channel that separated Sibiu from the mainland of Derlavai. His own kingdom remained under Algarvian occupation. Powers above, his own wife remained under Algarvian occupation. But he was fighting back again.

He tapped the leviathan in a pattern the same in the Lagoan service as it had been in that of Sibiu. Obediently, the great beast raised the front part of her body out of the water, lifting Cornelu with it so he could see farther. If an Algarvian ship glided down a ley line without his seeing it, he could hardly try to sink it.

Even with the added range to his vision, he saw nothing but sea and sky. He tapped the leviathan again, and it sank back under the water. By the way the beast quivered under him, he knew it thought rearing was part of an enjoyable game. That was all right with him. He would enjoy the game if it led him to Algarvians. King Mezentio's men wouldn't, but sending them to the bottom would only make Cornelu happier.

"Now," he muttered, "I think we've been traveling along a ley line, but I'd better make sure."

Like the skin-tight suit he wore, his belt was made of rubber. He took from one of the pouches on the belt an instrument of bronze and glass. Inside the hollow glass sphere that made up the bulk of it were two vanes of thinnest gold leaf. They stood well apart from each other.

Cornelu let out a satisfied grunt. That the vanes repelled each other showed they were in the presence of sorcerous energy – and the only sources of sorcerous energy out on the ocean were the ley lines that formed a grid on sea and land alike. If Cornelu waited here long enough, a ship was sure to pass close by.

But he had no idea how long *long enough* might be. And, loathing the Algarvians as he did, he was not in the mood to wait. He wanted to hunt. He was a coursing wolf, not a spider sitting in a web waiting for a butterfly to blunder along and give him a meal.

He turned his instrument this way and that in his hands, watching the gold-leaf vanes flutter as he did. He knew they spread wider when parallel to a ley line than when perpendicular to it. As he'd thought, the line on which he'd positioned himself and his leviathan ran from northeast to southwest. Without hesitation, he urged the leviathan in the latter direction, toward the coast of Algarvian-occupied Valmiera and of Algarve itself.

"If you don't go where the bees are, you won't get any honey," he told the leviathan. Talking to this new beast wasn't like talking with Eforiel. He'd told his old leviathan everything. With this one, he still felt a certain reserve. He wasn't sure how much it understood, either – after all, it spoke Lagoan, not Sibian. Cornelu knew that was an absurd conceit, but he couldn't get it out of his mind.

The leviathan swam along happily enough. It was doing what it would have done had it never made the acquaintance of mankind: foraging. When it got into a school of mackerel, its long toothy jaws opened and closed, snapping up fish after fish. The only notice it took of Cornelu on its back and of the eggs strapped beneath its belly was that they made it swim a little slower and more awkwardly than it would have otherwise. That let a couple of mackerel it should have caught get away. But it still caught plenty, and didn't seem aggrieved.

"Come on, my beauty," Cornelu urged it. "Come on. Bring me to a ship. It doesn't have to be a great big ship. Just bring me to a ship."

He was lying. He knew the kind of ship to which he wanted the leviathan to bring him: to a great Algarvian floating fortress, all bristling with heavy sticks and with egg-tossers. Sending a vessel like that to the bottom would be the beginning of revenge for everything Algarve had done to his kingdom and to his life.

But sending a vessel like that to the bottom wouldn't be easy. He knew as much. He would have to be sly. He would have to be sneaky. He would have to be lucky. The sailors aboard a floating fortress would always be alert against attack by leviathans. So would the mages aboard such a ship, though he didn't worry so much about them as he would have on land. He had his instrument for detecting sorcerous energy, but wasn't using any to speak of. That made his own sorcerous footprint very small and hard to note.

Sea . . . sky . . . sea . . . sky. Still nothing but sea and sky, as far as he could see. He muttered in frustration. And then he spied something neither sky nor sea, but not something to delight him as a hunter. Instead, he cursed and ordered his leviathan to dive. He hoped the dragon gliding through the air far above had not spied him.

His rubber suit and sorcery kept the cold of the southern seas from slaying him by stealth. Another sorcery let him get air from the water around him, so that he could stay down as long as the leviathan could. No mage had ever successfully applied that latter spell to a leviathan, to let it stay submerged without ever needing to come up and breathe. Nor had any mage ever made a spell to let a man dive as deep as a leviathan could without the weight of the water above him crushing out his life.

He had the leviathan stay submerged as long as it could. When it finally had to rise to spout, he anxiously scanned the heavens. If that dragonflier had spotted him before he took cover below the surface of the sea, an egg might fall out of the sky at any moment, or the dragon might come skimming low over the waves to flame him off his leviathan. He hated dragons and dragonfliers not least because they could hurt him and he couldn't hit back.

But, once more, he saw nothing but sea and sky. He breathed a sigh of relief at what had annoyed him only minutes before. He hated ley-line warships, too, but he hated them because they belonged to Algarve. Aye, they could hurt him. He could hurt them, too, though, if only he got the chance.

Patting the leviathan, Cornelu asked, "Now, which way did you swim when you went under?" The leviathan couldn't answer – and, by his own silly logic, wouldn't even have understood the question, being a Lagoan beast.

He pulled out the instrument he used to detect sorcerous energy. Both gold-leaf vanes hung limp, which meant the leviathan had swum away from the ley line. Cornelu turned the instrument in his hands. The vanes stayed limp. Cornelu cursed, loudly and foully. Why not? No one was around to hear him.

With a couple of taps, he ordered the beast to swim south. After what he judged to be about half a mile, he stopped the leviathan and examined the instrument again. If anything, the vanes hung closer together than they had before.

Cornelu grunted. He hadn't found the ley line, but he'd found where it wasn't. That gave him a better idea of where it was. He turned the leviathan back toward the north and swam past – he hoped he swam past – the point where he'd begun trying to reacquire it. Then he checked the instrument once more and nodded to himself. The vanes were separating.

Before long, he'd found the ley line again. He sent the leviathan south-west down it. These were Algarvian-controlled waters. Where were the warships with which the Algarvians controlled them?

Most patrols, by the nature of things – the ocean was vast, the targets upon it few and small and far between – ended in futility. Cornelu's whole war till now had been futile. He didn't know how much more futility he could stand.

That thought had hardly crossed his mind before he spotted a speck on the horizon. Hope flooded into him. If he could bring his leviathan back to Setubal after sinking an Algarvian ship, even the haughty Lagoans would have to give him his due.

Haughty wasn't quite fair. The Lagoans thought they were better than anybody else, but they didn't flaunt it the way, say, Valmierans did. For his part, Cornelu remained convinced one Sibian was worth three Lagoans any day. Nobody who talked through his nose the way King Vitor's subjects did was altogether to be trusted.

Well, now Cornelu had the chance to prove that of which he was convinced. He urged the leviathan toward the ship – and the ship was coming toward him, too. He couldn't have caught it from behind, not unless it was just lazing along.

He pulled a brass spyglass off his belt. A minor magic kept its lenses dry so he could peer through it right away. The ship seemed to leap toward him. He gasped. For a moment, he thought it *was* a floating fortress. Then he realized it was the next class down, a ley-line cruiser. His lips skinned back from his teeth in a savage smile. "It will have to do," he said.

Through the spyglass, he saw sailors on the deck of the cruiser. A jack of green, white, and red snapped in the breeze. Cornelu nodded. He wouldn't be attacking a Lagoan ship by mistake. That would be biting the hand that fed him.

Those sailors would be on the lookout for leviathans. If they spied him, he would never get close enough to plant his egg against the cruiser's flank. He fought the Algarvians, ironically, by keeping his mount at the surface. Mezentio's men would be watching for the big plumes of vapor that rose when a leviathan came up from the depths. So long as his beast kept breathing steadily, it wouldn't give itself away too soon.

Cornelu had to gauge when to dive for his attack. If he waited too long, Mezentio's men *would* spot him. If he dove too soon, his leviathan wouldn't be able to come alongside the cruiser. He would have to surface before it got there, and then he would really be in trouble.

When he judged the moment ripe, he tapped the leviathan, which slipped beneath the waves and sped toward the ley-line cruiser. It knew it had to swim alongside or under the ship long enough to let him attach the egg. He'd sometimes wondered if leviathans had any true notion why men did such things. The beasts fought among themselves, over mates and sometimes over food. Did they know their masters fought, too?

And then Cornelu had no more time to wonder, for the leviathan brought him up right below the cruiser. His lost Eforiel could not have done a finer job. All he had to do was pick the moment to signal the leviathan to swim belly-up beneath the Algarvian warship, so he could slide along the harness and release an egg. The egg clung to the hull of the ley-line cruiser. As soon as its shell touched the ship, a spell began to bring it to life.

Cornelu regained his position near the leviathan's blowhole. Urgently now, he ordered his mount away from the ship. The egg would burst whether he was close or far. He didn't want to have to endure a burst close by: this egg was far heavier and more potent than any a dragon could haul into the air. He also wanted to get far enough from the ley-line cruiser to let the leviathan surface safely.

He didn't quite manage that. The leviathan had to spout a little sooner than he'd expected. The Algarvians flashed mirrors in his direction. They weren't sure to which side he belonged. He took a mirror from his belt pouch and flashed back. His signal would be wrong, but, as long as they kept playing with mirrors, they wouldn't be lobbing eggs at him. And his leviathan swam farther from the cruiser with every heartbeat.

Before long, the Algarvians realized he wasn't one of their own. Eggs began flying through the air toward the leviathan. The first couple fell short, but the enemy's aim was liable to improve in a hurry.

Then the egg he'd planted burst. The ley-line cruiser staggered in the water, as if it had collided with an invisible wall. The Algarvians forgot all about him as they tried to save their ship. They couldn't. Its back broken, it plunged beneath the sea. Cornelu's bellow of triumph might have burst from the throat of a warrior from five hundred years before: "For King Burebistu! For Sibiu!" This time, he'd struck the enemies of his kingdom a heavy blow.

About every other Algarvian officer who came into the tailor's shop Traku ran took one look at Talsu working beside his father and told him, "You are lucky to be alive."

Each time, he had to nod politely and say something like, "Aye, I know it."

However polite he acted, he wasn't always sure it was a good thing that he was alive. The wound in his left side still pained him. When he walked, he wanted to bend his body to favor it as much as he could. When he sat, he kept twisting to find the position where it hurt least. He couldn't find a position where it didn't hurt at all. By what the healer said, that would be a while yet, if it ever came.

What made it hard to stay polite, though, was that the Algarvians didn't mean he was lucky to be alive after the redheaded soldier stabbed him. They meant he was lucky the occupying authorities hadn't seized him, tied him to a post, put a blindfold on him, and blazed him.

One of Mezentio's officers wagged a forefinger under Talsu's nose. "You are a fortunate fellow in that the military governor for this district is an easygoing old man who would sooner swive his pretty young mistress than do his job. With most of his kind . . ." And the fellow drew that finger across his own throat.

"Oh, aye, I'm about the luckiest man in the world," Talsu agreed. By then, he'd said it so often, he managed to sound as if he believed it. The Algarvian captain shut up and left him alone.

But what right did the redheads have to take any woman who struck their fancy? What right did they have to pick a fight with someone who happened to be a Jelgavan woman's friend? What right did they have to stab someone who didn't care for their lewdness?

The right of the conqueror. That was what they would answer. That Algarvian had proved his answer with the point of his knife, and had got off scot free. Talsu didn't have so sharp a counterargument.

"Well, Father, it will be a while yet before I can run around and get in trouble like I could before," he told his father that evening as Traku was closing up the shop.

Traku started to slap him on the shoulder, as he would have done before Talsu made the acquaintance of a blade. He stopped awkwardly, the motion half completed. Any jar hurt Talsu these days. Embarrassed at himself, Traku said, "I wouldn't mind if you did."

"I wouldn't mind if I did, either," Talsu said, "but I can't, not for a while. I haven't got the strength to haul rocks or break them, either. But you taught me the needle and scissors, so I can still bring in money."

"Once upon a time, the way fathers will, I hoped you'd make something better than a tailor of yourself," his father answered, barring the door. "But you couldn't hope to rise too far out of your class, and I'm glad you're content to stay where you are." That wasn't exactly what Talsu had said. Before he could tell his father so, Traku went on, "And if you want to right about now, I bet we could fix up a marriage for you that's in our class, and the arrangements would go like *that*." He snapped his fingers.

Talsu flushed. "D'you really think so?" he mumbled.

"Aye, I do," Traku said. "Gailisa's never hated you, you know, and now that you took on the redheads to keep them from doing whatever they would have done to her, she really thinks the sun rises and sets on your head."

A slow smile stretched across Talsu's face. "Aye, I had noticed that. She's come visiting a lot since I got stuck, hasn't she?"

"Just a bit," his father said solemnly. "Pretty girl. Good girl, too, and that counts for more in the long run, though you can't always see as much when you're young. She's grateful to you, sure enough." He nodded, agreeing with himself. "She shows it, too, in ways that count. We haven't eaten this well since before the war. If you end up deciding needle and scissors and tape measure and tailoring magic don't suit you, you might have yourself a grocer's shop instead."

"I'm not going to worry about that right now," Talsu said. A delicious smell floated down the stairs. He grinned. "I'd sooner worry about supper – stuffed cabbage, or my nose has gone daft."

"The rest of you, maybe. Your nose, no." His father held out a hand. "Do you want some help getting up the steps?"

"I can manage," Talsu said. "It doesn't hurt as much as it used to." Going up or down stairs, especially up them, made him raise his legs higher than usual, which meant the healing muscles in his flanks had to work harder. Up he went, slowly. Saying it hurt less than it had was true, but didn't mean it didn't hurt at all.

He made it, though, and made it without gritting his teeth more than a couple of times. That was a sizable improvement on the bent-over hobbling he'd done when he first came home. And once, a few days before, he'd stumbled going up the stairs. He'd thought he was going to come to pieces. He'd rather hoped he would, in fact; he hadn't hurt so much since just after he got stabbed.

He also had to sit carefully. Once he was at the table and had taken a couple of deep breaths, the pain eased. It didn't go away, but it eased. His sister Ausra set a heaping plate in front of him. He dug in. The sauce, sharp with vinegar and sweet with honey, livened up the cabbage and the mix of wheat and barley with which it was stuffed. "Good," he said enthusiastically – and blurrily, because he didn't bother swallowing first. "Thank you."

"Don't thank me – thank your lady friend," his sister answered. "She's the one who got us the ground mutton and the honey."

"My lady friend," Talsu echoed. "I guess maybe she is."

His father coughed. His mother smiled. His sister laughed out loud. "Of course she is, you dunderhead," Ausra said. "She's as much your friend as you want her to be."

Traku had said the same thing. Hearing it from another woman, though, made it somehow seem more real, more immediate. (Not that thinking of Ausra as a woman rather than as a brat and a nuisance of a little sister didn't feel strange.) "Well, maybe," Talsu muttered.

"No maybes about it – it's true." That wasn't his sister, but his mother – and Laitsina spoke with great certainty.

Traku coughed again. "What I told him was, he could stay a tailor if he chose, or he could go into the grocer's line if he didn't. Pass me that pitcher of wine, will you, Ausra?"

Talsu's ears burned. "Don't you think it's rude to run somebody's life for him right in front of his face?" he asked the rest of his family.

Ausra stuck out her tongue at him. "Would you rather have us run your life behind your back?" she asked.

"I'd rather you didn't try to run it at all," Talsu said. "I had enough of that and to spare in the army, even if the food is better here."

"The food wasn't much better here till a little while ago," Ausra said, not about to give in. "And why is it now? Gailisa, that's why."

If they'd teased him about Gailisa any more, he thought he might start hating the grocer's pretty daughter. Such irks always lasted till Gailisa came into the tailor's shop, at which point they blew away like fog in the Bratanu Mountains. So it was again the next morning, when she walked in while he was cutting the pieces for an Algarvian officer's cloak.

"Hello," she said, and then, "How are you feeling today?"

Waggling the palm of his hand back and forth, he answered, "Not bad. I am getting better." If he said that often enough, maybe he'd believe it was true.

"That's good," she said, nodding, hanging on his every word. "I'm glad to hear it. Those Algarvians have never been back since . . . since the day you had trouble."

"I'm glad to hear that," Talsu said. "Here's hoping they get sent to Unkerlant, or maybe to the land of the Ice People."

His father made a sour face. "They're winning both places, if you believe the news sheets. Even if you only believe a quarter of what's in the news sheets, they're still winning." Traku opened a drawer, rattled through it, and slammed it shut, then did the same with another. Shaking his head, he muttered, "Must have left the fool thing upstairs. I'll be back when I find it." Off he went, leaving his son alone with Gailisa.

Talsu was convinced his father had done that on purpose. By the way she smiled, so was Gailisa. "Your father is a nice man," she said, which, to Talsu, only proved she didn't know Traku all that well.

He laughed. Gailisa raised an eyebrow and waited to hear what he had to say. After a moment's thought, he said it: "I don't know but what we had more fun when you were snippy all the time. You keep treating me like I'm one of the powers above and I'm liable to start believing it, and then where would we be?"

"Here in Skrunda, probably," Gailisa answered. "It's hard to be snippy with you after you did what you did, you know what I mean? I liked you before, and then—" She stopped and turned red.

Before Talsu could say anything to that, his side twinged. He grabbed it and grunted. Sound and movement were altogether involuntary. After it eased a little, he said, "I'm glad it made you like me better, but I'm not so glad as all that, if you hear what I'm telling you."

"Of course I do," Gailisa said. "I thought you were going to die, right there on the floor."

"So did I," Talsu said. "Thanks for getting help so fast."

"You're welcome," she answered. Then she walked over to him, put her arms around him, and kissed him. "I like this better than being snippy. What do you think of that?"

"I think I like it, too," Talsu told her. "Kiss me again, so I can find out for sure." She did. When Traku came downstairs, neither one of them noticed him. He went back up again, chuckling under his breath.

After the narrow valley in which Kunhegyes lay, the vast expanse of western Unkerlant seemed all the more enormous to Istvan. And the forest of pine and spruce and fir ahead looked big enough to cover half the world.

Staring, Istvan said, "We spent more than half a year fighting our way through the mountains and down on to the flatlands, and now we have to go through *this*? We could be another year on the way." If anything, that was liable to be a low guess. The forest might swallow anything, up to and including a Gyongyosian army.

"It's not so bad as that, Sergeant." Captain Tivadar took a map out of a leather map case and pointed at the red lines snaking through the green on the paper. "Here, do you see? Plenty of roads going through."

"Aye, sir," Istvan said. He could hardly disagree, not when he was a sergeant, a cobbler's son, talking to an officer with a fancy pedigree. He did add, "What do you want to bet, though, that King Swemmel's men fight at every crossroads?"

"If it were going to be easy, we would already have done it," Tivadar answered. He pointed ahead, then to the map again, and nodded in satisfaction. "See? There's the highway we've been following."

"Aye, sir," Istvan repeated. The alleged highway wouldn't have been much of a road even in the Gyongyosian valley where he'd just spent his leave. It was narrow, twisting, altogether, unpaved, and at the moment muddy. It disappeared among the trees as if it had no intention of ever coming out the other side – if the forest had another side.

"Onward, then," Tivadar said. "This is splendid timber, some of the finest in the world. If we can find ley lines to take it away, it'll make Gyongyos rich."

If there were any ley lines in this stars-forsaken country, the Unkerlanters would have cut down the forest and hauled it away themselves. So Istvan thought, at any rate. Since they hadn't, ley lines were likely to be few and far between – or perhaps they really were just undiscovered out here on the edge of nowhere. But Tivadar had his orders, and had given Istvan his.

Istvan turned to his squad. "Forward!" he called. "Into the woods. We're going to take them away from the accursed Unkerlanters."

"Aye," the troopers chorused. They were warriors, of a proud warrior race. They would obey. Even bespectacled Corporal Kun, lean and knowing and gratingly sophisticated, said, "Aye," with the rest as they advanced on the forest.

Szonyi said, "I wonder if they've got egg-tossers in there, waiting for us to get right up to the edge of the trees before they let us have it." He sighed. "Only way to find out is the hard way."

"And isn't that the sad and sorry truth?" Istvan said, more in resignation than anything else. "Well, they haven't killed us yet, so we're still ahead of the game." As other sergeants and officers were doing, he raised his voice: "Come on, you miserable lugs, get moving. Somewhere in there, we've got Unkerlanters to flush out."

He and his men tramped across the meadow that led to the forest. The grass was a brilliant green, far brighter than the nearly black needles on the trees ahead. Yellow ox-eye gentian and red clover brightened the meadow more. Butterflies flitted from flower to flower. Some sort of ground squirrel, not long out of its burrow after a long winter's nap, stood up on its hind legs and chattered indignantly at the soldiers marching past.

And then, off to Istvan's left, the ground erupted in a roar. A trooper shrieked, but not for long. Istvan stared up at the sky. No dragons wheeled there, only a rusty-red jay like the ones he might have seen at home. And no more eggs were flying through the air to land on the advancing Gyongyosians.

Someone else shouted out what flashed through his mind: "Have a care, all! The stinking sons of goats have buried eggs under the meadow. Tromp on one and you'll never tromp on anything else."

All at once, Istvan wanted to walk above the grass. His bowels knotted with every step he took. Kun spat and said, "I wonder how much fun we'll have going down the highway that's supposed to run through the forest."

Istvan didn't like thinking about that, either. "Have we got any mages who can sniff out buried eggs for us?" He asked the question in a loud, hopeful voice. Nobody responded to it. Istvan rounded on Kun. "What about you? You were a mage's apprentice, after all."

Kun bared his teeth in what was anything but a smile. "If I could, do you think I'd be stomping along like everybody else?"

"No law against hoping, is there?" Istvan said.

"No, and there's no law against stupidity, either, though there cursed well ought to be," Kun retorted. That was insubordinate, but Istvan let it slide. He knew why Kun was unhappy. He was unhappy for the same reason himself.

Another egg burst, this one half a mile over to the right. Istvan couldn't hear whether the luckless Gyongyosian who'd trodden on it shrieked or not. He ground his teeth and kept going. Half a minute later, yet another burst shattered the morning calm. A magpie screeched annoyance at having its hunt for worms and crickets and maybe mice disturbed.

Higher and higher, the trees loomed ahead. But for the roadway that led into the forest, no one had ever taken an axe to it. Gyongyos had few woods like this, and none so vast. People were scattered thinly over this part of the world; it looked, Istvan judged, much as it had when the stars first shone down on it.

"Kun, walk point," he called as his squad went into the forest a little to the north of the road. "Szonyi, on the right. Fenyes, on the left. I'll take rear guard for a while. Keep your eyes open, everyone. Somewhere in there, the filthy goat-buggers are waiting for us."

The world changed when he went in among the trees. The sun disappeared, except for occasional dapplings sneaking through the thick branches overhead. The air got cooler and damper; spicy, resinous scents filled it. Istvan's boots scuffed on red-brown fallen needles. Here and there, especially at the bases of tree trunks, lacy green ferns sprang up.

On the meadow, Istvan had been able to see for miles. Here, the trees cramped his vision, and not just from side to side. When he looked up, those dark boughs hid the sky. He shook his head. He didn't like that.

"No stars tonight," he muttered, more to himself than to anyone else.

But one of his troopers heard, and answered, "They'll see us, Sergeant, even if we can't see them."

"Aye," Istvan answered, but he remained unreassured. He kept looking up. Every once in a while, he managed to spy a sliver of blue. When he did, he felt he'd won a victory.

A red squirrel holding a fir cone in its front paws peered down at him with beady black eyes and chittered in annoyance, as its cousin had out on the meadow. He raised a hand. The squirrel ducked back, putting the bulk of the branch – which was as thick as a man's leg – between itself and what looked like danger.

Seeing it put a new thought in his mind. "Keep watching overhead," he called to his men. "If the Unkerlanters haven't put some snipers in the trees, I'm an even bigger fool than you think I am."

Up ahead, Kun said something. Istvan thought he heard the word *impossible*, but he wasn't sure. He decided not to find out.

Heading east and not getting turned around in this dim, shadowless world kept the whole squad – and probably the whole army – busy. Kun's sorcerous training, though scanty, did come in hand there. From somewhere or other, he'd got a chunk of lodestone. He tied it on the end of a string and chanted over it. It swung in a particular direction. "That's south," he said confidently, and made half a turn to his left. "So *this* is east." He pointed.

"How does the lodestone know where south lies?" Istvan asked.

"Curse me if I can tell you," the former sorcerer's apprentice said. "But I know *that* it does, which is what we need."

"What we need is to bump up against the Unkerlanters, so we can knock 'em out of the way," Istvan said. "All this waiting is making my belly gripe."

"It'll loosen up when the fighting starts, that's certain," Szonyi said. "If you're anything like me, you'll thank the stars that you don't foul yourself."

That was no way for a member of a warrior race to talk, but Istvan just chuckled and nodded. Maybe some heroes didn't think about what might happen to them when they went into action, but he did. He couldn't help it.

Twilight under the trees was darkening toward real twilight when he and his countrymen ran into the first positions the Unkerlanters had built to block their path. "Down!" Kun shouted, and everyone in the squad threw himself flat. A beam zipped past above Istvan's head. Whether it would have caught him had he not gone down, he didn't know. It struck a tree trunk behind him, and blazed through the bark deep into the wood. Aromatic steam gushed from the wounded pine.

Istvan scuttled over behind another tree. Ever so warily, he glanced around it. He saw nothing but more trees ahead. "Where are they?" he called softly.

"Up ahead somewhere," Kun answered, which was doubtless true but imperfectly helpful. Sounding exasperated, the point man went on, "They're Unkerlanters, curse it. They're good at hiding to begin with, and they've had plenty of time to get ready for us."

Shouts and curses and screams rang out all through the forest, as the Gyongyosian army ran into the concealed Unkerlanter defenders. The Unkerlanters had egg-tossers hidden among the trees along with their soldiers, and started using them as soon as their foes collided with them.

And King Swemmel's men had left forces in the woods who'd waited and stayed hidden while the Gyongyosians went past, then attacked from the rear after Istvan and his comrades bumped into the main defensive line. Istvan found out about that when one of them blazed at him from behind. He'd thought he had good cover, but suddenly a charred hole appeared in the tree in back of which he was hiding, and only bare inches from his head.

He whirled and threw himself down on his belly. Where had the beam come from? Shouts of "Swemmel!" echoed through the darkening woods. For a moment, panic filled him. Was the whole Gyongyosian force surrounded and about to be cut to pieces? If it was, the Unkerlanters would have to go through a lot of stubborn men like him. Maybe there was something to springing from a warrior race after all.

Was that a rock-gray tunic? Istvan blazed. An Unkerlanter groaned and tumbled out from behind the trunk of a spruce. Istvan yanked a folding shovel off his own belt and began digging a hole in the soft dirt. He'd named himself rear guard for the squad. That meant he was the one who had to be first defender against threats from behind.

He smelled smoke. No matter how moist the forest was, all the blazes and bursting eggs had set it afire. He dug harder than ever, but wondered even as dirt flew whether he was doing anything more than digging his own grave. He also wondered whether anyone, Unkerlanter or Gyongyosian, would come out of the forest alive.

As Krasta came downstairs from her bedchamber, Colonel Lurcanio was pacing back and forth in the hall at the bottom of the stairway. His green eyes sparked as he glared up at her. "What took you so long, milady?" he growled. But then, however unwillingly, he bowed over her hand and kissed it. "You do look very lovely tonight, I must say, which almost makes the delay worthwhile."

Had he left off the *almost*, Krasta would have known she'd created just the effect she wanted. Lurcanio was difficult – sometimes impossible – to manage. But she didn't wish she'd got Captain Mosco instead, not any more. Off in the trackless wilds of Unkerlant . . . She didn't want to think about that.

"I'm sure your driver will be able to get us to the reception in good time," she said. "He doesn't dawdle over everything, the way mine does."

"He is an Algarvian, and he is a soldier," Lurcanio said. The angry rumble had left his voice; Krasta decided he'd put it there to see if he could make her afraid. This time, it hadn't worked. And he didn't push it, either, as he sometimes did. He slipped his arm around her waist. "Let us be off, then."

His driver was indeed an Algarvian and a soldier. The fellow proved that by leering at Krasta as Lurcanio handed her up into the carriage. He was tall and young and handsome, but surely had no breeding at all. Krasta did not believe in rutting with her social inferiors.

Lurcanio spoke to the driver in their own language. The driver nodded, flicked the reins, and got the horses going. Despite what Krasta had said about him, he didn't drive very fast, not when all the streets of Priekule were lit only by a sinking crescent moon. Lagoan dragons didn't fly up to the capitals of occupied Valmiera very often, but the Algarvians made things as hard as they could for them on principle.

Taking advantage of the darkness, Lurcanio set a hand on Krasta's leg just above the knee and slowly slid it higher and higher along her thigh. "You're in a bold mood tonight," she said, amused.

"I am in a happy mood tonight," Colonel Lurcanio declared, and moved his hand higher still. "And do you know why I'm in a happy mood tonight?"

"I can think of a reason," Krasta said archly, setting her hand on his.

He chuckled. "Oh, that, too, my dear," he said, "but I can get that any time I want."

Her back stiffened. "Not from me, you can't. Not if you talk that way."

"If not from you, then from someone else. Finding it isn't hard, not in a conquered kingdom." Lurcanio sounded annoyingly smug. The trouble was, Krasta knew he was right – and if she threw him out of her bed in a fit of pique, she would be left without an Algarvian protector. When she didn't rise to his bait, Lurcanio went on, "No, the chief reason I am happy tonight is that we have smashed the attack the Unkerlanters made on our positions south of Aspang."

"Good," Krasta said, though she couldn't have found the city on a map to save herself from the headsman's axe.

"Oh, aye, it is," Lurcanio replied. "Swemmel's men spent most of the winter smashing us, which is the main reason Captain Mosco's bastard will likely never see his – or even her – father. Had they kept on smashing us now that spring has come, it would have been a great deal less than amusing."

"They're only Unkerlanters, after all," Krasta said.

Lurcanio nodded. "Even so. And they are once more proving they are *only* Unkerlanters, if you take my meaning."

Krasta didn't, not altogether. She didn't trouble herself to go looking for it, either. Instead, she craned her neck for a better look at the skyline. "It still seems wrong, not to have the Column of Victory standing tall and white and pretty there."

"It wouldn't be lit up now, not in wartime." Lurcanio could be annoyingly precise. "Maybe one day King Mezentio will build a new and grander column in its place: an Algarvian Column of Victory, to last for all time, not just a paltry double handful of centuries."

"In Priekule? That would be—" For once, Krasta remembered in the nick of time who and what her companion was, and swallowed a remark that would have got her in trouble with Lurcanio.

A few minutes later, the carriage pulled up in front of the mansion that belonged to Sefanu, the Duke of Klaipeda's nephew. The duke had commanded Valmiera's beaten army in the war against Algarve. He'd since retired to his country estates. His nephew was quite happy playing host to the occupiers.

As usual at these affairs, Algarvian and Valmieran men were present in about equal numbers. All the women, though, were blondes, and all young and pretty: Krasta wasted no time before looking over the potential competition. Some of the Valmieran women were nobles like her, some commoners she'd seen at other functions, and some new faces. Her lip curled. The Algarvians could pick and choose and discard as they pleased, and they did.

Some of the new faces topped painfully thin bodies. Several of that type congregated at the buffet, exclaiming over meats and cheeses the likes of which they hadn't seen for a long time. No noblewoman would have stuffed herself as they did. But their Algarvian escorts stood around watching with amused smiles. *Probably brought them here just to fatten them up*, Krasta thought spitefully.

Rather more Valmieran noblewomen than commoners wore Algarvian-style kilts. Krasta scowled when she noticed that. Some of the Valmieran men had taken to wearing the Algarvian style, too. Krasta liked that no better.

Sure enough, here came Viscount Valnu, in a kilt so short, he would have had trouble staying modest if he bent over. His bonily handsome face wore a dazzling smile. "Hello, darling!" he said, fluttering his fingers at Krasta. He hugged her and kissed her on the cheek, then hugged Lurcanio and kissed him on the cheek, too. "Hello, my lord Count! And how are you?"

"Well enough, thanks," Lurcanio said, and kept his distance from Valnu from then on. Algarvian men were more apt to kiss than Valmierans, but they didn't usually do it quite like that – though Krasta recalled seeing Valnu at one party with an Algarvian officer who was definitely like that.

Valnu, to her certain knowledge, wasn't, or wasn't altogether. "What *have* you been doing lately?" she asked him, more than a hint of malice in her voice.

"Why, whatever I can, of course," he answered. "Come with me, and I'll tell you all about it." He turned to Lurcanio. "I wouldn't steal your lady without your leave, my lord Count. That were rude indeed."

"It's all right," Lurcanio said indulgently. By his tone, he thought he was safe enough entrusting Krasta to this creature of no obvious gender.

Krasta knew better, and the thought of being unfaithful to her redheaded lover suddenly looked delightful, not so much for Valnu's sake as to put one over on Lurcanio. She took hold of Valnu's arm. "Aye," she gushed, "tell me *everything*."

Valnu's smile grew brighter yet. "Oh, I will," he said, and led her off through the crowd. Behind her, Lurcanio laughed. Krasta was laughing, too, but inside, where it didn't show. *You don't know as much as you think you do.*

She steered Valnu over to the bar so she could collect a mug of ale, then let him steer her out of the mansion and on to the street. "You do need to know that I came here with Lurcanio's driver, not my own," she murmured.

"Oh, I do, do I?" Valnu said. "And why is that?"

"Because you can't have this fellow drive along some quiet road while we do whatever we want in the carriage," Krasta answered. "He'd blab to Lurcanio, sure as sure."

"While we do whatever we want?" Valnu laughed softly. "The last time we tried that, you shoved me out of the carriage and left me to walk home alone in the dark. I don't know about you, my dear marchioness, but that isn't what *I* had in mind when we started on the ride."

Krasta shrugged impatiently. "You deserved it, for picking just the wrong time to start chattering about shopgirls."

"I won't say a word about them now, I promise you." Valnu slid his arm around her. "Stroll with me. We can look up at the stars together, or do anything else we happen to think of."

There were more stars to look at than there had been when Priekule was at peace. With the city dark, they shone in great, glittering profusion:

multicolored jewels scattered across black velvet. After one brief glance, Krasta forgot about them. She hadn't come out with Valnu to stargaze. She'd come out to enjoy revenge on an Algarvian keeper who took her for granted.

But Valnu really did feel like strolling, or so it seemed. Fuming a little, Krasta went along for a block or so. Then she got mulish. Planting her feet firmly on the slates of the pavement, she took hold of Valnu and said, "If you brought me out here to trifle, what are you waiting for?"

"To get a little farther away," Valnu answered, which made no sense to her. "But this will do well enough." He gathered her in. She kissed him more fiercely than she'd ever kissed Lurcanio. The Algarvian was a skilled and pleasing lover, but he also held the whip hand, and Krasta knew it. Not here, not now.

Valnu was nuzzling her neck and nibbling her ear when a thunderous roar behind her knocked both of them off her feet. The first thing Krasta noticed was that she'd torn a knee out of her velvet trousers. Only after cursing at that did she proclaim, "Powers above! What happened!"

"If I had to guess, I would say an egg burst in Sefanu's mansion," Valnu answered. He rose and, with startling strength, hauled her to her feet. "Come on."

Because he sounded sure of himself and acted as if he knew what he was doing, Krasta followed him back toward the mansion. His guess had been right on target, and so, she saw, had the egg. The mansion's second and third stories had fallen in on themselves, and fire was beginning to spread in the ruins.

Shrieks from injured and trapped people inside made the night hideous. A few men and women, disheveled and bleeding, pulled themselves free of the rubble and came staggering away. Krasta yanked at an arm sticking out from under a pile of bricks. It came away, with no body attached to it. She dropped it with a horrified cry. Her stomach lurched, as if aboard a diving dragon.

"Lurcanio," she muttered. It hadn't been his arm – it had belonged to a woman. But what chance had he had to get away?

And then, from behind her, he said, "I am here." He'd lost his hat. He had a cut over one eye, and another on his forearm. He also had most of his aplomb. Bowing, he said, "Good to see you intact, milady. Your pretty popinjay picked just the right time to entertain you there."

"Aye," Krasta said, and realized for the first time that she might easily have been inside the mansion when the egg burst. Her stomach lurched again. "Curse the Lagoan dragons!" she exclaimed.

"Dragons?" Lurcanio shook his head. "No dragons tonight. That egg didn't drop, milady – it was smuggled in and left to burst. Plenty of ways to arrange such a thing. And when we find out who did it, we'll arrange his guts as pretty as you please. Oh, he'll take a *long* time to die." He sounded as if he looked forward to seeing that. In some ways, Algarvians remained barbaric after all. No matter how fine and mild the night was, Krasta shivered.

Vanai laid her hand on Ealstan's forehead. He was burning hot, as he had been an hour before, as he had been a day before, as he had been ever since he came down sick three days before. He thrashed and muttered and stared up at her from the bed. "Conberge," he muttered.

Biting her lip, Vanai soaked a wash rag in a bowl of cold water, wrung it out till it was nearly dry, and put it on his forehead. If he thought she was his sister, he was in a bad way indeed. No one in his right mind could have mistaken her for a swarthy, solidly made Forthwegian woman.

"What am I going to do?" she exclaimed. She'd managed to get occasional sips of water and broth down Ealstan, but that wasn't nearly enough, and she knew it. And he needed something more than a cold compress to fight the fever, too. She turned the compress over. Already, the heat that came off him had gone a long way toward drying the side that had touched the skin.

He needs a physician, she thought, *or at least real medicine.* She'd been thinking that for most of the past day, ever since it had become clear that the fever wasn't going to leave any time soon. He would have gone out for her. She knew that. But he didn't face capture and worse if he stuck his nose outside the door to the flat.

"Chilly," he said in conversational tones, and started to shake. He wasn't chilly; he was as far in the world as he could be from chilly. But he thought he was freezing. His teeth started to chatter. Vanai piled blankets on him, but he kept shivering underneath them. He'd done that before, too. It never failed to appall Vanai.

With a grimace, she made up her mind. Ealstan had to have more help than she could give here with what little they had in the flat to fight fever.

Taking care to speak Forthwegian so he wouldn't fret, Vanai said, "I'm going out now. I'll be back as soon as I can." She did her best to sound as if everything were perfectly normal, as if she could go out any time she chose, as if nothing could possibly happen to her when she went out into Eoforwic.

Maybe she even succeeded, for Ealstan said, "All right, Mother. Be careful out in the blizzard." Because he thought he was cold, he thought the rest of the world had to be cold, too.

"I will," Vanai promised. She took all the money she could find in the flat – a good deal more than she'd thought she and Ealstan had. Algarvians were famous for being bribable. She'd bribed Major Spinello with her body. Next to that, she didn't worry about silver.

Stepping out into the hall, seeing walls that weren't the walls of her flat, felt very strange. She wished she'd changed into the long tunic Ealstan had got for her, but it wouldn't disguise what she was, not on a fine, bright spring day. She hurried downstairs and out of the block of flats.

Street noise hit her like a blow. Eoforwic dwarfed Oyngestun; she'd forgotten how big and brawling the capital was. She'd seen it briefly when she and Ealstan first came here from the east. Since then, she'd stayed high up, looking out through window glass at the world but taking no part in it.

Seeing strange faces up close felt wrong, unnatural. And people stared at her, too. A Forthwegian with a face like a big-nosed ferret grabbed her by the arm. Even as she twisted away, he demanded, "Lady, are you out of your skull? You want the redheads to nab you?"

She needed a moment to notice that the question had come in Kaunian, a slangy dialect far removed from what she'd heard and used back on Oyngestun – the kind of Kaunian pickpockets and thieves would speak. This fellow had probably learned it from blond pickpockets and thieves.

"I need an apothecary," she said in Forthwegian – no use drawing attention to herself by ear as well as eye. "My . . . brother's sick."

"Uh-*huh*." The ferret-faced Forthwegian didn't believe that. After a moment, she understood why: a brother would have been as conspicuous as she was. That meant this fellow knew she had a Forthwegian lover. But he was saying, "Two blocks over, a block and a half up, and he won't ask no questions. Just stay invisible between here and there."

"My thanks," Vanai said. But the Forthwegian had gone on his way as if she really were invisible.

Few of the other dark, blocky men and women on the streets seemed to notice she was there, either. In Eoforwic, she remembered, Forthwegians and Kaunians had rioted together against the Algarvian occupiers when they learned what happened to the Kaunians the redheads sent west. It hadn't been like that in Oyngestun. It hadn't been like that most places in Forthweg. Had it been, the Algarvians would have had a harder time doing what they did.

"What do you need?" a gray-bearded Forthwegian asked her. He was grinding some powder or another with a brass mortar and pestle. As the fellow who'd recommended his place had said, he didn't seem to care that she was a Kaunian.

"A fever-fighter," she answered, and described Ealstan's symptoms without saying who or what he might be in relation to her.

"Ah." The apothecary nodded. "There's a deal of that going around, so there is. I'll mix you up some willow bark and poppy juice, aye, and a bit of hairy marshwort, too. It's got an ugly name, but it's full of virtue." He reached for bottles full of bark and a dark liquid and dried leaves, then mixed them together after grinding all the solids to powder. After that, he poured in something clear and sparkling. "Just a bit of grain spirits – for flavor, you might say."

"Whatever you think best." Vanai trusted him at sight. He knew what he knew, and was good at what he did. Had an Algarvian or a naked black Zuwayzi told him of the same symptoms, he would have made the identical medicine. She was sure of that.

"Here you are," he said when he was done. "That'll be three in silver." Vanai nodded and paid; she thought Tamulis, back on Oyngestun where things were cheaper, would have charged her more. As she turned to go, the apothecary showed the first signs of knowing what she was: he called after her, "Get home safe, girl. Get home, and stay there."

She looked back over her shoulder. "That's what I intend to do. Thank you." He didn't answer. He just went back to the medicine he'd been compounding when she came into the shop.

She clung close to the walls of shops as she scurried back toward her block of flats, as if she were a mouse scurrying along a baseboard to its hole. Again, most Forthwegians she saw pretended not to see her. She did hear one shout of, "Dirty Kaunian!" but even the women who yelled made no move to do anything about it.

Powers above be praised, she thought as she reached the last corner she had to turn before reaching her building. *I got away with it.* She turned the corner . . . and almost walked into a pair of Algarvian constables who were about to turn on to the street she was leaving.

Had Vanai seen them half a block away, she could easily have escaped; they were both pudgy and middle-aged. But one of them reached out and grabbed her even as she was letting out a startled squeak. "Well, well, what are we having here?" he said in fairly fluent Forthwegian.

"Let me go!" Vanai exclaimed. She kicked at him, but he was nimble enough despite his bulk; her shoe didn't strike his stockinged shin. Then she thought to use guile instead of force. "I'll pay you if you let me go." She reached down and made the silver in her pocket jingle.

The constable who didn't have hold of her leered. "*How* you paying us, eh?" His Forthwegian was worse than his partner's, but Vanai had no trouble understanding what he wanted from her.

Most of the horror that gripped her was horror at not feeling more horror. If that was what it took to get rid of the Algarvians, why not? Major Spinello had inflicted himself on her for months. After that, what were a few minutes with a couple of strangers? She should have been appalled at thinking that way. Part of her was, but only a small part. Spinello had burned away the rest of her sense of . . . shame?

In quick, almost musical trills, the Algarvians talked back and forth. One of them pointed to the dark mouth of an alleyway across the street from where they stood. If they took her back there, they could do what they wanted with her and no one would be the wiser unless she screamed. "Let's be going," said the one who had hold of her, and he gave her a shove in that direction.

She would have seized a chance to escape, but they offered her none. *Now I have to hope they'll let me go after . . . this*, she thought, grinding her teeth. Relying on the honor of men all too liable not to have any made her legs light and shaky with fear.

And then a Forthwegian loomed in front of the constables. "Turn her loose," he rumbled. "She ain't done nothing."

"Aye, that's right," a woman said from behind her.

"She is being a Kaunian," the constable answered, as if that explained everything. Most places in Forthweg, it would have.

Not here. "Aye, she's a Kaunian, and you're a son of a whore," said the burly man blocking the constables' path. A crowd started to gather. The Forthwegian repeated, "Turn her loose, curse you."

Had he shouted for Vanai's blood, he might well have got that. As things were, everybody in the growing crowd shouted for the constables to let her go. The two Algarvians looked at each other. They were time-servers, not heroes. The bold, the young, the brave, were off doing real fighting. These fellows couldn't hope to blaze everybody who was yelling at them. They would get mobbed, and a riot would start.

The one who had hold of Vanai's arm held out his other hand. "Ten silvers' fine, for being on street without permitting," he declared.

Vanai gave him the coins without hesitation. The other constable stuck out his hand, whereupon the first one split the money with him. They both beamed. Why not? They'd made a profit, even if she hadn't gone into the alley and done lewd things for them.

With a pat on the head as if she'd been a dog, the first constable let her go. "Run along home," he told her.

She didn't wait to let him change his mind – or for the crowd to disperse, which might have tempted him to do just that. And the crowd helped in another way, for it kept the Algarvians from seeing which building she entered. "Safe," she breathed as she got inside. She hurried up the stairs to give Ealstan the medicine. She clutched the jar tightly. It had ended up being expensive, but oh! – how much more it might have cost.

Waddo came limping up to Garivald as the peasant tramped in from the fields with a hoe on his shoulder as if it were a stick. The firstman grabbed Garivald by the elbow and pulled him aside. "It's gone," he said hoarsely, his eyes wide with fear.

"What's gone?" Garivald asked, though he thought he knew the answer.

"Why, the crystal, of course," Waddo answered, proving him right. "It's gone, and powers above only know who's got it or what he's going to do with it." He stared at Garivald. "*You* haven't got it, have you? We were going to take it out of the ground together, the two of us."

"No, I haven't got it," Garivald said. Waddo hadn't asked him if he'd dug it up. Had the firstman asked him that, he would have denied it, too, not caring at all whether he lied. The less Waddo knew, the less anyone – particularly anyone Algarvian – could wring out of him.

At the moment, Waddo seemed not far from panic. "Someone has it!" he said. "Aye, someone has it. Someone who'll use it against me. He'll tell the redheads, and they'll hang me. They're bound to hang me."

He wasn't a brave man. Garivald had known that since before he'd started to shave. The firstman had enjoyed his petty authority in Zossen while he had it. Now that he had it no more, he lived in constant fear lest the Algarvians make him pay for everything he'd done while the village was under King Swemmel's rule.

"Try not to worry," Garivald said, though he might as well have told the sun not to rise tomorrow. He thought about letting Waddo know the Unkerlanter irregulars who roamed the woods had the crystal – thought about it and put it out of his mind. The less Waddo knew, the better, sure enough.

"Don't tell me that! How can you tell me that?" the firstman said. Garivald only shrugged; no answer he gave the firstman would satisfy him. Wide-eyed, Waddo stumped away, digging the end of his stick into the ground at every stride.

"What's chewing on him?" Garivald's friend Dagulf asked.

"Powers above only know," Garivald answered. "You know how Waddo gets sometimes. It never means anything."

"I haven't seen him *that* heated up since the Algarvians came into Zossen," Dagulf said, rubbing the scar on his cheek. "And he thought they were going to boil him for soup then."

"They'd have to skin a lot of fat off before they could eat it if they did," Garivald said, which made Dagulf laugh. It also made the other peasant stop asking questions, which was what Garivald had had in mind.

As the peasants and their wives were going out to work the next morning, the Algarvian sergeant in charge of the little occupying force started beating on the lid of a pot with a hammer to summon them to the village square. He read a proclamation from a sheet of paper, which meant his Unkerlanter was grammatically accurate even if badly pronounced: "His Majesty, King Raniero of Grelz, announces that, with the help of his brave allies from Algarve, the wicked invasion of his domain by the forces of Swemmel the usurper has been beaten back, crushed, and utterly quashed. Now let us all give three hearty cheers to thank the powers above for this grand and glorious victory, the harbinger of many more."

Along with the rest of the villagers, Garivald dutifully cheered. He'd learned from experience that, if the cheers weren't hearty enough to suit the redheads, they'd keep the peasants there till the shouts suited them. He had work to do. Cheering loudly from the start let him go do it. He didn't have time to waste standing around.

He wondered how much truth the proclamation held. The Algarvians had been in the habit of announcing victories even in the middle of winter, when the irregulars made it clear Mezentio's men were getting pounded. But Algarvian soldiers had come forward through Zossen in the past few days, which likely meant things weren't going so well for Unkerlant.

Another squad of Algarvians, these men mounted on unicorns, rode into the village while he was out weeding. Garivald paid them no particular attention, even when they didn't go west right away. He'd grown too used to the redheads to worry about any one lot of them very much. A year before, he'd never so much as seen an Algarvian. He heartily wished he'd never see any more of them, either, but that wasn't the sort of wish likely to be granted right away.

When sunset came, he shouldered his hoe and trudged back toward Zossen, as he did every evening. Again, he noticed the Algarvians standing at the edge of the village without paying them any special heed. It was Dagulf who remarked, "Looks like that cursed long-winded bugger of a sergeant is pointing at you."

"Huh?" Garivald looked up in surprise. Sure enough the redhead who'd delivered the proclamation did have his index finger aimed his way. When he saw Garivald had noticed him, he beckoned.

"What's he want with you?" Dagulf asked.

"Curse me if I know." Garivald shrugged and sighed. "Guess I'd better go find out, though." He turned away from the shortest path toward his home and walked over to the sergeant, who stood with some of the newcomers to the village.

"You being Garivald, is not being so?" the sergeant said. His

Unkerlanter was much worse when he had to try to speak it without a script.

"Aye, I'm Garivald," Garivald answered. The question, plainly, was for the record; the sergeant knew who he was.

All the Algarvians who'd come into Zossen that day aimed their sticks at him. "By order of King Raniero and King Mezentio, you are under arrest," one of them said. His Unkerlanter was much better than the sergeant's. Even so, Garivald had trouble following what the fellow said through the roaring in his ears: "You are to be taken to Herborn for trial, the charge being treason through subversive songs. After the trial, you are to be executed in accordance to the law. Any resistance and you shall be blazed without trial. Now come along."

Numbly, Garivald came. Later, he thought he should have laid about him with the hoe, and with luck have slain a couple of the redheads before they did blaze him down. At the moment, stunned by the catastrophe that had overfallen him, he let them take away the hoe, let them tie his hands behind his back, and let them lead him to their unicorns.

With his hands tied, he couldn't mount one of the beasts by himself. A couple of Algarvians helped him get aboard. He'd never ridden a unicorn before. He would just as soon not have started riding one in this particular way. But he had no choice; he'd lost any possibility of choice once the hoe was gone. The Algarvians tied his feet together under the unicorn's barrel.

"What happens if I fall out of the saddle?" he asked.

"You get dragged to death or trampled to death," answered the Algarvian who'd announced his arrest. "We don't care. We can deliver your body. If you want to keep breathing a little longer, don't fall."

They wasted no time. Unkerlanters, at King Swemmel's urging, talked about efficiency. The redheads personified it. They – and Garivald – rode out of Zossen before Annore could burst shrieking from the house she'd shared so long with her husband.

Even after darkness fell, they kept on heading east, back toward the capital of Grelz. Garivald had heard the irregulars boasting of what they did to small bands of Algarvians they caught away from help. He'd believed those boasts. Tonight, he discovered that, like so many, they were nothing but wind.

The Algarvians treated him like a domestic animal, without either kindness or cruelty beyond what they needed to make sure he didn't escape. When he asked them to stop so he could ease himself, they did. Toward midnight, they rode into another village. They fed him then, from their own rations – spicier than what he was used to eating, but no worse – and gave him wine to drink. They let him sleep in a hut, but posted guards around it. He was too worn even to think about escape for more than a moment.

Not long after sunset, they – and, perforce, he – started off again. Had he been less weary and saddlesore and frightened, he might have marveled at the endurance of the unicorn he rode. That, though, wasn't what struck him. By midafternoon, he was farther from his home than he'd ever been in his life.

"Will you sing us one of your songs to pass the time?" asked the Algarvian who spoke Unkerlanter.

"I don't know what you're talking about," Garivald said stolidly. "I don't know anything about making songs."

To his surprise, the Algarvian nodded. "Aye, I'd say the same in your boots," he agreed. "But it won't do you any good, not once we get you to Herborn. They'll blaze you or hang you or boil you no matter what you tell them."

"Boil me . . ." Garivald didn't want to say that aloud, but couldn't help it. Everybody knew what had happened to Kyot at the end of the Twinkings War. To think of that happening to him . . .

On they rode, past meadows and woods and fields under cultivation and fields going to weeds, past villages that looked achingly like Zossen and past villages that were nothing but charred ruins. Garivald had heard about what the war had done, but he'd never really seen it, not till now. Words started to shape themselves inside his mind. He didn't know whether to laugh or to cry. Whatever songs he made now, he'd never have the chance to sing them.

No village was near when evening came. Confident as if in the middle of their own kingdom, the Algarvians encamped at the top of a low hill. They had three men up and watching all through the night: watching Garivald, watching their unicorns, watching for any trouble that might come their way. Garivald had kept hoping irregulars might use the cover of darkness to attack them, but none did.

"Herborn in a couple of days," the redhead who spoke Unkerlanter said to him the next morning. "Then your trial, then the end." He wasn't gloating. He was as matter-of-fact as if talking about the weather. That made him more frightening to the peasant, not less.

On went the unicorns, taking Garivald on toward the big city he'd never seen and would not see for long. Late that afternoon, the road went through a wood of mixed beeches and birches and pines. The Algarvians chattered back and forth in their own language and kept looking this way and that – they didn't like riding along so close to trees that they could reach out and touch them.

And they had reason to mislike it. When the ambush hit, it hit hard and fast. A barricade of logs and brush blocked the road. Mezentio's men had barely reined in before Unkerlanters started blazing at them from behind trees and bushes. Algarvians tumbled out of the saddle one after another. One of the redheads lifted his stick to blaze Garivald but crumpled, clutching at himself, before he could loose his beam.

Some of the unicorns fell, too, shrieking shrilly from the pain they couldn't understand. Garivald could only stay where he was. If anyone blazed his unicorn, it would crush him when it went down.

Before long, the irregulars came out of the woods to finish off the two or three Algarvians still groaning. One of them strode up to Garivald. "Who are you?" he demanded. "Why did the whoresons grab you?"

"To kill me, that's why," Garivald answered. "I'm Garivald the songmaker."

He wondered if the fellow had heard of him. When the irregular's eyes widened, Garivald knew he had. "Garivald the songmaker, in my band?" he exclaimed. "I will gain fame for that." He thumped his chest, then drew a knife. "I, Munderic, set you free. You are one of my men now." Far from home, suddenly saved from certain death, Garivald nodded eagerly. He was a peasant no more, nor a captive, either. As Munderic's knife bit through his bonds, he gladly became an irregular.